ABOUT THE AUTHOR

RUSTY YOUNG is the author *Marching Powder*, the story of a British drug-smuggler who was incarcerated in Bolivia's notorious San Pedro prison, and the presenter of *Wildlands*, an award-winning documentary about cocaine trafficking in Latin America.

After his four-month voluntary stay in San Pedro, Rusty lived in Colombia for eight years. For four of these years he secretly worked for the US government in counter-terrorism. At the time, Colombia suffered the highest rate of kidnapping in the world (on average nine people per day). As a manager of the Anti-Kidnapping Program, Rusty lived part-time on a military base, drove a Level III armoured vehicle, communicated with colleagues via encrypted radio and changed houses a dozen times.

Through police and army contacts, Rusty was able to interview special forces soldiers, including snipers and undercover intelligence agents, about their work. He also interviewed former hostages, their families and a broad cross-section of people from communities affected by violence, including priests, teachers and rural farmers displaced from their homes.

By far the most heart-wrenching stories he heard came from child soldiers recruited by the two main terrorist organisations – FARC and Autodefensas. At the peak of the war, an estimated 11,000 to 14,000 children were involved in the conflict, a third of whom were girls. The former soldiers, some as young as eight when they joined, described in detail their reasons for enlisting, their hatred of the enemy, their gruelling military training, their political indoctrination and their horrific experiences in battle. Once Rusty had earned their trust, they also opened up to him about gruesome tortures they were forced to witness or participate in.

Since 2011, Rusty's house has been the headquarters for a foundation that helps rehabilitate and resocialise former child soldiers. Ten per cent of his royalties from this book will go to assisting Colombian children affected by violence.

For more information about the author and how you can help, please visit www.rusty-young.com.

By the same author

MARCHING POWDER

COLOMBIANO

Rusty Young

BANTAM

SYDNEY AUCKLAND TORONTO NEW YORK LONDON

A Bantam book
Published by Penguin Random House Australia Pty Ltd
Level 3, 100 Pacific Highway, North Sydney NSW 2060
penguin.com.au

First published by Bantam in 2017
This edition published in 2018

Addresses for the Penguin Random House group of companies can be found at global.penguinrandomhouse.com/offices.

A catalogue record for this book is available from the National Library of Australia

ISBN 978 0 14378 154 7

Cover design by Jem Butcher Design
Cover images © Shutterstock.com and iStock.com
Internal design and typesetting by Midland Typesetters, Australia
Map by Ice Cold Publishing
Printed in Australia by Griffin Press, an accredited ISO AS/NZS 14001:2004 Environmental Management System printer

The paper this book is printed on is certified against the Forest Stewardship Council® Standards. Griffin Press – a member of the Opus Group holds chain of custody certification SCS-COC-001185. FSC® promotes environmentally responsible, socially beneficial and economically viable management of the world's forests.

To my loving parents, Marie and Peter,

and to

Simone Camilleri, fellow writer and lifelong friend

CONTENTS

Villavicencio and Bogotá
N
Javier Díaz's Hacienda
GARBANZOS
Sealed Road 15km
Brazil nut tree
Camila's House
Humberto Díaz's Finca
Pedro's Finca
Old Man Domino's Finca
LLORONA
Rope swing tree
Palillo's House
Puerto Galán wharf and market
PUERTO GALÁN
Dirt Road
PUERTO PRINCESA
Ferry
SANTO PARAÍSO
Guerrilla Territory
Guerrilla Territory

AUTHOR PROLOGUE

I FIRST MET Pedro Juan Gutiérrez González (not his real name) in Bogotá. It was during my initial visit to an *albergue* – a halfway house for child soldiers exiting the vicious civil war.

The children I was about to interview were participants in a government 'demobilisation' program that aimed to help them overcome their trauma and begin a new life by providing them with accommodation, food, education and psychological counselling.

As I pulled up in front of a large, ordinary-looking Spanish colonial house in the leafy, residential suburb of Teusaquillo, I noticed a well-dressed man in his early twenties standing outside the gate. He appeared to be waiting for me.

'You must be the journalist. Welcome!' he said, shaking my hand firmly as I exited my SUV. 'I'm Pedro. I'm a volunteer assistant here.'

In appearance, Pedro was typically Colombian – of medium build with straight dark hair, an olive complexion and brown eyes. He was handsome despite a prominent scar running down his left cheek. He glanced at my SUV.

'Level three armoured vehicle,' he stated confidently, tapping the bulletproof windscreen.

I nodded and tried to laugh it off. 'A potentially dangerous profession.' After all, Colombia had the highest murder rate of journalists in the world and armoured vehicles were common enough. However, it took experienced eyes to recognise one, and Pedro's narrowed.

'Which newspaper did you say you work for?'

'I'm freelance.'

Pedro nodded. As I followed him inside I noticed he walked with a slight limp. He gave no further indication of disbelieving me about my car or profession and quickly changed the subject, asking me whether I was married and mentioning his own wife and newborn son. However, if he did harbour any suspicions they were well founded – I wasn't a true journalist. I'd written only one book. Since publishing *Marching Powder*, I'd travelled to Colombia, fallen in love with the country and decided to make it my home. I was now working as a manager of a US government counter-terrorism program in anti-kidnapping. The work was interesting and satisfying. I felt we were making a difference. But in a country with two terrorist organisations whose members numbered in the tens of thousands, it didn't pay to advertise my job.

The first group was the FARC Guerrilla. In the 1960s, peasant farmers took up arms, aiming to fight poverty and social inequality by toppling the government and installing communist rule. To fund their revolution, they 'taxed' businesses and kidnapped the rich, appropriating their lands for redistribution to the poor.

The second group – the Paramilitaries – was created in response. Wealthy land and business owners, tired of the government's failure to protect them, formed their own private militias and 'death squads'.

Despite my absorbing job in counter-terrorism, the writer in me had remained restless; I was always on the hunt for interesting stories. Meeting these former child soldiers might be my first step towards at least writing an article.

'These kids have been through so much,' Pedro told me as we entered the *albergue*. 'You simply can't imagine. Here, we don't refer to them by their group. They need to stop thinking of themselves as Guerrilla or Paramilitaries. So please don't ask them that question.'

Pedro ushered me down a long corridor, knocked on a door and then pushed it open.

The scene inside reminded me of school camp. In an unpainted dormitory sat seven boys and five girls on bunk beds. Aged from thirteen to seventeen, they were dressed in jeans, T-shirts and sneakers. It was impossible to distinguish them from ordinary teenagers, let alone know which side they'd belonged to. However, they clearly knew who was who, and didn't seem happy sleeping in the same room with others who, only a month earlier, would have gladly slit their throats.

They were even more mistrustful of journalists, especially white-skinned *gringo* interviewers like me.

I greeted them individually and ventured a few questions. Their responses were courteous but contained nothing of substance. They restricted themselves to shrugs and mumbles, answering, 'I don't know, *señor*,' while glancing nervously at their roommates.

I left the dormitory and walked out of the house with Pedro, deflated and discouraged.

'You could interview me,' he offered as we reached my car.

'About what?'

'I was in the Paramilitaries for two and a half years. As a commander. I went through this same program four years ago.'

Suddenly his confidence and expertise made sense. I'd been thrown by his demeanour, maturity and his mention of a wife and child. I hadn't conceived that Pedro himself might have been a child soldier. He definitely had my attention now.

'Why do you want to tell your story?'

'For the same reason I'm working here: to help. People need to understand the truth in order to heal their scars.' He touched his cheek. 'I'm one of the lucky ones. I should be dead – the Guerrilla almost killed me several times – and I went down a dark path myself.'

I raised my eyebrows.

'This limp I have.' He chuckled ironically, lifting his right foot and shaking it. 'That was my own doing. I shot myself in the foot to avoid being captured and tortured to death.'

I shared similar concerns about avoiding kidnap. However, among the many precautionary measures recommended in the US Embassy security briefing, shooting yourself wasn't one of them.

'But this scar right here.' Pedro tapped his fist to the left of his sternum. 'The one I have here in my heart is the only scar that hasn't truly healed. This scar you'll only understand by listening. And that will require more than just the article you want to write. It will require a book.'

'If you're willing to talk,' I said, 'I have time.'

We began our recorded interviews that afternoon. Very quickly, I realised I'd been wrong to characterise Pedro as 'typical'. At twenty-one he'd already led an incredible life, one so far removed from anything I could ever invent, and yet one so horrific that I would not wish it upon my worst enemy.

Eventually, witnessing Pedro's trust in me, other child soldiers from the *albergue* came forward and shared their stories.

Making sense of their experiences and putting them in coherent order was difficult. Most didn't want their names mentioned for fear of reprisals – against themselves or their families. They were from different provinces, from different groups, and they'd joined and left the war at different times. Mostly, they were ordinary boys and girls simply wanting to make sense of what they'd been through. But they all had one thing in common: they were trying to *salir adelante*. Trying to *move on* and put their pasts behind them. Just like their country.

I also realised the complexity of attempting to chronicle a conflict that had raged over four decades. Many times I questioned my right as an *extranjero* – an outsider – to pass comment on a beautiful country I loved that had already been deeply maligned and stereotyped.

The more emotionally involved I became with the child soldiers' stories, the harder I found it to maintain any pretence of journalistic objectivity. Ultimately, I decided to weave their stories into a novel.

Some parts of this story are real. Most parts are fictionalised and informed by my own experiences and historical research. These children's pasts were complicated and painful. Their stories affected me deeply and changed my life. I felt they needed to be told.

Rusty Young

PART ONE

LITTLE PEDRO

1

THEY CAME ON a Wednesday to execute my father.

Looking back, I should have sensed something amiss during morning Mass three days earlier. The new priest's maiden sermon had left the congregation divided – some bored, some irate – never a good omen in a small Colombian town.

When the congregation rose to leave, Señor Muñoz, the father of my girlfriend Camila, paused briefly in the aisle and leaned towards Papá.

'May I talk to you outside?' Glancing at me, he added, 'In private.'

I was fifteen years old and in adolescent limbo: not old enough to be included in adult discussions yet not young enough to run off and play. While the grown-ups talked, I stood shiftily on the church steps with Camila and my best friend, Palillo, waiting for them to finish.

Palillo, or 'Toothpick' – whose real name was Diego Hernandez – liked provoking trouble. And he liked pushing others into it, then running around them in figure eights like a dog in long grass.

He now draped his arms over our shoulders, placed his hands behind our heads and twisted them towards our fathers. They were deep in conversation, breaking only to scratch their chins and cast significant glances our way.

'*¡Pillado!*' Palillo declared gleefully. 'You two are so *busted*!'

'Don't listen to him, Pedro,' said Camila, shrugging out of Palillo's grip. 'If my father was going to snitch, he'd have said something to us first.'

Camila was a year younger than us and as magazine-beautiful as always, despite a hangover from the previous night. While Palillo made it his mission to stir up my life, Camila worked to reassure me. She had a magical way of protecting me from the world without criticising anyone else.

'They're staring at you, Pedro,' Palillo insisted.

'At *all* of us,' I countered.

I was prepared to accept my share of blame for the previous night's party, although it was Palillo who'd demanded we drive down to the rope-swing tree, and Palillo who'd produced a bottle of Cuban rum and pressured Camila to skol 'just one more shot' six more times.

'They're probably trying to figure out who buried Farmer Díaz,' Camila said, using her thumbs to smooth out the creases on my forehead. 'Or discussing the new priest's sermon. Wasn't it pathetic?'

She continued speculating. I continued frowning. I knew Camila's father held me in begrudging esteem. So long as I respected his curfews and his daughter's chastity, he would tolerate me.

The trouble was, I hadn't obeyed last night's curfew. Palillo had insisted Camila would be fine; they'd lined their stomachs with milk. He said he would take personal responsibility. But come ten o'clock, I was the one left with an inebriated girlfriend and battling a dilemma: drive her home on time but stumbling drunk, or wait until she was at least somewhat sober. From his window, Señor Muñoz had watched me pull up two hours late.

'Busted,' gloated Palillo, leaning right into my face and tickling my cheeks with his long, black fingers.

'Fuck it!' I said, slapping his hand away. 'I'm going over.'

'No fucking way! They'll crucify you.'

'Yes fucking way. Watch me!'

I hated people who refused to confront things. I strode towards our fathers, emboldened by the fact that Camila was watching.

'Good morning, Señor Muñoz.' I greeted Camila's father politely, shaking his hand.

'Pedro.' He nodded and forced a smile.

'Is something wrong, Papá?' I asked.

'We'll discuss it later, *hijo**.'

Both men now stared at me without blinking. Although vanquished by the adults, I returned victorious to my peers, who looked at me questioningly for my conclusion.

'Camila's father knows she was drinking but he didn't snitch,' I stated confidently.

'Told you!' said Camila.

'What exactly did they say?' asked Palillo flatly, folding his arms. I couldn't tell whether he was unconvinced or simply disappointed.

---

* see glossary

'It wasn't anything they said. I can just tell. They were discussing town business. It was *political.*'

Papá signalled that it was time to leave. I kissed Camila goodbye and drove us home. Mamá was with us, so Papá still couldn't mention what was wrong.

Papá's conversation with Señor Muñoz on the church steps that day was merely the latest in a series of warning signs that had begun gathering like slow-circling vultures over an injured animal. First, the 3.30 am cylinder bombs that had rained down on Llorona's main street a month earlier. Second, the clandestine night-time burial of Farmer Díaz, who'd been kidnapped and then murdered by the Guerrilla. And third, the bullet through the church's stained-glass window that had prompted the old priest's transfer to Bogotá for reasons of personal safety.

It was all big news. It was all connected. And it was all leading up to something bigger.

2

I'M NOT SURE how my parents managed to keep the war from me for so long, but they did.

Of course, I had a vague awareness of what was going on from rumours I heard at school, late-night gunfire that my parents claimed was thunder, and the strain in Mamá's farewell every time I rode my bicycle into town.

I knew that the Guerrilla existed. And I knew they fought the government army. During primary school recess, we played *soldado* and *guerrillero*, using sticks as guns and rocks as grenades. We drew blades of grass because nobody wanted to be a soldier.

According to my classmates, the *guerrilleros* were the good guys. In the countryside, they kidnapped wealthy landowners and distributed the ransom monies to peasant farmers. In cities, they tunnelled hundreds of metres underground into army stores to steal weapons and they hijacked milk trucks, whose bottles they dispensed to people in the slums.

I did my best to feign comprehension, but really, I didn't know what either side was fighting for. To me, the war was like the front-page headline of *El Tiempo*, the big-city newspaper that Papá read: although bold and important, its underlying events reached me from a great distance and only involved people I didn't know. It wasn't until my late childhood that I realised the war was all around me, and always had been.

Llorona was a small but prosperous river town set in a gentle valley in the Colombian province of Vichada. Further south was the Peruvian Amazon and further east, the mountains and jungles of Venezuela and Brazil. I'd lived there since the age of four when we lost everything and moved from Armero.

Llorona had a church, a bullet-pocked police garrison and a dusty football field that doubled as the primary school yard. The central plaza had four inward-facing wooden benches where old men sat feeding pigeons and playing checkers. Family-run stores were located along Avenida Independencia, the main street and the only one that was sealed. It was a small town, but a magnificent town, at least to my innocent eyes.

When I was ten, I tripped during a weekend game of *soldado* and *guerrillero* with Palillo in full pursuit. I sat rocking back and forth on my haunches, hugging my scraped shins and staring at the blood. Then I began picking the dirt out, cursing Palillo for causing the fall.

Papá intervened.

'Leave it!' he said. 'Stand up, *hijo*.'

As I stood, I pointed my favourite gun-stick at Palillo. Papá grabbed its tip and diverted my aim away as though it were a real weapon. He explained that war was not a game. For over a decade, he said, the Guerrilla had controlled the three river villages to the south of Llorona. The army controlled Garbanzos, the nearest major town. But Llorona was different. The army patrolled inside the town's perimeter; the Guerrilla controlled the surrounding countryside. Over the years, the warring sides had reached an informal truce: the Guerrilla didn't attack Llorona and the army didn't go looking for them or their camps. Our *finca*, or farm, was four kilometres from the plaza. As such, we lived in the grey area on the border between two enemies and had to contend with pressure from both groups.

After Papá's explanation, I began seeing things properly. I'd always thought the soldiers who crossed our land were from the army's battalion in Garbanzos. Some of them were, but others were members of the army's enemy, the communist Guerrilla. The army and Guerrilla looked similar. Both had short haircuts, wore green camouflage uniforms and hats, and carried rifles. Papá, who'd always told me to go inside whenever they came, now kept me next to him.

Up close, I learned to distinguish between them; the army soldiers wore shiny black leather boots whereas the Guerrilla wore rubber rain boots and were younger, and their squads included women. But both groups acted similarly. When an army patrol arrived, they would ask, 'Have you seen the Guerrilla?' When a Guerrilla patrol arrived, they would ask, 'Have you seen the army?' Both sides wanted to know the number of enemy troops, what weapons and provisions they carried, and what their commanders looked like.

When I was eleven, during spring cattle sales, I saw my father arguing with the Guerrilla finance commander, Zorrillo. I arrived for the end of the dispute and kept my mouth shut as I'd been taught. It ended with Papá handing over cash.

'Are they working for you?' I asked when Zorrillo's twelve-man squad had departed.

'Other way around,' he responded dryly. When angry, rather than yelling, Papá became sardonic.

He told me the Guerrilla requested that every farmer and business owner pay them a special tax to support their revolution, which would overthrow the corrupt government and replace it with a communist regime. They'd even enshrined it in their Guerrilla tax legislation, calling it Law 002. Unofficially, they referred to the tax as a *vacuna*, which literally means 'vaccine'.

'What are they vaccinating us against?'

'Their own bullets,' Papá replied.

It was from Papá that I inherited my sarcasm. Padre Rojas, the town priest and Papá's best friend, often said my father was a devout Catholic with the cynicism of an atheist.

Witnessing Papá being forced to pay the Guerrilla *vacuna* was an important moment for me. It was the first time I'd seen him back down. After that I snapped my gun-stick and stopped playing at war, and Papá no longer hid anything from me. I was already very close to my father, but our deep bond grew deeper as the Guerrilla expanded their territory, bringing them closer and closer to our farm.

During my last year at Llorona primary school, the Guerrilla made us attend a community meeting at which Zorrillo – the commander who'd forced Papá to hand over cash – pontificated on government corruption, social justice and equal rights for everyone.

'Llorona at least has phone lines and electricity,' declared Zorrillo. But five kilometres further south, in Puerto Galán, he reminded us, the lines stopped suddenly. There was no garbage collection. No police station. No courthouse. No hospital. Just dirt roads and wooden shacks with tin roofs. Another ten kilometres south, in Puerto Princesa, Guerrilla soldiers were forced to stand on street corners and arbitrate disputes. Across the river in Santo Paraíso, there were not even dirt roads. Only mud, donkey trails and a thriving cocaine industry.

Mamá didn't like me talking to the Guerrilla soldiers who crossed our land. She'd been protective of me ever since my older sister, Daniela, died in a mudslide when I was four. I don't remember my sister much; however, according to Papá, Mamá never got over it. She rarely mentioned

Daniela – and she'd taken down the framed photos since they were too painful a reminder – but sometimes I'd find her in the kitchen, standing stock-still and crying for no apparent reason.

The best policy for dealing with the Guerrilla, according to Mamá, was simply not to see anything, not to hear anything and certainly not to say anything. This was known as *La Ley de Silencio* – The Law of Silence. It prevailed in Llorona and most Colombian villages. The army had a similar name for it. They called it the Law of Shakira, after her pop song 'Deaf, Dumb and Blind'.

Papá disagreed. Some day I'd have to talk to them – better if I learned now. Besides, things were never as simple as Mamá wanted them to be. The army and the Guerrilla knew every family along their patrol routes. They asked questions about your neighbours – seemingly innocuous questions, like the last time relatives had visited them, when they'd picked their harvest, or how many shopping bags they brought home. And although it was tempting to respond 'I don't know' to every question, if a neighbour answered differently, one of you was a liar.

So it was best to be definite on facts but vague on details. In rural Colombia, *definite vagueness* was a full-time occupation. Papá advised me to always tell the truth, but to pause and think before answering. Because if you didn't pause before an easy answer like your name, then your pause after difficult questions would be more noticeable.

Both the army and the Guerrilla would ask if you had milk, rice, sugar or cooking oil to spare. Sometimes even water. They were extremely polite about it.

'If it's not too much trouble . . .' they might begin. As if compliance were voluntary and it was okay to refuse. But there is nothing voluntary about a favour when the man asking it is brandishing an AK47 with his finger tapping the trigger guard.

If you said, 'Sorry, I have nothing to spare,' they might search your property and prove you were lying. But if you gave them something and your neighbour snitched, the other side could accuse you of collaborating with the enemy.

Traitor if you do, liar if you don't. Either way you were completely *jodido*.

That's what you foreigners and people from the big cities don't understand. No matter how hard you try, you can't remain neutral. Eventually, you have to pick a side. And if you don't, one will be picked for you. As it was for me.

3

ON THE CHURCH steps, when Camila had mentioned the secret burial of Farmer Díaz, I'd struggled not to reveal that I knew who'd buried him.

A week earlier, Papá had tapped lightly on my door at midnight.

'You awake?' he whispered.

'*Sí.*'

'Get dressed quietly! Don't wake your mother.' Although sleepy, I leaped out of bed at his next words. 'I need your help.'

Danger and adventure didn't appeal to me as they did to Palillo. However, assisting Papá and sharing a secret with him did.

'Where are we going?' I asked, trying to sound casual.

'To do some work.'

'What kind of work?'

'The work of other men.'

Papá never criticised people directly; he said it was unchristian. Instead, he became cryptic. I had no idea what he meant by 'the work of other men'. It was only in the garage, when he placed a blue tarpaulin, two torches and a shovel in the tray of our Mazda utility truck, that I guessed what was happening: we were going to bury Farmer Díaz.

Our main industries in Llorona were agriculture, cattle farming and river trade. Fertile ground, strong rainfall and a semitropical climate made it ideal for bananas, granadillas and guanábanas. Llorona was a wealthy town, although, if you judged by appearances, no one had any money. Fear of kidnapping and extortionate 'vaccines' by the Guerrilla meant even millionaires pretended to be poor.

Wealthy landowners wore old, tattered clothes and patched holes in their shoes rather than buying new ones. They rarely spent money, not even on their families. Bank statements were sent to alternative mailboxes. Wives' jewellery could not be worn outside the house. Their adult children lived in large city apartments, drove luxury cars and attended private universities while they themselves drove rusted tin cans that broke down frequently in full public view. To prove how poor they were, they neglected to fix leaks in their roofs and then performed a wailing show for repairmen when handed a quote. In Colombia, hiding wealth was a national art form long before cocaine traffickers perfected it.

In certain individuals, like our neighbour Humberto Díaz, the threat of kidnapping brought out their inner miser. Although Díaz attended church, Papá had little time for him. He owned an interprovincial bus company and a thousand hectares of land with seven hundred head of cattle, but even before Guerrilla *vacunas* he had a reputation for adding dirt to potato sacks to increase their weight and using hollowed-out weights on his scales. When his labourers demanded their pay, he'd shrug and say, 'There's no money.' When they quit, he'd simply hire new workers and do the same.

Foolishly, Díaz maintained he couldn't pay the Guerrilla *vacuna*. As a compromise, they offered to accept livestock or crops instead, but he refused to hand over even a single calf, declaring that his cattle were mortgaged to the bank. The Guerrilla discovered that he was lying and sent a squad to surround his property.

'Commander Botero wants to talk to you,' said the squad leader, frog-marching him from his *finca*. 'Let's go!'

Jorge Emilio Botero was Zorrillo's official alias, which he used in written communications and when dealing with civilians. Zorrillo was his *apodo*, or nickname, used by his group and by brave locals behind his back.

Humberto Díaz wasn't even allowed to pack a change of clothes. That night the Guerrilla phoned his wife, Eleonora, to say they would hold him until she paid. Although Papá abhorred kidnapping, he said the Guerrilla had no choice. If enough people followed Díaz's lead, an unintended social class would be spawned – the *nouveau* poor – whose members deliberately understated their wealth for the sake of social appearances. Then where would we be?

Padre Rojas was right: for a serious-minded Catholic, Papá could be very sarcastic.

The Guerrilla started the bidding at a million dollars. Ransoms were often in US dollars. Although communists hated North Americans, at least their currency was stable. Rumours spread that Eleonora Díaz had refused to pay that amount, instead countering with one hundred thousand – further proof her husband's poverty was a sham. Usually, the Guerrilla would have kept him longer to negotiate a better price. Once holding a hostage, they were never in a hurry. But this time they responded by executing Díaz.

The Guerrilla normally buried their victims and told the family where to look. However, on this occasion they dumped the body and refused to say where. The army performed multiple searches. Finally, a fisherman spotted Díaz on the riverbank at the S-bend one kilometre up from the rope-swing tree. Everyone knew where he was, but no one went to retrieve him. His two adult sons, Javier and Fabián, were too scared.

When Papá heard the news, he stopped making jokes. He sat glumly at the dinner table, shaking his head. In a decades-long conflict, we had reached a new low: neither side had ever obstructed the burial of the dead.

Alive, Humberto Díaz was not a man whose company my father sought. Dead, however, Papá had no choice but to help him. His religious principles forbade him from leaving a member of the congregation unburied. So that's why we were driving to the river after midnight, armed with two torches, a blue tarpaulin and a shovel.

We found Díaz at the S-bend, where the fisherman had indicated. He was covered in flies and maggots. I wasn't squeamish, having slaughtered cows and seen dead bodies before, but I was disgusted at what the Guerrilla had done.

'Why not bury him here?' I asked as we rolled Díaz in the tarpaulin and dragged him back to the truck.

'Without proper Catholic burial in consecrated ground, a man has no possibility of entering heaven.'

From the way Humberto Díaz had acted on earth, I didn't fancy his chances anyway. But at least we'd give him a shot.

At 2 am we reached the church cemetery. I held the torch while Papá broke the earth. Perspiring as he dug, he wiped his brow repeatedly. Several times I held out my hand for the shovel but he removed his shirt and waved me away. In the pale, flickering torchlight his muscles were like strips of rope under a sheet.

'Cowards,' he muttered as the digging got the better of him. 'Cowards!'

At first I thought he meant the Guerrilla for killing Humberto Díaz and not disclosing his whereabouts.

'Cowards!' he said again, and only then did I realise he was referring to Díaz's sons. Javier and Fabián were in their twenties. They should have been the ones doing this.

We lowered the body into the grave. Papá handed me the shovel. Pleased that I could finally help, I began scooping dirt back in.

'No!' he whispered, gesturing that he'd meant for me to take the shovel and tarpaulin to the truck.

Papá rapped quietly on the priest's door but returned without waiting for it to open. It was important that Humberto Díaz be commended to God. But it was also important that Padre Rojas could deny seeing whoever had dropped off the body. Papá didn't think anything would happen to the priest. At that stage of the war, the armed groups were still feigning respect for the church.

With Díaz's body out of our vehicle, the danger had passed. Papá tossed me the car keys. We arrived home safely. No one had seen us and no one saw Padre Rojas conducting the burial. We'd gotten away with it. Almost.

4

THERE WAS NO proof of who had retrieved Díaz's body, but people speculated. Every time the rumour that he was now in the cemetery came up, I feigned ignorance whilst tingling at the dangerous, shared secret that bonded me with Papá. At lunch, when Mamá mentioned it, Papá peered over his newspaper and suggested she lay flowers on the grave on behalf of Díaz's wife and sons, who'd now fled to the city. He didn't even glance at me. He didn't have to. I was his midnight accomplice and his midday vault.

But the Guerrilla knew for certain that Padre Rojas was involved. They would never dream of digging up a body – in those days, they were godless but not depraved. Instead, they sent an emissary, Ratón, to question the priest. Aged in his mid-twenties, he was a rat-faced commander with a pointy nose and thin, triangular ears. Padre Rojas informed Ratón that someone had knocked on his door at around 3 am and he'd come out to find the body already half-buried.

'I don't believe you,' declared Ratón.

'I'm not lying.'

'You're not telling the whole truth either.'

'I'll leave that for God to decide,' the priest said, peremptorily closing the presbytery door.

Ratón blocked it with his foot.

'Who helped you, old man?'

'God,' responded Rojas. 'And that's Padre to you, son.'

Never one to dip his words in honey, the Padre already had strained relations with both the Guerrilla and army. He was like the town's moral conscience; he pronounced judgments from the pulpit that everyone knew would never be enforced, but that they liked to hear anyway. In sermons, he never mentioned culprits by name, although he came razor close.

'Those parties responsible for kidnapping Lara Benítez,' he might say, 'should return her immediately to where she belongs.' Then he would adjust his reading glasses and peer over them before booming into the microphone, '*With her family.*' And everyone would know because he'd said 'those parties' and not '*that* party' that his message was intended for the Guerrilla units. But Rojas was equally unforgiving of the army. In response to their illegal searches and roughing up of peasant farmers at gunpoint to gain apparent confessions, he said, 'Those persons who falsely accuse, should refer to the eighth commandment, in which Moses was told not to bear false witness . . .'

As a priest with community influence, Padre Rojas was given religious leeway by both sides. Nevertheless, he was poking his tongue into beehives. Then a Guerrilla mortar bomb, aimed towards the police station, went astray by five blocks, crashing through the church roof and exploding in the aisle. Luckily, it was 3.30 am and no one was inside.

Señor Muñoz and my father led the work party to repair the damage. Extension ladders and labourers were borrowed from our *finca*. Even Colonel Buitrago, the head of the Garbanzos army battalion, came to show community support. On hands and knees, he patiently removed metal shards from the pews using tweezers, then relacquered them while Papá cut out the singed segment of carpet and dragged another section across to cover the gap.

After Colonel Buitrago and his twelve-man security contingent departed, the rodent-faced Ratón walked in, flanked by three bodyguards from the *Milicia Bolivariana* – the Guerrilla's plain-clothed urban militia that was in charge of their logistics, intelligence, recruitment and community liaison. He apologised for the mishap and offered compensation. Padre Rojas accepted the apology but refused their cash. Ratón eyed him fatally.

Then, two weeks after the cylinder bomb, we buried Humberto Díaz and Ratón visited Padre Rojas a second time. After slamming the presbytery door, the priest was sent a formally worded threat typed under official Guerrilla letterhead:

In furtherance of the mutual respect and esteem the church and the Guerrilla have for each other's humanitarian work carried out for the good of the people, the FARC Guerrilla hereby advises that further interference in our affairs will not be tolerated.

Daniel Joaquim Gómez, Comandante, 34th Unit

Daniel Gómez was Ratón's alias. A muffled phone call followed, demanding Padre Rojas leave town. He didn't. Finally, a single 9mm round was fired through the stained-glass windows. Rojas was obliged to inform the Bogotá diocese of any material event that affected the security of its personnel. The bullet was, as they say in these parts, the final drop that caused the cup to overflow. Padre Rojas was recalled to the capital, effective immediately. His maid could pack and send his belongings.

We did not know who the new priest would be, just as we did not know that one brave man leaving a town's decade-long tug of war would permit even greater acts of cowardice.

In a Catholic town where everyone knew the Bible by heart, the new priest's arrival stirred expectations. Padre Rojas would be a tough act to follow. The new priest certainly looked the part. Where Rojas had worn pleated pants and collared shirts, Guzmán wore a white robe and coloured sashes that contrasted with his thick, jet-black hair. He ascended the pulpit with pomp and solemnity and raised his chubby, porcelain-white hands in the air, ready to inspire a tumult of passion. Some anticipated the *eye-for-an-eye* sermon to provoke the government army into action. Some wanted Matthew's *turn-the-other-cheek* sermon in order to calm the situation. At the very least, we all expected a simple restatement of community values.

Instead, the weak-chinned Padre Guzmán opted for *love-thy-neighbour* in times of trouble. That might have worked in the big city, where not knowing your neighbours made it easier to love them. But in a town of four thousand people it fooled no one.

Bored and disappointed, the congregation spilled through the mahogany doors grumbling about the new priest. He'd already made the women irate by firing the presbytery maid, a local girl. He'd brought his own *mulata* maid with him from the city. In the car on the way home, even Mamá got in on the criticising.

'It's not because of her colour,' she said. 'I'm not a racist. You know I have no problem with Palillo coming to our house. But that *mulata* girl is *half his age.*' She whispered this last part. Mamá still tried to have coded conversations in front of me. She was referring to the *mulata*'s massive bosom and the fact that she was remarkably pretty.

'I think it's best not to judge until you know her story,' Papá said tersely. He was unusually tense that day.

'Let's not fight, *amor*,' said Mamá, resting her hand gently on his knee. 'I know how much you miss him.'

Most people don't think of priests as having dear friends. However, Padre Rojas and Papá were truly close. Before leaving for the capital, the priest had ridden his red motorbike to our *finca* to shake Papá's hand a final time. They nodded and exchanged pocket bibles.

'There goes a brave man,' my father said, and I never doubted it.

As we watched Padre Rojas recede from view, I looked skyward and a raindrop splattered onto my nose.

'Big change coming through,' said my father without looking up.

He was right. Until then, the changes had been gradual. However, the Guerrilla bombing of our town represented a significant shift. It meant their informal truce with the army had ended. The threats against the priest and the bullet through the stained-glass window were another tectonic shift – the church was no longer sacred. Not burying the dead was another step towards the abyss. And finally, Padre Rojas's departure itself caused a collective mood change. Ripping away a man profoundly attached to his community is like tearing a long stitch from a pullover. When that stitch is one on which all other threads depend, things behind him begin to unravel.

Anyhow, that was how I grew up until the age of fifteen. It was how many kids grew up in small Colombian towns. You tried not to see, hear or speak of things around you. Sometimes, it was best not to even think.

For the most part, that strategy worked.

Between the army and the Guerrilla, tensions flared up, then died down. One side advanced; the other retreated. The war was like a slow-burning campfire onto which both sides occasionally threw wood. And that's probably the way it would have continued, if not for the arrival of the Autodefensas.

5

ON THE FRIDAY afternoon two days before our conversation on the church steps, Camila raced up to the grain store where I was buying cattle pellets and clinked a coin against the window. I waved for her to come inside. She waved for me to come out.

'I've been looking for you everywhere,' she wheezed. 'Palillo's gone!'

'Gone where?'

Biting her lip, she looked up and down Avenida Independencia then whispered, 'With the *duros*.'

In Llorona, we didn't call them Autodefensas or Paramilitaries, or even *paras* or *paracos* like they did in newspapers. They were simply *los duros* – the hard men. The *duros* were the archenemy of the Guerrilla. Fearsome hit squads committed to wiping out communism, they'd been founded in cities and worked their way into towns and villages, then outwards into the mountains where Guerrilla bases were located. Recently, their recruiters had arrived in Garbanzos. In other parts of Colombia, it was an open secret that the Paramilitaries worked hand in hand with the army. In fact, there was speculation their leaders *were* the army.

'Shit!' I raced for the Mazda.

Camila followed. 'I'm coming with you.'

'What if someone sees you? Your dad will kill you.'

'Palillo's my friend too.'

I drove quickly. Palillo had wanted to join the army since he was seven. I remember his arrival at our primary school; it was the week before our tests, a strange time to be changing schools. He was also the first boy to volunteer to play the soldier in our game of war.

'Why do you want to be on the army's side?' I'd asked provocatively.

'Why not?' he retorted, sucking air into his lungs and stepping forward. 'It's good practice for eliminating Guerrilla.'

I called him a *fascista*. We fought. He knocked me to the ground. When he offered me his hand too quickly, I realised he'd gone easy on me and was giving me a way out. Once I accepted his hand, he hoisted me to my feet, hugged me and said softly so no one would overhear, 'Now we can be friends.'

Palillo hailed from the coastal port of Turbo. His father had been a boat captain. His mother made Palillo tell everyone he had drowned in a riverboat collision. But really, he'd been murdered by the Guerrilla for defying a ban on shipping medical supplies to Indian villagers. The family was ordered to leave Turbo.

His mother took up with a visiting mechanic, Diomedes Murillo, and they moved twenty-nine hours inland to Llorona, where Diomedes discovered a far more lucrative profession: picking the leaves from coca plants to be used in cocaine production.

Coca crops were grown in the mountains south of Santo Paraíso. Harvesting them four times a year required casual labourers who worked ten-hour days to strip the small, rounded leaves from the shrubs. It was gruelling, sweaty work in the roasting sun, but since the crops were illegal, the leaf pickers – known as *raspachines* – could earn a year's wage in a month.

On payday, when his stepfather got drunk, a skinny Palillo would follow him home on his bicycle.

'*¡Lárguese!*' warned Diomedes, his fist bulging. 'Get the hell outta here.'

But Palillo maintained a safe distance, hoping Diomedes would give chase and use up energy. As he got bigger, Palillo let himself get caught so Diomedes would take everything out on him instead of his mother. However, when his stepfather wised up to this, Palillo would be sent outside, from where he'd watch, seething, through the window. He thought maybe a witness might save his mother some trouble, even if the witness was just a kid. But it never did.

Hoping I'd have a better idea, he requested I join his vigil. We rattled bins and made a ruckus until Diomedes came thundering out like a bull.

'You kids scram!'

When Palillo turned nine, Diomedes decided his stepson needed a job. Children were often employed as *raspachines* since their nimble fingers were more adept at stripping the leaves. For two weeks, Palillo didn't turn up for school. His stepfather had taken him deep into the mountains and forced him to pick coca leaves until his fingers bled.

When Palillo's mother found out, she marched Palillo back to school by the ear. This earned her another beating, but she was adamant: no child of hers would participate in the drug trade.

Palillo hated the Guerrilla for causing his father's death. And since his father's death had caused his stepfather's arrival, he hated them even more. Not to mention how much he hated them for causing his move to Llorona. He said it was a shitty town with shitty people, where there was nothing to do except smoke cigarettes. He wanted out. But boys in Llorona knew there were only two ways to leave town – the Guerrilla or the army. Eighteen was the minimum age to join the army; Palillo had already presented himself twice at the gates of the army barracks, claiming to have lost his birth certificate, to no avail. Now, with the arrival of the Paramilitaries in Garbanzos, there was a third option.

The Paramilitaries had no minimum age; you simply had to be big enough to carry a pack and fire a rifle. Those who left rarely returned to Llorona – it was too dangerous if the Guerrilla found out – although some had been sighted in Garbanzos. They now cruised around in four-wheel drives or rode motorbikes. They wore new sneakers and jeans with the latest cell phones hooked to their belts. Under their shirts, many concealed pistols. They drank beer in public plazas. Their parents no longer told them what to do. Pretty girls pointed at them. Older men avoided them. They had respect.

'You'll get yourself killed,' I warned Palillo when he mentioned joining.

He shrugged. 'Better to die from a bullet than boredom.'

'You don't really mean that.'

'Easy for you to say.'

Although my family wasn't wealthy, the fact we owned land made us rich by Palillo's standards. Since I'd refused to enlist, he was waiting for me to realise there was no future in Llorona. But that Friday he must have grown tired of waiting. Camila's best friend, Carolina, had seen him boarding the *colectivo* to Garbanzos half an hour before, carrying a bulging backpack with tent poles poking out.

'There he is!' said Camila as we parked by the fruit juice stand in the central plaza. Palillo was sitting at a plastic table with three men. 'What are we going to do?'

'Wait in the car,' I ordered. Then I softened. 'I won't be a minute. Honk if you need me.'

'What are *you* going to do?' she asked, folding her arms grumpily.

'No idea.'

Palillo's beer arrived just as I did, which meant he hadn't been there long.

'Sorry I'm late,' I said, slapping him on the back and sitting down. I recognised two of his three companions – they'd attended my high school before dropping out. A couple of years above me, they now looked far older than seventeen.

'I'm Pedro,' I said, leaning forward and extending my hand to the third – a huge, cinder block of a man with a mean squint, who was known as El Tigre. He shook my hand and raised his eyebrows at Palillo, who hadn't mentioned a friend coming along.

'He's cool,' Palillo said without looking at me, and there was a pause while El Tigre studied me. With the waiter hovering, he couldn't ask questions.

'Drink, Pedro?'

I nodded. These were not people you wanted to offend. Besides, I needed El Tigre to think I was genuine. Eyes locked on me, he ordered another beer. The can hissed open and he slid it across. I took a tiny sip and, when the waiter stopped loitering, spoke quickly.

'Palillo said there was a job opportunity. Would you mind giving us more details before we decide?'

El Tigre again looked at Palillo – he'd believed they had a done deal. But he said nothing, instead nodding to his underlings. I listened courteously to their vague proposition. They called it 'work' – we would live on a *finca* and all food would be paid for – although they did not make clear what duties were entailed.

'I'd like to think about it, if that's okay?' I said, prodding Palillo under the table. 'I think we both need some time. Palillo, you need a lift back?' I stood gingerly.

El Tigre's eyes narrowed. He slapped the table. 'Wait!'

I sat back down.

'Take this phone number for when you're ready.'

Relieved, I took the business card – *Don Jerónimo's Taxi Service* – stood once more and shook hands effusively with El Tigre at precisely the moment a car horn honked twice. My eyes shot to the Mazda to see Camila surreptitiously sinking below window level. Scanning the plaza, I saw the blue Ford truck belonging to my Uncle Leo – Mamá's brother – swing into view. My stomach churned. Leo drove past slowly, pretending not to see me. But of course he had.

All the way home Palillo sat tensely in the back seat, a lit cigarette jutting from his lips like a smouldering fuse.

'At least open the window,' I said, not wanting Papá to smell the smoke.

'Thanks, Super-Pedro, you're my hero,' he responded, imitating the high-pitched voice of a rescued maiden. 'Now I can go back to our shitty town.'

'It's not that shitty.'

'Damn right it is,' said Camila, reaching for Palillo's cigarette. I didn't contradict her because I knew she was showing solidarity with Palillo as a reward for his not joining. Besides, I didn't want to upset her; she'd recently promised to sleep with me on my sixteenth birthday.

I bit my bottom lip and drove. It seemed everyone wanted to leave Llorona, and they wanted *me* to leave too. Palillo wanted me to join the Paramilitaries. As for Camila, she wanted to study fine arts in Bogotá. We'd been dating for two years but already she'd mapped out our lives. Top of her grade, she was going to university. If her family couldn't afford the tuition fees, we'd run away and live in a studio apartment in the capital, catch a bus to work in the morning, cook dinner over a tiny stove and scrimp and save for utility bills.

'This town is so *dull*, don't you think?' she'd say. 'We need a magic carpet.'

Back then, thinking of the city gave me stomach knots, as though I'd drunk too much coffee. Millions of strangers, rushing around impatiently. Skyscrapers of steel and glass, multi-lane highways and everything sold in plastic. Buses and red trams with turnstiles, traffic lights and pedestrian crossings. Things I'd only seen on television.

The tallest structure in Llorona was the church, which was three storeys high. I'd never ridden an escalator or an elevator. But Camila yearned for the city, and the prospect of her going without me gave me just as many stomach knots.

Even my parents wanted me to leave. They'd pressed me to sign a student loan application to study business when I became eligible for early graduation in a year.

'You'll be the first person in our family to go to university,' Papá told me.

'You'd make us so happy,' added Mamá. 'We'd be extremely proud.'

When you truly love your parents, there's not much you can say to that. I swallowed my disagreement. In the meantime, however, I was hedging my bets, studying hard enough to not look stupid, but not so hard that they'd think I was academic. So far, it was working. Every year, my teacher wrote in my report card that I needed to apply myself more but I *had potential.*

I liked having potential. Potential is good. As long as it stays as potential and doesn't get you accidentally admitted into university.

We dropped off Camila, and then I drove Palillo home. 'I guess I'll see you tomorrow,' I said.

Palillo could pretend to be mad for several hours, but I knew deep down he was grateful that I'd cared enough to stop him.

'Aren't you forgetting something?' He held out his hand.

I sighed and gave him the business card for *Don Jerónimo's Taxi Service*.

We may have rescued him temporarily, but he was still determined to join. I suspected that his getting drunk at the rope-swing tree with Camila the following night was his way of bidding us farewell. If I didn't find a reason for Palillo to stay, I'd lose him forever.

During our Friday night phone call, Camila suggested I find him a job. That's what I wanted to talk to Papá about that Sunday after church when we set off to go fishing, as we did every week.

On the river Papá was usually at his most approachable. But as we dragged the dinghy to the water's edge, I could tell he was still brooding over his earlier conversation with Señor Muñoz on the church steps. Brooding and fuming like I'd never seen him before.

6

ALTHOUGH PAPÁ WAS silent as I rowed, his lips moved, a sure sign he was composing a speech. We had several fishing spots along the river – some on the outer bends where fast-flowing currents brought nutrients that attracted fish, others in calmer stretches behind rock formations or mossy logs. Papá's fishing rod was a family heirloom. It had a varnished cedar reel seat, a cork grip and a shaft made of finely cut cane strips into which three sets of initials were burned: Papá's, his father's and his grandfather's. My own initials would be added on my sixteenth birthday. Until then, I'd have to content myself with a plastic hand reel.

I drew the bow of the dinghy up to a partly submerged fallen tree and secured it with a rope. We both cast and paid out the lines until they went slack and then we drew them up a little so the bait rested just above the bottom.

The sun sat high in the sky, its rays sparkling off the water. Papá leaned back with his elbow resting on the dinghy's side, steeped in private thoughts. From time to time, the sun ducked behind one of the high clouds and the resulting shadow sent a shiver up my spine and made the hairs on my arms stand on end.

Two hours passed like that, and I'd almost convinced myself that I'd been wrong about Papá's mood when finally he spoke.

'Anything you want to tell me, Pedro Juan?'

He only called me by my full name when a lecture was pending. Whatever Señor Muñoz had told him, he was trying to tease it out of me, like baiting an eel from its nest.

'No, sir.'

'Anything you think you *should* tell me?'

I hated that question. Rather than fishing with a rod, it was like using a net. He could just throw it out and pull in confessions about crimes he'd never even suspected.

'Nothing I can think of.'

Papá's voice hardened. 'What in Christ's name were you doing in Garbanzos plaza? Out in the open where everyone could see?'

It took me a moment to realise he was referring to Friday afternoon, when I'd gone to rescue Palillo from the recruiters.

'It was only half a beer, Papá. I didn't even finish—'

'I'm not talking about drinking, Pedro. Who were you *with*?'

Of course I couldn't mention Palillo or Camila.

'Old school friends.'

'Those boys are not your friends,' he said sternly. 'They're *killers*. They kill people!'

'I wasn't going to join. I swear I would *never* join.'

'Palillo can look after Palillo.'

'But I thought I'd never see him again!' I said, relieved that Papá had guessed my reason for going to the plaza. 'He's looking for any work he can get.'

'No *buts*, Pedro Juan. Did you ever stop to think how other people might view our family after what you did?'

'Why do you care what people think of us?'

'What I care about is this family! I care about the consequences for *this family* if people see you drinking publicly with killers. *Think*, Pedro! What happened three weeks ago? *Think!* What did we do last weekend? *Think!* What happened last August to Ariel Mahecha's father?'

Three weeks ago, we'd fixed the church roof after the stray mortar. Last weekend, we'd buried Humberto Díaz. The previous August, the Guerrilla had killed Ariel's father for being a *sapo*. *Sapo* literally means 'toad'. But it also means 'snitch' since both toads and snitches talk too much.

'But, Papá! I didn't tell them anything! All I said was—'

'What you did or didn't say doesn't matter. These men speak with bullets. You risked all our lives.'

Suddenly, I felt ten years old – the same age I'd been when Papá told me not to play at war. I bowed my head, waiting for more, but Papá stood, using my shoulder to balance while he untied the rope and pushed us out into the slipstream.

'Change seats,' he said. 'You row.'

It was the longest row of my life. We sat opposite each other in silence. Papá stared fixedly at a point on the bank. My own gaze remained locked on the transom. Papá was absolutely right. I'd put myself and my family in danger. The Guerrilla often killed innocent people to send messages to their enemy and anyone watching. To them, we civilians were like ping-pong balls they smashed back and forth at each other. It didn't matter that I had no intention of joining. Just by speaking to El Tigre, I'd risked being branded a *sapo*.

On the other hand, if Palillo had joined, he might have ended up dead. Papá had taught me that we have an obligation to others – to our friends, to people less fortunate, even to our enemies and sinners. Isn't that why we'd risked our lives to bury Humberto Díaz? Didn't we have an obligation to protect people from danger?

It was now the magical dusk hour, when the sun sank behind the mountains, the shadows of trees drooped across the river and the jungle came to life. Swarms of insects skimmed over the water's surface, bringing schools of fish up from the river depths. From time to time, a baitfish flew into the air, tail still flapping, its silver scales flashing momentarily in the fading light.

I barely registered any of this. Instead I felt the trembling of my hands on the oars as they made jittery strokes. My father's gritted words – *you risked all our lives* – felt like a brand seared unexpectedly on a calf by its kindly master.

By the time we reached the Mazda, Papá's silence was so deafening I felt like I'd committed murder.

'I'm sorry, Papá. I didn't think.'

He spread his arms wide. 'Come here.' He gave me a hug. 'I shouldn't have yelled at you. But you need to learn you can't force a man into doing right. He has to work it out for himself. Until he does, the best you can do is keep your own house in order.'

Although happy that our fight was ended, I pressed him softly.

'He's my best friend, Papá.'

Papá sighed. It was his *okay-I-surrender* sigh.

'Edgar is leaving on the first of December. Provided Palillo's mother lets him drop school, he can have Edgar's job on minimum wage. No leave until twelve months. And tell him *no drinking*!' Papá pinched my ear playfully. 'That goes for you too.'

7

THAT NIGHT, ON the phone with Camila, I resolved two mysteries: who had snitched on me, and Papá's strange conversation with Señor Muñoz at church. Rather than coming to me directly, or even going to Papá, my cowardly Uncle Leo had told Señor Muñoz he'd seen me with the Paramilitary recruiters. Señor Muñoz then had little choice but to inform Papá.

'Forgive him, Pedro,' said Camila. 'He was in a tough position.'

Señor Muñoz I could pardon. But I was livid at my uncle.

At forty-two, Uncle Leo was still a bachelor. Despite a paunch and baldness, he fancied himself as a Colombian Don Juan. Papá, being a strict Catholic who opposed sex before marriage, expressed his disapproval with subtle sarcasm.

'I don't know why your brother doesn't marry,' he'd once commented quietly to Mamá. 'He's certainly interviewed enough candidates.'

I asked Camila, 'Were you seen in the plaza too?'

'No,' she cooed, now grateful I'd made her stay in the Mazda. 'I owe my hero big time.'

'Bring forward my present?' Her virginity on my sixteenth birthday.

'*Amor*, March is only four months away.'

'Three months and twenty-six days.'

'Someone's counting.' She laughed and we said goodnight.

I awoke on Monday determined to triumph at mathematics because it would make Papá proud. Naturally, Palillo hadn't studied.

'I can count just fine,' he proclaimed. 'And I can do decimal fractions.'

Pointing at a group of girls, he scored their faces. 'Eight-point-two. Three-point-seven. Nine-point-one. Plus I can do size estimates.' His gaze moved lower. '32B. 30A. 34D.'

Palillo was determined never to be serious. *Never.* His real dream was to be an actor. He wanted to play the forbidden *negro* love interest in TV soap operas. I told him to be realistic – no black actors appeared on TV, except the washerwoman who does the soap powder commercials.

'Exactly,' retorted Palillo. 'There's a job vacancy. And I'm going to fill it.'

'In the meantime, perhaps if you took that *real* job you've been offered.'

I explained Papá's proposition and Palillo's face lit up. He began making a list of what he'd buy with his first paycheque: Nike shoes, Discman, gold chain, and Nokia cell phone. By 'pens down' he'd added twenty more items and was in debt until mid-next-century.

Having diverted Palillo's focus from joining the Paramilitaries, I felt relieved. The following day, Tuesday, I drove our Mazda to the garage for repair with my bicycle in the tray and then pedalled to my science exam.

On Wednesday, I woke to my alarm at 5.45 am, feeling good about that afternoon's geography exam, and crept barefoot to the kitchen to prepare Papá's morning *tinto.* I milked the cows beside Papá, and then spent two hours studying.

Just before noon, Papá walked me to the gate where I'd leaned my bicycle.

'Good luck with geography!' He pulled me into a hug. With my chin on his shoulder and my eyes closed, I felt that he'd fully forgiven me for being seen with the Paramilitaries in the plaza. Coming out of the hug, however, I tensed at the sight of several Guerrilla soldiers fanning out across our yard.

The cylinder bomb. Humberto Díaz's burial. The bullet through the stained-glass window and Palillo's recent attempt to join the Paramilitaries.

All big news. All connected. And all leading up to this moment.

8

THE TWO CLOSEST soldiers had their AK47s pointed at me and Papá. The rest crouched, their rifles scanning in arcs. I recognised none of them and knew from their grim expressions that this was no ordinary visit.

At first, I counted twelve *guerrilleros*: two covering us, four under the oak tree, four near the shed and two at opposite ends of the fence. Then I saw more soldiers in surrounding paddocks. And more still, hidden back near the edge of the forest. I'd never seen so many in one place. There must have been thirty or forty.

'What do I do, Papá?' I whispered, convinced it was me they'd come for. Papá must have thought the same. He looked alarmed.

'Stay close,' he said, pushing me behind him. 'Let me do the talking.'

When their point guard signalled, a group of ten more *guerrilleros* emerged from behind the shed.

'Name?' demanded a thickset boy with blond hair and piercing green eyes – rarities in a country of mixed Indian-Hispanic descent.

'Mario Jesús Gutiérrez Molina,' answered Papá.

'ID card, please.'

'Your commander knows who I am,' Papá said, nodding to the shed where he'd recognised Ratón. As head of the Guerrilla's urban militia, he normally wore civilian clothes. That day, however, he was in uniform and carrying a heavy Motorola radio.

'He's not in charge,' said the boy.

'Who is then?'

'Me.' A scowling, chimneystack of a man with arms as thick as saplings stepped from behind him. 'Know who I am?'

Papá nodded and handed over his *cédula*.

It was Caraquemada. It had to be. We'd never seen him in the flesh, but his horribly disfigured face was famous throughout the region. The left half of it looked like it had been eaten away by acid. A thin flap of skin half-covered a glass eye.

Papá averted his eyes politely. 'How can I help you, *señor?*'

Caraquemada glanced towards me. 'Your son . . .' he began, and my heart stood still. They were going to take me! 'Send him inside.'

I could breathe again. And my tension diminished further when I saw Zorrillo. Although three commanders in one place meant something big, Ratón and Zorrillo could vouch to Caraquemada that Papá had never given them any trouble.

But then Mamá ran out of the house, screaming. I later learned that, from her kitchen window, she'd seen our three farmhands tied up and led away. When four rifles were pointed at her, she froze and her hands shot into the air. As Papá moved to protect her, the blond boy raised his rifle.

'Go inside, Pedro,' Papá ordered. 'Take your mother with you.'

I remained riveted to the spot.

'What's all this about?' Papá demanded of Zorrillo. 'We paid last Wednesday.'

However, Zorrillo pretended not to know him. Stepping forward, he handed a written sheet to Caraquemada, who crosschecked it against Papá's *cédula*.

'Mario Jesús Gutiérrez Molina, you are charged with supplying the government army.'

Papá laughed – convinced there had been an error – and pushed the rifle tip away.

'That's not true.' But when the blond boy thrust it back, Papá sounded less confident. 'Supplying them with what?'

'Water.'

Papá sucked in air. I stood paralysed with disbelief. In a lawless, war-torn land where extortion, kidnapping and murder were rife, being accused of giving away water was like being fined for littering during a hurricane.

'Do you wish to speak in your defence?' Caraquemada asked.

Papá could have denied it, or claimed the army lieutenant had given him no choice. But he had the nerve of a bullfighter. Rather than lie, he defended his principles.

'It is a sin to deny a thirsty man water. You and your men are also welcome to drink from my pipes.'

Caraquemada took this as an admission.

'Please accompany us for further investigation.' His tone was businesslike, as though Papá had the option to refuse. But Caraquemada's face told another story.

'I will do no such thing.' Papá must have known that they'd already decided his fate. Once he'd admitted the offence, there was no need for further investigation.

Caraquemada handed the *cédula* to Ratón and nodded. The Motorola radio was on high volume as Ratón called through my father's details to their superior – yes, the prisoner's identity was confirmed, but the prisoner was refusing to co-operate. After a delay, a woman's voice responded: 'By order of Comandante Santiago of the Revolutionary Armed Forces of Colombia . . . *¡Ajustícialo!*'

I stood frozen with shock, believing I'd heard incorrectly.

Picking at his fingernails using my father's *cédula*, Ratón repeated the order as though he were relaying a weather forecast. 'Execute him.'

'The prisoner will kneel,' ordered Caraquemada.

'No! Stop!' I yelled. 'It's me you want.'

'Shut your fucking trap, Pedro!' snapped Papá. 'I said take your mother inside.'

Papá had never spoken to me like that. His white knuckles wrapped around his pocket Bible and his mouth would barely open. 'Please. Not in front of my family.'

Caraquemada nodded to the blond bodyguard. 'Take them inside.'

Two female *guerrilleras* bundled Mamá into the house. Sobbing, she offered no resistance. But when the blond boy motioned for me to follow, I backed away. He lunged for me, but I ducked out of his grasp.

'Come here, you little *bastardo*!' he hissed.

'The prisoner will kneel,' Caraquemada repeated, trying to shove my father down by the shoulder.

Papá raised his chin. 'I'll remain standing.'

Seeing Caraquemada draw his pistol, I dived forward desperately, aiming to grab it. But the blond boy crash-tackled me. Overpowered, I was pinned flat on my stomach with his knee grinding my cheek into the ground. I thrashed beneath him, scratching at his arms to make him get off. But he was too strong. And with my head immobilised, I was forced to watch every excruciating moment.

Still clutching his pocket Bible, Papá began reciting the Lord's Prayer.

'Our Father, who art in heaven, hallowed be thy name . . .'

The first time Caraquemada circled Papá, he paused to swat a fly. Then he continued with the stiff, legalistic language communists used to demonstrate they were fair.

'Mario Gutiérrez, you are hereby accused of the offence of material collaboration with the army of the Oligarchy, the natural enemy of the people. You have confessed your crime against the people's revolution, and therefore, by the power vested in me by the Revolutionary Armed Forces of Colombia, you are hereby sentenced to the maximum penalty.'

'Please, no!' I begged. 'He's done nothing wrong!'

On the second circle around, Caraquemada's good eye narrowed as he chose a spot at the base of Papá's skull. Papá ceased his prayers, looked at me and yelled, 'Close your eyes, Pedro!'

But I couldn't tear my gaze away. Unable to move, I begged God to intervene and save Papá.

On the third time around, Caraquemada raised the pistol and touched his finger to the trigger.

Papá cried out, 'Look after your mother.'

'No. No. No!' I screamed, bucking desperately from the ground. But Caraquemada fired. I heard the hollow pop of the pistol and watched my father's head jerk suddenly. Then he teetered on his feet for an impossibly long time before tilting forward slowly like a tree dealt its final axe-blow.

'Let's move out!' ordered Caraquemada, turning away.

How strange, I thought, that Papá did not try to break his fall. His knees buckled and I heard Mamá wailing as she dashed from the house, and then a terrible crack as Papá's skull struck the hard, dry earth.

9

'WAIT!' CALLED THE blond boy. 'What do I do with this one?'

I was still writhing beneath him, struggling with all my might to free myself so I could reach Papá. Tears blurred my vision.

After what seemed an eternity, Zorrillo returned. 'Feisty little bastard, aren't you?' he said, stroking his rifle along my cheek. 'How old are you?'

I barely heard him. Papá's blood was seeping slowly into the dirt. I had to get to him.

'How old?' he repeated, digging his rifle tip hard into my cheek, grinding it against my teeth until I tasted blood.

Unable to contain my rage, I spat blood onto his pants. 'Fifteen.'

Zorrillo's eyes turned murderous. However, to kill me he required authorisation from the *Secretariado*. Snatching Ratón's radio handset, he spoke into the microphone.

'The son's here too . . . Pedro Juan Gutiérrez González . . . Fifteen years old . . . No, *comandante* . . . No concrete proof.'

The faint order came from Santiago's radio operator. 'Let the boy live!'

Crouching, Zorrillo asked with counterfeit concern, 'And what will you do now that your Papá is gone? Fifteen's too young to join the imperialist army.'

'You heard my father. Take his place on the farm and look after my mother, you *hijo de puta*.'

Somewhere behind me, Mamá gasped.

Infuriated, Zorrillo raised his rifle butt as though to smash my face, but then appeared to change his mind. Standing, he crossed to the edge of our yard and dragged his heel through the dirt, carving a line across the entrance to our gate.

'The traitor Gutiérrez's property is hereby declared off limits,' he proclaimed smugly.

We were banned from our farm. Just like that! Hearing the prohibition, I should have stopped there. But I simply heard Papá called *traitor* and it sent me wild.

'Traitor? You can't betray something you don't believe in. Papá thinks you're fucking scum, *hijo de puta*.'

Mamá cried out, 'Pedro! No!'

'Furthermore,' declared Zorrillo, 'the traitor Gutiérrez's body is to be left untouched where it lies, as an example to all other *sapos*.'

'No!' Mamá screamed. 'No. You can't!'

Zorrillo looked from Mamá to me. 'We know your names. We know where you . . . ' he paused to smirk, '*used* to live. We have people everywhere watching. There's nowhere in this country we won't find you. The penalty for defiance is death.' He fired his rifle into the air. '*¡Viva la revolución!*'

The blond boy lifted his knee and I scrambled to Papá.

At first, I couldn't find the bullet hole in the tangle of hair and blood. And when I finally did find it, it seemed impossible that a wound that small could have done any major damage. Cradling his head, I turned Papá over. His eyes were open but they had no life.

'Mamá, phone an ambulance!'

Mamá dropped to her knees beside Papá. Tears were streaming down her face. She cupped her hand tenderly against Papá's cheek. 'Oh, Mario,' she sobbed, her voice catching. 'No! Oh, God, no.'

'Go and phone an ambulance,' I pleaded. 'Quickly!'

Mamá squeezed my hand. 'It's too late, Pedro. He's gone.'

'Call one, please,' I kept begging. 'Mamá, *please*.'

'It's okay, Pedro. Everything is going to be okay,' she whispered, even though it wasn't. She threw one arm over my shoulder and the other across Papá's chest. Pressing her cheek against his nose, she pulled us into a family huddle.

I must have been in shock. I could not shake the feeling of bright white disbelief. This hadn't happened and wasn't happening.

My heart pounded against Papá's rib cage. Warm blood from the back of his head leaked onto my hand. And although my ears rang from the gunshot, I could hear Mamá's breathing and my own, but not Papá's.

Gradually, Mamá's breathing thickened into loud sobs. She began rocking, moving me with her. I don't know how long I stayed like that, rocking with Mamá on our grief-struck seesaw. Moments passed in slow motion, as though happening underwater.

Finally, I resurfaced and stood. I had blood all over my white school shirt and, as I strode towards the house, wiped more of it from my hand.

'Where are you going?' demanded Mamá, looking up.

'To phone the police and an ambulance.'

'But you can't go inside!' She eyed the paddock the Guerrilla had crossed and the mountain trail they'd taken. She was frightened. They might still be watching.

'Mamá, we need to get help!' I looked around. The Mazda was up on blocks at the mechanic's, but my pushbike was against the fence. 'I'll go to Old Man Domino's.'

'You can't leave me here! Let's walk down together.'

'Someone has to stay with Papá. I'll be five minutes, I swear.'

'Pedro!'

I couldn't waste any more time. Pedalling like a crazed Olympian, I yelled over my shoulder, 'I promise you they're gone, Mamá.'

But what I meant was: *They're getting away. And I promise you they won't.*

10

I SKIDDED MY bike to a halt and hurled it down in the front yard of Old Man Domino, our half-crazy eighty-year-old neighbour. Normally, he spent weekdays in the plaza drinking *aguardiente*, playing checkers and feeding the pigeons. But today he was home early, drunk in his rocking chair.

'What's happened?' he demanded, eyeing the blood on my shirt as I stumbled up the steps to his porch. He set aside his solo checkers game.

'I need the police,' I gasped.

His wife, Gloria, appeared at the door, a wet plate and dishcloth in her hands. 'Pedro! Are you hurt?'

'Please,' I begged urgently, 'I need to use your phone.'

'It's on the wall in the kitchen.' She stepped aside quickly so I could enter. 'First door on your right.'

The house was immaculately tidy and smelled of lavender. I yanked the phone off the receiver and punched in 123 – the emergency number. I asked for the Llorona police station. From there, the police could get to our *finca* in less than five minutes.

'I want to report a murder,' I said when I was finally patched through.

'How many people killed?' asked a squeaky voice.

'One.' I gave my name and instructions on how to get to our farm. 'Please hurry!' I urged him. 'And can you inform the army? And order an ambulance?'

I called the army base myself, just in case, but the phone rang out. Next, I rang Uncle Leo at his hardware store and told him what had happened.

'*¡Dios mío!* Is your mother okay? Put her on.'

'She's with Papá. I'm at our neighbour's house.'

'You left her alone?'

'They banned us from burying Papá. They banned us from entering our property. I came here to phone the police. I can't get through to the army so I need you to go to Colonel Buitrago.'

'Pedro, listen! Get your mother out of there. I'll go to the barracks and then I'm on my way.'

When I went out to the porch, Gloria was sitting beside her husband in her identical rocker. They were holding hands and pretending they hadn't overheard. But the window right above them was open and their eyes were wide.

'Anything we can do, young man?' asked Old Man Domino.

'Thank you. You've helped enough already.'

I waited for a few minutes on the porch, pacing back and forth, expecting sirens and flashing lights. I cursed the police. Officially, thirty-two policemen with an armoury of assault rifles were charged with defending our town against the Guerrilla. Instead, they spent their time picking up schoolkids for truancy or taking statements about unpaid debts, lost *cédulas* and missing chickens.

Gloria looked sad. 'Sorry we can't drive you. We sold our truck last year.'

Old Man Domino wiped his board of pieces. 'Sons of bitches!'

Some people whispered that Old Man Domino was a communist sympathiser, but I knew as I mounted my bicycle that he wasn't. And I began pedalling downhill, away from our *finca* and away from my promise to Mamá.

11

ABOVE THE ROOF of the Llorona police station stood a five-metre high pole that had once flown the national flag but now supported the apex of thick black netting designed to deflect Guerrilla mortars. The station's brick walls were bullet-pocked from an attack five years earlier and covered with recently painted red graffiti proclaiming, *THE GUERRILLA IS COMING.*

Inside the dimly lit entrance, a young man sat behind an old wooden desk, typing.

'I need to see your station commander. Now!'

'I'm the only one here,' he squeaked. His pimple-covered face looked barely eighteen. His armband read *AUXILIAR*, indicating a national service conscript still in training. 'You're the Pedro Gutiérrez who phoned?'

I nodded. 'Where are the others? How far away is the patrol?' With every passing minute, Papá's murderers were getting further away.

He shrugged, still focused on his typing. 'I've radioed them three times.'

Behind him, I saw two dormitories that contained sixteen double bunks stripped of mattresses. After the Guerrilla mortar attack three weeks earlier they must have taken to sleeping at the larger garrison in Garbanzos.

I banged my fist on his desk. 'My father's been shot and you sit there typing!' I swiped the machine from his desk. It crashed onto the floor, keys clanking. 'Where's the patrol?'

When he jumped up angrily and went to the door, I noticed his belt didn't even have a pistol, only the wooden baton they issued to trainees. Leaning out the doorway, he looked up the street in the direction the patrol would come from. Then he looked the other way, towards our *finca*, where a Guerrilla attack would come from.

'How many were there?'

'Fifty. Maybe more. Three commanders.'

He radioed this new information through immediately, but he was shaking and pale, and I realised he was scared. Suddenly I felt sorry for him. It wasn't his fault that his superiors made him stay on his own while they remained in Garbanzos hiding behind the army.

But it was obvious the police weren't coming and I didn't trust Uncle Leo to bring the army. I couldn't sit idle so I set off north on my bike towards the Garbanzos army barracks.

Hearing the *colectivo* approaching, I dumped my bicycle against the church wall. I half-expected Palillo to be on board on his way to our geography exam, but when I got on the bus I found that he wasn't.

I stood near the door, watching oncoming traffic for the army, police or Uncle Leo's blue Ford, ready to jump off. We lurched and braked between pick-ups and drop-offs. As I listened to the gears grinding, speakers blaring *vallenato* and the swoosh of the doors brushing open and closed for each passenger, my impatience mounted.

'Please, hurry!' I urged the driver. 'I'll pay for all the empty seats. They killed my father.'

I didn't say who'd killed him. But judging from the passengers' suddenly-blank expressions, they guessed. Waving away my offer, the driver accelerated to a hundred and arrived at Garbanzos plaza in eleven minutes – record time.

As I alighted, I glanced up at the faces pressed against the *colectivo* windows. No one had spoken after my announcement, but in small towns, bad news spreads quicker than measles through a kindergarten. Once the passengers dispersed, everyone would find out. I figured that was a good thing. Villagers liked and respected my father; people would step in and help. However, I figured wrongly. Only one thing travels faster than bad news: fear.

12

THE ARMY'S XVIII Battalion in Garbanzos occupied an entire block opposite my high school, Colegio Santa Lucía. Each day, Palillo and I passed its three-metre brick wall topped with razor wire, gazing up at fierce, helmeted soldiers who peered grimly out of its eight observation towers. But now I found myself running up to the guard at the gates.

'I need to speak to Colonel Buitrago. It's an emergency.'

'The colonel's not available,' the soldier responded.

'Please! The Guerrilla just killed my father.'

He nodded that he already knew. 'I shouldn't say this to you, but the colonel and most of our men are away on a mission. They've been gone three days. It might be another three before they return. I'm sorry.'

'They can't all be on the mission. And they must have left a truck?'

The soldier looked like he really wanted to help. 'We're all doing double shifts to keep the barracks protected. I'd help you myself, but I can't leave my post. Would you like to go inside and make a statement?'

Why bother making a statement in Colombia? So the authorities could frame it and hang it on the wall to remind themselves of the job they weren't doing?

Storming off, I yelled back at the soldier, 'What if it was *your* father?'

He signalled for me to return.

'Here's Colonel Buitrago's personal cell phone number. If you can get through, maybe he can override the stay-on-base order.'

Sprinting to the Telecom cabins in Garbanzos plaza, I tried Buitrago. It went straight to voicemail.

'Colonel, it's me, Pedro Gutiérrez. The Guerrilla killed my father. I know which way they went. You have to get here immediately. Please!'

Realising the colonel would have no way of contacting me, I rang back and left the phone number of the Telecom cabin. No return call.

Five minutes later, I left a third, much angrier message for Colonel Buitrago. I yelled into the phone, letting fly with words Papá didn't approve of.

'You're supposed to be protecting our fucking town. You're supposed to be Papá's fucking friend. But you're an *hijo de puta* and a fucking coward!'

After that, I sat on the sidewalk of Avenida Bolivar in Garbanzos plaza with my head in my hands, and I felt like crying. I did cry, in fact, and I didn't care who saw me. By then, everyone must have known. But no one stopped to speak to me. No one did anything to help. Everyone went on with their food shopping, their lifting of boxes and their buying of *lotería* tickets as though nothing had happened.

Papá was dead and I was surrounded by the indifferent and cowardly. Papá would have done anything for any one of these people. For a friend, a fellow parishioner, a complete stranger, or even someone he disapproved of like Humberto Díaz. But no one was doing anything to help him. I cried until I felt a gentle hand on my shoulder.

Camila.

13

'PEDRO . . . BABY . . . I . . . I don't know what to say.'

Camila hugged me. Soon she was crying too. She was always friendly with Papá. She jokingly called him her *suegro*, and he called her daughter-in-law.

'I'm so sorry, baby . . . I have no idea how you must feel.'

But that wasn't true. Looking into my eyes, Camila saw my horror, my shock, and my frustration. But she also saw something else: my guilt.

'It's not your fault.' She clasped my cheeks in her hands. 'If that's what you're thinking, Pedro, it's not true.'

I knew she was trying to help, but of course it was my fault! Out in the dinghy, Papá had told me I'd risked all our lives. In the end I'd *cost* him his life. The Guerrilla didn't kill people for supplying water. They killed Papá to send a message. In response to my speaking to the Paramilitary recruiters, this was the ping-pong ball they'd smashed at me and the world:

Don't even think of joining our enemy. This is what will happen.

As for my rudeness to Zorrillo, I hadn't even begun to comprehend what it would cost us. Although I would soon enough.

I leaned into Camila and buried my nose deep in her neck. She stroked my hair, comforting me. I'd been growing it long for the school vacation. Little things like that, which had been important, now seemed ridiculous.

It must have been five minutes before I raised my head and wiped my eyes. I felt a little calmer. The urgency had gone. I'd accepted the Guerrilla platoons had gotten away. With over an hour's start, they would be deep in the Amazon by now. But Papá would be proud of how hard I'd tried to rouse the authorities into action. Then I remembered – he was no longer there to be proud.

'Pedro, baby,' Camila said, still stroking my hair. 'When you feel strong enough, we should be with your mother. She needs you.'

She was right. I'd been sitting in the gutter feeling sorry for myself while Mamá had probably been staring at the mountains, terrified. I nodded and Camila stood. Holding my hands and leaning back, she pulled me to my feet. Shaking and numb, I signalled a passing *colectivo*.

'It's okay,' said Camila. 'I've got money.' She indicated a waiting taxi.

The *taxista* must have known what had happened because he didn't comment on the blood or where we were going.

'Where's Palillo?' I asked Camila.

She shrugged. 'Geography?'

Reaching Llorona plaza, the *taxista* claimed he couldn't drive further because he had another urgent pick-up. He was obviously too afraid to go up the hill. Camila argued, but I said it was fine. Uncle Leo would be with Mamá by now, so a little more time wouldn't make much difference. Besides, there was one more place I could seek help.

14

WHEN THE GUERRILLA killed Ariel Mahecha's father for being a *sapo*, Padre Rojas had been among the first on the scene. He'd ridden the parish's 85cc Yamaha – affectionately dubbed Little Red Riding Hood – behind the army truck that transported the body through town and stayed comforting the widow until after midnight. Surely his replacement, Padre Guzmán, would perform the funeral rites and offer Mamá comfort?

Leaving Camila watching the highway for the police and army, I banged on the presbytery door. When no one answered, I peeked through the blinds and tapped on a window. A side door was unlocked. I hesitated, but it was an emergency.

Inside, it was dark and smelled of stale beer and cigarette smoke.

'Father Guzmán!' I called out, my foot crunching on an empty can.

Suddenly, a light flicked on and a chubby, bald man in pyjamas towered over me, holding a bronze candelabrum at shoulder height, as though ready to strike.

'Stay right there! I'm phoning the police!'

I didn't recognise Padre Guzmán at first without his toupée. When I finally did, I held up my hands. 'I'm sorry, Father. I knocked and called out. My name is Pedro Juan Gutiérrez González. I'm the son of—'

'I don't care if you're the son of God. You can't come barging in like this. I have a good mind to tell your father.'

'That's why I'm here, Padre. My father's dead.'

The priest lowered the candelabrum. 'I'm very sorry to hear that, son.' He spoke as though he were measuring out a goblet of communion wine, watching the level of his words scrupulously so as to pour into them the right amount of sympathy. 'Dead how?'

'Shot.'

'Guerrilla?'

I nodded. 'Padre, would you come up and say a prayer with our family? Then my father needs to be buried in his plot.' I gave directions to our *finca*.

'Shot, you say?' He massaged his scalp. 'Then the police are there?'

'Not yet.'

'I'm new to this. I'll phone Bogotá for instructions.'

'But you *will* perform the burial rites? And we'll need a truck to bring Papá to the cemetery.'

'A truck? Unfortunately, my superiors have only seen fit to furnish me with a motorbike.'

Suddenly, the bedroom door behind him crashed open and the *mulata* maid emerged wearing an emerald green nightgown. She was statuesque, with skin as smooth as milk chocolate. The priest flushed like blown coal.

'Señorita Mosquera, what are you doing in my room? I told you to vacuum it tomorrow.'

'Vacuum it yourself, Orlando!' she barked. Guzmán feigned outrage until she said contemptuously, 'The boy isn't stupid.'

'What would you have me do?'

'Phone one of your parishioners.' She unhooked the wall phone. 'I saw a dozen trucks here on Sunday.'

Placing his arm across my back, Guzmán ushered me to the door, mumbling tissue-thin promises about how he'd try to help. 'I trust to your discretion regarding Señorita Mosquera. We don't want her to lose her job, do we?'

I departed unconvinced, although unable to argue.

'Wait!' The *mulata* maid raced after me. 'You look pale, Pedro. You should eat something.' She held out a plate of pastry *pasteles*. Flashing a panda keychain, she whispered, 'His motorbike is in the shed.'

'Thanks, but I can't take it. You'd get fired.'

'He's a nice man underneath,' she said sadly as I turned away.

Underneath *what*? I wondered. Underneath three robes of cowardice, his toupée and thirty excess kilos of hypocrisy?

'Pedro, look!' Standing by the highway, Camila waved excitedly. 'Here comes your uncle.'

Pulling up in his blue truck, Uncle Leo leaned across Mamá and wound down the window. 'I told you to take your mother to my house.'

'Where's Papá?' I demanded of Mamá. 'Did the police arrive?'

But Mamá wouldn't look at me. Instead, she concentrated on shredding a tissue. I raced to the back of the truck and looked in the tray. No body. No shovel. Nothing.

'You left him! Mamá! How could you?'

Finally, Mamá spoke. 'You said five minutes.'

I flushed with guilt but controlled my voice. 'We need to go back up. He's all alone.'

'We thought we saw something,' said Leo. 'Strange men approaching.'

'Impossible! The Guerrilla are long gone. And anyway, you could have brought Papá with you.'

'I know it's hard, but we've done all we can. Leave this to the authorities.'

'Then get out! I'll drive.' I grabbed for his door handle, but he banged down the lock and scrambled to wind up the window.

'Don't you think you've done enough for one week?'

His message was clear. I was responsible for my father's death. He knew it. I knew it. And he could tell Mamá about my meeting the Paramilitaries at any time.

'Coward!' I spat. I ran to retrieve my bike from where it lay beside the church.

'Wait!' Camila sprinted alongside me, grabbing under the seat as I began pedalling off. 'We'll go up together.'

I unhitched her hands. 'Please, Camila! I need to get there quickly.'

'Then I'll find a truck. I'll steal one if I have to.'

I loved Camila so much. She was fearless devotion during a storm of treachery.

'And find Palillo!' I called back.

As I crossed the bridge and stood pedalling for the ascent, I saw what I most feared: black dots circling in the sky above our *finca*.

15

NORMALLY, THE UPHILL pedal took twenty-four minutes. I did it in thirteen. A wake of turkey vultures scattered as I launched my bike at them. Luckily, none had reached Papá.

I gathered a small pile of rocks and hurled them at the vultures. After I struck one in the neck, we established a fragile truce: the vultures wouldn't come within my throwing range and I wouldn't attack them. But if I strayed too far from Papá, they'd bob their purple heads and dart in with their hooked beaks raised high.

It was a hot, windless afternoon with blue skies and no cloud. I hadn't seen Papá for two and a half hours. All that time, he'd been lying on his back in the blazing sun. His face was pale, although a crimson splotch extended from his right cheek to his forehead. His mouth had opened slightly, which made it look like his jaw had become stuck mid-sentence.

I stomped on a trail of ants and sat beside him. Mamá had arranged a chain of dandelions around his body and placed a rock beneath his head as a pillow. I adjusted the rock to force his mouth shut. But then there was the problem of his eyes.

I kept looking away because I couldn't bear the sight of those eyes – dull, frozen, brown and unseeing – but neither could I stop myself from staring. I knew I should put two fingers over the lids and slide them down. I'd seen it done in movies. They always did it so gracefully, as though calmly and respectfully closing eyelids on dead people is a skill we're all born with. But not me. Hours earlier, I'd hugged Papá on my way to a geography exam. Now, I could barely bring myself to touch him.

As long as my mind had been occupied with doing something, I hadn't had to think about *why* I was doing it. And now, even with clear evidence in front of me, I kept thinking: *This has not happened. Not to me. Not to my family.*

I watched Papá for minutes on end, and he continued staring skyward with black wings reflected in his irises. I looked up. Above us, scores of vultures circled like a swirling black plague, waiting. Finally, I closed Papá's eyes and rested my head against his chest.

The stillness and silence shrouding Papá was the most complete I'd ever experienced. The silence came from where his breathing used to be. But it wasn't only his breathing that was missing. It was his presence.

Finally, I opened my eyes, sat up and listened for an approaching vehicle. But no one came. Not the police, not the army and not even Señor Muñoz's man with a truck.

After an hour, my arm was sore from pitching rocks at the vultures. Fierce sun was beating down on Papá's face. Reaching over the fence, I removed the scarecrow from Mamá's pumpkin patch and twisted its wooden pole into the earth so that it cast a shadow over him. However, within a minute, a vulture landed on it, knocking it over.

I looked around for shade. Only ten metres from the fence line stood Papá's favourite oak tree. Beneath it was a wooden bench he'd fashioned by hand, where he sometimes read to me while I looked out over Llorona. If I could move him there, we'd both be more comfortable.

However, I was afraid to cross Zorrillo's dirt line or move Papá's body. Straight after Papá was shot, I'd been willing to defy the Guerrilla. But my blood had now cooled. *We have people everywhere watching you*, Zorrillo had said. I was convinced that if I broke either of Zorrillo's prohibitions, he'd find out.

So even when the phone began ringing at four o'clock and I thought it might be Camila calling, I didn't dare go inside to answer. It might be the Guerrilla testing me. Instead, I stripped off my bloodied shirt and covered Papá's face.

As time wore on, hunger and thirst cleared my thoughts. I began talking to Papá, asking his advice. Normally, I could approach him with any problem. Even if he couldn't help me solve it, he'd always say something that made me feel better.

'True, Pedro,' he'd say, 'you don't know whether you'll pass your exams, but you can only do your best. If you fail, you can always resit them.'

'True, Pedro, you shouldn't have crashed the Mazda. You'll have to work hard to pay for the repairs. But luckily, it's only a car, not a person.'

'What if I don't know what to be when I grow up?' I once asked.

'There's no answer to that,' he responded. 'But that's okay. Not knowing is an important part of life.'

He always said something comforting, but this time he didn't. What do you do when the one person you've relied on your entire life suddenly isn't there?

By half past five the sun had lost its sting and the temperature dropped. I was still in my school shorts with my shirt off, but even when I began shivering I couldn't go inside for a pullover. Three hours had passed since I'd returned to Papá. The phone had rung numerous times, but I didn't answer for the same reasons that I didn't drag Papá down to the cemetery myself.

Fear was one reason, of course. But there was another, even stronger one: I still held out hope. The police or army would come. Buitrago would react to my messages. Uncle Leo would return, or Padre Guzmán would change his mind.

By then, the *colectivo* passengers would have spread the news throughout the region. Papá had friends with trucks. He had suppliers, contractors and buyers. He had fellow worshippers from church. All it would take was one adult to do what was right.

Even if everyone else failed, I knew Camila wouldn't rest until she'd hired a truck driver. But when the sun dropped, my hope wavered like a kite in flagging wind. I also began to wonder what had happened to Palillo. Maybe he'd skipped geography and gone to Francisco's Pool Hall. Then an even more worrying thought assailed me: Palillo had also been seen with the recruiters. What if something had happened to him or his family?

Darkness fell. Stars and a half moon emerged. I could make out the constellations of Orion and Capricorn. They were the same clusters I marvelled at most nights. Normally, they would have been beautiful, but the world had changed and everything now shone less brightly.

I talked to Papá again, telling him not to worry – I wouldn't abandon him. I would bury him in consecrated ground so that he could enter heaven. I still had faith. And finally that faith was rewarded when Palillo appeared, pedalling uphill on his bicycle.

16

STILL IN SCHOOL uniform, Palillo threw down his pushbike and satchel. He offered no explanation as to where he'd been or why he'd taken so long.

'Your family's okay?' I asked.

He nodded.

'I thought maybe the Guerrilla had gone after you too.'

He simply shook his head and his strong arms enveloped me. His hug was fierce and full of energy.

It was exactly what I needed – someone to squeeze the desolation out of me, if only for a few seconds. That was the sensitive Palillo: rare as a sun shower but well worth the wait. I could tell by his big, long, sorry hug that he knew everything.

Then, just as quickly, he let me go, and sensitive Palillo became Palillo the Comedian. For Palillo, sorrow was to be laughed away. Sometimes you had to ignore the obvious – like my dead father lying on the road in front of us – and replace it with the absurd.

'At least put some clothes on!' Palillo said, pretending to notice my bare chest for the first time. He covered his eyes, reached into his school satchel and tossed me his own sweater. I put my school shirt back on – Papá no longer needed it, and the blood had long since dried – and pulled on the sweater over the top.

Palillo's eyes lit upon the scarecrow.

'Friend of yours?'

From this opening, I sensed an impending comedy routine. Normally, Palillo's joy was infectious. However, I wasn't in the mood.

'Please don't start.'

'We had one of these when I was growing up in Turbo,' he said, standing the scarecrow back up. 'But in Turbo scarecrows are black.'

'Can you wait here?' I asked, trying to ignore his antics.

'On the other hand, in Turbo, vultures aren't black.'

'I'm serious! I need to phone Camila.'

'They're white. And they're not called vultures. They're called politicians. But I'm not racist.' He displayed his palms defensively. 'Some of my best friends are white.'

I laughed and Palillo knew he had me, but only for a moment because then I started crying and he had to hug me again.

'Please stop this!' I said. 'Help me phone Camila!'

'I'll help you, but first . . .' He took a chicken sandwich from his satchel. 'Eat!'

We sat next to Papá, sharing the sandwich. The food, the sweater and Palillo's company lifted my spirits like smoke from a rekindled campfire. I was no longer hungry. No longer cold. No longer alone. Filled with fresh hope, I grabbed my bicycle before he could detain me with more comedy routines. But then Palillo broke the news.

'Camila's not coming. She's in her room, grounded.'

'Why didn't you just tell me?' I said angrily, mounting my bicycle anyway. 'I still need to phone for a truck.'

'No trucks available. After geography, Principal Prada told me what happened. Then I spoke to Camila through her window. She told me you needed a truck. That's what I've been doing for the past five hours. I called you a million times.'

Palillo had been unable to persuade anyone to come with a truck because I'd stupidly alerted the *colectivo* passengers to the Guerrilla's involvement. I slammed the bike down, devastated.

'Does it have to be a truck?' Palillo asked.

Surely, Papá would fit in a car? Or on the back of a motorbike? We'd both seen entire families move house on a 125cc motorbike – first-born child and two suitcases between the mother and father, infant in the basket and the family dog yapping along behind. We could carry Papá to the cemetery. Or use that spare door in the shed as a sled. However, I rejected every suggestion, claiming I needed a truck, until Palillo reached his point.

'A truck, or an adult to drive it?' He let that sink in before adding, 'It's just us, Pedro. No one's coming.'

Palillo was right. I'd been holding out for an adult to take control. I believed that transporting and burying Papá would get done magically by someone who was in charge. I didn't want to do it myself because I was deeply afraid of the Guerrilla. They'd murdered my father in front of me, and when I thought about defying them I was terrified.

'Then I'll hire a truck and drive it myself,' I declared.

'Fine.' Even though Palillo knew about the prohibition on crossing the property line, he pointed to our house. 'The phone's that way.'

He was right again. It didn't matter which of the two prohibitions I broke first. If I moved Papá for burial, I'd have to flee.

For the next ten minutes I struggled to breathe. The thought of leaving Llorona was a noose tightening around my neck. I didn't want to go. I loved my town. Everything important to me was there. My mother. Camila. My friends. Our *finca*. In fact, everything I'd ever *known* was there. The people I'd grown up with. My primary school. Our Mazda. My bicycle. Even the road and fence posts and Mamá's scarecrow. They made up my world. I still hadn't grasped that Papá's death had changed everything anyway. I thought the rest of my life was still there, fully intact. I hadn't yet considered how we'd survive without Papá working, and without our land.

Palillo was patient. He gathered more rocks, adding them to my pile. We took turns throwing them at the vultures. Even in the dark I hit two out of three.

'Nice!' said Palillo. 'You've still got the magic touch. And your eye is *in*, brother.'

I stopped mid-throw. I knew what he was hinting at. The Guerrilla had killed his father. He'd always planned on joining the army or Paramilitaries. Now that they'd killed my father too, he wanted me to go with him.

'No! No fucking way! I can't join the Paramilitaries! It was my last promise to Papá.' Not only was any promise to my father sacred, I also remembered what Papá had said in the dinghy: '*They're killers, Pedro!*'

Palillo listed many valid reasons for me to join: I couldn't stay on the *finca* anymore; the Paramilitaries were the Guerrilla's enemy, so living with them I would be safe; I could send my salary to Mamá. But as much as I understood his logic, my fear was greater.

'What will you do then?' Palillo asked quietly.

Fortunately, I didn't have to answer. Headlights appeared in the distance. We heard the low growl of a diesel engine winding up the hill. I leaped up excitedly.

'I'd call that a truck!'

For a few happy moments I believed Uncle Leo had changed his mind about moving Papá's body, but he cut the ignition fifty metres short of where we stood. I heard the wrench of the handbrake, then the hot engine clinking and contracting in the cool air. Leo didn't even have the *agallas* to exit the truck. Instead, he sent Mamá.

Palillo bowed. 'I'm sorry for your loss, Señora González. You and Pedro probably need time alone.'

As Palillo reached the Ford, Leo patted the door to offer him a lift, but Palillo pedalled straight past with plans of his own. Then the real fireworks began.

'Why can't we use Uncle Leo's truck?' I demanded. 'We need the priest to bury Papá. Otherwise he won't reach heaven.'

Mamá used to be Catholic, but after the volcanic mudslide in Armero she claimed to have seen too much suffering to believe in God. In a single night, 23,000 people had perished, including my sister.

Losing Daniela may have erased her religious faith, but that didn't stop her from using whatever arguments she thought would get through to me.

'It's the soul that matters, not the body. Your Papá was a good man. God will look kindly on him.'

'You know what Papá would want.'

'Yes, I do. I love your Papá and I know him better than anyone. I know he'd want us to be safe. For you and I to look after each other. To be a family.'

I tensed at her mention of *family* – what kind of family leaves one of its members behind?

'I love you so much, Pedrito.' *Little Pedro* was what she'd called me until I was seven. Of course she knew it would affect me. But I would not let her get through to me.

'Then lend *me* the truck.' She could change her brother's mind, and we both knew it. 'I'll drive Papá to the priest myself.'

'I'm begging you, Pedrito. Please don't do anything foolish. You're all I have left; we're all each other has left – can't you see that?' She hugged me then sobbed into my ear, 'Come back with me.'

'Come back with you and then what?'

But the *then what* was obvious.

The vultures would pluck out Papá's eyeballs, nibble off his face, chew his innards and strip the flesh from his bones. He'd be left to bleach in the sun like a cattle carcass while I lived dependent on Uncle Leo, a man I no longer tacitly disliked but openly despised. I'd finish my exams and pray for good mathematics grades. Meanwhile, our *finca* would turn to ruin, the crops would wither, the pipes would burst and our cattle would die.

True, if I obeyed their prohibition, the Guerrilla would not touch me. But what sort of life would I be living?

'I'll leave the key under the pot plant,' Mamá said as Leo flashed his headlights.

'What kind of wife leaves her husband to vultures?' I called after her.

She spun viciously. 'How dare you! Maybe if you hadn't spat and provoked them we could have buried your father and stayed on the *finca*. I tried to stop you but now you're saying I'm a bad wife.'

Already nailed to my own cross, her blame was a dagger in my side. Hearing her truck door slam and the sound of Uncle's engine recede down the hill, I stood there, silent and drained.

Then, suddenly, I felt liberated. Without hope, everything became simpler. They had made a mistake killing Papá. But they were not coming to fix their mistake. Neither were they coming to take control of the situation, nor to look after me and Mamá. They were not coming to transport Papá and bury him in the cemetery. And they were not coming to capture Papá's murderers and bring them to justice. Why not? Because there was no *they*. *They* didn't exist. There was only *me*. Everything was up to me.

17

NO SOONER HAD Uncle's tail-lights disappeared than I scoured Zorrillo's dirt line with my heel until it was utterly obliterated. I peppered the vultures with rocks, scattering them like skittles. I strode to the shed and returned with a kerosene lamp and shovel.

Papá's body was stiff as I dragged him to his favourite oak tree. The earth beneath was hard and rocky. Perspiring profusely despite the cool night air, I stabbed and punched the shovel repeatedly through roots. Sweat trickled into my eyes and stung so much I had to close them.

As I dug, my father's execution replayed in my mind. I saw his killers' faces in minute detail and I heard their voices as clearly as gunshots.

I saw Caraquemada circling Papá, pausing to swat a fly before studying the place into which he'd fire his bullet. I heard Santiago's radio operator order: '*¡Ajustícialo!*' I saw Ratón's sinister nod to Caraquemada and suffered his indifference as he relayed the order like a weather forecast: 'Execute him.' I felt the blond boy's knee on my head as I flailed like a fish on dirt. I remembered Zorrillo's rifle digging into my teeth, and the taste of blood in my mouth before he banned us from our farm.

With anger searing through my veins, I dug furiously, driving the shovel in harder and harder. I barely noticed the blisters forming on my palms, or the hot tears streaming down my face. By the time the grave was deep enough, my shorts were drenched in sweat. I climbed in and slid Papá gently down.

As I took his pocket Bible and crucifix necklace, I heard a small motorbike engine struggling up the hill and a silhouette darkened the corner of my eye. Palillo. I saw a shovel across his lap and a pack over his shoulder.

'You should have waited,' he said when he reached me.

'Whose motorbike?'

He lit two cigarettes and held up the panda keychain. 'It's Little Red Riding Hood. The *mulata* was coming to find you.'

'Carrying a shovel?'

Palillo shook his head. 'Lights were off at Old Man Domino's. A shovel was leaning on the porch with a candle lit beneath so you couldn't miss it.'

I dragged hard on the cigarette. I was so touched by the actions of the *mulata* maid and Old Man Domino that my head spun. And then it was Palillo's turn; his proposal was the bravest of the day.

'Cemetery?' He pointed at Papá. 'There's only space for two on the bike. I'll take him down pillion passenger and do some laps of the plaza.'

It took several seconds for me to comprehend that Palillo was proposing to transport and bury Papá on his own. He'd take all the risks by making sure he was seen publicly. For a moment, I felt relieved. I wouldn't have to do it myself. But only for a moment. What had Papá muttered while digging at 2 am? *Cowards!*

Papá was *my* father; I had to bury him. Although I'd felt rejected at the time, I now understood why he wouldn't let me help dig Humberto Díaz's grave. He wanted to shield me. Just as I should shield my best friend.

'I'll take him down myself and get the priest to do the burial.'

'No point. He got called away somewhere.'

If the new priest was hiding, there was little point going to the cemetery. By then I didn't want Padre Guzmán to bury my father anyway. He wasn't worthy of consecrating a vegetable patch. I would be better off burying Papá where he was.

'Return the shovel and Little Red Riding Hood,' I said, scooping dirt into the grave. 'It's better if you're not here for this.'

Palillo blew three concentric smoke rings then spat defiantly through their centre. 'Your father was the best boss I ever had.'

'The *only* boss you *almost* had.'

'Same thing.' Palillo began ladling dirt too. 'Either way, I'm unemployed. Temporarily.'

'You phoned Don Jerónimo?'

Glad I'd taken the hint, Palillo lifted his backpack with the tent poles.

'Dawn pick-up. He has one seat left.'

Palillo looked at me questioningly, but I continued scooping dirt.

Wordlessly, we finished my father's new home, patting the earth tight with the flats of the shovels. Papá could be at rest now. One day, I'd have the ground consecrated and the rites performed by a proper priest. The only thing missing was a headstone.

'You coming?' Palillo asked, his eyes locked on mine.

I answered indirectly by pointing at the shabby skeleton of the scarecrow. 'Hand me that cross.'

Both hands at its neck, I lifted the wooden cross high in the air and drove it down into the ground at the head of my father's grave. However, it was not a cross I was thrusting into the earth, but a stake I was plunging into the hearts of my blood enemies.

PART TWO

LEARNING TO KILL

18

CROUCHING IN A ditch with Palillo, an hour before dawn, I realised my life was now divided in two. The time before Papá. And the time after.

My dream of running the *finca* with him and taking it over during his old age was shattered, and I replaced it with a far darker ambition: to track down and punish his murderers.

After burying Papá I had entered the house. I'd filled a bag with Mamá's jewellery, some of her favourite dresses and mementos, the family photo albums, the property deed to the *finca* and Papá's will.

But I also wanted to say goodbye to the house. I breathed in its smell, I buried my nose in Papá's pillow.

From my own room I took a change of clothes, my toothbrush, pocketknife and driver's licence. I removed several photos from their frames and slipped them inside the cover of Papá's pocket Bible.

Outside, I opened the chicken coop, preferring the hens to take their chances with foxes than starve. I also opened the gate into Old Man Domino's property – as the dry season progressed, the cattle would pass through it in search of food. Hopefully, the money from selling them would last Mamá a while.

I carried Papá's fishing rod to Camila's house on my bike, while Palillo rode Little Red Riding Hood. After taking aim at her second-storey window with a pebble, I changed my mind. Camila would only try to stop me. Or she'd cry and demand to come with me. I leaned the rod quietly against the door. The note took three attempts to write.

Thanks for trying. Leaving to find work. Please forget me.

I didn't have the stomach to write more. And I omitted my usual sign-off: *Te amo*. It would only confuse her and make her wait for me.

'Say goodbye to her face,' insisted Palillo.

I shook my head. While I longed to feel Camila's arms around me, it would only cause her pain. Besides, I wanted her to forget me. *Hate* me, if she had to. There was no point in saying goodbye to Camila. Goodbye is for people you'll see again.

After dropping Little Red Riding Hood back at the church, Palillo and I rode our bicycles fifteen kilometres to Garbanzos in darkness and chained them up inside Uncle Leo's yard. I slipped the deed and will under his door and left Mamá's things on the back step. Then Palillo and I went to wait for Don Jerónimo in the ditch beside our school sports ground.

Until then, the need for action had spared me from having to think. But as we crouched there waiting, there was no escaping the self-recriminations and regrets. If only I hadn't gone to save Palillo from enlisting in the Paramilitaries, Papá would still be alive. And in the end, I had merely postponed Palillo's joining by a few days.

Despite my own culpability, I still found it impossible to accept the reactions of people like Mamá, Uncle Leo and Father Guzmán, and the lack of response by the police and the army.

I'd studied for my history exam and I knew the old saying: *A los buenos siempre los matan*. Good guys always get killed. In 1948, they assassinated the presidential candidate Gaitán, right on the eve of the election. Decades later another honest candidate, Galán, was leading the polls when he too was murdered, just for being good. In fact, both men were executed precisely for *how* good they were, and because they stood as reminders to those who were not. And during his reign of terror, Pablo Escobar murdered Lara Bonilla, the Minister of Justice, to remind ordinary people how truly powerless they are.

When Guerrilla commanders brazenly commit murder and wander off into the hills with impunity, two types of men are revealed: those who want to help but can't, and those who could help but choose not to. And that was the choice most of the citizens of Llorona made on the day of my father's murder.

For defying the Guerrilla, I could no longer live in Llorona. But I didn't want to live there anyway, surrounded by cowards and hypocrites.

It was cold when first light appeared on the horizon. My watch alarm sounded. It was Thursday, 5.45 am. That day's exam was in history. I was still dressed for school in my blood-soaked uniform. I hadn't slept for twenty-four hours, but I didn't feel tired. The adrenalin was still pumping. The shock was still rattling. And the sadness was still burning, small and blue and quiet, like a gas pilot light that could burst into angry flame at the slightest twist of a dial.

19

DON JERÓNIMO WAS a kindly, moustachioed taxi driver in his fifties who moonlighted as a driver for the Paramilitaries. Palillo and I were his first pick-up, and he talked to us jovially about his two teenaged daughters. Owning a taxi licence allowed him to transport people across the country without raising suspicion. The Paramilitaries paid him one hundred dollars per recruit, and reimbursed his fuel and food expenses. If a third party referred a recruit to him, he split the commission.

We travelled north into the province of Meta. It was a clear day with a sprinkling of cotton clouds drifting across the blue sky, and I was glad of the silence and the beauty. The long, flat road sliced through verdant pastures and water-drenched fields like a dried river of tar. In shallow marshes, flocks of white storks lurched into motion. Long legs thrashing, they seemed to run along the water's surface, the tips of their feet leaving light ripples.

An hour into the trip, Don Jerónimo pulled off the highway behind a black SUV. The driver opened the back door and a skinny kid with glasses scrambled out. Jerónimo shook the man's hand, produced a crisp banknote from his wallet and guided the boy back to our car.

Palillo shifted into the middle, and the kid, who was twelve years old and named Eugene, perched awkwardly on the edge of the seat beside him. When Palillo told him to sit back and relax, Eugene lifted his shorts to reveal welts and purple bruises covering the back of his thighs. They'd been inflicted by his father, a violent drunk called El Machetero, who'd killed six men in separate cantina brawls using a machete.

Three days earlier, Eugene had walked in on his father kissing a woman who wasn't his mother, and his father had given him seventeen *planazos* with the flat side of his machete. Eugene hid under his aunt's porch. She brought him food, but his father continued looking for him, and he knew he wouldn't be able to go home. Instead, he begged the local Paramilitaries to take him. 'When I showed them my legs they said my father was a prick and I should never go back. That's when they called Don Jerónimo.'

Palillo shook his head. Even his stepfather had never hit him with a machete.

'What about you two? Why are you joining?'

'The Guerrilla killed our fathers,' Palillo said.

Eugene eyed the blood on my school shirt, waiting for me to elaborate, but Palillo and I had already agreed: no surnames, no place names and no identifying details. In order to protect our families, it was best that no one knew we'd joined.

Mid-morning, on the highway that led to Los Llanos – Colombia's eastern floodplains that border Venezuela – we stopped at a gas station to pick up two more boys. Tango, a dirty, unshaven boy of about seventeen, squeezed into the back. His younger brother, Murgas, took the front passenger seat. He had long hair and a missing tooth, and looked like he hadn't slept for days. When they saw the rest of us they exchanged glances as though doubtful they were in the right car. I wasn't sure we were headed to the same place either. Eugene was as skinny as a rifle. Tango and Murgas reeked of alcohol and cigarettes. None of them looked like soldiers.

'You guys going to be working at the *finca* too?' asked Tango while Jerónimo filled the gas tank.

'Same as you,' Palillo answered. Like me, he must have assumed 'working at the *finca*' was code.

We continued travelling west towards the city of Villavicencio, the capital of Meta and the biggest city in Los Llanos. By midday, the rising heat haze made headlights shimmer for minutes before oncoming vehicles became visible. Metre-long iguanas sunned themselves on the highway's shoulder, absorbing the road's accumulated heat.

'Anyone hungry?' asked Jerónimo. 'Everything is paid for by the company: transport, clothing and food.'

The others nodded ravenously. Don Jerónimo pulled into a restaurant that offered *mamona* – meat smoked over hot coals.

'But please,' he said, pointing to me, 'you can't go out looking like that.'

I could have changed but I shrugged and stayed in the car with my dark thoughts while Jerónimo bought the others all the beef, pork crackling and *chigüiro* they could eat.

The trouble began after lunch when Tango and Murgas took too long in the bathroom. Jerónimo honked repeatedly until they emerged, glassy-eyed and smelling of marijuana.

'Last fiesta before starting work,' stated Murgas, laughing unashamedly. He took a bottle of *aguardiente* from his bag, gulped some down and passed it to Tango.

Jerónimo's jaw clenched. 'Just don't vomit on my upholstery.'

Drunk and stoned, Tango and Murgas became talkative. I realised that recruiters had tricked them, offering them highly paid jobs as security guards on a private *finca*. None of us said anything. It wasn't our responsibility. As for Jerónimo, he'd already paid for their lunch and wouldn't receive his commission unless they were delivered.

Two hours later we entered Villavicencio. Concrete high-rise buildings towered over the streets. There were traffic lights on every corner, and dual carriageways of bustling trucks, fleets of yellow taxis and large, inter-provincial buses heading to the capital, Bogotá. I'd never seen anything like it.

'You guys look young to be working in security,' said Tango when Jerónimo stopped to check the tyre pressure. He poked Eugene in the chest. 'Especially you.'

'Maybe we're going to different places,' I said, trying to warn him surreptitiously. 'You should ask Jerónimo.'

Tango and Murgas looked at each other and seemed to sober up suddenly. When we set off again, they stopped drinking and began watching every passing road sign.

Fifty kilometres beyond Villavicencio there were no longer any roadside dwellings. There were no shops, no towns and no traffic. Just long, flat, grassy plains. We passed a municipal road sign: GUERRILLA ¡NI PÍO! – GUERRILLA, NOT A PEEP! – indicating we were deep in Paramilitary territory.

Murgas signalled Tango, who tapped Jerónimo's shoulder.

'I need to use the bathroom.'

'You used it at the restaurant. We're almost there.'

Murgas lifted his green sports bag to his knee. He produced a packet of crisps, which he shared around, but he left the bag open so we could see its contents: a tennis-ball-sized chunk of marijuana wrapped in plastic, a second bottle of *aguardiente* and a black gun.

'I don't want trouble,' said Jerónimo.

'Neither do we.' Tango clasped Jerónimo's shoulder and leaned forward to speak menacingly into his ear. 'So don't make me piss on your upholstery.'

While Tango and Murgas urinated by the side of the road, or pretended to, they argued back and forth. Through my open window I overheard Tango's last words as they returned to the car: 'If we go back, we're dead.'

Murgas opened the front passenger door but didn't get in. 'Listen, old man,' he said. 'You better tell us where we're headed.'

Jerónimo sighed. 'I'm dropping you off at a *finca* called El Filtro. You'll stay there for a few days. After that, you'll be doing a four-month Autodefensas training course. If you want to turn back, tell me now.'

Tango and Murgas stepped away and debated in a furious whisper. Finally, they got back into the car.

'We're in,' Murgas said tersely, but neither of them looked happy.

Soon afterwards, Don Jerónimo turned onto a minor road that led to a run-down farmhouse and a long, dormitory-style building where we'd be staying. We were introduced to the owner, Doña Amanda, a tough woman of about forty with crow's feet at the corners of her eyes and pink slippers on her feet.

Before departing, Don Jerónimo paid us fifty dollars each as an advance on our salary. 'Good luck, boys,' he said.

The money reassured Tango and Murgas. They now seemed resigned.

I remained silent. Palillo thanked Don Jerónimo and shook his hand. Eugene waved goodbye. They had full bellies and more money in their pockets than they'd ever had in their lives. I knew that to Palillo this seemed like the beginning of a grand adventure. But to me, it was the beginning of a long quest for justice.

20

EL FILTRO WAS where the first-stage filtering process for the Paramilitaries occurred – cutting out the unfit before training commenced. The next day, a doctor examined us for hernias, poor eyesight or illnesses that might prevent us from becoming good soldiers. Five other boys had already been waiting a week. One was covered in soot and blood.

'What's with him?' whispered Palillo to one of the others.

'We call him El Psycho. He won't talk or even wash. The Guerrilla killed his family.'

Apparently, the first thing El Psycho did after finding his family dead was torch his own house. Kicking through the ashes the following dawn, he uncovered his mother's china intact. He lined the pieces up and stomped on them one by one. Neighbours took him to the police, who handed him to the Paramilitaries.

Training couldn't commence until they had sufficient numbers. So for six days, we rested, ate well and talked little since we didn't know each other or what to expect.

While Palillo and the other boys treated El Filtro like a holiday camp, I hung back and brooded. The shock, adrenalin and anger that had been sustaining me wore off, and I began to grieve for Papá and for my old life.

To someone who has not had a parent stolen from them, I can only attempt to explain how it feels. It's like having part of yourself hacked off without warning. Afterwards, they become like a phantom limb: you're sure they're still present because you can feel them, you communicate with them, but you just can't see them.

When I was eight, the boy I'd sat next to in class was hit by a truck. Devastated, I refused to go to school. But knowing there had been a time before our friendship made it possible to imagine a time after. A parent is different. There is no time before a parent. A parent is *always*.

During that week in El Filtro, I had terrible dreams. Each night, Papá was executed by the Guerrilla right in front of me. I woke, gasping, with tears on my cheeks. Then I felt the sheets against my skin and a wave of relief washed over me. *It was only a dream.* I went from panic to elation. The worst possible event in my life hadn't actually happened. Then I'd look around and my mind would begin to focus. Slowly, very slowly, the wave sucked back out. When you've lost someone close, the most painful dreams are memories.

Tango and Murgas smoked their tennis ball of marijuana. We were supposed to remain at El Filtro, but they came and went as they pleased. Doña Amanda said nothing. Don Jerónimo must have told her about the gun.

Because I'd warned them in the car, the brothers trusted me with their story. They had six brothers and no sisters, and had been born ten months apart to two different fathers. At fifteen, after a few years spent committing petty crimes, they bought a gun and moved to armed hold-ups of jewellery stores and finally *sicario* work – killing people for money. They boiled their bullets in holy water stolen from a church so they'd fly straight and true. They observed their target for weeks in advance for the best time and place. Then they stole a motorbike and one drove while the other shot. They paid off the police, who finally warned them that local storekeepers and residents were pooling together money to perform a *social cleansing* – eliminating known criminals, drug addicts and undesirables from the suburb. If they didn't leave, they'd be *disappeared.*

However, to earn a recruiter's commission, these very same police had sent them here. Tango laughed and snorted some white powder from the webbed skin between his thumb and forefinger. He now felt stupid. They should have known – never trust the police.

'Want some?' Murgas asked, holding out the plastic bag.

I shook my head. I'd never tried drugs and didn't intend to.

'What about this?' Tango produced their gun. I later learned it was a Taurus PT92, a semi-automatic pistol.

I hesitated. I'd fired Papá's .38 rifle on the *finca*, but never a pistol.

'Come on!' urged Murgas. 'We saw the way you looked at it – like you wouldn't mind using it on someone.'

I stared at them. 'Says who?'

'Says someone who's seen that look a hundred times. On the faces of our clients.'

I took the pistol. Resting it sideways on my palm, I liked the feel of it. It was small but solid, and felt heavier than it looked.

'And how much would one of these cost?'

'A thousand dollars,' Tango said, snatching back the Taurus. 'If you knew where to go.'

Tango and Murgas had both been to juvenile prison, where they'd trained homing pigeons, sending them out in shoeboxes with visitors so they'd return with cocaine strapped to their feet. They could shoot. They were older than the rest of us. That made them the kings of our group. Kings, that is, until the seventh morning at El Filtro, when Culebra arrived.

21

CULEBRA WAS AN ex-policeman who would be our junior trainer. He'd arrived in a mini-van to collect us for the remainder of our journey. He was five foot eight with a wiry build and a crew cut. A tattoo of an anaconda wrapped around his neck and slithered over his right shoulder, its broad head ending at his elbow.

He was friendly but firm. He waited until Tango was climbing into the van and then caught Murgas's wrists in an unbreakable grasp and deprived him of the green sports bag, from which he extracted the pistol. The whole thing took five seconds.

Murgas looked at me. I shook my head. I wasn't a *sapo*. Doña Amanda must have snitched.

'When do we get it back?' he asked Culebra.

'When your training is over. Now everyone get in the van!'

Tango and Murgas looked sheepish as we set off.

Culebra had a Smith & Wesson Sigma 9mm in a hip holster. Approaching a military checkpoint, he slipped it under his seat. Slowing, Culebra kept his eyes on the road. The soldiers peered at us through the windows but waved our van through.

An hour into the drive, Culebra showed his kinder side during a stop to buy us all a snack of *buñuelos* at a roadside stall. The twelve-year-old kid, Eugene, started feeding scraps to a stray dog.

'You want to keep her?' Culebra asked.

I was surprised. Missing half of one ear, with patchy yellow and brown fur, she was the last dog you'd choose for a pet. But Eugene's eyes lit up.

'Really? But how will I feed her?'

'No shortage of food on the farm.'

'Can I call her Mutley?'

Culebra shook his head. 'We'll call her . . . Daisy.' He opened the trunk and unfolded a tarpaulin already covered in dog hairs. 'Up, Daisy. Up!'

After driving for another hour, Culebra stopped to collect his superior, Beta, and six more boys. Beta was a burly, muscle-bound former drill sergeant from the army, with a python tattoo coiled around his forearm. As I'd soon learn, he wore the same outfit every day: aviator sunglasses; army-green T-shirt; camouflage pants; lace-up, shin-high leather boots; and a .44 Remington Magnum in a thigh strap. With Beta's arrival, all kindness ended.

'Cute backpack,' he said to Palillo, holding out his hand. 'Show me!'

Palillo passed it to him, but rather than admiring it, Beta tossed it out the window.

'Hey! What did you do that for?' Palillo turned to witness his backpack sailing through the air then bouncing into a ditch.

'You won't need it where you're going.'

'Don't worry, boys,' Culebra said reassuringly. 'Everything will be provided for you at the *finca*.'

I looked at my own backpack, with its Mickey Mouse logo. Suddenly it seemed childish. Winding down the window, I lobbed it out, keeping only my pocketknife and Papá's Bible. The photos, my driver's licence, and Papá's gold cross and chain were in my pocket. I didn't turn to watch it spin and tumble.

'That's the spirit!' laughed Beta.

Palillo stared at me like I was crazy. But I wasn't. For what I planned, I needed to be as tough as granite. I wanted no ties to my old life. I would not phone my mother. I would forget Camila. I would watch and imitate the trainers' every move, because it was from them that I would learn how to kill without mercy.

Three hours from El Filtro we turned off the highway onto a bumpy dirt track.

'There she is,' said Culebra.

Situated at the base of a rocky mountain was La 50, the Paramilitary training school. We were in the middle of nowhere. Sprawling away from the mountains for miles and miles were flat, open fields dotted with African oil palms shimmering in the heat.

As we drew closer, I spied men with rifles standing under trees. We passed through two cattle gates that were opened by heavily armed men wearing webbing, grenades, ammunition belts and face paint.

In those days, La 50 was simply an old farmhouse with five tin-roofed sheds that served as barracks. Fifty metres up the slope was a block of four toilets. When the van stopped, Palillo raised his eyebrows, as if to say, *Well, this is it.*

Outside the van, I stood still for a moment, taking in my surroundings. I was pleased to have finally arrived. On my face I felt the vicious sun that strikes the floodplains during the dry season. I listened to the soft wind and bent down to touch my palm against the parched, baking ground.

'Quickly! In you go!' urged Culebra, holding the third cattle gate open. 'Alfa 1 is not someone you want to keep waiting.'

About a hundred other recruits were already formed up on the parade ground. Confronted by unfamiliar buildings, new authority figures and so many unknown faces, I was reminded of my first day at school. Seeing all those weapons, my excitement was tinged with trepidation. However, for anyone who may have had misgivings, it was already too late. We had accepted their food, their money and their hospitality. We had journeyed hundreds of kilometres deep into their territory. There was no turning back.

We had joined the Paramilitaries.

22

'NEW RECRUITS, I bid you a very warm welcome to the *Autodefensas Unidas de Colombia*!' boomed Alfa 1, the senior commander of La 50.

However, there was nothing warm about him or his welcome. An ex-military officer with cold, steely eyes, he was tall and muscular. There was neither an ounce of fat on his body, nor an ounce of friendliness in his heart. Like the other two trainers, he had a snake tattoo: a rattlesnake inked on his forearm. Among Paramilitaries, a snake tattoo was a badge of honour and a symbol of rank.

'The United Self-Defence Forces of Colombia were created for one reason and one reason only. Because the Colombian Army is incapable of removing the communist cancer. So we must do their work for them.'

I later learned that Alfa 1 had been a promising army captain in charge of training eighteen-year-old conscripts when a conscript drowned in a foot of muddy water. There were boot prints on his neck, and an internal investigation judged Alfa 1 to have presided over systematic human rights abuses. He'd only done what had been done to him during his own training – practices his superiors were well aware of. However, he was made their scapegoat and discharged in disgrace.

Alfa 1 never got past the injustice, the shame and the massive hole left in his life. The army had been everything to him. He could no longer associate with his friends for fear of jeopardising their careers. Unemployed but with advanced military training, Alfa 1 had only one place he could go – the Paramilitaries. Although they paid more and he was still fulfilling his patriotic duty, it was not the same as the army. He could no longer return home in uniform and hold his head high in neighbourhood shops.

'In the Autodefensas,' he continued, 'you will be treated fairly. You will be treated with respect and dignity. Here, you will learn to become men. You will learn to fight. You will learn to kill. You will learn to obey orders.'

Then he added ominously, 'Unfortunately, not all of you will make it through the training. It is a sad fact that in every course I have conducted some men are simply not strong enough, physically or mentally, for war. Make sure you are not one of the weak.'

Alfa 1 concluded, 'Each one of you arrived of his own free will. However, if you do not wish to be here, now is the time to leave.' He pointed to the gates. When no one moved, he said, 'Good. Your pay is one hundred and fifty dollars per month. Fall out and line up for your kits.'

That amount was the minimum wage. Not having joined for money, for me this was a bonus. However, many recruits grumbled. They'd been tricked by recruiters. Tango and Murgas were the most disappointed – they'd each been promised four hundred dollars a month – but said nothing aloud. At least, not then.

There were one hundred and four recruits – ninety-nine boys and five girls. They came from all over Colombia. Eyeing each other warily, most stuck near those from their home province as we queued for Beta to shave the boys' heads and issue our kits – two uniforms, rubber boots, hat, belt, backpack, mess canteen and a hammock. Culebra set up a table of sandwiches and cans of Coke. Alfa 1 called us forward one by one and, during a brief interview, wrote down our personal details, including full name, address and our reason for joining, before assigning us an alias, which we could choose ourselves.

The aim was to give us new identities. We were not allowed to use our old names or discuss our previous lives so that, in the event of capture, no one could be identified.

Following each boy's registration, Alfa 1 assigned him a pay number. He then yelled out the boy's new alias so we could get to know each other's names. Our group included Pirata, Armani, R6 and Escorpión. Some chose TV and movie characters they admired, such as Terminator or Rambo. The prettiest girl was dubbed Piolín, which meant Tweetie Bird. The boy who pushed in behind her in the queue called himself Silvestre. The slowest girl was called Tortuga, meaning 'Turtle'. Tango and Murgas were allowed to keep their nicknames. Palillo kept his. El Psycho was already El Psycho. The trainers were Alfa 1, Beta and Culebra, but we were to call them *comando* – meaning commander – when addressing them.

Waiting in line, we got our first taste of military discipline. One of the boys must have been thirsty. He went back for a second soft drink and then a third, at which point Alfa 1 noticed.

'You like Coca-Cola, do you?' he boomed. 'I said one drink per man. But since you're so thirsty, you can drink the rest. Go on!'

A dozen cans were left. The boy's punishment was to drink one, sprint up the hill then back down, do ten push-ups, ten sit-ups, drink another Coke and then run back up the hill. The boy vomited after nine and claimed he couldn't go on. Alfa 1 increased the punishment, forcing him to wear a raincoat and carry a backpack containing four bricks.

It was a clever variation on the punishment known as *El Volteo* – The Knockdown. Normally, the recruit had to drink water, but making him drink Coca-Cola turned it into a group punishment. Fourteen other recruits missed out on a soft drink, which caused resentment against the boy and taught him that an individual's actions always affect others. Finally, Alfa 1 gave him a permanent reminder of the experience. From then on, he was to be called Coca-Cola.

Eugene's alias was also imposed on him. He wanted to be called El Machetero, as a reminder of his father. However, by the time he reached the front of the queue the name had already been claimed. He could have chosen something different, but stupidly admitted to hating his real name.

'Why don't you like Eugene?' Alfa 1 asked, his pen poised above the registration book.

'It makes me sound like a *ñoño*.'

Alfa 1 laughed. 'Then that's what we'll call you. *Nerd*.'

I liked Alfa 1 already. He had a practical, no-nonsense wisdom and was extremely tough. But he also had a sense of humour. I felt sure that once I told him the story of my father, he'd take me under his wing.

When my turn came, I spoke clearly and confidently, calling him *comando* and standing tall. However, Alfa 1 barely looked up. I gave my father's name as my own and, when he asked what alias I wanted, I gave my own name – Pedro. Papá had named me after Saint Peter. It was a sacred name and I wasn't going to change it.

'Pedro, your reason for joining?'

'It happened a week ago, *comando*. I live on the outskirts of a small town called Llorona. Both the Guerrilla and the army sometimes pass across our property. My father, you see, he never refused water to anyone. He said—'

'Everyone here has hard luck stories, Pedro,' Alfa 1 cut in, already impatient. 'Get to the point and don't think you're special.'

He dismissed me after summarising the most important events of my entire life in his notebook, using only three words: *Guerrilla killed father*.

To Alfa 1, neither my story nor my father's was important. In fact, *I* was not important. I was just another recruit, one of a hundred he would train that season. I resolved to change that.

Five minutes later, however, my first effort ended in failure.

23

'ARE THERE ANY questions?' asked Alfa 1 once we were kitted out in camouflage uniforms and lined up in parade formation. Keen to show my enthusiasm, I raised my hand.

'When will we be issued rifles, *comando*?'

'When I say so,' he barked. 'Name?'

He'd forgotten me already.

'Pedro, *comando*.'

'Pedro, give me fifty push-ups.'

My arms gave way after twenty-seven. Alfa 1 added another ten push-ups and told the whole group they'd wait until I finished. It was a lesson I wouldn't forget: when a commander asks for questions, he doesn't really mean it. We were there to obey orders.

'You like weapons, do you?' asked Alfa 1 when I couldn't complete the sixty.

Moments before I'd seen Coca-Cola fall into a similar trap, but I had to answer.

'I'm not sure, *comando*.'

'Then I'll help you find out.'

Alfa 1 assigned me to the armoury – a forty-foot shipping container where provisions and weapons were stored. It was considered the worst job on La 50. Having no windows, the container heated up like an oven. I was the first to start work and the last to finish. Since the inventory system took time to learn, the position wasn't rotated. My punishment would last until training was completed.

I cursed my own stupidity. Rather than coming to Alfa 1's attention for outstanding conduct, I'd started terribly. From then on, I resolved to keep my mouth shut unless spoken to. If I had to ask anything, I would obey the chain of command, first speaking to Culebra, who'd then go to Beta, who in turn would go to Alfa 1.

During our first week in the Autodefensas, we said little and did exactly what we were told. We eyed each other suspiciously, trying to distinguish ally from enemy. Friendliness was weakness. To speak out of turn was to risk sounding stupid. Choosing the wrong group could prove disastrous.

The hierarchy became obvious at our first mealtime. The three trainers sauntered to the front of the queue, followed by the four gate guards who were permanently stationed at La 50. The twenty-four perimeter guards huddled together at two tables. They were here to do an advanced training course after being promoted. But Alfa 1 had timed their course to coincide with ours so that they could act as perimeter security until we were trained to use rifles and could do it ourselves. Being more experienced, they weren't going to socialise with raw recruits. In fact, they resented us. Babysitting us meant that their three-week course would take six weeks.

The rest of us jostled for our places in the hierarchy. At the top were those with prior military or police training. Then it descended according to age and size. MacGyver, at age twenty-one, had already passed Autodefensa training, but he'd been sent back for 'retraining', making him the unwilling senior of our intake. Although he could easily have asserted himself using his size and experience, something must have shaken him. He sat quietly at the corner of an empty table. I sat down next to him. Palillo plonked down opposite me, with Tango and Murgas at the other end. Meanwhile, those who hadn't established a group tried different tables before the gaps filled and the glue dried on our seating arrangements.

Ñoño, as the youngest and smallest, was at the bottom of the hierarchy. He had yet to reach puberty or understand the social dynamics of a group.

'Mind if I sit here?' he asked at the trainers' table.

'Reserved,' Culebra stated coolly. But the seat remained empty until the trainers had finished eating.

Arriving at our table, Ñoño looked at me hopefully. In the registration queue, he'd heard my story. I'd heard his story too, and he must have assumed this was a bond between us.

'Reserved,' I said, barring the chair beside me with a straight arm. I didn't want the obligation that a friendship with a small, weak boy would bring. But Ñoño was as stubborn as a mule. He placed his plate on the table, obliging me to shove it aside.

Palillo glared at me. With two siblings and three half-siblings, he was used to looking after children. He tapped the adjacent seat. 'This side isn't.'

Palillo's kindness earned him instant admirers. The five girls – Piolín, Tortuga, Mahecha, Paisa and Mona – descended on our table, nodding to Palillo. Piolín sat next to Palillo, diagonally opposite me. Although she was the prettiest of the five, I kept my eyes down and slurped my soup loudly. I didn't need any reminders of Camila. Palillo, however, relished having a female audience. He directed his first question to the table.

'So if we were in combat and had exactly five minutes to live, what's the last thing you'd do before dying?'

'Eat chocolate!' exclaimed Tortuga.

'No candy stores in the jungle,' replied Palillo.

'Get drunk,' said Mona.

'In five minutes?'

Of course the girls knew where Palillo was headed, but they seemed to enjoy watching him get there.

When all eyes were on him, he said, 'I'd make love.' He leaned closer to Piolín. 'To the nearest beautiful woman.'

'Me too,' she declared, blushing defiantly at her friends' laughter. 'But with my boyfriend.'

Placing his hands on the table, Palillo half-stood, craned his neck and looked around. 'I'm not seeing him anywhere.'

She folded her arms. 'Well then, I wouldn't.'

'Then you'd be missing out. You know what they say about long-distance love.'

'What?'

'In long-distance love, all four are happy.'

This time Piolín joined in the laughter until MacGyver stood suddenly, drained his bowl and departed, creating an awkward silence. I also stood, tipped back my soup and followed him.

'You did right,' he said as we crossed to the dormitory. 'Don't get involved with those girls. They're *princesas intocables*.'

I had no intention of getting involved. But neither did I think they behaved like untouchable princesses.

'They seem friendly enough.'

'You're not understanding me,' he said seriously. 'They're for the commanders. Tell your black friend if you want. Although it didn't come from me.'

Theoretically, the girls weren't owned. They were free to choose whom they wanted to be with. However, they were earmarked, like calves that had shown early potential but weren't yet ready for market. Eventually, the commanders would make their interest known, and in the meantime they were off limits to the rest of us.

I did warn Palillo. 'Even if one of the girls chooses you, what makes you think the trainers will allow it?'

'Mathematics, Pedro. Simple mathematics.' He placed his palms against each other and paired off three fingers of his left hand against three on the right, folding down his right thumb and forefinger. Then he wiggled the two spare fingers. 'Five girls minus three commanders leaves two for Toothpick.'

Since Piolín had a boyfriend, Alfa 1 trained his sights on Paisa, the second prettiest girl, which forced Beta and Culebra to choose the third and fourth prettiest respectively.

To Palillo, this meant that Piolín was not a danger. She was a challenge.

Since the trainers banned us from discussing our past lives, it took a long time to get to know anyone. The first boys we learned about were those who never wanted to go home, or who had no home to go back to, such as El Psycho and Ñoño. But gradually I heard the others' reasons for joining. Some were escaping violent homes. Others had joined for the same reason I had: their happy home lives had been destroyed by the Guerrilla. A few were homeless kids who'd been collected off the street by recruiters. However, the overwhelming majority were ordinary boys who had two simple reasons for joining: poverty and unemployment. The money they earned went straight to their families.

Quickly, we settled into our daily routine. After rising at 5 am, we did an hour's physical training, including sit-ups, push-ups, star jumps and a six-kilometre jog. We bathed in the river before breakfast started at 7 am. After washing our mess tins and cutlery, we formed up on the parade ground and were assigned camp duties, such as sweeping the barracks and scrubbing kitchen pots. Mid-morning we did classes in military tactics – attacking in L-formation, attacking in V-formation, constructing an ambush and detecting an ambush. Lunch was at midday. More military classes followed – orientation, map reading, camp hygiene and survival skills. Each of us was given a length of plywood sawn into the shape of a rifle. These pretend rifles would be our personal weapons until we were taught to use real ones. We had to carry them everywhere and keep them within arm's reach, even when sleeping.

Towards sunset, we ran the obstacle course. We climbed a rope net, dropped to the ground and crawled on our bellies through twenty metres of mud and a seven-metre-long concrete pipe. We squeezed through five tyres, climbed a brick wall, balanced along a thin, wobbly log and crawled through a square concrete pipe. After wriggling beneath a canopy of barbed wire, we swung along monkey bars and sprinted to the jetty, from which we launched ourselves into the creek – known as La Quebrada – to cool off. Daisy, who ran up and down barking while we did the obstacle course, splashed into the water with us.

The course had to be completed within a set time. To add pressure, the trainers yelled in our ears and struck us with wooden sticks. The stragglers quickly picked up their pace. Each day, Culebra shaved three seconds off the time permitted. Anyone who didn't make it received extra duties. Ñoño was by far the slowest and regularly incurred fines and punishments, which only made him more tired and nervous the next day.

'I can't help it if my arms are too short to reach the monkey bars,' Ñoño complained to Culebra, the most sympathetic of the trainers.

'Tell that to enemy bullets. You think they'll listen?'

'War is war,' declared Alfa 1. 'The enemy doesn't make allowances for age or size. Neither do we.'

El Filtro had weeded out the sick. The trainers were now filtering out the weak. It didn't matter that Ñoño had begged to join. He'd been warned: weak was weak, in all its forms. The second time we did the obstacle course, Palillo lifted him to reach the bars, but he was reprimanded. Ñoño was running out of options.

Beta made it worse for him. He had a cruel streak and enjoyed tormenting Ñoño. Crossing the mess hall one night towards the end of the first week, Beta stopped at our table, leaned down beside Piolín and said discreetly, 'Let me know if any of you need women's stuff. We have a box in the container.'

'Thank you.'

'That goes for you too, Ñoño.'

Ñoño flushed. In the awkward silence that followed Beta's departure, he turned to me. 'They'll send me home. I can't go back. Can you teach me to jump like you?'

'Sure.' I pointed towards the river. 'The pier's that way.'

MacGyver snorted with amusement. Piolín winced.

I felt bad, but I couldn't let myself start caring for Ñoño. He would come to depend on me, and in the end I wouldn't be able to protect him. Besides, helping him would bring me into direct conflict with the trainers.

Publicly, Palillo said nothing. Privately, he was disappointed.

'That's not like you,' he said as we brushed our teeth before bed.

I shrugged. 'Not like the old me.'

Like an autumn tree stripping itself to grow strong again, I had to let the leaves of kindness and compassion fall.

24

FOR FREE TIME after dinner, the common room boasted satellite television, a VHS player, board games and playing cards, although most recruits went straight to their hammocks. I was unable to join them, owing to my punishment. While others relaxed, I worked alone in the shipping container, listening to the slow thump of the diesel generator, organising shelves and making supply lists.

What Alfa 1 had intended as a punishment, I was determined to convert into positive learning. I enjoyed being on my own. I learned about weapons and improved my logistical skills. More importantly, it kept my mind occupied.

Working logistics in the armoury was similar to ordering and inventorying supplies for Papá's storage shed, although on a grander scale. Both entailed predicting needs and planning for contingencies. The camp required building materials, diesel for generators, medical supplies and various hardware products. We also needed food for a hundred and thirty-five people, including pallets of rice and gallons of cooking oil that were delivered to the gate every week.

One of the ways the government tried to prevent supplies reaching the Guerrilla was restricting the purchase and sale of certain items. Guns, bullets, camouflage fabric for uniforms, green fabric for police uniforms, VHF and UHF radios with more than two kilometres range, and even armoured civilian cars were all considered 'war matériel' and required a licence from the Defence Ministry. Legitimate importers and distributors would be taking a risk selling on the black market. But for the right price, people will do anything.

The container also had a desk and two tall, grey metal filing cabinets. Culebra was in charge of the armoury, and I was glad to be working with him rather than Beta. I soon noticed his weakness, which was laziness. He appreciated my diligence since it meant less work for him.

'If you trust me to lock up,' I said, 'I'll finish the count. You sleep.'

I fell easily into the role, organising my own system, placing orders for spare parts and writing shopping lists for Culebra's supply runs into Puerto Bontón. We had our trusted black market suppliers for restricted items, and phoning them to place orders became my responsibility. I kept a petty cash float, a ledger of purchases and, eventually, Culebra even told me the safe combination. The only unpleasant thing about working in the armoury was the heat. One sweltering day, when Culebra complained about it, I tentatively said, 'Why not cut a small window above the desk to let hot air escape?'

He cut the window that very day, a thirty centimetre by thirty centimetre square that he covered with wire mesh. Culebra might have been lazy, but not when it came to his own comfort.

Another of my jobs was to help repair weapons. When a weapon malfunctioned, Culebra consigned it to the repairs box. There it might remain for months until replacement parts were imported or, if it had only a minor fault, until Culebra had time to fix it using a part from another decommissioned weapon. A tiny component could prevent an entire pistol from working. One might have a broken firing pin, another a magazine that jammed or a faulty trigger spring.

Culebra taught me how to disassemble the damaged weapons and search for the required part. Most of the pistols were Taurus PT92s – the same type Tango and Murgas had shown me at El Filtro. Manufactured in Brazil, they were inexpensive and had few working parts.

'When will we learn to fire one of these?' I asked Culebra.

'You won't,' he said. 'Not during basic training.'

As recruits, we'd use Galil rifles. Pistols were only for commanders; the perimeter guards were being taught to use them as part of their advanced training course. But I needed to learn to use a pistol before I went after my father's killers. A rifle was too large to steal, and anyway, I wanted Papá's murderers up close.

'Would you teach me to shoot one?'

He laughed. 'Maybe one day.' He was just brushing me off, but I resolved to change his mind.

Ten days into the training, Culebra had just returned from purchasing supplies in Puerto Bontón. I was helping him unload the bags from the camp's Chevrolet Blazer SUV when Alfa 1 approached us.

'We need more electrical tape urgently,' he said to Culebra. Tape hadn't been on Alfa 1's shopping list. I could see Culebra wanted to roll his eyes, but instead he took a deep breath and opened the Blazer door.

'I can drive,' I offered.

Alfa 1 laughed. 'You're fifteen.'

'I've been driving on our *finca* since I was twelve. And I have a licence.'

'Is it valid?'

They waited while I went to my locker to fetch it. On my way back, I realised that if Alfa 1 examined it closely he'd know I'd lied about my name. I was sweating as I handed it over, but he merely glanced at it before handing it back.

'No recruits allowed off La 50 alone. Prove you can be trusted. Then we'll see.' My heart sank until he turned to Culebra and added, 'Pedro will drive. You supervise and report back to me later.'

I now accompanied Culebra whenever he bought supplies in Puerto Bontón. Culebra was content as I was the one driving and carrying heavy bags of provisions while he 'supervised'. And I'd come to the attention of Alfa 1. After that, I sometimes saw him watching me thoughtfully, and I wasn't sure whether to be happy or nervous. On the one hand, Alfa 1's attention might put me in line for a promotion. But he was also more likely to notice if I deviated from the rules, and that could be very dangerous.

There were many rules in the Paramilitaries and many punishments for breaking them. Some were financial punishments in which fines, called *multas,* were deducted from your wages. Accidentally dropping your weapon, for example, might cost ten dollars. Most punishments, however, involved forms of physical torture.

'Think you're here for a romantic holiday?' Culebra yelled at Silvestre, simply for whispering to Piolín. 'Fifty push-ups.'

Once the commanders singled a boy out for punishment, they waited for him to make more mistakes. When Silvestre was overheard by Beta joking that he had a destiny to eat some Tweetie Bird pie, he was punished with *El Suplicio Chino* – The Chinese Torture. Facing down, he had to support his weight on his toes and forearms and keep his body straight like a plank for two minutes. The moment a knee touched the ground, the trainers struck him hard with his own wooden rifle and the clock started again.

Seeing Silvestre being beaten by the instructors, I worried about Palillo. At school, Palillo had played the class clown. I feared that his impulsiveness, rebelliousness, or interest in Piolín would get him in trouble. During class I sat next to him tensely, ready to nudge him to keep quiet.

In the second week, on payday, we were permitted a three-minute phone call from the office. This was a great privilege, Beta told us. Guerrilla soldiers were banned from ever contacting their families again.

Beta sat nearby to make sure we didn't give away information about our location. Most recruits said they were working on an African oil palm plantation. They'd see their families at the end of sixteen weeks and would phone again when they could.

When my turn came, I considered calling Mamá but was still too angry with her.

'Don't you want to let her know you're okay?' asked Culebra.

Instead of calling, I arranged to have my salary deposited into my parents' account at the Agricultural Bank. That way, Mamá would know I was alive.

Later, during question time in Alfa 1's political class, Tango raised his hand. Perhaps after contact with the outside world he'd grown overconfident.

'Murgas and I were told we'd be paid four hundred dollars per month.'

Alfa 1's face flashed menacingly like lightning on the horizon. 'On the first day I told you the pay and asked if anyone joined against his will. And now you two dare question me?'

For insubordination, Alfa 1 gave the brothers the harshest punishment to date. Two days tied to wooden posts in their underwear in the blazing sun, a punishment known as *El Soleado* – Sunstroke. They received no food but enough water to keep them alive. Blistered and weak, they rejoined our table on the third morning.

Punishments were given arbitrarily and were often completely disproportionate to the offence. But the commanders' message was clear: there was nothing we could do to question or defy them. They owned us completely.

Of course, the girls were treated leniently. They talked and giggled without being reprimanded, and the commanders went easy on them during physical training. This was part of the system of penalties and inducements used to win them over. Although Tortuga always finished the obstacle course long after Ñoño and outside the maximum time permitted, nothing was said.

Whenever I saw a new punishment meted out to another boy, I tried to train myself to survive that punishment. During free time, I practised push-ups, sit-ups and pack runs with bricks. Some days I refused to eat, giving my food to Palillo. Other days I didn't drink, no matter how hot and thirsty I became. To practise for when we'd have to do guard duty, I kept my eyes open all night.

I wanted to make myself tough enough to handle anything they threw my way. If Alfa 1 punished me, I'd take it and thrive. I aimed to be the best recruit of my intake and earn promotion. The faster I rose through the ranks, the sooner I'd gain the skills and the opportunities to go after Papá's killers.

I tried to occupy every waking minute so I wouldn't have time to think. But when I did have a moment's rest, my thoughts invariably returned to Papá. I liked to remember him in our happy times, fishing on Sundays, sitting in our pew at the church or at the family dinner table with Mamá serving roast beef.

I still woke from nightmares, covered in sweat. In my dreams, Papá now died in different ways: drowning in the river where we fished, while I desperately tried to pluck him from the rapids, or thrown head-first through the windscreen of our truck when I ran a stop sign and collided with a bus.

There were only two constant elements to the nightmares: Papá always died violently and the fault was always mine.

In connection with my work in the armoury I sometimes had to go to the office, where I overheard the trainers' phone calls, radio communications and snippets of conversation. By staying as still as a spider, I could get them to forget I was there and talk freely.

Culebra grew careless and left files open. One day, when I was alone in the container, I passed the desk and saw a face I recognised: Ratón's. The photo was slightly blurry, as though taken through a long-distance lens. It was lying on a sheet of paper in an open manila folder on the desk.

I looked over my shoulder guiltily. Then I slid the photo across and scanned the words on the page below:

CHAPA: Daniel Joaquin Gómez.
APODO: Ratón
UNIT: 34th Unit, Vichada Province
RESPONSIBILITIES: Recruitment, logistics, and community liaison
LAST REPORTED SIGHTING: 2nd November 20—, seen buying supplies in Villavicencio by a civilian informant

Finally, I'd found the first useful clue in the hunt for my father's killers. It hadn't occurred to me that I could trace the Guerrilla using their supplies. Necessities such as food, oil and antibiotics they could buy from any corner store or marketplace. But provisions such as camouflage uniforms, military hardware and specialised batteries required authorised distributors. That was how I'd get to Ratón. According to the file, he'd last been sighted buying supplies in Villavicencio only six weeks earlier. And I already knew what one of his regular purchases must be – batteries for the Motorola radio through which he'd received the order for Papá's execution.

25

NOW WHENEVER I awoke from a nightmare, I lay awake listening to the deep breathing and occasional snores of the other boys and fantasised about taking my revenge. After seeing Ratón's file, my thoughts focused increasingly on him.

December the 17th marked one month since Papá's death. In my locker, I built a small shrine containing Papá's pocket Bible and a plaster statuette of Mary that I'd bought in Puerto Bontón. On either side of Mary, I propped up photos. The first was of Papá and Mamá, taken two Christmases ago, smiling as they embraced on the sofa, surrounded by presents and torn wrapping paper. The second was of Camila, beautiful in a blue summer dress. The final photo was one I'd taken of Papá on a Sunday afternoon six months earlier. It showed him sitting comfortably in the dinghy with his foot braced against the gunwale and the fishing rod resting against his knee, enjoying his afternoon of relaxation. Wearing Papá's crucifix around my neck, I prayed and wrote him a letter.

There were no locks, so I was careful not to give away anything specific about the Autodefensas. But I wrote about my feelings, how things were going with Palillo and the thoughts I had at night. After writing, I took off the chain with the crucifix and stored everything in a shoebox under the statuette of Mary.

Over the coming weeks I would write more letters to Papá and also postcards to Camila, which I never posted. Maybe one day I'd send them – one day when all this was over. But that day seemed a long way off. I had yet to fire a gun. I didn't have a vehicle, a pistol or bullets. All I had was my anger.

Meanwhile, I kept my head down and tried not incur the commanders' wrath. But I worried more than ever about Palillo, who continued to flirt with Piolín behind their backs.

We could all see how the commanders wooed the girls with privileges. The hair conditioner, tweezers and underwear a girl needed could be delayed or accelerated depending on her attitude. If she were friendly, she might get the body lotion she requested the next day; if she weren't, it might take two weeks to arrive.

The girls played the commanders' game cautiously – not asking for much, but not refusing privileges either. They knew their rights under the Autodefensa Statutes – extra lip balm didn't oblige them to have sex.

Piolín, their leader, ensured they protected each other. If one was summoned to the commanders' dormitory on an errand, a friend went with her. Piolín was smart and read widely, so Alfa 1 kept her onside with a reading lamp and books. Although she'd announced she had a boyfriend, she was still the most beautiful of the five and he hadn't completely given up on her.

Training, meanwhile, increased in difficulty. On the obstacle course, Culebra continued reducing the maximum time, Alfa 1 shouted at us through a megaphone, and Beta hit us harder. Ñoño spent his free time practising on the monkey bars and now, after one or two failed leaps, he was usually able to grab the first rung and swing across. But he was always the last of the boys to finish and his punishments accumulated.

The physical demands were almost too much to bear. But the harder the trainers pushed us, the harder I tried. On the first day I'd finished the course in the middle of the pack. Eventually, though, the additional training I did in my free time began to pay off.

'Relax!' whispered Palillo as I did my nightly sit-ups after locking the armoury.

'I'm still working.'

'That's not work,' he whispered. 'You're punishing yourself.'

As long as I controlled the pain I could stay focused on the future and stop wishing for my old life. I could forget that my own mistakes had destroyed everything. I also believed this extra training would protect me against every possible eventuality. However, there were some punishments so brutal they were impossible to train for.

26

ONLY THREE WEEKS into the course, we were thoroughly exhausted. With just one rest day per week, our muscles barely had time to recover. The relentless yelling, sleeping in uncomfortable hammocks as well as pointless exercises – such as being woken in the middle of the night and ordered to stand at attention for an hour – had also worn us down. Tango and Murgas were still angry at being tricked and even angrier at their recent *El Soleado* punishment.

However, it wasn't easy to leave the Autodefensas. MacGyver told me a discharge was occasionally granted to men who'd proven themselves to be good soldiers and who would keep their mouths shut. But this was up to individual commanders and only considered after four years.

Tango and Murgas knew this but couldn't wait. They were fed up. A week before Christmas, they decided to do something about it.

'We're leaving,' whispered Murgas, slumping down beside me at breakfast, while Tango sat opposite him. 'Want to join us?'

'Are you crazy?' I lowered my voice even though the table was still empty. 'Where would you go? There's nothing for fifty kilometres in every direction. The commanders have vehicles, binoculars and boats. How far do you think you'll get on foot?'

'We wouldn't be on foot. And we only have to get as far as that army base we passed at Puerto Bontón.'

Their plan was for me to drive them there. Although the guards at the gate searched the Blazer thoroughly on the way in and out, personnel in the vehicle were assumed to have permission.

'Then what?'

'We'd hand ourselves in.'

Being under age, they hadn't broken the law by joining the Autodefensas. Provided they didn't return to their old neighbourhood – the scene of previous crimes – Tango and Murgas wouldn't do prison time. But even if they did, anything would be better than La 50.

'And what would *I* do?'

'The same as us. Or just keep driving.'

'Pass the salt!' said Tango loudly. I looked up and saw Ñoño approaching with Daisy trailing behind him. He was the one who fed her and she followed him everywhere, even sleeping under his hammock at night.

I stood, leaving a half *caldo* with fried egg on the table.

'You eating that?' squeaked Ñoño.

'I'm full,' I lied. After the midnight sprints I was as hungry as a packhorse, but I slid the tray to Tango and Murgas. If they were planning to leave, they'd need to build up their strength.

Tango approached me again that afternoon. Following the obstacle course, we had free time until dinner. We'd somersault from the pier into shoulder-deep water. Those who could swim would paddle twenty metres upstream to a metal pole, the tip of which poked out of a two-metre high waterfall. We'd hang on and let the water strike our faces until the fierce current tore us off.

The five girls bathed twenty metres downstream. The unwritten rule that the girls were off limits didn't stop Palillo from sneaking looks or a hundred boys from splashing, wrestling and teasing to show off.

Neither Tango nor Murgas could swim. Waist-deep in water, Tango sidled up to me. I didn't even want to be seen talking to him, but he put a hand on my shoulder to detain me.

'Not interested,' I said. There was no way I was going to desert. La 50 was exactly where I wanted to be.

'Think about it, Pedro. You'll never find your father's killers stuck in a shipping container in the middle of nowhere.'

I froze. 'What do you mean?'

'We're not stupid! We heard you telling Alfa 1 at registration what happened to your father and saw the way you looked at our gun. Murgas has a master key to both the container and the weapons rack. I'll steal a pistol for you myself!'

'Don't do it!' I hissed, horrified. 'Be patient! At least wait until we've finished training!'

We were interrupted by Silvestre, who was splashing closer. 'In you come, Ñoño!' he cried. 'What's wrong? That time of the month?'

I looked up and saw Ñoño standing on the pier with his arms folded awkwardly. Daisy sat beside him. Perhaps she sensed his discomfort because she whined and licked his knee. It wasn't so much getting into the water that was the problem, it was getting out – he didn't have a hair on his body and our standard-issue white boxers turned semi-transparent when wet.

Jump! I thought. If he dived in now, that would be the end of it. He could remain in the water until everyone was out – or until the girls got out, when the boys' attention would be focused on them.

'Girls aren't watching,' Silvestre comforted sarcastically.

'Hey, girls!' called Rambo. 'You're not watching, are you?' But now, of course, they were.

I exchanged a glance with Palillo. Then I swam towards the pier and climbed out of the water.

'*¡Mierda!*' yelled Palillo suddenly. Thrashing through thigh-deep water, he waded towards the bank. 'I think I saw an anaconda.'

'Where?' demanded Silvestre above the splash of panicked swimmers racing towards land.

'Down there.' He pointed between his legs. 'It was huge.'

The other boys' panic turned into laughter.

Grabbing Ñoño's shoulder, I spoke in his ear. 'Climb out when the girls do!' Then I hurled him off the pier.

Palillo winked at me. With one neat manoeuvre he'd distracted attention from Ñoño and shown the girls what lay captive in his boxers.

After lights out, as Culebra checked our hammock ropes, Palillo made a loud enquiry. He felt he'd outgrown the name Toothpick. Was it possible, *please comando*, to change his alias to a much longer and thicker word starting with 'A'? Hilarity ensued, to Culebra's considerable bemusement.

Lying awake that night, I worried about Tango and Murgas's plans to desert. My refusal to drive them to Puerto Bontón wouldn't deter them for long. At the moment, their inability to swim meant that they couldn't cross the river, and it would be too risky to break through the closely guarded perimeter. But the water level was dropping. Another week or two without rain and they'd be able to wade across the causeway.

I didn't really believe that they had a master key to the weapons rack, but if anything went missing from the container, the trainers would assume I was responsible.

The next day I suggested to Culebra that we put a second lock on the top eyelet of the container door. I was always making suggestions on how to improve things and he didn't think anything of it.

'You'll need to bring out the stepladder twice a day to open and close it,' was all he said.

'I don't mind.'

It was a small price to pay to ensure I wasn't accused of stealing weapons. I didn't anticipate that Tango and Murgas wouldn't wait until the water level dropped. Or that my suggestion about the padlock would lead suspicion exactly where I hadn't wanted it: directly back to me.

27

TANGO AND MURGAS left that very night, breaking through the perimeter security rather than trying to cross La Quebrada. Every changeover, the new perimeter guard performed a count of those sleeping. But Tango and Murgas had stuffed their blankets with newspaper and positioned stolen boots at the foot of their hammocks, and as a result their absence wasn't detected until the following morning's parade. Pandemonium overtook the camp. They weren't the only deserters. Jirafa, Pele and Armani were also missing.

Training was suspended immediately. Following a flurry of radio and phone calls, a full-scale search began. Three additional SUVs were called in, two flat-bottomed boats began patrolling through the reeds in the river, and Alfa 1 sent out the recruits in groups of five in different directions with radios.

I avoided eye contact with Culebra. I'd been stupid to suggest the padlock. I had no idea they'd escape that very night. The commanders were already analysing the possibility that the deserters might have received inside help. Six perimeter guards were interviewed, and when the escape path was found, the two guards on either side of it were tied up to the wooden posts for *El Soleado*.

'We didn't help them,' insisted one of the guards to Alfa 1.

'You didn't stop them either.'

Even for unintentional acts of omission, someone had to be held responsible. We were all put on half-rations because, according to Alfa 1, someone should have noticed the boys leaving, even at night. I was sure that suspicion would soon fall on Palillo and me. We'd arrived in the same van as Tango and Murgas. Their hammocks were hung near ours and they sat at our breakfast table. If anyone had known about their plans, it was us. I wasn't worried about Palillo; not only was he innocent, he could act his way out of anything. But my suggestion about the padlock was too much of a coincidence for the trainers to ignore.

There was only one way for the deserters to go – inland – and MacGyver had no doubt they'd be found.

Several times while we were searching, a helicopter flew overhead.

'Army?' I asked MacGyver.

'Too small. *El Patrón*.'

El Patrón was Don Carlos Trigeño, the owner of La 50, who lived fifteen kilometres uphill at La 35, his other property. In Puerto Bontón, I'd heard it said that not a leaf fell without his permission.

I waited all that first day for the commanders to question me, but they didn't. However, at breakfast the next morning Beta spoke the words I was dreading: 'Culebra wants to see you in the armoury.'

I now had exactly seventy paces – from the mess hall to the container – to finalise what I was prepared to divulge. If I admitted knowledge of the escape plot, I would not only be punished for failing to inform the commanders, but also forced to confess that the deserters were headed to Puerto Bontón, making their capture more likely. If I denied knowing anything and Tango and Murgas were caught and implicated me, I'd be in even worse trouble for lying.

When I entered the container, Culebra was leaning over the radio. He straightened as I came in, and I noticed that he had something concealed in his right hand.

'*Buenos días*.' His tone was casual but he was watching me intently. 'Notice anything different?'

I scanned the equipment racks carefully. Everything appeared to be in order. Then I saw the window. The mosquito mesh had been punched through and was hanging by a thread.

'I guess your window wasn't such a great idea after all.'

I'd been so focused on my request for the extra padlock – something that was at least designed to keep the deserters *out* – that I hadn't realised my innocent suggestion of a window might lead Culebra to think I'd actively helped them to get *in*.

However, I tried to remain cool as I inspected the damage. 'What did they take?'

'Compasses.' He paused significantly. 'The ones you left on the desk.'

'I'm sorry. I never imagined . . .' Unlike Palillo, I was a terrible actor.

Culebra smiled slightly at my discomfort. If he'd previously suspected that I knew of the deserters' plans, he was now certain of it.

'Don't apologise. The window was a bad idea, but the padlock wasn't.'

He opened his hand to reveal the two padlocks. The padlock from the bottom eyelet had been filed through. But the lock I'd suggested for the top eyelet was intact.

'They couldn't get to it without the stepladder,' he explained. 'The compasses were all they could reach. And energy bars.'

I realised that Culebra wasn't accusing me – he was *thanking* me. He'd only mentioned the window as a test, to find out whether I'd known about the escape plan.

I eyed him warily. 'So we're good?'

'If the weapons are safe, *I'm* safe. And if I'm safe, *you're* safe.' He patted me on the back. 'And I now know you're not a *sapo*.'

It was a simple lesson in loyalty. By not revealing the deserters' plan, I'd proven I wasn't an informant. At the same time, I'd protected Culebra by suggesting the second padlock. If they'd stolen weapons, he'd be the one crumpled against a pole shrivelling like an apricot in the hot December sun.

'Remember that pistol shooting lesson you asked for?' he said. 'Consider it a promise.' From the spares box, he tossed me a silver key. 'And when the Blazer gets back, we need double-sided tape from Puerto Bontón.'

He was making it clear that I was now trusted enough to drive out of La 50 by myself. I was so relieved at not being punished that I didn't consider the opportunities this would present, but they wouldn't be long in coming.

28

FROM THAT DAY on, I was regularly sent off base alone to buy supplies. Soon, the commanders also had me running personal errands.

'Drive into Puerto Bontón and buy a box of batteries for the flashlights,' Culebra would say. 'And while you're there, get me a soft drink and some cigarettes.'

To demonstrate my discretion, I stapled their personal packages closed since they contained liquor bottles, porn magazines and letters from their wives and girlfriends. Palillo thought my helping them so attentively was undignified. Other recruits whispered that I was the teachers' pet, but I didn't care. I had my reasons for being there, and they didn't include status or popularity.

Three days after the deserters' escape, training resumed. It was tougher than ever, especially since we were still on half-rations. Nevertheless, our collective punishment drew us closer together. And at least we weren't suffering like the two perimeter guards, still tied up in the sun.

At the end of the fourth day, the search was terminated. We all breathed a collective sigh of relief. It was Christmas Eve and our spirits were high since the deserters had made it. Although they'd let the group down, we'd feared the consequences for them if they were captured. In the barracks following evening political class, we were light-hearted – flicking towels and tipping each other out of hammocks.

While everyone else joked around, Ñoño wanted to continue the class discussion about communism. Few of us properly understood the doctrine. Most hadn't studied beyond the sixth grade. But Ñoño, who was probably the brightest of our group, insisted on giving us a dissertation on communism, using big words like 'proletariat'.

'You need to get outside more often,' Palillo told him. 'You've spent too much time reading the encyclopaedia.'

'You're just intimidated by my intelligence,' said Ñoño. 'Do you even know what that word means? In-tim-i-date.'

Palillo, being twice Ñoño's size, couldn't retaliate. Instead, he unbuttoned his trousers, saying, 'You think I'm intimidated by you? I'll show you intimidating.' He pulled out his dick at the exact moment Alfa 1 walked in.

'Everything okay?' asked Alfa 1, immediately detecting from the direction of everyone's gaze some dispute between Palillo and Ñoño.

'Yes, *comando*,' said Palillo in a casual voice. He had his back to Alfa 1 and he did not turn around or make any sudden movements that would have raised suspicion. He left his big, black dick hanging out. 'Ñoño here is just giving me a spelling lesson.' Palillo ticked off the letters on his fingers. 'I-N-T-I-M-I-D-A-T-E. Jesus, Ñoño. That word must be ten inches long.'

Everyone laughed except Alfa 1, who shook his head and walked out. Palillo grabbed Ñoño by the neck, lifting him off the floor.

'Put me down, Toothpick,' protested Ñoño.

'Who you calling Toothpick, Harry Potter? Show me that little white wand of yours. Because you better have some magic in that thing for me to be intimidated.'

Funny moments like that broke the gruelling monotony of training, but they never lasted long. And as training continued, short moments of hilarity were often followed by lengthy periods of horror.

Christmas Day was free time. However, breakfast rations were still half and the two guards were still tied to the poles in the sun. We played a football game against a team of trainers and guards, although only half-heartedly. Their side won, but they knew we hadn't tried.

At noon the same day, the two punished guards were brought in from their poles and made to stand before the recruits at afternoon parade.

'This is what's called a second chance,' Alfa 1 told us. He turned to the guards. 'Plank position. Backs straight. Three minutes. If one knee touches the ground,' he added, training his revolver on them, 'you're dead.'

It was *El Suplicio Chino*.

After two minutes of planking, the guards' bodies began to tremble. After two and a half, they seemed to be convulsing.

'Breathe!' advised Culebra.

For the last ten seconds, Beta counted down and we joined in. 'Ten, nine, eight . . .'

The guards made it to three minutes and then collapsed.

Alfa 1 announced that guard duty would now be added to our camp chores, even though we only had wooden rifles. He paired us up with the real perimeter guards for one-hour shifts. Although it was only an hour per day, if we were assigned a night shift our sleep was interrupted and there was no time to catch it up.

After seeing what had happened to their colleagues, the guards were jittery and this new task only increased their resentment towards us. However, we had to practise – soon we'd start rifle training and, when the guards finished their advanced course, we'd be responsible for our own security.

After seeing how harshly the perimeter guards had been punished, I added planks to my nightly exercise routine.

Ñoño came out and did planks beside me. I moved back inside. Although I felt sorry for him, I couldn't be associated with weakness.

On the second morning after Christmas, I was called to the gate because a tarpaulin-covered army supply truck had arrived, honking its horn.

'Delivery for Alfa 1,' the lieutenant who was driving informed me. He said I couldn't sign for it so I radioed Alfa 1 and was close enough to overhear their conversation. Evidently Alfa 1 knew Lieutenant Alejandro, but from the way they shook hands I could tell the lieutenant was neither expected nor welcome.

'What can I do for you?' asked Alfa 1 warily.

'Special delivery,' Alejandro answered, holding up typewritten documents. 'Courtesy of General Itagüí.'

'We haven't ordered anything.'

'We have some property that might interest you. Some lost property,' said the lieutenant, flinging open the tarpaulin.

I don't know who looked more surprised – Alfa 1 or the five boys. I guessed they'd climbed into the truck voluntarily, having been told a destination different to La 50. But their faces went from calm to panicked in an instant.

'*¡Joder!*' Alfa 1 swore then shook his head. 'Where did you find them?'

'They wandered in through our front gate,' said the lieutenant, handing the documents to Alfa 1. 'They had some rather interesting stories to tell. We wrote them down, but of course we didn't believe them.'

The documents were witness statements signed by the boys denouncing the Autodefensa training school at La 50.

'You lot. Out!' Alfa 1 jerked his head. Terrified, the boys obeyed.

Lieutenant Alejandro delivering the deserters confirmed what should have been obvious. The indicators were already there long before: the official sign on a government highway – GUERRILLA, NOT A PEEP! – and the army waving us through the Puerto Bontón checkpoint. The Autodefensas worked hand in hand with the police, army and provincial government. Even if you made it off La 50, there was no higher authority to escape to. In Los Llanos, the Autodefensas *were* the highest authority.

We all expected the deserters to be punished immediately. But they trained with us that day. They ate with us at lunch and dinner. They slept in their usual hammocks. The fact that nothing was said or done only compounded their sense of dread. Their punishment did not come until the next morning when we were introduced to Don Carlos Trigeño, the supreme commander for the entire region of Los Llanos.

29

COMANDANTE TRIGEÑO FLEW in by helicopter from La 35. At six foot two, Trigeño stood half a head taller than Alfa 1. His shoulders were broad and he wore an immaculate, tight-fitting camouflage uniform. A grenade hung from his belt, along with two side-arms, both in leather holsters – a revolver and a Colt .45 pistol. His sideburns were greying and he looked to be in his mid-forties. Trigeño's eyelids drooped like a lizard's while the steel-grey eyes beneath them darted everywhere.

He observed our morning training session and afterwards, as we stood at ease in parade formation, he mounted a wooden crate in front of us and delivered a rousing speech. My first impressions of Trigeño were positive. He was articulate, purposeful and had a sense of humour. Where Alfa 1 called the Paramilitaries by their military title – Las Autodefensas – Trigeño had a different name: *La Empresa,* meaning 'The Company'.

'New recruits, I bid you a very special welcome to *La Empresa,*' he began. 'You are now members of one of the biggest firms in our great nation and, as such, you will influence Colombia's history. *La Empresa* has thousands of employees but, unlike most companies, does not discriminate based on your family name, where you come from or your education level. All we care about is how hard you work. Each one of you has an equal opportunity to advance within this group. Your own capabilities and efforts will determine how quickly you ascend.'

Trigeño stepped from his crate, opened the lid and took out two empty green glass bottles. He strolled ten paces to the right and placed them side by side on a tree stump. Then he began to walk up and down between the rows of boys, as though conducting a parade ground inspection. By the time he passed me in the third row, I realised he was scrutinising faces not uniforms. I also saw that he'd removed his revolver from its leather holster, and as he continued his speech, he flourished it to emphasise his points. The effect was unsettling. Even without it, his presence and his voice commanded our complete attention.

'Unlike many companies,' he continued, '*La Empresa* pays in full and on time.' His booming voice, with its staccato words and melodramatic pauses, was now coming from behind me. 'You will be given rest time as deserved. You may occasionally receive bonuses for outstanding work. We do not deduct money for food. We do not deduct money for uniforms or housing. And best of all, you do not pay taxes.'

Here he received a few chuckles.

'In return, what do we expect from you?' he asked rhetorically. 'We expect loyalty.' *Crack!* went his revolver.

I jumped. My heart began pounding. I heard the sound of a body hitting the ground but kept my eyes to the front. Nobody turned. We stood immobilised, like frightened rabbits cornered by a fox. I glanced towards Alfa 1, Culebra and Beta, but their expressions were stern. None of them intervened.

The silence was absolute except for the crunch of Trigeño's boots on dried grass.

'We expect hard work,' he boomed. His footsteps stopped. *Crack!* went his revolver a second time. Again, I heard the soft thud of a body striking the ground.

'And we expect you to obey orders.' *Crack!*

A third body fell.

I held my breath and continued to stare straight ahead, but it was easy to guess the identity of Trigeño's victims: Jirafa, Pele and Armani, three of the five deserters. Tango and Murgas were standing side by side at the end of the row in front of mine. I couldn't see their faces, but Tango's legs were trembling and Murgas was gripping his wooden rifle hard enough to turn his knuckles white.

Trigeño continued speaking, and his voice didn't alter in pace or tone. It was entirely lacking in emotion, as though killing three boys had merely been a fitting way to punctuate his speech. But the sound of his voice was moving closer. He was returning to the front.

'There are many valuable lessons you will learn with us. You will learn self-discipline, self-respect and respect for others, which are fundamental for rebuilding this great nation of ours.'

He appeared at the edge of my field of vision and paused to glare at Tango and Murgas. I tensed, waiting for him to raise his revolver, but he didn't.

'You two. Out the front.'

Tango and Murgas emerged nervously from the ranks, their faces ashen. They must have been caught between fear and a faint trace of hope from still being alive.

'You!' Trigeño said to Tango, handing him the revolver. 'Have you fired a weapon before?'

'Yes, *comando*.' His voice was steady. I marvelled at his composure.

Trigeño drew his other weapon, the Colt .45, and pointed with it towards the stump with the bottles.

'Do you see those bottles over there?'

'Yes, *comando*.'

'I want you to shoot the left bottle. Can you shoot that bottle?'

'Yes, *comando*.'

'Then do it!'

Tango took careful aim and fired. The glass exploded.

'Good!' yelled Trigeño. Taking the revolver from him, he handed it to Murgas. 'Now it's your turn. I want you to shoot the other bottle.'

Murgas fired and missed. He looked at Trigeño, wondering whether to try again.

'Missed. Not so good.' Trigeño's tone was deliberately comical this time and we laughed, more from a release of tension than genuine amusement. Surely this meant there would be no more killing.

Taking the revolver, Trigeño handed it back to Tango, put an arm around his shoulder and walked him five paces further away from the tree stump before swivelling him around.

'Do you see that boy over there?' He pointed to Murgas.

'Yes, *comando*.' Tango looked as though he was going to be sick.

'I want you to shoot that boy. Can you shoot that boy?'

There was a soft sound among the ranks, a collective intake of breath at Trigeño's cruelty. This was much worse than the three executions he had just committed.

Tango looked at Murgas. He was trembling but he didn't raise the revolver.

He looked away. 'I can't, *comando*. He's my brother.'

'Then you just missed. Not so good.' He grabbed the revolver and forced it into Murgas's hand. 'Let's see if you can do any better. Shoot him!'

When Murgas hesitated, Trigeño pressed the muzzle of the Colt .45 against his temple. Hands shaking, Murgas pointed the revolver at Tango and screwed up his eyes.

'I can't either, *comando*.'

'We're going to wait here all afternoon until one of you pulls the trigger. I'm in no hurry.' He turned to the assembled recruits. 'Are any of you in a hurry?'

We were too stunned to answer, so he repeated the question louder and this time the chorus came back, 'No, *comando*.'

On his next turn, Tango once more refused to shoot his brother. Now angry, Trigeño fired a shot next to his ear. Tango jumped. Trigeño then dug the Colt .45 tip into his cheek.

'It's him or you. Who's it going to be?'

Tango began crying. He raised the revolver and pointed it at Murgas's chest. His hand was shaking.

Trigeño fired next to his ear again, closer this time, and then screamed, '*Who's it going to be?*'

Tango squeezed the trigger and a shot rang out. Murgas's face was distorted for an instant, and then he crumpled to the ground. I heard him groan.

Tango dropped the revolver and stood there quivering with his head bowed and tears running down his nose. He began to sob, breathing in great gulps that racked his body.

'Good!' Trigeño picked up the revolver and wiped it on his trousers. 'You're no longer schoolboys. You need to learn. This is war, men. In war, we have rules. The first rule is that you must obey orders. If you don't obey orders . . .' He fired two rounds into Murgas's prostrate body, ending his groans. 'You will be killed. The second rule is that if you can't kill the other man, he'll kill you.'

He spun on his heel and walked back to Tango, who was still sobbing.

'And the third rule is . . .' He placed a consolatory arm across Tango's shoulders and leaned into his ear as though about to give him some fatherly advice. 'No deserting!'

He fired a round into Tango's ear and Tango dropped.

'Lunch is at twelve,' said Trigeño, walking off. He turned and pointed at the bodies. 'Nobody eats until this mess is cleaned up. You, you, you and you,' he said, pointing to Silvestre, Pollo, Ñoño and El Psycho in the front row. 'Chop 'em and pack 'em, boys. Fifty by fifty.'

30

THE TROOP FELL out and wandered silently towards the sleeping sheds, still in shock. Most of them probably felt like I did. The knot in my stomach was not caused solely by the loss of Tango, Murgas and the others, or even by witnessing Trigeño's brutality. Having not intervened or said anything, I felt complicit in their deaths. I'd even laughed at Trigeño's showmanship and answered his question about not being in a hurry.

The four boys selected stood by the bodies under Beta's supervision to carry out Trigeño's order.

Picar y Empacar – Chopping and Packing – was the usual method by which the Autodefensas disposed of bodies. It was an expression I was to hear many times over the coming years, but that afternoon few of the recruits knew its meaning.

Beta handed Ñoño a machete and a shovel and pushed him towards Tango's body. Ñoño froze at the sight of blood. I'd lingered nearby, hoping for the opportunity to volunteer. Now I stepped forward.

'I'll do it,' I said, taking the shovel, although I still didn't see the purpose of the machete.

I'd buried two bodies in two months – Humberto Díaz's and Papá's. I was no priest and La 50 was not consecrated ground, but I knew the prayer that needed to be recited. Besides, I wanted Beta to know I could dig a grave.

He watched curiously for five minutes then stopped me. 'Hole's big enough. Get on with it!'

My prayer lasted ten seconds before Beta interrupted. He believed in black magic, not God, and claimed a spirit called the Big Red Boy protected him.

'You can pray later,' he said, stabbing the machete into the ground next to my foot. 'Chop him first.'

'What?'

'Chop!'

Finally, I understood. He wanted me to hack the body into pieces so it fitted in the hole.

'Honestly, I don't mind digging,' I offered, careful not to show my horror.

Beta picked up the machete and swung the blade downwards, embedding it in Tango's shoulder.

'He's dead already,' he said. When I still hesitated he aimed his Galil rifle at me and took it off safety. 'Don't think I won't.'

I studied his eyes. They were two marbles in concrete. He had four combats and thirteen dead *guerrilleros* to his name. There was no doubt he'd pull the trigger.

As a boy, I used to help my father butcher animals. The principles were the same. *Detach. Think about something else. Or someone else.* This wasn't Tango, I told myself – it was Ratón. I imagined his weasel face and pointy ears, his bored tone as he relayed the order to execute Papá. I took hold of the machete and pulled it out of the flesh.

The other boys took their lead from me. Silvestre picked up the second machete. El Psycho took the third.

Following Beta's instructions, we stripped the clothes from Tango's body and rolled him onto his back. Beta told us that the intestines and internal organs would expand in the days after death, so we'd have to remove them. I grimaced as I cut into Tango's belly, and was careful not to look at his face.

We took turns with the machetes. While the rest of us stood back to avoid getting blood on our uniforms, El Psycho kneeled beside the body with a look of fascination. The work was disgusting and smelly. But while we turned away, groaning or holding our breath, El Psycho stared without blinking and his nostrils flared as he inhaled the stench.

'Hurry up!' I told him.

We all wanted to finish quickly, but he made small incisions, peeled back skin and perforated tissue. At first I assumed he'd frozen up like Ñoño, but when I offered to take his place, he shoved me back and growled like a wolf protecting a carcass.

I shrugged and exchanged glances with Beta, who shrugged back. There was something very wrong with El Psycho.

Working mechanically, we hacked through the spinal cord and disconnected the head. Then we quartered the body and chopped the arms and legs into smaller pieces. The most difficult parts were the knees and elbows. If the machete wasn't heavy enough to split the joints, we had to dig around in the sockets with a knife, cutting the tendons and then pulling the bones apart with our hands.

In fifteen minutes, Tango, a healthy boy, was reduced to an unrecognisable pile of bloodied limbs that we scooped into a black garbage bag and dumped into a hole not much bigger than fifty centimetres by fifty centimetres. We buried the internal organs separately.

When we'd finished with Tango, I crossed myself, finished my prayer for his soul and commended him to God.

'You lot are dismissed,' declared Beta. 'Pedro, bring me four more workers. You choose.'

I nodded, glad he'd recognised my efforts. I decided that I'd also help with the next body. Then maybe Beta would recommend me to Alfa 1.

'Thanks,' whispered Ñoño as we walked towards the water trough to wash our hands. 'You saved me.'

A short time later, I helped the second group of boys chop and pack Murgas. Three of the four vomited. Two cried.

'The first time is always the worst,' Beta comforted. 'Just get on with it.'

Coca-Cola refused to continue until Beta cocked his rifle as a reminder of the second rule of the Paramilitaries: he who cannot kill will be killed himself.

31

AFTER BURYING FIVE bodies, I felt sure I would be on Beta's promotion list.

'Do you want us to make crosses?' I asked. 'To mark the graves.'

'Are you stupid?' Beta's hands shot to his hips. 'That's exactly what we *don't* want. Now empty their lockers!'

But I wasn't stupid. Papá and I had risked our lives to give Farmer Díaz a dignified Catholic burial. Doing the same for Papá was part of the reason I'd had to join the Autodefensas. But Beta had no respect for God or religion. I felt an impulsive anger towards him. Like an overstretched rubber band, my self-control finally snapped. When Beta turned his back, I pointed my wooden rifle at him. In my fury I forgot why I was there and all my carefully laid plans.

It was MacGyver who slapped it down and glared at me.

'They like you,' he hissed. 'Don't ruin it.'

I was unsure why MacGyver had taken such an interest in me. He certainly didn't care about the deserters. Together, we untied their hammocks and burned their clothes. Since stealing from a dead man was bad luck, we even burned their money. But I disobeyed Beta's instruction to throw their crucifixes in the river. When no one was looking I put them in my pocket and later transferred them to Papá's shrine.

As we returned to the mess hall, MacGyver offered me a further warning: 'Don't ever mention those boys again. They no longer exist.' To MacGyver, dismembering and burying the deserters had been an unpleasant chore, like cleaning toilets – you simply screwed up your nose, turned your head away and got on with it.

In the mess hall, Piolín wore make-up for the first time and the other girls' eyes were swollen from crying. Twenty-one of us had participated, and the others regarded us with a combination of sympathy for what we had been through and guilt that they had been spared.

Of course, the full impact of what we'd done would take weeks to absorb, but for the moment we sat staring at our uneaten meals in shock. The boys were not just dead; they'd been completely effaced from the earth. Between them being shot and buried, little more than an hour had passed. We had no time to adjust to the fact that they were no longer with us; they went straight into the ground.

I felt disgusted with myself. Never in my life could I have imagined mutilating a dead body. If threatened, I thought I'd refuse. But when it came down to saving my own life, perhaps I was capable of anything.

They're killers, Papá had told me in the dinghy.

I'd known that when I joined. In fact, I'd wanted to learn how to do it. I just hadn't thought we'd be killing people from our own side.

During my nightly prayers, I added an 'Our Father' for the five boys. Throughout the night I heard others sobbing. In the morning, a puddle of urine lay below Silvestre's hammock.

'Careful!' I warned Palillo the next day when I saw his eyes wandering towards the burial spot. The earth was packed down so tight you couldn't tell five bodies were below.

'I just can't believe . . .' said Palillo, shaking his head.

'Keep it to yourself.'

MacGyver had advised us never to mention deserting. Attempting it, planning it, suggesting it, discussing it or even joking about desertion was punishable by death. Silence shrouded our approach to the boys' place. Our primary feeling once the initial shock abated was undoubtedly the same: fear that it would happen to us. Scanning the ground, I saw 50 by 50 graves everywhere. My eyes played tricks on me. Every raised mound of earth covered a dead boy beneath. How many more were buried on La 50?

From that day on, there were no more thoughts of mutiny. No thoughts of escape. No answering back. Each time I passed the graves, I thought of Papá. At least he was resting under his favourite oak tree with a view over a town he loved rather than out in a baking field far from home. At least he had a cross marking his grave. And at least Mamá and I knew where he was. The deserters' families might never hear of them again. As time passed and grass grew over the graves, who would remember where they were?

Two days after the executions, I left breakfast early and, when no one was looking, I pushed a 200-peso coin half-a-finger deep into each patch. It wasn't much, but maybe one day someone would find those coins and keep digging.

'Lost something?'

I turned. Culebra was there, holding two empty bottles and his Smith & Wesson Sigma. He'd crept up on me, stealthy as a jaguar. I flushed, certain he'd seen the coins.

'No, *comando*.'

'Come with me!' Placing the bottles on a stump, he held up the pistol.

An image flashed through my mind: Trigeño placing two bottles on the stump and handing Tango his revolver. My gut twisted with fear.

'You still want to learn how to fire one of these?'

I thought Culebra was toying with me and that I was about to be punished. I looked around, but we were alone.

It took me several minutes to relax completely and accept that Culebra hadn't seen the coins. He was simply making good on his promise to teach me how to shoot.

32

THE SIGMA SW9F felt comfortable in my hands. Ammunition was contained within a seventeen-shot magazine. Before bringing me to the firing range, Culebra had used two of those shots to show his skill by shooting the bottles on the stump from twenty metres, but that still left fifteen rounds for me. I doubted he'd give me more since black market bullets were expensive.

We stood eight metres from the target – a human-shaped plywood cut-out. I focused my mind, trying to memorise Culebra's instructions. I might not get another pistol-shooting lesson and I needed to absorb every piece of knowledge.

'Feet shoulders' width apart, arms straight but elbows not locked, right hand on the pistol grip, left hand supporting the right wrist. Breathe normally. A single, steady squeeze. No jerking or sudden movements.'

I closed my left eye and took aim, aligning the top and rear sights. The target was a solid black bullseye surrounded by concentric circles in the centre of the human cut-out. Following Culebra's advice, I dropped the front sight slightly, just below the desired point of impact. I could see the sharply focused front sight touching the bottom of the blurry bullseye. I took a deep breath and began to exhale. Then I squeezed the trigger.

The silhouette target flexed with the bullet's impact.

'Not bad for a first try. How does it feel?'

'Good.'

It felt better than good. I could finally see my goal within reach. A pistol would allow me to get close to Ratón before exacting justice. He would hear the speech I'd been composing in my mind for weeks.

'Now step back and take your next shot.'

I backed up, took aim and fired again. I liked the pistol's kick and the weight of it in my hands. The bullet hit the target closer to the bullseye.

Each time the casing ejected and the plywood target rebounded, Culebra pointed out small things I was doing incorrectly, and then told me to step back before taking my next shot. He taught me to fire standing, crouching and kneeling.

'And always count your shots.' He raised an eyebrow. 'How many?'

'Sixteen, including your two with the bottles,' I responded. 'One left.'

I aimed and fired from ten metres. The bullet hit the edge of the bullseye, my best shot of the day. But that was it. Culebra took back the pistol.

He told me to collect the spent 9mm casings and throw them into a pit beside the rifle range that was already half-filled with empty shells. I obeyed, but kept a handful of casings to add to the shrine in my locker.

'Keep working hard. Keep me informed. And stay loyal.' Culebra tapped the pistol's barrel against his tattoo. 'And one day you might get one of these.'

I smiled. I was definitely on the promotion list.

Culebra tossed me the keys to the Blazer.

'I need batteries. Not the usual kind – the radio ones. The supplier phoned to say they've arrived. And I want some personal supplies. From Villavicencio.'

Villavicencio was the city we'd passed through on the way to El Filtro. It was four hours away.

My mind raced. A truck with tinted windows. An entire day on my own. Stores where the Guerrilla might purchase specialised supplies. Ratón in plain clothes thinking no one would recognise him in a city of three hundred thousand people.

'Sure. What do you need?'

Apart from batteries, Culebra wanted crates of beer, rum, porn DVDs, generic Viagra and condoms. New Year's Eve was the following day.

'Will I miss class?'

'Yes. A technical class on the parts of a rifle. I'll give you the handbook and you can catch it up later. But Alfa 1 wants to speak to you first.'

Culebra was using me since he had to teach class and couldn't leave base. But I didn't mind being used. I was learning about his brand of loyalty. While I scratched his back, I'd scratch my own too. In Villavicencio, I had a few errands to run myself.

33

NO MALE RECRUIT had ever been inside the commanders' dormitory – only the girls. Beyond the open door, Alfa 1 sat writing at his desk and did not look up as we entered.

Culebra slipped sideways and retreated against the wall. 'Here he is, *comando*.'

The trainers' shed was the same size as ours, only ours slept twenty-four. Two beds – presumably Beta's and Culebra's – stood against the far wall. Alfa 1's space had two roof-high partitions and included a kitchenette. In the centre of the room stood a weights bench and dumbbell rack. On the desk sat a television, several cell phones and chargers, and a radio.

Alfa 1 continued writing while we stood waiting.

'Tell me about the broken padlock,' he said finally.

Surprised, I glanced at Culebra. He'd implied the padlock would stay between us. Alfa 1 looked up and intercepted my glance.

'Soldier, if you think my men don't inform me of everything that occurs on my base, then you've learned nothing about chain of command. Eyes to the front!'

'Yes, *comando*.'

'Now, I want to know why you requested an additional padlock for the armoury right before five boys deserted.'

'To protect the container, *comando*. It's my job.'

I was trying to be succinct, but my response seemed to infuriate him.

'If you drive to Puerto Bontón, soldier, it's because I authorise it!' he barked. 'If you shoot a pistol, it's because I permit it! And if you're still standing here breathing after not reporting those boys' desertion plans, it's because I'm allowing you the oxygen.' He slammed his hand on the desk. 'Why did you request the padlock when you could have said nothing and gotten away with it?'

I was shocked by how much he knew, but I answered honestly.

'I didn't know anything for certain, *comando*,' I said. 'I'm not a *sapo*, but I did want to protect the weapons.'

Alfa 1 stood from his desk and began to pace across the room.

'Luckily for you, I judge a man by his actions and not by his thoughts.' He lit a cigarette. 'I've seen Trigeño kill boys just for discussing desertion. He might have killed you along with them, just for knowing. Your failure to inform us of their plans wasted a lot of man-hours, training time and aviation fuel.' He laughed ironically. 'Personally, I'm glad they escaped. I wouldn't want boys like that on my team during combat. And now the others understand that there are consequences. But you still did wrong.'

'Yes, *comando*.'

He took a long drag on his cigarette. 'I know you joined the Autodefensas because the Guerrilla killed your father. But tell me this: are you in for the long haul, or are you simply angry?'

That would have been the moment to tell him about my father's killers. However, if Alfa 1 guessed my intention to go after them, he might become suspicious and that could jeopardise my plans.

'I'm loyal, *comando*,' I lied, meeting his eyes. 'I'm here for as long as it takes.'

'Culebra has told me about your hard work in the armoury. And Beta reported that you volunteered to help dispose of the deserters. Keep leading, Pedro, and you'll be in line for promotion. But remember: being loyal to the Autodefensas means being loyal to *me*. I want no secrets on this base, no matter how small.'

With that, Alfa 1 dismissed me.

I went to my locker breathing a sigh of relief and changed into my civilian clothes, covering my military haircut with a cap. It was important to keep a low profile when venturing outside our territory.

I took the bullet casings from the pockets of my uniform and tipped all but one of them into the box with my letters to Papá. The remaining casing I put back into my pocket, deciding to take it with me to test the thoroughness of the gate guards' searches. Since it was a spent casing, without an actual bullet, I wouldn't get into trouble if they found it.

Alfa 1 might consider keeping secrets on La 50 a form of disloyalty, but by authorising me to drive alone to Villavicencio, he'd enabled me to keep far bigger secrets from him off the base.

34

AS USUAL, THE guards noted the time and purpose of my journey, and scrutinised the interior of the Blazer. They pulled out everything, from the emergency triangle to the tyre jack. On a vehicle's inbound journey, the guards were looking for cameras, hidden recording devices, telephones, weapons or explosives. On the way out, they searched for anything that might be stolen or seemed out of place.

When I'd driven to Puerto Bontón with Culebra, the search had been quick and friendly. But since the deserters' escape, La 50 had become like a prison compound in lockdown. The gate guards searched as though their lives depended on finding something. They even patted my groin and turned my pockets inside out.

The guard raised an eyebrow at the single bullet casing. 'What's this?'

'Trash,' I said casually, but I felt disappointed. If I couldn't get so much as a spent cartridge off base, what chance did I have with a pistol?

The guard pointed to twelve garbage bags lined up against the fence. 'Then you won't mind helping us again with those.'

At the end of their shift, the gate guards were supposed to carry the camp garbage five hundred metres to the dump. On my previous supply run to Puerto Bontón, I'd driven it there for them, saving them several trips. I loaded the bags into the back of the Blazer. It couldn't hurt to keep the guards onside.

The dump was an excavated pit three metres deep and ten metres across, with the extracted dirt piled beside it. It stank like an open sewer.

I backed up close to the pit and swung the bags in. A swarm of flies swirled into the air, rats scuttled over the edges and rancid air wafted skyward.

I was glad to get back onto the long, flat highway. At the Puerto Bontón army checkpoint, I readied my licence but the soldiers recognised the Blazer and waved me through. Once I got past Puerto Bontón a weight lifted from my shoulders and my mind became clearer.

Driving across the floodplains, I noticed that the water levels in the ponds and rivers had dropped, forcing the white storks into denser clusters. *Cebu* – specially bred cattle with high, protruding backbones – stood in fields with tiny egrets perched on their shoulders. I felt free, with a long, sunny day ahead of me.

For five weeks I'd been obeying orders under threat of severe punishment, even death. But outside the gates of La 50, an entire world had been going on without me. In that world you didn't follow orders. You didn't request permission to use the bathroom. You weren't told what time to sleep and wake up. Being off La 50 reminded me of what had once been normal. With fresh air blasting against my face and the stereo volume up, I pretended I was back in Papá's Mazda, happy and in control.

On the other side of Monterrey, I passed the same sign we'd seen on the way to El Filtro: GUERRILLA, NOT A PEEP! Half an hour later, a large road sign listed the distances remaining to upcoming towns. At the top of the list, twenty kilometres ahead, was Villavicencio. At the bottom was Garbanzos: 517 kilometres away, only a seven-hour drive.

My thoughts turned to home. It was the 30th of December. Mamá would be at Uncle's cooking stuffed pig with rice. Camila would be trying on dresses for tomorrow's salsa party. Perhaps I could just keep driving. I had hundreds of dollars that Culebra had given me for supplies. But the temptation lasted only until I reached the city centre of Villavicencio, where on every corner and in every passing face I saw Ratón. I remembered the file on Culebra's desk. Ratón had been sighted here on the 2nd of November, buying supplies, only two weeks before Papá's murder.

I knew Ratón needed batteries for his Motorola radio and, from the evidence in his file, he'd probably come to pick them up himself. I purchased everything on Culebra's list, leaving the radio batteries until last. All the electrical stores in town, including our own supplier, were located on the same block on Third Avenue and sold nearly identical merchandise.

I approached a shoeshine man who was squatting on a wooden stool at the corner of Third Avenue and 16th Street and offered him some coins to enter six of the seven stores and collect a business card from each. Meanwhile I'd visit our own supplier, Don Harold.

Harold was busy with another customer. I stood waiting in the doorway, fingering the bullet casing in my pocket and studying the faces of passers-by. It was to this street that Ratón would come. Would I be capable of shooting him?

On a firing range, ten metres from a stationary plywood cut-out, my aim had been good. But I'd only fired fifteen shots. I envied the perimeter guards who were allowed to fire hundreds every week. They were given so much ammunition that they usually came back with unused bullets, the numbers of which it was my job to record in a large inventory book.

Suddenly I realised how I could get the pistol bullets: I could under-report the number of bullets that were returned to the armoury after shooting practice. One day a number '6' could be turned into a '5'. Another day a '9' could become an '8'. With more bullets in actual stock than were recorded in inventory, I could then remove them without Culebra noticing a discrepancy.

Don Harold's customer left and I introduced myself. Our battery order was ready, packed in four boxes, and Harold was helpful, answering all my queries about our current radio model. What was the best way to keep the contacts clean? Would keeping the handsets on low volume extend the battery life? However, this was merely a lead-in and soon I began asking about the Motorola line. Knowing I was keen to save money for my bosses, Don Harold showed me a VHF and UHF catalogue. I recognised Ratón's model – the Motorola CP200.

'How much would this cost?'

'Two hundred dollars.' He winked. 'But if you bought enough units, I could give you a special price.'

'How long would they take to order in?'

'Two weeks. Three to be on the safe side.'

'And the batteries?'

'The same.'

The Guerrilla would have the same lead times for their orders. If I could find out when Ratón placed an order, I'd also have an approximate pick-up time. I thanked Don Harold and paid him in cash.

I carried the boxes to the Blazer. On the corner of 16th Street, the shoeshine man was waiting for me with the six business cards. I paid him too and departed.

Before leaving Villavicencio, I bought a city map, a cheap Nokia cell phone, a prepaid SIM card and a phone charger that could be plugged into the Blazer's cigarette lighter. Culebra had the connections to buy anonymous SIM cards, but I had to fill in a form and show identification. However, the storeowner gave me the code for blocking caller ID on outgoing calls.

Of course, I couldn't smuggle any of these things back onto La 50. I'd have to hide them in the one place I knew no one would look – the dump.

So I also bought two large zip-lock bags to protect my purchases from the weather.

The four-hour drive back passed quickly, and by the time I reached the dump it was 6 pm and my hands were trembling. The feeling of doing something unauthorised was now very real. By hiding a phone outside the Autodefensa base, I was risking my life. I would need to be careful. In fact, I would need to be *meticulous*.

I removed the battery from the phone so that it wouldn't run down. I searched the Blazer – even a receipt could give me away. Then I sealed everything inside the zip-lock bags and buried them in the south-east corner of the dump. I kicked a large stone down from the field above and covered the place so that I could find it again. After wiping my hands and knees and patting myself down, I was left holding the 9mm bullet casing.

Although the empty cartridge was harmless, new guards would be at the gate and bringing it back onto the base would be hard to explain. But neither did I want to throw it away. It was my lucky casing – the one that had given me the idea about under-reporting the inventory of bullets. I decided to keep it with the other items. And bending down a second time towards that pestilent stench to retrieve my zip-lock bag, I had another inspiration.

The guards searched everyone and everything that left La 50 as though their lives depended on it. Everything, that is, except the garbage.

That night, lying in bed, I thought of the deception I was now guilty of and what could happen to me if I were found out. I remembered Tango and Murgas, and how they'd been killed before my eyes, chopped, packed and completely erased from the earth. But then I pictured Papá's face and the risks meant nothing. My fantasy of killing Ratón came strongly into focus – now that I'd seen the electrical stores in Villavicencio, I could imagine exactly how it would be.

It is early evening when Ratón arrives. Few people are on the sidewalk. I approach quietly from behind as Ratón exits the shop. I grab his arm and stick my pistol between his ribs, telling him not to try anything stupid. He recognises from my voice and demeanour that I am professionally trained and does not resist. We walk calmly to the Blazer, which is parked around the corner. Once in the car, I make Ratón tie his own blindfold, which I've placed in the glove box.

Ratón begs to know who I am, where I am taking him and what I intend to do. I tell him to keep his mouth shut if he knows what's good for him.

We drive out to the field I have chosen, park the truck behind a large tree and walk a kilometre from the road. I command Ratón to kneel. I remove the blindfold and tell him who I am and why I have brought him here. It has only been four months. I know he recognises me and remembers what he did. But he pretends it wasn't him – he is innocent; I have the wrong person. I tell him there is no use denying it and eventually he changes tactics, now arguing that it wasn't his fault – he was merely a junior radio operator who conveyed messages between commanders. He says he is sorry for my father's death and he begs for mercy. I then deliver my speech while Ratón remains silent with his head bowed.

I have practised this speech many times in my mind. It is the same speech I will deliver to each of my father's killers when their turn comes. I know precisely how long it will take, the voice I will use and the exact words. Words like justice and suffering and right and wrong.

This is war, I tell Ratón. A war that the Guerrilla started and that they continue to wage on Colombia. It is their rule that you must choose one side or the other and so they must surely realise the consequences arising from that choice.

I reason with Ratón and, gradually, I see in his eyes that he accepts justice must be done. Killing him is now the only thing to do – it is the right thing, the moral thing. I promise to make it quick provided he tells me where to find the others, which he does

Finally, I circle Ratón slowly, just as Caraquemada circled my father. I pronounce the crime he has been found guilty of. The crime of killing a good man – a community man, who attended church and went fishing every Sunday – on the flimsy pretence of supplying water to the government army. The crime of making an innocent woman into a widow, of leaving a son without a father and of banishing them from the land they depended on to survive, thereby adding to their sorrow and preventing them from continuing life with any shred of dignity.

On the third time around, I place the pistol at a point I have chosen at the base of his head and pull the trigger. Ratón's skull thumps on the ground and I walk away, not looking back. And it is done.

35

THE FOLLOWING DAY – New Year's Eve – I began stealing 9mm rounds. After range practice, the twelve perimeter guards lined up at the container to hand back their pistols and boxes of unfired ammunition. While I wrote, Culebra called out each man's alias, the last three digits of the pistol's serial number and the number of unfired bullets he was returning.

'Valderrama, number three-seven-one, returning eight bullets.'

At first, I was too scared to under-report the bullets. In the end, I only changed one numeral, writing a '5' instead of a '6'. If Culebra checked my list, he might notice. However, his thoughts were on that night's celebration. There would be music, and each of us would receive four vouchers that could be exchanged for cans of beer. Culebra gave my list only a cursory glance before opening the brown paper package of Viagra and condoms I'd bought for him.

Once I'd added up the column of numbers and tipped the returned bullets into a bucket, I relaxed. The fraud was buried. During any future inventory count, the bullets would be out by one, but it would be impossible to determine when or how the error had occurred. Nevertheless, I needed many more bullets to fill a pistol's magazine. And I needed them within ten days, before the promotion course ended. Next time I'd have to be braver.

As we locked up for the afternoon, Palillo came to the container to ask me to swap my 6 pm guard duty shift for his 10 pm shift. Since drinking was not permitted until after guard duty, this would allow him to start partying earlier.

'Sure. Take these too,' I said, handing him my beer tickets.

When Culebra realised I wasn't drinking, he pressed the container keys into my palm.

'Guard these with your life. And no matter how much I beg, don't give them back to me until tomorrow.'

'Why not?'

'When I drink, I get crazy. On New Year's Eve two years ago, I opened the container and fired eighty-two rounds into the air at midnight.'

If he'd been a recruit, he might have been executed. Instead, Alfa 1 fined him twenty dollars per bullet – several months' salary. But this year, with me minding his keys, he could get properly drunk.

After dinner, the party began. Music blared from the office loudspeaker. Recruits and guards became more raucous as the night wore on. Meanwhile, the commanders were having their own private party in their dormitory, where they'd retreated with four of the girls and several bottles of rum.

I tried to join the festivities, but the effort to appear cheerful was exhausting. Guard duty came as a relief, although the perimeter guard who was partnered with me kept grumbling. Standing under a *copaiba* tree, listening to the music blaring and looking across at the brightly lit mess hall where a hundred soldiers were celebrating, I felt more alone than ever.

I prayed to God and told Papá I missed him like a *loco* and that I knew he missed me too. I told him I was working on a plan to get justice against his killers.

Although I'd left my lucky bullet casing at the dump, I had put another in my pocket. Rolling it between my fingers, I started analysing how to get my stolen bullets off the base. I couldn't simply throw them into a trash can then collect them at the dump. Earlier, when I'd inspected the black bags of garbage lined up against the kitchen wall, several were ripped and leaking. My bullets, being small and heavy, might drop through the holes when the guards carried them to the dump. The bags were also identical, and it might be a week before I could next get to the dump. How, among hundreds of bags, would I recognise which was mine?

When my hour was up, I returned to the mess hall to find the others drunk. Palillo was on a table, trying to impress Piolín with an invented dance he called *crossover,* which involved tap dancing to *regaetón* with two spoons in his mouth. Ñoño was demonstrating how a magnet affects a compass needle. Only MacGyver remained on the group's edge, looking pensive. Then the commanders sent Tortuga out of their dormitory with a message: beer rations were now doubled. The dormitory door slammed shut, the lights went out and a cheer went up for the commanders – Paisa, Mahecha and Mona were still inside.

'At least someone's getting some action,' muttered Silvestre.

Only a few days earlier, after the deserters were chopped and packed, the girls had bawled. Now, three of them were having sex with the perpetrators.

In a way, it made perverse sense. The girls were frightened and being with a commander implied protection. No matter what mistakes they made from now on, the commanders would presumably not execute their lovers. Tortuga, having just been excluded from the dormitory, appeared worried. Whereas Piolín, with her boyfriend back in Barranquilla, looked serene.

That night, Paisa, Mahecha and Mona's decision might have seemed good. But now that the commanders had gotten what they wanted, they wouldn't need to work so hard for it in future. The girls didn't know the many things they'd have to endure in order to maintain that protection. And if they protested, the protection could be withdrawn at any time, making them worse off than before.

I went to the kitchen to look again at the garbage bags. It occurred to me that wrapping the bullets in newspaper or food scraps would prevent them from falling out. Ñoño was passing around a plate of watermelon slices – their thick rinds would be ideal.

Marking the bag, however, was riskier. More identifiable marking would be easier for others to notice too. Then I remembered the heavy-duty garbage bags Culebra kept in the container. They were identical in size and colour to those used for kitchen waste but had bright yellow ties. The yellow ties would be distinguishable from hundreds of others at the tip but not suspicious. And I had the keys to the container in my pocket.

Although I didn't yet have all my bullets, I could start experimenting with the empty casings right away. Everyone was drunk. The commanders were out of the way. It was the perfect opportunity to execute a dummy run.

'Cheer up,' said Ñoño, offering me the fruit platter. 'It's New Year's Eve.'

I snuck away from the mess hall with two slices of watermelon on a paper plate, stopping only to collect the other bullet casings and my pocketknife. In the container, moonlight shone brightly through the mesh window, throwing a trapezoidal patch of light onto the floor. The garbage bag took only a moment to retrieve.

I was about to leave when it occurred to me that this was the most protected place on La 50 to conduct my trial. I bit into the watermelon, chewing the fruit until only a bite and the thick white rind remained. Then, crouching on the floor, I inserted my pocketknife, twisted it, and slid the empty bullet casings in, just as I'd seen Mamá do when she stuffed garlic cloves into turkey.

Suddenly, I heard footsteps crunching on the gravel outside. Keys jangled. I froze, too panicked to think where to hide the watermelon and remaining casings. Then Ñoño's voice sounded nearby.

'*Comando*,' he called. 'They're asking if they can open the rum you keep in the office.'

'Who is?' It was Beta. He was right at the container door.

I looked up at the desk and saw the brown paper package containing the Viagra and condoms that Culebra had forgotten to take with him. In another second, Beta would find the padlocks unlocked, the container door open and me crouched inside. But Ñoño's drunken response confused him.

'The rum in the office. They want it. And the *aguardiente*.'

'What? Who's asking?' demanded Beta.

'Up at the office,' rambled Ñoño. 'The lights are on.'

'Shit!' Beta's footsteps sprinted away.

I quickly slid another two casings into the watermelon rind and pushed both bits into the bottom corner of the garbage bag. Then I slipped out of the container and closed the padlocks.

I was shaking. If Beta had walked in, who knows what punishment he'd have ordered? If he thought I was stealing, that was punishable by death. Quite possibly, Ñoño had inadvertently saved my life.

Still trembling, I rejoined the group and began collecting beer cans and other rubbish to fill the bag.

'Stop being so responsible,' yelled Palillo. 'It's New Year's!'

I dumped the garbage bag with the others and headed towards La Quebrada for some air. After a short while, I heard footsteps again.

Piolín sat down beside me with two cans of Aguila, the beer from her home city of Barranquilla. Beta must have landed her best friend, Mahecha, since he'd lent Piolín his cell phone. She balanced the phone on her knee and offered me a can, flicking her fingernail against its side.

'Happy New Year.' The aluminium clinked and her voice sounded lonely. Two beers hissed open, but I didn't take mine. 'You escaped from the party too?'

I'd seen Palillo annoying her earlier. They seemed to be getting close, although he was doing all the talking. I shrugged.

'You don't talk much,' she said.

'Don't you need some privacy to phone your boyfriend?'

She glanced at my lips. 'I made him up.'

I could see she wanted me to ask her why. Instead, I accepted the beer and looked at my knee.

'Girlfriend?' she asked.

I nodded. 'Camila.'

She slid her arm across my back and held it there for an entire minute, leaning her forehead against my ear. I could hear her breathing. Then she placed a hand on my knee, kissed my cheek gently and whispered, 'What I'd give to be Camila.'

Girls are such wondrous creatures. In six weeks I hadn't spoken to Piolín. I'd barely even looked at her. She was beautiful as a tower-bound princess. She could have her pick from her three jailers or the hundred men beneath her with skyward eyes and lolling tongues, many of them taller, older, funnier and better looking than I was. As her footsteps receded, I noticed she'd transferred the phone to my knee.

Holding it, I looked up at the black sky with stars splashed against it like specks of silver sand. There was a half moon and I could distinguish my favourite constellations of Orion and Capricorn. I wondered whether they could see Camila and what she was doing right then. I had her photo in my pocket. I wondered whether there was some wild party that she'd snuck away from for fresh air, and whether the most *guapo* guy from the dance floor had followed her out, and then what she'd think and say as his hand inquired against her knee.

My thumb hovered over the phone's keypad. The temptation to call Camila was overwhelming. I reached into my pocket for her photo, but my fingers touched instead the one remaining bullet casing. My resolve strengthened and I turned the phone off.

The feeling would pass. It was simply New Year's Eve nostalgia. It *must* pass. I had a job to do and that job was like grief. Six weeks in. Painfully hard. And only just beginning.

36

ON JANUARY 1st, we exchanged our wooden cut-outs for proper rifles – Galils and AK47s – which we called our *novias*.

'Think of your rifle as your new *girlfriend*,' said Culebra, our firearms instructor. 'Do not let another man get his hands on her. You must sleep with her, know how to undress her in the dark and keep her well lubricated at all times.'

He paused until Palillo's laughter died down. Palillo still laughed the loudest, but he no longer interrupted with stupid questions, instead saving his comedy for when the instructors weren't around.

'Have any of you fired a rifle before?' Culebra asked.

Ñoño raised his hand. I didn't, although I'd fired Papá's .38 Winchester many times. The Winchester was good for scaring foxes or for putting a dying cow out of its misery. But firing a farm rifle – a .22, a .38 or even a shotgun – was nothing like firing a military assault weapon. Thinking that one qualified you for the other was plain dangerous.

The first shot knocked Ñoño backwards. He dropped the rifle and was punished with a two-hour pack run in place of dinner.

The Galil was heavier than Papá's gun, required a bigger cartridge and had a bigger kick. We learned to fire on semi-automatic mode, in which one round was fired per trigger squeeze. From the start, accidental rifle discharge earned us an instant day of *El Soleado*. A week later, simply being caught with your rifle off safety earned the same.

Beta encouraged us to give our new *novias* names. Silvestre called his rifle Piolín 'after a girl he once loved, but who didn't love him back'. Officially, Piolín still had a boyfriend back home. But thanks to me, Palillo had inside information and now worked on her with greater intensity. She liked him, but he ruined it by playing the clown.

'You don't always have to be the centre of attention,' I told him. 'Ask her about *her*.'

But Palillo thought winning a girl was about being funny, spending money on her, telling her she was beautiful and hoping she'd cave in. Since our shoulders became stiff from the rifle strap, Palillo offered to massage Piolín's knots. She arched her spine, leaned back against him and closed her eyes. Palillo proclaimed loudly so that everyone would hear, 'Did you know that ninety per cent of massages lead to sex?'

Piolín's eyes shot open and she stood. 'Then ten per cent of men are inept.'

Carrying four-kilogram rifles strapped to our shoulders also made the obstacle course harder. Beta reduced the minimum time by three seconds per day and added a creek crossing, during which we had to hold our *novias* above our heads.

Ñoño's speed had improved, but the addition of the Galil and the creek triggered a major setback. By the time he reached the monkey bars, he was exhausted. He leaped but kept missing the bars until Beta shouted at him to continue with the course and punished him afterwards with extra kitchen duties.

After training ended one day, Ñoño again sought my help. All his previous efforts seemed in vain; he was right back where he'd started.

'Teach me to jump like you,' he pleaded.

Since I secretly owed him for New Year's Eve, I agreed to help him practise. But after ten failed attempts on the bars, I could see no amount of training would be enough.

'What if I don't graduate?' he asked despondently.

'Perhaps your father has forgiven you,' I suggested, trying to put a positive spin on being sent home.

But that wasn't Ñoño's worry.

'The trainers hate me. Do you really think they'll let me go home alive?'

'Why not? Everyone's allowed to go home for two weeks' leave once we've . . .'

'Once we've graduated.'

He looked at his boots. I shook my head sadly. If Ñoño had short arms and couldn't jump high enough, it wasn't my fault.

Midway through the first week of January, Culebra sent me to Puerto Bontón for supplies, giving me a chance to stop at the dump. The garbage bag with yellow ties was easy to find. And when I ripped off one of its bottom corners, the two pieces of rotting watermelon rind tumbled out with the bullet casings still in place. I was now ready for the real thing.

I continued falsifying the bullet inventory, and by the time the perimeter guards finished their pistol training I'd under-reported sixteen of them – even more than I'd hoped. I'd remove all sixteen from the armoury in one go, insert them in watermelon rinds and place them in a single, yellow-tie trash bag.

I'd also need to steal a pistol, which I'd send out via the same route. But a pistol was larger and riskier to smuggle and would require more ingenuity to obtain. In the forty-foot container there were enough pistols to start my own shooting range, but each one was registered in the inventory with a unique serial number, and Culebra looked after them like they were his babies.

By mid-January, the trainers were calling us *soldiers* rather than recruits. The perimeter guards had finished their advanced course and departed, and we were now solely responsible for guard duty. It was the thick of the dry season, and training days were long and hot and gruelling. During breaks we gulped down litres of water and watched lizards skirmishing over scraps of shade. Afternoons ended with the obstacle course. We were more careful leaping from the jetty now since the water level had dropped, leaving shallow rocks exposed. When we returned to the mess hall at dusk, mosquitoes descended and crickets flitted through the browned, withered grass.

My muscles no longer ached and I no longer felt tired. The cement had dried around our routine and our bodies had moulded to the expanding training regime like new school shoes around growing feet. We woke automatically at 5 am without an alarm. We ate at the same table and sat in the same seats. We knew our places and we knew the rules.

My only worry was Ñoño, who continued to fail on the monkey bars. Each punishment wore him down, making him even less likely to succeed the next time.

'Thanks for trying,' said Ñoño at the end of one practice session. 'I owe you.'

'You don't owe me anything,' I said. Then, without thinking, I added, 'We're even.'

'You mean because of New Year's Eve?' He seemed embarrassed to mention it. 'It was nothing. I didn't want Beta to catch you.'

'Catch me?' I tried not to sound defensive. Whatever Ñoño knew, or thought he knew, I couldn't admit anything. 'I was just working.'

'With the lights off? I don't know what you were doing with those watermelons, Pedro. And I'm not asking. But you should be careful. If *I* can see what you're doing, the trainers might also.'

And he walked off, leaving me to contemplate the monkey bars and whether I'd truly done my utmost to help him. I knocked my forehead repeatedly against the wooden pole and then kicked the pole hard.

This was exactly the reason I'd avoided being friends with Ñoño. I knew I'd end up taking on his problems and that he'd eventually get in the way of my plans. Besides, what did he expect me to do? Lower the monkey bars? Beg the trainers to make an exception for his height?

Seven thick rusted nails jutted outwards from the wooden upright. If I repositioned just three of them together on the inside, they wouldn't look out of place and Ñoño might use them as a foothold. I'd have to do so without anyone knowing, not even Ñoño. If the trainers discovered the nails, he'd be the first to be blamed and would need to deny everything convincingly.

That night, I took a clawed hammer from the container and swapped shifts with Palillo, who was on the guard post closest to the monkey bars. Before tapping in the rusted nails, I hesitated. Repositioning nails was no big crime, but helping the weak was a risk I'd sworn never to take. People had to save themselves and make their own decisions. Once I'd started, where would it stop?

But the trainers did hate Ñoño. Beta's bullets were getting closer and closer. And while hammering in three nails might mean nothing to me, they were three nails that could save a boy's life.

37

DURING THE NEXT afternoon's obstacle course, Ñoño made three failed leaps for the monkey bars. On his fourth attempt to shimmy up the wooden support pole, his left boot found the nails. Having tried to clamber up that same pole many times, he must have been surprised to find a new foothold, but cleverly, he didn't glance down.

I stood on the wharf, dripping wet, and observed Beta's reaction.

'Well done!' he cried. 'Finally.'

Although short and weak, Ñoño was a good sprinter. He punched his fist in the air as he finished fourth-last.

Clapping slowly, Beta squinted at the pole. 'Your training paid off.'

I was relieved, but the nails would only be a temporary measure. Once Ñoño's strength and confidence were high enough to do everything on his own, I'd reposition the nails lower and eventually remove them altogether.

The following afternoon, Culebra came to the container looking stressed.

'Alfa 1 is in a filthy mood. He's been snapping at us all morning. Now he's ordered a spot inventory count.'

My heart skipped a beat. If I didn't separate out my bullets before the spot count, the discrepancy would be discovered, corrected and the bullets re-absorbed into inventory. Hiding them in the container for removal another day wasn't an option – Culebra was working right beside me. I told him I needed to use the bathroom urgently. But to prevent the bullets knocking audibly against each other in my trouser pocket, I had to walk slower than usual. Culebra noticed.

'Pedro!'

I froze. 'What?'

'You shit your pants or something?'

I paused. 'Not yet. But I will if you keep me here much longer.'

Culebra laughed and threw a rag at my back.

As I pissed against the side of the container, I dropped the bullets onto the ground and kicked them underneath. Then I ran my hands through my cropped hair and dug my fingers into my scalp. This time, there was no doubt about what I was doing: stealing from right under the trainers' noses. The penalty for being caught would be death.

However, two days later when the inventory count was completed, Culebra relaxed, enabling me to steal another yellow-stringed bag, insert the bullets into watermelon rinds and add the bag to the ordinary kitchen trash.

One good thing did come out of the surprise inventory check: I noticed that the only pistols not counted were the damaged weapons in the decommissioned box – their sole purpose was to be stripped for spare parts as the need arose.

When a pistol malfunctioned, Culebra now left the fiddly, time-consuming task of searching for spare parts to me. And if none could be found, the malfunctioning pistol would be added to the box and could remain there for months.

No record was kept of the parts already used from the stripped pistols. In fact, the box was a jumble of half-disassembled weapons. But there were three Taurus pistols in the box, and if I took the good parts from each, I could create a perfectly functioning weapon.

For eight weeks, I'd had my pistol without knowing it. I stripped the recoil spring from one Taurus and the firing pin from a second and added them to a third. I dry-fired it quickly to ensure it worked. Then I disassembled it, wrapped the parts in toilet paper and removed them from the container one by one.

Everything was falling into place, and the trainers still had no suspicions. In fact, when I drove Beta to Puerto Bontón, he himself lifted the garbage bag containing the Taurus parts and hurled it into the dump.

On my next solo trip to the dump, I reassembled the Taurus, cocked it and dry-fired it. It worked just as before, only now, away from the base, the click of metal sounded more satisfying. Then I placed the Taurus with the bullets in one of the two zip-lock bags and removed the phone and battery.

Back in the Blazer, I lined up the business cards from the electrical stores on the dashboard. I took out my photo of Papá. Although I'd already taken a million risks, I was willing to take a million more.

One by one, I called each of the electrical stores, inquiring about the Motorola CP200 lithium-ion battery.

Each store gave the same response: 'That's restricted war matériel! Who are you and where are you calling from?' When I persisted nicely, they explained that an over-the-counter sale of long-range VHF radio batteries without a licence from the Defence Ministry was illegal.

I hung up, dejected.

But a few days later, on my next visit to Puerto Bontón, I phoned each store a second time, claiming I had a licence and needed five batteries – could they quote? This time, four storeowners said they could get them in. I'd have to attend the store in person with the licence and identification. Of course, I couldn't go through with this, but at least my search was narrowed. One of those four stores must be the Guerrilla battery supplier. But which one and how could I find out when Ratón would next visit?

I couldn't phone, claiming to be Ratón – his supplier might know his voice. Nor could I claim to be one of his subordinates – the Guerrilla probably had specific greeting codes. But it occurred to me that I might be able to find out more by visiting the stores and impersonating a junior *miliciano* working on Ratón's behalf.

Why not? I looked the part: I was young and had a shaved head and a military-trained physique. By visiting, I could watch their reactions closely. Even if my ruse was detected, I might at least discover which store Ratón used.

Unfortunately, being sent to Villavicencio depended on the whims of the commanders. Since we were in the thick of training, there were no upcoming parties. And with Mahecha, Paisa and Mona making nightly visits to their dormitory, the trainers had no need for porn videos. As for Piolín, she continued pining after her phantom boyfriend while Palillo played along.

Rejection hadn't made Palillo change strategies with Piolín; it made him determined to be funnier and earn more money.

'This country has resources,' he said on payday, eyeing trucks from Trigeño's Agricultural Co-operative as they rattled towards La 35 with yellow barrels of fertiliser and departed an hour later laden with cattle. Palillo counted his salary three times, curling up his nose. The envelope always looked thicker than what came out of it. 'We can't be employees forever.'

At the time of Papá's job offer, Palillo's shopping list of what would make him happy had been modest. Now, he'd seen greater wealth and his dreams had grown accordingly. His Discman was now a solid platinum watch. His childhood slingshot was a Colt .45. His Yamaha 250cc was a Toyota Blazer. All of it belonged on a splendid ranch.

I humoured him. 'How much would you need?'

'Approximately two hundred and fifteen thousand dollars.'

'On the minimum wage, that would only take . . .' I counted on my fingers. 'Three and a half lifetimes.'

I refused to spend my salary, taking out only the small amount I needed and sending the rest to Mamá. But Palillo's envelope was always empty before the next one arrived.

Two days later, returning from the rifle range, a voice yelled from the back of the group, 'Everybody down!'

We hurled ourselves to the ground. For ten seconds the only sound was that of twenty soldiers scrambling towards the trees. Crawling was painful now that we carried rifles that weren't to be scratched.

'What was that?' asked Piolín.

I looked up. Palillo was lying on top of her. Somehow, his limbs were sprawled across Tortuga, Mahecha and Paisa. The fifth girl – Mona – had escaped his grasp, although he was reaching for her ankle.

'I thought I heard enemy,' claimed Palillo.

Gradually, we realised what he'd done.

'Get off me!' cried Piolín.

'What do you mean?' His lips were centimetres from hers. 'I practically saved your life.'

'Get your hands off me!'

'And that's my thanks?' Palillo stood and slapped his thighs to brush the dust off. 'I take a grenade for you and no reward.' He adjusted the anaconda. 'No gratitude. Not even a kiss.'

Palillo made me laugh. Seeing him happy made me happy too. Through a rare combination of luck and grace, Palillo could do cartwheels along a cliff edge and not even a hurricane would make him fall. He could dance hopscotch through a minefield. And while everyone around him was blinded and shell-shocked, stumbling around in search of missing limbs, he'd emerge from the blast zone smiling, swinging his anaconda and singing, 'What's the time, *mi corazón*?'

Neither had he given up on his acting dreams. The Paramilitaries was simply his toughest role yet – the audience came from all over the nation and the critics had guns. But seeing him happy also made me realise I should never have gone to Garbanzos plaza that Friday. Palillo would have ended up in the Paramilitaries eventually. Even if Papá had given him a job on the *finca*, he'd have joined the army when he turned eighteen. Either way, Palillo would have been fine.

And Papá would still be alive.

38

THE SIXTH EXECUTION occurred in the first week of February. A strong hand covered my mouth and shook me awake. Using field signals, Beta formed twelve of us into a squad and laid out our mission. He pointed to the motionless silhouette of a man at the south-east guard position and ordered us to sneak up and surround the post. I assumed it was another night training exercise.

In the prone position, we inched warily forward. Reaching the guard, I saw that it was Pollo. Beta stood and waved a hand in front of his face. I'd never seen anything like it. Pollo was snoring on his feet, completely unsupported. Ñoño stifled a giggle. Beta touched his finger to his lips, stood behind Pollo and unsheathed his serrated hunting knife. Until the last moment, I believed Beta was demonstrating his stealth. But he gripped Pollo's jaw and wrenched back hard, slitting his throat all the way around. Pollo woke instantly, clutched his neck and fell kicking to the ground, gargling blood. He bled out in less than a minute.

Beta gave the order: 'Chop him and pack him, boys. Fifty by fifty.'

By morning parade, everyone knew. Alfa 1 backed Beta up.

'If you're tired before guard duty, the coffee urn is always full.'

Culebra explained their rationale: there were one hundred and six lives to protect at the base. One man falling asleep could cost all of them. So now there were only one hundred and five.

Nerves began to fray. Daisy's howling vigil over Pollo's grave made it worse.

'Shut that dog up,' Rambo yelled. Pollo had been his best friend. Ñoño held Daisy tightly in his hammock. During class, he tied her to a tree.

The girls looked the most tired. Cushy guard shifts and lighter chores no longer seemed a fair exchange for their frequent call-outs to the trainers' dormitory. But they wouldn't leave the commanders. Through Palillo, I heard Mahecha invented women's problems to avoid sleeping with Beta.

Palillo concentrated on our upcoming leave – he was trying to convince Piolín to go on a beach vacation with him. But for me, every injustice was a reminder of Papá's death. MacGyver joked that I was the commanders' golden boy. For almost four months I'd done everything right. I played their game and I played it better than any other recruit. I made them think that I was working on their side. But there was only one side I was working on: my own.

Lying in my hammock at night, I ran through different scenarios of what I'd say to the four storekeepers and how they might respond. Unlike Palillo, I was no great actor. However, I did have one advantage when it came to impersonating the Guerrilla's urban militia: having observed them collect *vacunas* from Papá, I knew their mannerisms and how they spoke. And more importantly, I knew their names.

Ideally, I wanted information that might lead to a time and location where I could find Ratón. It might be an invoice from a previous order, a docket for future delivery, a contact name or a transport company. But first I needed to discover which store he used. At a minimum, that would allow me to observe the store during my two weeks of leave in mid-March. After that, my plan was vague. I might go through the storeowner's rubbish. I might break in at night and steal his client list and customer orders. But to do any of these things I needed to get to Villavicencio.

Culebra ignored my hints about needing more supplies, instead sending me to Puerto Bontón. Even when I hid the double-sided electrical tape, he said we could survive without it until the end of the course.

Then, on February 20th, he required something that was unavailable locally.

'Fireworks,' he said. 'Lots of them. And smoke flares.'

He gave instructions on where to purchase them, as well as money for alcohol for our graduation party and a list of 'personal items' for the three trainers.

Finally, I was to drive to Villavicencio.

This time, when I stopped at the dump, I tucked the fully-loaded Taurus into my trousers. I needed to practise carrying it. It might also come in handy. On the million-to-one chance I saw Ratón, I'd take him on the spot.

Before setting off, I creased and rubbed dirt on all four business cards to make them look older. On the reverse side of each, I wrote the name DANIEL JOAQUIN GÓMEZ.

I arrived in Villavicencio before midday. Culebra's purchases took less than an hour, and then I drove to Third Avenue.

At each of the stores, I told the owner the same story: my boss needed five Motorola CP200 batteries, for which he had a government permit.

'They're hard to get in,' said the first.

'We don't keep them in stock,' said the second after flipping through a catalogue.

To each objection, I shrugged like an innocent errand boy who didn't know what he was buying.

'I just do what I'm told.' I held up the store's dirtied, creased business card. 'This is where he said to come.'

The first storekeeper frowned. 'Who's your boss?'

I flipped over the card to reveal the hand-written name DANIEL JOAQUIN GÓMEZ – Ratón's political alias. This name was Ratón's bond; it struck fear into people who knew it, including his suppliers.

'Should I know him?'

'He's a regular customer.'

Frowning, he looked up his database but found nothing. From his confusion and lack of fear, I could tell he was genuine. The next two storekeepers didn't recognise the name either. However, the fourth storekeeper, Boris Sandoval, nodded.

Sandoval was a respectable-looking man in his mid-forties with a neatly trimmed moustache. A girl of about nine years old, wearing a school uniform – presumably his daughter – sat quietly behind the counter doing her homework. This man couldn't possibly be Ratón's supplier, I thought. But he was.

'Why didn't he include them in last week's order?'

I couldn't believe my luck. I'd expected to have to coax information out of the storekeeper or threaten him, but Sandoval had voluntarily jumped a few steps ahead.

'Like I said, comrade,' I removed my cap so he'd see my military haircut – the same one worn by *guerrilleros*, 'I just follow orders and deliver messages. My boss said to combine both orders. When do you think they'll be ready for pick-up?'

'Same as usual – two to three weeks. Why didn't he come himself?'

Obviously, the haircut wasn't enough. I lifted my shirt to let him see the Taurus.

'Phone him when they're ready. You have the correct number?'

Suddenly wary, Sandoval nodded. He looked at his daughter, who hadn't seen the pistol.

'Go finish your homework in your room, *cariño*.'

She closed her books obediently and disappeared through the door behind the counter. I heard her feet pattering up a staircase. He waited until the sound of footsteps faded before consulting a blue folder. 'A 310 number?'

'That's the old one,' I told him. 'It's now a 312.'

Switching on my phone, I read out the new number: mine. As Sandoval wrote, I read the previous number he had for Ratón upside down and memorised it. 'My boss keeps it switched off for obvious reasons. Just leave a message.'

My plan was simple. When both orders were ready for pick-up, Boris Sandoval would leave a message on my phone, thinking he was calling Ratón. Now that I had Ratón's number, I'd phone him, pretending to be Sandoval, and leave the same message, word for word, in case it contained hidden codes. Ratón would come to pick up his order, just as he normally would, but with one important difference: I'd know he was coming.

'Why didn't your boss phone to place the order himself?' Sandoval looked down at the old number. He'd put a tiny cross next to it and written NEW beside the one I'd given. 'How come he sent you?'

'The 310 number was compromised. One of our suppliers snitched. The police were intercepting several lines. Three other suppliers were arrested – all of them are now dead.'

Sandoval's eyes widened. He snatched up his pen and scrubbed out the old number like it was diseased. He wouldn't be dialling that number ever again.

Outside, I crossed the street to the *Residencia Royal* – a small hotel diagonally opposite Sandoval's store – and asked to see a room on the second floor. I didn't know exactly when the batteries would arrive, so I made a reservation for the entire two weeks of my leave. I paid four days' deposit in cash. But I wanted no mistakes – number eight, the room I'd been shown, was the one I needed. From behind the curtains there was a clear view up and down both sides of Third Avenue. I had no way of predicting what time of day or night Ratón would come, or from which direction. But he had to enter via the storefront – there was no back entrance. I'd approach him from behind with my Taurus, disarm him and make him accompany me to my vehicle.

Of course, there was nothing to stop Ratón phoning or dropping by to check whether his original order was ready. And unless I could somehow use the Blazer, renting a truck would be complicated and expensive. There were other risks too: What if the batteries arrived early, before our course finished? How would I then get off La 50? Or what if the batteries arrived late, after my leave was over?

I thanked the *residencia* manager then drove around the block several times, searching for public parking lots and the quietest route back to the highway. I filled in additional details on my city map – the location of traffic lights and road works – and I identified two contingency escape routes. Afterwards, I purchased a shovel.

On the drive back to La 50, I turned left into a disused side track immediately after the GUERRILLA, NOT A PEEP! sign in Monterrey. After a kilometre of bumpy driving, I crossed a rise and spotted a giant saman tree two hundred metres from the track. No dwellings were visible. The location was perfect. I hid the shovel in a bough of the tree then returned to the highway. This time, I smiled at GUERRILLA, NOT A PEEP! It would be the last sign Ratón ever read.

Suddenly, a new song by Juanes came on the radio and I felt ecstatic. I honked madly at the storks huddled together in shallow ponds and swerved playfully towards the metre-long iguanas as they dashed from the road's shoulder. It was a wonderful afternoon – I was speeding towards clear blue skies with warm, fresh air whipping across my face and uplifting music filling my ears.

In a single day, I'd gone from sketchy speculations and vague hopes to having a concrete plan. Ratón was finally in my sights. And once I had him at my mercy, I was certain that he would lead me to the rest of my father's killers.

Thirteen weeks of training were now over. There were only three to go. All I needed to do now was regularly check my phone for messages and continue doing exactly what I'd been doing.

In the first week of March, Daisy went missing. For ten days, Ñoño was inconsolable. Despite her barking, we'd all grown fond of her too. We searched for her during lunch breaks, calling and whistling. Maybe wild pigs had got her, maybe she'd fallen into La Quebrada, or maybe she'd simply run away. But to Ñoño, our explanations made no sense.

'She'd never leave me,' he said.

He didn't give up searching until Rambo grabbed his collar during kitchen duty and yelled at him to stop complaining about a stupid dog. Beta overheard and sentenced both to another week's kitchen duty.

'That's not fair,' muttered Rambo.

Instantly regretting what he'd said, he fell to apologising. But Beta raised his pistol to Rambo's eye and fired. This time, I didn't flinch. Rambo's crime: being tired and saying three words without thinking. It was unfair and cruel and unnecessary. Rambo had been friendly to everyone. Beta killed him simply because he could. And afterwards he smirked because there was nothing we could do about it.

When there was just one week left in the course, I persuaded Culebra that the Blazer needed a new alternator. It could be installed in a single day but the part would take two weeks to arrive. I offered to drive the truck to our mechanic in Villavicencio at the beginning of leave and pick it up on my return. But in reality, I'd ordered the part a week earlier and booked its installation for the first day of my leave, which would give me two weeks using the Blazer.

Now, all I had to do was keep my mouth shut and pass the final obstacle course. But then, with one stupid, split-second decision, I ruined everything.

39

MARCH 11 WAS to be our final training day. I guessed Alfa 1 was planning something big because ten additional commanders had arrived at La 50 the day before to assist with modifications to the obstacle course.

All afternoon, they cleared the long, dry grass with machetes, dug canals and hosed the ground until it turned to mud. They stacked five large piles of wood between obstacles and divided the fireworks I'd purchased in Villavicencio into ten plastic bags.

After the obstacle course, Alfa 1 would announce promotions. I had no doubt I was on the short list to become a junior commander, but I aimed to cross the finish line in record time. I was the fittest I'd ever been in my life and wanted to prove that my discipline had paid off. My only concern was Ñoño.

'What are they planning with all that barbed wire?' he asked anxiously.

'You'll be fine,' I reassured him. 'You've done the course a hundred times. Tomorrow will be no different.'

The next day at 7 am we returned from bathing in La Quebrada to find Beta and the ten extra commanders standing in a line with their arms folded, blocking the entrance to the mess hall. In place of breakfast, Beta announced, we would do a four-hour endurance pack run, jogging continuous laps around the camp's perimeter. Although March was the hottest time of the year in the flood plains, we received no rest breaks and no food, only water. Since it wasn't a race, I jogged in the middle of the pack with Palillo and Ñoño to conserve energy.

By 11 am, when we stumbled across the finish line in front of the mess hall, our pack straps were sweat-welded to our shoulders and we were pale with strain and fatigue. Legs trembling, we collapsed backwards onto our packs and lay on them like overturned turtles, opening our eyes only when we smelled roasting meat.

Outside the mess hall, we saw a calf spit-roasting over hot coals. We lined up with plastic plates to receive a white-bread sandwich with a single sliver of meat drowned in spicy *ají* sauce. Although the beef tasted strange, fresh bread and meat were rarities at La 50 and we were ravenous. A second, much larger portion followed – this one tasting like proper, succulent beef – accompanied by potatoes and *Postobón* soft drink. After lunch, we lay on the grass, massaging our twitching thigh muscles and digesting the food.

'Don't eat any more,' I warned Ñoño when Culebra offered a third helping.

We hadn't done the obstacle course yet, and I guessed from the trainers' continuing preparations that our ordeal would be tougher than expected. By then, they'd wrapped barbed wire around every obstacle. The smell of diesel drifted through the air.

'On your feet, soldiers!' yelled Beta.

We lined up for the start. It was now midday and the sun was at its fiercest. Usually, we would set off in groups of fifteen at one-minute intervals in order to avoid congestion. Since the fifteen-man groups hadn't changed in four months, we'd become complacent, establishing an unofficial order of who went first, second and third, up to fifteenth. This made tackling the obstacles easier and more efficient for everyone; rather than pushing and fighting, we politely waited and gave way before competing in the final stretch.

This time, however, all ninety-seven soldiers were to start together. Nevertheless, we had to finish the course within the same time.

'Go hard at the beginning,' I advised Ñoño. I knew the starting sprint would be brutal – getting caught behind others at the first obstacle would cost valuable seconds.

Ñoño nodded. We both understood what was at stake. Failing to complete every obstacle in the allocated time meant not graduating. Although the exact consequences of not graduating were never stated, we'd seen the trainers' barbarity.

'On your marks,' Culebra shouted. He fired his Galil into the air. Ninety-seven pairs of boots pounded the earth. Ninety-seven sets of shoulders barged against each other as we elbowed, pushed and sprinted our way towards the first obstacle, the rope-net climb.

Immediately, I understood the purpose of the additional trainers. With this final course, Alfa 1 aimed to test our limits by simulating gruelling, war-like conditions. As we climbed the net, the trainers stuck our backs, calves and feet with wooden rods. One blow landed on my leg and

I swallowed a yelp of pain. From the top of the net we dropped down and crawled along the ground. The trainers fired live rounds, the bullets striking the ground only centimetres from us, kicking up the earth. They tossed fireworks among us – spinning pinwheels shooting sprays of searing, white-hot sparks. Flares tumbled and rolled, pouring out coloured smoke. We coughed and choked, blindly bumping into each other.

As I dragged myself through the first concrete pipe, tear gas flooded my lungs and burned my eyes. I emerged from the pipe disoriented, only to find thick black smoke from the five diesel-soaked woodpiles billowing across the remaining obstacles.

The gunfire, explosions and swirling smoke infected the race with life-or-death urgency. Adrenalin-charged, panicked and short of breath, we became hunted pack animals in a race for survival. When Coca-Cola tripped at the foot of the brick-wall climb, rather than helping him up, several boys stomped over him.

I was in the leading group. As we balanced along the wobbling-log, Beta lobbed flash-bang grenades beneath it – each one exploded with a deafening roar and a blinding flash of light. During the rope-net mud crawl, Alfa 1 fired bullets so low that I could hear them zinging over my ears.

'Heads down!' he screamed. 'Lift them and lose them.'

I was now in the lead. As I elbow-crawled my way through the square concrete pipe – the third-last obstacle – I heard the hum of flies buzzing ahead. At the tunnel's midpoint, a single shaft of light penetrated the pipe and I found myself looking directly into the eyes of the dead calf I'd just seen roasting on the spit. I recoiled in shock. Then I noticed a strong smell of faeces. Shit had been smeared over the pipe on either side and I had to place my hands in it to climb over the severed head. The concrete pipe led upwards at a thirty-degree angle. I hoisted myself out and sprinted towards the second-last obstacle – a belly-crawl through mud beneath a roof of criss-crossing barbed wire.

The crawl space was narrow, and the trainers had hung the calf's intestines from the wires. I closed my eyes as slimy, bloody innards slid against my cheeks. I pressed on, but when I finally made it to the end of the mud-crawl, I found myself looking into the eyes of another severed head: Daisy's.

My stomach lurched. Daisy had trained with us the entire course. She had been more than our mascot; she'd been one of us, and the trainers had killed her just to give us something to think about between the barbed-wire crawl and the monkey bars. Later, MacGyver explained their logic: battle was not merely physical but also psychological and emotional. So the trainers beheaded a different 'Daisy' every course, aiming to replicate what it felt like to suddenly see someone you knew killed in the midst of battle. The trainers may have had their logic, but at that moment I was revolted by their calculated cruelty.

Detach, Pedro. Detach! Daisy is not a person. This is war. This is what you wanted.

The monkey bars were slippery with Daisy's blood, but I didn't stop. I flew off the final bar and landed with bent knees, as behind me I heard soldier after soldier crying out at the sight of Daisy.

I was the first to launch myself from the wooden jetty into the cool, knee-deep water of La Quebrada. Panting, I washed off the mud, blood and shit. I lay floating on my stomach, allowing myself an underwater smile and a brief moment of self-congratulation while the next finishers splashed in beside me. *I'd done it!* Only then did I remember Ñoño. Daisy had been his dog more than anyone's.

I scrambled onto the jetty to see Ñoño three-quarters of the way back in the pack, just beginning the mud crawl. At the sight of Daisy's head he froze momentarily but then lifted himself out of the mud.

Having made it past Daisy, I assumed Ñoño would be fine. He simply had to swing across the monkey bars and then sprint to the finish line. When Culebra yelled, 'Two minutes remaining!' I was certain he'd make it easily.

However, when he reached the monkey bars, his foot went automatically for the three rusty nails and he slipped, landing facedown in the mud. He tried again, but the nails were gone. He tried twice more, but each time his foot slid against the pole, his fingers slipped on the blood-splattered bars and he fell.

Twenty soldiers backed up behind Ñoño, screaming for him to hurry. No one thought to calm him; they were too intent on not failing themselves.

'Move forward!' Alfa 1 bellowed, striding towards the group while firing into the ground repeatedly. 'Forget him! We're an attack force. Go around him!'

Everyone pushed past Ñoño except Silvestre and Palillo. They knew they weren't allowed to assist him, but neither would they abandon him. Time was running out. As Culebra commenced the sixty-second countdown, Alfa 1 began firing at the monkey bars.

'Go around him!' When a bullet glanced off the wooden post, Silvestre obeyed. Palillo stayed, even as the bullets struck closer, until Alfa 1 fired between his feet. 'Leave him! He's already dead.'

Palillo swung along the monkey bars as Alfa 1 stomped towards Ñoño.

'Come on, soldier! You've got no cover. Get yourself out of there! You're a stationary target. Here comes the enemy.'

Mud splatter from the bullets got closer and closer until Ñoño must have felt the bullet thuds vibrating in his fingertips. He lifted himself to his elbows, readying himself for one last try, but then Beta dropped Daisy's head in front of him, eyes open, tongue out.

'You ate your own dog for lunch,' Beta yelled at Ñoño. Then back at the rest of us. 'All of you ate Daisy with *ají* in that sandwich.'

Hearing this, several people retched and vomited. Ñoño, however, placed his hands over his ears and his strength deserted him. Collapsing facedown in the mud again, he remained as still as a carcass.

'Ñoño. Run!' I yelled. 'Ñoño!'

But he could no longer hear me above the rifle shots. Alfa 1 was only ten metres away.

The others stood on the wooden jetty in horrified silence, hands pressed against their mouths, listening to Alfa 1's successive gunshots. Paisa covered her eyes. Mahecha turned her back. We could all sense what was coming. It had been coming for four months: this was the final day of training; Alfa 1 was eliminating the last of the weak.

'Thirty seconds,' announced Culebra.

'You have to do something,' Piolín whispered to Palillo. 'They'll kill him.'

I looked at Palillo. His face was strained with anguish, but he clenched his jaw and shook his head.

'If we interfere, they'll kill us too.'

I wanted to turn away like Mahecha or cover my eyes like Paisa, but I couldn't. A strange feeling welled up inside me, beginning in my stomach and surging into my throat. A similar feeling had surfaced briefly when Beta made us chop up the deserters' bodies. And it had come again – although in smaller, shorter bursts – after every execution, every torture and every act of cruelty that I'd witnessed.

I realised that it came from the soft part of me that believed people sometimes needed protecting, and it was provoked by witnessing strong, powerful people abusing those who are weak. Of course, this softness had not died completely with Papá, although it had been savagely severed.

During my four months at La 50, I'd deliberately tried to kill off its remaining roots. In order to track down and kill Papá's murderers, I told myself, I had to learn to bear all forms of suffering – not only my own, but also the suffering of others. I'd forced myself to observe others in pain, and I had done so without interfering.

But now, seeing Alfa 1's bullets splashing closer to Ñoño, I was surprised to discover the emotion welling up inside me stronger than ever, threatening to spill out in mutiny against my will.

'Twenty seconds,' announced Culebra.

'He's just a kid,' I said.

And then somehow I found myself sprinting towards Ñoño without remembering the first step I'd taken, or the exact moment I'd decided to help him. The calculating part of my brain had been overridden by something more deeply ingrained – something that resided in my gut and that told me what to do even when my rational mind and the world around me was arguing the exact opposite.

'Stop, Pedro!' Culebra yelled. I was aware of him chasing after me, although only vaguely. 'Come back!'

But by then I'd sprinted the fifty metres from the jetty to the monkey bars, and although my heart was pounding and I was struggling for breath, I couldn't stop no matter how much the trainers screamed at me or how many bullets they fired.

I pushed Alfa 1's rifle away and threw myself into the mud next to Ñoño. When Alfa 1 kept firing, I covered Ñoño with my body. I wouldn't let him kill Ñoño. He'd have to kill me first.

Alfa 1 stopped firing.

'What the *fuck* are you doing, Pedro?'

We stared at each other. Alfa 1 seemed as surprised as I was. There was silence for a moment.

Then Ñoño came alive. Struggling beneath me, he dug his elbow into my ribs. 'Leave me alone!'

'It's me! Pedro!' I slapped him hard and ripped him to his feet by the collar. 'Now run!'

In the final straight, Culebra's countdown was deliberately slow. Ninety-five soldiers chanted with him, slowing the count further. Even then, we crossed the line two seconds late. However, as we splashed into the water, the others gave an almighty cheer.

Only then, with the sudden rush of cold and enveloping wetness bringing me to my senses, did I properly realise what I'd just done. As I clambered onto the wooden jetty, I knew rescuing Ñoño was a decision I would shortly regret. In fact, seeing the trainers' furious faces, I regretted it already.

I wished I had stuck to my plan. I wished I had maintained my self-control. I wished I had calculated the risks and the consequences. And I wished that I had never laid eyes on Ñoño.

40

AS SOON AS Ñoño was on the jetty, he rushed towards me.

'I knew you were my friend. I *knew* it!' He hugged me tightly and said quietly in my ear, 'I owe you my life.'

But Palillo prised Ñoño's hands apart and shoved him hard in the chest so he almost fell backwards into the water.

'Pedro, the trainers are pissed at you,' he said anxiously, leading me away from the small group that was gathering to congratulate me. 'You need to keep a low profile. Don't make eye contact with anyone. And *you*!' He pointed back at Ñoño, who had regained his balance and was already trotting after us. 'Shut the fuck up, stop being so happy, and disappear!'

As we passed the girls, Piolín whispered, 'That was the bravest thing I've ever seen.'

But it wasn't. It was a moment of weakness. Now that my normal thinking had returned, I realised my true mistake dated back two months to January when I'd hammered in those rusty nails. The nails were meant to be temporary, but Ñoño had come to rely on them. I should have removed them as planned. In fact, I should never have helped Ñoño in the first place.

As the three trainers departed in a huddle towards their dormitory, I felt Alfa 1 glaring at me. Right then, the group mood was on my side, so he didn't take action. But my punishment would not be long in coming.

While the others dried off and changed into fresh uniforms, Palillo led me out of sight behind the container. I had to prepare myself mentally for every possibility, he said. My punishment might be anything from a fine of several months' salary, a few days of *El Soleado*, the Chinese plank, or even worse. He didn't need to spell out what he meant by *even worse* – disobeying a direct order could mean execution.

I kicked the container. 'How could I be so stupid?'

I went to Papá's shrine to pray and seek strength, but when I opened my locker it was empty. The Virgin Mary statuette was gone. The unsent postcards to Camila and letters to Papá – gone. The photos – gone. I turned. Piolín was standing behind me.

It must have been something important for her to enter the male dormitory. Her head was bowed and she could barely look me in the eye.

'The trainers need to see you in their quarters,' she said.

'Thanks.'

'Pedro, be careful! They're drunk.' She stepped forward and hugged me tightly, pressing her fingertips into my back. It was the type of goodbye hug a condemned man might receive before walking towards the gallows.

My first knock on the flimsy wooden door was drowned out by the sound of death metal music blaring from inside. The door was unlatched. Hesitantly, I pushed it open. Inside, the three trainers appeared to be celebrating the end of the course. They didn't notice my arrival.

With their shirts off, Beta and Culebra were straddling the weight benches in the middle of the room, doing arm curls with twenty-kilogram dumbbells. The veins swelled around their snake tattoos – Culebra's anaconda slithering over his clavicle and down his bicep and Beta's python curling around his forearm. As they paused between sets, Culebra poured two shots of *aguardiente* from a bottle on the floor beside them, which they downed instantly.

Alfa 1 was sitting at the kitchenette table, perusing a list of names. On the table sat another half-empty bottle of *aguardiente*, a shot glass and a scrunched up bedsheet.

'You wanted to see me, *comando*?'

Culebra dropped his dumbbell, stood slowly and turned off the music. He looked at me apologetically and I wondered whether he'd tried to defend me to Alfa 1. Over months of working closely together, we'd become friends. But if it came down to it, there was no question of where his loyalty lay.

Beta glared at me maliciously before pointing to the chair across the table from Alfa 1. Both he and Culebra moved to stand behind Alfa 1 so that all three were ranged opposite me, as though I were a prisoner in the dock facing three judges. I sat with growing trepidation.

Seated, I could make out the names on Alfa 1's list – they belonged to the one hundred and four recruits who'd begun training in November. Some names had one or two ticks beside them – presumably those being considered for promotion. Most had crosses. And some names were struck through with a dark line: Tango, Murgas, Pollo, Rambo, Armani, Pele and

Jirafa – all of them dead. My own name had three ticks beside it, which had been changed to crosses, and a line through it. However, there was also a question mark in the margin; perhaps they hadn't yet condemned me.

For a long time they said nothing. Alfa 1 sat drinking silently – his face was hard to read. Culebra looked uncomfortable, but Beta's scowl hid nothing – he wanted me dead. It was he who lifted the sheet to reveal the possessions from my locker, including my letters to Papá, which had been opened. I flushed with anger and embarrassment – they'd sifted through my private world. Then my embarrassment was overtaken by panic at what they might have discovered in the letters.

Although I'd been careful not to mention any specific plans, or even my intention to seek justice for Papá, Alfa 1 might easily read between the lines. However, it seemed that searching my locker had been Beta's idea. He began to read excerpts from the letters to humiliate me and see how I'd react.

'Dear Papá,' he began in a sneering falsetto, 'I miss you so much and I'm so sorry for what I did. I know I can never take it back . . .'

I knew he was baiting me so that I'd leap at him and give him the perfect excuse to kill me. I kept my fists clenched by my side, eyes front and locked on the horizontal, reminding myself that I was a soldier and this was a test.

Beta handed a letter to Culebra, who accepted it without enthusiasm. 'Dear Papá,' he read, 'I have your Bible, and I pray every night as you taught me.'

Now two voices mocked me, mocked my father and humiliated me with my darkest thoughts and most painful feelings. One after the other, they dove in and tore strips from me, like hyenas taking chunks from a fallen lion cub.

'Whenever I feel weak, I think of you and I know you're protecting me. You give me strength to go on . . .' Beta raised his eyebrows in challenge, perhaps believing he'd lit upon my most intimate disclosure.

But I held strong, and when Alfa 1 saw their mockery wasn't working, he clapped his hands as a signal to desist.

'Think that was clever what you did this afternoon?' he demanded.

'Definitely not, *comando*.'

'Think that was brave?' demanded Beta, copying him.

'No, *comando*.'

'Do you think I would have shot Ñoño?' asked Alfa 1.

'I don't know.'

'Well, I *would* have. You want to know why? Because one boy like Ñoño cannot override the military objective of an entire unit. You were at the front, Pedro. You'd reached your goal. Why turn back for someone who was already dead?'

'I was weak,' I said. 'I felt sorry for Ñoño. It was wrong and I apologise.'

'Weak is exactly right,' said Alfa 1. 'You were told not to go back. You disobeyed our orders and you did so publicly. Make no mistake, recruit, there must be consequences.'

I bowed my head. I was no longer *soldado*; he was back to calling me recruit.

'We trusted you, Pedro,' said Culebra sadly, tapping his pen against the list of names. 'You were first in line for promotion.'

I bowed my head lower. 'It was one mistake, *comando*. I promise it won't happen again.'

'One mistake?' repeated Alfa 1 sarcastically. 'This was not an isolated incident.'

Beta stepped forward and dropped three rusty nails on the table. His smile was now sinister.

'Did you really think I wouldn't guess who was responsible for these nails appearing the day after you changed guard shifts with your best friend?'

So they'd known about the nails all along. But rather than confronting me in January, they'd allowed me and Ñoño to get away with it in order to later teach us both a lesson.

'Forgive me, *comando*. I shouldn't have interfered.'

'Damn right. We're the trainers. We know best how to turn boys into men and men into soldiers.'

Alfa 1 scratched his head and tapped his pen tip against my name. Now that I'd confessed, fully submitted and given him nothing further to criticise me for, I hoped he could see that I was truly humbled and meant every word of my apology.

He turned to Beta for his final input.

'You know my position,' Beta said. 'Culebra's gone soft. Any other recruit would be chopped, packed and underground by now.'

'Leave us, both of you!' Alfa 1 commanded, frowning. Clearly, he had yet to decide.

Alfa 1 now stood, skirted the desk and leaned into my face. He grabbed the back of my neck and forced me to look at the tattoo on his forearm.

'Do you know what this is, Pedro?' he demanded through gritted teeth.

'A rattlesnake.'

'Yes! But do you know what it *means*? To be part of a team? Do you understand what it means to be a true Autodefensa? You may think that you know better than your commanders, but you don't. You need to be a team player. You need to trust in the Autodefensas. You need to have faith in its leaders and faith in me. There's no room in a military chain of command for individuals to do whatever they like. In a battle, that costs lives. And there's no room for pity either – our enemy will have none for you.'

Alfa 1 paused, folded my letters and placed them in a bag with the statue, photos and postcards. He breathed out heavily and slid the bag towards me.

'Hand back the Blazer keys. Your leave is suspended. You will remain on La 50 until further notice. And not a word of this conversation to the others or I might change my mind about giving you a second chance.'

I waited for more. But that was it! My body flooded with relief.

'Yes, *comando*,' I said, taking my possessions and heading quickly for the door. 'Thank you.'

My relief lasted only until I closed the door and comprehended the full consequences of having my leave revoked. When I did, Alfa 1's punishment seemed almost as bad as execution. I would have preferred a week tied naked in the sun, two Chinese planks and a fine of six months' salary.

During my confinement to base, Sandoval the storekeeper would ring my phone, which was switched off and buried at the dump. I wouldn't be able to listen to his message. When Ratón didn't show, Sandoval might try a few times more. Eventually, he'd contact Ratón some other way, or Ratón would contact him. Once they communicated, Ratón would realise something was wrong. He'd probably change numbers and suppliers. He might even disappear altogether.

I might never get a chance at Ratón again. And maybe not at Papá's other killers either. After my confinement, who knew how long I'd be stuck on La 50? Moments earlier I'd been glad to be alive, but what did that matter if everything I'd planned and worked so hard for was now completely destroyed?

41

WHEN I RETURNED to the dormitory, everyone seemed amazed that I was alive. They wanted to know my punishment.

'I can't say,' I told them glumly.

I had all afternoon to dwell on my own stupidity. I would have given anything to take back what I'd done. But our course was now over. Our rifles were cleaned, oiled and shelved in the container. That night there would be a party with a blessing ceremony and the following day our two-week leave would begin. There would be no more classes, no more exams and no more opportunities for me to prove to Alfa 1 that I was a tough team player.

While everyone around me cleaned out their lockers and happily discussed vacation plans, I lay in my hammock, depressed and angry with myself. From our course, six boys had been chosen for promotion – Silvestre, Escorpión, Indio, Kamagra, Pirata and Johnnie Walker. Right then, they were lining up in the office to have their snake tattoos done.

That should have been me, I thought. *I should have been with them in the office.*

When the others left for dinner, Palillo and Ñoño were still trying to guess my punishment. I was so depressed that I no longer cared about Alfa 1's orders. I confided in them.

'That's all?' exclaimed Ñoño. 'No pay cut? Not even a single push-up?'

To Ñoño, my punishment was fantastic news. He'd been feeling guilty because this was all his fault. He couldn't understand why I was so upset about losing my leave. Neither could Palillo – I'd told him that I didn't want to return to Llorona anyway, so what did it matter?

'I'll stay behind with you tomorrow,' he offered.

'I'd rather be alone.'

Ñoño also tried to comfort me, offering to bring me food and my beer ration from the mess hall. I told him to go away.

When Ñoño left, Palillo shook his head.

'Your punishment's too light,' he said. 'You need to stay on guard, Pedro. Remember when the deserters were captured and returned?'

Of course I did. They'd been sent back to training and ordinary duties as though nothing had happened.

Palillo was right. There had to be more. And there was. It came that very evening in the form of a Venezuelan witch doctor.

42

LA BRUJA BRAVA – the Fierce Witch – stepped from a motorised canoe onto the bank of La Quebrada wheeling a leather suitcase and surveyed the assembled graduates.

She was short and squat, with thickly matted black hair threaded with condor feathers. Her wizened face might have belonged to an old-looking thirty-five-year-old, or a well-preserved seventy-year-old.

'She doesn't look so fierce to me,' said Ñoño. 'And I'm betting that suitcase is full of dried llama foetuses.'

'I doubt it's soap or a change of clothes,' joked Palillo, referring to her pungent odour.

La Bruja Brava laid her suitcase at the water's edge and flipped open the lid; it was empty. She lit a small pipe that she produced from the folds of her voluminous skirts. Then, fully-clothed, she waded into the river until the water was waist-deep. She lifted her face skyward, her eyes rolled back and she began to chant unintelligible words in a thick, masculine voice.

'What's she saying?' I asked.

'It's an Indian dialect,' answered MacGyver, who'd pushed his way to the front. 'She's invoking the Big Red Boy.'

'The who?'

'The devil. You make a pact with him and he saves your life.'

Alfa 1 stood on the riverbank and ordered us to strip to our underwear. He announced that making a pact with the Big Red Boy was compulsory. The devil's spells protected you against enemy fire. Provided you obeyed the individual spell given to you, bullets could hit your body but never penetrate. A *right* spell meant that your right side was protected in battle. A *left* spell meant that your left side was protected. Those given an *even* spell should not advance with an odd number of troops in their squad and vice versa for *odd* spells. Other spells required you to repeat a special saying or throw a handful of rice over your shoulder after the first bullet was fired.

Beta went in first. Since spells expired after six months, he needed his renewed. He liked to display the keloid scarring on his abdomen that proved he'd already been saved once. His spell involved chewing on a piece of *mutamba* bark before battle then reciting a phrase that only he was allowed to know. The Fierce Witch guided his head underwater and inhaled smoke from her pipe, blowing it into his face as he resurfaced.

While Beta dressed, MacGyver strode in and I slunk to the back of the queue where I hoped to be less visible and perhaps even avoid receiving a spell. Papá had told me God could forgive everything except making a pact with the devil. It meant you'd lose your soul and couldn't enter heaven. Palillo saw my discomfort and followed me.

'Don't worry. It's perfectly fine to have two religions,' he assured me.

To him, faith was like ice-cream: ordering a double scoop allowed you to mix contradictory flavours. However, like Papá, I was a one-flavour man.

Palillo told me I couldn't refuse – white magic was common throughout Los Llanos, so we were surrounded by believers. Besides, the trainers were watching me closely. Ñoño also had his reservations, although for different reasons.

'This is uneducated bullshit,' he crowed. 'Do they really think stupid chants will block bullets travelling at a hundred metres per second?'

'Quiet!' hissed Palillo. 'Remember to stay on guard.'

The line advanced rapidly. Hemmed in on one side by the river and on the other by twelve trainers, I felt like a bull being corralled towards a matador.

As Ñoño entered the water, Alfa 1 eyed me attentively. Palillo went next. When my turn came, I followed Palillo's advice and stepped forward without protest. Before holding my head underwater for five seconds, the Fierce Witch told me my spell. I should always move forward and face my enemy; the moment I turned my back or took my eyes off him, he would kill me.

As I came out of the water, Alfa 1 eyed me again. But I wasn't his true target – he must have overheard Ñoño's earlier snideness about the Fierce Witch.

'You don't feel protected by this uneducated bullshit?' he asked with apparent concern.

Ñoño, who was buttoning his shirt, seemed startled. 'I have my spell, *comando*.'

'And yet you don't sound convinced,' replied Alfa 1. Then he yelled to the troop assembled on the bank, 'Does anyone else here *not* believe in the Big Red Boy?'

Although most Colombians are raised Catholic, not a single hand went up.

'And yet I'm sensing doubt,' observed Alfa 1, no longer needing to shout. The troop was so silent that I could hear water trickling off nearby rocks. 'I think we need an example for the doubters.' He aimed his Galil at Ñoño's chest. 'Kneel.'

Ñoño remained standing. He was half Alfa 1's size. He clasped his hands and looked up pleadingly as though praying to a giant god.

'Please, no, *comando*! Please.'

Alfa turned the Galil away from Ñoño and fired his entire magazine into the creek. The rifle cracked repeatedly, a line of bullets splashed across the water and the air filled with smoke and the smell of burned sulphur. Ñoño was trembling. Alfa 1 gripped his shoulder and pushed him down.

'I said *kneel*!'

The rifle was now empty. Alfa 1 removed a single round from his breast pocket and held it up before inserting it in the chamber and cocking the rifle, which he then trained back on Ñoño's chest, waving it from left to right. 'Left or right? Which side is your spell?'

Ñoño was too shocked to answer. The Fierce Witch came out of her trance and answered for him.

'His left.'

'Then hold still,' said Alfa 1, digging the muzzle under Ñoño's left collarbone, the side that was protected, 'and you won't feel a thing.'

Ñoño's eyes now pleaded silently with mine. However, Alfa 1 caught the direction of his gaze. Smiling sarcastically, he raised his eyebrows at me in challenge.

'Pedro, any objections?'

Of course, he was testing me. Would I make the same mistake I'd made that afternoon? Would I dive once more in front of his rifle to save Ñoño?

'No, *comando*,' I answered. 'I learned my lesson.'

This time, I wouldn't interfere. After the obstacle course, Alfa 1 had asked me, 'Why turn back for Ñoño if he was already dead?' I was an Autodefensa and Alfa 1 was my commander. And if my commander wanted Ñoño dead, then it was simple – Ñoño had to die.

'Good!' said Alfa 1. Keeping his left hand on the barrel and the muzzle tip buried under Ñoño's collarbone, he lifted his right hand from the butt and signalled for me to stand in his place and hold the Galil. 'Then perhaps you'd like to demonstrate for everyone exactly what that lesson is?'

Finally, I saw the trap he'd laid. Alfa 1 wasn't making an example of Ñoño for doubting the Fierce Witch – that was simply a pretext. He was making an example of us both for the obstacle course: I was to shoot Ñoño.

It all made sense now – the perverse logic of Alfa 1's lecture to me on teamwork and trust, as well as the lightness of his punishment. This was Alfa 1's true punishment: having to do myself the very thing that I'd prevented him from doing at the obstacle course – eliminate the weak.

Ñoño began begging loudly. 'Pedro, no. Please! No.'

Alfa 1 spoke louder. 'That's an order, Pedro.'

I looked at the rifle and then at Ñoño. I didn't believe for a second that the Fierce Witch's magic spell had made him bulletproof. But I knew that if I didn't shoot him, Alfa 1 would anyway. Besides, wasn't this what I'd wanted? An opportunity to undo my mistake and prove to myself my own toughness and commitment?

As I gripped my right hand underneath the rifle butt, Ñoño's eyes grew wide with disbelief.

'Sorry, Ñoño,' I said, touching my finger slowly against the trigger. Breathing in deeply, I focused my eyes on the tip of the muzzle and emptied myself of all thought and feeling. And without further hesitation, I squeezed.

43

WHAT HAPPENED NEXT I remember as keenly as my father's execution. The muzzle flashed, the rifle cracked and Ñoño's hand went up in belated protest. He flew backwards, his left elbow striking the ground and his body twisting over. He looked up at me, pained and completely bewildered. Alfa 1 took the Galil from me, actioned it, and the ejected casing arced through the air, clinking and spinning against rocks.

'*¡Médico!*' I yelled, cutting my shirt in two with my knife. From that range, the 7.62mm round might have tunnelled through cleanly. I lifted Ñoño's shirt to locate the entry and exit wounds and staunch the bleeding.

'No medic,' Alfa 1 countermanded.

Ignoring him, I rolled Ñoño onto his back. The front of his shirt was singed, but there was no blood.

'Does it hurt?'

'Of course it fucking hurts! You shot me.'

'You and you!' Alfa 1 pointed at Coca-Cola and Silvestre. 'Chop him and pack him, *muchachos*.'

Ñoño sprang to his feet and leaped back. 'But I'm not dead.'

He unbuttoned his shirt. Beneath, I saw severe bruising and seared flesh from the muzzle blast. But still no blood, and no bullet wound.

'Let me look properly!' I said.

But Ñoño pushed me in the chest. 'Get the fuck away from me!'

I was no longer his saviour and he was no longer my loyal servant.

I'd shot Ñoño. The fact he'd survived was no thanks to me. It was now the Big Red Boy he worshipped.

That night, as everyone got drunk on *aguardiente* to celebrate the end of the course, Ñoño refused to talk to me. He'd drilled a hole through Alfa 1's spent cartridge and hung it on a leather thong around his neck. Displaying his bruise and burns, he skipped sideways from group to group like a river crab, re-enacting how the bullet had bounced off his skin. But whenever I approached him, Ñoño turned his back and walked away. I wanted to explain what had happened. It was perfectly logical. I'd even found proof.

Alfa 1 had inserted a blank – a training round that simulates ordinary gunfire. Almost everything is the same. The muzzle flashes and the rifle cracks, but the spent casing must be ejected manually and there is no recoil because no bullet leaves the barrel, only a heavy blast of burning-hot air. Ñoño had never been in danger. Afterwards, I had retrieved Alfa 1's empty ammunition box from the trash as evidence.

'You going to ruin it for everyone?' asked MacGyver when he saw me heading back towards the group. 'They all think they're bulletproof.'

To join the army you needed a school certificate, but most Autodefensa soldiers could barely read and write. They didn't know about blanks. They believed what they saw and what the trainers told them. Should I tell them the truth?

As everyone continued celebrating, I slipped off to La Quebrada to be on my own and think.

Staring into the swirling waters, I replayed the shooting in my mind and tried to justify to myself what I'd done. Most people believe they'd never shoot someone, especially not a friend. Even with a gun pointed at their head and given the choice between their life and the other person's, they believe they'd simply refuse. However, until it comes down to it – until they're actually in the situation – they don't truly know.

But Alfa 1 had shown me differently. He was like a doctor displaying to me an X-ray of my own skull. I'd seen myself properly now – not my face in the mirror but the bare bones beneath. Although I had yet to kill anyone, I now knew I was a killer, and I was glad. A killer was what I needed to be. However, Ñoño hated me and I wondered what the others thought. As the Fierce Witch had closed her suitcase – now packed with watches, necklaces and money donated by soldiers to the Big Red Boy in exchange for his protection – I noticed them looking at me differently.

I knew I shouldn't have been so worried about other people's opinions, but I was. Over sixteen weeks, although I'd made few friends, I had established a reputation.

So when Palillo found me sitting on my own at La Quebrada, I decided to lie. I would claim that I'd known about the blanks in advance. It was believable that I'd been part of Alfa 1's act – I'd worked in the armoury and was close to the trainers.

'Don't cut yourself to pieces, *hermano*,' said Palillo, putting his arm across my shoulder. 'Something like that was bound to happen to Ñoño. He brought it on himself.'

'They were blanks,' I said, holding out the evidence.

Palillo nodded without needing to read the box. 'I know.'

'Ñoño was never in any real danger,' I said. 'None whatsoever.'

'I know what blanks are.'

Rather than lying, maybe it was better to avoid the subject altogether.

'Is Ñoño okay?'

'One minute he hates you, but the next he's so busy retelling the story that he forgets. Come back to the party. Try talking to him.'

As we walked towards the mess hall, a group of soldiers stepped out of my way. Although our usual table was full, four boys stood to make space. As I sat, the girls wouldn't look at me and the volume of conversation increased.

'Does everyone hate me that much?' I asked Palillo.

'No,' he said. 'They respect you. Although they're also a little afraid.'

'Afraid of what?'

'That you'll shoot them next.' Palillo laughed, which made me laugh too. He had a magical way of cheering me up.

We sat a while longer, watching Ñoño re-enacting his near-execution and proudly displaying Alfa 1's spent cartridge. I called him over, but he wouldn't come.

'And what do *you* think, Palillo?'

'Ever since Tango shot Murgas,' he said, 'I think all of us have been praying we wouldn't be selected to execute someone. But at the same time, every one of us has also been wondering what they'd do in that situation. Whether they'd be capable of pulling the trigger. Unlike us, you now know.' He took the box from my hand and stood. 'I'll tell Ñoño that you knew about these beforehand. Otherwise he'll never forgive you.'

'I'll tell him myself.'

'No, the trainers want you in the office.' He winked. 'Something about a tattoo.'

44

LEANING AGAINST THE inside office wall was a short, bespectacled man holding a leather satchel. I didn't have time to look at him properly before Beta called me to attention.

'Eyes front, soldier.'

Alfa 1 sat at the desk. At the river, he'd proven his point – that he could make me obey any order he gave – and he'd proven it publicly. He now seemed back in control and relaxed.

'Don't look so worried!' He signalled for the man with the briefcase to step forward. 'I'm promoting you, Pedro. You'll get your own squad of eight soldiers. You can choose four, the other four I'll decide. And get used to the idea of protecting Ñoño. You wanted him alive, you keep him alive.'

Culebra added his congratulations. 'I asked this man to wait. I was sure you'd prove your worth.'

The bespectacled man with the briefcase was their tattoo artist – every graduation he was driven in from Puerto Bontón. Immediately following the obstacle course, he'd done six tattoos – one for each new commander. He now opened a book crammed with designs for me to choose from – page after page of variations, but all of them snakes. There were striking taipans, flat-headed cobras, poised rattlesnakes, dangling tree snakes and African mambas, each with the letters AUC beneath.

From the moment I'd seen Culebra overpower Murgas at El Filtro, I'd dreamed of getting my own snake tattoo. The tattoo meant that I'd made it. To the Guerrilla and those civilians who knew what the letters AUC stood for, the snake inspired fear and respect. I was now not only part of a group, but an important member. I was a commander and I had my group's full backing.

But a tattoo also locked me in. It meant one hundred per cent commitment. Once the ink had stained my skin, there would be no turning back – I'd be a Paramilitary for life. And once people saw it, there would be no denying who I was.

After flipping the pages back and forth, I chose an eyelash viper. I'd seen them south of Llorona – small, yellow and deadly with scales over their eyes that looked like eyelashes. They were an ambush predator, waiting for prey to come within striking distance. Local Indians said they winked after they'd bitten you but before the poison sank in. I liked the idea. I wanted Papá's killers to know, between when I struck and when they died, that it was me doing it. They'd underestimated me and I'd give them time to regret it.

I requested the viper coiled around my shoulder blade where it would be covered most of the time.

As the tattoo artist prepared the ink, Culebra poured me a shot of *aguardiente*.

'Drink up!' said Culebra.

'No, thanks,' I said. 'I don't like the taste.'

'It's an acquired taste,' said Beta. He slammed the shot down on the table. 'Acquire it!'

'That's an order, *comando*,' said Culebra, laughing.

To those raised in Los Llanos, a man who didn't drink was not to be trusted.

I downed the shot, grimacing as my lips and throat burned.

Culebra poured another. 'Drink!'

'*To the Autodefensas!*' Beta said.

Culebra poured shots one on top of the other like he was dealing cards. Alfa 1 and Beta pressured me to keep going while my tonsils burned and my veins coursed with hot lava. After a few minutes, my head was spinning and I couldn't feel my tongue.

'Go on,' urged Culebra. 'It'll numb the pain.'

'No more,' I said. 'I want to feel it.'

I wanted the tattoo to feel satisfying.

When it was done, the blood soaked up with gauze and my shoulder bandaged, Alfa 1 slapped my back. 'You're one of us now, Pedro. But when you come back from your leave, you need to show more respect. Maybe having other men's lives in your hands will stop you from thinking so much about yourself. Because whatever self-indulgent shit is going on inside that head of yours, this group is bigger than that and being in this group will save you.'

The following morning, I awoke hung-over, sick and confused. I was still in the office, fully clothed. Beta pressed something cold and metallic against my cheek – a black Smith & Wesson – a present for my promotion, although it would have to remain in the armoury until I'd completed the advanced training course.

'Happy birthday!'

It was 12 March. I'd been looking forward to turning sixteen. I'd been looking forward to my present. But instead of making love to Camila, I got a tattoo, a pistol and toughness.

'Alfa 1 must really see something in you,' said Culebra. 'In six intakes, we've never seen him give anyone a second chance like that.'

'You should go celebrate,' said Beta.

I groaned.

'We'll see you in two weeks,' said Culebra, returning the Blazer keys to me and taking back the Smith & Wesson. 'And I'll teach you how to shoot this properly.'

'Sure, see you then.'

But I wasn't so sure I would. I knew how to shoot. And I already had everything I needed: the Blazer keys, a cell phone with Ratón's number, a Taurus pistol loaded with bullets and a heart once filled with love for Papá still baying ferociously at his death.

Maybe Palillo was right. Maybe Alfa 1 had done me a favour, after all. If I was capable of killing a twelve-year-old boy, then I was capable of killing anyone. And although I wasn't sure of much, there was one thing I knew with absolute certainty.

I was going to shoot Ratón.

PART THREE

TRAPPING A RAT

45

THE RULES FOR leave were simple: keep our mouths shut and return in two weeks. Changing back into our civilian clothes felt strange. Those clothes now belonged to previous lives, and in many cases no longer fitted. Coca-Cola's T-shirt barely stretched over his muscles, and Tortuga's jeans slid from her hips.

When I got through the gate search, Palillo was waiting on the road, his pack slung over his shoulder. The other recruits were piling into two Ford F350 trucks that would ferry them to Puerto Bontón for their onward journeys.

'Where are we going?' Palillo asked, helping me hoist trash bags into the Blazer.

'We? What about your beach holiday with Piolín?'

I glanced at the F350 where Piolín was talking and laughing with Mahecha and Paisa. Ensconced happily between the two, she'd left no space for Palillo.

'Piolín can wait,' Palillo said flippantly, and I wondered whether the trip had ever existed outside his imagination. 'I'm with my *hermano*.'

'I'm not going to La Llorona, if that's what you mean. I told you already, I'm having the Blazer repaired in Villavicencio.'

'Come on, brother. We're on vacation and I've got money to burn!'

As much as I'd have liked us to spend our leave together, my plan to go after Ratón was dangerous, and I didn't want Palillo involved.

When I still refused, Palillo shrugged – surely I could at least drive him as far as Villavicencio, where he'd catch a bus to Llorona?

At the dump, I unloaded the garbage bags quickly, hoping Palillo wouldn't offer to help. Luckily, he was too busy flicking through radio stations. I jumped into the pit and retrieved my zip-lock bags, tucking the Taurus into the back of my pants.

But by the time we reached the Villavicencio bus terminal, Palillo had changed his mind. He'd decided to stick around for a few days – driving through the city, we'd passed bars, shopping centres and a cinema. At the *Residencia Royal*, he announced he'd share my room in order to save his money for shopping and girls. This severely compromised my plans, but it was impossible to say no.

We dropped the Blazer at the mechanic's and all Monday afternoon I humoured Palillo, eating lunch with him and going to a shopping centre to buy clothes. However, I was distracted. More than three weeks had passed since Ratón had placed his original order. What if he came to the store to check on it in person? In that case, I needed to be at the hotel window, watching, with my Taurus ready.

Finally, I told Palillo I was tired and returned alone to the *residencia*, stopping to purchase a pair of binoculars together with the rope, blindfold and gag I'd need once I'd forced Ratón into the Blazer. I planned to approach him posing as an unthreatening delivery boy whose hands were occupied by a heavy load, so I also obtained a large box filled with styrofoam, which I stored under the *residencia* stairs.

The following morning I woke ready to begin my stake-out of the electrical store. I told Palillo I was sick and urged him to go out and have fun. After he left, I placed the fully loaded Taurus wrapped in a T-shirt under my pillow and sat by the window with my binoculars, scanning up and down the street.

The storekeeper, Boris Sandoval, rolled up the shutters at 9 am. No rear access meant customers and deliveries came through the street entrance. Sandoval purchased coffee from the passing *tinto* girl at 10 am and ate lunch at the counter. Standing in the doorway, he smoked two cigarettes every hour, flicking the butts onto the pavement. His daughter arrived from school at 3 pm and did her homework until her mother came to collect her two hours later. The store closed at 6 pm when Sandoval retired upstairs.

Palillo checked on me twice during the day, bringing me antibiotics and soup. Each time I heard him climbing the creaky wooden stairs, I quickly hid the binoculars and slipped back into bed. I left the room only once, to pick up the repaired Blazer, which I transferred to a public car park around the corner, leaving the rope, blindfold and gag in the glove compartment.

'You should get some air,' Palillo told me when he returned laden with shopping bags. He exuberantly laid out his purchases – a cell phone, a Discman, a gold chain and a fake Rolex. 'Have you even been outside today? We could go to the park.'

I shook my head and buried my face in the pillow. Perhaps if Palillo grew bored enough he'd depart for Llorona.

That evening, Palillo announced he was going to a *discoteca*. After he left, I raised my binoculars and squinted at Sandoval in his tiny apartment above the store. Of course, Ratón probably wouldn't just drop by outside of business hours, but by then I was hooked.

Ten minutes after Palillo's departure, the storekeeper was eating dinner when suddenly I heard the key rattle in the lock behind me. I turned to see it drop to the floor and heard the lock click.

Before I could reach for the Taurus, the door flew open. Palillo burst into the room to find me standing by the window clutching my binoculars. He must have tiptoed up the stairs.

'What the hell is this?' he demanded, striding angrily towards me.

'None of your business, is what it is.'

I glanced instinctively at my pillow. Palillo lunged towards it. Unwrapping the T-shirt, he held the Taurus high above my head. 'I'm your best friend. Of course it's my business.'

I held out my hand, demanding the pistol. 'I didn't ask you to babysit me.'

When I grabbed for it, Palillo gripped me by the throat to keep me away. I was shocked; he hadn't laid a hand on me since we were seven. I tried to pry his fingers from my neck, but even with one hand occupied with the Taurus, he was far stronger. He wrestled me to the floor, pinned my arms with his knees and slapped me.

'Wake up, Pedro! Whatever you're getting yourself into is dangerous. You need to tell me what it is. Now!'

Straddling me, Palillo refused to let me up. I struggled until I was out of breath. Suddenly, I felt exhausted from the strain of a full day waiting on edge for Ratón to arrive, listening for my best friend's footsteps and hiding everything from him.

'Ratón,' I told him. 'The radio operator. He buys batteries at a store opposite.'

Palillo allowed me to sit up.

'So you're going to shoot him on a busy public street right in front of where we're staying?'

'Of course not. I know what I'm doing.'

I hadn't even begun to explain the details, but Palillo shook his head.

'This is *stupid*. And dangerous. What if Ratón shoots first? What if the storeowner tries to play the hero? You could get caught or killed.'

He told me that this wasn't me; I was smarter than this. Was this what my father would have wanted? I stared at the Taurus and didn't answer.

'I know you're still angry, but this thing will consume you. You need to forget the past and move on with your life.'

'I can't,' I said stubbornly. 'And this is exactly why I didn't tell you – I knew you'd do this. Now give me back my pistol and get out.'

'What about your mother? She needs you, Pedro. Don't you think she's suffered enough?'

'Leave my mother out of this!'

'Then think of Camila. Have you even called her?'

Of course, he already knew the answer to that. I'd deliberately not contacted Camila. I'd thought about her all the time, but it wouldn't have been fair to make her keep thinking of *me*. For a decent girl like Camila, the life she'd lead with me would be no life at all. Camila was beautiful and smart. She'd easily find someone else, if she hadn't already.

'I'll make you a deal.' Palillo proffered the Taurus just out of reach. 'One phone call. Talk to her for five minutes. Afterwards, if you're still determined to do this, you can have your pistol back and I'll help you.'

'No deal.'

'You can't do this on your own. The job needs at least two people.'

Palillo was bluffing, but his bluff had merit. I could use a lookout in case something went wrong. I was already tired. What if I fell asleep and Ratón came? What if I couldn't run down to intercept him in time? While I drove Ratón to the saman tree, it would be easier to have an accomplice sitting behind him, training the pistol on him. In fact, now that I thought about it, the Blazer was a stick shift. How would I steer, point a pistol and change gears?

Palillo was right. Two people would be better than one.

I knew Camila's number better than my own. Using his new cell phone, Palillo placed the call. Disguising his voice, he apologised to Señor Muñoz for phoning so late, gave another student's name and claimed they had an urgent group assignment. He nodded excitedly, handing me the phone as Camila's confused voice came on.

'*¿Hola?*'

She knew there was no assignment, and when I froze up she guessed immediately who it was.

'Pedro, is that you? Pedro, *cariño*. If that's you, please talk to me. I know it's you. Why won't you talk?'

Palillo made desperate signals for me to speak. But the words wouldn't come. I hung up.

'What did she say?'

'Nothing.'

But I was lying. Just by saying my name she'd said everything. She was still thinking of me. Four months after I'd abandoned her she was still thinking of me and waiting for my call. Palillo smiled gloatingly. He'd known that the mere sound of Camila's voice would splash water on my fiery resolve and cool the burning coals of my angry heart.

'Call her back!' he demanded. I refused so we grappled over the phone. But Palillo had the reach of a champion boxer. Holding me at arm's length, he pressed REDIAL and then spoke into the phone.

'No, it's me, Palillo . . .' His face turned ashen. '*What?* When? Is she okay?' He stared at me intently, then dropped his voice. 'Just a moment.'

He stepped into the bathroom, clicking the door behind him, and I could hear his low murmuring punctuated by higher notes of surprise. Finally, after two minutes, he emerged.

'It's your mother,' he began, placing a hand on my shoulder. 'Don't worry, she's fine, but five days ago she was having trouble breathing and collapsed. The doctors think it was a heart attack, and she was hospitalised for three days. She's back at your uncle's place now, resting.'

Hearing this, I felt both shocked and ashamed. Immersed in my own bitterness, I hadn't bothered to think about how Mamá was coping. When I'd thought of her at all it had been with resentment. By not phoning, I'd been punishing her, knowing how much even a single call would have meant. But now I saw my actions for what they were – selfish and petty.

It broke my heart to think of Mamá in hospital, all alone and not even knowing where I was. I sat on the bed, my head bowed, caught between my instinct to race home and be by Mamá's side, and the likelihood that Sandoval would call at any moment, putting Ratón within my grasp. If I departed, I might never get a second chance at him. After all the hard work and immense risk I'd undertaken, abandoning my plan to get Ratón at this crucial moment would be like ripping a tightly glued bandage from a still festering wound.

Finally, I looked up.

'Pack your things,' I said. 'First thing in the morning, we're leaving for Garbanzos.'

46

WE DEPARTED THE *residencia* before dawn. I'd spent a restless night and wasn't happy about abandoning my stake-out.

'You're doing the right thing,' Palillo insisted as we drove out of the public car park. 'Abducting Ratón here in Villavicencio is too risky. There are regular police patrols and hundreds of potential witnesses. Better to do it in a remote location closer to his home territory.'

'You mean in Llorona?'

'I'm thinking Santo Paraíso.'

'But that's deep in Guerrilla territory.'

Papá had never allowed me to visit Santo Paraíso. Everyone knew it was the haunt of emerald smugglers and drug traffickers. The village furthest south from Garbanzos, it was also the nearest to the Guerrilla camps. Despite its seedy reputation, however, Palillo had been to Santo Paraíso many times – first as a kid, when Diomedes put him to work picking coca leaves, and later on errands for his mother or to collect his inebriated stepfather after three-day drinking binges.

'That's my point – it's where Ratón is most confident, and that makes him vulnerable. Maybe we ambush him on a trail to the coca fields. Maybe we take him one night after he's been drinking at Flora's Cantina. Either way, the jungle is so dense that we won't have to transport him far.'

'What if someone recognises us?'

Palillo shrugged. 'You'll have to stay out of sight. But the Guerrilla don't know I helped bury your father or that I've joined the Autodefensas. Think about it, Pedro – I'm your biggest asset!'

Hearing this, I felt better about my decision to abandon my stake-out. Palillo could infect anyone with his optimism, and having him on my side halved the risks.

On the way to Garbanzos I confessed everything, including how I'd obtained the gun and bullets, and the details of my plan for Ratón at the saman tree. Palillo apologised for slapping me and I apologised for lying.

'How did you find me out?' I asked.

'You were acting strangely, and then I saw the Blazer in the *parqueadero*. I asked if you'd been out, but you said no.'

'Clever.'

'Clever? You're the one who stole a pistol and bullets from three psychopaths without being noticed. Anything else you've stolen?'

I had to tell him.

'You're sitting in it.'

Palillo removed his safety belt, lifted himself from the seat and looked around. It took several seconds before he comprehended.

'You mean you stole this truck? I thought you had permission. You stole the whole fucking Paramilitary truck!' Laughing, he gave me a high five. 'Right on!'

With Palillo in such high spirits and his newly purchased *regaetón* CDs blaring, the 500 kilometres of winding road flew beneath our tyres in no time. On the inbound highway, I began to recognise familiar details – the colour of mailboxes, the angle of crooked fence posts, and landmark trees by the side of the road. Even the air had a distinctive odour.

I imagined what my return home might have been like, if not for Zorrillo's prohibition. At our farm, I'd find Mamá in the garden hanging clothes on the line. She'd embrace me and we'd both say how sorry we were. The dream continued until Palillo turned down the music.

'What are you going to tell everyone?' he asked, furrowing his brow. 'Our stories have to match.'

In our new job, I informed him, we stood each day at the base of African oil palms, holding a long stick with a rope coil to hook the fruit. Work started at 5 am and ended at 3 pm. The pay was lousy, but it was tax-free and we were given meals, work clothes and lodging. The Blazer belonged to our boss, who'd sent us to pick up tractor parts and permitted us to visit home.

'You're a better liar than I am!' exclaimed Palillo.

In all likelihood, Mamá would not believe my story. There were many wives and mothers of Paramilitary soldiers in Garbanzos. It was impossible they didn't talk. However, most knew better than to stir up trouble. With such high unemployment, income from husbands and sons saved families from poverty.

'And what about Camila?' asked Palillo.

Since the phone call, I'd been sure I wanted to see Camila. But now I started having doubts. We might rekindle our love only for me to leave her again. A bigger fear was also gnawing at me. Camila had called me 'sweetheart' on the phone, but deep down I was afraid she was with someone else.

Entering Garbanzos, I noticed tiny changes wrought during my absence: a freshly painted house door, a new billboard advertisement and shops with changed window displays. It had only been four months, but I now felt much, much older.

We should have taken side streets to the plaza where the cheap *residencias* were located. Instead we paraded down Avenida Bolivar with the windows down, our elbows out and the music pumping. We wanted the town to know we were back. We had made it, and although we were only sixteen, we were men now.

Everyone knew everyone in Garbanzos. Seeing our unfamiliar vehicle, they looked up. It was a reckless thing to do, attracting so much attention. But I liked being in that truck. I wanted people to think that maybe it was mine. Maybe I had an important job now. I also liked having the Taurus within arm's reach. It made me feel that no one could ever mess with me again.

Every Paramilitary soldier dreamed of returning home triumphantly with enough money to buy his mother a house. In the meantime, he might pay her rent a year in advance. But the very minimum a Paramilitary son returning home should do was fill his mother's refrigerator and pantry.

It was only 10.30 am so I had time to check into our *residencia* with Palillo and stop at the *supermercado* before I drove to see Mamá.

Gripping five bags of groceries, I knocked on Uncle Leo's door. I knew he wasn't home. I'd seen his blue truck parked in front of his hardware store on the main street.

Mamá opened the door and her hand shot to her mouth.

'Pedro! *¡Por Dios!*' She hugged me tightly. 'How I've missed you!'

I lowered the shopping to the floor and returned her embrace. 'Me too, Mamá.'

'Let a poor old mother take a look at her son!' Pushing my shoulders back to appraise me, she looked me over, skipping my military haircut and concentrating on the rest of me. 'New clothes! And you must have grown two inches.'

In contrast, Mamá seemed to have been whittled away by sadness. Grief and illness had ravaged her face like drought, leaving her eyes parched and her skin as mottled as a dried creek bed.

'What happened, Mamá?' I asked, carrying the shopping inside. 'Camila said you were in hospital.'

Mamá avoided my gaze. 'The doctors aren't sure. They thought it was a heart attack, but now they're saying it was angina, brought on by stress. I'm meant to rest and then get checked again on Monday.'

I didn't need to ask the cause of her stress. Papá's death was still imprinted deeply on us both. Being banished from her home and not knowing where I was had also taken their toll. We hugged again and her affection tempered my remaining bitterness like sugar meeting coffee.

'Mamá, I'm sorry I wasn't here for you.'

On the day of Papá's death I'd treated her too harshly. I'd blamed her excessively because I was actually blaming myself. At the time, I'd been unable to put myself in her shoes. Although the decision to leave Papá unburied would have been an agonising one to make, perhaps any woman in her position would have done the same to protect her son and brother.

I stacked the pantry and refrigerator as, against my protests, Mamá prepared me *caldo*. Looking around the cramped living room, I noted she slept on the fold-out sofa. I saw new clothes but none of her possessions from the *finca*.

'You got my salary?' I asked.

Mamá closed her eyes and nodded her blind acceptance of my new job. If she suspected I'd joined the Autodefensas, she didn't let on. 'It was the only way we knew you were alive. Thank you, Pedro. I couldn't survive without your and Leo's generosity.'

Uncle Leo! I bristled at the mere mention of his name. Mamá I could forgive, but nothing could excuse Leo leaving Papá to the vultures and refusing to lend me his truck.

Mamá ladled *caldo* into my bowl then sat at the table with me while I ate.

'Have you visited the *finca*?' I asked.

She dabbed at her eye. 'I went up twice . . . but only to the fence line. I saw the cross you made.' Suddenly, she broke down. 'Pedro, please! Promise me you won't go to the *finca*. The Guerrilla killed three *campesinos* last week. Colonel Buitrago checks on me sometimes. He says our property isn't safe—'

'Colonel Buitrago? What's he done about the killers?'

But she never got to respond. Uncle Leo's arrival cut our conversation short.

'Pedro!' He smiled unconvincingly. 'Good to have you home.'

'Uncle Leo.' I glared at him and got to my feet. 'I was just leaving. I only came to see Mamá.'

'You're welcome to stay.' He scratched his head nervously. 'There's not much space here, but we'll manage.'

'I won't impose. I already have a hotel.'

As I walked towards the door, Leo followed me, determined to show up my ingratitude with more offers. 'Do you need a lift? Or I could lend you the truck.'

'A bit late for that, isn't it?'

Without turning, I jangled the Blazer keys and gave him the finger. After he retreated, I bade goodbye to Mamá, who'd also followed me to the door, and promised to come again the following day.

'Try to be nice to him,' she said. 'He means well.'

'I'm sorry because he's your brother, but I can't be around him. It reminds me of that day.'

'I know it does, Pedrito.' Mamá hugged me.

She stood on the doorstep, watching me go, and called out after me.

'Please, Pedro, I'm begging you. Don't go to the *finca*. It's too dangerous.'

47

BACK IN THE Blazer, I breathed a long sigh of frustration. I'd intended to drive straight to Llorona and visit Papá's grave; now it seemed I couldn't. Not only was the Guerrilla prohibition still in place, but it would upset Mamá, which was the last thing I wanted.

Instead, I picked up Palillo and drove to our old school, Colegio Santa Lucía. We parked opposite the wrought-iron gates, near the grassy football field where I'd played Saturday football with Papá barracking from the sidelines. There, we waited for the principal to ring the lunch bell and Camila to emerge.

I'd wanted to give Camila warning – meeting after school and seeing her on my own. But Palillo had argued persuasively for a group attack using the element of surprise – it would give her less time to think.

At 12.30 pm, the principal, Rector Prada, emerged from the main building with his wooden-handled bell. He'd never missed a day of school nor rung a single bell late.

As Prada shook his bell, a swarm of students streamed onto the playing field. Palillo's eyes lit up at the sight of the fresh-faced schoolgirls in their blue plaid dresses, black shoes and knee-high white socks.

He rubbed his hands together and made kissing sounds. 'Succulent and ripe for the picking!'

They were the same girls Palillo had been staring at lustfully for years, but fruit that had once been out of reach was now within his grasp. Four months older, an inch taller and having left school, he'd climbed several rungs of the attractiveness ladder and his confidence had ascended with him.

News of our arrival spread like wildfire. A crowd of curious students quickly gathered, their fingers poking through the cyclone wire fence. I spotted Camila a moment before she saw us. She hesitated at the gate and looked directly across the road at me. Leaving school grounds during lunchtime was forbidden, but that wasn't the problem. I could read her face. It told me that despite having hoped for this moment, she was suddenly dreading it.

I smiled and waved, but she continued to stand there uncertainly until her best friend, Carolina, snatched up her wrist and dragged her across the road.

We hugged. Holding her, I felt tingles down my spine. I'd missed her so much. Coming out of the embrace, I tried to kiss her but she turned her face, and all the nice things I'd been meaning to say melted in my mouth.

I searched Camila's face. 'Is something wrong?'

'You cut your hair.' There was an implied question – my hair was military-short.

'It was getting long. But I can grow it again for you.'

'Don't! Short hair brings out your cheekbones.' She ran her fingers down my cheeks and gave me a half-smile, but still no kiss.

'We're going to shoot some billiards at Francisco's,' I ventured tentatively. 'Want to come?'

I thought going to one of our usual haunts would remind Camila of the old days; but her eyes fired with anger. 'Pedro, you're acting like we saw each other yesterday. You can't just turn up after months of silence and expect everything to be the same!'

Behind her, dozens of noses poked further through the cyclone fence.

'Can we talk in private?' I held open the back door for her to get in. Surprising her at lunchtime had definitely been a mistake. 'Please. I'll explain everything.'

On his side of the truck, Palillo was faring much better with Carolina. During that same interval, he'd flashed his fake gold necklace and imitation Rolex, made passing mention of his high-paying job and established legal ownership of the Blazer.

Suddenly, our spectators dispersed. Rector Prada appeared in the playground, reaching for his whistle. Palillo slid into the front passenger seat and turned the sternly-approaching principal to our advantage.

'*¡Rápido!* Jump in!'

The girls obeyed, slammed the door, and we sped off. In my rear-vision mirror, I saw the principal standing in the middle of the road blowing his whistle. Palillo and I tapped knuckles while Camila and Carolina shook their heads, laughing.

Speeding towards the pool hall, I felt invigorated. Seeing Camila in person – hearing her voice, smelling her hair and touching her – silenced my doubts. I couldn't ignore how I felt when she was near me. Of course, I didn't know what future we had or what would happen when I had to leave. But I wanted her. I needed her. And I had to win her back.

48

FRANCISCO'S POOL HALL had been our usual after-school haunt when it was too rainy for the rope-swing tree. We'd spent more afternoons here than I could count, bribing older boys to sneak beers and cigarettes to us.

As I lined up the break for our second game of billiards, Camila perched on a stool beside the billiard table.

'So, tell me about this new job,' she said.

'Not much to tell, really.' I averted my gaze, plucking at my T-shirt. 'Harvesting the fruit from African oil palms. After the first day my muscles were so sore I could hardly move. But you get used to it. Whenever I want to quit, I think of the money I'm sending Mamá.'

I didn't like lying and I was no good at it, but Palillo chimed in with details about our *hijo de puta* boss and Camila seemed satisfied.

She sighed. 'I would've come with you.'

'And done what for money?'

'The same as you.'

'It's not work for a girl.'

'That's not the point, Pedro. After you left I cried for a month.'

'I'm sorry I didn't call. I kept thinking about you the whole time. And I'm sorry about the note. You know I'd never have left you. *Never.* But . . .'

I stopped, since I didn't want to use Papá's death as an excuse.

'You must miss him.'

I nodded and my eyes filled with tears. Camila hugged me to change the subject.

That was our pattern for the rest of the afternoon – creeping in close and then pulling away. We were treading lightly over old territory, testing to see if we still had our connection.

In two and a half hours, Camila didn't let me kiss her. We avoided the big subjects. How long I could stay. Whether she knew anything about the Guerrilla and our *finca*. Whether she still loved me and wanted any future with me. I asked none of the questions I wanted to about other guys. I had no right. I'd hurt her and she was still making up her mind.

It was hardly the homecoming I'd imagined. All afternoon my mind played tricks on me. One minute I felt like I was in the right place, the next like it was all wrong. And if it felt like this in Garbanzos, what would it be like in Llorona, where my memories of Papá would be even stronger?

Palillo and I drove Camila back to *colegio* before the final bell. Carolina had stayed at the pool hall to meet some friends. It felt strange parking among the waiting parents of the younger students. Normally, we were on the other side of the fence.

'You'd better go,' Camila said. 'My father's picking me up.'

'Since when does he pick you up?'

She bit her lip. 'Since the Guerrilla destroyed the Llorona police station last month. He insists on knowing where I am at all times.'

So, the Guerrilla had come back to finish the job they'd started the previous October. I wasn't alarmed; mortar bombs didn't mean they'd taken control of the town. However, the bombing was symbolic: the Guerrilla were growing stronger.

Unfortunately, Señor Muñoz's protectiveness meant I'd have to get his permission to see Camila – no easy task since he knew I'd defied the Guerrilla and broken his daughter's heart.

'*¡Mierda!*' Camila exclaimed suddenly, sliding down the seat. It was 3.14 pm. Rector Prada had appeared in the playground, his head turning while his nose twitched like a bloodhound's. Camila eased the door open and I watched her skirting behind cars.

Rector Prada's glare landed on our Blazer.

'Fuck!' I turned to Palillo. 'He's seen us.'

Palillo laughed, honked the horn and impersonated the principal. 'Pedro Juan Gutiérrez González, correct your posture or you'll grow up twisted.'

Rector Prada began to cross the road, signalling for us to wait. Before Palillo could honk again, I grabbed his wrist and turned the ignition.

Palillo pulled up the handbrake and held it. 'What's he going to do? Make you pick up litter during recess?'

It was too late; Prada tapped on the window and I wound it down. He nodded politely to us both. 'Gentlemen.'

I nodded back. 'Señor Rector.'

'Gutiérrez, you topped the mathematics exam.'

It took me several seconds to process what he meant. Exams came from a completely different planet. In that world, I should have been pleased by my result. I remembered studying hard for that exam two days before Papá's death.

'Would you like your exam papers returned?'

I shook my head and Rector Prada didn't press me. I was no longer his student and he respected the new state of play. 'For what it's worth, Gutiérrez, I was very sorry to hear about your father.'

For five years he'd stood over me like a giant stop sign, telling me only which lines I was prohibited from crossing. Now, unexpectedly, he'd lowered his guard and given me some open road.

'Please don't punish her.'

Rector Prada sighed. 'Just don't let it happen again.' He crossed back to the school and rang the bell at 3.18 pm – three minutes late.

Palillo had been wrong about approaching Camila at school, but he'd been right about speaking to the principal. I'd needed to face him, just as I'd eventually have to talk to Señor Muñoz, whose car I saw approaching from the opposite direction. But I wasn't ready for that yet; I was still bitter at him for preventing Camila from getting a truck to transport Papá's body. Besides, there was someone else I needed to see – and an apology that I needed to make.

49

DESPITE HAVING PASSED the army barracks countless times on my way to school, the following morning I went beyond the three-metre high walls topped with barbed wire for the first time.

At 9 am I was ushered into Colonel Buitrago's office to find him sitting at his desk, writing. He was in his mid-fifties with a round face, thick silver hair and a grey-flecked moustache.

'Colonel, I apologise for the voice messages,' I said, stepping up to his desk.

'You were angry,' he stated matter-of-factly, continuing to write. 'But I wasn't ignoring you that day. My phone was out of range. I didn't get your messages until two days later.'

I felt ashamed as I remembered my last message: *You're an hijo de puta and a fucking coward.*

'Thank you for looking in on my mother.'

He finally put down his pen and acknowledged my thanks with a nod. 'It's the least I can do.'

'I want to make a statement, Colonel. I know some of the names of Papá's killers – and I can describe the others in detail.'

'There'll be time for that later. Let's take a walk.'

He led the way out of the barracks and down the street towards the central plaza, nodding to street vendors and storekeepers. Despite the Guerrilla having a price on his head, he displayed no fear, eventually perching on a bench in full uniform while having his shoes shined by a young boy wearing a grimy hat. He flicked lint from his three-starred lapel, perhaps wondering whether, despite my apology, I still believed he'd neglected his duty or feared the Guerrilla.

'I'm sorry about Mario Jesús, Pedro. He was a good friend and a good Catholic.'

'*Gracias.*'

'I see you're wearing his crucifix.'

Buitrago fingered his own silver cross. Although I was still resentful, I remembered him kneeling with a pair of tweezers beside Papá, pulling shrapnel from the church pews, and my resentment diminished.

'I started battling the Guerrilla two and a half decades ago, Pedro, long before you were born. The hardest part isn't the gunfights but the funerals. I've lost count of how many I've attended.'

'Papá never had a funeral. I buried him myself on the *finca*.'

The colonel sighed. 'Believe me, if I'd been here that day, I would have pursued the men who killed him. I'd have ensured he received proper burial. But I can't be everywhere at once. Each time the Guerrilla place a collar bomb on an oil pipeline, I have to send a platoon to secure the area while engineers mend the leak. Meanwhile, the *guerrilleros* blow a phone or electricity tower as a further distraction and take advantage of my overstretched resources to kidnap a new victim, move a cocaine shipment or kill a good man like your father.'

I nodded.

'It mightn't feel like it, but I'm one hundred per cent on your side.'

'Then go after them, Colonel. I told you, I know who they are.'

'It isn't that simple. The Guerrilla camps are five days' march away. We can't just walk in. The approaches are sown with landmines. They have scouts.'

'You have helicopters.'

'Which make noise. They have hostages, and they threaten to kill them if we come too close.'

'Their urban militia don't. The commander who operated the radio—'

'This is not an overnight job. And there's a correct way of doing things.'

He glared at three Autodefensa recruiters seated at the cantina then flicked two fingers towards them as though they were marbles. The recruiters catapulted from their seats, abandoning their beers on the table.

I was about to tell him exactly where he could find Ratón, but seeing this, I stopped myself. Not every army officer in Colombia was willing to collaborate with the Autodefensas. Buitrago tolerated Autodefensa recruitment since the Guerrilla was their common enemy. But the Autodefensas weren't going to run the town. Not on his watch.

'The fact is, Pedro, we have undercover operatives throughout the region, gathering intelligence on enemy activities. This war against the Guerrilla will be won through persistence, and by winning the hearts and minds of civilians. Not by stooping to their level. Or *worse*.' He glared once more at the recruiters' table – now empty – then looked significantly at me, and I realised he knew exactly where I'd been for these past four months.

The colonel was a stainless steel cog in a rust-ridden machine. But his *correct way of doing things* was frustrating. He didn't approve of the Autodefensas, but he lacked enough soldiers himself to make Llorona safe for ordinary people.

'When can we return to our *finca*?'

He gave me a pitying look.

'Not yet, Pedro. My patrols have been monitoring the situation. Trust me. It's not safe.'

'When then?'

'My lieutenant will take your statement whenever you're ready.' He patted my waist where the Taurus was concealed. 'Right now you're on the wrong path. But if you decide to change your life, my battalion gates will be open to you when you turn eighteen.'

50

AFTER MEETING WITH Buitrago, I was satisfied that the army was at least trying to find Papá's killers. However, they were slow and I wasn't ready to give up our budding plan to abduct Ratón.

'Are you absolutely sure you want to go ahead with this?' Palillo asked back at our *residencia*. 'Kill a man in cold blood? You might start World War Three.'

'Two hundred per cent sure,' I declared. 'Besides, the Guerrilla are the ones who started it. We'll be doing society a favour. Did your friend know anything?'

While I'd been talking with Buitrago, Palillo had gone to visit a boy he used to pick coca leaves with when he was a kid.

Palillo nodded. 'He said Ratón changes safe houses regularly and tries to avoid routines. But every Saturday he has to be at Flora's Cantina in Santo Paraíso to oversee the workers' market.'

'Won't Ratón have bodyguards?' I asked.

'At the market, yes. But afterwards, no. My friend says that when he leaves, they stay behind. That's when Ratón is at his most vulnerable.'

The tiny settlement of Santo Paraíso lay diagonally across the river from Puerto Princesa, where the dirt road south from Garbanzos stopped. It was the wildest of places, a collection of primitive huts huddled amid dense jungle. The only access was by private boat or the river ferry that glided with glacial slowness back and forth between the two villages, transporting two cars at a time, together with pedestrians and supplies.

Santo Paraíso's remoteness from the authorities made it a *contrabandistas'* paradise. The mountainsides above the town were blanketed with thousands of hectares of waist-high coca plants, and the entire local economy was dedicated to the production, wholesaling and transport of cocaine.

Flora's Cantina was a notorious drinking den on the settlement's outskirts, a favoured haunt of *narcotraficantes*, coca-leaf pickers and Guerrilla commanders when they came down from their mountain camps. Restricted chemicals were bought and sold. Bar brawls erupted with a flurry of punches or a clash of machetes, and often ended in exchanges of pistol fire.

But the clearing beside the cantina was also the site of the weekly workers' market, a place where honest day workers – *jornaleros* – gathered to be hired or paid by respectable landowners for tending food crops. The Guerrilla set wages and ensured workers were paid fairly by farmers and *narcotraficantes* alike.

Each Saturday morning, Palillo told me, Ratón was transported to and from the workers' market by Anaufre, an old boat driver who lived in Puerto Princesa. Anaufre had worked for the Guerrilla for years. At 9 am, he'd ferry Ratón across the river and drop him off near Flora's Cantina, then return to Puerto Princesa until it was time to pick him up again at noon.

'That's when we strike,' Palillo said. 'Anaufre waits for Raton at a small, rarely used jetty. It's wooden and half-rotting, so most boat traffic stops at the newer concrete wharf nearer the village centre. Trust me, it's perfect.'

The narrow path from the jetty to the cantina cut through thick jungle. However, we couldn't simply ambush and kill Ratón on the spot – someone might hear the shot and, even in our own hired *lancha*, we mightn't be able to motor away in time. Instead, Palillo had hit on a brilliant idea: we'd offer to ferry Ratón across the river ourselves.

'We'll go to Puerto Princesa before Anaufre is due to pick up Ratón and I'll sabotage his motor. Fixing it will delay him by at least an hour. When Ratón arrives at the jetty, I'll claim that Anaufre is sick and has sent me in his place. With no phone lines or cell phone reception, Ratón will have to take my word for it.'

Since Ratón might recognise my face, I'd hide under a canvas cover in the boat's bow. When we were far enough out into the river, Palillo would distract him by pointing back to the jetty and say, 'Look there!' – my signal to emerge with the Taurus.

We'd then travel further upstream to a remote patch of jungle where I could deliver my speech and interrogate him about Papá's other killers.

Palillo's plan sounded feasible. But Saturday was two days away, and I could barely constrain my impatience.

'Relax, *hermano*!' Palillo said while I paced up and down. 'You're home. Why not make peace with this shitty town and enjoy yourself?'

Over the next two days I tried to follow his advice. I ate lunch each day with Mamá. On Thursday morning, I made my statement to Buitrago's lieutenant. Late afternoons, I'd meet Camila in the plaza. Since I didn't want Señor Muñoz knowing I was back, Palillo would phone Carolina, who'd phone Camila so that she'd have an alibi for her visits to Garbanzos.

However, I felt like I was living a double life. The whole time I was playing the roles of doting son and repentant boyfriend, my thoughts were preoccupied by Ratón.

As I waited for Camila in the plaza on Friday afternoon, I saw the Díaz brothers – the cowardly sons of the man Papá and I had buried – sauntering towards their offices at the bus terminal. Physically, the brothers couldn't have been more different. Javier Díaz, at twenty-eight, was solid as an ox and short in stature with a soft, chubby face and a penetrating gaze. His brother, Fabián, was four years younger but much taller and better looking. He had high cheekbones, perfect white teeth and long black hair that drooped across his eyes.

It was strange that the Guerrilla had killed Humberto Díaz, banished his wife from the region but allowed their sons to return. I figured Fabián and Javier must have come to some arrangement with them. Their *colectivos* and trucks continued to run the route all the way south to the Puerto Princesa wharf, whereas most other bus companies had to stop at Llorona. Although accompanied by bodyguards, Fabián and Javier were back to walking the streets of Garbanzos like they owned it.

Their name was plastered everywhere, including on the outside of the bus terminal and on the TRANSPORTADORES DÍAZ *colectivo* that now screeched to a halt in front of me. Hanging from the steps, the *busetero* boy called out the bus's destinations.

'Llorona, Galán, Princesa. Llorona.'

He waved to me. They had an extra sense, these boys. They often knew where passengers were going before they knew themselves. He beckoned to me.

'*¡Suba!* Llorona?'

If only it were that easy. To catch the bus, ride my bicycle up to our *finca,* kiss Mamá and then help Papá finish work in the remaining light.

My old life was over. However, now that I was back, I had to keep reminding myself.

Camila had grown tired of our deception. I was tired of it myself. I wanted to spend every moment with her and was annoyed that I couldn't visit her at home like before.

'I can't stay long,' she said, climbing nervously into the Blazer and glancing over her shoulder. 'I told my father I was going shopping.'

'Does he suspect?'

'Not yet. But this can't go on. I hate lying. You need to talk to him.'

We hugged, and I felt her warm breath against my neck. I'd given up trying to kiss her, hoping she'd make the first move when she felt comfortable.

'If you like, I'll phone him tonight.'

'Better face to face.' She broke our embrace and gave me a peck on the cheek before opening the door. 'He'll be at church on Sunday.'

I realised Camila wasn't simply requesting that I make peace with her father – it was a condition. If I could win him over, I was hopeful she'd come back to me. However, before the appointment with Señor Muñoz, I had another special appointment with an old but soon-to-be-deceased friend: Ratón.

51

THE FOLLOWING MORNING Palillo cycled to Puerto Galán to pick up the seven-metre *lancha* he'd arranged to rent. However, he returned to Garbanzos wharf in an old, two-seat dinghy with a ten-horsepower Yamaha outboard. There was barely enough space for our legs, let alone for me to hide under my canvas.

'The stupid owner decided to paint his other boat!' said Palillo angrily as the boat puttered to a stop. 'There was nothing I could do.'

Palillo revised our plan: I'd hide amid the dense jungle lining the path from Flora's Cantina to the river. After Ratón passed me on his way to the jetty, I'd follow cautiously, pausing at the edge of the trees until I saw Palillo give his explanation about the old boat driver being sick and Ratón climb into the boat.

'But once I emerge from the jungle, Ratón will see me,' I protested.

'I'll tell him you're a porter bringing me fuel. If you carry a jerry can, I doubt he'll look closely. But if he recognises you and makes a fuss, we'll finish him on the spot.'

I was already nervous, but this change of plan rattled me further. So much could go wrong. What if Ratón drew his weapon? If I had to shoot him immediately, I'd miss out on my valuable interrogation. And if his men heard the gunshot, how would we escape in such a snail-paced boat?

On the journey downriver, the sky was grey and ominous. Palillo stared pensively at the boat's prow as it sliced through the water and I watched the riverbanks glide by. The Santo Paraíso side to our left was deep-green virgin jungle, while on the Llorona side I saw cleared land and houses propped on stilts as protection against flooding. Five kilometres beyond Llorona, we passed Puerto Galán. Ten kilometres further on we reached Puerto Princesa.

Pulling up alongside Anaufre's boat, Palillo, ever the consummate actor, opened our motor and pretended to fiddle with a screwdriver. Once he was certain no one was watching, he stepped confidently across the gunwale and hacked off the rubber barb on the female fuel line fitting. Disintegrating rubber was a common problem in the tropics, so Anaufre wouldn't suspect sabotage.

We puttered across the slow-flowing river towards Santo Paraíso, a ramshackle collection of huts nestled amid the lush tropical jungle. Ahead of us, the small car-ferry was docking at the new concrete boat ramp. Two black SUVs drove off and pulled up on the edge of a grassy clearing where vehicles were parked haphazardly under the trees. Colourful *lanchas* lined the riverbank. We cut the motor two hundred metres before the ramp and coasted in towards a small wooden jetty.

'This is it,' Palillo declared, jumping out to wade through the mud and reeds. He dragged the dinghy the last few metres. 'There's the path.'

I followed his gaze and saw a tiny gap in the vegetation.

'Wait here. I'll go up and do some reconnaissance.' Palillo jogged up the path. He returned after ten minutes, tense with excitement.

'I saw Ratón! He's in the clearing beyond Flora's, supervising workers lining up for their salaries. I didn't get close, but I only saw four plain-clothes *milicianos* and none of them are shadowing Ratón.'

This reassured me; our plan was back on track. Palillo passed me the jerry can and I walked up the trail, looking for a hiding spot on the bend so I'd have a clear view of Ratón as he approached. For several minutes I scouted unsuccessfully. Although the foliage was dense, none of the tree trunks was thick enough to conceal me.

Suddenly, I heard the tramp of boots from the direction of the river, and a thunderous voice booming, 'Get me five porters!' Before I could leap into the undergrowth, the same voice shouted, '*¡Oiga!* You!'

A tall, moustachioed man wearing a cream poncho strode towards me. From his belt hung a Colt .45. Following him were two fierce-looking men, each with a twenty-kilo bag of cement balanced on his shoulder.

'Want to earn some quick money?' he demanded.

'No, *gracias*. I'm here for fuel. We're almost out.'

'The village is completely dry. We've brought Flora's gasoline delivery in our boat. Carry up some cement and I'll sell you half a tank.'

I was terrified at the thought of going anywhere near Flora's Cantina with Ratón nearby. But trapped by the logic of my own cover story, I had no legitimate reason to refuse. My further excuses sounded feeble and the man became irritated.

'*Muchacho*, it's our fuel or nothing. Tito, give him your sack and go back for another.'

One of the workers heaved his cement onto my shoulder and turned back towards the river, while I stumbled up the path after the man in the poncho and the other worker. With only twenty minutes before Ratón was due to meet Anaufre, I hoped I'd be able to drop off the sack and scurry back in time.

After a hundred metres, the trail opened into a large clearing surrounded by towering trees. To our left stood a long rectangular hut with a thatched roof and open sides, elevated from the ground on stilts. Stairs led up to the entrance. Painted in large white lettering over the doorway were the words DOÑA FLORA.

In front of the cantina, wooden tables and chairs were set out on the bare earth. There, a motley assortment of about forty coca-leaf pickers, ordinary day labourers and *cocaleros* – men who worked in the cocaine laboratories – sat drinking bottles of beer. Young, skinny girls and older women wearing piles of make-up – Doña Flora's *muchachas* – moved languidly from table to table, sitting on customers' knees and flirting.

On the far side of the clearing a queue of workers snaked up to a man seated at a table. My view was obscured, but it must have been Ratón. I felt furious just knowing he was there, and I bristled with impatience to return to the river.

I followed the ponchoed man up the stairs and into the cantina, and almost choked at the sight of a wiry, dark-skinned figure at the bar, drunkenly demanding a *canasta* of beer. It was Diomedes, Palillo's stepfather. Quickly, I swivelled and lifted the sack to my other shoulder, pulling it in tightly against my cheek.

Diomedes tossed a transparent bag containing white powder on the counter and the bargirl scooped some of it out with a shot glass. Only then did I notice a chalkboard propped up behind the bar listing the prices of drinks not in pesos but in *gramos*.

I could hardly believe what I was witnessing: cocaine was accepted as hard currency. I'd only seen cocaine once in my life – the minuscule amounts snorted by Tango and Murgas. But once I'd snuck past Diomedes and into the large, dimly lit back room, I realised Santo Paraíso wasn't a place for small-time consumers; it was a wholesale cocaine supermarket.

'Over there,' ordered the man with the poncho, pointing to the far wall where rows of plastic barrels were stacked two deep and three high. Along the side wall, dozens of waist-high hessian sacks overflowed with coca leaves. The leaves would be sold to nearby jungle laboratories to be crushed and stomped on by workers in a pit, then soaked in gasoline to leach out the valuable ingredients.

To reach the wall I had to pass several tables where more drinkers sat, including a fat man wearing a loose-fitting shirt, gold chains and a cowboy hat. He was heating a white substance in a spoon over two candles, presumably cocaine base produced by the jungle laboratories. The deferential silence of the two men seated opposite him made it clear he was the *patrón*.

When the substance bubbled and cracked, the *patrón* nodded and pairs of workers began lifting huge barrels out a side door, past a short, weaselly man who stood counting them.

I stopped dead in my tracks. It was Ratón! I'd have recognised that pinched nose and those pointy ears anywhere. How had he finished so quickly with the queue of workers? Unfortunately, my sudden halt caused the worker behind to bump into me, which in turn caused me to knock against the fat man's chair and almost drop my cement.

'*¡Gonorrea!*' he cursed, staring up at me. 'Who *en putas* are you?'

With Ratón so close, I didn't dare say my name. Instead, I spun away from him, towards the man with the poncho, who shrugged.

'He's a boat boy I found by the old jetty, *patrón*.'

'I haven't seen your face before. You new?'

'I don't work here, *patrón*,' I said humbly, bowing my head. 'I was promised fuel.'

The ponchoed man nodded. 'Two of them came on a boat, *patrón*.'

'But you live here?'

'In Llorona.'

'Can anyone here vouch for you?'

With the sack pressed even tighter against my cheek, I went through the pretence of looking around the room, neither expecting nor wanting to recognise anyone.

Imagine my shock when I saw Javier Díaz drinking beer with a respectable cattle rancher from Garbanzos. I tried not to stare; Javier was the last person I'd expected to see. How could he risk being here, in a village controlled by the men who'd murdered his father? I almost caught Javier's eye but thought better of it. Javier was a coward who, if it suited him, would disown his mother.

'I don't think so, *patrón*.'

But the *patrón*'s eyes were sharp as an eagle's; he'd noted my glance and lengthy pause.

'Javi!' he called out. 'You know this *pelado*?'

Javier turned, his mouth slightly agape, but then thankfully came over, out of Ratón's earshot.

'Don Miguel, he's not with me.'

'I asked whether you knew him.'

'Not well.' Javier paused. 'He's from Llorona.'

'He's not *policía*?'

Javier's hands fidgeted. 'I only recognise him because my father knew his father.' Clearly, Javier was afraid of Miguel and wanted nothing to do with me. 'As far as I know, he's a cattle farmer's son.'

This appeased Miguel slightly. He returned to testing the next batch of cocaine base. 'Give him his fuel,' he said to the man with the poncho. And then to me: 'Put down that sack and wait over there where you can't do any damage, you clumsy *idiota*!'

'I'll keep an eye on him, Don Miguel,' offered Javier.

Javier now made a show of greeting me with a polite but distant handshake, as though our families hadn't been next-door neighbours for a decade.

'What the hell are you doing here?' he said in a low, angry voice. 'This place is swarming with Guerrilla. You could get me killed.'

'I'm buying fuel to go fishing.'

'Aren't you afraid of them? After what happened to your father . . .'

'Aren't *you*? After what happened to yours.'

'Of course I'm afraid. But I need to hire yucca and banana workers for my fields. The Guerrilla insist on witnessing me make payments in person. One word from them means no labourers for me. My crops will rot and my buses can't run. But that's my business, not yours.'

During this conversation, my gaze flitted between Ratón and the siphoning of the fuel, which seemed to take an eternity. The appointed worker had to first wait for the fuel to arrive from the boat. Then he searched for a hose and took several sucks to get the gasoline trickling. When it finally flowed, the thin hose filled my jerry can with the speed of a leaking tap. Javier noticed me eyeing Ratón. And although I couldn't be certain, I thought he noted the outline of the Taurus tucked into my trousers.

Ratón finished counting barrels, nodded to Don Miguel, and left via the side door. I was itching to follow him. But I couldn't leave, not with Don Miguel right there and the ponchoed man blocking the main door, arms folded. Departing without my jerry can would reignite his suspicions. Instead, I waited, counting every precious second. Each step I imagined Ratón taking placed him a step further from justice.

Finally, they returned my jerry can.

I walked briskly out into the main room of the cantina, down the stairs and across the clearing, and then sprinted down the track, arriving at the riverbank, pistol drawn, thirty seconds too late.

Palillo was already motoring out with Ratón seated in the bow, waving his arms impatiently. Palillo looked back at me and shrugged, as if to say, *What happened?*

I hid in the undergrowth, and when Palillo returned I explained everything, including my encounter with Javier Díaz.

He spat his disgust. 'I don't trust either of those Díaz brothers.'

'What did Ratón say?'

'He called me a stupid *negro* then turned his back. If I'd had the Taurus, I would've done the job for you.'

'What do we do now?'

'Ratón has seen my face. And when he speaks to Anaufre . . .' He kicked his heel into the transom. 'We need a new plan.'

52

BACK AT OUR hotel Palillo drank half a bottle of Havana Club to steady his nerves. His hand shook as he stubbed out his cigarette – a delayed reaction to being trapped on a boat with the wily Ratón, who'd been armed with a pistol, whereas the only weapon Palillo had within reach was an oar. Palillo had been convinced Ratón was onto him and at any moment would turn and shoot.

But, unlike Palillo, I was gaining my nerve, not losing it. Seeing Ratón again had injected fire into my blood. And although my hands trembled too, it was from anger at coming so close to the prize and then having it ripped away.

Since we couldn't reuse the same strategy, Palillo was working on a revised plan. But I was irritated that it would be another seven days before we could try for Ratón again.

'We'll get him,' Palillo insisted. 'Just relax, be patient and don't do anything rash.'

That afternoon, Palillo temporarily moved out of our *residencia*, as his stepfather had gone back into the mountains to pick coca. Palillo planned to spend the rest of the day with his mother and siblings, and to stay with them on Saturday night.

On Sunday, I went to morning Mass in Llorona with Mamá, hoping to regain Señor Muñoz's approval. Colonel Buitrago sent two armed soldiers to escort us. Mamá was delighted and dusted off her best dress.

'It feels like old times,' she cooed as we set out in the army vehicle.

Leaving Garbanzos, I felt relaxed. In the daylight I recognised familiar landmarks – trees, rocks, small hills and even potholes. My body felt comforted as it swayed with the curves of the road, recalling years of daily trips to and from school on the *colectivo*. And then, as we entered Llorona, we saw it: the destroyed police garrison – the one I'd visited to report Papá's murder.

The netting had failed to repel the cylinder bombs. Four large craters were strewn with the bricks from two collapsed walls. Across the remaining bullet-pocked structure was written a piece of blood-red graffiti: PEOPLE'S ARMY ARE HERE.

'Anyone killed?' I asked.

'Just one. A junior conscript.' The senior bodyguard shook his head. 'The others were lucky. They were eating dinner in Garbanzos.'

So that's what things had come to. A single death was lamented by no more than a headshake; failing to defend a town under attack was considered lucky.

'The dead conscript,' I said, 'was he the boy with pimples?'

The bodyguard nodded.

It made me furious. The boy had tried to do his job honourably, but his superiors had left him alone and defenceless, like a donkey tethered to protect a village from a jaguar. Similar levels of cowardice were infecting the nation. That week the government had raised the possibility of a ceasefire so it could enter into peace talks with the Guerrilla.

When I mentioned the ceasefire proposal, our escorts snorted their derision. In the last month, Caraquemada's 34th Unit had stepped up its local campaign. Farmers had been forced to pay higher *vacunas*. There had been two kidnappings. Three *campesinos* had been ordered from a bus then shot in full view of the other passengers, their bodies dragged into a drainage canal. The Guerrilla were masters of perfidy – talking peace while waging war. Government propaganda was little better. Elected officials came and went, leaving behind a graveyard of broken promises. Their announcements gave one version; Llorona and the river villages lived another.

Reaching the church steps I looked south to the hills and, when I saw our *finca* still standing, relief rushed through me like water through an unblocked drainpipe. I could make out the house, the shed and even the fence line. Although reassured, I was frustrated to be so near to home yet unable to return. We left the junior bodyguard pacing nervously on the church steps while the other soldier escorted us inside. The Guerrilla considered anyone in uniform a legitimate military target.

My entrance into church provoked murmurs. Camila, seated with her parents and two older brothers, Sebastián and Nicolás, turned and smiled. Señor Muñoz looked from me to his daughter and frowned. I was surprised to see Palillo escorting his mother and younger siblings in through the side entrance. He winked at me.

Another family was seated in our usual pew, but they stood to change seats. Everyone knew I'd defied the Guerrilla, but I couldn't tell whether they were being respectful or distancing themselves.

Our pew was soaked with Papá's memory. I smelled him in its red cushion. Where I knelt on the wooden kneeler, I imagined indentations from the pressure of his knees. However, as the chubby Padre Guzmán ended his sermon without condemning even one of the recent incidents, I was reminded of how much things had changed since the days of Padre Rojas.

After Mass, I waited on the church steps while Mamá, escorted by the senior bodyguard, went into the cemetery to lay violets on Humberto Díaz's grave. This was one of Papá's last requests of her, and she made a point of doing it each time she visited.

'*¡Vámonos!*' the junior bodyguard said to me, scanning the hills. 'It's safer for you to wait in the car.'

I shook my head and surveyed the plaza in front of the church. It brought back more memories. I looked at the familiar *mini-mercado* and street-side stores selling soda bottles filled with gasoline for motorbikes. Our former neighbour, Old Man Domino, sat on one of the plaza benches drinking *aguardiente* and feeding pigeons.

A small crowd of Papá's old friends and acquaintances crowded around to pat my shoulder and express their condolences for his death. Finally, Señor Muñoz approached me gingerly, like one of Old Man Domino's pigeons edging towards a dangerously located crumb. For him, this spot must have roused strong memories of his last conversation with Papá.

Aware of Camila watching anxiously, I stepped forward. 'Señor Muñoz,' I said, holding out my hand.

'Pedro, I'm truly sorry about your father.' Señor Muñoz shook my hand warmly. 'Mario Jesús was a dear friend. I apologise for not doing more to help on that tragic day. But I hope you understand my duty as a father.'

I nodded.

'Come to dinner tomorrow night. It will give us a chance to talk.'

His wife, who had returned from their car with Papá's fishing rod, offered it to me, adding, 'Your friend . . .' she glanced at Palillo and hesitated, realising she didn't know his proper name. 'Your friend, *The Toothpick*, is also welcome.'

'I'd enjoy that,' I said, accepting the rod.

'*Vamos*,' urged the bodyguard a second time, tugging at my wrist.

Mamá had returned and we scrambled into the car, which now contained an additional passenger: Palillo.

Sunday afternoon had been my favourite afternoon of the week. It broke my heart having to return to Garbanzos after Mass. All the way back I looked over my shoulder, thinking that I should have been fishing with Papá.

'Francisco's Pool Hall, driver,' Palillo instructed the bodyguard after we'd dropped off Mamá. 'Pedro, you coming?'

'On a Sunday?'

Palillo frowned, not understanding. 'You don't have to drink.'

I spun the centrepin of the fishing rod and Palillo finally caught my meaning.

'Will the dinghy sink if I invite someone special?'

'Depends how fat he is.'

'*She*, Pedro. She.'

53

IT WAS HOT on the river. The sun reflected off the water brilliantly. Removing his shirt, Palillo offered to row, wanting to impress Carolina with his military-trained muscles. Camila and I sat in the bow holding hands.

As we reached my favourite fishing spot, I felt myself relaxing. While I fished, Palillo smoked cigarettes, drank rum and struck tanning poses. I feathered my line and tilted my face up towards the immense blue sky. Strangler figs clung to the trees along the banks, their branches interwoven like twisted fingers. In the riverside tree canopy, a tribe of howler monkeys screeched and hurled leaves and fruit into the branches below.

Above the trees, the mountain peaks rose boldly, their slopes steep and green and rocky. Watching the slow-moving cloud riding the light breeze, listening to the *slap-slap-slap* of the boat's hull against the water as it tugged against its mooring, and with my fingers dangling in the cool water, I had the impression we were bobbing in a vast cauldron of nature.

With the Taurus in the bait box, I felt invincible. Let the Guerrilla come, I thought. This was now their territory. But I would be ready for them.

Of course, fishing here wasn't the same as with Papá. But with our gang back together, it began to feel like old times. At *colegio*, they'd dubbed us the three *mosqueteros*. Now, with Carolina, there were four of us.

Suddenly, my cell phone rang shrilly. All of us were surprised. There was rarely phone reception in Llorona – we must have hit a lucky patch on the river.

Camila frowned.

'Who else has your number?' she demanded, folding her arms. She was sometimes jealous.

Only three people had my number: Camila, Palillo and Boris Sandoval in Villavicencio.

I shrugged. 'It's probably work.'

Palillo knew 'work' didn't have my number, and I avoided looking at him in case our faces gave away the lie. We both knew what that call meant – the storekeeper had received Ratón's batteries.

The phone continued ringing and vibrating in my hand.

'Well?' demanded Camila. 'Aren't you going to answer?'

I shook my head. 'I'm on vacation.'

'Until when? Maybe they need you back early.'

My thumb hovered over the keypad. Ratón was suddenly within my grasp, but being with Camila had made me feel happy for the first time since my father's death. I wanted that feeling to continue. Over four days I'd felt her anger thawing, although I'd resisted committing to a departure date in case I changed my mind when I got the call from Sandoval. But now I pressed REJECT CALL.

'Until next Sunday, *mi amor*. Seven more days,' I announced.

Camila threw her arms around my neck. 'Oh baby, that's wonderful!'

Driving back to our hotel after dropping Camila and Carolina home, we were stopped at the main traffic lights in Garbanzos when the Díaz brothers spotted us. They were exiting the Agricultural Bank and Javier raised his hand in polite greeting. When I ignored him, Fabián stepped in front of the Blazer and banged the hood.

'Pedro! Pedro! Pedro! How are you, my friend?'

Insincerity dripped from them thicker than the gold chains around their necks. Both brothers shook my hand through the window, rudely ignoring Palillo seated beside me. My family lacked the Díaz wealth, but owning land at least made us acceptable to them, whereas Palillo's family rented a shack in the poorest area of Puerto Galán.

Still, I was confused. At the cantina Javier hadn't wanted to know me, but both brothers were now acting as though I were one of their oldest friends.

Javier must have noted my scowl of scepticism.

'I'm sorry I couldn't vouch for you to Don Miguel,' he said apologetically. 'As I told you, my position is delicate. But let me make it up to you. We're having a party next weekend.'

'Blue Label whisky,' Fabián chimed in. 'Pork *lechona*. A live *vallenato* band. Important people from Bogotá. You and your beautiful girlfriend should come.'

'*Gracias*, but the three of us are busy that night.'

'We didn't say which night.'

'I know. But thank you anyway.'

Insulted, Javier kept his cool. 'You must at least drop by for a drink. We'll toast to our fathers. May their souls rest in peace.' He crossed himself loosely then handed me his business card. His brother did the same.

The mention of our deceased fathers was so sudden and casual it left me speechless. Accelerating away, I felt like the electric window couldn't go up fast enough. Only months after their father was brutally murdered and they were throwing parties. The Díaz brothers wanted something, but I didn't know what. Was Javier trying to make up for the fact that he'd failed to vouch for me at the cantina? Were the brothers merely being sympathetic neighbours? Or did they suspect it was Papá and I who'd buried their father? But that was impossible. Not even Palillo knew about the burial.

'What was that all about?' I asked.

'Don't be stupid. They've discovered exactly who you are.'

'And who exactly am I?'

'A commander in the United Colombian Autodefensas. And they're long-term cultivators. One day, they might need you.'

54

BACK AT OUR *residencia*, Palillo and I listened to the voicemail that had been left after I'd pressed REJECT CALL in the dinghy:

'*Hola*, it's Pacho speaking. The chickens are ready for pick-up.'

'Motherfucker!' exclaimed Palillo.

I played it again. Despite the fake name and code, I recognised Sandoval's voice. In one way, this was a relief: my original plan was still on track. However, the knowledge that with a single phone call I could have Ratón in my sights in less than twenty-four hours was almost too much for me.

'Delete it! And Ratón's number too,' Palillo advised me. 'Don't worry, we'll get him next Saturday.'

While Palillo showered, I listened to Sandoval's message four more times. Finally, as I heard the water stop running, I deleted it. I had to get ready. Dinner with Camila's family was in two hours, although my friend The Toothpick had no intention of attending.

'Good luck with the in-laws,' said Palillo, emerging from the bathroom with a white towel wrapped around his waist.

'Thanks.'

'When you get back, knock five times like this.' He demonstrated his secret tap.

'What for?'

'Because Palillo might have company. Naked company.'

I laughed. Only five days since he'd seen Piolín, and already she was ancient history. I wished I could forget and move on like him. But once something was in my head I couldn't let it go.

As I was driving to Camila's house, Sandoval's voicemail continued to plague me. Finally, I forced myself to relax. After all, I didn't need to phone Ratón to pass on the message immediately. I had their code now. And if our plan to take Ratón at Santo Paraíso miscarried again, I could use it at any time.

Señor Muñoz sat at the head of the table. His giving me the place of honour to his right was pressure enough. Camila's not-so-subtle sideways glances and under-the-table nudges only added to it: the future of our relationship was contingent upon my withstanding a thorough analysis under the family microscope.

The main course passed uneventfully with Camila's brothers ignoring us. As her mother served dessert, Señor Muñoz asked me casually, 'Is your job dangerous?'

Camila must have repeated the African oil palm story.

'It can be.' I cut a strawberry with my spoon then looked him in the eye. 'A tractor tipped on one of the workers in January.'

That was all that was needed. An honest-to-God denial.

'I know your Papá would be proud of the way you're looking after your mother.'

I beamed. But then I felt guilty because his praise was based on a lie.

After dinner, Señor Muñoz invited me to speak privately in his study. He produced a bottle of Johnnie Walker, still gift-wrapped, and two tumblers.

'Whisky? I've been saving this.'

I nodded and we clinked glasses.

Señor Muñoz sipped his whisky and was silent for a moment. 'My daughter cried for a month after you left,' he said finally, choosing his words carefully. 'She hardly ate. She didn't do her homework. In fact, she barely left her room. I know you had your reasons, but I don't want to see her get hurt again.'

'Señor Muñoz,' I said, 'I'll be honest – I can't offer Camila stability right now. I need to be away earning money. But I do love her.'

He nodded; there was something else eating away at him. 'I'm also worried about the Guerrilla. You being back here and going out so publicly might provoke them. And if Camila is with you . . .'

'I understand. But I'm only here for another week and I'll be careful.'

Sighing, he placed his hands on the armrests and pushed himself wearily to his feet. 'At your age, my wife and I were engaged. So who am I to stop young love?'

55

AT 3 PM THE following day, Palillo and I drove to Colegio Santa Lucía to pick up Camila. Palillo was glowing like a blacksmith's poker fresh from the coals. He'd slept with Carolina the night before, making him an instant expert on the female species.

'Could be your turn soon, *hermano*,' Palillo declared, casually adjusting his crotch. 'Girls never want to be the first in their group to fall. But once one has fallen, they don't want to be the last either.'

Camila burst through the gates, looking beautiful with her hair in pigtails and her uniform riding high. Marcia, another of the girls from Camila's year, was crossing the road behind her, blowing kisses to Palillo as she headed for our truck.

'But what about Carolina?' I asked.

'Supply and demand.'

'What?'

'There are plenty of pretty girls.' He smoothed Moroccan oil into his hair. 'But there's only one Palillo.'

With Palillo's newly lost virginity came a newfound cockiness. He'd persuaded Juanita to skip lunch on Tuesday. Wednesday recess he had a date with Olivia.

Palillo made me laugh, but we were so different. I was glad to see him happy, although I didn't envy his growing appetite. The only girl I wanted was Camila.

Palillo began his Monday 3.30 pm appointment with a kiss. 'Marcia, I believe you've met my chauffeur, Pedro.'

His banter, however, met with fierce opposition. Camila was Carolina's best friend.

'*You!*' She grabbed his ear. 'Out of my seat. Pedro's *mine*.' She dragged him from the car. Locking the doors, Camila leaned in and kissed me with her tongue. My body flooded with pleasure as I felt her coming back to me.

It was our first proper kiss. Then she pulled a bikini from her backpack. 'Rope-swing tree please, driver.'

Camila was pleased with me for winning over her father. At Llorona River, she cast aside her shoes, stripped off her knee-high socks and began slowly unbuttoning her blue plaid uniform. Then she slipped it off entirely as she sashayed towards the water. I'd seen her in a bikini, but the way she disrobed now was far bolder than I remembered.

'Wait!' I stalled while I thought up a reason not to take off my shirt. If Camila glimpsed the tattoo, it would ruin everything. 'I haven't got a towel.'

'Who said anything about swimming?'

She unclipped her bright-blue bra. Then she shook her shoulders so the straps slipped down her arms.

'What are you doing?'

'What does it look like I'm doing?' Holding the bra in place, she turned and came back towards me. 'I believe somebody is owed a birthday present.' She smiled, letting the bra slip down her body. 'Or have you forgotten our promise?'

The first time Camila and I made love, I was nervous. I kept thinking someone might see us. Her overprotective brothers might come sprinting down the road. Or school kids might be spying from the bushes.

I was quick the first time. I tried to stop it but my body let me down. Camila said it didn't matter; she'd heard it happened to all guys. Besides, there was no rush. We could do it again, that day or the next day, or whenever I wanted. When she said that, all pressure disappeared.

The second time was everything I had imagined and more. We removed the rear seat cushions from the Blazer and laid them on the ground. Halfway through we swapped so she was on top, controlling the rhythm. Afterwards, I had never felt so contented in my life. The sun was descending and I lay there looking at her, caressing her face, smiling and laughing, and relieved because we'd finally done it. There was no need to ask about other guys. I knew there weren't any. And there was no need to ask about her feelings or intentions for the future. We both knew we were back together. In fact, in our hearts, we'd never really been apart.

When Mamá told me I looked exhausted, I blushed. For three afternoons in a row, Camila and I had made love by the rope-swing tree. I couldn't get enough of her. She couldn't get enough of me. I was always vigilant about not exposing my tattoo and Camila had noticed nothing.

If I dropped Camila home late, Señor Muñoz no longer complained. There were no more curfews. Provided I had a respectable job and honoured his daughter, there would always be a chair at his table for me and an after-dinner whisky.

Every moment I couldn't spend with Camila, I spent with Mamá. My anger at Uncle Leo dissipated. On Tuesday, I ate lunch with him. On Wednesday, I minded his hardware store while he made deliveries. As long as he and Mamá didn't interrogate me about my comings and goings, I made sure I was on time for meals. Palillo was happy, showering his mother and siblings with gifts, drinking, smoking and luring schoolgirls to Francisco's Pool Hall. If I hadn't missed Papá so much, I would have been happy too. For the first time since his death, however, I did feel peaceful. I had money of my own, I'd reconciled with Mamá, and I was more in love than ever.

The potential Guerrilla threat against me receded in my mind. Strangely, the temptation to phone Ratón and tell him his chickens were ready also receded. I began to reconsider whether Palillo and I should make our second attempt against him the following Saturday. Palillo had yet to come up with a new plan. Even if he did, the idea of abducting and killing Ratón now seemed naïve and unrealistic. A blindfold, gag and twenty minutes of pistol training didn't qualify me as a kidnapper.

Besides, after making my witness statement I was satisfied that Colonel Buitrago would keep his promise to bring Papá's killers to justice. I'd done all I could – burying my father and assisting with detailed descriptions of the murderers. I was sixteen years old. My obligation was to my mother and my own future.

By Thursday afternoon I was dreading Monday – our return to La 50. Camila and I drove to the rope-swing tree and made love. In that hour afterwards, the world seemed new again. Camila was where she belonged: in my arms. When she whispered in my ear that she loved me, a million new possibilities flooded my mind.

I could leave the Autodefensas and return to the *finca*. The house had enough rooms for Camila and me not to disturb Mamá. Of course, for Señor Muñoz to accept us living together, we'd need to get married. It mightn't be safe to move back immediately, but even if we had to wait a year or two until Buitrago drove the Guerrilla out of Llorona, we could do it. Collecting Camila from school earlier that afternoon, I'd waved to Rector Prada and requested my exam papers. One day, I might return to school or enrol in university like Papá had wanted. Meanwhile, I'd take a job in Garbanzos, even a shitty job with miserable pay. If Alfa 1 wouldn't discharge me right away, I'd work hard until he did. If he refused, I'd write to Trigeño. Colonel Buitrago's offer might be a last resort; I could join the army when I turned eighteen. Anyway, a year or two more with the Autodefensas would mean more money to invest in the farm. And at some point in the future, Camila and I could start a family of our own.

Distracted by dreamy thoughts, I dropped my guard. I stood lazily, stretched and then sauntered towards the river. That single error split my fantasy like a machete blade through bone.

'Swim, *mi amor*?' I called to Camila.

She didn't answer. I turned to find a look of horror on her face. She'd seen the tattoo.

56

'I KNEW IT. I fucking *knew* it. How could I be so stupid? They told me what you were doing. That's why I asked you about your work. But you lied to me, Pedro, and the worst thing is I believed you!'

'I'm sorry. I should have told you the truth. But I didn't want to hurt you.'

I tried to put my arms around her; however, she recoiled from me as though the viper on my shoulder were real.

'Have you killed people?'

'No. I promise on my father's grave.'

'That's something, at least. But . . .' She shook her head. 'This isn't you. You *hate* tattoos. You said—'

'I know. Look, Camila. I've made a mess of things. But give me another chance. I'll ask to quit and I'll make things right with you.'

'And what if they don't let you? I heard the minimum was four years.' She dressed quickly as tears welled in her eyes. 'I don't think I can do this. I can't wait four years wondering every day whether I'll see you again. Wanting the phone to ring, but when it does, not wanting to answer for fear it will be bad news. Besides, how can I trust you after you lied to me and to everyone?'

'You're right,' I said, pulling on my pants. 'This was a stupid idea.'

'What was?'

'Coming down to the rope-swing.' Grabbing the seat cushions, I got in the truck, slammed the door and flung open the passenger side. 'Get in! I'll drop you back home.'

When she refused, I started the engine and accelerated rapidly so the door jerked shut.

'Pedro! Wait! Where are you going?'

I opened the passenger door again, gently this time.

'I'll drop you back home. Then I'm going to the *finca*.'

'Don't!' she said sadly, looking down. 'It's too dangerous.'

Her warning only made me more determined. 'Are you coming or not?'

I counted aloud to three then sped away, tyres churning earth.

It was the rudest I'd ever been to Camila. She'd waited four months for me, not knowing if I'd return. When I did, she gave me her virginity. She told me she loved me and I left her behind in a cloud of dust, hands covering her eyes, and she had to walk four kilometres home, ashamed and distraught, with dirt-blackened tears streaking down her face.

57

DUSK WAS FALLING as I skidded the Blazer to a halt in front of our farm. At first I noticed nothing out of the ordinary. In fact, I paused to admire the sparkling lights of our little town. From that distance, it looked majestic. Below, I could see the church with its tall steeple, the well-trodden football field, the criss-crossing streets and the plaza, and I felt the tension seep out of me. Then I caught glints of smashed glass. Turning the truck to face our house, I switched to high beams. The words POR SAPO were graffitied five times across the white boards in blue paint. The phrase meant FOR BEING A SNITCH.

I pounded my fist furiously against the steering wheel and exited the Blazer, slamming the door behind me. Caraquemada had accused Papá of supplying the army with water, not of being an informant. So this message could only be for me.

I was angry not only at the Guerrilla for defiling our family home and slandering my father's good name, but also at everyone who had kept this news from me – Camila, Mamá, Uncle Leo and Colonel Buitrago. I was even angry at Papá's friends who'd expressed their condolences. Their strange, pitying looks and vague warnings about it being *too dangerous to visit the finca* now made sense. Everyone had known, but no one had told me the truth.

The fact that no one had been brave enough to clean off the graffiti reminded me of how cowardly people were and how little they'd helped on the day of Papá's execution. And I was insulted at everyone getting together behind my back and agreeing to treat me like a reckless child who needed protecting from himself. I felt thoroughly betrayed.

I sprinted up the steps. All the windows were broken. The front door was smashed. I ran inside. Even though the electricity must have been cut off long ago, I tried the light switch. It wouldn't have made a difference; the light fittings were shattered. Taking a flashlight from the Blazer,

I flicked its beam over the devastation inside. Everything was toppled, broken or destroyed – the sofa upended; the kitchen table and chairs thrown against walls; cutlery, utensils and Mamá's crockery strewn across the floor. I wrinkled my nose at the strong odour of urine. This was not the work of thieves; the television was still there, and I could see nothing missing. Neither was it spontaneous vandalism; the destruction was too systematic. *Everything* had been damaged, including objects whose value hardly warranted the effort, like clothes that had been shredded and forks that must have been bent by hand. This was my punishment for burying Papá.

As I entered my room, a floorboard creaked underfoot. The bedsheets smelled of sweat. Someone had slept in my bed. When another floorboard creaked on the way out, I bent down and peeled away several boards. In the floor cavity lay a wooden crate filled with military supplies – AK47s, AK45s, RPGs, camouflage uniforms, rubber boots and binoculars. The Guerrilla trashing our house was not only a punishment and warning; it was meant to disguise the fact that they were using it as a storage and supply point and also, owing to its isolation and strategic view over the town, as a lookout post.

By some miracle, Mamá's glassware from the sideboard had survived. Taking it with me, I stormed from the house and lined it up on the front porch. I went to the shed where we stored the five-gallon gasoline cans. I poured fuel over the wooden crate, doused my bed then splashed some over the floorboards for good measure. Twisting some old newspaper into a crude fuse, I wedged it between the slats of the crate. The only thing I lacked was a match.

I went outside to the Blazer and depressed the cigarette lighter. Only then, as I waited for the coil to heat, did I notice something was indeed missing: the cross at the head of my father's grave. I searched the ground wildly in the semi-darkness and finally found it flung far from the oak tree, broken in two and bullet-riddled. The Guerrilla had used it for target practice.

As I nailed the cross together I found myself back there on the day of my father's death. Flailing on the dirt with the blond boy's knee on my head, I watched Caraquemada circle Papá. The gunshot popped in my ear and Caraquemada walked away. Papá's skull cracked on the dry ground. Wave after wave of hatred surged through me as I drove Papá's cross into the ground. I wanted the Guerrilla dead. All of them. I wanted to burn everything down. Not only our house but the whole town.

The ejected lighter had gone cold. I depressed it again. As it heated a second time, my breathing calmed enough for me to think clearly. What was happening to me? I loved that house. I had grown up in that house. It meant everything to me and to Papá; he had spent every spare minute of the last eleven years maintaining and improving it. And I'd never doubted that it would some day be mine. Only an hour before, lying naked and peaceful by the rope swing tree, I'd dreamed of restoring the farm and living there with my mother and Camila. But now I was planning on torching it. And why? Because I was like a child, acting out of spite. If I couldn't have it, then no one else could.

I needed to get a hold of myself. I went to the bathroom. The mirror was cracked and the face that stared back at me was that of a stranger. I bent down and splashed water on my face, willing myself to regain control. When I was calm enough, I filled buckets with water, tipped them on the fuel and mopped my bedroom floor. I heaved the heavy wooden crate out of the floor cavity and, in short bursts, dragged it to the Blazer. Using paint from the shed, I whitewashed the Guerrilla graffiti and wrote a new message by its side:

¡AUC PRESENTE!

THE AUTODEFENSAS ARE HERE!

I returned to the Blazer and took one last look out over Llorona. It was no longer majestic. It was a wretched town with dirty streets, a church with a bent spire, a dusty football field and a decrepit plaza.

Stopping only to deposit my mother's glassware on Leo's doorstep, I drove furiously out of town, taking curves at speed and not deviating for potholes. I knew it was wrong to have considered burning down our family home. But I also knew that the world would never be right while men who committed acts of barbarity were alive and roaming free. I was heading back to Villavicencio. And I would make the Guerrilla pay.

58

ON THE ROAD to Villavicencio, I called Ratón's number and left a message: it was Pacho calling and his chickens were ready for pick-up. It was after midnight when I arrived and parked the Blazer one block south of the electrical store, leaving the crate of weapons and explosives concealed beneath a blanket in the trunk.

When I asked the sleepy *residencia* manager for my key back, she wasn't surprised to see me. In fact, since we were paid up until Sunday, she probably hadn't even noticed our absence.

'Where's your friend?' was her only question.

I shrugged and smiled. 'Out with a *chica*.'

I found Room 8 exactly as we'd left it – curtains drawn, Palillo's half-filled ashtray on the floor and our beds unmade. It was as though the entire week in Llorona had never occurred.

The next day I resumed my stake-out; after my phone message, I was now certain Ratón would come. My plan remained unchanged: watch from the window, wait for him to appear and then sprint downstairs. Before Ratón reached the electrical store, I'd cross the street diagonally, carrying my Styrofoam-filled box, intercept him from behind, disarm him and then march him to the Blazer.

For most of Friday, I watched the comings and goings at the electrical store. I'd filled the Taurus magazine with 9mm rounds from the stolen cache, figuring it would be a fitting end for Ratón to be killed by a Guerrilla bullet. The Paramilitary bullets I'd stolen from the armoury were lined up on the windowsill. I tapped and spun them as I waited, scanning the street. Palillo called my cell phone several times. Each time I let the call ring out.

Finally, in the early afternoon, I saw a man of Ratón's stature at the northern end of Third Avenue, walking coolly but resolutely in the direction of Sandoval's store. I snatched up the binoculars. They were zoomed in too far to locate him within the dense crowd of lunchtime shoppers, and I struggled with the focus dial, trying to get a visual on him. For a few seconds, I thought I'd been mistaken, but no, there he was, dressed in jeans and a black T-shirt, with the same skinny face and pointy nose I'd seen last Saturday.

My fist clenched and I had to drop my binoculars and place my palms flat on the desk to regain control.

'Son of a bitch!'

Cocking the pistol, I switched it off safety. I swiped the extra bullets from the windowsill into my pocket, bounded down the stairs two at a time and grabbed my box from under the stairwell. I supported it with one hand; with the other I gripped the pistol.

As I stepped from the pavement to cross the street a policeman on a motorbike cruised slowly past. From the other side of the *avenida* Ratón noticed him too – he slowed, lit a cigarette and leaned casually against a wall. Five metres behind him, a man dressed in a collared shirt and pleated trousers stopped also and took out his phone. He nodded discreetly to Ratón.

My heart raced. I hadn't factored in a bodyguard. It would be impossible to disarm two men and control both while forcing them into the Blazer. I had to quickly recalibrate my plan.

The police patrol departed. Ratón stomped out his cigarette and signalled to his bodyguard; they were on the move again. A parking space had opened up close to the store entrance, and Ratón waved to the driver of a small yellow taxi double-parked at the north-eastern corner of the block. I realised that, rather than arriving on foot, the two men had arrived by car. The driver flashed his headlights and started the engine.

I drew a deep breath and crossed the street as the taxi pulled in. The driver honked and slammed on his brakes.

'Watch where you're going!' he yelled, bringing me to the attention of Ratón and his bodyguard.

The bodyguard held up his hand. 'I'm sorry but this taxi's reserved. I'll flag you another.'

I detected the slight bulge of a weapon at both his and Ratón's waistlines. Adrenalin flooded my body. I looked up and down the street. With scores of potential witnesses in both directions, shooting the bodyguard in broad daylight and then trying to abduct Ratón was not an option.

'Thanks,' I said, 'but I'm going into this store.'

'Do you need a hand? That looks heavy,' said Ratón, glancing at my box and addressing me with a crooked-toothed smile. I had a moment of panic as he squinted, as though trying to place me. 'Open the door for the *muchacho*,' he ordered his bodyguard.

The bodyguard obeyed, and I walked through with the two of them following closely.

Boris Sandoval was seated at the glass display counter at the far end of his store, punching buttons on a calculator. Behind him was the staircase that led up to his apartment.

As we entered, Sandoval looked up from his accounting, recognised me and smiled in greeting, perhaps relieved that I'd arrived in the company of my 'boss', Ratón.

'Good to see you again!'

Luckily, it wasn't clear to whom he was speaking, but I had to act quickly. Sandoval's next utterance might give me away. Walking towards the counter with my enemy at my back, the narrow aisle seemed to contract, hemming me in on all sides.

I quickly scanned the two-metre-high metal shelf running down the centre of the store and among the light fittings and transformers saw what I needed: a roll of electrical cable. I'd disarm Ratón and the bodyguard, make Sandoval lock down the outside shutter, and then bind the bodyguard with electrical cable before interrogating Ratón.

'After you,' the bodyguard said to me as we approached Sandoval. However, I wanted to surprise them from behind.

'No, I insist,' I said, stepping aside so I could put two metres between us – close enough to aim, but too far for them to grab at the Taurus. 'You go first.'

When Sandoval frowned in confusion, I got ready to drop my box and point the Taurus at Ratón. Suddenly, the upstairs door clicked open and Sandoval's daughter padded down the stairs carrying two plates of food. For some reason, although it was Friday, she wasn't at school. Immediately, I began to panic. I couldn't shoot anyone in front of a little girl. I edged towards the door, preparing to abort the mission.

'You won't need that box, *compa*,' Sandoval said, using the Guerrilla's term for friend. 'I packaged the batteries for both your orders together.'

Ratón stared at my face, finally recognising me. He looked stunned and horrified.

I dropped my box. The bodyguard looked at me in astonishment as Styrofoam spilled onto the floor. I advanced, crunching it beneath my feet, raised the Taurus and aimed at Ratón's chest.

The bodyguard went to draw his weapon.

'Leave it!' I shouted at him. 'Put your hands on the counter or I put a bullet in your boss.'

Reluctantly, the bodyguard obeyed. Ratón held up both palms and started retreating.

'Easy, *muchacho*. Put that thing away. We can work this out together.'

The little girl began crying.

'Close your eyes, *cariño*,' Sandoval said.

'Stand still,' I yelled at Ratón. 'Throw your pistol on the floor.'

He glanced at his bodyguard but then reluctantly complied.

However, he'd created a critical distance between himself and his bodyguard so that it was impossible for me to keep my pistol trained on both.

'Sandoval,' I ordered. 'Lock the shutter and cut me some electrical cable.'

When Sandoval went to move, his daughter latched onto his thigh, screaming, 'No! No! No!'

'It's okay, *cariño*,' he said, bending down to comfort her. But then, rather than fetching the cable, Sandoval bundled her into a hug and pulled her down behind the counter.

With my attention momentarily distracted, the bodyguard reached for his weapon. I aimed for his chest and fired. In the confined space of the electrical store, the shot sounded like a thunderclap. The pistol recoiled, jerking my hands upwards.

I'd missed, striking his arm. The bodyguard dived towards the shelves, firing back at me. I fired two more rounds – one missed but the other hit him in the stomach as he disappeared behind the metal racks of electrical goods.

Almost at the same time, Ratón lunged forward to retrieve his pistol, but before he could get his hands on it I fired at him and missed. He scrambled out of sight as his injured bodyguard let loose from between the stacked boxes with a volley of shots. I dropped flat onto the floor and scrambled behind the glass counter. We exchanged fire, but neither of us had a clear view of the other. Bullets ricocheted off the wall behind me and the glass cabinet exploded into flying shards.

Next to me, the little girl was crying while Sandoval hugged her, repeating over and over, 'Don't hurt my daughter, please don't hurt my daughter.' Then he yelped in pain and blood spurted from his thigh.

I was now trapped behind the counter with no safe way out of the store or even up the stairs. I heard whispering and then the bodyguard fired again.

I fired back repeatedly until his pistol clinked against the tiled floor and he fell silent.

I heard footsteps sprinting towards the door. I got one shot away at Ratón as he fumbled with the door handle, but it, too, went off-target, striking him in the lower back and causing him to trip and stumble as he rushed onto the street.

I raced out and found him on the pavement, crawling towards the taxi. The taxi driver leaned across the passenger's seat to open the door for Ratón. He reached into the glove box and raised a pistol. But before Ratón could climb in, I fired three shots, splintering the rear windscreen. Ratón changed direction, scrambling instead under a truck where I could no longer see him. Tyres squealed as the taxi sped away, its open door swiping two parked cars. The gunshots, screeching tyres and scraping metal had brought shoppers to doorways. Pedestrians hid behind cars. All of them were watching me. But I had to finish the job.

Gripping Ratón by the ankles, I dragged him out from beneath his truck. Bleeding, he clutched at my trousers.

'No. Please. No. Please, no.'

I placed the pistol against his temple. 'You killed my father. Why, when I was the one who spoke to the recruiters?'

'That was Caraquemada, not me.'

'Not true and not good enough.'

'I'm a radio operator. I have nothing to do with making the orders or carrying them out.'

That wasn't true either – he'd been more than happy to extort money, oversee drug transactions and write a threatening letter to Padre Rojas. If I'd had more time, I could have argued. But dragging Ratón to the Blazer was now out of the question. I pressed the muzzle of the Taurus against his head.

'*Why?*' I demanded angrily.

'I don't know. It wasn't up to me. I liked your father. We were friends.'

Ratón's claim of friendship with Papá infuriated me. It was the last lie he'd ever tell.

I pulled the trigger. The pistol clicked. I was out of bullets. Seeing his opportunity, Ratón tried to wrestle me down. I fought to stay on my feet, reaching into my pocket for the extra bullets, but Ratón punched my wrist, spilling them across the pavement. Although bleeding heavily, he was strong. He grappled me to the ground, climbed on top of me and strangled me as my left arm flailed about the pavement, grasping for the bullets that remained just out of reach. Using my right hand, I struck at him with the Taurus butt.

Ratón choked me harder and harder with one hand while the other struggled to prise the pistol from my grasp. My left hand alternated between unhooking his grip from my neck and groping for bullets. Each time I saw one and reached for it, Ratón kicked or slapped it away. Just as I was about to pass out, I thought of his bored expression as he repeated the order, 'Execute him!' With a sudden burst of anger my fingertips stretched out and lit on a bullet. Inserting it in the chamber, I held Ratón in a fierce hug and fired into his side. His chokehold went limp. I rolled him off me. He was dead.

Panicked, I sprinted down the block towards the Blazer. Then I had second thoughts: the numberplate could be noted down by witnesses. Instead, I ran around the corner, planning to blend in with lunchtime shoppers. But I wasn't thinking straight. How could I blend in, covered in blood and holding a pistol? I hailed a taxi. The driver slowed down but then sped past me. I heard sirens. On foot I wouldn't get far so I ran back to the Blazer. Pulling out, I scraped the rear bumper of the white sedan in front.

My hands were shaking uncontrollably and I breathed in deep gulps of air. Since I hadn't arranged a safe house in case things went wrong, at first I didn't know what to do or where to go. Then I reverted to my original plan, taking the quiet back streets out of the city and driving towards the *Ni Pío* sign in Monterrey. I didn't stop until I reached the saman tree.

I sat there, forehead against the steering wheel, heart still racing, breathing hard. I'd killed Ratón. Everything had gone wrong. But at least I'd killed Ratón.

Five minutes later, through the shock, the gravity of my new predicament dawned on me. Although safely out of sight, I was covered in blood with no change of clothes, sitting in a vehicle whose numberplates might have been noted. I'd been seen by Sandoval, his daughter, the taxi driver and scores of passers-by. The binoculars with my fingerprints on them were still in the *residencia*, but I couldn't return.

Police would be searching for me and the Blazer. Maybe they'd already identified me through the *residencia* manager. I had no doubt they'd catch me shortly. But if I drove back onto the highway, they'd catch me immediately.

My phone rang. I flinched. Had they tracked me already? I scrambled to remove the battery, intending to throw away the SIM card. But then I saw the caller ID: PALILLO.

59

'WHERE ARE YOU?' I asked urgently.

'On a bus heading to Villavicencio. Camila told me what happened. I've been calling you since yesterday. Don't do it, Pedro!'

I paused. 'Too late.'

'*¡Mierda!* Where are you now?'

'At the tree.'

'Bury him then come back and collect me at the *residencia*. It will be less suspicious.'

'I can't. Things went wrong. There were witnesses.'

'Then I'll come to you. Don't move!'

When Palillo arrived on foot from the highway two hours later with our bags, he saw me sitting with my back against the wheel of the Blazer, head on my knees, and he sprinted the last fifty metres.

'Fuck!' he exclaimed. 'We need to get you to hospital. Where are you shot?'

Still in shock, I was shivering so much I could barely shake my head.

'Not my blood,' I stammered.

Now that Palillo knew I wasn't injured, I braced myself for another lecture about my mother, my father, Camila and not letting go of the past, but Palillo had said everything he'd wanted to a week earlier. We both knew what I'd done – I'd fucked up badly.

'We had a deal, Pedro,' was all he said.

After that, Palillo was coolly detached and practical. He retrieved the shovel from the saman tree and handed it to me.

'Strip down and make yourself useful,' he ordered.

While he looked through my bag and found jeans and a clean T-shirt for me, I dug a hole and buried my bloodied clothes, the blindfold, gag, rope, maps and cell phone.

'Everything!' he demanded.

I threw in the Taurus then filled the hole.

Afterwards, my hands were trembling so much that I couldn't drive.

'Give me the keys,' said Palillo, even though he didn't have a licence. The Blazer stalled several times before he got it moving. We sped towards the highway in first gear.

'What's that smell?' he asked, crinkling his nose.

Not wanting to mention the crate of weapons, I pointed to the five-gallon gasoline container I'd taken from the *finca*. With Palillo now in control my mind began to clear.

'Where are we going?' I asked.

'To the only place in this country you'll be safe from the police and the Guerrilla – La 50.'

Of course Palillo was right. But it struck me as ironic that only the day before I'd dreamed of leaving the Autodefensas, whereas now I was officially a criminal, fleeing to them for protection.

'What happened to your lip?' I asked, noticing that a scab was forming.

'Stepfather came home.'

'Your mother okay?'

'Shitty town.' Palillo spat out of the window. 'We should never have gone back.'

Since I was still shivering, Palillo reached into the back for the blanket. In doing so he uncovered the wooden crate and discovered the true source of the gasoline smell.

'What's this?'

I didn't answer, so Palillo pulled over and got out to check. Lifting the lid of the crate, he cast me a sharp look then dragged it from the trunk.

'No!' I said. 'The Guerrilla had that stored in my bedroom. I want to take it back to Alfa 1.'

For the first time since rescuing me, Palillo raised his voice.

'Do you know how many police and military checkpoints we passed between La 50 and here? And if by some miracle we're not stopped and searched because this vehicle stinks of diesel, do you think you can just walk up to Alfa 1 and say, "Hey, thanks for the vacation! Do you want this crate-load of weapons and explosives I happened to find whilst driving the truck I stole from you?"'

Splashing fuel over the crate, Palillo snatched the blanket from me and added it to the pile. He held out newspaper and a cigarette lighter.

'Your one-man job,' he said, nodding towards the weapons crate. 'You finish it.'

When I refused to take them, Palillo tossed me his cell phone.

'Either you blow it, or you phone Buitrago with the location. Your choice.'

60

I CALLED COLONEL Buitrago's secretary with the location of the crate. Although it was out of his operational area, I hoped he'd get credit for the find. If his patrols saw the graffiti I'd left on our *finca* and bothered to go inside, he'd probably guess where the weapons were from. Maybe then he'd realise who was on the wrong path. And he'd also owe me.

Reaching La 50 at dusk, we passed through the gate search as if nothing had happened. It was Friday and we were back two days early. The trainers were still on leave. No one asked about the Blazer. We cleaned it, aired it, replaced the door handle, filled the gasoline tank and sandpapered the white paint off the bumper scratch. I was still convinced I'd get caught, but Palillo was relaxed.

Before arriving at the saman tree, he'd stopped at the *residencia* to collect my possessions. Police across the street had been taking witness statements, but evidently the killer's description hadn't yet reached the manager. Palillo had played it cool when he entered, acting surprised when she told him there'd been a triple shooting out front. Rather than sneaking out or paying her a tip to keep quiet, he'd demanded a refund for the two remaining nights, claiming we were both moving to a safer hotel.

'This never gets mentioned again,' he declared, handing me the refund. 'Keep your mouth shut forever and nothing will happen.'

Despite Palillo's reassurance, for the next two days I was convinced that any moment police would descend in helicopters with a warrant for my arrest.

I shivered when I thought about what I'd just done. I'd killed two men. One of them without wanting to. I hadn't expected killing a man to be so difficult and so messy. Trigeño and Beta had made killing look easy – graceful even. They did it in one simple motion that took a fraction of a second and seemed painless to the victim. But man does not die easily. And no matter how much you tell him he has to die, or even *show* him he has to, he will never accept it. Man wants to go on living, and he will fight and grasp and plead to his last breath because his life is what is most precious to him.

Each night I fretted about witnesses and evidence – the taxi driver, the storekeeper, the *residencia* manager, ballistics tests on the eighteen 9mm shells left behind on the pavement, forensics tests on hair strands in my cap, the skin under Ratón's fingernails and even the Blazer's paint scratches on the white sedan.

Palillo laughed. 'You've been watching too much American TV,' he said. 'This is Colombia.'

I couldn't have asked for a better friend than Palillo. I'd cut his vacation short, broken our agreement to abduct Ratón together and made him complicit in a double homicide, but he was cracking jokes. And he was probably right.

I'd read in the newspaper that the previous year over 30,000 homicides had been recorded nationally. During Pablo Escobar's reign of terror, dead bodies lay unattended for hours, sometimes days, because police didn't have enough resources to collect them, let alone identify victims, open an investigation file and pursue the killers. After all, what had they done about Papá's murder? And if three presidential candidates had been assassinated without a single charge brought, why would authorities bother with a simple street killing? If anything, when investigators identified the victims as *guerrilleros*, they'd realise I'd done them a favour. Or even if they miraculously discovered who I was, they'd never come to a Paramilitary base looking for me. La 50 was the perfect refuge for criminals.

Palillo's arguments calmed me. By Sunday, when no police had arrived and no news of the killings reached the base, I began to believe him – maybe I wouldn't be caught. But that didn't stop me from being haunted by the memory of Ratón tugging at my trousers, begging for his life. At night, I'd wake suddenly, gasping for breath with the full weight of Ratón's body on top of me as he bled out. My hammock had become twisted about my body, wrapping around me like a dying man clinging desperately to life.

On Sunday afternoon, I grew anxious about Alfa 1's return. He had a way of finding out everything. Paramilitary recruiters in Garbanzos plaza might have seen us in the Blazer. Alfa 1 might notice the scratches on the bumper. I suggested we invent a cover story for where we'd been, but Palillo said to tell him the truth, although only if asked.

This was the truth according to Palillo: 'The alternator was repaired early, so you didn't think Alfa 1 would mind if you took the vehicle to visit your sick mother. You paid for the gasoline yourself and you're sorry for the scratch – you're happy to pay for it.'

My first conversation with Alfa 1 went exactly as Palillo predicted.

'Welcome back, Pedro,' he said, slapping me on the back. 'Nice vacation?'

Seeing the commanders' faces, I realised Palillo was right – I'd gotten away with it. *I'd gotten away with murder.*

With my anxiety gone, I had time to reflect clearly on what I'd done. Of course, I didn't regret killing Ratón – not for a single moment. Nor did I regret killing his bodyguard – he was a *guerrillero* and deserved to die. But I didn't feel satisfied. I hadn't killed Ratón the way I'd planned – the same way the Guerrilla executed Papá. I hadn't performed my ritual. And Ratón had died too quickly. There had been no chance for him to acknowledge the wrong he'd done or to accept that he needed to die for justice to be served.

Even worse, I'd been unable to extract information on where to find Papá's remaining killers.

Now, as the others started returning to base, it occurred to me that in my search for Caraquemada, Zorrillo, Santiago and the blond-haired boy I was back at the very beginning. I knew their names but little more. However, I knew where the Taurus was buried. And I vowed that next time I would not make the same mistakes.

complete in the [illegible] paid [illegible] quality [illegible] and [illegible] for the [illegible] happy as [illegible]

My first conversation with [illegible] was [illegible] I [illegible] predicted.

We [illegible] and [illegible] the [illegible] the back [illegible] the commander [illegible] Father [illegible] away with a [illegible]

With [illegible] I had [illegible] Because I didn't [illegible] for a [illegible] moment. Not [illegible] killing [illegible] deserved to [illegible] killed [illegible] the same way [illegible] except [illegible] had been [illegible] chance for him to acknowledge the wrong he'd done [illegible] he deserved to die [illegible] deserved.

Even worse, [illegible] and [illegible] killing [illegible]

Not [illegible] It [illegible] back in the very beginning [illegible] And I [illegible] would not make the same mistake.

PART FOUR

WORKING FOR THE COMPANY

61

ON SUNDAY EVENING, I watched truckloads of returning troops pour onto base. It was late March – the final month of the dry season. The earth was brown and hard and parched, and the water level at La Quebrada was low enough for heavy trucks to cross.

Soon we'd form our squads and start patrolling the countryside, but in the meantime the base was being expanded to accommodate a larger intake of recruits. A forklift was unloading a blue forty-foot shipping container from a semi-trailer. It contained an industrial deep-freezer, gas cookers, toilets, washbasins and bags of cement. But my work provisioning the camp was over and a new boy had been assigned as Culebra's assistant.

While ordinary soldiers helped construct two new dormitories and another toilet block, we junior commanders would complete a ten-day crash course in pistol handling. After that, we'd receive the rest of our advanced training during breaks between patrols.

Commanders now treated us more civilly. We no longer had to salute them constantly or say *comando* twice per sentence. Gone also were their punishments. Alfa 1 was almost polite.

'Please form up!' he yelled on Monday morning after breakfast. 'Commanders out the front.'

I lined up with the other newly promoted soldiers – seven from our course and five who'd been chosen from existing ranks. We stood expectantly, facing the troops.

'Attention!' yelled Alfa 1. 'Eyes to the front! Salute!'

The salute was for Trigeño. He'd come by road, accompanied by fifteen bodyguards. As he strode onto the parade ground, I remembered him on his first visit, weaving between lines of recruits and shooting boys to punctuate his speech.

Today, however, Trigeño was not the crazy-eyed lunatic who had forced Tango to shoot his own brother. He was light-hearted, even jovial, shaking hands with each of us junior commanders in turn.

Then he leaped dramatically onto a crate to address the assembled troop.

'An army without leaders is like a headless snake,' he announced, his voice carrying easily across the still, dry air. 'It will thrash about wildly, but eventually die. These men will guide you and, in return, you must obey their orders and be willing to sacrifice yourselves in their defence.'

These words had a profound effect on me. Surveying the rows of fierce-looking soldiers, I felt completely safe for the first time in months.

'Can anyone tell me a man's greatest weakness?' asked Trigeño.

Silvestre raised his hand. 'His carotid artery.'

Trigeño shook his head.

'His pressure points,' guessed Pirata.

'His testicles,' cried Palillo from the safety of the back row.

'No,' Trigeño said, smiling and holding up his hands until our chuckles subsided. 'A man of war's greatest weakness is also what he values most – *his family*. Every Guerrilla commander hides behind a *chapa* and an alias. But if we discover his full name, it will lead us to his date and place of birth, to his parents and his friends. Maybe he has an ex-wife he phones at Christmas. Maybe he writes to his children who attend university in Mexico.' Trigeño scanned our faces to ensure we were following. 'Family is your enemy's greatest weakness. *But it is also yours*.'

Trigeño continued his speech, exalting the virtues of loyalty, courage and service to the nation, but I was only half listening. His words about family had struck a nerve, and I couldn't stop thinking of Mamá, and of the mess I'd left behind in Llorona. I'd upset a Guerrilla nest and run off, leaving others to suffer the consequences.

Of course, the Guerrilla had no proof against me. One of Buitrago's patrols might have discovered their weapons. The graffiti might have been painted by the Autodefensas recruiters from Garbanzos. Nevertheless, my presence in Llorona and sudden disappearance made me a suspect. And if they'd killed Papá simply because I'd spoken to Paramilitary recruiters, what might they do to Mamá if they deduced I'd stolen their weapons?

After Alfa 1 ordered the troop to fall out, Trigeño led the twelve new commanders on a walking tour of La 50.

'This farm is where I grew up,' he began. He pointed to one of the boys' dormitories. 'That was the milking shed.' Then he pointed to the girls' dormitory and the trainers' quarters. 'That was where farmhands slept, and that was the stable. And here . . .' He stopped on the bank of La Quebrada and his face became grave. 'Here was where the Guerrilla shot my father. They'd come to kidnap him, but he and my brother saw them and fled. They were running through this creek when the Guerrilla opened fire. The bullet struck my father in the spine. *Gracias a Díos*, he died instantly and my brother escaped, hiding in scrub over that hill. But they left my father's body in the dirt like that of a dead dog.' Trigeño's voice faltered. 'Not a day goes by that I don't think of him.'

None of us said a word. But after hearing this I felt we had something in common. Every time he crossed that creek, he must have relived his father's death, just as I relived Papá's.

'I had two choices,' continued Trigeño, regaining his composure. 'Stay here and fight, or flee. The land and house had been in our family for generations. How could I turn it over to men who would rather steal at gunpoint than do an honest day's work?'

Trigeño suspected some of his own farmhands had tipped off the Guerrilla about his father's movements. He hired loyal men to infiltrate them and identify the culprits. Meanwhile, he convened a meeting of local landowners and asked them to join his fight against the communist *subversivos*. Trigeño paid farmhands double wages to risk their lives as armed security guards. He enlisted the army to assist with military training. Word reached the Guerrilla, making him a target. However, Trigeño found the traitors one by one and drove the Guerrilla out of the region. He didn't specify how he achieved this, merely saying that *one led to another* and the region was *cleansed* of communists.

'I was protecting not only my family's land but the entire community. Witnessing my success, many landowners sent me money, rifles and men. There was no shortage of volunteers, especially among those who'd lost relatives to the Guerrilla.'

I now found myself admiring Trigeño. Starting with nothing except anger and willpower, he'd formed his own private army. When I'd joined, it had numbered only five hundred soldiers but was growing rapidly. Of course, all around Colombia, other landowners were building similar militias to defend themselves against Guerrilla incursions. However, Trigeño's real genius was not in multiplying his own forces but in uniting these disparate, independent armies under one single banner: *The United Self-Defence Forces of Colombia*. He was doing exactly what I wanted to do, only on a far grander scale. Trigeño's pursuit of justice was not personal. It was national.

That night, I called Mamá from my new cell phone: each junior commander had been issued with one, together with an untraceable SIM card. From these we were allowed to make personal calls, provided they didn't clash with our duties.

'With privilege comes responsibility,' Culebra stated as he handed them out. 'So please, *be discreet*.'

I rang Uncle Leo's number and felt relieved when Mamá answered.

'Pedro? Are you okay?' Her voice sounded small and hurt, and my relief turned to guilt.

'I'm sorry, Mamá. There was an emergency at work. They needed the truck.'

The lie tripped uneasily off my tongue. After discovering her glassware on Leo's doorstep Mamá must have known I'd visited the *finca*. Possibly she'd heard about the graffiti I'd written.

'You got your glassware?' I asked coolly. 'Everything else was destroyed, as I'm sure you know.'

'I'm sorry, *hijo*. I should have told you. But I knew you'd do something foolish.'

'So you heard about my tidying up at the *finca*?'

Mamá paused, perhaps wondering whether this was a conversation she wanted to have. If she acknowledged my graffiti, she'd be openly recognising that I'd joined the Autodefensas. And then she'd either have to agree to support me or try to stop me.

Her sigh of resignation told me she preferred to continue feigning ignorance.

'Just as long as you're safe, Pedro. That's all I care about.'

Camila was not so easy to pacify. It was worse than last time. Last time I'd had good reason to leave. Last time I'd at least written her a note. This time, I'd driven off in anger and without making up for our fight. When I phoned, Camila's father told me she was out, even though it was a school night. She was also 'out' when I called the following afternoon, and again after dinner.

Finally, I told Señor Muñoz I wouldn't take no for an answer. When Camila came to the phone she was angry, but there was no question that we were still together.

'Why did you lie to me, Pedro?'

'Why did *you* lie to *me*?'

She, too, had known about the Guerrilla vandalism and kept it from me.

'I was afraid of how you'd react. I was trying to protect you.'

'Exactly.'

That helped her understand. We'd both lied. We were both trying to protect each other. Deep down she'd always known that I'd joined the Autodefensas with Palillo.

'I thought that after you spoke to Colonel Buitrago . . .'

'Buitrago's useless.'

I told her how the Guerrilla had used our *finca* as a lookout post – probably in order to bomb the police garrison and kill the police boy – and about the weapons cache hidden in my bedroom that could have been used for further attacks against our town. When Camila heard how I'd resurrected Papá's cross because they'd shot it up, she had no further argument.

'This is something I have to do,' I told her. 'It's not going away by itself.'

Camila understood. With Guerrilla power growing in Llorona and starting to affect the whole population – not just landowners and businessmen – something had to be done. She just wished I wasn't the one to be doing it.

Of course, things would be difficult for us. I had only two weeks leave every four months. But we reached an agreement that was the opposite of the one I had with Mamá.

'No more lying?'

She sniffed her acceptance. We'd wait for each other.

'But, Pedro, aren't you worried about the cross? They might guess it was you.'

'It's done now. Anyway, I'm here. They're over there. They can't touch me.'

Uneasily, I remembered Mamá but quickly quashed the thought.

'Be careful. And call me whenever you can. I need to know you're alive.'

With forgiveness from Mamá and Camila, perhaps I, too, should have forgiven. But I couldn't forgive. Neither Papá's killers, nor myself.

62

AFTER TALKING WITH Camila, I felt very alone. Hearing her voice at the end of a phone line reminded me that I was again hundreds of kilometres from the people I loved, and it took little time for my mind to turn to the men responsible for that separation.

Ratón was dead, but the other four were still breathing. There was the blond-haired boy who'd tackled me and forced me to watch my father's death – I'd recognise him if I saw him but knew nothing else about him, not even his name. Santiago, the commander who'd ordered my father's execution, bore the ultimate responsibility, but to me he was merely a name relayed through Ratón's radio.

My most intense hatred was for Caraquemada, the man with the glass eye and half-burned face. With a single shot, he'd stolen Papá from me, and I would make him pay. But I hated Zorrillo, Caraquemada's second-in-command, with almost equal ferocity. It was Zorrillo who, from sheer spite, had forbidden Papá's burial and banned us from our *finca*. He was responsible for my having to flee. And he was the reason Mamá was living in poverty, sleeping on her brother's sofa.

I loathed Caraquemada and Zorrillo with every lungful of air and every painful throb of my heart. During Beta's first pistol-shooting class I superimposed mental images of both men's faces onto the life-size plywood targets at the shooting range and dedicated alternating bullets to each of them.

'Your pistol will be of no use during battle,' Beta instructed us. 'But keep it on you at all times. Never get caught alive by the Guerrilla. They kill ordinary soldiers on the spot. But if you have one of these . . .' He pushed up his sleeve to reveal his python tattoo. The implication was obvious. If captured by our enemy, my viper tattoo would guarantee a protracted and painful death.

I fired three times in rapid succession. *Bang!* I shot Caraquemada in the wrist. *Bang!* I shot Zorrillo in the knee. *Bang!* I shot Caraquemada in the shoulder.

'No! No! No!' screamed Beta. 'You're doing it wrong.'

But I'd hit where I'd aimed. The wrist. The knee. The shoulder.

I'd learned from my mistakes. In future, I'd shoot to immobilise Papá's murderers until I could drag them somewhere quiet and deliver my speech. Unfortunately, without the information I'd expected from Ratón, I had no leads on where to find them.

My only hope was that there might be something on Caraquemada or Zorrillo in the Autodefensa intelligence files. After all, that was how I'd found Ratón.

That night, I checked the safe. Since my promotion, I no longer had to ask permission to enter the office. The commanders trusted me – I was one of them.

I removed the pile of manila folders, laid them on the table and flipped through them one by one, slowly at first, and then with increasing desperation. There was nothing on Zorrillo or Caraquemada. It shouldn't have surprised me. They operated well outside Trigeño's protectorate. In Ratón's case, I'd been lucky: since he travelled to Villavicencio for supplies, he'd appeared on our radar. I replaced the files, slammed the safe shut and slumped into a chair, holding my face in my hands.

It was only a week since I'd shot Ratón, but already I was brimming with frustration. And that frustration continued to mount as I was told to choose half of the squad that I was to lead into the remote regions of Los Llanos – hundreds of kilometres in the opposite direction from Papá's killers.

63

ALFA 1 INSISTED THAT each squad contain a mix of new graduates and more experienced soldiers. He'd already chosen four members of mine. Ñoño had been selected before my leave – since I'd saved him during the obstacle course, he was now my responsibility.

Fortunately, Ñoño had forgiven me for shooting him. Palillo's explanation that I knew about the blanks made sense. Ñoño even seemed embarrassed to have believed a witch's spell could stop bullets.

'So we're good?' I asked Ñoño, feeling guilty about lying.

'You saved me then you shot me,' he joked, 'so I guess we're even.'

Alfa 1's other picks for my squad were Yucca – a boy from our course who was slow to learn and kept mainly to himself – and Giraldo and Veneno, who I'd yet to meet. They were older than me and had already been patrolling for three years.

When it came to my own choices, the first two were easy. Palillo I could count on without question. He was in good spirits as he helped construct the new dormitories, flirting and joking with Piolín.

'Did you miss me?' he asked her.

'Why would I miss you? I hardly even know you.'

'If you knew me, you'd miss me. I'm addictive, like chocolate,' he said, sliding a Snickers bar into her breast pocket, which made her smile.

MacGyver was my second choice. Before joining the Autodefensas, he'd served two years in the army, so he had experience with weapons and had a few battles to his credit. MacGyver had no leadership aspirations and wasn't envious of my promotion. He simply wanted to keep a low profile and stay as far away from the senior commanders as possible. I still didn't know what he'd done to be sent back to basic training, but it must have been serious. All he'd said was that repeating four months of your life was better than losing it altogether.

My third choice was Coca-Cola. He was my age, and ever since his *El Volteo* punishment on the first day, he'd obeyed every command.

I hesitated over my fourth and final pick. I needed a team player who was intelligent and capable and wouldn't flout my authority. Finally, having made my decision, I went to see Alfa 1 and had my choices approved.

At lunch I fell in step with Palillo as we walked towards the mess hall.

'Ever since you helped me in Villavicencio,' I said, 'I've wanted to make it up to you. And now I have.' There was someone who'd be perfect for my squad, and whose selection would make Palillo happy. 'My fourth pick is Piolín.'

'Impossible!' he exclaimed, his eyes lighting up. 'And they approved it?'

I shrugged. 'None of the other commanders wanted her. They said girls are useless in combat. And pretty girls cause distractions and rivalries.'

Palillo gave me a high five then began singing lyrics from one of the only songs he knew in English: *Nowhere to run to, baby. Nowhere to hide.*

In the first week of April, we set off to patrol a remote region of the Meta province. After travelling by truck for several hours over bumpy, dusty roads, we set out on foot from a *finca amiga* – a friendly cattle station that required protection.

For the next seven days, we trekked through shoulder-high grass, stopping only to rest beneath trees or to scan the distance with binoculars and relay our location and observations back to La 50 via radio. Every day was the same as the last – long, hot and dry. We ate the same food for breakfast and dinner – beans, rice and chickpeas – and the same Maggi packet soup for lunch. At dusk, an army of mosquitoes descended, plundering our skin with an arsenal of invisible needles.

The region had been 'cleansed' of Guerrilla years ago, but locals were reluctant to explain how Trigeño had achieved this. Only one man – the seventy-year-old owner of a *cebu finca* – gave a straight answer.

'*A fuego y sangre*,' he told me. *With fire and blood.*

Farmers greeted us with friendly waves. Children rushed out to meet us, wanting to hold our rifles. Wives and daughters offered us food. Some were pretty, but the rules for dealing with civilians were very strict – we were to be polite, but never too friendly.

Maintaining discipline within my squad in the remote savannah wasn't as easy as I'd expected. Petty arguments erupted simply because everyone had excess energy and limited ways to expend it. As commander, I became the bullseye for my squad members' darts of frustration.

Veneno – whose alias meant 'Poison' – was the most troublesome. At twenty, he was the second oldest after MacGyver. He was half a head taller than me, and there was barely concealed bitterness in his every look, in his surly tone of voice and in the way he carried out my orders with deliberate slowness, as though daring me to reprimand him.

One evening, as we were lifting the packs from our shoulders, I asked Veneno to fetch firewood for cooking.

'But I did it yesterday,' he protested.

He was right – normally I rotated each duty, but this time I'd forgotten. However, now that I'd given the order, I couldn't back down.

'It doesn't matter. Do it again.'

Veneno strolled towards me, still wearing his pack, and stood centimetres away, breathing heavily into my face with his hands on his hips.

'Why should I obey a teenager who's barely taken off his training wheels?'

Before I could answer, MacGyver grabbed Veneno by the throat, lifting him onto his toes.

'Because he's your commander. End of story.' MacGyver let go, shoving him backwards, and Veneno fell onto his pack with a thud. 'If you've got a problem with Pedro, take it up with Alfa 1 and see where it gets you.'

The argument occurred on the last day of our first patrol, and I hoped they'd both cool down after some time apart. During our rest leave between patrols, I continued my advanced training course on La 50, but my squad was given the option of paying to stay at La María, a nearby *finca* owned by Trigeño that boasted a swimming pool, ping-pong table and kiosk. Those who preferred not to spend their meagre wages could stay on La 50, where they received free food and accommodation but had to wear uniform and do three guard shifts per day.

Either way, our respite didn't last long. After only two days of rest we were collected by truck and transported to a new 'friendly farm' to start another assignment.

In mid-April, the wet season commenced. Rain came down in sheets that swept across the landscape. With no dry campsites, everything got wet and stayed wet. Damp socks caused our toes to go soggy then blister. But despite these privations, being out in open space made me calmer. My mind was occupied with leading my squad. I began to think of its members as *my* men. They were soldiers, but after a few weeks they were also like brothers, even Veneno. A brother you dislike is still a brother. Alfa 1 had been right – being responsible for other men's lives removed a lot of selfish, self-indulgent shit from my head.

Of us all, Palillo was the happiest – Piolín couldn't evade his attentions. After four months training outdoors, her muscles were lithe and she had a golden tan. Yucca, Giraldo, Veneno and Coca-Cola all watched her longingly. I even caught myself staring at her without meaning to.

At first, we found Palillo's overtures towards her entertaining. No one took him seriously, least of all Piolín. But during our third rotation in north-eastern Casanare, the two began to lag behind, deep in conversation and dragging their feet. When I read out the guard roster, I'd catch them winking or smiling at some private joke.

One lunchtime, when they sat together on a log away from the group, Veneno finally voiced what the others must have been thinking: 'I thought she had a boyfriend in Barranquilla.'

MacGyver approached me one evening as we were setting up camp. He'd seen Palillo and Piolín holding hands, and Palillo trying to steal a kiss, which she'd turned away from.

'Remember what I told you,' he said. 'I like Palillo – he's funny – but do you really think the prettiest girl in the history of the Autodefensas can go to a nobody *negro* from Llorona?'

'I don't see the problem,' I said. 'The commanders already have their girls.'

'That's not the point. If those two get together, the commanders will take it as an insult. And the others in our squad are getting jealous. You need to inform Alfa 1.'

'I can't. Palillo is my best friend.'

In fact, I'd never seen Palillo so dedicated to pursuing one girl. I was glad to see him happy. At the same time, I was beginning to think I'd done all three of us a disservice by including Piolín in the squad.

I warned Palillo privately. 'What you're doing is dangerous. If MacGyver knows, others might guess too.'

'So what if they do? She can be with whoever she likes. Love isn't against the rules.'

I was amazed to hear Palillo mention love. The word just slipped from his mouth. This was more serious than I'd thought.

Seeing Palillo and Piolín so happy made me envious of the simple things they took for granted. They'd known each other less than six months and yet they could talk every day. They could wake up next to each other. And although they couldn't kiss openly, they could at least look into each other's eyes. Camila and I could only talk by phone. I called her whenever

I could, but in remote regions there was usually no signal, and we only returned from patrolling every eight days at best. Sometimes we went directly from one patrol to the next.

In May, I went more than three weeks without hearing Camila's voice. But when we finally did speak, she told me something that fanned the flames of my vengeful thoughts to white-hot fury.

64

WE HAD RETURNED to La 50 after three back-to-back rotations. At night, as soon as my duties ended, I called Camila. She was overjoyed to hear from me; however, once the initial burst of excitement subsided, her voice turned serious.

'Pedro, there's something I've been meaning to tell you. But I don't want you getting angry. Do you promise?'

A hundred possibilities raced through my mind: she'd kissed someone else; she wanted to break up with me; her father had discovered I was an Autodefensa. But I held my voice steady.

'That depends on what it is.'

Camila hesitated. 'After you told me what you did at the *finca*, I snuck up there and took down your father's cross. I've hidden it under our house. Please don't be mad!'

'You *what*?' I exclaimed. 'Why would you do that?'

'Because he would have known it was you.'

'Who would have known?'

'Zorrillo.'

There was a long silence before I trusted myself to speak.

'Why? What do you know about Zorrillo?'

'My father made me swear I wouldn't tell you . . .'

'Too late now. You have to!'

Camila finally told me everything she knew about the events following Papá's murder.

Two weeks after I'd buried Papá and left Llorona, Camila's father had collected our cattle and herded them to the Sunday markets in Puerto Galán. The Guerrilla presided over the markets and usually extracted a ten per cent commission from both buyers and sellers – they'd done this for decades and everyone accepted it as part of business. However, that day, Zorrillo himself had been present. When he recognised the brand on the cattle as Papá's, he raised the *vacuna* to fifty per cent as punishment for my burying Papá, adding, 'Tell that *muchacho* next time he crosses us, it won't just be graffiti.'

I listened, cold with shock.

So it had been Zorrillo who trashed the furniture inside our house. Zorrillo who sprayed graffiti on our walls. Zorrillo who pissed on our rugs. And Zorrillo who shot up Papá's cross. My blood boiled. For that alone I could have killed him.

Hadn't they punished my family enough for me talking to the Autodefensa recruiters? Wasn't it sufficient that they'd killed my father and driven us off our land? Did Zorrillo have to keep tormenting us?

'My father refused to sell at half price,' continued Camila, 'but Zorrillo drew his pistol and forced him to. Zorrillo bought the cattle himself, throwing the cash on the ground. He said his men would enjoy a fine meal, care of a dead man. Afterwards, Papá felt responsible for not transporting the cattle to a different market. He wanted to cover the loss. But your mother wouldn't accept his money. She said that we should never tell you or let you see what Zorrillo had done to your *finca*.'

I now understood why Mamá had so little money. She'd explained it by claiming she'd had to repay the bank, but the sale of our cattle should have more than covered our small debts, leaving plenty over for her to start a new life.

Trigeño's warning now rang in my ears. A man of war's greatest weakness is his family. Zorrillo had exploited that weakness: to get back at me, he'd struck devastatingly at my mother.

I should have thanked Camila for taking down Papá's cross – she'd run a huge risk to protect me. And she'd also broken a promise to her father by telling me the truth. But I was angry.

'You shouldn't have gone to the *finca*. I don't want you involved.'

'I'm already involved. And I did it for your mother too. She has nightmares about bumping into Ratón in the streets. She's suffering, Pedro.'

'You think I don't know that? But since we're being honest, there's something I haven't told you either. Ratón is dead.'

'What? How do you know?'

'Because I killed him.'

There was a long silence. A very long silence.

'Killed him how?'

I told her about Villavicencio. Camila went quiet while she processed everything. It took only seconds for her to guess my intentions.

'Don't even think about going after Zorrillo! My father says he's surrounded by bodyguards. You won't get within ten metres of him.'

But I wouldn't need to get within ten metres. The Galil's effective range was 400 metres.

'I love you, Camila,' I said. 'I'll talk to you tomorrow.' Then I hung up.

I now knew for certain that Zorrillo hadn't left the area. In fact, I knew exactly where to find him: at the Sunday cattle markets in Puerto Galán.

65

UNFORTUNATELY, KNOWING WHERE to find Zorrillo and being able to do something about it were two very different things. Camila's revelations only increased my frustration because until my next leave I'd be stuck patrolling or on La 50. I considered inventing a family emergency and asking Alfa 1 for a few days' special leave.

But almost immediately, developments at La 50 rendered that hope futile. The next day, Alfa 1 was teaching our advanced group how to use a 40mm grenade launcher when we were interrupted by Culebra.

'There's something on the news that you need to see,' he said to Alfa 1. 'In fact, you should all come into the office. This affects everyone.'

On the small television attached to the wall, the President was announcing that the government had officially entered into peace talks with the Guerrilla's high command.

The President's face was clean-shaven and unlined, but his expression was weary.

'The Colombian people are tired of war,' he said, 'and I am confident that a ceasefire and eventual disarmament will lead to lasting peace for our great nation.'

The government's proposal required the Guerrilla to release thousands of hostages currently held in their camps. A one-for-one humanitarian exchange was under consideration – releasing captured *guerrilleros* held in prisons – but only provided all military hostilities ceased.

The RCN news report crossed to a secret jungle location where a tall Guerrilla spokesman with grey sideburns, dressed in camouflage and wearing a red beret, outlined their expectations for the proposed talks. Unlike the *guerrilleros* in Llorona, whose speech was peppered with *campesino* slang, he was articulate and intelligent, and he gesticulated passionately as he spoke. Within a minute, I was so drawn in by his arguments about equality, social justice and government corruption that I almost forgot he was the enemy.

Then his name appeared in white text at the bottom of the screen: SIMÓN SANTIAGO.

I froze in shock. I was looking at the man who'd ordered Papá's execution.

It was the first time I'd seen Santiago's face or heard his voice.

I kicked a metal wastepaper bin hard. It hurtled through the air, knocking a gaping hole in the plaster wall and spilling trash everywhere.

'Pedro!' yelled Alfa 1. 'What the hell? That comes out of your salary!'

'That's him!' I pointed at the screen. 'The man who—'

'I don't care. You need to control yourself—'

He was interrupted by the shrill ringing of his phone. He glanced at the caller ID and held up his hand for silence.

'Yes, of course I'm watching the news,' he responded tersely to the caller. Suddenly, he gestured for Culebra to turn down the volume.

'Don't joke with me! That's not funny.' Alfa 1's face went pale and he turned his back to us, swearing then whispering something before stepping slowly from the office and clicking the door quietly behind him.

I straightened out the dinted wastepaper bin and placed it back beside the desk, although my attention remained locked on the news piece.

Not only was Santiago refusing to disarm the Guerrilla, he was making ridiculous demands of the government, including a massive demilitarised zone – an entire municipality of Colombia that was to be cleared of all police and government soldiers, since the Guerrilla commanders feared assassination. Santiago also demanded that the government disband the Paramilitaries, which he called 'the army's secret right-wing death squads who murder peasant farmers, teachers and union leaders with complete impunity in a dirty war against the nation's poor'.

'That's pure *mierda*!' Beta yelled at the television. The others also began yelling until Alfa 1 re-entered the office. We immediately fell silent. The RCN anchorman was summing up the official response to these demands:

'The President has indicated that the government will investigate these serious allegations and, if they are true, take action against the people responsible.'

'Fucking politicians!' Alfa 1 shouted, booting the metal wastepaper bin. His kick was so powerful that it blasted the bin right through the wall, leaving a hole twice the size of mine. 'They're all cowards!'

I was reminded of Papá's midnight pronouncement on the Díaz brothers – they were cowards for not doing their job as men, thereby forcing us to do it for them. Alfa 1 continued destroying the office – hurling phones and even snapping the screen of a laptop over his knee.

Beta, who was normally the short-tempered one, had to restrain him in a headlock.

'What? What is it?'

Alfa 1 broke free.

'That was Trigeño who phoned. The government might be issuing an arrest warrant.'

'For Trigeño?'

'No, for me.'

66

ALFA 1 CLAIMED he was a scapegoat in the government's campaign of public appearances – designed to appease the Guerrilla and prevent negotiations stalling. Of course, the Autodefensas still had considerable power to protect Alfa 1. The investigation against him could be sidetracked. Evidence could be made to disappear. Judges could be bribed and witnesses coerced.

However, his potential arrest warrant changed the atmosphere at La 50 as well as our operational focus. New orders came from Trigeño. We were to assume every radio exchange was recorded; we were never to mention our location or the commanders by name, especially not Alfa 1, who'd be confined to base. The training course for new recruits, which was due to commence in June, was postponed indefinitely. Worse still, the junior commanders' phones were confiscated. Not only could I not call Camila or Mamá, I couldn't even phone to tell them why.

My squad's next assignment in north-west Casanare was cancelled – instead, we were ordered to patrol the countryside surrounding La 50 in a clockwise direction at a radius of five kilometres. Six other squads were also recalled, two to circle at ten kilometres and another four at a radius of twenty kilometres. The Autodefensas were no longer defending the outer regions of Los Llanos; we were defending ourselves.

When the army battalion at Puerto Bontón stopped taking Alfa 1's calls, he instructed Beta to give a new class to the junior commanders: what to do if caught by government forces.

'If captured, don't say anything!' Beta instructed. 'Just sit tight. We'll find you and get you out.'

Culebra added his agreement. 'We're in this together. And remember that *this*,' he said, slapping two fingers against the anaconda tattoo encircling his neck, 'is forever.'

That night I turned my back to the mirror and looked over my shoulder at my own tattoo. Although it was permanent I didn't want my life in the

Autodefensas to be forever. If the government's plan succeeded and the Guerrilla demobilised, it might be safe for Mamá and me to return to the *finca*. The problem was that I didn't think the plan *would* succeed. And in the meantime, we were all stuck protecting our senior commanders rather than fighting the Guerrilla like we were supposed to.

Over the next week, whenever I returned to base, I read newspapers, watched television and listened to radio reports, hoping to see or hear Santiago again. The country was awash with the news of the potential peace talks. The international community was showing interest in brokering the deal.

According to Alfa 1, in thirty years of fighting, this was the Guerrilla's smartest play yet. They'd convinced everyone that they were ready for peace and eventual participation in the democratic process. But we knew better. The communists' power was growing, and if the President granted them their demilitarised zone – a land area the size of Switzerland – he might as well hand them Colombia on a plate.

I cut out a photo of Santiago from the newspaper, enlarged it several times on the office photocopier and stapled it to a plywood target on the pistol range. Alfa 1 found me shooting at dusk. Rather than scolding me for wasting *La Empresa*'s resources, he'd brought his own rifle and box of ammunition.

'Good idea,' he said, taking aim at Santiago. 'Tomorrow, make me a hundred more copies.'

We stood side by side, taking it in turns to shoot until it was dark.

'You've come a long way, Pedro,' he said to me as we gathered our empty shells and headed back. 'And you hate the Guerrilla almost as much as I do.'

'If we catch Santiago,' I said, 'let me kill him myself.'

'Fine.' Alfa 1 sounded amused. 'He's yours.'

'Is that a promise?'

We'd reached the container, and in the overhead light he saw that I was serious.

He nodded. 'As a reward for your loyalty.'

But I wasn't as loyal as he thought. Inside the armoury, I now identified various spare parts from decommissioned Galils and readied them for assembly into a complete, functioning rifle – exactly as I had with the Taurus.

This time it was easy. I knew my way around the container and spare parts box better than anyone. I outranked the new recruit assigned to the container – he had no right to question me.

In fact, the next time I was sent on an errand to Puerto Bontón I walked out of the container carrying the assembled Galil in plain view of the commanders and placed it openly in the back of the Blazer next to mine. Culebra waved to me. I smiled back. The gate guards didn't comment on the second rifle.

But as I wrapped the Galil in plastic and buried it in the garbage pit, I realised why I didn't feel as happy as I had when I'd succeeded in stealing the Taurus.

This time I wasn't breaking the commanders' rules; I was breaking their trust.

While the commanders fretted about being raided and arrested, my own greatest fear concerned Palillo and Piolín. At La 50 they were careful, but when we were patrolling they now did everything together. Veneno, in particular, paid close attention, perhaps looking for an opportunity to undermine my authority.

One night Piolín had a headache and Palillo promised to do her guard duty for her without first requesting my permission. To make a point and not show favouritism, I refused to allow it. Around midnight, however, I was woken by her giggling. Palillo was sitting with her at the guard post, whispering. I took him aside.

'I specifically said *no*.'

'There's no rule against doing voluntary guard duty. Two sets of eyes are better than one.'

'Not if both sets of eyes are distracted.' With Palillo completely unrepentant, I could no longer turn a blind eye. I needed to find out how far their relationship had progressed. 'Palillo, have you slept with her?'

'Not yet.'

I felt relieved – maybe he would listen to reason. But his next comment made my jaw drop.

'Adriana isn't easy like other girls.'

'Adriana? Her name is Piolín. You need to call her Piolín.'

'She doesn't like being named after Tweetie. She's not a cartoon character.'

'I'm sorry, Palillo. You're losing focus and it's jeopardising everyone's safety. I'm going to have to tell Alfa 1 about this.'

'You can't be serious! I've done nothing wrong.'

Then Piolín arrived from her guard post. She placed a hand on Palillo's shoulder. 'I'm free to choose who I want. And I've chosen Palillo.'

Seeing the two of them standing there together, backing each other up, I couldn't do it – I couldn't risk Alfa 1 splitting them up simply because they were making my job difficult.

'Okay, but this is your final warning. If either of you disobey me again, I'll ask Alfa 1 what he thinks of your relationship.'

'Fine!' said Palillo. 'We'll be more careful.'

However, four days later, still patrolling the perimeter of La 50, Palillo fell and landed hard on his back. Piolín rushed to offer him her hand.

'Are you okay, *mi amor*?'

At least six people heard those words – *my love*. Immediately realising her error, Piolín gasped and flushed. Palillo tried to cover for her by making a joke.

'Do you mean the love of your life or the love of your week?'

But the damage was done. Those two words had given Veneno all the evidence he needed.

67

AT FIRST, NOTHING happened. We continued our patrol, there were no more slip-ups, and we were granted two days of rest leave. Culebra was now the senior-ranking commander at La 50, while Alfa 1 and Beta remained hidden uphill at Trigeño's personal farm.

One afternoon, an army truck covered with a green tarpaulin – the same one that had been used to return the five deserters – arrived at the gates. Behind the steering wheel sat the same flat-faced man, Lieutenant Alejandro.

Culebra told me that the lieutenant wanted to speak privately to Alfa 1 on a matter of national security. Culebra had sent for Alfa 1, but in the meantime I was to show our visitor to the commanders' quarters.

I climbed into the truck's cabin and Alejandro drove around the camp's outskirts before reversing up to the door of the dormitory. Without asking permission, he searched inside the room before returning and peeling back a tiny corner of the truck's tarpaulin.

'It's clear,' he whispered.

I watched in astonishment as a wrinkled male hand emerged from the dark interior and gripped the wooden grill. Then the corner of the tarpaulin was thrust outwards to reveal a silver-haired man wearing an immaculate green officer's uniform. His buttons shone and his black leather shoes were polished to perfection. My mouth fell open as the sun glinted off a row of medals pinned to his chest and the metal stars that graced his epaulets. Standing before me was a three-star general of the Colombian National Army.

Even for a three-star general, there is no dignified way to climb out of the back of a truck. Lieutenant Alejandro offered his hand. The general waved him away and jumped down. Once on the ground, he preened himself like a fussy bird, brushing imaginary dust from his sleeves and pulling down his jacket to straighten it. Then he removed his hat, tucked it under his arm and stepped into the dormitory, followed by Alejandro.

I introduced myself and offered the general a chair.

'I'll stand, *joven*,' he stated defiantly. 'Where's Captain Murillo?'

Alfa 1's voice boomed from the doorway. 'That's Alfa 1, General Itagüí, now that I'm no longer under your command.'

I realised who the general must be – Alfa 1's former chief, the one who'd discharged him from the army for human rights abuses.

'Good to see you, Alfa 1,' said the general cautiously.

Alfa 1 sauntered into the room, followed by Beta and Culebra. 'It's good to see you too, General, being smuggled around in the back of a truck. Ever heard of a phone?'

'It's this peace process. Our phone lines are monitored and I can't be discovered communicating with the Autodefensas at such a critical juncture.'

Itagüí told us that the President had forbidden the army from going after the enemy. Eighteen generals had already resigned.

'But I've spent thirty years risking my life for this county. I have to keep fighting the Guerrilla in any way I can.' The general nodded to Lieutenant Alejandro, who left the room and returned with two heavy cardboard boxes. 'To that end, I'm providing you with our intelligence on the Guerrilla. Details of their command structure, transcripts of radio and phone intercepts, and satellite images from the North Americans.'

I was stunned. My hopes of tracking down all Papá's killers, not just Zorrillo, reignited.

The general unfurled an aerial photograph of dense jungle with several rivers cutting through it. 'Somewhere in this area, our analysts believe there's an important base that may house up to five hundred *guerrilleros*. We're under strict orders not to attack while peace talks continue, but you, on the other hand . . .'

Since the Autodefensas didn't legally exist, the peace process didn't bind us. We could do the army's dirty work for them while they obeyed the ceasefire.

Itagüí had one condition for his offering: no copies were to be made. He'd already photocopied his originals and marked a green triangular stamp over the text in the middle of each page. If our copies fell into the hands of the *Fiscalía* – the Public Attorney's Office – or the press, the general would know the leak had come from us.

'If all goes well, you can expect more of this, One good thing might come of this peace process after all. For thirty years we've known next to nothing about the Guerrilla high commanders. But if the politicians grant them their demilitarised zone, they'll have to show their faces. And we'll be there recording every intonation of their voices, collecting each fingerprint left on a mug and storing every hair that falls from their heads. Anything we find we'll pass on to you. Someone has to continue this war while we can't.'

The general extended his hand to be shaken. 'Do we have a deal?'

Alfa 1 paused, and I remembered how proud he was. His discharge from the army had scarred his life. 'You come here asking for my help,' he began, 'and yet . . .'

Itagüí's hand became a fist. 'I won't beg, Captain Murillo, you son of a bitch!'

Alfa 1 laughed and gripped his hand around Itagüí's fist. 'That's what I like. A bit of the old fight!' Their eyes met and they smiled then shook hands.

Alfa 1 ordered Beta to fill two glasses with *aguardiente*.

'To peace,' Alfa 1 proposed, holding up his glass.

'To peace and war,' countered General Itagüí, clinking his glass against it. 'Since one can only be purchased at the price of the other.'

They drained their shots. Then Alfa 1 walked his guests outside to their truck.

'I have one more present for you,' said the general. He ripped back the truck's tarpaulin. A man in camouflage uniform lay flat on his stomach with a blue pillowcase over his head. His wrists were bound and a long rope was tied around his neck. A soldier sat with a rifle trained on the prisoner and a boot on his spine.

'We captured this *hijueputa* in Puerto Vallarta waiting for a food drop that we intercepted,' explained the general. 'He's admitted to being a *guerrillero*, but hasn't said much else. We think he might know about that big base, or at least a smaller, half-way base that supplies it.'

The guard now ordered the prisoner out, jabbing him in the ribs with the muzzle of his rifle and forcing him to grope his way blindly over the back of the truck.

The general nodded to Alejandro, who removed the pillowcase to reveal a blindfolded man in his twenties. He had a thick beard and smelled as though he hadn't washed for several weeks. The general ripped off the blindfold.

'He hates us taking this off. The Guerrilla have brainwashed him into thinking that if he sees our faces, we'll have to kill him. But after thirty days, the law requires me to either hand my prisoner to the *Fiscalía* for charges or release him. Those thirty days are up.' The general cut the man's bindings. 'I'm hereby releasing him from government custody without so much as a scratch on his face.'

The general held the front page of that day's newspaper under the man's chin while Lieutenant Alejandro took a photo as proof that their prisoner was in good condition on the date they released him.

'What do you mean I'm released?' said the *guerrillero*. He opened his eyes and blinked repeatedly against the light.

'I mean you're free to go wherever you can!' declared General Itagüí, patting him on the back. Then he climbed into the truck and drew the tarpaulin across.

As the *guerrillero* heard the truck rattling towards the gate, his eyesight began to adjust. He squinted around cautiously, taking in the vast plains and rustic farm buildings. Joy spread across his face. He must have thought he'd been dumped on a *finca* in the middle of nowhere and could walk to safety. Then he saw us. When he spotted our black armbands with the white letters AUC, all colour drained from his face.

Suddenly, the *guerrillero* bolted, sprinting after the truck's dust trail, his rope leash swishing in the dirt behind him like a startled snake. Beta gave chase and stamped on the rope, jerking the prisoner to a halt by his neck. The man fell backwards, choking. Beta tightened the rope and forcibly marched him over to stand before Alfa 1.

'What do we do with this one, *jefe*?' he asked, drawing his serrated hunting knife. 'I think he saw my face. Yours too.'

But Alfa 1 shook his head. He didn't go in for unnecessary cruelty.

'Put that away! We phone Trigeño. If this man knows about their mother base, it could change everything.'

An hour later, as Trigeño's helicopter landed, the President was announcing the appointment of a High Commissioner for Peace who would ensure that negotiations were fair, transparent and free of corruption. But with the Autodefensas and army backed into a corner, the start of the squeaky-clean peace process signalled the beginning of an even dirtier phase of the war.

68

TRIGEÑO'S EYES WERE red-rimmed and his face looked haggard. On seeing the assembled junior commanders waiting outside the office, he frowned.

'This had better be good!' he said to Alfa 1, who beckoned him into the office.

'It is, *comando*.'

Five minutes later, Trigeño opened the door smiling and invited us inside.

We crammed into the office, perching on chairs and desks, leaning against the wall or sitting on the floor. Trigeño stood against the far wall next to a large whiteboard. Alfa 1, Beta and Culebra were ranged alongside him.

'I have exciting news,' he began. 'We've received new intelligence about the existence of a large Guerrilla base. With your help, I've decided to restructure *La Empresa*. Our aim is to expand operations, locate this base and launch an attack.'

The junior commanders murmured amongst themselves – this was indeed big news. For the past month we'd been bunkered down. Now Trigeño was ordering us to go on the offensive.

He asked us to call out suggestions and assigned a scribe to write them on the whiteboard. Then Trigeño catapulted into action – talking, pacing, questioning and spinning on his heel. It was hard not to get caught up in his enthusiasm. We hadn't even located the base yet, but his certainty made everything seem possible.

To attack the base, we'd need more soldiers. Recruiters were to double their efforts – he'd pay fifty per cent more per boy delivered. Additional trainers would be recalled from patrolling remote villages since Trigeño required three more intakes to be trained by the end of the year.

'Impossible, *comando*,' protested Alfa 1. 'It's already June and each course takes four months.'

'Then shorten the courses or double the intake sizes. Just get me more soldiers!'

'Even fully trained soldiers will be useless without weapons.'

To the list of suggestions were added rifles and munitions, more pistols for commanders and two additional shipping containers.

'We'll also need four new dormitories, piping and showers, hammocks, chairs and tables, uniforms, boots, two more SUVs . . .'

Once Trigeño had started, he didn't pause for breath and the scribe struggled to keep up. He leaped from one idea to the next like a monkey swinging through the high canopy, launching himself clear of one branch without knowing where his next handhold was, but with the supreme confidence that he would never fall.

'And someone call my accountant! I need these expenditures approved.'

Two minutes later, Silvestre relayed a message for Trigeño: his accountant wanted to know where the money for all this was coming from.

Trigeño snatched the phone from his grasp. 'Find it!' he yelled into the handset. 'I don't care how! Call around for donations.'

I'd never heard anyone talk like that. And I'd never heard of money just being 'found'; Papá always said *plata* didn't grow on trees. But for Trigeño, the word 'no' didn't exist and the phrase 'I can't' might be a man's last. Within thirty minutes, he'd filled three whiteboards.

From now on Alfa 1 would dedicate his energies to military strategy: analysing the army's data, supervising reconnaissance to find the Guerrilla base and planning an operation against it. Culebra was appointed head trainer at La 50. Beta would become head of 'intelligence gathering'.

'What are my new responsibilities?' Beta asked Trigeño.

'You can start by telling me where you're holding this *guerrillero* son of a bitch.'

'In the container.'

Trigeño opened the office door, signalling for his three senior commanders to follow. I raised my eyebrows questioningly at Culebra and he nodded that I could come.

It was mid-afternoon and baking hot outside. As the soldiers stationed at the door unlatched the bolts and opened the container, I wrinkled my nose at the sour smell that poured out on a wave of stagnant air.

Inside, two sweat-drenched soldiers were guarding the prisoner, who was tied to a chair with his hands and ankles bound. Perspiration glistened on his forehead, and his neck was already ringed by a purple bruise from the rope Beta had stomped on. His eyes were closed, but he licked his cracked lips.

Trigeño unholstered his Colt .45, pressed the front sight into the man's throat and used it to lift his chin.

'I need you to open your eyes and look at me.' He spoke softly and gently, like a nurse ministering to a disoriented patient.

The man blinked his eyes open. When he saw the gun at his throat, his knee began trembling.

'There are two ways we can do this,' Trigeño said. 'One: you give us full, truthful answers that we can crosscheck. That way, you earn a quick death. Or, two: you play tough or tell us a story that doesn't check out. In that case, you'll die slowly, like a snail in salt.' He bent down so he and the prisoner were eye to eye. 'So . . . whose camp were you supplying?'

The prisoner spat in his face. A gob of saliva stuck to Trigeño's nose and began to ooze downwards.

Perhaps he'd hoped to provoke Trigeño into shooting him immediately. But Trigeño simply stared at the man and shook his head.

'Wrong answer, comrade.' He removed a white handkerchief from his breast pocket and raised it, as though to wipe his nose, but instead he swung his fist swiftly and powerfully, striking the *guerrillero* across the face.

The blow knocked the man sideways, capsizing the chair and slamming his head against the metal floor. He lay there unmoving.

Trigeño doubled over in pain, cradling his fist in his left palm. He stamped on the container floor. '*¡Hijo de puta!* I think he broke my fingers,' he said through clenched teeth. 'I'm getting too old for this. Fetch that strange boy you told me about – El Psycho. And prepare a truck for the Palace of Truth.'

'Already done, *comando*,' replied Beta, proud to have pre-empted Trigeño's wishes. 'I've radioed his squad. He'll be here by tonight.'

Trigeño crouched beside the fallen *guerrillero*, who was lying on his side with the chair still attached, groaning. His cheek was cut and blood trickled from his mouth. With his white handkerchief, Trigeño dabbed at the blood.

'I do apologise,' he said. 'Sometimes I lose my temper.'

Trigeño wedged his boot against the chair leg and hauled the *guerrillero* upright.

To my amazement, the prisoner looked defiant. 'It's easy to hit a man with his hands tied,' he said, slurring and forming the words with difficulty.

'You're absolutely right.' Trigeño bent down and began untying the man's bindings. Alfa 1 shot him a look that said, *Are you sure that's a good idea?* But Trigeño hoisted the prisoner to his feet.

'Hit me!' he said. 'Go on! I deserve it.'

The prisoner looked around the container – sizing up the guards, measuring the distance to the door and even taking in Trigeño's two pistols.

Trigeño stepped closer. '*¡Vamos!* This might be your last chance to punch an Autodefensa.'

Finally, the prisoner clenched his hand into a fist and drew back, readying himself to strike. But then both arms dropped by his sides, limp and defeated. Trigeño smiled, and I saw the sinister genius behind what he'd done. By giving the man the freedom to strike, he'd forced him to accept the futility of any type of resistance.

'Okay. I'll talk.'

'No, you'll *sing*,' said Trigeño viciously, shoving him back down into the chair. 'If you think you're suffering now, wait until you get to the Palace of Truth.'

He turned to leave.

'Wait!' the *guerrillero* called after him. 'I'll tell you everything right now. Why take me elsewhere?'

Trigeño paused at the door. 'Because I'm a very busy man. And because *everything* can take a very, very long time.'

69

AS TRIGEÑO'S HELICOPTER lifted off, a renewed energy swept through the camp. Since the peace announcement, we'd been mired in fear and uncertainty. But with the army back on side, Alfa 1 announced we were no longer in lockdown.

Culebra phoned the recruiters with a message: the cancelled training course was back on, commencing in three weeks. Culebra wanted twice as many boys as before and offered recruiters incentive payments for reaching their quotas.

Meanwhile, the *guerrillero* remained imprisoned in the container, although Beta was already planning the construction of a concrete holding cell embedded in the hillside.

The boxes of intelligence files were still locked in the office with Alfa 1, who stayed up all night studying them. The next morning, he summoned me to the office. Manila folders were arranged in neat piles on the desk.

'I need your help, Pedro. You're a better reader than I am. But this stays strictly between us.'

'What am I looking for?' I asked, trying to hide my excitement. I was convinced the files held the key to trapping Zorrillo and Papá's other killers.

He slid across a piece of paper on which four words were written: Jader Sebastián Murillo Fuentes.

'That's my real name,' he said. 'If there's a reference to the Autodefensas or an informant, photocopy it and place it in this folder. If there's a reference to me or my warrant, tell me immediately.'

Alfa 1 wanted the investigation against him quashed and any informants silenced. Of course, it was a long shot that I'd find anything. The investigation was being conducted by the *Fiscalía* and the police, whereas these were army files.

The folders contained a mix of unconfirmed intelligence data, analysts' compilations, witness statements, security incident reports and Executive

Security Reports compiled by battalion commanders. The Guerrilla then numbered approximately 20,000 soldiers, and there were personnel dossiers on about 500 commanders, listed by their real names. I only knew Zorrillo and Caraquemada by their aliases and political names, but luckily many of the files also contained a photo in the top right corner. Surely Caraquemada's horrifically scarred face would be instantly recognisable. The blond boy's lighter hair colour should also be easy to distinguish, and I had a clear mental image of Zorrillo. Skimming quickly through the files, however, I saw none of them.

Finally, I located a report from the Garbanzos Battalion compiled by Colonel Julius Orlando Buitrago on April 15.

INTRODUCTION: Over the past 12 months, major security incidents include the bombing of the Llorona police station, multiple kidnaps and murders of local citizens, 43 engagements with the enemy, ambushes of our patrols resulting in the death of 17 troops, and the destruction of two vehicles via remotely detonated explosive buried under the unsealed highway.

LLORONA: In March, weapons cache (15 AK47s, 18 grenades, 5 MGLs and 1000 rounds of 5.56mm) discovered during a routine patrol hidden in the residence of a murdered cattle farmer. Threats and intimidation against local businessmen continue, including micro-business owners previously ignored by extortionists.

PUERTO GALÁN AND PUERTO PRINCESA: Intensified recruitment drives and troop build-ups. Letters and pamphlet drops to citizens demanding compulsory attendance at Community Meetings hosted by communist political commanders.

SANTO PARAÍSO: Narco-traffic activity continues with weekly open-trade cocaine markets protected by Guerrilla.

CONCLUSION: Readers are referred to previous quarterly reports containing requests for more troops, vehicles, mine detectors, radio handsets, VHF repeater towers and increased aerial surveillance as well as cash funds to pay intelligence sources. If these requests are denied or deferred, a continued deterioration in the security situation is highly probable.

I noted that Buitrago had reported that the weapons crate was discovered inside our house *during a routine patrol.* Camila had told me that my AUC graffiti had been whitewashed by the army shortly after she took down Papá's bullet-riddled cross. I presumed the colonel had ordered these measures to protect me and prevent retaliation by the Guerrilla, and I felt grateful. Perhaps there would be no further consequences for my impulsiveness after all.

Next in the file came specific 'Incident Reports'. Of course, I longed to analyse each page meticulously, but that was impossible with Alfa 1 sitting opposite. If I didn't flip the pages regularly, he'd look up and ask me what I'd found. So I skimmed ahead in search of what I most wanted – information on Papá's execution and his killers.

It felt strange to see events that I'd lived through and seen with my own eyes described in dry, factual documents devoid of emotion.

A copy of the threat letter to Padre Rojas was on file, although there was no mention of how our beloved priest had been torn away from long-standing friends or of the upheaval within the demoralised congregation.

There was a lengthy report on Farmer Díaz's kidnapping, but I skipped over it since its ten pages contained only dates, times and transcripts of phone calls.

The file on the church bombing in Llorona the previous October reported it as follows:

Army response time: 17 minutes
Property damage: minor

There was no mention of the thunderous noise and ground-shaking explosions of the mortar bombs waking thousands of families and causing them to cower in terror.

Finally, I came to the report on Papá. It felt slightly surreal reading my own witness statement:

He fired and my father's head jerked then he fell to his knees and collapsed face-forward onto the dirt.

It was also horrific to realise someone I loved was now referred to by a case number and called simply *el difunto* – the deceased. However, it seemed that Buitrago had kept his word. Correspondence with the *Fiscal* prosecutor's office showed he'd succeeded in securing convictions against Zorrillo and Caraquemada in absentia. An *orden de captura* – an arrest warrant – had been issued for each man. Unfortunately, all warrants against Guerrilla commanders had been temporarily suspended to facilitate the peace talks.

It made me furious. By what right could politicians declare convicted murderers temporarily *not* to be murderers, just so they could sit down with them to talk peace?

If you want justice in this country – real justice, I mean – you can't wait for the government to do its job. You have to pursue justice yourself. I slammed the file shut and retrieved the original folder containing the personnel dossiers.

'Find anything?' asked Alfa 1, looking up hopefully.

'Not yet.'

However, my witness statement and Buitrago's diligence had in fact served for something. From their warrants, I now had Zorrillo and Caraquemada's real names, which allowed me to locate their personnel dossiers.

Zorrillo had been born EDGAR ROBERTO HURTADO JUNÍN. As a minor, he'd been arrested for car theft and aggravated assault. Later, he'd worked as a bodyguard, driver and assassin for the Medellín cartel, led by Pablo Escobar. Then, at the age of twenty-five, he was convicted for possessing fifty kilograms of cocaine concealed in the spare tyre of a vehicle he was driving.

By losing the cartel's merchandise, Zorrillo fell foul of them and in La Picota prison was forced to seek protection in the Guerrilla-controlled wing. Upon his release, he raised funds for the Guerrilla by turning against his former organisation.

From his years as a driver, Zorrillo knew the names and faces of mid-level traffickers, their accountants and political associates. With Guerrilla backing, he phoned former colleagues and demanded they pay *vacunas*. Anyone who refused was kidnapped, ransomed and, while in captivity, forced to reveal trafficking routes, the location of laboratories and the names of chemical suppliers.

The Medellín cartel put a price on Zorrillo's head and fed the Colombian authorities information on his whereabouts. However, each time the authorities closed in, the Guerrilla moved him to a different part of the country with a changed identity. His current field of operation was Santo Paraíso and Puerto Galán, where he was the 'Commander of Finances' under Caraquemada.

In addition to his extortion of cartel members, Zorrillo was suspected of masterminding thirty-two kidnaps. He was believed to have ordered forty-two homicides and issued countless extortion demands. Ten of his most recent extortion victims were cattle farmers and businessmen in Llorona and Garbanzos, including Humberto Díaz's sons, Javier and Fabián.

In the file were photocopies of four ID cards and two passports belonging to him, all of which carried different names. In successive photos he had short hair, long hair, no hair, a beard and a moustache.

I'd always thought of Zorrillo as a local, small-time *vacuna* collector, not much different to Ratón. But 'Zorrillo' was simply the latest of his many aliases designed to conceal the extent of his criminal enterprise, the amount of money he'd stolen and the incredible damage he'd caused around the country.

The report ended with a psychologist's profile:

> The subject's major weaknesses appear to be greed and vanity. Photos and receipts seized from his penthouse in Medellín at the time of his arrest reveal a predilection for designer clothes, prostitutes and sports cars. Hostages report that he continues to wear a gold Rolex even while sleeping in the jungle. He carries a Gucci wallet filled with cash that he displays in front of field workers and wears leather shoes. And, while his rank-and-file soldiers trudge through the mud, he travels by car whenever possible.
>
> In the opinion of this analyst, the subject manifests symptoms of Narcissistic Personality Disorder, characterised by a long-standing pattern of grandiosity, an overwhelming need for admiration and a lack of empathy towards others. The subject is unlikely to be a true communist. His relationship with the FARC is one of mutual self-interest.

I remembered how Zorrillo had referred to my father as 'the traitor Gutiérrez'. But he was the one who'd repeatedly betrayed his friends.

Zorrillo's demise could not come quickly enough. I only hoped I could reach the Puerto Galán markets before his superiors relocated him again. But whatever the case, I was certain of one thing: the key to trapping Zorrillo was money. Extorting money was how he lived. Extorting money was how he'd die.

When I began reading Caraquemada's file, however, I knew immediately he'd be much harder to track.

Caraquemada had no legally registered name or date of birth and no record with government entities – the Department of Births, Deaths and Marriages, the police, schools or even hospitals. The reason for this was bizarre: his parents had been Guerrilla commanders and their son was born in a mountain camp in the late 1960s. I'd located his file under 'A', since the name on this arrest warrant was 'Son of Alvaro Alvarez'.

Alvarez had been a dynamite technician in an emerald mine in Arauca when, as a union leader, he was targeted for assassination by the mine's owners. After hiding his wife in a remote village, he joined the recently formed Guerrilla, who prized him for his organisational skills and expertise with dynamite and soon made him a commander.

During a secret visit to his wife, the army tracked him down. Husband and wife fled back to camp, with one complication: she was pregnant. The Guerrilla did not allow infants in their camps – they made noise, required feeding and took a fighter out of action. Normally, women who fell pregnant in the ranks were forced to abort. But for the partners of important commanders, exceptions could be made.

When the child was born he was not given a name, instead being referred to as *Sardino*, a common nickname for young boys. *Campesino* sympathizers raised the boy until the age of eight, after which he lived in the camp as an ordinary revolutionary. Sardino cleaned weapons, attended communist classes and learned to shoot. He committed his first murder at the age of eleven; the victim was a landowner who'd laughed at him.

According to the file, by his early twenties the man I knew as 'Caraquemada' was a fearless commander and an expert in military tactics, masterminding and leading several raids on remote police garrisons.

As to the cause of his horrifically scarred left cheek, there were three competing versions: a jealous lover who poured acid on him while he slept, a 40mm army grenade that also killed his *socia*, or an accidental explosion while he was wiring a landmine.

After this incident he became even more committed and vicious. His alias changed to Caraquemada – meaning 'Burned-Face' – and, since he was now highly recognisable, he rarely left the mountain camps, from which he launched increasingly violent and successful campaigns against the army.

He became expert at moving large numbers of troops undetected. He trained junior commanders from other *bloques* to emulate his tactics. He also mastered the art of escape. During several battles he was the only member of an entire troop to return alive. Because of his face and these escapes, rumours circulated that he'd made a pact with the devil and could not be killed. Local *campesinos* and his own men feared him. When attacked, they claimed, he could change form, becoming a pig or a chicken or simply vanishing into thin air.

Caraquemada was ruthless. He was disciplined. The jungle was his home, the Guerrilla was his family and the revolution was his life. All this would make capturing him difficult.

However, the psychological profile did mention one potential weakness: a voracious appetite for women. *Guerrilleros* weren't permitted wives or girlfriends; however, they were allowed a 'sentimental partner' or *socia*. As a senior commander who frequently moved between units, Caraquemada kept multiple *socias*, all of them under fifteen years old. When he saw an attractive *campesina* girl, he pressured her parents until they let him have her. If she was pretty, he forced her to join so he could enjoy her regularly. The parents of one girl taken from her home had travelled for days by foot to the camp, where they complained to another commander. They were later found murdered.

At that moment, Beta knocked on the door and requested Alfa 1 step outside for a quick meeting.

Seizing my opportunity, I photocopied the entire 150 pages, praying the machine wouldn't overheat. I inserted the copied pages into an unopened ream of paper, which I resealed and placed at the bottom of the stack for later retrieval.

As I closed the cupboard, the door was suddenly flung open and Alfa 1 strode in brusquely.

I concentrated on not looking guilty, which only made my pulse race harder.

'Pedro, is there something you need to tell me?'

70

IT WAS PAPÁ'S old trick – the fishing net question – and, whatever he was angling for, there was only one way to play it.

'Not that I'm aware of, *comando*.'

Alfa 1's eyes narrowed. 'Very well. I've authorised Beta to transfer Piolín out of your squad, effective immediately. Tortuga will replace her.'

There could only be one reason for the transfer: her previous week's slip-up.

'As her squad leader, don't I get a say in this?'

'Not when a trusted commander like Beta comes to me with legitimate concerns about safety. You were warned when you chose her; Piolín is a distraction.'

'But no rules were broken.'

Alfa 1 scowled, obviously irritated. 'Pedro, you need to respect not only the rules but also the people who enforce them. If you'd come to me rather than keeping secrets, this might have turned out differently. You need to be loyal to me above everyone else, including your best friend.'

'Yes, *comando*.' I bowed my head.

So it was my fault. Perhaps, if I'd acted when MacGyver suggested, Alfa 1 would have simply reprimanded them.

'You can finish reading the files later. Right now, you'll inform your soldiers that Piolín is being transferred as part of restructuring. Patrols commence tomorrow morning at six.'

My squad had spent the weekend at *La María* and had just returned to base. I only hoped that during their time off, Palillo and Piolín hadn't become closer. However, as I led Palillo behind our dormitory, he told me that they'd shared a room.

'So if you spent the night together,' I said, 'then you two have . . . ?'

Palillo shook his head. 'Not yet. We're planning to. But I want it to be special. Like you and Camila.'

He was really excited.

'There's something I have to tell you.'

'Sounds serious.' He smiled awkwardly. 'Has someone died?'

'Piolín is being transferred from the squad.'

At first he looked at me in disbelief. Then his face dropped and he kicked the wall of the dormitory. 'Fuck! I'll kill Veneno. I'll fucking kill him. Dirty *sapo*.' He breathed out heavily through his nose. 'What will happen to her?'

I shrugged. 'I don't know yet. Trigeño has ordered a major restructuring and the commanders are on edge, so it's best if you two aren't seen together for a while.'

I tried to comfort him, telling him it would take time but he'd get over her. He insisted he wouldn't – there was no one like Adriana. He told me he'd written her poems.

'You know, Pedro, I can hardly spell so they were nothing great. But I was just telling her how I feel. The next day, she'd composed them into a song, which she sang to me.' Palillo was crying now, leaning forward against the dormitory wall with tears streaming down the bridge of his nose. I'd never seen him cry. Not even after the fiercest beating from his stepfather. 'No one ever sang to me. Not even my mother. She was always too busy with my brothers and sisters.'

I knew it was no use telling him about meeting new girls in the future. He only wanted Piolín. 'Even with the transfer, maybe there's some way . . .'

'Don't be naïve! Defying the commanders could get us both shot.' He shook his head. 'But she was the best thing that ever happened to me.'

When I told Piolín the news about 'restructuring', her face turned white.

'I'm truly sorry, Piolín. There was nothing I could do.'

'No, *I'm* sorry, Pedro. We should have listened to you.'

Before dinner, Piolín sought me out privately. Her eyes were red and swollen. She handed me a thick, white envelope.

'I want you to give this to Palillo,' she said. 'It was meant to be a present.'

Inside were two plane tickets from Villavicencio to Cartagena, on the Caribbean coast. She'd purchased them by phone and had them delivered to *La María*.

'When I bought these,' she said, 'I thought maybe the war was over, or *our* war at least. We could fly away and, if we kept our mouths shut, maybe they wouldn't come after us.'

'Does Palillo know?' I asked.

Piolín shook her head. 'I wanted to surprise him.'

I tried to hand them back. 'They're expensive. You should request a refund.'

'No, maybe he can use the money to help his siblings. They need protection.' She looked at me meaningfully. 'He told me how you two used to wait outside his house on your bikes, throwing stones to distract his stepfather.'

I was surprised Palillo had discussed his family problems with Piolín. There'd been an unspoken code in our childhood: we both knew what happened in his family but talking about it wouldn't change a thing.

Piolín sighed. 'It's funny – when I ran away from home I never expected to meet someone like Palillo. To everyone else he's a clown. But to me, he's a giant black lamb. I probably shouldn't tell you this, but I trust you. The other night, we were sharing a room at *La María*. I was drunk and I finally told him I wanted to do it. So when he was in the shower I took my clothes off, lit a candle and waited under the sheets. But you know what? Palillo never laid a hand on me. He said he didn't think I was ready. And afterwards I realised he was right. I probably wasn't.'

'Why not?'

She looked at her feet. 'Last year, when my mother was away for weeks at a time working as a cleaner, my father raped me. Not just once. It went on for two months.'

'You mean your stepfather?'

She shook her head. 'No, my father. That's why I ran away and joined up. This might sound stupid, Pedro, but I wanted to kill men. All men. That's why I invented a boyfriend. I didn't want anyone coming near me.'

Later I found out that stories like Piolín's were not uncommon – most of the Autodefensa girls had horrendous pasts – but at the time I was shocked.

'Who else knows about this?'

'After Palillo, you're the second person I've told.' Then she laughed ironically. 'Actually, the third if we're counting my mother. She didn't believe me. That hurt worse than what my father did.'

Finally, I gleaned the depth of connection between Palillo and Piolín. Both had joined the Paramilitaries simply to get out – it didn't matter where. Somehow, despite the horrors surrounding them, they'd found each other. But now, right at the very moment they'd dreamed of something better than the life they'd been dealt, the commanders had separated them.

I considered waiting to give Palillo the envelope until after we'd departed. He might do anything: beg Alfa 1 to intercede, confront Beta or even fight

Veneno. However, he took it well, praising Piolín's generosity and hiding his disappointment.

He said nothing more until we heard further news later that night: Beta had transferred Piolín into his own unit, the one responsible for 'intelligence gathering'. From now on, she'd be directly under his control and constantly within his reach.

'*Son of a bitch,*' Palillo muttered.

Our eyes met and I knew we were both thinking the same thing. On La 50 Beta was ruthless enough, but out in the grassy savannah with no one watching and no higher authority than himself, could such a man be trusted to respect Piolín?

71

FOR OUR NEXT patrol in July, we'd expected a normal rotation lasting eight days, but on the sixth day we were recalled to La 50. We arrived late on Saturday night to discover that several other squads had also been called in. There were rumours of an intelligence breakthrough on which we'd be briefed the following day.

Early on the Sunday, I found Piolín by La Quebrada, crying. Assuming she was still upset about her separation from Palillo, I sat by her side, as she had with me on New Year's Eve nearly six months earlier.

'Are you okay?' I asked.

'I can't believe he sent me there and made me watch!' she cried.

'Who?' I asked, realising this had nothing to do with Palillo.

'Beta.'

Her new squad had been in charge of transporting the captured *guerrillero* to the Palace of Truth, an isolated cluster of trees far out in the north of Casanare where suspects were interrogated. But once the prisoner was delivered and her squad was reassigned to other duties, Beta had ordered Piolín to remain and hold the tape recorder during the interrogation.

El Psycho had tortured the *guerrillero* for four days, slicing him up and down his arms and legs with a surgical scalpel, and then banging the tree branch to which the prisoner's wrists were tied to make fire ants descend and feast on his congealed blood. Beta had done the questioning. Each session went on for hours. They stopped only for meal breaks and to change the batteries on the voice recorder.

Piolín was traumatised.

'He was like a scarecrow, with bits of flesh hanging off him,' she sobbed. 'At one stage, he offered to go undercover for them with a satellite transponder. Beta held up a mirror and showed him his own mangled face, laughing. "But they'll never recognise you," he said. After that, the man begged to be killed – but El Psycho wouldn't kill him. He sewed the cuts up again to keep him alive longer.'

Tears trickled down Piolín's cheeks. 'The *guerrillero* was called Efraín, and he told them his life story even before the first cut. After he'd confessed everything, they insisted he tell them more about the layout of the mother camp. He tried to invent something just to stop the pain. But when they asked him for details, he couldn't supply them because he truly didn't know. So they tortured him for lying. I never thought I'd say this, but I was happy when he died.'

Piolín broke down before I could ask what had caused Beta to station her there. I guessed it was punishment for rejecting his advances.

I placed my hand on her shoulder while she regained her composure. I felt sickened by what she'd told me, but I kept wondering what Efraín had revealed. Could the camp possibly belong to Santiago?

Her gaze remained fixed on the water. 'I read somewhere that there is only one thing worse than the most horrible acts of evil men: the silence of good men. But whoever said that was wrong. They never heard a man trying to scream but gurgling instead because his lungs were filled with blood. Over that sound, give me the silence of good men any day.'

Turning, Piolín looked wistfully at the La 50 gate and the single road that led back to Puerto Bontón then to Bogotá and then to her home town of Barranquilla.

'I know what you're thinking,' I warned. 'Don't!'

'I won't, but . . .'

'But what?'

'I think I made a mistake joining.' She stood resolutely, wiped her eyes and took out a make-up compact. 'It was good to see you, Pedro. You're one of the nice ones.'

72

FIVE WEEKS HAD passed since Trigeño ordered us to hand in our phones. Only now did Alfa 1 return them. He was in excellent spirits – apparently Trigeño had pressured one of the witnesses in the case against him into retracting her statement.

I phoned Camila immediately. She was relieved to finally hear from me, although frustrated at having a boyfriend she rarely saw and who she wasn't able to phone. As I listened to her grumbling about everyday problems – her overprotective father, a bad result in her mathematics exam and a girl who had been spreading gossip about her – I could feel my mind being cleansed of the things Piolín had told me.

Camila and Piolín were the same age. Both were pretty. But their lives were so different. Whatever problems Camila had, she was still extremely lucky.

As for Mamá, she must have become worried by my lack of communication, because she'd sent me a postcard that had been delivered to La 50 by Don Jerónimo the taxi driver while I was away patrolling.

Mamá had been careful. The postcard had no addressee. It was unsigned and undated, and it mentioned no names.

> *Mi querido*, I hope this finds you well. I've found work during the day. I listen to the radio and watch telenovelas at night, when I most miss talking to your father. Of course, I miss you too. And I know a little someone who is very much looking forward to seeing you. Please call me when you can.

I rang Mamá, intending to thank her for the postcard and to urge continued caution. Uncle answered gruffly, told me she was now living elsewhere and gave me her new number. Hearing Mamá's voice, I felt relieved, then immediately went on the offensive.

'Why move out, Mamá? I didn't like you living with Uncle Leo, but we can't afford it.'

At first Mamá gave evasive explanations about earning extra money by sewing and ironing at nights, but when I pressed harder she finally admitted the truth.

'Eleonora Díaz offered to let me stay in the guesthouse at her sons' *finca* near Garbanzos.'

'*What?* How are you even talking to her? I thought she was in Bogotá.'

'She came to see Colonel Buitrago to discuss her own *finca*. He said our properties still aren't safe. Eleonora saw the position I was in and insisted on helping.'

'Mamá! We're Gutiérrez! We don't accept charity.'

I hated the thought of us owing anyone. It was undignified for Mamá and reflected badly on me. A son should look after his mother. If he couldn't, then the job fell to the males of the extended family, in this case Uncle Leo.

'It's not charity, Pedro. They're family friends. Eleonora has also suffered tragedy. We talk by phone almost every day. Her sons send their regards to you. You remember Javier and Fabián?'

'You know Papá never approved of Humberto Díaz.'

'I've got to live somehow, Pedro,' Mamá pleaded, her voice starting to strain. 'And your uncle needs his privacy. If I'm there, he'll never find a wife.'

So that was it! Leo and his little *amigas* needed somewhere to get private.

'Please, Mamá, move back to Uncle Leo's.'

'I can't do that, Pedro. It's rude to Eleonora when she's been so kind. I need friends. You're gone. Leo has his work. You have Palillo with you. Who do I have? Tell me! Who do I have?'

Mamá began crying and that always got me. Once a woman starts crying, the man has to back down. We're tougher than they are. Mamá wasn't one of those women who use crying as a weapon. Neither was Camila. They only cried when they meant it. Hearing her upset, I tried to see Mamá's perspective. She'd gone from her parents' house straight into marriage. For twenty years, Papá was all she had known. Without him, she was adrift, a riverboat cut loose from its mooring.

'Don't cry, Mamá. Everything will work out fine. My leave is in two weeks. I'll find you somewhere else to live.'

Mamá sniffed. 'Things are complicated right now. Phone me before you arrive, Pedro. And don't bring that truck. You need to be . . . discreet.'

It was on the tip of my tongue to ask her what she meant. But Silvestre was signalling to me urgently. Alfa 1's briefing was about to commence.

'Fine. I've got to go, Mamá.'

I hung up and strode towards the office. The other squad commanders were already taking their seats on the rows of folding chairs that had been set up in the middle of the room.

I resolved to somehow find the money to rent Mamá her own place. I didn't like her depending on anyone else, especially the Díazes. Although we'd been neighbours for eleven years, they'd never shown any interest in us while Papá was alive. We'd done our duty by burying their father, but they didn't know that. They owed us nothing. And I found their sudden generosity suspicious.

The sons had handed me their business cards when I'd visited Llorona. At the time, I'd brushed them off. However, now that my mother was accepting their hospitality, things had changed. I needed to talk to them. I could have called Javier or Fabián – I still had their cards in my locker. But that conversation was one I'd prefer to have face to face.

73

ALFA 1 SAT behind us in the back row, allowing Beta to conduct the briefing. At the front, a map was taped to a corkboard. Beside it, a poster-sized photograph was covered by translucent brown paper that concealed the details of a man's face.

Beta cleared his throat to signal that he was ready to begin. When Silvestre and Johnnie Walker continued talking, he glared at them until a hush fell over the room. This was Beta's chance to dominate, and he was revelling in it.

'New intelligence has come to light,' he announced. 'An informant has kindly volunteered information about the Guerrilla's mother base, which we suspect is located near the border with Venezuela.'

Beta stressed the phrase *kindly volunteered*, smirking as he said it. I remembered Piolín's description of Efrain's final days.

'Our informant has been with the Guerrilla for only two years and is not privy to military strategies. However, he was able to give us details of food drops made along the Cristal River that he and his squad transferred to other locations, usually three or four days' trek towards the Venezuelan border. We believe the food's ultimate destination was the Guerrilla camp.'

Beta explained that the food drops were always *dead drops*, meaning the location was known to both parties but there was a deliberate time gap between drop-off and pick-up. Therefore the informant never saw the faces of those who dropped off the food he picked up, or of those who collected the food after he left it. However, he'd confirmed the quantities of food, revealed the frequency of the deliveries and listed his drop locations. He'd also given up the alias of his squad commander and twenty names and descriptions of various *compañeros*.

'Unfortunately, this man's information is five weeks old. His sudden absence will have been noted and his commanders will have broken up his squad and rotated them to different parts of the country. However, our informant also gave us the names and descriptions of five civilians – boat drivers or donkey drivers who transport food into the jungle accompanied by Guerrilla squads. These men are poor, but because they own boats and donkeys they can't change locations as easily as the *guerrilleros*.'

Beta pointed behind him to the map into which several red pins were inserted.

'We now have seven known drop locations near fishing settlements along the Cristal River, and we plan to hit all seven simultaneously. Your squads will go door-to-door, questioning locals about these five men, their current whereabouts and the names of any family members, associates or friends. If anyone you question runs, shoot them in the leg and bring them in. If you suspect any person of concealing the whereabouts of these men or other significant information, bring them in. I want these people alive . . .' Beta smirked again. 'At least alive enough to talk.'

'Remember,' said Alfa 1, coming to the front, 'these temporary river settlements are occupied by indigenous populations, seasonal workers and fishermen. Make sure you have solid evidence before bringing in a civilian.'

I understood his implication – once the Autodefensas began interrogating a suspect, that person would never be released.

'If we start killing innocent people,' added Alfa 1, 'we'll have a catastrophe on our hands.'

He looked squarely at Beta as he said this, as though challenging him to disagree. We could not afford any public relations blunders.

I raised my hand.

'*Comando*, is there any indication of who owns the large camp?'

'How did I know you'd ask that?' Alfa 1 laughed. 'Good news, men.' He tapped the brown paper that concealed the enlarged photograph. 'We are now certain of the camp's owner. You have all seen this *hijo de puta* recently on television, pontificating articulately about peace and poverty and the good of the nation while prancing around like he's the next president of Colombia. But make no mistake! This man is a killer, a drug trafficker, a kidnapper and a criminal of the highest order.'

As he tore back the brown paper my pulse raced with excitement. I was certain he was referring to Santiago.

But instead I found myself looking at the face of another famous *guerrillero*: Tirofijo, or 'Sureshot'.

Several commanders exclaimed aloud and we looked at each other openmouthed. Tirofijo was the grand prize – the Guerrilla's supreme commander who'd started the insurgency in 1965 by arming peasants and organising them into militias. Eliminating him could change the course of the war, as well as Colombian history.

Despite that, I was bitterly disappointed. To me, Tirofijo was merely a face – more a historical myth than a real man. My hopes of finding Santiago plummeted.

Beta distributed copies of Tirofijo's photo, which we were to show to everyone we questioned. Long after the others had departed, I sat staring at the photo. All my hopes now rested on a vague plan of finding Zorrillo in Puerto Galán and then somehow tracking Papá's other killers during my future leave periods. But there was no guarantee of capturing Zorrillo and, with only two weeks' leave granted every four months, the hunt for the others might take decades.

I stood sluggishly and dragged my heavy boots towards the door.

Alfa 1 called me back. 'Close the door!' he ordered.

I obeyed.

'Did Piolín tell you about the captured *guerrillero*?'

I wasn't surprised that Alfa 1 knew about our conversation. He kept himself informed of everything that occurred on his base.

I nodded cautiously.

'It's a shame she had to witness that,' he lamented. 'The Palace of Truth is no place for a pretty girl.' Leaning back in his chair, he asked me philosophically, 'You know the worst thing about torture?'

I shook my head.

'It works.'

Alfa 1 slid a facedown photograph across the desk, his palm covering it. 'The photo I asked Beta to distribute of Tirofijo is part of our counter-intelligence. We ask the Guerrilla sympathisers some pertinent questions, but we also throw in some misleading questions to keep our enemy guessing about what we know. The last thing we want is *this* man,' he slapped the back of the photo, 'the *real* target, moving his base.'

He lifted his hand and I turned the photo over. It was Santiago. My smile stretched from ear to ear.

74

WITH INFORMATION FROM the tortured *guerrillero*, Alfa 1's patrols now had purpose and direction. Leaving a reduced guard protecting the *fincas amigas*, he ordered squads to each of the dead drop locations identified by Efraín. We hoped that with seven squads asking questions along a thirty-kilometre stretch of the river, one of the collaborators might lose his nerve and try to flee. Alfa 1 had set up hidden checkpoints on the road and placed an undercover man on every bus. The army would monitor unusual boat movements.

By sending in small squads as deliberate provocation, we'd also test the Guerrilla reaction times and assess which of their drop zones they guarded most strongly, hoping to find a weakness in their defences and a possible route into Santiago's camp.

My squad reached the ramshackle fishing settlement of Puerto Pescador at dawn.

In the gathering light, we saw a few dozen wooden shacks strung out along the bank of the Cristal River. The settlement wasn't marked on any map and most of the shacks were only occupied during the rainy season.

As the fishermen pushed their boats out into the river's slow-flowing waters, we began our first round of 'door knocks', targeting the women. They regarded us with suspicion, hanging back in the shadows of their doorways with their naked, brown-skinned children crowding around their skirts. They must have been accustomed to armed men asking questions – perhaps from the army or Guerrilla passing through – and claimed not to recognise the names we read out or the photo of Tirofijo.

Around midday, when the fishermen returned, we visited each dwelling a second time. The men were scaling fish and mending their nets, while their wives washed clothes in the river and stretched them out to dry on the rocks. The fishermen shook their heads, grunted and responded to our barrage of questions with perplexed looks and few words.

When shown the photo of Tirofijo, some said they'd seen him, but only on television.

After a day of door knocking, we set up camp approximately five hundred metres west of the riverbank, in a thicket of jobo trees atop a small knoll. The knoll itself was in the centre of a treeless, grassy field, giving us clear views for two hundred metres in all directions. Now that we'd questioned the fishermen, we needed to be on high alert. We were on the border of Guerrilla territory and they might retaliate. In the event of an attack, the trees would provide cover, and the elevation would give us superior firing positions as well as a strong radio signal back to base.

By late afternoon, dark clouds had gathered and it began drizzling, decreasing visibility. I sat against a tree trunk, thinking, while half my men remained on watch and the other half stretched out and tried to sleep. Even with confirmation that the base belonged to Santiago, I realised we were only beginning to scratch the outer perimeter of his security rings. The base itself was deep in the jungle, towards the Venezuelan border, through fifty kilometres of wide rivers and dense jungle. But at least we were advancing.

Suddenly, I heard Palillo hiss twice – the signal for danger. I hissed back and belly-crawled towards his tree. While Palillo leaned his forehead against the trunk and aimed his Galil, I peered through his binoculars east towards the river. At the limit of our grassy field I could see little at first. Then I caught flashes of movement in the woods and the metallic glint of rifles. After I made out the first shadowy human figure, the others became easier to spot. There seemed to be dozens of them, scurrying through the trees in all directions. With the fading light and the stress, it was hard to estimate their number, but I guessed around forty.

'Ready,' whispered Palillo, confident he had them in his sights.

'Wait,' I answered, tossing a rock to wake MacGyver, who shook the others by the ankles. I took aim also and waited tensely as my men wriggled towards their assigned positions, but the enemy must have realised we'd detected them. They opened fire first.

The noise of their rifles was like a jet engine. Bullets hurtled towards us, kicking up sprays of earth, sending bark flying and causing shredded leaves to cascade down upon us. Palillo returned fire, but my heart pounded and I froze up completely. During training, we'd always fired one shot at a time to conserve ammunition, but the deafening roar of rifles on automatic disoriented me until, finally, I recalled Alfa 1's advice about a soldier's first battle: 'Fire as soon as you can, even if you don't have a clear shot. Your fear will discharge with the rifle.'

I fired without aiming properly and the Galil jolted against my chest. The impact on my ribcage knocked out my breathing, but Alfa 1's advice worked – the jolt stemmed the overload of adrenalin in my body. I suddenly felt calm and clear-headed. We needed to hold our positions, radio for backup then conserve ammunition.

But before I could give the order we were already in trouble.

'I'm hit,' yelled Veneno. 'Help! I'm hit.'

He lay on the ground, clutching his back and rolling around. I scrambled to him and grabbed his pack straps to roll him onto his stomach. His pack blocked my view of the wound, but I saw a dark, wet patch spreading quickly down the back of his right leg. I touched his pants – the cloth was already saturated. I fumbled through my own pack for the first-aid kit and unravelled a tourniquet and bandage. MacGyver crawled over to us.

'We can't stay here,' he warned. 'Once it's dark, they'll surround us and we'll have nowhere to run. We need to get off this hill or we'll be stuck here all night dodging their grenades.'

As though to confirm his words, there was an explosion thirty metres downhill at the base of the knoll.

'Shit!' MacGyver said. 'They must have an MGL.' A Multiple Grenade Launcher.

We also had grenades, but they were hand grenades – completely useless against an enemy at two hundred metres. Another explosion sounded on the other side of the knoll. Our protective fortress of jobo trees now felt like a prison. A single fragmentation grenade landing among our trees could kill us all.

Nevertheless, retreating across open ground carrying an injured man would be difficult. Then it got worse. Coca-Cola gasped, stumbled and clutched his calf.

'I think they got me,' he stated calmly.

His hand came up covered with blood. He looked horrified and confused. Ñoño scrambled to his side and dragged him to safety behind a tree.

I yelled to Tortuga and signalled for her to come over. 'Radio it in! Major battle. Two men down. We're under siege by a large enemy force. We need reinforcements urgently.' I tossed her the bandage, tourniquet, iodine and morphine syringe. 'Fix Veneno! I want both injured men together. Then you and Ñoño help return fire.'

MacGyver pointed west – the opposite direction to the approaching enemy. 'I can take two men down that way and circle around into the woods to stop them spreading out.'

I didn't like splitting the squad, but when another grenade exploded nearby, it seemed like our only option. 'Okay! Go!'

MacGyver waited for the next grenade and then led Yucca and Giraldo down the back of our hill, which was still protected from their line of fire. Tortuga and Ñoño attended to Veneno and Coca-Cola. Palillo and I continued firing to slow the enemy's advance. But since they were still hidden among the trees they were well protected.

Within two minutes, we heard rifles cracking from the northern edge of the grassy clearing. I had no idea how MacGyver had managed to reach the trees and then cover so much ground so quickly, but the Guerrilla mustn't have expected it. MacGyver's fire coming at them from forty-five degrees now destroyed their cover. They turned on their heels and ran back towards the river.

Palillo and I sprinted down the open slope while MacGyver's group gave chase through the trees. The Guerrilla stopped frequently to return fire, but neither we nor they had a clear shot through the thick woods. Ahead, I heard a boat engine roar to life.

We emerged into a clearing to see the river two hundred metres ahead. Twelve *guerrilleros* were sprinting towards a boat that was being pushed out into the current by a man wearing a black T-shirt and red shorts who was knee-deep in the reeds. Since they were in the open, they no longer returned fire, instead concentrating on reaching the boat. Palillo stopped running and fired.

'Come back here, you fucking *gallinas*!'

Now that we had them on the run, he seemed to be enjoying himself, swearing and calling them chickens. They were a hundred and fifty metres ahead of us – a difficult standing shot, but well within the Galil's range. Palillo switched to automatic and sprayed them with bullets without altering his aim. I dropped and lay flat, taking aim and breathing deeply as we'd been taught. I fired at the end of a long exhalation. My rifle cracked but the enemy kept running. I readjusted the rifle's position, nestling it firmly against my shoulder and placing my right cheek ten centimetres back from the rear sight. I took more time to aim. I fired. Nothing. But my third shot caused one to fall.

Two turned and rushed back for him. Now that I had my aim, I fired four more shots at them in rapid succession. A second man went down. The third man tried to drag both his fallen comrades to the river, but the rest of his squad was already scrambling into the boat and pushing off. He abandoned the two dead, raced to the river, splashed through the water and was hauled over the side of the boat.

I fired at the boat. They were getting away.

'Missed,' called Palillo, who had dropped down beside me and was observing with the binoculars.

I fired again.

'Missed. Splashed to the right and a metre too high.'

I fired yet again.

'Hit the bow. Aim a little up and to the left.'

I lined up a fourth shot, but by then the *lancha* was motoring away swiftly and they returned fire on automatic, forcing us to cover our heads with our forearms as bullets whizzed overtop. I snatched the binoculars from Palillo and got a glimpse of the boat driver, who was crouching behind his outboard. He was skinny with dark skin, shoulder-length hair and a moustache.

Tortuga flopped down beside us. She'd sprinted from our knoll on her own but was hardly puffing. She crawled forward with the radio pack still on her back, firing at the boat as it rounded the river bend.

'Call it in!' I ordered. 'Two enemy dead. Ten escaped by boat. Might be more coming. We need those reinforcements. And two of our men are down.'

Tortuga repeated my order through the radio but changed the last part: 'One of our men down.'

I looked at her, wondering what she meant, but she had no time to explain. MacGyver belly-crawled in beside us with Yucca. 'We need to move quickly. We're exposed here.'

I nodded. We retreated into the woods. The order came back from Alfa 1: he would send a truck with reinforcements and notify the two nearest foot patrols, but they might take two or three hours to arrive. In the meantime, we were to evacuate immediately, carrying our injured to the army checkpoint five kilometres upriver. They'd be notified to expect us. We were to leave the enemy bodies but take their rifles if we could reach them safely.

75

ONLY TWO KILOMETRES into our upriver journey, Alfa 1 radioed us that the army was sending a boat. They transported us to their river checkpoint and then transferred us into the Autodefensa truck.

Back at La 50, we were hailed as heroes: Palillo for detecting the enemy's approach early; Ñoño for his rapid first-aid response; Tortuga for her calm and accurate radio communication; MacGyver for his quick tactical thinking, leadership and bravery; and me for my marksmanship.

'We haven't seen shooting like that for years,' said Alfa 1. 'Two confirmed kills from two hundred metres using only nine rounds. Incredible!'

For the next few days I felt elated. I was also proud of my squad. I remembered Trigeño saying soldiers should be prepared to give their lives for their commanders. At the time, they were only words. But now I believed them.

It is a strange and powerful feeling to know that the man beside you would sacrifice his life for you without a second's hesitation. It's a feeling few people will ever know, and one that is almost impossible to explain to those who have not served in the military.

The only person not to receive the commanders' praise was Veneno. The dark, wet patch on the back of his right leg had not come from a bullet wound but from a burst water bottle in his pack. He swore he'd felt the impact and gone into shock. But over the coming days he was teased mercilessly by soldiers walking past him and tipping water on themselves, falling to the ground and calling, 'I'm hit! *¡Socorro!* I'm hit!'

The joke never got tired and Veneno had to keep quiet or risk further ridicule.

Meanwhile, Coca-Cola was laid up with a shattered tibia in the Villavicencio military hospital, where Lieutenant Alejandro had registered him as a regular government soldier injured during training exercises.

It would be at least six weeks before he was able to walk, and even longer before he returned to active duty.

Culebra, who was about to commence his basic training course with one hundred and sixty new recruits, offered to take on Coca-Cola as a *punto*. This involved sitting in the doorway of a shack along the highway from Puerto Bontón, holding a radio and reporting suspicious traffic movements. It was ideal for incapacitated soldiers – they continued to receive full pay and be of service to *La Empresa* – but it was also the most boring job imaginable. The only human interaction came when fresh batteries arrived. Besides, I didn't want any replacements – the skirmish had made our unit tighter and I wanted to keep it that way.

'Thanks, but I need him,' I said.

'Let me know if you think of anybody else who's suitable.'

I nodded and then left to seek out Alfa 1 privately in the office.

'Did they find anything on the two bodies?' I asked, hoping the slain *guerrilleros* might have had maps or phone numbers in their pockets that would give us a lead on the mother base.

'*Nada*,' he said. 'The army arrived within the hour, but the bodies were gone.'

I was disappointed. I wished I'd searched them myself when I took their rifles. Alfa 1, however, insisted I'd acted correctly. He'd ordered me to evacuate immediately. Besides, my description of the long-haired boat driver might prove useful. Of course, he might flee the area or join the Guerrilla for safety, depending on whether he believed he'd been seen by us. My recollection of the boat itself was vague, but Palillo had grown up around boats and promptly told Alfa 1 that we were looking for 'a faded-green wooden *lancha*, six metres by two, with four seats and a forty-five-horsepower, long-tillered Mercury outboard.'

'So what happens next?' I asked Alfa 1.

'We'll pass on the descriptions of the boat and its driver to the army. Their river patrols will be on the lookout.'

'There must be a hundred boats matching the description.'

'But only one with a 5.56mm round lodged in the right bow.'

'Won't they scuttle and sink it?'

'If the Guerrilla pays the owner for it, yes. Otherwise, that *lancha* is someone's livelihood. Let's see. In the meantime, take your men and relax. Five days leave. Go!'

Trigeño's accountant must have found some money. All of us were paid a month's salary as a bonus and given five days fully-paid rest and recuperation leave at the Puerto Bontón Military Club, which boasted a swimming pool, a bar and two tennis courts. I received an additional two months' salary for the confirmed kills and one month for the two AK47 rifles, which Culebra added to the container inventory. Alfa 1 handed me my bonus in cash. I'd never held so much money in my life.

'And if you have any other requests, now is the time to ask,' he said.

'I'd like a scope for the Galil. All we had were binoculars. But if I'd had a scope . . .'

'That might be difficult.' Alfa 1 scratched his head. 'But I'll ask Lieutenant Alejandro if he can make one go missing.'

'And there's one more thing, *comando*. It's about Piolín . . .'

The first night at the Puerto Bontón Military Recreation Club, we drank Costeña beers until late and traded stories with the government soldiers who were on leave with their wives and girlfriends. They weren't at all surprised by our skirmish – all over the country both sides were breaking the ceasefire, although nothing was reported publicly that might jeopardise the delicate negotiations. In fact, the soldiers were envious that we'd engaged the enemy. They felt betrayed by the government – the ongoing peace process was only giving the Guerrilla breathing space to fortify their defences and supply routes, increase recruiting and training, and move their civilian and army hostages.

At midnight, MacGyver was drunk and wanted to take Palillo to Don Otto's *puteadero* to celebrate. But Palillo refused, claiming he preferred to save his money. I guessed the real reason: he was still stuck on Piolín.

The next day, as we lazed around the pool, hung-over, the fun and teasing continued. I had to take my share for having radioed in a 'major battle' in which we were 'under siege from a large enemy force'. I laughed it off, glad I hadn't said aloud that I'd seen forty enemy soldiers when there were really only twelve. Besides, my teasing was nothing compared to the ongoing humiliation shovelled upon Veneno.

Ñoño renamed him, diluting his *apodo* from 'Poison' to 'Water Bottle'. Tortuga initiated a debate over which was a more masculine drink – Coca-Cola or Water? We laughed at how, crawling awkwardly forward with the radio on her back, she had truly resembled a turtle. But since she'd come out firing, Palillo affectionately renamed her 'Ninja Turtle', which eventually stuck and got shortened to 'Ninja'. Veneno's new nickname would probably also have stuck if he'd continued on with us. However, before our next patrol he'd be receiving some unexpected news. I'd recommended he be assigned to permanent *punto* duty.

I had an even bigger surprise for Palillo. 'Do you still have those plane tickets to Cartagena?' I asked him.

'Why?'

'Piolín's out of Beta's unit. She's now under Silvestre. And she's on leave right now.'

Palillo hugged me in joy and disbelief. 'You asked Alfa 1?'

I nodded. 'But this isn't an official sanction of your relationship. You still need to be discreet.'

Seeing Palillo so ecstatic, I immediately phoned Camila. For once, everything had gone right and I wanted to share my happiness with her.

'Great news, *amor*,' I began.

'*¡Qué bueno!*' she exclaimed excitedly. 'What?'

Then I stopped, realising exactly what that great news was and how it might sound to her. What, precisely, was I going to tell her? That I'd killed two men with a rifle from two hundred metres and been commended by my superiors for confiscating their weapons? That if our friends in the army could track down the boat driver, he might give up valuable information that could then lead us to Santiago's camp, and that I wanted to be in the front line when we raided it?

No! These were the exact things that would make her worry. Although we'd sworn to each other *no more lies*, I realised this was an impossible promise to keep if I wanted Camila to feel safe and keep loving me. And as much as I wanted to share every part of my life with her, for as long as I was in the Autodefensas there would always be important things I'd have to shield her from.

'I got paid a bonus!' I said instead. 'I want to buy you a present. Choose anything!'

'Well . . .' she began coyly, 'we've both been invited to a party next Friday, and there's a green dress I like—'

'Buy it!'

'Oh, *amor*! I miss you so much. When are you coming?'

I looked at the date on my phone. We had four more days' accommodation paid in advance at the Recreational Club before our second leave officially started.

'Right now,' I said. 'I'm boarding a bus right now.'

PART FIVE

LOS NARCOS

76

THE FIRST LEG of the journey, to Villavicencio, took six hours. My bus passed through two government checkpoints, and at each I tensed, hoping the army searches would not be thorough. The stolen Galil that I'd retrieved from the dump was dismantled in a black sports bag deep in the undercarriage of the bus, my own Smith & Wesson pistol was taped under my seat, and the photocopied intelligence files – which I'd collected from among the reams of paper in the office – were in my backpack. However, my fears of discovery were unrealised; the soldiers merely asked us for identification and did not bother examining our luggage or asking us to disembark.

At Villavicencio, I changed buses and phoned Mamá to inform her of my arrival time. I was sure she'd be overjoyed to learn about my bonus. It would be enough to get her out from under Javier Díaz's roof and into her own rented place. I would no longer be under any obligation to the Díaz family. And when Uncle Leo found out, I hoped he and his little *amigas* would feel ashamed.

During the final leg, the overnight trip to Garbanzos, I passed the time by plotting Zorrillo's demise. That Sunday's market in Puerto Galán would be the first of the month – always the biggest for cattle sales – so I figured he'd attend in person. I'd find a well-concealed ambush point at a reasonable distance from the market that was within my shooting capability. There, I'd wait until Zorrillo arrived and then disable him with a bullet in the knee, stomach or wrist. I'd dispense with his two or three bodyguards and then sprint in, disarm him and begin circling for my ritual interrogation.

I became so absorbed in my planning that I hardly noticed the bus's arrival. When its doors swished open, it was 8 am and I was the only passenger left on board.

Normally, the multi-levelled Garbanzos Bus Terminal pulsed with activity. Street hawkers and overzealous porters would compete to be heard above crackling loudspeaker announcements. That morning, however, the arrivals hall was so quiet that I could hear my own footsteps echoing off the dusty concrete floor. The food and souvenir stores were closed. Boards were nailed across the windows of six of the eight bus company offices lining the eastern wall. Only two ticket counters were staffed – TRANSPORTADORES DÍAZ and RÁPIDO VELASQUEZ.

I spotted Mamá immediately among the rows of vacant plastic chairs. On either side of her stood two broad-shouldered men. Judging by the bulges at their waistlines, both were carrying pistols. Mamá rushed towards me with open arms.

'Pedro, I've missed you so much!'

'I've missed you too.' We hugged. 'But who are they?'

'Javier's driver and bodyguard.'

'You won't need them anymore,' I said confidently, draping my arm across her shoulders and guiding her towards the exit. 'I got a promotion and salary increase. I'm finding you a new place to live this afternoon.'

I'd expected Mamá to be surprised, but not to stop dead and stare at me. She hesitated and glanced around the empty terminal. 'Pedro, I can't move house right now. It's too dangerous.'

I remembered things Mamá had said over the phone – that the situation was 'complicated' and that I would have to be 'discreet'.

'What do you mean?'

She looked out to the car park and gestured to a black Mercedes SUV with tinted windows. 'I'll explain in the car.'

When I insisted I wasn't going anywhere until she told me, Mamá reluctantly opened her handbag and handed me an envelope. 'This was slipped under Leo's door three months ago. I didn't want to discuss it over the phone.'

Inside was a letter printed under the Guerrilla's logo – crossed rifles and an outline map of Colombia against a yellow, blue and red background – the same logo that had appeared on the threat addressed to Padre Rojas. I read it with increasing alarm.

Esteemed Señora Gutiérrez:

I am hereby communicating with you on behalf of Frente 34 of the People's Army, The Revolutionary Armed Forces of Colombia. You are required to attend a meeting in Puerto Galán next Saturday to discuss recent developments in local security.

It was signed 'Jorge Emilio Botero', which I knew from the army's intelligence files was Zorrillo's latest political alias.

My hand began shaking. If Mamá had attended the meeting as demanded, the Guerrilla might have kidnapped her. But by failing to attend, she would have been declared an *objetivo militar* – a military target.

The letter was dated May 5th.

'A month after my last leave?'

Mamá bit her lip and nodded. We both knew what that meant: after seeing the AUC graffiti, the Guerrilla had investigated and linked it back to me.

I was so angry I wanted to ram my fist into Zorrillo's face and pummel it to a pulp. However, my anger at Zorrillo paled beside my guilt and concern that I'd put Mamá in danger.

'What happened when you didn't go?'

'They phoned me twice at your uncle's. I hung up both times. After that, we unplugged the phone. Leo didn't want to leave the house. That was when Eleonora offered me a place to stay.'

Finally, everything made sense: Mamá not answering Uncle Leo's phone for weeks; her moving out; her fretful, guarded voice during recent conversations; and now the bodyguards. None of this was Leo's fault; it was all mine.

'Mamá, I . . .'

'It's okay,' she said softly, taking my hand. 'I'm safe where I am.'

It seemed that not only would Mamá have to remain with Javier Díaz, but that I had reason to feel grateful to him.

'Colonel Buitrago thinks it's best if you stay with us. Javier has electrified fences, an armoured vehicle and guard dogs . . .'

I gritted my teeth and waited for her to finish. Though I couldn't object to Mamá continuing to live at the Díaz *finca*, I didn't have to accept any favours from them myself. I told her to thank Javier but that I was staying in a hotel. Although Mamá looked disappointed, she didn't try to argue.

'At least come next Friday. Javier's having a party. Eleonora and Fabián are flying down to attend. The family has been good to me, Pedro. It would be rude not to show your face.'

Luckily, I had a perfect excuse. 'Sorry, but I've already committed to a party that night with Camila.'

As I kissed Mamá goodbye, she gripped my hand tighter.

'Be careful, *hijo*. Our *finca* is fine, but things have changed since your last visit. The colonel asked that you not contact him directly. But he said to warn you that there's now a Guerrilla roadblock on the highway entering Llorona. Apparently they have two lists of names. One for people who are permitted through. The other for people considered military targets. Three people have been taken hostage in the last month, including a young girl.'

Mamá didn't say it outright, but I could guess what she was thinking: what if I was on their list? And I didn't say what I thought either: I didn't care. If Zorrillo and Caraquemada had added me to their list, *good*. They were on mine. Nevertheless, I promised Mamá I'd be safe, and I meant it.

I decided not to stay at the Hotel Pandora, where I'd stayed on my previous leave, choosing instead a different *residencia* two blocks closer to the police garrison. I checked in using the name on the fake *cédula* provided by the Autodefensas – Jhon Jairo García Sanchez. I took a second-storey room with a window overlooking the plaza and another window that backed onto an awning, from which I could jump if I needed to make an emergency escape.

I left a message on Camila's phone with details of my new hotel and check-in name before walking to Uncle Leo's hardware store four blocks away.

As I entered he gave a start and then nervously looked around, as though he were suddenly harbouring the world's most wanted man.

'You can't be in here,' he hissed. He turned to his new 'assistant' – an attractive girl with a vacant look on her face who probably didn't know the difference between a nail and a screw. 'Amelia, pull down the grill and padlock it.'

'Nice to see you too, Uncle. I won't stay long. I'm here for my bicycle.'

'You have some nerve showing up here. Everyone knows what you've done,' he said, becoming more aggressive once the grill was down and he was safe from prying eyes. 'That graffiti could have got me killed! Not to mention your mother!'

I glanced deliberately at his pretty shop assistant. 'At least now you have your privacy back.'

I left via the back exit but took my time, helping myself to a hammer, nails and rope – all of which would be crucial to my plan of getting Zorrillo – and leaving the money for them in the back storeroom. I wasn't going to owe Uncle Leo anything.

If he wanted to avoid me, that was fine. However, if it were true that everyone knew what I'd done, this vacation would be very different to the last. I would be disciplined about security – eating my meals and meeting Mamá indoors. When I was outside, I'd wear a hat to cover my short hair.

All morning and afternoon I sat alone on my hotel bed, looking out over the dreary plaza, feeling deflated.

Thanks to the ceasefire, the Guerrilla's operations were expanding and they were becoming more daring – hand-delivering letters inside Garbanzos, establishing roadblocks to control the movement of people and goods, and snatching motorists from cars. No wonder the bus terminal was as deserted as a graveyard. Brazen kidnappings deterred travellers, which in turn caused business closures and unemployment. Eventually, the Guerrilla might paralyse our local economy.

Without Palillo to cheer me up like last time, I felt lost and alone. It was not until 3.30 pm when I heard a faint knock at the door that my mood suddenly lifted: Camila.

77

CAMILA SWEPT INTO the room like a fresh summer breeze. She dropped her school satchel and the shopping bag she was carrying and launched herself at me, wrapping her legs around my waist. She kissed me over and over, covering my cheeks, neck and ears, and began unbuttoning my shirt. But when I slid my hands up her thighs and under her school uniform, she slapped my wrists away.

'Not yet, *señorito*. First I have a surprise.' Taking the shopping bag with her, she locked herself in the bathroom and called through the door, 'You're going to love this.'

Secretly, I hoped it was lingerie. Pink lingerie. Or maybe blue, like the bra she'd been wearing the first time we made love. Finally, Camila flung the door open and waltzed out wearing an emerald-green cocktail dress.

'Well?' she said, twirling nervously on bare feet. The dress opened in a V-shape halfway up her spine, revealing the flawless olive skin of her back and her delicate shoulder blades, which jutted out like budding angel wings. 'Do you like it?'

I stood from the bed, held her hips at arm's length, appraised her fully and then slid my hands slowly up her body. 'Almost as much as what's inside.'

'Tell me what you think! Honestly!'

'I think you look absolutely stunning, baby. I think you're the most beautiful creature in the solar system.'

'Really?' Camila blushed and looked down. 'But which shoes match best?' She held up two well-used pairs, crinkling her nose at each.

'I'll buy you new shoes.'

'Are you sure?'

Camila's parents were humble storekeepers. They'd brought her up to believe expensive gifts were an unnecessary extravagance. But I wanted to give her not only the things she needed, but also the things she desired.

'I've been working hard.' I kissed her. 'Who else am I going to spoil?'

She kissed me back. 'Carolina will be *so* jealous. Her new boyfriend never even takes her out.'

It felt good seeing Camila so happy and knowing I was the cause. It even felt good to make her friends envious. None of their boyfriends had jobs. Of course, giving Camila presents didn't make up for the months I'd been away. Nor would it compensate for our future separations. But while I was there I wanted to treat her like a princess.

We smothered each other with kisses. This time, when I launched a follow-up attack on her hemline, she didn't resist.

We spent all afternoon making love. Afterwards, beaded with perspiration, Camila traced a fingernail over the skin of my shoulder blade, circling the snake tattoo.

'I'll see you tomorrow after school, and on Saturday we can look for those new shoes. This party is going to be amazing! Important people are flying in from Cali, Medellín and Bogotá. They'll have caterers and they're hiring a famous band.'

'Who is?'

Camila reached across me into her satchel and flipped a green cardboard invitation onto the pillow with a smile of satisfaction. Our names were written at the top in silver calligraphy. The date was next Friday and the invitation was signed:

With Compliments, Javier and Fabián Díaz.

I stared at the invitation, feeling as though I'd been tricked, even though it was no more than a misunderstanding. Not for a moment had I imagined Mamá and Camila were referring to the same party. But Camila was so excited she didn't notice my frown. Her parents had also been invited.

'Papá was so honoured. The Díazes have always ordered their groceries from our store, but he never expected an invitation delivered *in person* by Javier. My mother's been dieting to fit into her formal dress. And no one else from school is going. You should have seen Carolina's face.' Finally, Camila noticed I hadn't said a word. 'What's wrong?'

'I'm not sure we should go.'

'But I've already accepted.'

'You go with your parents. Tell them I'm sick.'

'What?' Camila sat up in bed, not even bothering to cover her breasts with the sheet as she normally did. 'Why would I go without you? I'll hardly know anyone.'

'I just . . . I don't know.'

I couldn't understand why Camila and I had been invited. The Díaz brothers were much older than us and from a completely different world. And it seemed even stranger that they'd invited Camila's parents, who they'd probably never spoken to. Rather than feeling flattered by their attentions, I felt pressured. It was bad enough being indebted to them for looking after Mamá, but now they were making it impossible for me not to attend their party.

Camila assaulted me with a barrage of reasons for attending: she'd already bought the dress, it would be rude not to go, and my mother would be disappointed.

'This is important to me,' she pleaded. 'And they're nice people. Look!' She produced a second green invitation. 'They even invited Palillo. You know what everyone thinks of his *borracho* stepfather. But they didn't want Palillo to feel left out.'

Camila always thought the best of people, but I doubted Palillo would agree with her assessment of the Díaz brothers' motives. Last time they'd invited me to a fiesta – while barely deigning to look at my best friend – Palillo had told me I was naïve; they were cultivating me because I was an Autodefensa commander. However, I had no valid reason to refuse Camila.

She pestered and begged and even sulked a little until I was on the verge of capitulating. Then her cell phone vibrated. It was her father. I expected her to lie about who she was with – Señor Muñoz was a strict Catholic; she was fifteen years old and naked in a cheap hotel room – but to my surprise she said proudly, 'Yes, he's right here next to me.' She covered the mouthpiece and turned to me. 'Papá says *hola*.'

'Say *hola* back.' I rummaged through my suitcase and held up a bottle. 'Tell him I brought him some palm wine.'

Camila relayed my message and then came back with an invitation. 'Papá insists you help him drink it. Lunch on Sunday after church? What time should he pick you up?'

I hesitated before accepting; Sunday was market day in Puerto Galán. 'One o'clock.'

'My father really likes you, you know?' Camila said after hanging up. 'Please don't let him down.'

As far as she was concerned, once I'd said 'yes' to lunch, I was definitely going to the Díaz fiesta. But in my mind, I hadn't technically agreed.

Camila left me with a lingering kiss. After she departed, Trigeño's warning about family echoed in my mind. I'd already put Mamá in danger. By dining with Camila's family, would I be endangering them too? However, I quelled my concerns. They didn't affect my plans for the following day while Camila would be at school.

I turned off the lights at 8 pm and set out at four o'clock the next morning, heading towards Puerto Galán to begin my preparations against Zorrillo.

78

THE RISKIEST PART of the journey was the fifteen-kilometre bicycle ride from Garbanzos to Llorona. If I were caught by the Guerrilla with the fully-loaded Galil and binoculars in my sports bag, it would be all over for me.

Few people were awake that early, but, just as the Autodefensas had *puntos* posted in dwellings along the road to La 50, the Guerrilla would have twenty-four-hour lookouts with two-way radios safeguarding their newly claimed territory. Instead of taking the main highway, I pedalled along dirt tracks and through privately owned fields I'd known since childhood.

At the rope-swing tree, I unchained Papá's dinghy and quickly attached the Galil beneath its hull using the nails and rope from Uncle Leo's hardware store. Once out on the river, I began to feel safer. It was still dark but I could make out the silhouettes of fishermen, lit from below by candles flickering inside plastic bottles. I lit my own candle, waved to them, cast my rod and began drifting south with the strong current pulling me towards Puerto Galán, five kilometres downstream.

With fishermen surrounding me, the risk of being caught was lower. The Guerrilla had boats for searching river traffic, but I hoped they'd be watching for motorised army patrols, not a lone boy in old clothes fishing from a rowboat. Besides, if anyone stopped me midstream, it was unlikely they'd demand I flip the dinghy.

By the time the sun began to rise, my disguise was complete. I'd caught, scaled and gutted three sierra fish. My hands were grimy and bloody, and I was wearing a broad-brimmed hat. I now relaxed and even reminisced about long, happy Sundays out fishing with Papá.

Finally, I spotted the old wooden wharf jutting out from the empty Puerto Galán food market – a sloping concrete floor bordered by ten wooden pylons supporting a corrugated-iron roof. The market operated on Sundays, selling fruit and vegetables, river fish and fresh meat from the adjoining cattle market and abattoir. I rowed towards it and pulled the dinghy up onto the riverbank. Then I recast my line from the bank and stood fishing with the early morning sun blazing into my eyes and the sprawling village behind me.

My knowledge of Puerto Galán was vague. I'd visited as a boy when helping Uncle Leo with deliveries during school breaks, but most of my trips had been in the company of Palillo, who'd grown up there. Forty years earlier, this area had been virgin jungle. Settlers had simply arrived; each cleared a plot with axes and machetes, erected a dwelling on stilts, constructed a chicken coop and declared it his own.

Papá had often herded his cattle here to the saleyards – it saved on trucking costs to Garbanzos – although he never let me accompany him. The men who lived here worked as *raspachínes*, like Palillo's stepfather, or as *cocaleros*, who produced the barrels of cocaine base I'd witnessed being traded at Flora's Cantina. Floods of illicit cash meant that in a village of only two thousand inhabitants, there were three whorehouses, six cantinas and four nightclubs that pumped out music all Sunday afternoon.

In time, electricity and phone lines were extended from Llorona. But Puerto Galán remained a lawless, forgotten village with pot-holed roads that turned to mud in heavy rains, no hospital, no bank and not a trace of government.

I was now deep inside enemy territory. Nevertheless, I felt calm. There wasn't a single uniformed *guerrillero* in sight, only ordinary people going about their morning business. Of course, I didn't doubt the Guerrilla had *milicianos* disguised among the civilians. But the only visible evidence of their presence was a prohibition painted on a wooden board:

NO PUBLIC DRINKING
NO DRUGS
NO LITTERING – PROTECT THE ENVIRONMENT
BY ORDER OF THE REVOLUTIONARY ARMED FORCES OF COLOMBIA

Besides, if anyone stopped me and asked what I was doing, I had a good excuse: I was visiting Palillo's family. They lived in a shack along the riverbank five hundred metres to the north, which was the cheapest area to rent because of mosquitos and flooding. I found the door broken off its hinges and Palillo's mother kneeling with her back to me at the small iron stove, blowing coals to boil a pot of coffee. Before I could knock, Palillo's eldest sister stepped in front of me with one index finger pressed to her lips and the other pointing to a single bed where her stepfather, Diomedes, slept. He was snoring in his underwear. His gigantic belly, glistening with sweat, heaved up and down with each strained breath, and his hand gripped an empty bottle of rum.

Palillo's mother turned and looked anxiously from me to her husband. She tiptoed across the dirt floor to the doorway, pulling her hair down across her face in an attempt to hide two maroon bruises below her left eye.

I wanted to stay and give them news of Palillo, but knew it would be dangerous for them if Diomedes awoke and found me whispering outside. He might beat Palillo's mother again, and he'd probably find the money Palillo had sent, which she took from me and hid inside her bra. Mother and daughter both hugged me, and I slipped away.

I returned to my dinghy and dragged it south through knee-deep water, scouring the bank for an optimal vantage point. I found a thick tangle of scrub one hundred metres from the market with no dwellings nearby. I didn't know how Zorrillo would arrive – by road from Puerto Princesa, by foot or by boat – but from my position I could cover all three approaches. I'd have a flat, clear line of sight into the market and would be camouflaged by the scrub.

I scanned the plaza and food market a final time before digging a small trench with my hands. Then I flipped the dinghy and unhooked the Galil. It was a hardy rifle and would still fire properly after immersion in water, but I cleaned it with a rag and oil to remove grit from the barrel and firing mechanism. Then I dried the bullets, wrapped everything, including the binoculars, in a hessian sack and buried it. Finally, I covered the spot with leaves and rowed steadily back upstream, arriving at my *residencia* in time to phone Camila during school recess. I was satisfied by my practice run and by what I'd seen in Puerto Galán and confident that on Sunday I would be ready for the real thing.

79

ON SATURDAY I bought Camila her shoes and then we spent the entire day in my hotel room. I would have liked to visit my old friends and shoot billiards at Francisco's Pool Hall, but the fewer people who knew I was home the better.

On Saturday evening, I prayed with Mamá at the Garbanzos church. It wasn't the same as Llorona, but Colonel Buitrago had recently lost a twelve-man squad in an ambush near Puerto Galán and could no longer justify sending two soldiers to accompany her, especially not after the threat letter from Zorrillo. Mamá would have preferred us to attend Sunday morning Mass, but I'd lied and told her I had plans with Camila.

On Sunday, I followed the same routine as I had on Friday: cycling to the dinghy at 4 am and rowing downstream while fishing. To avoid suspicion from Camila, I'd been deliberately vague about my plans. I hadn't told her about having gone to church on Saturday night – instead, I told her that on Sunday morning I intended to sleep in or go to Mass with Mamá in Garbanzos, which would give me an excuse for leaving my phone switched off.

I'd have plenty of time to get down to Puerto Galán, eliminate Zorrillo and be back for her father to pick me at 1 pm as planned. Since Camila would be attending Mass in Llorona, I doubted she'd call before midday anyway.

By 6 am I was in position on the western riverbank next to the buried Galil. The sun rose, revealing clear blue skies. In the marketplace, *campesinos* were already arriving, their backs bent under sacks of corn and potatoes. After shedding their burdens, the men set up wooden stalls. Their wives laid out tomatoes, bananas and onions on colourful cloths and hung strips of dried meat from overhead strings.

A stream of diesel trucks began arriving too, spewing black exhaust into the air, their brakes squealing as they rolled to a stop at the cattle yard beside the food market. Their doors were thrust open and the cattle driven down ramps into holding pens. By 7 am, both the food and cattle markets were awash with the first wave of buyers.

Slowly, I scooped away mounds of soil and unwrapped the Galil. I had yet to see any Guerrilla soldiers, but to a distant observer I wanted to look like a fisherman lying on his back, lazily dangling his line in the river. I dug the handle of the fishing rod into the ground next to me at a forty-five degree angle and put my shirt on back-to-front. I removed my boots, placing them near my feet with their toes pointing skywards. Then I lay flat on my stomach with my hat pulled down low over the back of my neck.

Looking along the Galil's sights, I had a clear view into the market. The bright sunlight streaming from directly behind me would give me an advantage when Zorrillo arrived – casting light onto him while making me difficult to spot. Nevertheless, I affixed two cardboard toilet rolls to the binocular lenses and wrapped the sack around the rifle to prevent reflections that could reveal my position.

By 8 am, the market was full but Zorrillo hadn't arrived. At 9 am I imagined Camila entering church with her parents. By 10 am, I calculated that getting back to my *residencia* in time for her father's pick-up would now be difficult.

Finally, a green SUV with tinted windows pulled up beside the vegetable market. My heart began to pound.

Through the binoculars, I could see Zorrillo perfectly as he emerged from the vehicle. He was dressed in the same camouflage as ordinary *guerrilleros*, but I would have recognised his thin moustache, sloping shoulders and arrogant swagger anywhere. I'd been studying Zorrillo's file for weeks and thinking about him for months. Seeing him in person, however, I felt a surge of anger and had to remind myself to stay calm.

Heart still racing, I switched from the binoculars to the Galil, lining up its single front sight between the two-pronged rear sight. Immediately, however, three bodyguards emerged from the SUV and another eight surrounded the vehicle. They formed a ring around Zorrillo, blocking my shot as he strolled casually into the market.

I raised the binoculars again and watched in frustration as he weaved among the shoppers and stall keepers, joking and patting their backs like a benevolent feudal lord checking on the good health of his peasants. But their unsmiling faces and his accounting logbook told a different story: he was there to levy taxes. Pen in hand, he moved from seller to seller, noting down takings and inspecting cash tins and even pockets.

Then Zorrillo zigzagged his way to the gate adjoining the cattle yards, where trade was now winding down. He signalled to Don Mauricio, the cattle yard owner. Mauricio nodded and then handed over a bulging plastic bag, which must have been filled with cash – a *vacuna* on the day's combined sales. When Zorrillo signalled for more, Mauricio displayed his open palms until Zorrillo pointed his finger sharply in his face, forcing Mauricio to pay extra from his own wallet. As Zorrillo pocketed the cash and disappeared back into the market, Mauricio leaned against the metal rail and remained motionless for a long time, staring at his boots.

Witnessing this made me furious. I imagined Zorrillo doing the same thing to Señor Muñoz on the day he'd sold Papá's cattle – stealing fifty per cent of the money that Mamá needed to survive. I also remembered Zorrillo banning me from burying Papá and then banishing us from our land.

My hands were shaking and I could no longer calm my breathing. Unfortunately, shooting Zorrillo in the knee in order to capture and interrogate him would be impossible. Not only would it be ineffective – at my first shot some of his bodyguards would throw themselves over him – but it would also be suicide. Even if I made every bullet from my thirty-round magazine count, how would I defend myself against eleven *guerrilleros* sprinting towards me, firing?

No! I would not rush the job and risk my life. Instead, I'd forget the interrogation and kill Zorrillo while I had the chance. It pained me that he would die without knowing who'd brought him to justice or why. But it was better to shoot him while I had the opportunity.

I rowed across the river and lay in a new position on the opposite bank. I was now one hundred and thirty metres from my target but still confident I could make the shot. After all, the Galil was accurate up to four hundred metres and I'd shot men from two hundred metres. I'd take a single shot and then escape into the jungle, with the water between us buying me valuable time.

But the sun was overhead now, casting everyone beneath the market roof into shadow. Furthermore, Zorrillo was surrounded by hundreds of hardworking *campesino* farmers and women shopping. Children of all ages darted about. From that distance, I didn't trust my own marksmanship. For a bullet that needs to travel over a hundred metres in a light wind like the one that was currently rippling the river's surface, even a millimetre's inaccuracy as it leaves the barrel can multiply out to a metre's deviation at the target.

With so many innocent people nearby, I couldn't fire. Nevertheless, I held my position with the safety switch off and my index finger poised against the trigger, hoping Zorrillo would move clear of the civilians. He only had to step two metres to the left and I could take a clean shot. I glanced at my watch. It was almost midday. Camila would be calling my cell phone, worried. When I didn't answer, she'd probably phone the hotel receptionist and ask him to bang on my door.

Finally, Zorrillo pocketed his pen, slapped his accounting notebook closed and signalled to his driver.

As he moved into the light, out of the protective circle of his bodyguards, I lined him up and slowly curled my finger, feeling the trigger digging lightly into the soft skin below my fingertip. Suddenly, a woman walked in front of him carrying a baby. I straightened my finger and drew breath. But when the woman had passed, the moment had also. Zorrillo was once more surrounded by guards.

Seething, I watched him re-enter his SUV. It had been a busy day and the *vacuna* takings must have been good. After slipping a few banknotes to the two men closest to him, Zorrillo farewelled half his bodyguards, laughing and waving like a visiting dignitary. Although it was illogical, I felt it was me he was laughing at.

Four months earlier I might have switched the Galil to full automatic and sprayed the departing vehicle with fire, hoping a lucky ricochet would kill him. But I resisted the childish impulse and afterwards was proud of my self-discipline and patience.

Five minutes later, rowing hastily upstream with the Galil at my feet, I was even gladder of my decision. As I drew level with the wharf, I had a direct view into Puerto Galán plaza. Uniformed *guerrilleros* were stationed on every street corner, stopping vehicles and searching shoppers. And on the opposite bank, only two hundred metres north of where I'd been, I saw a Guerrilla squad resting among the trees. If I'd taken the shot, I'd never have gotten away. The Guerrilla had survived for over thirty years. How could I have thought they wouldn't cover both sides of the river?

I had failed yet again. I'd been so close – I'd had Zorrillo in my sights – but that only made it worse. Deep down I knew the crowded public markets were no place for an ambush.

I needed to lure Zorrillo away from civilians to a remote location where he had less protection. And for that I would need outside help – someone I could trust; someone who had regular contact with the Guerrilla, but someone who hated them nonetheless.

My first approach would be to Don Mauricio.

80

I REACHED MY hotel reception at 3 pm, two hours later than agreed, expecting to find Camila and her father pacing in the lobby impatiently They weren't. I checked my phone. My luck was in. Camila had left three nearly identical messages: her mother wasn't feeling well. Could we make it dinner instead of lunch?

Señor Muñoz picked me up that evening at 5.30 pm. He was in a cheerful mood, and since Camila hadn't accompanied him, I was forced to make future-son-in-law conversation. He thanked me for giving Camila a cell phone.

'It gives me peace of mind to know where she is during the day and when to expect her home, although I wish the signal worked south of Garbanzos.'

I half expected a fatherly lecture from Señor Muñoz on the security situation. But, unlike Uncle Leo, he treated me as an adult. We spoke man to man, and he was even open about his reason for coming early – dinner wasn't until seven o'clock, but it was safer to travel during daylight hours.

At least, he said, we didn't have to worry about passing through the Guerrilla roadblock because it was located four kilometres south of his house, at the northern entrance to Llorona.

'But my brother, who lives in Cali, told me that in his region the Guerrilla sometimes erect surprise roadblocks on lonely stretches of highway to kidnap rich people for ransom. Of course I'm sure that won't happen here, especially with the peace talks, but I'd rather you stay the night.' Señor Muñoz turned his head and winked at me. 'In the spare bed, of course.'

I was surprised at how relaxed he was. It seemed he'd become accustomed to the Guerrilla's proximity, even enough to have me in his car despite knowing that I'd defied their ban on burying Papá. I enjoyed him sharing these confidences with me – security issues weren't something to discuss with women.

Dinner with Camila's brothers and mother went smoothly. I talked about Ñoño and Coca-Cola as though they were work colleagues, and I even managed to crack a few jokes. When Señora Muñoz talked excitedly about the upcoming Díaz family fiesta, I didn't have the heart to tell her I wouldn't attend.

After dessert, I agreed to stay the night on the fold-out cot beside Camila's eldest brother, Sebastián, in order to show Señor Muñoz that I, too, was cautious about safety.

When her brother was asleep, Camila pushed the door open slightly and signalled to me from the corridor. Placing her fingertip to her lips, she led me outside and under the house using a small flashlight.

The floorboards were thin and we had to whisper so as not to wake her parents. At first, I was expecting an illicit midnight tryst. Instead, she led me to a corner and handed me two pieces of wood.

'I thought you might like to see this.'

'What is it?'

She twisted one piece so it was perpendicular to the other. I drew breath, recognising my father's cross.

I ran my hands along the splintered wood. My fingertips found the bullet holes and memories flooded back: making the cross from the scarecrow on the day they executed Papá; returning to the *finca* to find it bullet-riddled under the oak tree; driving it back into the ground before setting off to kill Ratón.

'Thank you for rescuing this,' I said, although Camila removing it to protect me hadn't changed anything – according to Uncle Leo, everyone knew I was the one who'd written the pro-Autodefensa graffiti on our *finca*.

I looked up and saw that Camila's arms were folded.

'I don't want you going back to the *finca*. It's not safe. Promise me you won't.'

'*Bien*.' I shrugged, since I had no intention of visiting our *finca*. 'I promise.'

'And promise that you aren't going after Zorrillo or your father's other killers.'

'What?' The space beneath the house suddenly shrank. I felt claustrophobic, hemmed in by the overhead floorboards and nearby concrete support columns.

'Pedro, please! I'm worried about you. I *know* you. You're planning something. I can feel it. I want you to promise me on your father's cross.'

'Promise you what?' I hoped she wouldn't mention Zorrillo again – that was a promise I could never make.

'That you won't do anything stupid like last time.'

I took her in my arms and hugged her tightly. 'I promise, baby. I won't take any unnecessary risks.'

The next morning I accompanied Camila to school on the *colectivo*. I kissed her goodbye at the school gates and waited until she had passed inside the cyclone wire fence, turned to wave goodbye and passed out of sight.

Then I took out my cell phone and prepared to make a call. I'd told Camila the truth – I wouldn't take any unnecessary risks. But that wouldn't stop me from taking the necessary ones.

81

DON MAURICIO TORRES, owner of the Puerto Galán cattle markets, had been a friend of Papa's, and I knew him to be a direct man. However, after observing him the previous day through binoculars, I also knew he was a frightened man. So when I phoned him, I didn't dare mention that I'd been present at yesterday's markets or my true purpose. Instead, I said I needed to talk to him about a problem we had in common. I'd be happy to explain the details if he could meet me at my hotel.

I remembered Mauricio as a tall and proud father of four – a happy, successful businessman whose leathery skin spoke of a lifetime of hard outdoor work. However, the man who knocked on my door looked tired and stooped. He was also as skittish as a horse before a thunderstorm. To make him feel safer, I partially drew the curtains. But once we'd shaken hands, he sat on the very edge of his chair as though ready to bolt.

After a few formalities – Don Mauricio enquiring after my mother and asking how long I'd be in town – I approached my subject circuitously, saying I'd heard what Zorrillo had been doing at the cattle market and about the way he'd levied a fifty per cent tax on the sale of Mamá's cattle. Things had deteriorated significantly since Zorrillo's arrival in the region, I argued, and surely a lot of people would be better off if he weren't around.

'The whole world would be,' he responded. 'Is that what you meant by a common problem?'

'Yes it is.'

His expression didn't change. 'I'm listening.'

I described how Zorrillo was behind the recent increase in kidnapping and extortion, and detailed every incident I knew involving him. 'Something needs to be done,' I concluded, before inching my chair closer to Don Mauricio. 'He has to go.'

Mauricio leaned back and folded his arms. 'And how does this involve me?'

'I know he's robbing you blind. I was there yesterday.'

Don Mauricio's eyes widened. 'Doing what?'

I lifted the sports bag onto my lap and unzipped it to reveal the folded Galil. 'I couldn't get a clear shot. There were too many civilians. I need someone to help set up a meeting with Zorrillo at a remote location. I'll do the rest.'

Finally, Mauricio must have realised that it was *his* help I wanted.

He shot to his feet. 'They told me the graffiti was yours, but I didn't believe it. This conversation is over.'

'Wait!' I stood and clutched his elbow as he turned to leave. 'At least hear me out. No one would know it was you.'

Don Mauricio stared into my eyes pityingly. 'Twenty years ago, when I was younger and braver, I might have said yes. But I'll tell you the same thing I told Colonel Buitrago a year ago when he asked me to set up an ambush: I have a family.'

'All the more reason to remove Zorrillo.'

'You don't understand. Three weeks ago, when I couldn't pay Zorrillo, they kidnapped my daughter, Cecilia. She's only thirteen, still a child. It was that blond boy you might have seen – Buitre they call him. He stopped her bus on the way back from *colegio*. A man phoned that night and spoke to my wife. He told her the price. He said if we called the police, they'd kill her. Every day that I didn't pay, the ransom would go up.'

'What did you do?'

'I rang everyone I knew, borrowed the money and paid immediately. I handed the cash to a young boy on a motorbike wearing a helmet. I'd given them everything, but I wasn't even sure Buitre would release her. It was three more days before he did – the worst three days of our lives. The police found her at midnight by the side of the Villavicencio highway, dirty, sobbing and still in her school uniform. I've sent Cecilia, my wife and my other children to stay with my sister in Medellín. But I can't join them yet. I'm now in debt and I'd lose my business.'

I was truly shocked by this news. At the transport terminal, Mamá had mentioned a girl being kidnapped. I hadn't known it was Don Mauricio's daughter.

'I had no idea,' I said. 'I'm very sorry.'

Don Mauricio's expression softened. He patted my shoulder and mumbled something about being sorry for my family too; we'd all suffered. 'Believe me, I'd do anything to get back at the men who did this – anything except risk my children growing up without a father. Tell me, Pedro, do you still believe in God like your father did?'

'I do.'

'Then remember that our lives are not our own to sacrifice. Rather, we must live humbly in service to others. The Guerrilla have a long memory. You of all people should know that.'

As Mauricio let himself out I pondered his words. In seeking justice for Papá, was I going against the values he had instilled in me? The previous day, when I should have been praying beside my mother in church, I'd been training a rifle on a man, itching to squeeze the trigger. I chased after Mauricio, catching hold of his arm at the top of the staircase.

'Wait! There must be someone else you can suggest.'

Mauricio shook his head – I was incorrigible. 'Try Javier Díaz. Or his brother, Fabián. I hear they're being squeezed hard on every one of their business fronts.'

'Anyone else?' I followed him as he hurried down the stairs.

Mauricio waited until we reached the wooden hotel door. His fingers touched the handle, but he didn't turn it. He must have been afraid of being seen with me in public.

'Don Felix Velasquez,' he said finally. 'Last week, when he couldn't pay the Guerrilla *vacuna*, they torched one of his buses.'

82

BACK IN MY ROOM, I lifted the loose floorboard under which I'd hidden the intelligence files and started flipping through them. 'Buitre' was the name Mauricio had mentioned as belonging to the blond boy who'd kidnapped his daughter. I had no doubt it was the same blue-eyed *guerrillero* who'd knelt on my head and forced me to watch my father's execution. Feverishly, I paged through the personnel dossiers on Guerrilla commanders to 'B', but there was no mention of Buitre – not surprisingly, because the files were arranged by real name, not alias. However, that didn't stop me. I spent the next two hours scanning every page and still came up with nothing; the name 'Buitre' wasn't there.

That night Palillo phoned. I told him that I'd handed his mother the cash as promised, although I agonised over whether to inform him about her bruises. He was on vacation, enjoying the throes of new love with Piolín, so I decided against it.

I explained the weekday routine I was beginning to establish and would more or less follow for the rest of my leave – having lunch with Mamá at the hotel restaurant, waiting for Camila to visit after school and escorting her home on the *colectivo*, then spending my nights alone.

However, I wondered whether Palillo had spoken to Camila when he said, 'I hope you're keeping your promise. I'm not coming to save you again.'

Of course I lied, omitting my intention to visit Don Felix Velasquez, the owner of Rápido Velasquez – the only bus company still operating out of the Garbanzos transport terminal aside from Transportadores Díaz.

Originally a cattle rancher, Don Felix had started a transport company with a small fleet of *chivas* – the colourful, open-air buses used by *campesinos*. The company had grown rapidly, and, until recently, had been the region's biggest. Three years before, Don Felix had even run for mayor.

The following day at midday I went to the terminal and peered through the glass-fronted ticket office, ignoring the disapproving glance of the female ticket clerk who sat at the sales window.

'Can I help you?' she asked.

I didn't ask for Don Felix, even though I could see him seated at his desk inside a small office off to the side. He was in his mid-fifties, with a full head of dark, curly hair, a moustache and a fedora that never left his head. I figured if there were no witnesses, he'd be more likely to agree to my plan.

I waited half an hour until the clerk closed the ticket booth and left, having placed a sign in the window that read: AT LUNCH UNTIL 2PM.

I circled around behind the row of ticket booths and easily found the back entrance. I knocked then tried the handle, expecting to find Don Felix alone.

The door opened, a hand shot out and grabbed my collar, and a pistol was pointed in my face. I hadn't counted on bodyguards. One held me while the other frisked me.

'Where's the usual kid?' the first bodyguard demanded. 'Who are you?'

'The bravest man in town,' said Don Felix, emerging from his tiny side office. 'Pedro Gutiérrez González. The question is: what does he want?'

'A private meeting with you, Don Felix.'

He nodded for his bodyguards to wait outside and invited me into his office, indicating that I should take one of the seats in front of his desk.

'I heard how you buried your father,' he said. 'That Autodefensa graffiti was also yours?'

I nodded. Nothing was to be gained by lying or prevaricating.

'I need your help, Don Felix, and you need mine. I heard what Zorrillo did to your bus. If he's allowed to continue, every business in the region will go bankrupt.'

'Not every business,' Felix said coyly, nodding towards the neighbouring office belonging to Transportadores Díaz. 'Certain people will benefit from my closure.'

'But surely they pay more *vacunas* than anyone. How do they survive?'

'Survive? They're expanding. As to *how* . . .' Don Felix shrugged cynically, 'you tell me.'

I knew there was no love lost between Don Felix and the Díaz clan. Aside from being business competitors, Felix and Humberto Díaz had been political rivals in the same local elections three years earlier, until Felix withdrew as a candidate suddenly and without explanation.

'You must hate the Guerrilla.'

'You don't know the half of it.'

Don Felix explained that when he'd fallen behind in his *vacuna* payments to the Guerrilla, they'd banned his buses from the routes south of Llorona. Felix defied the ban – how else could he repay them if he couldn't work? – and in response they torched his *colectivo*. Felix had vehicle insurance, but it didn't cover *Force Majeure* or Acts of Terrorism. The loss of that one vehicle was catastrophic enough. Another would be fatal to his business. He wanted to sell up and leave but couldn't. While the Guerrilla controlled the highways, he couldn't even sell his remaining fleet – fifteen of his *chivas* and *colectivos* were locked in a yard in Puerto Princesa. Assuming he could persuade fifteen drivers to risk their lives by defying the ban, how would they drive them out? As soon as the ignitions started and Felix opened the gates, Zorrillo's lookouts would know. In other parts of the county, the army set up security convoys to escort long lines of cars from town to town. But in our region, the army no longer ventured that far south.

This meant Felix was completely *jodido*, but it also meant he didn't hide his hatred for the Guerrilla. In fact, from the way he talked so openly and angrily about them, I figured he might be prepared to take risks. And luckily, since he'd never married, he had no family to worry about.

I leaned forward and lowered my voice. 'Zorrillo needs to go.'

He leaned forward also. 'How would you do it?'

'One man: me. One shot: from a distance. No risk to you.'

'But exactly how and where?'

'You'd phone him and set up a meeting.'

'I'd call that a risk. If you fail, he'll know it was me. If you succeed, his commanders will investigate.'

'Then tell me when and where he comes to collect the money.'

'He no longer does. They phone me to say how much I need to have ready. A courier comes to collect it – usually a kid.' Felix reached under his desk and lifted a shoebox. He flicked open the lid to reveal wads of small denomination bills wrapped in rubber bands. 'Stick around for a while and you'll see for yourself.'

I spent the next twenty minutes with my forehead pressed against the interior window of Felix's darkened adjoining office, peering through a narrow slit between the venetian blinds. I was disappointed that Don Felix couldn't help me set up an ambush for Zorrillo, but curious to see what would happen next. Finally, I heard a knock and one of the bodyguards opened the door. The *vacuna* collector was a boy of about eleven, wearing ripped jeans. Felix's bodyguards frisked him, but he was unarmed and far too small to be a soldier.

I doubted they'd send a child without someone at least watching over him. Through a gap in the curtains of the office's external window, I scanned the bus terminal wondering where his senior was. Another boy of about thirteen was standing back against the far wall, sipping a can of Fanta.

Don Felix handed over the shoebox. The boy was so confident and cheeky he even shook hands and said *gracias*. The whole process took less than thirty seconds. Felix and his bodyguards watched him go. It disgusted me. Three grown men – two of them armed – defenceless against a little boy. Felix shook his head wretchedly.

Later he explained everything. The Guerrilla had refined extortion to factory-line efficiency. One squad conducted intelligence on a business – watching its offices, counting customers and estimating turnover. Another squad phoned the owner to quantify the payment amount. A third squad collected, although the Guerrilla's urban militia were too shrewd to do the collection themselves – they outsourced it to children. And a fourth squad did 'enforcement' in the event of default.

Felix could do nothing in response. Informing the authorities or shooting the collectors would only get his offices bombed, more of his buses torched or Felix himself assassinated. Even in Garbanzos, where the Guerrilla weren't as strong, he still had to pay. It was a clever system. Striking at any one of the independent parts of the chain – particularly a child who wasn't even part of the Guerrilla – would have little effect and yet would have severe repercussions.

Witnessing this from the neighbouring office was like being trapped behind steel bars watching someone slowly drown. Only it wasn't a person drowning. It wasn't even a family business. It was an entire country. And I felt powerless to stop it.

I followed the boy with the shoebox, hoping he might lead me to Zorrillo. He cut around the corner behind the bus terminal and squeezed through a gap in the crumbling wall of an abandoned lot. Then he must have sprinted into the trees, because when I reached the gap he'd vanished. When I returned, the boy in the terminal was gone also. I knocked on Don Felix's door, figuring he'd been helpful and hoping he might know more.

'Where else can I find Zorrillo?'

'Try Santo Paraíso. The cocaine markets operate there every Saturday at Flora's Cantina. You'll probably find Caraquemada too.'

'Too risky,' I said, recalling my abortive attempt on Ratón.

'Then I can only suggest you follow the dirty money trail.'

'Which dirty money trail?'

'The one that flows to and from the region's most illustrious businessmen.'

And for the second time that day, Don Felix tilted his head towards the neighbouring office belonging to his competitors – Javier and Fabián Díaz.

83

ALL ROADS, IT seemed, were leading me to the Díaz brothers' door. Mamá was living with them. Camila wanted me at their party. Don Mauricio had recommended I speak to them. And now Don Felix had too. Even the southbound bus heading towards Camila's house that I signalled bore the brothers' surname – TRANSPORTADORES DÍAZ.

I boarded the *colectivo*, but after travelling three blocks it braked suddenly. Through the window, I saw the boy in ripped jeans sprinting to catch up. With him was a boy of about twelve, whose T-shirt stretched over the bulge of a concealed pistol.

Tensing, I felt for my Smith & Wesson. As the boys took seats directly in front of mine I flicked it off safety. They peeked in the shoebox then tapped knuckles like Palillo and I often did. I couldn't believe it. Two little criminals working for Zorrillo were sitting right in front of me, laughing.

Gripping the pistol, I stood, sliding it up the back of their seat towards their necks. Once you've killed a person, you know how easily it is to repeat.

'Stop!' I called. 'Driver!'

I'd take the next bus to Camila's house. I had to. Otherwise I'd shoot those boys.

I knew I'd done the right thing; I couldn't have followed them – they were heading south, probably through the Guerrilla roadblock to deliver the money to Zorrillo. Beta would have disarmed them, taken them off the bus and tortured them. But I wasn't Beta. I didn't torture people, or even send them to be tortured.

Nevertheless, that night back in the hotel, I was more depressed than ever. How on earth had Trigeño convinced an entire community to assist him in hunting down his father's killers? He'd made it sound easy, but I couldn't persuade even a single man.

As I was drifting off to sleep, my cell phone rang. It was Padre Rojas.

'How are you holding yourself up there, prodigal son?'

'With two feet and a shovel. You?'

The priest laughed. 'Cheap communion wine and a stack of Bibles.'

I felt complicit with Rojas. He, too, had paid heavily for defying the Guerrilla.

One day I would tell him how I'd caused Papá's death by drinking with the Autodefensa recruiters. From the priest's friendliness towards me, I was certain he didn't know.

'Pedro, you're doing a marvellous job of looking after your mother. I know Mario Jesús is proud.'

We shared that too – Papá existed for us both in the present tense.

'I saved your pocket Bible, Padre.'

'Keep it! One day we'll swap them back.'

'One day when?'

I was sceptical he'd ever return. If events over the past nine months hadn't spurred the government into action, then what would?

But Rojas was philosophical. 'God works in mysterious ways. Things won't always be this bad.'

I no longer shared his faith. What I'd seen of life convinced me God was no more in charge of the planet than extraterrestrials. No sane being would permit what was occurring. However, Padre Rojas's conversation inspired and motivated me, although probably not in the way he'd intended.

I threw back the sheets, swivelled out of bed and knelt, although not to pray. Instead, I lifted the floorboard. When skimming through the files at La 50, I'd seen several pages about Humberto Díaz's kidnapping. And since I'd decided to attend Javier's party in two days' time to request his help setting up an ambush against Zorrillo, I wanted to know exactly whom I was dealing with.

As soon as I began reading the file on Humberto Diego Uribe Díaz, I regretted not doing so earlier. It contained a wealth of information, but certain facts stood out as being more significant than others.

For one thing, Díaz may not have been solely a cattle rancher and businessman. He was on DEA and Colombian National Police watchlists. The army file stated:

> Díaz is suspected of transporting and/or supplying ether, sulphuric acid and potassium permanganate found in barrels at a jungle laboratory raided by Colombian Anti-Narcotics Police and traced via airway bill

back to a vendor in Florida, USA. Suspected links with Alias Zorrillo, former member of Medellín cartel, currently finance commander for Guerrilla's southern block.

For another thing, Díaz was not ultimately killed over the failure to pay a million dollar ransom, as I'd believed. As soon as his wife had reported the kidnap Colonel Buitrago had requested intercepts on every phone line used by family members. Eleonora had consented, although Javier and Fabián had refused to have their cell phones monitored, claiming the kidnappers had told them not to speak to the authorities.

The Guerrilla had contacted Eleonora by phone on the day after the kidnap. The call had been recorded and transcribed, and a copy placed in the file. Voice recognition software had confirmed the caller's identity: Zorrillo.

MONDAY 7.02 pm – Call to Díaz Property in Llorona – Duration: 9 seconds

Zorrillo:	'We need a million dollars.'
Sñra Díaz:	'I'll get it ready. But I want to speak to him. How do I know he's alive?'
Zorrillo:	'Tell your son, Javier, to be at the Garbanzos hacienda in one hour.'
	[END CALL]

MONDAY 8.07 pm – Call to Díaz Property in Garbanzos – Duration: 1m 15s

Javier Díaz:	'Papá?'.
Zorrillo:	'I'm passing him to you.'
Humberto Díaz:	'*Hijo*, I want you to listen carefully. I need you to look in the office floor safe. You remember where, right?'
Javier Díaz:	'I'm running upstairs now . . .' [sound of footsteps] 'I'm with Fabián. We're here at your desk!'
Humberto Díaz:	'The combination is 7812B.'
Javier Díaz:	'7 . . . 8 . . . 1 . . . 2 . . . B . . . It's open.'
Humberto Díaz:	'Now look inside. There's a small white book. A man will arrive in an hour to collect it and the money.'

Javier Díaz: [sound of rustling] 'There's no white book in here.'

Humberto Díaz: 'Look harder! My life depends on it.'

Javier Díaz: 'I am! I'm looking.'

Humberto Díaz: 'It's a little book. A book of names.'

Javier Díaz: 'There's no book.' [sound of scraping] 'And there's nothing white.'

Humberto Díaz: 'You're as useless as your *puta* mother. Pull everything out, you *idiota*!'

Javier Díaz: 'I have. There's no white book.'

Zorrillo: [sounds of struggle] 'It's me again. Find it or your father's dead.'

Javier Díaz: 'I'm telling you it's not here.'

Zorrillo: 'Then we'll kill him.'

Javier Díaz: 'Then kill him, you *hijo de puta*. Because I haven't got it.'

[END CALL]

That must have been the second-last time the brothers ever heard their father's voice. A day later, Zorrillo phoned again, and this time Fabián answered.

TUESDAY 6.03 pm – Call to Díaz Property in Garbanzos – Duration: 12 seconds

Fabián Díaz: 'Papá?'

Zorrillo 'No, it's me. Did you find it?'

Fabián Díaz: 'No.'

Zorrillo: 'You're lying.'

Fabián Díaz: 'I'm not. Put my father on.'

Zorrillo: 'Last chance. You'll never even find the body.'

Fabián Díaz: 'Go fuck yourself.'

Humberto Díaz: [screams] 'No. No! Please.' [sound of gunshot]

[END CALL]

I dropped the pages, unable to read on. I could almost hear that gunshot, ringing as loudly as the one that killed my own father. I could only imagine Javier and Fabián's reaction upon hearing it, followed by the dial tone when Zorrillo hung up. It must have roused in them the same feelings I'd experienced, seeing Papá fall to the ground – fear, disbelief, powerlessness and anger. And afterwards, guilt.

Like me, they'd been impulsive and aggressive under extreme pressure from Zorrillo – but I bet Javier and Fabián had later regretted their words. It was a small mercy they hadn't witnessed their father's execution like I had.

One thing that surprised me was the mention of a separate *finca* at Garbanzos where Humberto had his office. I presumed this was the home Javier and Fabián now occupied, but I'd never known that our miserly neighbour owned another property.

Resuming my reading, I found that although Colonel Buitrago had respected the sons' wishes not to have their personal phones intercepted, he had requested a list of their call logs from Telecom.

These records revealed that Javier received five calls on his cell phone from the same number used by Zorrillo. Each call lasted approximately three minutes. They occurred during a six-month period *after* his father's death. No conclusions were drawn from this in the army file.

The end of the file contained a handwritten addendum, presumably penned by Colonel Buitrago:

> A five-day search for Díaz's corpse was conducted by the army. The search was suspended when two soldiers were killed during an ambush on the western bank of the Llorona River. Rumours from multiple sources claim Díaz's body is now in an unmarked grave in Llorona Cemetery, buried by persons unknown.

[END FILE]

I finished reading with a mixture of shock, curiosity and sadness. The fact that, officially, Humberto had been buried by *persons unknown* meant that no one had ever discovered that Papá and I were responsible. However, I was astounded that we'd buried a man involved in the cocaine trade. Papá must have known about Díaz – what else could explain his deep-seated disapproval of our neighbour? He detested cocaine *traficantes*; he said they'd corrupted the entire country and that profits from trafficking fuelled the war. But why, then, had Papá risked our lives to bury such a lowlife? After further reflection, I decided that Papá's decision was proof of his deep principles and immense bravery. At great risk, he had done his religious duty – even sinners like Díaz deserve a decent burial. And he'd also stood up to the Guerrilla on behalf of the man who least deserved it. That took courage.

At the same time, I was curious about the phone calls Javier had since received from Zorrillo. Why would he speak to the man who'd murdered his father? Perhaps he'd had to negotiate the family's safe return in order to operate their businesses. Although Javier was forced to rub shoulders with cocaine traffickers like Don Miguel in Santo Paraíso, there was no evidence the mother or sons were involved in the cocaine trade themselves. The companies they now ran – cattle, transport, fertiliser production, and construction – were legitimate.

Javier, Fabián and I were all victims of the same despicable killers. I'd imagined an ulterior motive behind the Díaz brothers' attentions towards me where none existed. Besides, those phone calls demonstrated that Javier had direct contact with Zorrillo. Potentially, that made him my perfect ally. But then what had Don Felix meant by *follow the dirty money trail*?

I wanted desperately to phone Colonel Buitrago to quiz him. I figured he owed me in return for tipping him off about the weapons crate. However, if he discovered the Autodefensas possessed copies of his files, word might get back to Itagüí and Alfa 1.

On Wednesday, I met Camila after school in Garbanzos plaza and we boarded a *colectivo* headed towards her house. Camila was in a good mood. However, I was still distracted by what I'd read about Humberto Díaz and debating whether I should confide in Camila and ask her opinion.

After several bus trips to and from her home, I'd also become complacent. And seven kilometres into the journey, I would pay for that complacency when disaster struck.

84

WHEN WE BOARDED the Transportadores Díaz bus it was half full. Old Man Domino and his wife were sitting on the right-hand side towards the back. Although I hadn't spoken to them since the day Papá died, I hadn't forgotten what they'd done for me, or my vow to repay their kindness.

Camila and I sat across the aisle from them and I nodded politely. 'How have you been, *señores*?'

'You're on the wrong bus,' muttered Old Man Domino without looking at me.

'I'm going to my girlfriend's house. Have you met Camila Muñoz?'

'Pay attention, young man! Your bus goes in the opposite direction,' he insisted, still not meeting my eyes. 'You should get off.'

I shrugged at Camila. Maybe he was drunk. Or perhaps he was going senile. Camila winked back at me and her eyes motioned downwards to Old Man Domino's wrist, where I saw a white medical band. There was also a circular sticking plaster on his forearm, and I guessed he'd been to the Garbanzos clinic for a blood test. With the amount he drank, it was a miracle he was still alive.

I smiled at his wife, but she turned her head to stare out the window. Her jaw was tense and I assumed she was embarrassed by her husband's behaviour. But Old Man Domino wasn't drunk or senile; he was attempting to secretly warn me.

Rounding a blind corner halfway to Camila's home, the bus braked suddenly. Through the windscreen, I saw a line of six cars stopped ahead of us. A soldier in the middle of the road was using a fluorescent baton to direct us towards a diagonal line of orange traffic cones that led to the highway's shoulder. Beside him was a green metal sign with white lettering: *National Army – Security Check.*

'Not again!' The driver cursed under his breath.

I had my Smith & Wesson tucked into my waistband under my shirt, but I wasn't concerned. I'd passed two government checkpoints a week earlier without incident.

However, when the bus pulled to a halt, I got a better look at the twenty or so soldiers who stood beside it gripping rifles. Their uniforms were exactly the same as those of the army, but with one crucial difference: these soldiers wore black rubber boots.

The Guerrilla! They'd moved their roadblock north – perhaps to provoke the army, or perhaps to net people like me who usually got off before the roadblock. My heart began pounding furiously. I nudged Camila in the ribs.

'They're *guerrilleros*,' I whispered.

'*¡Mierda!*' Her hand gripped my knee. 'What should we do?'

'We'll be okay. Just let me do the talking.'

The automatic doors swished opened and two *guerrilleros*, aged about fourteen, stormed up the stairs, brandishing their AK47s. Adrenalin surged through my body. Camila's grip on my knee tightened.

One boy watched the driver while the second addressed us. '*Buenas tardes*, ladies and gentlemen. Please place your hands on the seat in front of you.' The boy walked unhurriedly down the aisle, his boots squeaking as he eyed the passengers one by one. When his gaze met mine, he held it for a moment and then thankfully moved on. 'We're from the 34th Unit of the FARC. This is a security check. We're making the region safer for everyone.'

I began to panic. A security check meant there would be a full-body pat down.

'Everyone please stand, leave your cell phones on your seats and exit the bus.'

Before obeying, I had a quick choice to make: take the pistol with me or leave it on the *colectivo*. I remembered Beta's lesson: a commander should never get caught alive by the enemy. The pistol was for defending myself to my last breath. If I left it behind and they discovered who I was, an agonising death awaited me. On the other hand, if I took it with me and they discovered it, it would be one man with a pistol against twenty soldiers with military assault rifles.

I decided to chance it unarmed – I'd rely on my fake ID and hope no one recognised me. I lifted my sports bag to my knee as cover, extracted my Smith & Wesson from my waistband and wedged it into the gap between our green vinyl seats. Camila's eyes widened but she said nothing.

'What are you doing?' the boy demanded, detecting my movement.

'Leaving my bag here on the seat.'

'Bring it with you! All belongings need to be searched.'

As I filed down the stairs in front of Camila and Old Man Domino, I heard a third boy outside yelling commands to the passengers alighting ahead of us: 'Hands against the windows! Feet spread apart! Have your identification cards ready.'

Hearing this, I realised I'd been right to leave my gun behind – their searches would be thorough. Nevertheless, I felt truly frightened. To walk unarmed towards the enemy went against my every soldierly instinct. I felt naked and powerless. All it would take was one of the twenty *guerrilleros* to recognise me.

I mentally revised the name and date of birth on my fake identification. I knew the types of questions they'd ask: Where was I from? Where was I going? What for? With whom was I travelling? Where did I work? My answers needed to sound confident. If they detected nerves and my story didn't hold up, they'd overpower me in seconds.

Behind me, Camila gave my hand a gentle squeeze. Both our palms were clammy, but her simple touch calmed me. As we descended the final step, she interlocked her fingers with mine. I'd never been so glad that she was with me. Of course, Camila didn't know the full details on my fake *cédula*. But she knew the name I'd registered under at the hotel. And providing I was questioned first, she would go along with whatever I said. She would not falter and we'd get through this together.

However, as soon as Camila's foot hit the asphalt, a female *guerrillera* seized her wrist and jerked her away from me.

'Women this way,' she barked. 'Other side of the bus.'

With no chance to align our stories, my panic escalated. Would Camila say we were travelling together? Would she remember to use my fake name and say that my job was picking the fruit from African oil palms?

Stay calm, I told myself. *Breathe deeply and stay calm.*

I stood in line to the left of Old Man Domino, facing the bus with my hands touching the window, my back to the Guerrilla squad and my brain racing faster and faster. I couldn't believe this was happening only seven kilometres from Garbanzos. Where was the army? If Old Man Domino had known about the roadblock, surely word had reached Colonel Buitrago.

Through the window I could see Camila being questioned on the other side of the bus. Our eyes met briefly. Her face was ashen. I now wished I'd told her to pretend not to know me. She would have been safe then. But the most important thing now was for our stories to match. I tapped my *cédula* against the window and she nodded that she understood. I was relieved when her interrogator finally moved to the next passenger.

In the bus's side mirror, I caught glimpses of the scene behind me. Seven *guerrilleros*, working as a team, were making their way down the line of male passengers. They looked about twelve or thirteen years old, and three of them were girls. One of the boys squeezed and patted each man from shirt collar down to socks, a girl rifled through bags, and the eldest looking boy checked IDs and asked questions. Three metres behind us, the remaining four stood covering our backs with their AK47s. By the time the interrogator reached me, even my fingertips were perspiring, leaving smudges on the glass.

After studying my *cédula* and comparing my face to its photo, the boy slid the edge of the card down an alphabetical list of names on his clipboard. Halfway down, I read my own name: Pedro Juan Gutiérrez González. I tensed, but he went past it in search of my assumed name – Jhon Jairo García Sanchez – which, of course, wasn't there.

'Occupation?'

'Field worker. I cut fruit from African oil palms.'

'Take off your hat.'

I obeyed. I didn't dare turn around, but I could feel his eyes studying my military haircut. Suspicion entered his voice.

'Your *cédula* says you're from Meta. Why are you so far from home, Jhon Jairo?'

'I'm visiting family.'

Hearing my story aloud, it sounded flimsy. The boy stepped in closer, tapping my ID card against his clipboard, and his eyes bore into me with increasing distrust.

'Who exactly are you visiting? I need full names and an address.' He turned and looked back, as though debating whether to call over a superior. Tilting my head around under my armpit, I followed his gaze back to a tall, well-built man, the only soldier who looked fully-grown.

By then, three cars and a Rápido Velasquez bus had been detained behind us.

'This one's on the list, *comandante*!' cried a girl, jabbing her rifle muzzle into the back of an overweight man with a moustache and herding him and a woman, who was probably his wife, away from their vehicle.

'Bring him over,' replied the commander. 'That makes three from the list plus the oligarch driving the BMW.'

I thought I recognised his voice, but his face was partially concealed by a hat. He was interrogating three men who were kneeling before him with their hands behind their heads. Two of the men were young and casually dressed. The third was an elderly gentleman wearing a suit. The fat man with the moustache was forced to kneel too.

At that moment, the commander removed his hat and wiped sweat from his brow.

I froze. It was the blond boy – Buitre. He was standing only three metres behind me, next to the four guards. Heart racing, I bowed my head lower and pulled my arms in tightly against my cheeks.

I knew I had to answer the soldier's question about who I was visiting, but I couldn't. Whatever I said would only sink me deeper and endanger Camila. All I could feel was the blood thumping through the tight veins of my forehead. *If Buitre sees me, I'm dead – tortured . . . and then dead.*

The interrogator shook my arm, demanding again, 'Who are you visiting?'

'Me!' came a voice from beside me. It was Old Man Domino.

'And who are *you*?' asked the boy.

'His grandfather.' Old Man Domino handed over his ID card. 'And you can call me "sir", *muchacho*.'

His rudeness was deliberate. The boy was thrown off balance, clearly unaccustomed to challenges from civilians. I was thankful for Old Man Domino's intervention – it strengthened my cover story and diverted the boy's attention. But for how long? If he asked more questions, our responses would never align.

The boy held the two ID cards side by side, looking indecisively from one to the other. Then he stiffened. 'Your surnames are different. I need to check this with my *comandante*.'

Heart in my mouth, I tilted my head again and my eyes followed his footsteps towards Buitre. I looked sideways, gauging the distance to the bus door, planning to sprint for my pistol.

However, Old Man Domino turned abruptly, drawing the ire of the four guards, who pointed their rifles and yelled at him to stand still.

'*¡Oye!* Buitre, tell this *muchacho* you know me!' he called out.

'I think that man's drunk,' said our interrogator. 'His breath stinks.'

'Him!' Buitre laughed and waved the boy away. 'He's always drunk.'

'But—' the boy protested, holding up the ID cards.

Buitre pointed at our bus. 'Finish that one quickly. Move on to the next bus.'

As the soldier returned our ID cards and ordered us back on board, I smelled gasoline and saw two *guerrilleros* using a hose to siphon fuel from the gas tank of the bus behind us. The boy followed us inside, still suspicious. When he saw me sit down next to Old Man Domino, he shook his head and jumped off.

I collapsed back against my seat, shaking. Old Man Domino had saved me. No words could ever express my gratitude.

Camila boarded, pale and perspiring. I moved across the aisle to sit beside her, but we didn't look at each other. I had no idea what she'd been through on her side of the bus. I wanted to comfort her but didn't trust myself to speak.

I sat on my shaking, sweaty hands, trying to breathe evenly and not look out the open window. Only metres away was one of my father's killers – a man I had dreamed of killing but who had been only seconds away from killing me.

Suddenly, cries came from the *guerrilleros* outside.

'*¡Los Chulos! ¡La Ley!*'

The Vultures and *The Law* were the Guerrilla's terms for the army and the police. Whistling and hand signals passed along the line of *guerrilleros.*

'Take these three enemy away,' Buitre ordered, pointing at three of the four kneeling prisoners.

'No!' screamed the wife of the overweight man with the moustache.

She clutched at his shirt, but two *guerrilleros* prised her off. She dug around inside her handbag, pulling out a white plastic bottle, which she rattled.

'Please, *señor*!' she said to Buitre. 'He needs these for his heart! He could die without them.'

But Buitre waved her away.

She began crying. 'It's only medicine. Please take it! It's only medicine.'

The three hostages were led away – hands bound with plastic ties, rifles digging into their spines – leaving the elderly man in the suit still kneeling.

'Do you have your car keys?' Buitre asked him.

'Of course.' Hope flashed across the man's face as he reached into his pocket. 'I can drive you wherever you like. Or better still, just take the car—'

Without even letting him finish, Buitre shot him in the side of the head. He slumped sideways and a collective gasp came from the passengers on our bus.

'I will.' Buitre scooped up the keys from the dirt and tossed them to a subordinate. 'Turn the oligarch's car sideways and block the road. Then torch it.'

'Army!' The call came again – louder and more urgent this time. At that moment, there was an explosion. They'd set the Rápido Velasquez bus on fire, sending flames licking up its sides.

Our driver swore and slammed his foot on the accelerator. As the bus sped off, we looked through the back window with our hands covering our mouths at the scenes of chaos and panic on the highway behind us.

The dead man was facedown beside the highway with a grey-haired woman slumped over his body, wailing. Motorists were scrambling for their cars. Several passengers from the torched bus stood watching it go up in flames. Others ran for cover. A line of vehicles extended in both directions, blocked by the burning bus. Panic spread as dozens of drivers attempted three-point turns at the same time, honking and screaming at each other. We rounded the bend and lost sight of them.

Behind us, I heard a second explosion – that must have been the dead man's BMW. A second tower of thick black smoke billowed upwards. I hugged Camila. She was trembling violently and her chest was heaving as she emitted small, staccato gasps.

'It's okay, baby,' I said. 'We're safe now.'

85

ONCE OFF THE bus and back inside her house, Camila raced up the stairs to her room. I found her lying on her bed. At first she wouldn't look at me and I assumed she was in shock. When I caressed her hair, she curled into the foetal position.

'Your fake *cédula* I can understand,' she said. 'But why do you need the gun?'

'For protection.'

'But if they'd found it, they would have shot you. You could have been killed. You could have got us both killed.'

'They wouldn't have touched you. But there are worse things they could do than shoot me.'

I'd answered truthfully and my reason for carrying a pistol was logical. But sometimes truth and logic don't win an argument. Sometimes, they make it deteriorate.

Camila opened her eyes. They were filled with tears. 'Worse things like what?'

'Nothing happened, *amor*. We're both fine. And you know what I do for a job. It won't be for much longer, I promise.'

I tried to see things from Camila's perspective. Four months earlier, she'd reluctantly accepted what I did. But she'd only known in theory. Seeing my pistol and having rifles pointed at her at the Guerrilla roadblock had suddenly made it real.

'Maybe you shouldn't be here,' she said.

I was stunned. Was she saying she wanted to end our relationship?

'Don't you see?' she rushed on. 'I'm putting you in danger. None of this would have happened if you weren't back here to see me. You'd be on the coast with Palillo or staying safely with your mother.'

'Don't be silly! You're not putting me in danger! And it's my choice to be here.'

Camila was silent again. At least she hadn't said she wanted to break up. But what she *was* saying almost amounted to the same thing. Of course, I'd have happily paid for us to travel and meet in a different town. But Camila had a year and a half of school remaining, and it would be impossible to time my leave periods to coincide with her vacations. Our relationship was already strained by distance and time apart. Not being able to visit her at home would end it completely.

'We'll be fine.' I brushed the hair back from her cheek. 'They didn't see me. And I won't travel on that bus route ever again.'

Camila buried her face in the pillow. 'I just want a normal life like the girls at school. I want a normal boyfriend.'

'That's not fair, *amor*. You know why my life is like this. You know what they did to Papá.'

She sat up and hugged me tightly. 'I'm sorry. What I meant was I just want to feel safe.'

'You are safe, baby. I love you and we're not going to lose each other. I promise.'

I felt her hot, wet tears against my neck. I knew she loved me deeply. But we'd left the underlying argument unresolved – the difficulty of her being the girlfriend of someone wanted by the Guerrilla while she lived in a town that they controlled.

I left Camila on the bed, hoping she'd be calmer by morning. Señor Muñoz drove me back to Garbanzos. Three hours had passed by then and they'd cleared the dead body, but we saw the patch of blood and the debris, including the burnt-out hulk of the bus belonging to Felix Velasquez, its lettering still visible. Several windows had melted in a strange pattern down its side, the glass resolidifying like stalactites. Beneath them on the asphalt I saw pools of hardened black rubber that must have belonged to the tyres.

By the time I reached the hotel, I had moved on from my shock and now felt angry. I kept seeing the faces of the young boys and girls at the roadblock. If the long-promised communist revolution ever succeeded, our country would be governed by fourteen-year-olds brandishing AK47s and their eleven-year-old henchmen in ripped jeans who collected taxes for them. I watched television, convinced that the roadblock would be national news. An incident like this was clear proof the Guerrilla had violated the ceasefire. It could not go unreported, especially when there were at least fifty witnesses.

But there was nothing.

Fucking coward journalists! I thought. *Fucking big-city media companies!*

Like many Colombians, I suspected this was part of an organised political conspiracy; they were deliberately suppressing the news. But it wasn't.

I've since learned the truth about journalists in Colombia. We have the bravest reporters in the world. Many have given their lives to tell the truth about the war and cocaine trafficking. Some live in exile overseas. But those living closest to the conflict zones are warned to keep quiet or be killed. The armed groups know their phone numbers and where they work and live. Even those who publish articles anonymously in big-city magazines like *La Semana* and *Cambio* can be traced. Or their families can be. So they report selectively.

Nevertheless, right then and there, I resolved that one day I'd tell my life story to someone who would be willing to publish it. I know I've done terrible things – killed people and even worse. I know I've lied to those I love. But people need to know that this is not a lie. The things I've witnessed with these eyes – these stories I'm telling you – they're too horrible for anyone to invent. This is the truth about Colombia and I want people to know it.

The following afternoon, when Camila came to my hotel, I could see she was still upset. She was quieter than usual, and after only an hour, she said she was going home.

'Are you okay?' I asked.

'I'm fine, *amor*,' she said. 'I just need to be alone. I need time to think.'

I said nothing. We were still together, and that was what was important.

On Thursday night, there was still no news about the roadblock. I switched off the television, picked up my Galil and began cocking and uncocking it. I pulled the rounds from the chamber and then re-inserted them one by one into the empty magazine before reattaching it and starting again. I would not lie idle while Zorrillo, Buitre and their men committed atrocities. Something had to be done, and with the government's continued inaction, Javier Diaz might be the only one who could help me do it.

86

ON FRIDAY, JAVIER'S driver collected Camila and me from my hotel for the five-kilometre drive into the hills. It was a hot, humid evening but the electric window wouldn't go down.

'It's fixed in place. Bulletproof glass,' said the driver, tapping the thick windscreen with his knuckle. 'But I'll turn up the air-conditioning. Perhaps you'd like some music or television?'

Twin screens flickered on in the seats in front of us. We looked at each other. That car must have cost more than most houses. Camila's wide-eyed fascination increased when we reached a high stone wall overrun with creepers and two large wrought-iron gates parted as if by magic.

As the tyres crunched slowly up a winding gravel driveway, Camila pressed her forehead against the glass. Along both sides, a continuous box hedge was punctuated by palms planted at intervals and floodlit from below.

Finally, the car rounded a marble fountain and pulled up in front of a palatial two-storey mansion. Camila stepped out and turned in a full circle, her lips parted in amazement. On one side of the house was a spacious car park filled with late-model Mercedes and BMWs. Beyond it, three helicopters perched on the grass. On the other side was a fishpond and, in the distance, an artificial lake with a speedboat moored to a jetty.

I'd always thought of Humberto Díaz as a humble cattle rancher whose sole residence was the modest *finca* next to ours. This exotic hacienda hidden behind high walls told a different story.

I still had no idea of the nature or extent of Humberto Díaz's involvement in the cocaine trade. There were many parts to the business that went on south of Santo Paraíso. As the intel file stated, Díaz may simply have imported, transported or sold chemical precursors, many of which were expensive and difficult to obtain in wholesale quantities. He may have owned fields where the coca plants grew or simply owned the crops themselves – paying *campesino* farmers to plant, tend and harvest them. He may have controlled the jungle processing laboratories where the leaves are stomped on and broken down into paste, or the refining laboratories where the crude coca paste is converted into crystal. He may have sold and exported the final crystallised product or he may simply have been a middleman. I had no way of knowing and it was not a question I could ask his wife and sons. In fact, with so many guests vying for their attention, it would be hard enough getting Fabián or Javier alone.

We ascended a sweeping staircase. The sounds of a bass guitar and snare drums reached my ears and the smell of roasting pork *lechona* filled my nostrils.

Just past the entrance a waiter appeared wearing white gloves and carrying a silver drinks tray. He indicated a short queue where arriving guests stood, waiting their turn to be welcomed by Eleonora Díaz and her son Javier.

'Would the *señores* care for a beverage?'

Camila accepted a glass of champagne before whispering to me, 'Where did all these people come from?'

Not from Llorona, that was for sure. The women were dripping with jewellery and the men wore tailored suits. Most of them were older; some had silver hair. The younger women looked like they'd stepped off a fashion shoot.

Most guests had driven to Garbanzos with bodyguards and police escorts. Others had flown down for the weekend. Not everyone could be accommodated in the guest bungalows, so Javier had booked out every room in the town's best hotel.

Camila pointed out a pretty woman with blonde hair and unnaturally large breasts. 'I've seen her on TV,' she whispered. 'I think she's a newsreader.' Camila adjusted her dress nervously and gulped her champagne. 'Does my make-up look okay? Maybe I should fix it.'

Camila had applied extra-thick mascara and black eyeliner, and her hair was tied up in a chignon with two curled tendrils dangling playfully around her ears. She might have been only fifteen but already she looked like a woman.

'Don't worry,' I reassured her. 'You're the most beautiful girl here.'

I hoped that we could have fun that night. It would help Camila forget the roadblock incident. I only had four more days of leave and after that I wouldn't see her for another four months.

At the front of the queue, Eleonora Díaz, whom I barely knew, greeted me as though we were intimate acquaintances.

'Pedro! How delightful to see you,' she said regally. 'And this must be your beautiful girlfriend.'

In the months since Humberto Díaz's death, Eleonora's face had hardened over, evidently as a result of plastic surgery. However, her new swimsuit-model breasts, bee-stung lips and designer eyes that stretched wide like those of a goldfish, rather than recreating the façade of youth, only emphasised that the rest of her had not fared so well. Consulting her hands for her true age – which must have been almost fifty – I noted diamonds and emeralds: the exotic knuckledusters of a wealthy widow who'd fought hard to get where she was and even harder to stay there. A thin white scarf was wrapped around her neck like a loose hospital bandage, completing the look. She was as sexy as a Peruvian mummy.

Nevertheless, it was common courtesy to pay the hostess a compliment.

'Your dress is very beautiful, Señora Díaz,' I said, lighting upon the only sincere praise available. I expressed my condolences for the loss of Humberto Díaz. 'And I see you're still wearing your wedding ring. My mother also swore never to take hers off.'

Eleonora exchanged glances with a meek man lingering beside her, whom I assumed to be another guest. He stepped forward and extended his hand.

'I don't believe you've met my new husband, César Lamprea, the former mayor of Popayán,' she said. 'We married in a small ceremony in Bogotá two months ago.'

I flushed from cheek to cheek, but Eleonora didn't even look embarrassed. Only nine months had passed since her first husband's execution and already she'd remarried. I mumbled my apologies and was glad when Camila tactfully shuffled us along to greet Javier.

Attired in a suit, he presented a very different face than he had at Flora's Cantina. Here, in his natural environment, he was polite and sophisticated. Thick, curly hair sprouted from beneath the unbuttoned collar of his silk shirt. He'd put on weight and looked tired and stressed.

'Welcome, my friend.' He shook my hand with curtness and efficiency, flashing a manufactured smile. 'It's been too long. Please, make yourself at home.'

I complimented him on his picturesque grounds and the party, and thanked him for inviting us. 'Perhaps, when you have time, we could—'

'Yes, later we'll talk properly. Now if you'll excuse me . . .'

Leaving Javier, we crossed the lushly appointed foyer – which boasted glass tables, ornamental vases and paintings displayed in specially designed alcoves – to the French doors on the other side. Stepping outside again,

I noted that the mansion was U-shaped, designed around a stunning centrepiece: an enormous, kidney-shaped swimming pool. In Garbanzos and Llorona, such luxuries were unheard of. We lived on a river; we swam in that river.

In a marquee beside the pool, the party was in full swing. Waiters wearing tuxedos and serving canapés circulated among the elegantly dressed guests.

Mamá spotted us and hurried over. She looked happy and excited for the first time in months.

'Oh, Pedro,' she said, hugging me, 'you look so handsome dressed up. You remind me of your father.'

But I didn't feel handsome. Among this rich and glamorous crowd, I felt young and stupid and out of place.

For the next hour, I danced with Camila – salsa, merengue and vallenato – but I didn't feel comfortable for a single moment.

Outside the hacienda's high stone walls a war was going on. Yet the other guests seemed completely oblivious to it. A kid like Ñoño was proud when he could afford to buy his mother a bag of groceries. The men here wore expensive cologne and had their nails manicured. I doubted any of them had fired a rifle. National military service was compulsory for every male aged over eighteen, but they'd probably bribed their way out.

The night took a turn for the worse when I returned from the bathroom to find Camila standing by the pool chatting to the younger Díaz brother, Fabián. He was stylishly dressed in tailored pants and a tight-fitting shirt that displayed the muscles of his chest. His straight black hair was tied back in a ponytail, and he wore a diamond earring that I thought made him look like a girl but which was probably all the rage in the city. I had to admit he was good-looking. He had clear olive skin, an athletic build and large, confident eyes that gave him the look of a man to whom women came easily.

'*Mi amor*,' Camila said, turning to me with a smile, 'you already know Fabián?'

I nodded and held out my hand, which he shook.

'Of course!' he said. 'We've known each other for years.' In fact, Fabián had spent most of the last ten years in Bogotá – first at an exclusive high school, then at university. He laughed and added, 'I remember when you were only this high and running around naked on the grass.'

'Have a whisky, *amor*,' Camila said, signalling to the waiter. 'Go on! Just one!'

'It's Blue Label,' prompted Fabián.

'I don't drink,' I said pointedly, taking a soda water from the tray.

Fabián picked up a whisky and drained it in a couple of gulps. I hoped to bring the conversation around to the political situation and the Guerrilla, but soon realised Fabián wasn't interested. He was drunk and trying to impress Camila.

With his tongue loosened, he became critical of his own family. According to him, Javier was controlling, bull-headed and deaf to reason. 'But we're stuck with each other,' he said, 'since Papá left us equal shares of the business. Javier would love to buy me out, but he can't. Mamá holds the controlling stake.'

'Your mother lives in Bogotá now, doesn't she?' asked Camila, politely turning the conversation. 'Did she fly down specially for the party?'

'Yes. I'm trying to persuade Javier to put in a runway. It's time I got my pilot's licence. What about you, Pedro?' He turned for a moment and smiled condescendingly. 'You'll be old enough to drive soon?'

The hairs on my neck bristled. *I drove your father's remains to the cemetery, you son of a bitch* were the words that sprang to mind. Instead, I shrugged and said, 'I've been driving for years.'

From Fabián we learned the names of several guests from the Colombian *farándula* – politicians, models, actresses and artists – all personal friends of the family. Camila asked about the gorgeous blonde newsreader she'd seen earlier.

'You mean Andrea? I'll introduce you. But right now, perhaps you'd like to . . . ?' He indicated the dance floor, and then looked to me for permission. 'Mind if I borrow your girlfriend? I promise to return her when you get jealous.'

I could see that Camila was torn. She wanted to dance but didn't want me to feel left out. 'It's your party too, *amor*,' I said to her. 'Dance all you like.'

I was left holding their empty glasses while Fabián led Camila onto the dance floor. When they'd finished the first song, Camila looked at me and shrugged – did I mind if they danced again? She seemed to be enjoying it.

I nodded, but Fabián's behaviour began to irk me. He had a dark-eyed defiance, like a spoiled child who always got what he wanted and then rubbed it in. I didn't like the way he held Camila tightly while dancing. I didn't like him whispering familiarly in her ear, nor the way his hands lingered on her waist for several seconds after a song finished. But his blatant flirtatiousness annoyed me less than the fact that Camila played up to it, laughing and smiling and playfully touching his arm.

I suppose she felt flattered. At twenty-five, he was ten years her elder and there were plenty of pretty women his own age to choose from. But it left me with the feeling of being too poor, too young and simply not good enough.

Some of the younger guests – city types with easy manners and confident smiles – tried to include me in their conversation. But all of them referred to bars, clubs and restaurants in suburbs of Cali and Medellín as though everyone knew them. I found myself fidgeting, at a loss for what to do. Camila, however, fitted in graciously, laughing and dancing with Fabián's friends, and drinking too much.

'Slow down, baby,' I warned her between songs.

'I'm fine.'

'I just don't want you to get drunk.'

Camila was happy. She was meeting people: older people, glamorous people, educated people. Fabián was her guide into this world that was so far from everything we'd ever known. Neither of us had ever flown in a plane; these people owned helicopters. Fabián even inveigled himself into meeting Camila's parents, who were also on the dance floor.

Finally, I tired of watching Camila dance with Fabián and approached the only other person who looked out of place: Colonel Buitrago.

Buitrago was sitting alone at a table wearing a blue shirt. He had loosened his tie and was nursing a crystal tumbler of whisky.

'Mind if I sit?' I asked politely.

'Please do. I hoped to bump into you tonight.'

After exchanging pleasantries, the colonel updated me on my father's case.

Of course, I already knew about the capture order issued for Zorrillo and Caraquemada from the files, but I feigned surprise and thanked him for his hard work. I longed to ask him about the follow up to Humberto Díaz's case and whether he suspected the sons of involvement in *narcotráfico*. Why else would Buitrago continue tracking their phone calls long after their father's death?

'I'm sorry I couldn't meet you this time in an official capacity,' he said. 'The current political situation is delicate, as I'm sure you know.'

'I understand. But you found the crate?'

Buitrago hesitated. 'I did, thank you. Although it might have been wiser to skip the graffiti, leave the crate where it was and just make the phone call.'

'There were people I thought might want the weapons. People who could put them to good use.'

'The Colombian Armed Forces is the only organisation legally empowered to fight the Guerrilla.'

'So you still think I'm on the wrong path?'

'I think this whole country's on the wrong path. This peace process is a mistake. The army needs money. The government should be raising taxes to fund the war, not appeasing the communists.'

I'd heard similar sentiments from General Itagüí, but at least he'd done something about it, delivering to us the intelligence files and his *guerrillero* prisoner. As a result of his long collaboration with the Autodefensas, General Itagüí presided over a province cleansed of insurgents, whereas Buitrago had the Guerrilla running rampant on his doorstep.

'What will you do next time Buitre advances his roadblock, Colonel? What will you do when Caraquemada is close enough to launch mortars into your main plaza?'

'My duty.' He sat upright in his chair, puffed out his chest and adjusted his tie. 'I'll defend this town to my very last man. Sacrifice my own life, if necessary.'

'What if that's not enough? Wouldn't outside help be better?'

'I've seen what happens to other regions once *outside help* arrives.'

'And so have I.'

I don't know what Buitrago had seen, but Trigeño's success in Los Llanos spoke for itself.

'Be careful, Pedro. Sometimes the cure is harder to remove than the cancer.'

There was an uncomfortable silence. I looked up and noticed that Camila had vanished, as had Fabián.

I stood, excused myself and left the colonel there with his whisky, his bravery and his stubborn principles that soon might cost many lives and the government's already-fragile control over the region.

I entered the house but it was deserted, except for a maid who scurried past me with lowered eyes. The kitchen, with its polished granite benches, was empty. A maze of corridors led to multiple doors. I switched on the lights in two or three rooms – guest bedrooms and bathrooms with double showers and gilded taps – but there was no sign of Camila.

In the upstairs corridor, I heard the low murmur of a television. All doors were closed except one, from which light streamed. I entered and found myself in a study with a white woollen carpet, a black leather sofa and a glass coffee table bearing a crystal decanter of whisky. When I saw the large mahogany desk I realised this must be Humberto Díaz's office – the one mentioned by him in his second-last phone call to his sons.

The walls were hung with elegantly-framed photos of Humberto. There he was, aged in his early thirties, wearing a leather riding hat and mounted on a purebred *paso fino* that must have been nineteen hands high. There he was, several years older, behind the controls of a helicopter. In his forties, now balding, he posed with his wife and two young sons at Disneyland.

In a more recent shot, an ageing, pot-bellied Díaz stood on the deck of a yacht with men wearing ties who looked like politicians or businessmen. A newspaper article about a former vice-president was framed with the final photo, showing Díaz shaking the same man's hand.

During his lifetime, Humberto Díaz had cultivated the persona of a struggling, respectable cattle farmer. But meanwhile he and his family had lived an entirely different life outside Llorona – a life of wealth, travel and unbridled opulence.

Had Papá known the full extent of his other life? My curiosity was fully aroused now, and neither considerations of propriety nor the risk of getting caught could have deterred me from what I did next.

After checking that the staircase was empty, I switched off the corridor light – it would flash on if someone approached. I knelt beneath the mahogany desk and ran my fingertips through the carpet until they detected a ridge. The carpet peeled back to reveal a large concealed floor safe. Knowing what I was doing was wrong, I felt my senses on full alert.

Keeping one eye on the door, I punched in the combination I remembered from the phone transcripts: 7812B. Each beep sounded in my ears as shrilly as a fire alarm. After the fifth beep, a dull metal thud announced that the bolts had released. I hesitated, listening intently for approaching footsteps. Then I yanked the heavy metal lid upwards and stifled a gasp.

The safe was jam-packed with US bills: twenties, fifties and hundreds. It was the kind of money you only ever see on TV, too much for me to count. I lifted several stacks to see if the white book Zorrillo had demanded lay beneath, but it was pure cash.

My original suspicions resurfaced, this time as near certainties. The brothers had obviously continued their father's illicit activities. Legal businesses keep their money in banks. It also made the depth of their involvement clearer: no one makes that much money from owning a coca field or transporting barrels of ether.

Suddenly, the corridor light came on and I quickly closed the safe. When Javier pushed open the door, a crystal tumbler of whisky in his hand, I was standing once more, innocently admiring the row of photos.

'Pedro! I was wondering where you'd escaped to.'

'I was looking for Camila. I think she's with your brother somewhere.'

'I apologise. When Fabián's drunk, he can be a painful *pendejo*. But they'll turn up.' He extracted a beautifully engraved silver cigar case from his pocket, flipped it open and held it out to me. 'Cigar?'

'I don't smoke.'

From Papá and Trigeño, I'd inherited a natural mistrust of anyone involved in *narcotráfico*. Under normal circumstances, I'd have left the party immediately and taken Camila with me, never to speak to the brothers again. But Mamá still needed the Díaz family's protection. And their being criminals didn't change the fact that I needed their help to get Zorrillo. In fact, it made it more likely that Zorrillo's death would be in their business interests, especially if he was squeezing them hard, as he had their father.

I touched my finger against the photo of Javier and his father posing with Mickey Mouse. 'You must miss him.'

Javier lifted the frame from its hook and stared down at it for a moment. 'I loved him very much,' he said. 'But to tell you the truth, I never knew him well. We were sent away to school very young. And even during our vacations, he was rarely home. Of course, we never lacked for anything. All this,' he indicated the luxurious surroundings, 'comes from his hard work. But he wanted us educated so we could have better lives than he did. That was his thing – his life's goal. He'd grown up poor so we had to be better than he was. Not just better educated, but *better*.'

'And your mother?'

'She drinks too much. We were raised by our maids.' He looked down at the picture again and then replaced it on the wall. 'When Father died I hardly had time to grieve. I had to take over his affairs immediately or we'd have lost everything. A week before the Guerrilla took my father, he made me promise that if anything happened to him, I'd keep my brother in line. I've tried to do as he asked, although Fabián hates me for it.'

I thought of *my* last promise to Papá – not joining the Autodefensas. At least Javier was keeping his.

'You must hate Zorrillo and Caraquemada.'

'We do,' he said simply. 'But life goes on.'

I thought his remark callous. My father had been killed shortly after his. But my life hadn't simply *gone on*. It had been slammed sideways then dropped off a cliff.

'Javier, why did you invite me here?'

He seemed surprised. 'We used to be neighbours. We've known you since you were a little sardine.'

'But why look after my mother?'

'She was good to our family. After our father was killed, the entire community turned their backs on us, as though we were somehow to blame for what the Guerrilla did. Your mother defied them and placed flowers on Father's grave.'

Since hedging and subtlety were getting me nowhere, I said, 'Why not tell me what you really want?'

Javier smiled ironically and calmly flicked his polished fingernail against his crystal tumbler. 'Why not be open yourself, Pedro? What did Felix Velasquez say about me when you visited him?'

'Who says I did?'

'Come now!' Javier chuckled. 'My bodyguards talk to Felix's bodyguards.' He sipped his whisky. 'What you're proposing is dangerous, Pedro. I'm not saying *no*, but afterwards, there would be consequences. If you and I can't trust each other, this conversation should end now.'

I was stunned. All that week, I'd been sneaking around Garbanzos asking questions and searching for information. That night, I'd snooped around Javier's house, hunting for clues. I even had secret government files on his father and the combination to his office safe. But Javier had been several steps ahead of me. Since he'd pre-empted me, I followed his lead.

'It would only take one man. *Me*. And you to set up a meeting at a remote location.'

Javier threw back his head and laughed.

'Zorrillo didn't kill my father, he merely pulled the trigger. The men who killed my father – and yours – sit atop an organisation numbering twenty thousand. So killing Zorrillo won't make a difference; he's a medium-sized branch on a gigantic tree. To fell that tree, you'd need to sever its trunk and then chop away every root so it doesn't grow back again. *Ever*. And to do that, you'd need an entire army. A tougher one than Buitrago's. An army that fights the Guerrilla using their own tactics.' When he looked back at me, Javier's face had become sinister and I saw a flash of his brother's arrogance. He glanced down at my belt where the Smith & Wesson was concealed, raising his eyebrows. 'Do you know such an army?'

I never got to answer.

From a nearby room, I heard Camila's laughter. It was too shrill, unnaturally so.

'It's my hair!' came her muffled squeal. 'My stupid hair!'

I covered the distance to the door in three long strides.

'Wait!' Javier called, following me. 'I'm sure it's nothing.'

Behind a closed door on the opposite side of the corridor, I heard voices. I tried the door, but it was locked, so I barged my shoulder against it. The flimsy lock gave way instantly and I burst into a palatial bedroom with a king-size bed.

Inside were three good-looking men in their mid-twenties together with Fabián, the blonde newsreader called Andrea and Camila. Fabián was seated on a waist-high bureau, legs apart with his hand extended towards Camila, who was standing in front of him, her head bent forward and her mouth centimetres from his extended hand, as though she were about to lick it. Andrea stood behind Camila, holding her hair bunched above her head. A pornographic movie was playing on an enormous flat-screen television embedded in the far wall.

As the door crashed back against the wall, everyone stopped and turned to me.

'What's happening here?' I demanded. 'What are you doing to her?'

In the awkward near-silence that followed, the only sound was the groaning of the naked woman on the television.

'She's fine,' Fabián said. 'We're just having a little fun.'

One of the men tried clumsily to nudge a silver tray under the sofa with his toe. On it was a solid white brick – the size of a toaster – wrapped in plastic. A scalpel lay beside it and a triangular corner of the block was chipped away, broken into powder.

Fabián lowered his hand and I saw the same white powder in the webbing between his thumb and forefinger. They were giving Camila cocaine.

The woman on the television groaned louder.

'Turn that off!' commanded Javier angrily. Andrea fumbled around for the remote but was too drunk to find the STOP button.

'Camila?' I asked. 'Are you okay?'

'*¡Perfecta!*' She stood to full height and faced me, smiling radiantly, her hair dishevelled and her cheeks flushed with alcohol. She seemed completely unashamed, as though it were perfectly normal to be bending over between the knees of a man she barely knew in a bedroom with a block of cocaine while watching pornography.

'Everyone, this is Pedro. Pedro, these are my friends – Fabián and . . . sorry . . . what were your names again?'

The others mumbled their greetings. Fabián slapped the powder from his hand.

'Join us, Pedro! Have a drink.' He picked up a whisky bottle and raised his eyebrows. His pupils were dilated and his teeth grinding together.

My eyes returned to Camila. 'We're leaving.'

'*Ay*, come on, Pedro!' she said. 'Let's have some fun. These people are *fun*.'

Perhaps to her they were. Perhaps she thought them decadent yet sophisticated. But I could see them for what they were and I wasn't standing for it. Camila might have thought I was embarrassing her in front of her new best friends; however, she'd given no thought to the danger of getting drunk and taking drugs with strangers. Her parents were right downstairs. What would they have thought?

'I said we're leaving.' Camila could see how angry I was but made no move to leave. 'Now!' I snatched her wrist and yanked her away from Fabián.

Fabián leaped furiously from his bureau. 'This is our house and our party. Who are you to break through a locked door and start giving orders? And Camila can do what she wants. She's not a child.'

'She's fifteen!' I dragged Camila towards the door.

Behind me, I heard Javier reprimanding his younger brother. 'You idiot!'

And Fabián's indiscreet response: 'You said we didn't need him anymore. You said he probably didn't even know Trigeño.'

So Palillo had been right all along.

I led Camila around the edge of the sparkling pool, stopping briefly at Colonel Buitrago's table. I was now angry at him. He shunned me for being an Autodefensa when *he*, an upstanding officer in the national army, was at a party hosted by men he surely knew were *narcotraficantes*.

'If it's money you need,' I said, 'there's about a million dollars upstairs in the safe. I believe you have the combination.'

I no longer cared if he knew we had the files. It might be another wake-up call for him and a spur to action. Because as long as he refused to get the job done, other men would have to do it for him.

I dragged Camila past the crowd of stylish guests, thankful not to see her parents or my mother, down the gravel driveway and through the gates. Even though I'd rescued her, Camila wanted to go back. She was high on cocaine and drunk, and that made her sarcastic and insulting. She'd never mocked me before. But she began mocking me now.

'Yes, Pedro, I'm fifteen. But you're sixteen and *so* mature! Where do you think you're taking me?'

'Home.'

'*¡Fantástico!* On your bicycle? I'll sit on the handlebars.'

'We'll take a taxi from the plaza.'

'And drive past the Guerrilla roadblock? Very clever. I hope you have your gun?'

I released her wrist.

'You want to go back? Fine. Go!'

I escorted her safely inside the security gates before stomping downhill towards the town, booting pebbles and swearing and cursing.

I tossed and turned all night seething and thinking about Camila. I knew her parents would ensure she reached home safely, but in the meantime she was still at the party.

After the scene I'd caused and Javier's reprimand, I doubted Fabián would try anything more with Camila. But she'd keep talking to his handsome, drug-dealing friends in that beautiful green dress that showed her cleavage. They might ask for her phone number. After I'd left Garbanzos, they might invite her to the big city, picking her up in one of their helicopters. And the next party she attended, I wouldn't be there. If Camila decided to try cocaine again, I wouldn't be there to stop her.

PART SIX

THE BATTLE OF JAGUAR RIVER

87

AFTER A SLEEPLESS night, I phoned Camila's house at 9 am, hoping to make peace. Even though Camila had behaved irresponsibly, I'd overreacted with jealousy. But there was no answer. I tried her cell phone and left a message, but signal coverage in Llorona was weak and I doubted she'd get it. Determined to make amends, I decided to visit her.

I was unlocking my bicycle when my phone rang – a blocked number. I expected it to be Camila returning my calls from a Telecom cabin. Instead, to my surprise, Culebra's voice came on.

'You need to get back here now.'

'What's happened?'

'Our cousins found your boat and its owner.'

Culebra was being deliberately cryptic – probably because of Trigeño's paranoia about telephone intercepts. But I realised immediately that by 'cousins' he meant the army. They'd captured the boat driver who had helped the Guerrilla escape after our skirmish.

'The boat has a recent repair to the bow, but our cousins need one hundred per cent certainty that the owner is the man you saw.'

Since the suspect was a civilian, the army was playing strictly by law; they needed me to identify him.

'There's a bus departing this afternoon.'

'No, this is urgent. I'm sending Jerónimo. Be in the plaza in twenty minutes.'

I hurled my clothes into my bag, hid the Galil and binoculars behind a pile of old timber in Uncle's yard and called Camila, again without success. This time there truly was a work emergency, but she'd never believe me.

Don Jerónimo pulled up in the same dark-windowed SUV with the same statuette of Jesus hanging from his rear-view mirror.

'Look at you!' he exclaimed. 'All grown up! You must be important to deserve a pre-paid pick-up.'

As we sped along the highway towards Villavicencio airport to collect Palillo, who'd also been recalled as a witness, Jerónimo was friendly and talkative, but I was in no mood for socialising. Eventually, when I remained unresponsive, he switched on the radio.

It was 1 am when Jerónimo, Palillo and I finally arrived at the metal gates of the Puerto Bontón army garrison. A serious-looking greeting party awaited us next to the floodlit guard's booth.

Beta stood in the glare of the car's headlights with his arms folded. Alfa 1 was pacing and smoking. A dark figure stepped briskly out of the shadow of a tree. It was General Itagüí.

The last time I'd seen him he'd considered me a *muchacho* barely worthy of eye contact. Now he shook my hand as he slid into the seat beside me.

'Pedro, thanks for cutting short your leave.'

I exchanged uneasy glances with Palillo. Until then, I'd assumed identifying the boat driver would be a mere formality. But it must have been something far more serious if it had kept a three-star general waiting until after midnight and persuaded him to allow the Autodefensas onto his base at a time of politically sensitive peace talks.

Judging by the orderliness of his base, the general was a strict man who ran a tight ship. The garrison was peaceful. Rotating sprinklers sprayed fine mist onto the lawn and two soldiers patrolled with a German shepherd. Jerónimo drove us slowly along a narrow asphalt drive bordered by white-painted rocks and neatly arranged flowerbeds.

We stopped beside a brick building with a sloping tin roof. Two guards saluted the general. A grave-faced Lieutenant Alejandro appeared and dismissed Jerónimo. Then he gave us a short briefing.

'Yesterday, one of our boat patrolmen noticed a green vessel matching your description pulled up on the riverbank near Puerto Pescador. A hole in the bow had been recently sealed with resin. We identified the boat's owner and raided his house before dawn, taking him captive. But we need you to confirm that he's the man you saw.'

'Is this necessary?' interrupted Beta impatiently. 'The prisoner has admitted to owning the boat and repairing the bullet hole. End of story.'

'The suspect is a civilian. And he denies knowledge of how the damage occurred.'

'I didn't see the boat driver's face,' Palillo said. 'I only saw him from behind.'

'But you saw the boat.' Alejandro shone his torch onto a photo of a green *lancha*, which he handed to Palillo. 'Is this it?'

Palillo studied it carefully. 'It's the same colour and size, with the same motor. And the repair is exactly where the bullet struck. But I can't swear it's the same boat.'

This meant that identifying the man would be solely up to me. Alejandro heaved open the heavy door and used his torch to lead us down a dark staircase that stank of urine. My hands slid along the cold handrail and my knuckles brushed slimy bricks. From behind me, Palillo squeezed my shoulder. He'd offered to look at the prisoner anyway, in case seeing him triggered recognition, but I knew he was really coming as a gesture of solidarity.

At the bottom of the stairs, one of the guards flicked on a light, illuminating a corridor with four metal doors. Alejandro slid back an observation hatch in one door and gestured for me to look through it.

Inside, a single bulb lit up a bare concrete holding cell. A man lay curled on a thin mattress under a brown blanket.

The two guards entered the cell, gagged the prisoner, lifted him by his armpits and dragged him to where I stood in the doorway.

'Well?' said General Itagüí, his hands on his hips. 'Is it him?'

'A simple yes will do,' said Beta.

'If you're not sure,' warned Alfa 1, 'they'll have to release him.'

The man was now only an arm's length away and must have guessed why I was there, because he began begging me with his eyes and making desperate, inarticulate sounds into his gag.

I'd expected either an instant jolt of recognition or to be sure I'd never seen this person before in my life, but I experienced neither. Three weeks had passed. And I'd only seen the boat driver for a few seconds through binoculars.

'Can I see his whole face?'

Alejandro sighed and then nodded for the gag to be untied. Immediately, I understood the reason for his reluctance.

'I own five identical boats that I rent out,' blurted out the prisoner. 'I don't remember who used that particular boat that day. I fixed the hole but thought nothing of it because my boats get damaged all the time—'

'Cover his mouth!' ordered Alejandro angrily before turning to me. 'Well?'

'I need a moment.'

I now wished that they'd never removed his gag. Knowing the facts for and against him, my mind turned to the likelihood of his guilt. If he'd rented out his boat only three weeks ago, wouldn't he remember to whom? Wouldn't he at least offer up a list of possible names?

On the other hand, if he were guilty, wouldn't he have sold the boat? Or at least painted the vessel so the repair wouldn't be obvious?

I stepped away to confer with Palillo.

'I know you want it to be him,' he whispered, 'but tell the truth. That you don't know.' I understood Palillo's reasons for siding with the boat driver. His own father had driven boats and was killed by the Guerrilla following a false accusation.

'What if he's guilty and they let him go?' I whispered back. I turned to Lieutenant Alejandro. 'Does his family know he's here?'

'He's single and lives alone,' said Alejandro. 'No one knows he's here.'

If I said yes and the suspect was innocent, he would spend thirty days isolated in this holding cell being interrogated by the army. But the fact that he didn't have a wife and children at home worrying about his disappearance meant he'd be the only one affected by my decision. On the other hand, if the man was guilty, he might lead us to Santiago.

I later realised the significance of the choice I made that night, but at the time I was simply tired and hungry, stressed from the previous night's fight with Camila and, most of all, frustrated at not getting Zorrillo.

'It's him,' I said.

'Good!' exclaimed Beta. Then he barked at the guards: 'Throw him in the Blazer.'

'What?'

'This *guerrillero* son of a *puta* is coming with us.'

It took several moments to process what was happening, and when I did, I froze in disbelief, my stomach sinking and my skin crawling. The boat driver would not spend thirty days with the army; they were handing him straight over to the Autodefensas.

'But . . . why not keep him here?'

'This investigation is time-sensitive,' answered Alfa 1.

Alejandro clarified: 'Once the Guerrilla notice his absence, they'll flee and any information he gives on this case will be outdated.'

Beta was far blunter: 'A proper interrogation needs to occur immediately.'

Alejandro called it a 'case'. Alfa 1 used the word 'investigation'. Beta said it was an 'interrogation'. But my heart filled with dread at the events I'd just set in motion: what all three of them meant was torture.

88

ALL THE WAY back to La 50, I was reeling with shock. Palillo's angry glare made it worse. He shook his head at me, as if to say I should recant my claim. But it was too late for that. I'd made my decision and couldn't have taken it back even if I'd begged. Worse still, I had to listen to the thumping and kicking of the bound, gagged and blindfolded prisoner in the back of the Blazer.

When we arrived at 2 am, we were greeted at the gate by two members of Beta's hand-picked 'intelligence-gathering' team. Beta drove us past the newly constructed dormitories, where Culebra's one hundred and seventy fresh recruits were sleeping, and uphill to the new holding cell, which had also been completed in my absence.

The bunker jutted out of the hillside fifty metres from the dormitory where Palillo and I would sleep. Electricity wasn't yet connected, but otherwise the bunker was ready to receive its first inmate.

I shuddered as Beta's two assistants took hold of the prisoner's arms and lifted him out of the Blazer. The boat driver thrashed as fiercely as a freshly caught fish. He had to be dragged over the last few metres of stony ground and into the cell.

'Bring batteries and a voice recorder,' Beta ordered a third assistant. 'And fill that barrel with water.'

I headed downhill, my stomach queasy. *What's done is done*, I told myself.

Palillo was no longer speaking to me. We were the only two in the dormitory but he lay in his hammock and turned his back.

It was a warm, still night, which allowed sound to carry. When I heard the first blood-curdling scream, I reached for the yellow foam earplugs that we used on the rifle range. Palillo rolled over, slapped the earplugs to the floor and finally spoke his mind.

'You caused this,' he said. 'If you don't want to go in and watch, you can at least have the fucking *cojones* to listen.'

'I never meant for this to happen. I thought the army would keep him.'

'That's not the point. You lied. The Pedro I grew up with would never have lied like that.'

'Then you're saying I should stop them,' I said, twisting out of my hammock. But Palillo came after me, grabbing my shoulder and jerking me back.

'Don't!' he said as a second agonised scream pierced the air. 'That's a dead man you're hearing.'

I stood with Palillo, leaning against the doorframe, listening. A dim light now shone from under the bunker door. I noticed several extension cords running from the kitchen. There were muffled moans, followed by wailing – 'No, no, no!' – and crying.

The prisoner's screams echoed through my body. Were they applying electrical cables to his wet skin or holding his head underwater in that barrel until he sucked water into his lungs? Were they cutting him with a scalpel and then sewing up his wounds to prolong his agony?

I knew Palillo was right. Innocent or guilty, the boat owner would never be allowed to walk free. I'd condemned a man to be tortured to death.

After two more hours and four more earth-shattering screams, Beta emerged from his bunker for a coffee break.

'Has he confessed?' I asked, striding across the grass.

Beta shook his head. 'He's a tough *cliente*. But some people take time.'

'Then what's happening in there?'

'The Law of War is what's happening.'

I was already familiar with the Law of Silence. Now I was learning how to break that silence, and it was called the Law of War. When Beta read the anxiety in my face, he splashed the dregs from his cup onto the ground.

'Either come in and help, or go to bed. It's too late to be developing a conscience, soldier.'

I returned to my hammock, but sleep was impossible. Instead, I prayed that the man was guilty. That was the only thing that could justify what I'd done. After another scream – by far the loudest of the night – there was a lengthy silence and I changed my prayer.

'Please, God, let him die. End his suffering. *Please*!'

However, if I'm completely honest, it was more my own suffering I wanted to end.

When the first traces of murky light seeped through our doorway, I was delirious with tiredness. But at least the screams had stopped. I must have drifted off to sleep because I awoke to Alfa 1 shaking my foot.

I sat up in my hammock. 'Is he dead?'

He smiled. 'Put on your boots! I think you need to come and hear this for yourself.'

With Alfa 1 beside me, I entered the bunker. The only light inside came from early-morning rays streaming through the doorway behind us. The prisoner lay motionless on a stained mattress, covered with a blanket.

He was facedown with his limbs spread-eagled and four thick ropes tied to his wrists and ankles. Three of the ropes extended to heavy metal hooks embedded in the walls, presumably designed to limit his struggles. However, the prisoner's convulsions must have been titanic because the fourth hook lay on the floor in a pile of concrete dust and brick chunks.

'Lift the blanket,' ordered Alfa 1.

If not dead, I at least expected the prisoner to be battered, bruised and bleeding. But when I slowly peeled back one corner of the blanket, wincing, he was snoring peacefully and there was no blood. Only then did I notice the half-eaten steak on a plate beside him. There was also an empty mug, and packets of painkillers and sleeping tablets.

'He's still alive?'

'For the moment,' said Alfa 1.

The man was wearing only boxer shorts. Clearly visible on his naked skin were six large, red triangular-shaped welts: two on the back of each thigh and two larger ones in the middle of his back containing tiny white dots. I smelled scorched flesh and looked around for what they'd used to burn him.

My gaze followed the extension cord to its end, where it was connected to an electric clothes iron. The tiny circles on the man's skin mirrored the iron's steam outlets.

Alfa 1 kicked the prisoner in the ribs. He wakened, propped himself drowsily onto one elbow and looked up at us. There were two more triangles – one on his cheek and one in the centre of his forehead.

'I'm sorry,' I gasped as the man blinked and recognised me from the barracks.

'Don't be,' said Alfa 1. 'He had a choice. He could have co-operated. But instead he chose to lie to us for over three hours.' He booted the prisoner's ribs again. 'Tell him!'

The man's eyelids drooped as he looked at me. 'You were right. That was me you saw in the boat. I work for the Guerrilla.'

Alfa 1 filled the prisoner's mug with water and led the way outside. There, he summarised everything Beta had taped on the voice recorder during the interrogation. As it turned out, the innocent civilian boat driver was not so innocent after all.

The boat driver wasn't a Guerrilla soldier, but he drove riverboats for them and they paid him handsomely. He also ran a legitimate boat-hire business as a front, although he made little money from that, and he lived humbly, like the other inhabitants of Puerto Pescador, so no one would suspect.

Several times a week, he transported Guerrilla supplies to the camp. Mostly his cargo consisted of food and other provisions such as batteries, toiletries, oil, salt and medicine. There were tanks of diesel for powering the generators and barrels of outboard gasoline for the Guerrilla boats located further upriver.

Sometimes he transported bales of cocaine and garbage bags full of cash. And occasionally he carried passengers: a squad that needed to move quickly, or a mid-level commander travelling incognito. He'd delivered Proof of Life videos downriver and letters from the hostages' families back to the camp. Once, he'd even transported five hostages – lying flat on the bottom of the boat under a tarpaulin – right past the army checkpoint.

The boat driver confirmed the existence of a large Guerrilla base belonging to Santiago near the Venezuelan border. It had been there for five years and, judging by the cement, nails and wire he'd delivered in the first twelve months, it had taken a year to construct.

'Based on the weight of food delivered weekly, the camp must house at least three hundred soldiers,' Alfa 1 concluded. 'Possibly more if this man isn't their only supplier.'

Although the boat driver had been close to the camp, he'd never been inside. On a map, he identified four locations where he parked on the riverbank. Each time, a team of *guerrilleros* would quickly unload his cargo then send him further upstream into smaller tributaries to fool the US satellites and spy planes.

'That took five hours to tell?' I asked Alfa 1.

'Two. For the first three he resisted. Only after the second burn to his face did he confess.'

The man also gave up the names of men who drove trucks for the Guerrilla, a driver of gasoline tankers who siphoned off petroleum for them and companies that sold them food. He even offered to take Beta to some buried Guerrilla money – hundreds of thousands of dollars, proceeds from cocaine sales and ransom payments.

Alfa 1 patted me on the back, opened the door slightly, and we peered in at the boat driver. 'I know you weren't sure about this. But you did right, Pedro.'

The man was snoring once more. Knowing what he'd done, I no longer pitied him. True, he hadn't killed anyone – he didn't even carry a gun – but he'd betrayed his country for cash. And all around Colombia there were many more like him, profiting from other people's misery. I was almost glad he'd tasted a few hours of suffering.

'What will happen to him?' I asked.

'He'll spend a few more days with Beta. After five years working with the Guerrilla, he must have plenty more to tell. Then, if his stories check out, he'll live. When the time comes, he'll be the guide to Santiago's camp.'

'When will we attack?'

'It could be weeks, maybe months. This is only the first step.'

When Beta returned with his two assistants, Alfa 1 ordered them to get the prisoner antibiotics.

'And maybe some magazines and a television,' he added. 'He has a long wait ahead of him.'

'He's a fucking *guerrillero*!' Beta exclaimed. 'Why give him privileges?'

'Because we're not tyrants.'

Alfa 1 didn't see himself as a tyrant. Nor did I see myself as one. Nevertheless, bit by bit, I was becoming more like my commanders.

The previous night, by fingering a civilian for interrogation without being certain of his guilt, I'd stepped across a line. Now, after deciding the boat driver deserved it, I looked behind me and that line had vanished. And when I turned and looked to the future, I knew the lines ahead of me would be easier and easier to cross.

89

ALFA 1 WANTED ME to attend a meeting that was to be held as soon as Trigeño arrived by helicopter. In the meantime, I returned to the dormitory, where I found Palillo throwing movie punches and rehearsing lines in front of the mirror.

'You still angry with me?' I asked.

'Was he guilty?'

'Yes.'

'Then, no, I'm not.'

'So what's wrong?'

Palillo nodded to a postcard he'd tucked into the folds of his hammock. It was from his eldest sister, who was twelve, and had been delivered while we were away. In it, she'd mentioned that his stepfather's drinking was becoming worse.

Palillo threw another punch, flexed his muscles and then sized himself up in the mirror. 'My mother will never leave him.'

'Why not?'

'Lack of money.'

Every time there was trouble at home, Palillo fantasised about being rich and famous. Money would buy him safety, comfort and the power to help his mother and five siblings. But what he really wanted was for his stepfather, Diomedes, to disappear from their lives.

'I honestly think I could kill him,' said Palillo, striking the wall. I guessed the only thing stopping him was concern over how his mother would live afterwards with so many mouths to feed. Otherwise, I was sure Diomedes would be top of his 'to do' list.

I knew that Ñoño also harboured dreams of saving his mother from his father and faced the same obstacle: money.

'When I've saved up enough I'll buy my mother a house far away,' Ñoño had told me. 'And if my father interferes I'll know how to deal with him. Even the finest *machetero* is no match for a bullet.'

Palillo stopped throwing shadow punches and tossed me my cell phone. 'This has been ringing constantly.' There were several missed calls from both Mamá and Camila. I stepped outside and phoned Mamá first.

Mamá said nothing about my leaving town suddenly. Obviously, no one had told her about my storming out of the party or my argument with Camila.

'I'm so glad you met Eleonora and talked to her sons. Javier asked me to tell you he's sorry your conversation was cut short. He says that if you're ever interested in working closer to home, he'd be happy to assist.'

Javier had at least been subtle, but after the disastrous fiesta I had no interest in further contact with him or anyone else from his family.

Next, I phoned Camila. I explained my work 'emergency' and apologised for my overreaction, expecting her to do the same. Instead, she immediately went on the attack.

'What got into you, Pedro, dragging me out by the wrist like that? You've never laid a hand on me before.'

'You were drunk. I was trying to protect you.'

'Protect me from what? Fabián was the host. Nothing happened.'

'What do you mean *nothing happened*? They were giving you cocaine. Do you know what that shit is doing to our country? Where do you think the Guerrilla get their funding from?'

'It was only a little bit,' she said defensively. 'Besides, I don't need a jealous boyfriend embarrassing me in public. I'm fifteen. I can do what I want.'

Until then, I'd taken her reprimands and insults patiently, like a boxer trained to absorb body punches. But now I lost my patience and lashed out.

'Not if it's dangerous. And not if it makes you rude and selfish. You're the one who invited me to that party. In fact, you insisted I go. Then you disappear without telling me and I find you in a locked room with Fabián. How do you think that made me feel?'

Camila was silent for a moment. 'You're right,' she said at last, chastened. 'I shouldn't have left you alone like that. And I shouldn't have said those horrible things. I was angry, but it was totally wrong of me.' She sniffed. 'It's just . . . after what happened at the roadblock I wanted to forget everything . . . I do love you, Pedro. I'm sorry.'

I softened. 'Gracias, *amor*. But I need to ask one thing: did you give him your number?'

'He asked, and I refused. But I did give it to Andrea – the newsreader,' she added with a touch of defiance. 'I might need contacts when I'm in Bogotá.'

'Bogotá?'

'You never asked me how I did in my exams, but I came top of my class. My teacher says I should apply for an early admission scholarship next year. The *Nacional* university has places for students from rural areas.'

I was silent. I'd always known Camila wanted to leave Llorona. But whenever she'd spoken previously about moving to the capital, it had always been in terms of *us*. Her dream was for us to live together, sleeping on the floor of a rented room while scrimping and saving to get by. But now she spoke in terms of *her*.

Her voice brightened. 'Living in Bogotá will be great! There's a suburb called *La Candelaria* with artists, theatre festivals and galleries. You can visit me whenever you like . . .'

Of course, the possibility of Camila attending university was a long way off. The application date was months away, and the university semester wouldn't start for a year and a half. That was assuming she actually won the scholarship and that her father could help with living expenses. Nevertheless, it scared me to think of Camila beginning a new life that I wasn't part of.

'That's great, *amor*. I'll cross my fingers you get it.'

Our relationship was changing – it was becoming more on her terms – but I didn't want to lose her. Nor did I want her going to Bogotá on her own, or with Andrea and Fabián, which meant I had to track down Papá's killers faster. And with the boat driver's confession and Trigeño's military briefing about to begin, that was now a real possibility.

Fifteen senior commanders attended the briefing with Trigeño in the new office. I was the only junior commander present. Arguments erupted over what to do with the boat driver's information, although everyone agreed we had to act quickly before the Guerrilla noticed his absence.

'Let's intercept the food and gasoline trucks, shoot the drivers and leave their bodies by the side of the road,' said Beta. 'We'll torch the boat driver's house and five boats to send a message to other Guerrilla collaborators.'

Alfa 1 preferred a more measured approach. 'We should occupy Puerto Pescador and set up a roadblock to prevent supplies getting through to Santiago's camp. We'll weaken them before launching an attack. As for the boats, we should confiscate them and use them ourselves to patrol the river.'

Trigeño waited for his senior commanders to finish.

'We'll do none of that,' he stated quietly. 'The base is close to the Venezuelan border, so cutting off their supplies from this side won't starve them.'

In army circles, it was an open secret that the socialist government in Venezuela had long supported the communist insurgency in Colombia. The border was porous: weapons, munitions and supplies flowed one way from Venezuela; cash and cocaine flowed the other way as payment.

Trigeño had developed a plan, which he now outlined to us.

First, we'd transport the boat driver to Bogotá, from where he'd phone his girlfriend and say he was away visiting a supplier. The Bogotá number would be recorded in her telephone billing. He'd then apply for a passport. A one-way ticket to Costa Rica would be purchased in his name and someone would be paid to impersonate him and take the flight. Meanwhile, Beta's men would secretly visit his house to pack clothes and valuables. Under cover of darkness, they'd also dig up the Guerrilla's crate of cash.

The Guerrilla had IT experts and intelligence operatives embedded in phone companies, airlines and government agencies. All clues would point to the boat driver absconding with their money.

'The operation against Santiago needs to be covert,' explained Trigeño. 'Otherwise he'll flee, evacuate his troops and move the base. The Guerrilla will be looking for signs the boat driver has talked. But when there are no raids and no arrests, they'll relax. Of course, they'll change their codes and personnel as a precaution. But after that, we want them to go back to business as usual.'

'So we keep quiet,' said Alfa 1, folding his arms. 'Then what?'

'Phone your army friends. The army can use its one advantage – air power. Once we've pinpointed the base's location . . .' Trigeño paused dramatically. 'Boom! A five hundred pound MX-82 bomb will leave a crater the size of a football field. Santiago won't know what hit him.'

The other commanders seemed impressed, relieved even, murmuring among themselves and nodding enthusiastically. Bombing the base would inflict maximum casualties on the enemy with no risk to us.

However, I was disappointed – Santiago's death would be quick. I'd have no chance to interrogate him about how to find Papá's other killers. And I wanted Santiago to look into my eyes and understand why he had to die.

But when Lieutenant Alejandro arrived in response to Alfa 1's phone call, he dismissed Trigeño's plan.

'The generals will never authorise bombing,' he said. 'We're still in peace talks. Plus we're negotiating billions of dollars in aid from the EU and the

US government to fight drug trafficking. A bomb dropped on the border of Venezuela would be disastrous. We can provide aerial surveillance, radio communications intercepts and photographic data from US satellites, but you'll have to amass your own ground forces and go in yourselves.'

Trigeño kept his temper tightly controlled. 'So you want the victory, but the bloodshed will be ours?'

'The army will do its part,' the lieutenant said crisply. 'For one thing, we can help you determine the camp's coordinates.'

We all looked at the large map pinned to the corkboard. The boat driver's information had narrowed the likely location to a six-by-six-kilometre area right on the Venezuelan border. However, it wasn't possible to plan a coordinated attack on thirty-six square kilometres of dense jungle.

'How?'

'With a state-of-the art satellite transponder. The police can detain a Guerrilla truck driver, secretly insert it into his supplies and wait for it to reach the camp.'

Beta shook his head. 'The boat driver says everything is scanned daily by electromagnetic detectors.'

'Then we'll send in a *zorro solo*.'

'*Zorro solo*' literally translates as 'lone fox'. I imagined some kind of remote-controlled robot disguised as a furry mammal with a camera inside. But Alfa 1 later explained to me that *zorro solos* were highly disciplined, elite soldiers with special training in hand-to-hand combat, physical endurance, jungle survival and psychological control.

A *zorro solo* is taught to detect and disarm anti-personnel mines and crawl over trip-wires. To build up his tolerance for pain, he is covered with fire ants and not allowed to scream or scratch. Camouflaged, he can survive up to two months in the jungle, eating berries, fruit, tree roots and wild animals – anything he can find or kill.

Wearing only black boxer shorts and with his body covered in burned motor grease so that no skin pigment shows, he is inserted secretly into the jungle with a plastic-bladed knife and two energy bars for emergencies. His mission: to penetrate the Guerrilla's defences, gather intelligence and sometimes carry out acts of sabotage.

Trigeño nodded his agreement to Alejandro and then stood to give his final orders.

'Contact the commanders from other regions and ask them to lend us troops. We'll amass eight hundred soldiers, while our generous cousins here contribute *one*. We pinpoint the camp and study its defences. We plan and simulate an attack. And we obtain confirmation that Santiago is present. I'll leave the details up to you, Alfa 1.'

Trigeño strolled from the room and Alfa 1 dismissed us with a jerk of his head. He, too, was annoyed at how little help the army had offered.

As for me, a ground force attack renewed my hopes for getting proper justice against Santiago. Nevertheless, I was dead tired. As I trudged towards the dormitory, my limbs felt like concrete and my eyelids like lead weights. I rounded the shower block and Trigeño stepped in front of me, blocking my path.

'Pedro! The boy with the eagle eyes and viper tattoo. Walk with me!'

I froze, instantly wary. I'd been the most junior commander in the room. What could he possibly want with me? Falling into step beside him, I wondered nervously whether this 'walk' was an interview, a friendly stroll or an interrogation. Had he somehow heard about my mentioning the intelligence files to Buitrago at the Díaz fiesta?

As Trigeño led me along La Quebrada, I looked behind me for reassurance that someone had at least witnessed my departure.

But the sight of ten heavily armed bodyguards trailing us closely only exacerbated my unease.

90

TRIGEÑO STRODE ALONG the creek bed in silence, although I knew he must have had some purpose. He wasn't a man who wasted time. He worked until midnight and kept a laptop nearby at all times, 'in case he had a spare moment to do some work'.

Finally, he stopped beside the small, peaceful pool above La Quebrada.

'You know, Pedro, if you hadn't shot those two enemies and identified the boat driver, none of that briefing would have been possible.'

'*Gracias.*' I blushed, glad to be recognised.

'You're from Llorona?'

'Yes, *comando*.'

'We had plans to enter it three years ago but they came to nothing. And now the Guerrilla are too strong. We'd have to launch a large-scale invasion and I'm a poor soldier, not a banker. Besides, there's one stubborn man who refuses to collaborate.' He studied my face. 'Do you know Colonel Buitrago?'

'He and Papá were friends,' I answered hesitantly. 'I gave him my witness statement after Papá was executed by—'

'Caraquemada and Zorrillo, who received orders from Santiago. You want all of them dead.'

Astonished, I stared at him.

'I studied your personnel file and Alfa 1 told me about your little deal . . . and your recent request.' He handed me a velvet pouch containing a Bushnell 6500 – a zoom scope with nine times magnification that affixes to most rifles. 'However, a telescopic scope is of no use without professional training. We're conducting an advanced sniper training course in a few months – I want you to be a part of it.'

I could hardly hide my delight. 'Thank you, *comando*!'

'Santiago's base will be protected by expert snipers. We'll need sharpshooters too.' Trigeño waved to his head bodyguard, and his three-vehicle security caravan roared towards us. 'Once you're trained, you'll receive a salary increase. And if there's anything else you need, feel free to ask.'

I immediately thought of Palillo.

'*Comando* . . .' I began cautiously. 'There *is* something – actually, two things.' He raised his eyebrows and I felt heat rushing to my cheeks. 'When I shot those two *guerrilleros*, Palillo was beside me with binoculars. He reported where the bullets struck and that allowed me to adjust my aim. We've always been a team.'

'And the other thing?'

'Ñoño. He's only a kid but he's as brave as men twice his age. If given an opportunity . . .'

Trigeño opened the car door and nodded his farewell. 'Consider it done.'

I assumed Palillo would be grateful that I'd recommended him for the advanced course. But he was livid that I was bringing him closer to Trigeño.

'He's a psychopath. Have you forgotten Tango and Murgas? One wrong move and that could happen to us.'

'But I thought you needed extra money for your family. And I wanted us to stick together.'

'And then what? After sniper training, do you think they'll pay us to sit around watching movies?'

Palillo was content patrolling cow paddocks, receiving three free meals a day and a monthly pay packet, and enjoying quarterly leave. Being promoted would entail greater responsibility and bring him a step closer to the front line.

I'd deliberated over which aspects of my visit home to share with Palillo. My sightings of Zorrillo and Buitre would only worry him. Instead, I told him how Fabián had given Camila cocaine at the fiesta.

'The Díaz brothers are bad news,' Palillo said. 'Steer clear of those two.'

'I can't avoid them entirely. Mamá is living with them.'

'*What*?'

I explained how my mother had received the letter from the Guerrilla. Palillo was dismayed, but at least it caused him to back off a little.

After a few days he calmed down and settled into a contented rhythm. He did, however, remain sceptical of Trigeño. And a week later, his scepticism seemed justified.

Trigeño hated cocaine and *narcotraficantes* almost as much as he hated communism and the Guerrilla. According to him, the two went hand in hand.

'Traffickers are the scourge of Colombia,' he said, addressing us all during an evening political lecture at La 50. 'Cocaine corrupts every person it touches: senators, judges, lawyers, bankers and ordinary citizens. The easy money creates laziness and lawlessness. Field workers become accustomed to quick cash; women become prostitutes. Peasant farmers rip up their traditional food crops and plant coca seeds instead, leading to food shortages and rising prices.'

Ñoño raised his hand to ask how exactly the Guerrilla was involved.

'Traffickers need to be protected from the government and from us. The Guerrilla act like a private army, posting sentinels to guard coca leaf pickers while they work, and positioning machine guns at the edges of fields to shoot down the US fumigation planes sent to destroy the crops. Guerrilla soldiers guard jungle laboratories and markets in small villages where cocaine is traded. Of course, they claim they do this to protect coca farmers' rights. But it's really so they can collect taxes: ten per cent from buyers, ten per cent from sellers, ten per cent for precursor chemicals entering their territory, and a set fee for every kilo of crystal that goes out. An army of twenty thousand men requires funding. But if we destroy their trade, it'll be like switching off their life-support system.'

In accordance with Trigeño's instructions, civilians caught taking drugs were given a three-day grace period to leave town. However, for those who *trafficked* in drugs, the penalties were severe.

Violent proof of Trigeño's hard-line policy was not long in coming. The boat driver provided Beta's intelligence team with the name of a pig-truck driver who'd delivered cocaine to him for transportation along Guerrilla-controlled rivers and the truck driver in turn gave up his boss, Giraldo Gil, a farmer who lived on the outskirts of Trigeño's protectorate.

When Beta's platoon surrounded the farmhouse, they were surprised at what lay behind the crumbling walls of the dilapidated estate: an elaborate security system with four CCTVs, electrified fences and two patrolling guards who were easily persuaded to lay down their shotguns.

It was a Sunday and Giraldo Gil was eating lunch with his two younger brothers. Beta brought in all three for questioning. For a week, the Gil brothers and the pig-truck driver were accommodated in Beta's bunker, which now boasted two extra rooms.

The following Sunday, when Trigeño arrived, Beta led the four men out into the sunlight and tied them to separate wooden poles.

All three brothers were of the same stocky build, slightly overweight with short hair and a week's facial growth. The dark circles under their eyes told of sleeplessness and stress, but since all had talked frankly, none had been tortured. Nevertheless, Beta had El Psycho at the ready.

'I believe them,' Beta reported to Trigeño. 'But if they've told the smallest lie, this genius will gouge it out of them.'

Trigeño raised a palm. 'That won't be necessary. What's their story?'

Beta described how, for fifteen years, the truck driver had worked for the brothers' father, a humble pig farmer. When he died, the eldest son, Giraldo, inherited the farm. The truck driver hadn't liked it when his new boss required him to transport concealed trays beneath the pig cages and hand them over to the boat driver at Puerto Pescador. He didn't know what the trays contained, although he guessed it must be contraband. But Giraldo said, 'Do it and keep your mouth shut if you want to keep your job and feed your family.'

Giraldo's two younger brothers claimed no knowledge of his illicit business, even though both lived in palatial houses on neighbouring plots of land and drove brand-new SUVs – gifts from Giraldo, who'd also paid for their university educations.

The middle brother, Gentíl, was a recently graduated attorney who supported two children and an ex-wife. He was frightened.

'If you're going to kill me, please let me make one last phone call to my children,' he pleaded.

The youngest brother, Paolo, was an accounting student, unmarried with no children. He, too, was petrified. 'I'm a good Catholic. I'd like a Bible.'

The eldest brother, Giraldo, admitted to trafficking but begged Trigeño to set his brothers free. 'Please! They're innocent.'

Trigeño pointed to the youngest and then the middle brother. 'Get this man a Bible and this one a two-minute conversation with his children. Then kill them.'

While Beta's minions sprinted for a Bible and telephone, the condemned men protested vociferously, 'We've done nothing wrong! You have to believe us.'

Alfa 1 seemed shocked. 'But those two aren't traffickers.'

'They're not a pair of parish priests either. A lawyer and an accountant. Looks like Giraldo was grooming them for his growing empire.'

'*Comando*, you hired me for one reason – to rid the region of communists.'

'And their financial collaborators.'

'Which these two clearly are not.'

'Not *yet*. But how long do you think it would take for one or both of them to slip into their brother's shoes?'

Alfa 1 folded his arms. 'Since when did we start killing people for the crimes they *might* commit?'

Trigeño threw his hands up in exasperation. 'Fine. I won't force you to act against your conscience. Besides, I'd never ask you to do something I wasn't prepared to do myself.' He unholstered his weapon.

'That's not the point. I don't think we should be doing this *at all*.'

Trigeño lowered his weapon and his voice. 'You think I like killing? Well, I don't. But tough decisions require brave men to make them. The millions the Guerrilla make from drug trafficking taxes buy them weapons, food and uniforms. Take away cocaine and it will prevent uneducated *campesino* children from being recruited into their ranks. It will stop the car bombs they explode every week in crowded city streets. It will stop the roadside kidnappings. Defeating the Guerrilla will save countless lives, help poor people find an honest day's work and improve the lives of millions of people.'

Alfa 1 looked down and stabbed the toe of his boot into the dirt. 'I still don't agree.'

'Then there's only one fair way to settle this.' Trigeño removed a 200-peso coin from in his pocket. 'We let God decide. Tails they live. Heads they die.'

I could see Alfa 1 didn't agree with a coin toss as a fair way of administering justice, but he said nothing.

While the younger brother prayed furiously and the middle brother cried over the phone to his ex-wife and children, Trigeño flipped his coin high in the air. It twinkled as it caught the afternoon light and then dropped to the dirt.

Beta peered down at it, delighted. 'Heads it is!'

Without another word, Trigeño shot one brother and then the other in the temple. Both men slumped forward. The Bible given to Paolo thudded to the ground and the phone dropped from Gentíl's lifeless hand with a woman's voice wailing, '*¿Alo? ¿Alo?*'

The eldest brother, Giraldo, turned away with tears streaming down his cheeks.

Alfa 1 was frowning, but Beta hadn't flinched. As Trigeño strode towards his vehicle, Beta called after him and pointed at Giraldo. 'And what do we do with this one, *jefe*?'

Trigeño turned and glanced at El Psycho. 'I need you to send a clear message that will reach every corner of the province: no more trafficking.

We do this once and we do it properly. Then we won't have to do it again.'

'And the truck driver?'

'Drop him at the bus station.' He addressed the driver. 'Keep your mouth shut and find yourself a new employer.'

'*Gracias, jefe,*' the truck driver repeated over and over. '*Mil gracias*, I'll never say a word.'

Beta seemed surprised. 'But he knew he was transporting contraband!'

'We're after mid- and top-level traffickers. That man is a loyal employee with a family to support. Poverty is not a crime.'

I later learned more about Trigeño's political philosophy on cocaine *traficantes*. Not only did he want every last one of them dead, he wanted to exorcise the corruption and black money surrounding the drug industry. As with removing the communist cancer, it was preferable to extract too much of the surrounding tissue than too little, in order to prevent it rejuvenating in the future. He termed this 'preventative justice'. At the same time, he felt empathy for the underclass of workers who were exploited by *traficantes* simply because unemployment was so high in Guerrilla-controlled regions.

Of course, Trigeño doubted the driver would keep his mouth shut. In fact, he hoped he and the disarmed security guards would tell as many people as possible. The driver was witness to not only the Autodefensas' hard-line justice, but also to their capacity for mercy.

'You heard him,' barked Beta to El Psycho as he signalled his minions to release the truck driver, and return Giraldo to the bunker.

El Psycho's work as a maestro of human pain was already infamous. Soldiers avoided him like the plague. They said he was simply *wrong* and *not human* and that you shouldn't look him in the eyes because an evil spirit inhabited his body.

His 'message' utilising the brothers was one of his boldest works. After Giraldo gave up his suppliers, money and trafficking routes under torture, he was shot and the body parts of all three brothers were strewn across Meta-Vichada with dozens of tiny plastic bags of cocaine sewn into the skin. After two days – enough time for the flesh to begin rotting and flies to lay their eggs – the dead men's relatives were sent instructions and had to travel from village to village collecting the body pieces in a trash bag to eventually form the entire cadavers, rather like a treasure hunt combined with a human jigsaw puzzle.

They were then given three days to pack up their homes, finalise their affairs and leave – forever. This ensured complete degradation of the culprits as well as providing a strong deterrent for anyone considering trafficking cocaine. Imagine the psychological effect on locals who saw and smelled the sun-baked body parts infested with flies and maggots and then witnessed the faces of the distressed relatives as they discovered a head in a ditch, an arm in a tree and a leg or a foot tied to a fence post with ants crawling between its bloodied toes. No one would ever consider trafficking drugs after that.

Palillo raised his eyebrows at me as if to say, *I told you so.* But I didn't react.

Witnessing and hearing about these horrific deaths, you might think I'd be scarred for life. But I was quickly becoming inured to violence and the spectacle of blood.

When I applied Trigeño's arguments about preventative justice to my own experience, they were even more compelling. If cocaine trafficking had never been allowed to flourish south of Llorona, the Guerrilla wouldn't have grown so strong and Papá would never have been executed. By killing *narcotraficantes* before they spread into every region of Colombia, how many lives and families were we saving?

When I thought of the brothers' deaths in those terms, the fact that my own actions in identifying the boat driver had started the chain of events that ultimately led to their execution faded into the dark sky.

In fact, as I absorbed Trigeño's Autodefensa philosophy, what had once seemed cruel now seemed completely justified.

91

LESS THAN A week later, in early August, it was time for the boat driver to assist the army's *zorro solo* to penetrate deeply into Santiago's territory with the aim of entering his base. We assumed Trigeño's ruse of sending a man to Costa Rica impersonating the boat driver had succeeded.

As we waited for the *zorro*'s return, the next ten weeks of patrolling passed quickly, without a single skirmish or even an enemy sighting. Thanks to her bravery during the skirmish, Tortuga was now a respected member of the squad. With Veneno gone, Giraldo and Yucca quickly fell into line. As for Ñoño, my mentioning him to Trigeño resulted in him being offered training as a medic.

Coca-Cola returned to us after two months' convalescence. Unfortunately, several bone fragments remained lodged below his knee, making him a liability on long treks. He longed to be an *urbano* – one of the plain-clothes Autodefensas posted permanently in small villages. But since there was no opening at present Trigeño offered him a job as a *punto*, watching the highway with a radio. Coca-Cola accepted.

In late September, Ñoño learned that his aunt – the one who had fed him while he hid under her porch from his machete-wielding father – was sick. Her appendix was inflamed and if it burst she might die. But no hospital would operate without proof of health insurance or an upfront payment that was much more than Ñoño's savings.

'Tell her to phone this number to arrange a pick-up,' Trigeño told him, handing over a slip of paper. 'The driver will take her to Santa Margarita Hospital. Don't worry! Everything's paid for.'

Ñoño was eternally grateful and completely won over by Trigeño's gesture. Even Palillo couldn't deny the obvious benefits of being associated with the highest commander. Via the proper chain of command, he requested permission to conduct a relationship with Piolín, which Alfa 1 granted after talking to Trigeño. Piolín wasn't allowed back into our squad, but whenever their rest weekends coincided, she and Palillo were permitted to share a cabin at La María.

In late October, the recruits who'd begun training in July graduated. I was promoted a second time and given my own platoon – known as a *contra-guerrilla* – which contained four squads of eight men. Palillo and MacGyver were made junior commanders and given leadership of two of the squads under my command.

Before receiving his tattoo, MacGyver got drunk and finally revealed why he'd been sent back to basic training.

'My platoon was ambushed while we were out patrolling in Soap Canyon. The enemy opened fire when we were trekking through a narrow ravine. The fire fight lasted less than an hour. Everyone around me was dead. Amid the smoke, I could hear the *guerrilleros* scrambling closer. So, I took all the rifles I could carry and waded downstream, making my way to safe territory. I thought I'd be given a hero's welcome for saving our rifles from the Guerrilla. But Alfa 1 said an Autodefensa never retreats, and I should have fought to the bitter end.'

MacGyver had been sentenced to a punishment called La Quebrada – the creek. His eyes glistened as he stared into the campfire and described how he was tied to a metal pole – the one we'd always swum out to after the obstacle course – with the water up to his neck. It was raining hard, and the creek rose higher and higher until it reached his lips and he had to stand on tiptoes to breathe.

'Alfa 1 left me there all day and all night. All sorts of thoughts went through my head: the mistakes I'd made in life; the things I wished I'd done; whether my family would find out I was dead; and what I'd say if I could speak to them one last time.'

'But you lived!' I interjected. 'How did you get out?'

'Trigeño heard I was in La Quebrada and ordered me dragged from the water. I was like a half-drowned rat. Another hour, *mi amigo*, and I wouldn't be here. Alfa 1 was furious, but all Trigeño said to me was, "You've now had time to think. I'm sending you back for retraining so you can become a proper soldier." Ever since, I've kept my head down and avoided Alfa 1 like the devil.'

MacGyver paused and his eyes closed. 'Twenty-three boys died in that ambush. Trigeño sent their families their back salaries together with a few thousand dollars extra and a condolence letter, which he signed personally. He was taking a risk putting his name on paper. But he did it, and paid the compensation out of his own pocket, because he thought it was right.'

Hearing this, I was even more convinced Palillo's initial misgivings about Trigeño were wrong. Trigeño had changed the entire region, and everyone who'd met him only told positive stories. Finally, in the second week of November, our advanced training commenced.

While the rest of my platoon continued ordinary patrolling duties, Palillo and I were transported by SUV fifteen kilometres uphill to La 35, Trigeño's personal *finca*. I clutched the pouch containing the Bushnell scope. I'd been playing with it – looking through its zoom – but soon I'd learn how to use it properly.

After passing through three separate heavily fortified cattle gates, we found Trigeño waiting to greet us in front of a dozen rustic wooden dwellings. Beside him were sixteen older-looking soldiers who'd be doing the course with us.

'Welcome!' he said, sweeping his arm across the commanding views behind him. It was the end of the wet season and the verdant valley was covered with bright yellow flowers.

Trigeño explained that this 'satellite farm' had once housed his workers back when La 50 was dedicated to cattle and rice production. Their dwellings were now our dormitories and classrooms. The largest house, where Trigeño now lived, had four permanent guards. Although the agricultural co-operative he ran was profitable, Trigeño lived modestly. He permitted us a brief look at the interior of his house, with its old furniture and faded curtains. One of the farm's buildings stood out as newer than the rest: a wooden chapel embedded in the hillside.

'Those of you who are religious may use the chapel, which I built for my mother. She lives further uphill. And now I must leave you in the capable hands of Alfa 1.'

Alfa 1 leapt onto a rock to address the group. 'What you've seen in Hollywood movies about the lone-wolf sniper who, wearing jeans and a T-shirt, arrives undetected at a perfect position, screws together his rifle in three minutes, takes a one-in-a-million shot, then escapes at a brisk jog with a smirk of satisfaction, is *pura mierda*. It's bullshit, for a start, because there's never one sniper. Snipers go in two-man teams. One is the spotter, the other the shooter, and they swap roles every four hours. It's bullshit because sniper teams need to be in position and fully camouflaged before the target arrives. And it's bullshit because rifle and scope need to be zeroed on a shoot range and left fully assembled for optimal accuracy *before* setting off on an assignment.'

Here he broke off to introduce three bulky, tough-looking men who were standing behind us with their arms folded. These were our three foreign trainers – two Israelis and one Briton – who'd assist Alfa 1, communicating through translators.

'Over the next six weeks,' Alfa 1 continued, 'you'll acquire three primary skill sets: stealth penetrations, positioning and camouflage, and advanced marksmanship. But you'll also learn about leadership, teamwork and communication. Most of you think you already possess those abilities in abundance. This course will therefore serve as a lesson in humility.'

Advanced training was intense. Morning classes involved field craft and weaving ghillie suits – clothing made of burlap designed to resemble heavy foliage – and embellishing them with leaves and twigs from local vegetation. In the afternoons, we learned how to select a concealed shooting position, known as a 'hide', and how to set up ambushes or conduct defensive retreats in shadow. Beta even gave classes on how to resist torture, which included a three-night stint in his bunker being kept awake and yelled at with wet pillowslips tied over our heads.

During our very first practical lesson, Alfa 1 announced that six snipers were concealed within our field of vision. We were divided into two-man teams to scan for potential hides, and I was paired with Palillo. Snatching up my Bushnell scope, I rattled off a list of potential locations where I myself would have hidden.

'It can't be that easy,' whispered Palillo, frowning. Rather than picking up his binoculars, he scanned the nearby ground with his naked eye. However, I ignored him, sure that I was right.

We'd barely handed our lists of hides to Alfa 1, when, all of a sudden, a nearby bush, a rock that Alfa 1 had stood on and a log he'd sat on jumped up and bounded towards us, yelling. Every soldier gasped and threw his hands up for protection. Every soldier, that is, except Palillo, who sat calmly with his legs crossed.

Three sniper teams had been camouflaged the whole time only five metres away.

During his debrief, Alfa 1 gave each team sparing praise before tearing strips off them. 'Despite all you were taught in basic training, you still know nothing! But after basic training your errors could cost only your own lives.

Now that you've attained positions of responsibility, your errors might cost the lives of many others.'

'You may be a good shooter, Pedro,' he growled, ripping up my list. 'But without your spotter, you're nobody. You need to rely on your partner and develop communication that goes beyond words, extending into intuitive understanding.'

That night as I ate dinner, I reflected on what Alfa 1 had said. I knew he was right. No matter how much technical knowledge I absorbed, I failed continually at the most important lesson of leadership: recognising my own weaknesses and trusting that other people's strengths might be enough to compensate for them.

92

WHILE WE TRAINED, Trigeño came and went via helicopter, visiting different parts of the country for meetings, always carrying his laptop. Trailing two paces behind him was a journalist who was putting the finishing touches to a book about his life. Judging by his sycophantic laughter and the fact Trigeño called him *his* journalist, I imagined the portrayal would be favourable.

Trigeño was collaborating on the book because he wanted the AUC to become a publicly recognised political organisation that had articles of association, media spokesmen and, ultimately, representation in Congress. This would end the cycle of fear and allow people to speak out against the Guerrilla. Thanks to the peace process, Santiago and his Guerrilla cohorts were in the spotlight. The Autodefensas needed to give their version too.

On Sunday mornings I prayed in the chapel, often crossing paths with Trigeño's mother, who nodded to me solemnly. Once or twice, Trigeño prayed at the same time. Exiting the chapel, he smiled at me and touched his finger to his necklace, which carried a similar cross to mine. I was surprised that his mother acknowledged me, but not her son. I sensed strong tension between them.

During my free time, I visited La 50 to catch up on news of my platoon members. Culebra's second fast-track course was now in full swing. With a record intake of 250 recruits, La 50 was now an assembly line, the recruits jammed side by side in their hammocks like tinned sardines. Ñoño was completing his first-aid course. Coca-Cola was undergoing physiotherapy for his shattered leg.

Every dawn at La 35 I jogged alone, since that was the time of day at which I did my best thinking. One morning I found Trigeño jogging beside me, with a three-car security convoy trailing behind.

'Where's your journalist?' I asked jokingly, falling into step.

He laughed. 'He can't keep up! Nor can anyone else for that matter.'

I took this as a challenge and matched him stride for stride. At the end of ten kilometres we stopped and doubled over, panting breathlessly beside a slow-flowing creek.

An insect skittered across the water and a large fish surfaced to take it, sending ripples outwards. 'A pirarucu,' I said automatically.

'You fish?' Trigeño asked.

'I used to. Every Sunday with my father.'

'We should fish together one of these days,' he said. 'I keep the dam stocked with bream.'

'Whenever you have time, *comando*.'

Now that I'd ascended to platoon leader, I became privy to the commanders' private conversations and began to notice personality differences that hadn't been obvious during basic training.

A young soldier, Abel, was brought to La 50 with his hands tied. The previous day, on his birthday, he'd gotten drunk by the pool at La María and gone into the local village carrying his rifle to impress a girl he liked. He'd banged loudly on her door, causing her panicked father to phone the *urbano* commander, who captured and disarmed him. Alfa 1 had Abel bound naked in the sun, ready to be executed after three days of *El Soleado*. Trigeño, however, set him free.

'What about the statutes you wrote?' Alfa 1 said quietly to Trigeño at the commanders' dinner table, where we junior commanders were also permitted to sit.

'Relax!' said Trigeño. 'It was the kid's birthday.'

'Every day is someone's birthday,' Alfa 1 mumbled.

Trigeño heard him and retorted loudly, 'You're a hell of a soldier, Alfa 1, but you're also inflexible.'

Inflexible. That was the exact word for Alfa 1. He never wavered; he never bent. But neither did he adapt. I found myself being drawn towards Trigeño and away from Alfa 1's rigid, black-and-white way of thinking.

Beta seemed to delight in these disputes between Alfa 1 and Trigeño. Perhaps he figured that, as third in command, he might one day become their main beneficiary. He was also ambitious and sly. He'd state his opinion if asked, but once his superiors overruled him, he said no more, although he did seem to sulk a little and I noticed the occasional look of resentment cast towards Alfa 1, who was constantly reigning in Beta's violent tendencies.

With Alfa 1 busy overseeing our advanced training, Beta ensured that the recruits' basic course became more vicious and gruesome. Men in civilian clothes were delivered to La 50 blindfolded and gagged. After a week in

Beta's Bunker, they were dragged into the daylight, blinking, burned and beaten. Recruits were told that these men were captured *guerrilleros* and to practise their killing on them, and then their 'chopping and packing'. But I wasn't convinced that they were enemy combatants, particularly since Trigeño wanted the Guerrilla to return to 'business as usual'.

One day a man caught raping a six-year-old girl was brought to camp. Beta strapped him by the torso to an African palm. He tied one end of a rope around the man's stomach and the other end to the Blazer's tow bar, and then sped off, ripping the man in two.

'We have no government prisons out here,' stated Beta, 'but if we did, and that was your daughter, would you pay taxes to feed, clothe and house that bastard?'

His aim was a society with no Guerrilla, no cattle rustlers, no car thieves, no muggers, no drug addicts, no cocaine-traffickers, no rapists and certainly no child molesters.

'We don't want people like that in our community. Think of all the money wasted on courts and prisons for criminals who then get released and reoffend. Wouldn't it be better if those people just . . . disappeared?'

Slowly, I found myself agreeing with him. One day, I planned on having a family with Camila. Men who raped children simply didn't deserve to be alive. Making them *disappear* seemed the right thing to do.

By the end of the third week, I could strip, clean and reassemble my Galil while blindfolded. We'd memorised windage charts, learned to calculate the lag time for a fast-moving target and could estimate a man's distance from us using his crouching, sitting or standing height.

However, as mid-November approached, I began to dread the anniversary of Papá's murder. The day before his anniversary, I felt hollow as I ran my fingers over his photo. Many things had happened in my outside world, but I felt that my inner life hadn't moved forward at all. In fact, it had stagnated back there, exactly 364 days ago.

'You seem upset,' Trigeño said to me between classes. 'Is anything wrong?'

'It's nothing,' I said, looking down at my feet.

'Thinking about your father?'

I nodded, surprised that he'd guessed. 'Tomorrow will mark one year since his death.'

'Then tomorrow morning you will train extra hard to keep your mind occupied. And in the afternoon, we'll do something fun.'

That 'fun' thing was fishing at his dam. Trigeño was a busy man who had meetings with dozens of people every week, and yet he made time for me.

Standing barefoot in the mud, I felt myself relaxing as we fished side by side, overlooking the valley. Throwing out my sinker and then teasing in the line took me back to happier days with Papá. Below us, the lush plains stretched peacefully to the horizon.

Our conversation flowed smoothly. We talked about our common interests. Prayer. Jogging. Our favourite species of fish to catch. I told him about my father's rod, which had both Papá's and my grandfather's initials engraved in the handle. We also talked politics.

For Trigeño, there was one simple test of a political system: whether people wanted to join it or leave.

'You don't see North Americans desperately paddling tyre inner tubes through shark-infested waters to reach Cuba,' he declared.

Finally, as the sun descended, I told him how, following Santiago's radio order, Caraquemada had executed Papá while Buitre held me down. I told him how, because of my hot-headedness, Zorrillo had banned us from our *finca*.

Afterwards, I felt peaceful and lighter, as though expressing the unbearable weight of my pain made it a burden shared.

'But your mother's okay? She has somewhere to stay?'

I nodded cautiously, feeling my cheeks burn. Perhaps I'd been too honest with Trigeño, opening myself up to tricky questions. Having seen what he'd done to two innocent men simply for receiving benefits from their cocaine-trafficking brother, I certainly couldn't let him know that Mamá was staying with Javier Díaz.

Luckily, he didn't press me. Instead, he slipped some cash into my breast pocket. 'Call her and send flowers.'

'*Gracias*,' I mumbled.

'You need to be strong and stay focused, Pedro. Don't let your sadness distract you.'

'I *am* focused. I want Santiago dead. And all Papá's other killers.'

'Then trust me. You'll have your shot at Santiago – I'm sure of it.'

When a man like Trigeño expresses certainty, there is no reason to doubt. His certainty became my certainty, and the anniversary of Papá's death ended calmly with Trigeño and me fishing side by side.

After I returned from fishing, Alfa 1 sent for me. He was alone in his dormitory with two shots of *aguardiente* sitting on the desk before him. His eyes were sparkling, as though they were dancing their own little jig.

'Help me celebrate,' he said, sliding a shot towards me.

'What's the occasion?'

'My no longer being a fugitive.' He raised the shot glass. 'The witness won't testify. So there's no more arrest warrant. Gone!'

'So you know who the witness is?'

'Who the witness *was*.' Alfa 1 made the sign of the cross. Then he laughed. 'A son of a bitch with a mouth bigger than his brain – that's who he was.'

We drank and I felt privileged that he'd chosen me, and me alone, to share this news. In recent months, Alfa 1 had taken me under his wing. Even when he was hardest on me – singling me out for disproportionate and sometimes unfair criticism – I suspected this was also a perverse token of his affection and belief in my potential. He was holding me to a higher standard than the others.

Later, as I opened the door and bade good evening to Alfa 1, I noticed the strange dusk, with the sun and moon out at the same time, inhabiting opposite ends of the sky, and the difference between Trigeño and Alfa 1 struck me starkly.

The two men were loyal allies, intertwined links in a cast-iron chain of command. But Trigeño was a colourful performer, a man of ideas who wanted to take those ideas beyond himself and convince others in order to instigate social change. Alfa 1, on the other hand, was private and solitary. He lived his life in black and white. He judged men by their actions, and his personal sacrifice was his loneliness and a lack of gratitude from others.

Who was the greater man? I wondered as I walked back to my dormitory. Who would I follow, if forced to choose?

Papá wouldn't have liked either of them. *They're killers*, he'd said of the Autodefensas. But then again, I was now a killer too. A precision killer. And at the markets in Puerto Galán on the Sunday before Christmas, Zorrillo would not escape the justice of my bullet.

93

MY VISIT HOME in December was very different to my previous one in July. I arrived by bus on the Monday before Christmas, but Mamá couldn't meet me because she'd accepted work as a cook inside Buitrago's army garrison. She'd also requested more money from me the week before, so my salary would have to stretch.

I sent Camila a text with my hotel and room number. An hour later, she tapped at the door and slipped into the room like a frightened shadow. Instead of joyously launching herself at me, she stepped quietly into my arms and nestled her head under my chin.

'What's wrong?' I asked when she finally released me.

Camila's gaze slid away guiltily. 'I had to tell people we broke up.'

'What?' The news was like a slap in the face. 'Why?'

'Because my brothers found out you're an Autodefensa. Before they left town to find work, they informed Papá. He's furious with you. I had to lie and say we'd had a fight.'

Camila had heard of people quitting the Autodefensas before the obligatory four years of service, and that's what she wanted me to do. 'When I go to university, you can come with me and get a job in Bogotá. I'm sure Fabián would give you a reference.'

'Let's talk about it later, *amor*.'

But there were only so many times I could postpone the inevitable discussion. Camila was still devoted to me, but her patience was wearing thin.

It was 8 pm when Mamá called past my hotel still wearing her blue uniform, having just worked a ten-hour kitchen shift at the army barracks. Her eyelids drooped heavily with exhaustion.

'I can only stay for half an hour, *hijo*,' she said, kissing my forehead. 'Javier's driver is waiting downstairs.'

It was a strange state of affairs. Mamá was working galley-slave hours for a pittance and yet living in a mansion with an armed bodyguard to pick her up. But the extra money wasn't for her; it was for Uncle Leo. His hardware business was in trouble, thanks to a new Guerrilla checkpoint south of Garbanzos.

'No deliveries past this point,' a teenage *guerrillero* had informed Leo the previous month. He'd offered no reason and could not say how long the new policy would last.

Mamá shook her head. 'Without deliveries, half Uncle's business is gone.' She'd given him money to repay his suppliers and even buy groceries.

In fact, the entire region was in the grip of an economic crisis. South of Garbanzos, Caraquemada's unit now controlled everything. Declaring a regional strike, Zorrillo forced *campesinos* to march and chant with placards. He publicised this as 'a peasant-organised rally against environmental damage caused by US crop fumigation', but he fooled no one. Coca was the Guerrilla's cash crop, and he was protecting it.

Nevertheless, his strike was effective. People couldn't get to work. According to the hotel owner, the river towns were the worst affected. But even in Garbanzos plaza, stores were empty. Rather than spend money in restaurants, wives made packed lunches for their husbands, or families skipped meals altogether.

'I'm hungry,' I heard a little girl complain.

'Drink more water,' replied her mother.

Many times, I heard people mention how *la situación* was *mala*. People had stopped openly criticising the culprits. It wasn't the Guerrilla who were bad. It was *the situation*.

The only ones seemingly unaffected were the Díaz brothers. Somehow, their bus routes continued to operate.

What I'd predicted during my last visit was coming true: the peace process wasn't working. Slowly, the Guerrilla were consolidating their power and strangling the local economy. Determined to prove themselves the solution to poverty, they were prepared to become its cause.

After the latest spate of attacks – a daylight kidnap in Llorona and a homicide in Garbanzos plaza – locals were circulating a petition to remove Colonel Buitrago. They wanted a *duro* – a 'hardliner' – to replace him; someone who could protect them, perhaps someone not so opposed to the Autodefensas.

I saw the colonel the day after my arrival, his face tense, striding purposefully through the plaza surrounded by a dozen uniformed men. Since he'd requested I not contact him, I didn't wave, although I know he saw me because the following day he sent me an envelope via Mamá.

Inside were several photographs of our *finca* and a shot of Buitrago clutching a Bible as he stood under the oak tree near Papá's grave. On the back, he'd written: 'I said a prayer for Mario Jesús on your behalf.'

It was a thoughtful and conciliatory gesture after my heated outburst at the Díaz fiesta. I sent a short, unsigned, thank-you note in return.

Among Buitrago's many critics, the most scathing was Felix Velasquez, whose transport business had deteriorated further. Mauricio Torres also continued to struggle at the cattle yards under the Guerrilla's tightening yoke.

I was still determined to take a shot against Zorrillo at the Puerto Galán markets on Sunday, with my new scope and sniper skills. However, sneaking into the town in my previous disguise of fisher boy would be impossible. Every boat now had to report to the Guerrilla at the wharf.

I heard this news from Old Man Domino when I visited him in hospital. He was suffering liver complications and looked jaundiced, although his eyes retained their sparkle.

He must have noticed my disappointment and guessed I was up to something because, when his wife stepped outside to speak to the nurse, he clutched my wrist fiercely.

'You've got your whole life ahead of you,' he said. 'Don't ruin it by getting yourself killed.'

I was grateful to Old Man Domino, although his advice meant I'd have to think of another way in. I thought that perhaps Don Mauricio could smuggle me close to the market in a cattle truck, but he wouldn't take my calls. And without assistance, my plans for eradicating Papá's killers amounted to nothing.

94

IT WAS 6 PM on Christmas Eve and I missed Papá worse than ever. I sat alone on the edge of my mattress, staring down at his photo on my knee. It was my second Christmas since his death and the most miserable yet. At least the previous year I'd been angry at Papá's killers. This year, I was simply depressed.

I looked out of the window remembering how, when I was younger, the townsfolk would erect an enormous Christmas tree in the plaza. People would leave gifts underneath for distribution to the poor. Fairy lights flickered everywhere. Families would walk through the streets holding hands.

But that year, not a soul walked the plaza. It seemed everyone was with their family, dining together. Everyone, that was, except me.

Mamá was with the Díaz clan at Javier's hacienda. She'd offered to cook them dinner – they'd been good to her. I couldn't tell Mamá about Fabián giving Camila cocaine or my conviction that the brothers trafficked drugs, so when I refused to attend she assumed I was being rude and stubborn.

'When you're ready to be civil,' she said, 'I'll send our driver to collect you.'

Camila was with her parents and brothers. Unfortunately, I was no longer welcome in her home, and, anyway, it was too dangerous to visit. As for Uncle Leo, he was probably drinking with one of his teenage *perras*. I couldn't even bring myself to answer when Palillo's name flashed on my phone because I didn't want to infect him with my sadness.

I turned on the television. Caracol News was running a segment on the latest piece of Guerrilla villainy: they'd celebrated Christmas by hijacking a plane and forcing the pilot to land on a public highway. Then they'd kidnapped all twenty-two passengers, including a senator.

Andrea, the simpering newsreader from the Díaz party, urged us on this holiest of nights to spare a thought for the thousands of men and women living in captivity around the country. Her voice-over continued while the television displayed images taken from Proof of Life videos showing hostages at the Guerrilla's jungle camps. Imprisoned in cyclone wire cages, they slept on hardwood planks under thin blankets and ate from metal dishes like dogs. Their original clothes had rotted away thanks to the humidity, so they now wore Guerrilla camouflage. Many suffered from malaria or diphtheria, and their skin bore ulcers that never healed. Some had been trapped there for ten years.

The reporter crossed to a plaza in Medellín where the hostages' families huddled in groups, holding a peaceful vigil to lobby the government to seek a negotiated solution rather than attempt dangerous rescue operations. They held candles and waved placards.

One placard – in red, childish writing – simply read: HOLA, PAPÁ! I LOVE YOU!

It was held by a little boy who'd never laid eyes on his dad. His father, a doctor, had been kidnapped at a Guerrilla roadblock while doing volunteer aid work in a remote indigenous community. His wife was pregnant at the time. The boy was now five, and his mother had shown him photos and explained how much his father loved him. She'd also instilled in him the hope that his Papá might one day come home.

'We live with that hope,' said the mother softly, barely whispering into the microphone. 'Hope is the only thing that keeps us breathing.'

It was touching. It was gut-wrenching. And it almost flattened me to the floor with fury when they cut to an excerpt from an interview with Santiago, recorded months ago. In response to a question about the hostages' horrific living conditions, he'd replied, 'Our prisoners of war live in the same conditions as my soldiers. Here, everyone is equal.'

Was this how the Guerrilla, after their revolution, would make us all equal: equally poor, equally sick and equally miserable? In comparison to Santiago's callousness, the mother's dignity and defiance were inspiring.

The final interview was with a twelve-year-old boy suffering from leukaemia. I'd seen him on the news six months before. Lying in a hospital bed in a white gown, he was bald from chemotherapy and had a drip in his wrist. His last wish was to hold his kidnapped father before he died.

'I'm sorry for interrupting your television viewing and for being so ugly,' he'd joked, patting his bald head. 'But I only want to see my father.'

Every week for three years he'd written two letters: the first to his father, telling him how much he loved him; the second to Santiago, pleading for his father's release. In his most recent letters he'd begged simply for a temporary visit. However, since he didn't know whether the letters were reaching either man, he'd called the television station, which had sent a reporter to his bedside. Although the boy was sick, he told the reporter that he'd trek into the jungle if he had to. Santiago should just tell him where and when.

That was six months earlier. Now, for this special Christmas follow-up episode, the boy had finally received a reply. He held up a letter on light-blue paper from the Guerrilla. Santiago was considering a unilateral release of his father on 'humanitarian grounds'.

Smiling, the boy declared, 'This is the happiest day of my life since Papá left us.'

Since Papá *left us*, he said, presumably to avoid aggravating the Guerrilla. He didn't say, 'This is the happiest day since terrorists chopped down trees to block a narrow road late at night, pointed their rifles at a line of innocent motorists and crosschecked their ID cards against a list of *kidnappable* people.' He didn't mention, although it had been written about in the papers, that his mother had been forced to plead with her relatives to hand over their life savings for the ransom. Nor that she'd suffered a nervous breakdown trying to pay their mortgage, feed two children and cover her dying son's medical bills. Nor that his older sister had twice attempted suicide.

Stories like this moved me deeply. They formed a lump in my throat and made tears come to my eyes. But when Andrea, the sexy, lip-glossed newsreader, came back on, I tensed as she turned from her co-host to pout at the camera.

'And let's hope Santiago releases him.'

'Yes, Andrea.' Her co-host frowned and shuffled her papers before shooting back a similarly empathetic look. 'Let us hope.'

As for me, I despaired. I wanted to scream at them, 'Are you completely fucking insane? Can't you see what's happening?'

Santiago orders his men to hijack a plane and take twenty-two hostages. Then, with his next breath, he kindly offers to release one man whose son is dying, cunningly timing his response for Christmas to pluck at the nation's heartstrings. How could this tiny, manipulative act of apparent kindness be hailed as a beacon of hope? It sickened me to the marrow of my bones and the tiny fibres of my existence. And I wanted to shout the truth:

It was not *hope* they were showing. It was tragedy. Pure fucking tragedy.

I snatched up the remote and fumbled for the OFF button before they could depress me even more. Silence filled the room. I stared at the blank screen, listening to my own breathing.

It was Christmas, but the world was not right. The world was simply not right.

And with Santiago alive, it never would be.

95

THIRTY MINUTES LATER, a soft tap sounded at the door. I leaped up and flung it open, convinced that Camila had found a way to visit. Instead, Javier and Fabián Díaz stood before me.

Javier drew himself up to full height. Fabián looked sheepish and resentful, as though he'd come under duress. They glanced from my unshaven face to the unmade bed, the half-eaten meal in a polystyrene tray on the bedside table and the crumpled clothes strewn across the floor.

'How did you find me?' I demanded.

'Our driver knows where your mother comes each day. Please come and join us,' Javier urged. 'We've put a plate of food aside for you.'

'You drove all this way to collect me?'

'And to apologise face to face,' said Fabián. 'My behaviour at the party was unacceptable.' He was trying to sound sincere but I doubted he meant a word of it.

'Thanks, but no thanks. Now, if you don't mind,' I said, beginning to close the door.

'Please, Pedro! At least hear us out,' Javier begged. 'I've been thinking about what you said about Zorrillo and Caraquemada. You were right. This month, Zorrillo raised our taxes to fifty per cent. The Guerrilla are bleeding us dry . . .'

'We know we're being followed,' Fabián added. 'We think Zorrillo is doing to us exactly what he did to our father before they kidnapped and killed him. But if we flee, we'll lose everything.'

'And?' I interrupted.

'And we need to speak to Trigeño,' Javier said.

So there it was again! Palillo had guessed their motives eight months earlier and I'd heard it confirmed by Fabián's indiscretion at their party. Whatever crooked deal they'd struck with their father's killers wasn't working out so well after all. But if Javier and Fabián had seen what El Psycho had done to the three *traficante* brothers in Los Llanos, they mightn't be so keen on meeting Trigeño.

'Why come to me? Other people could get you Trigeño's phone number.'

'We've heard Trigeño is suspicious of outsiders. Our other friends mightn't be as . . . reputable. Whereas you've known us all your life.'

'I've heard you out. My answer is no. Now, goodnight.'

'Wait!' Javier jammed his foot in the door. 'We can give you Zorrillo. Set up a meeting in a remote place, just as you asked.'

This made my choice tougher. Although I didn't trust Javier, I had no doubt he could arrange a face-to-face meeting with Zorrillo. He might even persuade Caraquemada to come along too.

But as tempting as it was, my fear of Trigeño's reaction was greater. After his vehement pronouncements against the *narco-guerrilla* and his upcoming book, any connection with traffickers would torpedo his credibility. And once Trigeño discovered that I'd known their true profession, not even the deepest, darkest cavern on earth could shelter me from his rage.

'My answer is still no. Now please leave!'

When the brothers departed, I lay back on the bed, alone once more.

And that was Christmas! The second after Papá's death and the most depressing one I've ever spent.

Over the coming days, I saw Camila and Mamá regularly, but I couldn't get the image of that boy with leukaemia out of my head. I, too, hoped Santiago would release the father in time, but the selfish part of me was also envious of the boy. Maybe, just maybe, he would see his father again.

On December 30th, I boarded the bus to return to La 50 and slumped into my seat, watching sullenly as smiling and laughing passengers entered, chattering gaily about their vacations. How could people laugh and joke at times like these?

Optimistic people are fond of saying, 'Cheer up! Things could be much worse.'

But right then, my tent was not pitched in the optimists' camp. It was the lowest ebb of my life. The men who'd killed Papá were not only taking my beloved town but the rest of the country too. Worse still, people around me – ordinary, everyday people whose perceptions, actions and common sense I'd assumed had always determined the course of our country's history – accepted all this as if it were inevitable.

Against this, I had only one thing: my fight. I would not be passive like them. I would continue to battle, no matter what, even if it cost me my life.

When I changed buses in Villavicencio my stoicism was finally rewarded. A breaking newsflash appeared on the television screen above the driver's seat.

The Guerrilla had liberated eleven of their twenty-two hijacking hostages, with more expected to be released over coming days. The newsflash cut to a press conference with the President, who made a surprise announcement: 'Not good enough! They must release *all* the hostages.'

He had dark circles under his eyes and his hand was trembling. As a result of the hijacking, the President's political career was all but over. He'd pledged a peaceful solution to the three-decade-long conflict by convincing our nation that the Guerrilla leaders were capable of compromise. But the Guerrilla had made fun of him for months – recruiting, buying weapons, fortifying defences and moving hostages to more secure locations while gaining worldwide publicity for their cause. And now there was this plane hijacking.

'Today,' the President read sombrely, 'I've signed instructions to the nation's Attorney-General to legally annul the demilitarised zone. I've also directed the Minister of Defence to use the army to retake the area by force. Sadly, but necessarily, the peace process is over. The war against the communist Guerrilla must now recommence.'

'Thank Christ for that!' I yelled, clapping three times and rattling the headrest in front of me. To me, this announcement was like a belated Christmas present – a present from the Guerrilla themselves, tied with ribbons of their arrogance and flagrant disregard for human dignity.

I assumed everyone would be with me, cheering, applauding and whistling. Outside, patriotic motorists would honk their horns, fly flags and scream from windows as they did whenever Colombia made the first round of the World Cup.

But other passengers turned to stare coldly. The old lady in the seat beside me looked at me like I was crazy.

'Why would you say that? Why would you be pleased?'

'The Guerrilla killed my father,' I said. 'In front of me.'

That shut her up, although her disapproving expression didn't disappear entirely.

To the old lady and most other Colombians, the failed peace process was another sad episode in the tragic history of our nation – a cause for lament, not celebration. Yet while everyone else rallied for peace, I was cursing their stupidity and praying for war. Only years later did I look back and realise that the way I thought and acted back then was not normal.

But right then I was glad. Glad the war was back on. Glad that when Lieutenant Alejandro pulled up in his army truck at the La 50 gate two days after my return he was not alone.

General Itagüí was perched proudly beside him, smiling and waving like a touring monarch. Now that the peace process was over, he no longer needed to hide his friendship with Alfa 1.

'Welcome back, General,' said Alfa 1.

'Feels like I never left,' responded Itagüí, his shiny medals jangling as he bounded from the cabin like a dog let off its leash.

He'd been instructed by the President to make up for lost time. As a result, there was a third man in the truck's cabin – a man we'd all been waiting for: the *zorro solo*. He'd found Santiago's camp.

96

LOOKING AT THE *zorro solo* as he climbed from the truck, I felt disappointed. I'd envisioned a bronzed, shirtless warrior with twelve-inch biceps, a barrel chest and raised abdominal muscles like the panels of a turtle-shell. His killer stare would harpoon me against the wall.

However, the man before me was short and compact. He was wearing old jeans and a loose, faded T-shirt, and his upper body was slight. I had trouble imagining him as a barehanded assassin.

'Don't be fooled by appearances,' Lieutenant Alejandro told us as we walked towards the office. 'Judge him by his work.'

Only Alfa 1, Beta, Itagüí and I attended the meeting. After placing a large crate marked 'Classified' on the table, Lieutenant Alejandro reported on the mission.

'A helicopter lifted the *zorro solo*, the boat driver and one other soldier into the jungle to within thirty kilometres of the camp,' Alejandro explained. 'The boat driver guided them another fifteen kilometres closer along intricate tributaries and then turned back with his guard, while the *zorro solo* continued alone until he detected movement through the trees – a small Guerrilla patrol. Crawling, he followed their trail to the base, which was located on a triangular spit of land where two north-flowing tributaries join to form the Río Meta. His satellite transponder pinpointed it as being eight kilometres inside Venezuela.'

With water to the north, east and west, Alejandro explained, the base was like a castle protected by a broad moat. From the south it was accessible by foot but was heavily fortified by trenches, machine guns and guard posts, making a stealthy entry impossible. The *zorro solo* slipped into the river and let the current drag him to the base's northern tip. There, he scaled a tree, where he hid for five days, sharing it with a three-toed sloth and a family of squirrel monkeys. Although the taller trees of the rainforest canopy protected the base from aerial detection, the smaller trees had been felled, affording him a clear view over the camp.

The *zorro* estimated that the base housed five hundred soldiers, who moved about on raised pathways made of wooden logs bound together using vines.

'And after his return he made us this,' said Alejandro, lifting the lid of the crate and motioning for us to gather round. He lowered its side flaps to reveal a three-dimensional scale model of the camp.

I was astounded by its intricacy. Constructed from matchsticks, glue, rocks, dirt, thread and wire, the model was covered in neatly affixed labels indicating the latrines, commanders' cabins, armoury bunker, food storage areas, cooking tents and sentry posts, including two high up in the trees. The *zorro solo* had even recreated the overhead netting and tarpaulins designed to fool satellites and prevent soldiers rappelling from helicopters.

Three words beside a large tent at the northern tip of the camp set my heart racing: SANTIAGO AND PARTNER.

We'd found Santiago! As Alejandro continued, I hung on his every word.

The *zorro solo*'s tree was only fifty metres from Santiago's tent. Each day at 5 pm he watched Santiago giving orders to his *socia*, a beautiful girl who was also his radio operator.

Before leaving the base, the *zorro solo* had decided to test how the Guerrilla would react during an attack. At midnight, he stole a rifle magazine and placed it in the dying embers of a cooking fire. Ten minutes later, when he was safely back in his tree, the twenty-five bullet casings exploded like gunfire.

The troops grabbed their weapons and scrambled for the perimeter trenches. Ten guards rushed into Santiago's tent, but no one emerged. Two minutes later, the *zorro solo* was surprised to hear the squeak of metal directly below his own tree.

A hatch, perfectly concealed by the leaf litter of the jungle floor, flipped open. Five of the bodyguards climbed out. They stripped away nearby palms and ferns to reveal three wooden dugout canoes, which they dragged to the water's edge. They all piled into one canoe and paddled north-east, disappearing into darkness.

A minute later – presumably when the first group had radioed their safe landing – a sixth guard emerged from the hatch with Santiago's young girlfriend, who was carrying a laptop. They, too, sprinted to the water and paddled the second canoe in the same direction as the first.

Santiago and the remaining four guards never emerged. The *zorro solo* was convinced that Santiago was waiting in a tunnel beneath the hatch, ready to sprint to the third canoe. However, by then the Guerrilla had discovered the false alarm and the camp quickly returned to normal.

'Incredible!' exclaimed Alfa 1, shaking the *zorro*'s hand.

Luck had played a part in his observations. If he'd chosen a different tree, he might never have spotted the hatch and we'd never have known about the tunnel. But we now had everything we needed: the precise location of the base, its troop numbers and defensive layout, as well as knowledge of Santiago's probable escape route.

Alfa 1's excitement died suddenly when he noticed Alejandro's blank expression.

'We've almost captured Santiago and his base. What's the problem?'

'In this tiny cage here,' said Alejandro, pointing to a cube of barbed wire glued to the eastern part of the model, 'are twelve civilian hostages.'

97

IMMEDIATELY, ALFA 1 phoned Trigeño, who entrusted him with devising an operational plan. The location of the base inside Venezuela would, of itself, preclude the army from attacking. However, the presence of hostages made their open involvement impossible.

The Guerrilla's stated policy was to execute all prisoners in the event of an attempted rescue. They claimed that the army ignoring this policy made them responsible for the loss of innocent life during government assaults on their bases. But Trigeño argued that buying into this cynical reasoning allowed the Guerrilla to use kidnap victims as human shields, effectively holding a nation of forty million people to ransom. The Autodefensas would take all possible steps to evacuate the hostages as part of our attack plan, he said, but their presence wouldn't stop us from going in.

Alfa 1 ordered the erection of a life-sized reconstruction of Santiago's camp in a mountain forest upriver from La 50 to serve as our training ground for simulated attacks. To maximise our chances of approaching the camp undetected and successfully negotiating the river crossing, he studied rain charts from the previous ten years, as well as moon charts for coming months. The mission would proceed in April, he decided, when the river would be at its lowest.

We'd need to time the attack carefully. Waiting until the first rains fell would reduce our visibility and muffle the sound of our boots crunching over dried leaves and twigs. But too much rain would cause the river to rise, making the crossing treacherous.

According to Alfa 1's battle plan, our troops would circle wide around the base and assault it from the east, the least fortified flank, at 3 am when the *guerrilleros* were asleep. The army would monitor all radio signals emanating from the camp using US spy planes circling high above the clouds. This would allow us to confirm that Santiago was present on the attack day.

Meanwhile, Trigeño struck a deal with General Itagüí. If the Guerrilla fled during our attack and crossed back into Colombia, Itagüí would have soldiers positioned to cut them down and Air Force planes ready to bomb them. However, if they stayed in Venezuela and defended the camp, we were on our own.

Alfa 1 assigned specialised tasks to different teams. The first priority – assigned to Team A – was rescuing the hostages. Team A would cut open the cage and extract them to a nearby safety point. As the first into the camp, Team A soldiers faced the greatest risk of death. For this task, Alfa 1 selected his bravest, most experienced soldiers who were experts in close-quarters battle.

The second priority – assigned to Team B – was destroying the communications tower. Team B would sever the power supply to the antenna or deliver a heavy explosive to the battery source. This would prevent the Guerrilla from radioing the Venezuelan army for backup and also weaken the signal between their hand-held radios, severely diminishing their commanders' ability to coordinate a defence.

'In other words,' said Alfa 1, 'our aim is to arrive undetected, penetrate their perimeter, catch them unawares and sink them into deep confusion.'

Teams C, D and E were tasked with securing the base's munitions store and taking out the M60 machine guns along the eastern flank to allow the main body of troops to storm across the dry riverbed safely.

Finally, Team X, of which I was a member, was tasked with taking down Santiago. Exact details of *how* were given later, during a private briefing since the ordinary troops weren't to know our target's identity.

Team X was comprised of three two-man sniper teams. Palillo and I were the first. We'd cover Santiago's escape hatch from a camouflaged position across the Jaguar River. Palillo would observe the hatch using night-vision binoculars. I'd line up the shot through a night-vision scope. But I was not to fire until Santiago and his bodyguards were five metres clear of the hatch – that way, if I missed, I'd have time to line up a second shot before they scrambled back into the tunnel.

If I couldn't get a clear shot, however, I was to leave Santiago to the second team, which was covering the canoes. If the second team could not get a clear shot, a third team embedded to the north would cover the canoe's predicted landing spot.

Of course, there were no guarantees, but three teams covering three separate points of Santiago's likely escape route would maximise our chances of success.

This plan assumed we were not detected during the five-day jungle trek across the Venezuelan border. But if the enemy did detect us, Alfa 1 believed they'd storm across the Rio Jaguar to fight. Either way, we'd have a large-scale battle on our hands, which was precisely what Trigeño wanted.

At last, we were attacking the Guerrilla where they'd least expect it – within their safe haven. No matter what, Santiago would flee. And that was when the snipers from Team X would take him out.

98

DURING THE SIMULATED attacks on the replica Guerrilla base, I was finally able to apply the skills I'd learned during advanced training.

To represent enemy soldiers, Culebra ordered hundreds of human-shaped figures to be sawn from plywood. Beta divided the troop in two – while one team attacked, the other defended. Then everyone swapped teams. Everyone, that is, except me and the other snipers.

My role was always the same: shoot Santiago in the chest.

To simulate his escape through the hatch, five of our new recruits crouched in a ten-metre long trench, holding five plywood cut-outs nailed to broom handles. To distinguish him from his four bodyguards, the cut-out figure of Santiago had a black moustache and green epaulets. At various points during the main assault these recruits would suddenly raise the five cut-outs. While the figures danced about, my task was to quickly identify Santiago, line up a shot, then fire.

Each day I repeated this exercise under varying conditions. I shot Santiago from different angles and distances. I shot him partially obscured by his bodyguards and I shot him through trees. I shot him under moonlight and then under the light from flares launched skyward by Palillo. During an uncharacteristic dry-season storm, I even shot him through wind and rain.

And the more I repeated the exercise, the more confident I became that I'd get Santiago and the more faith Alfa 1 had in my abilities.

'You've come a long way since that day at the obstacle course,' he said, '*comando*.'

Calling me 'commander' was the closest he'd ever come to expressing approval of me. He was not like other commanders who freely dispensed praise to their juniors like candy to children. In fact, by withholding his approval, he made you want it more. And now that I finally had it, it felt like I'd climbed a tall mountain.

Alfa 1 looked into my eyes. 'I'm trusting you, Pedro. Don't let me down.'

Alfa 1 wasn't the only one observing me closely. Trigeño and I now fished together regularly after Sunday prayer. In my company, he was always friendly and calm.

'Maybe you don't see it now, Pedro, but you and I are very much alike – even though you didn't tell me the whole truth.'

'About what, *comando*?'

'About how close your family is to the Díaz clan.'

Suddenly alarmed, I didn't know how to respond. Trigeño had obviously been checking up on me. It wouldn't take much for him to discover that Javier was a cocaine trafficker, especially if he'd read the intelligence files. I didn't want him knowing about Mamá living with Javier, or even that I'd attended their fiesta. But neither did I want to tell a lie.

'We were neighbours. Growing up, I had little to do with them,' I said, trying to sound nonchalant. 'The two sons, Javier and Fabián, were ten years older than me and went to school in Bogotá.'

'Your mothers are close friends,' countered Trigeño. 'She laid flowers on Humberto's grave on their behalf. You chose not to mention those details.'

'I wasn't aware that you knew the Díazes. And I didn't think it right to mention another family's grieving.'

'Very modest of you. Very discreet,' said Trigeño without sarcasm.

'Is anything wrong, *comando*?'

'We're trusting you with an important mission, Pedro. I like to know about the men I'm trusting.'

As for Palillo, he now recognised the benefits of us being snipers. During the attack, we would not risk our lives crossing the riverbed to enter the camp. In fact, we'd be concealed at a safe distance from the main action; our only task was to take an accurate shot at Santiago and then retreat.

Using his influence as a commander, Palillo persuaded Piolín's superior to ensure she would be in the third wave to cross the river, removing her two steps from the front line. Of course, he was frustrated that he couldn't tell Piolín what was in store, but at least she'd be safe.

The shared responsibility of keeping the battle plan a secret also brought Palillo and me closer.

'I know how badly you want this, Pedro,' he said one night as we walked back towards the dormitory after dinner. 'And I want it for you too. I was against you killing Ratón in Villavicencio because it was stupid and dangerous. But I guess if I'd known who murdered my own father, I'd have gone after them too.'

He lowered his voice to a whisper.

'I'll help you with this, *hermano*. But once it's over, it's *over*. You understand me? No more promotions. No more special courses. Santiago was the one who gave the order that day. Once he's dead, you need to let go of this obsession and we need to find a clean way out of the Autodefensas.'

It was early March and the launch of our offensive was approaching rapidly. Our troops were almost ready.

When I'd joined, Trigeño's branch of the Autodefensas had numbered a mere three hundred soldiers. Since then our numbers had increased to eight hundred. The Autodefensas had expanded rapidly, perhaps too rapidly. Recent training courses had been rushed. The majority of soldiers were 'green', with only three months training and hardly any experience. The recruits currently training were due to graduate in late March. They'd go straight into battle.

On March 12, Mamá phoned to wish me a happy birthday. I rarely checked a calendar and was so busy that I'd forgotten. Afterwards, I stood in front of the same mirror as when I'd turned sixteen, looking over my shoulder. I'd grown two inches and my chest had filled out. It was exactly a year since I'd graduated as an Autodefensa, a year since I'd got my tattoo, and almost a year since I'd committed my first murders. I was now seventeen, but felt much older.

Camila phoned too.

'How's Llorona?' I asked.

'Worse than ever.'

Because the President had ended the peace process, the Guerrilla were exacting their revenge – committing atrocities and increasing their recruiting and training. Further pressure was mounting on Colonel Buitrago because a low-flying plane had been detected by US satellites dropping crates attached to parachutes into the jungle south of Santo Paraíso. The crates contained thousands of Kalashnikov rifles destined for the Guerrilla.

An *El Tiempo* journalist asked, 'Will you resign over this?'

Buitrago responded tersely. 'I don't control the skies. I've been posted here for four years to do a job. And I'm not leaving until it's done.'

Attendance at Camila's school was down by fifty per cent, but she'd triumphed in the recent scholarship exam at the Universidad Nacional, making her dream of leaving Llorona a near certainty.

'I start next February. Andrea's going to help me find a decent place to live and a job. I've been watching her on TV. She's amazing and *so* beautiful.'

She reiterated her plan for me to leave the Autodefensas and come with her.

All this gave me more reason to hate the Guerrilla and train even harder for the coming battle. The pressure from Camila and Palillo to end my obsession didn't work – it only made me want to speed things up. I didn't care about the trust Trigeño and Alfa 1 were investing in me. And I didn't care about obeying their instructions.

My fantasy about Santiago was far stronger than any direct order they could give.

On the night of the attack I shoot Santiago in the stomach – an excruciating wound, but one that takes a long time to cause death. I dispense with his bodyguards and walk coolly but purposefully across the dry riverbed. Santiago lies writhing on the ground. I kick away his pistol, crouch down and calmly tell him who I am and my father's full name. He begs me to spare him. He can give me anything I want.

'The only thing I want is something you can't give me – my father back,' I say.

I remind him of the propaganda he has spread, of the farce that his long-promised revolution has become, of the children he has recruited as canon-fodder and the eleven-year-old boys to whom he outsources his extortion racket.

He tries to justify himself with arguments about the greater good, equality for all, and the courage and beauty of the peasantry's struggle against the oligarchy.

'Was my father a wealthy oligarch?' I ask. 'No! He was a humble, hard-working farmer whose land provided food for us and employment for our workers. And I would have followed in his footsteps, had you not given that order. Death is what you have sown, not revolution. You, with your charm, your educated façade and your plethora of well-meaning ideas. But it has all been for nothing. Because now, you too must die.'

I can see in his face that he knows his cause is lost and he was indeed wrong to have murdered Papá. I order him to face death like a man and, finally, after all these years of cowardice – of hiding behind a female radio operator while guarded by an army of brainwashed children – Santiago pulls himself to his knees. I shoot him once in the head. He slumps forward then falls sideways.

And as I look down at his corpse, I know that, although the war is far from over, the forces of good, which for so long have appeared weak, will now begin to rise.

99

THE FIRST RAINS of the season, which would signal our departure, were late in arriving that year.

La 50 was packed beyond capacity with eight hundred Autodefensa troops – two-thirds of them Trigeño's, the other third 'on loan' from other Bloques – many of whom were sleeping in tents, hammocks slung between palms or simply on the ground. My own platoon knew very little about the mission. However, those from other Autodefensa units knew even less. From the replica base they could guess why they were here, but they had no idea where they were going or what they'd be confronting.

In mid-April, Mamá phoned me.

'What's wrong, Mamá? Why are you calling me at work?'

'That nice man. Jerónimo. The one who drives the taxi. They killed him! Right in front of Uncle's hardware. There was blood everywhere. It was horrible . . .'

I was stunned. With his jovial nature and sense of humour, Jerónimo had somehow seemed disconnected from the violence. Later, I learned that after dragging him from his taxi and shooting him before horrified onlookers, his killers spray-painted DEATH TO FASCISTS on the side of his car. Someone must have tipped off the Guerrilla about his work for the Autodefensas.

'When was this?' I asked, saddened and wondering what would now become of his two daughters.

'Yesterday.' She sniffed. 'They also torched one of Javier's buses. He'd really like to speak to you, Pedro.'

'Mamá, I can't. I'm very busy.'

'He's right here. It will only take a minute.'

'I said I'm busy.'

'*Pedro*,' she said in a quiet but stern voice – the one she'd employed to reprimand me as a child. I heard footsteps. I imagine she'd been standing next to Javier and was now walking away so he wouldn't overhear. 'The servants are packing up the *finca*. I think Javier and Fabián are fleeing for Bogotá. I don't know what to do. I'll have nowhere to live. I could go back to Uncle's, but—'

'Don't! It's not safe. What about Buitrago? Can't he help?'

'Impossible! Today they exploded a car bomb outside his garrison gates. Two soldiers were killed.'

'Let me speak to Javier.'

Javier's voice came on. As always, he laid on the charm, thick as *guanábana* juice.

'Pedro. How are you, my dear *amigo*? A thousand apologies for interrupting your work, but it's an emergency. Zorrillo demanded a million dollars in return for allowing us to keep our bus route. When we refused, he blew up one of our buses. But if we do pay, the same thing will happen to us as to our father.'

No bus route was worth a million dollars. More likely it was a cocaine trafficking route.

'And?'

'I need you to vouch for us to Trigeño.'

'Can't help you, sorry.'

'Wait! We can pay. We'd rather give the million to Trigeño than to the Guerrilla.'

My answer to Javier Díaz would always be no, but since Mamá needed his protection, I had to be diplomatic until I could find her somewhere safe to live.

'Now's not a good time, Javier. I appreciate you looking after my mother. I promise I'll get back to you within two weeks.'

I hung up before he could beg anymore, but Trigeño never missed a beat. He was beside me in a flash, his face half-concerned, half-inquisitive.

'You look worried. Bad news from home?'

I nodded. I was extremely anxious about Mamá but didn't want to mention the Díaz brothers or their offer.

'The Guerrilla killed Jerónimo the taxi driver.'

Trigeño gaped at me and turned pale.

'You know him?' I asked.

'He's my cousin.'

This news was almost as much of a surprise as Jerónimo's death itself. I'd had no idea about their kinship. Both men had kept it secret for obvious reasons, but it made sense – Jerónimo needed extra money and Trigeño needed someone trustworthy to ferry new recruits to La 50. Who better than a family member? It also explained how Trigeño knew so much about Llorona and Garbanzos.

'I'm sorry. I didn't know him well, but he seemed like a very decent person.'

Trigeño gritted his teeth. 'Those cocaine-trafficking communist *bastardos*! I'll make them pay.'

Hearing this confirmed that I'd made the right decision not to pass on Javier Díaz's offer. Although Trigeño could use every dollar he could 'find', it would only have been a matter of time before he discovered the true source of the Díaz funding. However, I began to worry that if Javier became desperate enough he would find some other way to get in touch with Trigeño. And then he might mention me and the fact that my mother had been living at his *finca*. I thought of the two innocent men Trigeño executed simply because they knew what their brother was doing and had benefited from his wealth.

As we waited for the rains to commence Alfa 1 kept us occupied with training exercises. During simulated attacks on the Guerrilla camp, we revised our specific roles.

These first-aid and evacuation exercises made me think of death. At seventeen, even being surrounded by violence, you don't think you're going to be the one to die. Of course, I'd told my friends I wouldn't care if I did, but I'd only said that because I was convinced it wouldn't happen.

But I was no longer convinced. Seeing the grim expressions on the commanders' faces, I knew we weren't attending a football final. Thinking of death every day made me despondent. As platoon commander, however, I couldn't let that show.

Following another rainless week, the Venezuelan witch doctor renewed our spells in La Quebrada, which, by then, was only knee-deep. Culebra repeated Alfa 1's trick with the blanks, this time shooting a small boy from Bloque Bananero who was teased for wetting his bed. The boy's survival was declared a miracle. Half my platoon knew the trick. The other half felt invincible.

A few days later, I gathered the six soldiers I most cared about – those from my original squad. I decided to be blunt.

'What if one of us dies?' I asked them. I held up pen and paper and eyed each of my men seriously. 'Do we trust each other?'

They nodded blankly. Although we'd known each other less than eighteen months, we'd patrolled together, eaten together and guarded each other's lives. During the Guerrilla skirmish not one man had lost his nerve.

'Then what happens if we die?'

'Who cares?' said Palillo flippantly. 'Providing it happens quickly, we'll never know.'

I changed my question. 'What do you want your families to be told?'

Yucca bit his lip. 'Tell my parents I died bravely in battle. Tell them I died quickly and painlessly. And tell my girlfriend that my last words were, "I love you."'

I handed him paper and pen. 'Tell them how, *alias* Yucca?'

I emphasised the 'alias'. Everyone understood immediately. Each soldier wrote his alias followed by his real name, his address and what he wanted his family told in the event of his death. He then folded the paper over and handed it on. We were taking a big risk – it was strictly against the rules to reveal your real name. That had been clear from day one.

I placed the list in a jar and buried it in front of them. Whoever lived could dig it up. Despite the risk, contacting each other's loved ones in the event of death seemed an obvious thing to do. The harder question, however, I saved until last.

'What if you get shot, but don't die?'

They studied their boots. Although we'd practised dragging injured comrades to first-aid posts and improvising stretchers using two rifles inserted through camouflage shirts, Santiago's camp was several days away by boat and then by foot. There were no hospitals in the jungle. There were no medical helicopters. And of course, no one wanted to slowly bleed to death. Or even worse – be captured and tortured.

Finally, MacGyver broke the silence.

'Put me out of my misery.'

Looking up, the others nodded slowly. Shooting a friend would be difficult, but that was what had to be done. Passing around my pocketknife, we each pricked two of our fingers and swore two different pacts, both beginning with the words '*If necessary . . .*'

The first: *to die for each other.*

The second: *to kill each other.*

That night, I twisted in my hammock. I imagine everyone did. These were not things anyone wishes to contemplate. At midnight, MacGyver shook me awake. He'd written a farewell note to his brother. He needed the jar. As I dug, lightning flickered on the horizon.

Reading down the list of six names, my former squad no longer comprised fearless fighters with nothing to lose. They were no longer soldiers named Yucca, Ñoño, Giraldo, MacGyver, Tortuga and Palillo. They were ordinary people with ordinary-sounding names – Juan Pablo, Eugene Jaime, Oscar Giraldo, Eduardo Yecid, Ana María and Sebastián Diego. They were people who had parents, siblings and lovers with addresses and phone numbers. However, that wasn't what kept me awake until dawn.

I hadn't written a will.

It was a ridiculous thought since I owned nothing of value, but that's what I kept thinking: *I should have left a will.*

Around 3 am, the sky flashed like a camera, thunder rattled the dormitory's zinc roof and I stopped worrying about my last will and testament. What I'd really meant to think of was my family.

If I died, my efforts to achieve justice for Papá would amount to nothing. Four of his killers would remain free. Mamá would be condemned to lifelong poverty, having lost not only her husband but also her son. Camila would be grief-stricken. I needed to call her and tell her I loved her. I'd tell her I wouldn't be home for my scheduled leave in May. And she should know that if I hadn't phoned by June, I wanted her to move on.

Barefoot, I snuck across damp grass towards the office. As I clasped the handle, thunder cracked overhead. It was dawn on the 26th of April – exactly six weeks after my seventeenth birthday – and the grey skies opened, dumping rain as loud as falling gravel. The long, tense days of waiting were over.

100

ON THAT FIRST rainy day of April, eight hundred Autodefensas changed into civilian clothes and were divided into groups of twenty. Since Guerrilla spies were hidden everywhere, the transport operation had to be conducted clandestinely. Soldiers were ferried across two provinces in tarpaulin-covered trucks. Weapons, uniforms and ammunition were transported separately. It would only take one sighting of abnormal troop movements to jeopardise the entire invasion.

Boats dropped us across the Venezuelan border, forty kilometres to the south of the camp, and we began the arduous journey towards Santiago's base. We trekked at night without torches, stumbling over moss-covered buttress roots. As we travelled deeper into the jungle, the moonlight penetrating the canopy grew dimmer and the tropical rains continued to pour down.

When daylight came, we lay down in our wet uniforms and tried to sleep on the decomposing leaves of the forest floor. Ants crawled across our faces and stifling humidity filled our lungs. Since any sound or smell could give us away, we weren't permitted gas cookers or even insect repellent, and by the second night my skin was covered in scratches and mosquito bites. If not for the *zorro solo*'s testimony, I'd never have believed humans could live in such inhospitable terrain.

It was almost 3 am on day five when Alfa 1 consulted his GPS and confirmed we were only one kilometre from Santiago's base. He'd timed our arrival perfectly and the torrential rains now bucketing down were a godsend, reducing our visibility to the enemy.

We slipped our packs from our shoulders, removed the additional ammunition and checked our rifles for dirt that could cause a cartridge jam. Palillo and I donned our ghillie suits. No one spoke. We all knew this was it.

I looked at my platoon members. MacGyver, who would take command in my absence, was relaxed, sitting with his back to a tree. Ñoño stared vacantly ahead. Tortuga paced in circles. Yucca and Giraldo bit their nails. The newly graduated soldiers looked grim. I imagined they had butterflies in their stomachs, whereas I felt curiously elated, imagining Santiago asleep in his base, about to get the shock of his life.

Alfa 1 gave the order for the three Team X sniper pairs to take up our assigned positions. Palillo and I wriggled slowly towards the riverbank.

I heard the water before I saw it. Rumbling mountains of it, swirling through the jungle. When finally we wormed our way into a good hide beneath a thick, fallen tree trunk, what I saw made my heart sink.

The river was far wider and deeper than we'd expected. We had trained for a one-hundred-metre sprint to their base, across a riverbed no more than ankle deep. But the river was now fifty metres wide and flowing fast.

My plan of injuring and then interrogating Santiago was now impossible. In fact, I was sure that we'd have to turn back altogether. Wading through the river while carrying a weapon was not only dangerous, it would extend the crossing time by two or three minutes – more than enough time for the Guerrilla lookouts to spot us.

'There's too much water,' I radioed through to Alfa 1.

Over the headset I heard him order three scouts to wade out and gauge the water's depth and speed. Through my night-vision scope, I watched their dark figures emerge from the trees on our side of the bank and creep slowly to the water's edge at two hundred metres separation. Although the scouts were sure-footed and cautious, I began to worry: if I could see them, so too might our enemy.

Fortunately, they returned without incident. However, the water had reached their waists. Although I couldn't see Alfa 1's reaction, I knew that despite his claim that the Autodefensas never retreated, he would not risk the lives of eight hundred men. After many months of planning and the huge expense of recruiting and training, the mission had been a failure – thwarted at the last minute by nature.

I imagined Alfa 1 now searching for a gap in the canopy in order to transmit the bad news via satellite phone to Trigeño and General Itagüí back at base.

As the long, slow minutes ticked by, Palillo and I scanned the opposite bank for movement. The thick jungle on the other side seemed eerily still. Finally, I saw movement: two *guerrilleros* were changing guard. Their smiles and relaxed hand signals confirmed that they were not aware of us. Palillo nudged me. He'd located the *zorro solo*'s tree, below which was Santiago's hatch.

Seeing how close we'd come, however, only increased my disappointment. Fifteen minutes passed with no order to retreat. The delay could only be explained by two things: cloud cover blocking the satellite phone connection to Trigeño or disagreement among the commanders about how to proceed. I suddenly had a dreadful suspicion: Trigeño, not being on the ground, might overrule Alfa 1's judgment.

A second later, it was confirmed via radio when Alfa 1 grimly relayed Trigeño's order: 'Prepare to cross.'

101

EIGHT HUNDRED AUTODEFENSA soldiers spread out along the six-hundred-metre stretch of riverbank. I had strict orders not to take my eye off Santiago's hatch, but I knew Palillo was watching the hatch and that two groups of bodyguards would emerge before Santiago. Besides, how could I not watch the river when my own platoon would be in the third group to cross?

Rather than storming across as they'd been trained, the first group waded into the waist-deep river in pairs. Each soldier held his rifle above his head in one hand while, with the other, he gripped his partner's wrist in case either slipped on the mossy rocks.

Unease welled up in my stomach. *They're sitting ducks*, I thought, my index finger tapping the trigger guard. I held my breath until the first group reached the opposite bank and fanned out into the jungle. They'd made it.

I imagined Team A sneaking towards the hostage cage and Team B going for the communications tower. Presently, my radio clicked twice – the signal for the second group to cross. They waded in more confidently than the first.

The radio crackled as the leader of Team A reported back from the Guerrilla camp: 'Hostages aren't here. Cage is empty.'

'Any signs of recent habitation?' asked Alfa 1.

'No bedding or blankets. No locks on the door. Hostages are not on the base.'

I breathed a sigh of relief and caught the white gleam of Palillo's teeth as he smiled. I'm sure all the commanders hearing this over their headsets felt the same – knowing our attack wouldn't jeopardise the lives of civilians lightened our anxiety.

The second group were almost across the river. Through my night-vision scope I witnessed the first soldier set foot on the opposite bank. I felt euphoric; we'd crossed two groups undetected.

Suddenly, a single shot rang out and the soldier fell back in the water. A flare soared into the sky, lighting the river and everyone in it, and the Guerrilla opened fire from two machine gun emplacements upriver and two downriver.

Leopardo, the leader of Team B, shouted over the radio, 'It's an ambush. We're—'

Gunfire crackled over my headset and then the transmission was cut, and that was the last we heard from the groups that had crossed.

It was a clever ambush, even though the Guerrilla had had little time to set it up. Perhaps their lookouts saw our scouts wading into the water. Or perhaps they simply saw the first group crossing. Either way, they had divided us perfectly – allowing a quarter of our men onto their side of the bank, trapping a quarter in the water and leaving the remainder on our bank.

In that first thirty seconds, the Guerrilla took advantage of our temporary disorientation to scurry into position. I caught glimpses of their movements – silhouettes darting between trees. Their trenches were so well concealed behind logs, sandbags and vegetation that they'd be difficult to detect even in daylight. The first flare died out and, as the next flare went up, hundreds of automatic rifles began their mad barking.

The troops still on our bank entrenched themselves and started firing back. But for those caught in the ghastly, flare-lit river, there was no place to hide. They did the only thing they could: took a deep breath and sank beneath the water, letting themselves be washed downstream while bullets sliced into the water around them. If anyone raised his head, he was picked off by the machine gunners. Most pretended to be dead, but the bullets did not discriminate between the bodies of the living and the dead; they pounded into both relentlessly. Even for those already shot, I flinched as their lifeless bodies shuddered with every impact. Soon, bodies were floating past Palillo and me, washed along by the fast-moving current. I was horrified.

Through my scope, I focused on the closest machine gun emplacement. It was manned by two *guerrilleros*. I was sure Santiago wouldn't risk coming out into the open with bullets whizzing everywhere. Not when they were slaughtering us from the safety of their base. In any case, I couldn't bear to see men I'd eaten with and bathed with, men I'd laughed with, being carved up like fruit in a mixer. I radioed Alfa 1.

'Permission to take out the M60s downriver, *comando*?'

My muzzle flash would give away our position; we both knew this. But Alfa 1's priorities had changed: he was now intent on saving his men.

'*¡Adelante!*'

I took aim and killed the two *guerrilleros* manning the machine gun closest to me. The second machine gun was further away, and I didn't have a clear view of it, but I shot anyway. The second M60 fell silent.

In response to my shots, a hail of bullets rained in on our position. Palillo and I ducked lower. Pressing our stomachs to the ground behind our tree trunk, we heard bullets whizzing overhead like angry hornets. After a minute the bullets stopped and Palillo was back in position with the binoculars fixed on the hatch.

However, our respite was brief. Alfa 1 was shouting over the headset to the troops: 'Move north. Repeat, move north.'

Hordes of Autodefensas streamed northwards, swarming around us, all of them firing across the river as they came. Their arrival drew more fire on our position.

The bullets ripped bark off trees. Twigs and torn leaves fell constantly from above. Small shells threw up mounds of earth. Bigger shells left man-sized craters, and the largest shells knocked over trees.

My eyes were burning from the smoke, my ears deafened by gunfire. I smelled burned sulphur and everything about me was confusion. This was not the war I imagined. I never expected the shouts of fear, the desperate pleas for assistance or the groans and screams of the injured. The second set of flares went out and, finally, there was a lull while everyone's eyes adjusted.

My own platoon flopped to the ground around us.

'We can't leave them,' MacGyver said to me, pointing to the bodies floating downstream. 'What are your orders?'

'Leave them,' I said 'They're dead.'

In the very thick of battle, however, training is often forgotten and very little goes to plan. Discipline breaks down and orders are sometimes disobeyed.

'Not all of them,' said MacGyver.

He sprinted to the river and dived in with Ñoño on his tail and Tortuga following.

They grabbed the arms and legs of the injured soldiers as they floated past and dragged them ashore. The rest of the platoon wrenched them to safety behind the trees.

They saved around ten lives before MacGyver was shot in the head as he ran back to the river. Tortuga was ankle-deep in water as bullets began buffeting her body. She started to fall forward but the continued impacts held her on her feet long after she was dead. She appeared to be dancing.

When the firing stopped, her knees finally buckled and she slumped into the river and was washed away.

Seeing this, Ñoño lost his mind. He stood on the riverbank – completely exposed to the enemy – and fired and fired. Long after the magazine was empty, he kept swivelling his rifle back and forth. Palillo and I ignored our own orders to watch the hatch and began shooting to provide Ñoño covering fire. Everyone did.

I stood and emptied an entire magazine. Palillo stood and emptied his. Yucca threw a rock at Ñoño, who came to his senses. As he sprinted back towards us, he fell and clutched his right buttock. He was hit. Giraldo rushed out and dragged him to safety.

Ñoño was limping so Giraldo took over, attempting to treat the injured soldiers they'd saved using the médico kit, before others ferried them back to the first-aid station.

'Get down!' I yelled to Yucca, who I could see standing in the open. Struck in the stomach, he was in shock, turning in circles. 'Get down, *idiota*!'

The fighting stopped suddenly and there was silence. I never expected this – silence at the peak of battle. I could hear Yucca's excruciating groans and wanted him to stop, but when I started crawling towards him, a volley of bullets whizzed around me. Yucca wouldn't stop groaning. When I failed to reach Yucca a second time, I aimed my rifle at him and had to stop myself from pulling the trigger. 'I said, *get down*!'

He sat down, looking at his forearm. Giraldo couldn't reach him either; he crawled to another injured boy – the bed wetter – and strapped a tourniquet around his arm.

I could only save Yucca by leaving the safety of my tree trunk. I signalled my intention to Palillo, edged out on my stomach and fired blindly across the river. No sooner had I fired than I'd given my position away and had to roll sideways a few metres to avoid being hit by the retaliatory fire that bounded back at me like an echo.

At least Yucca was now lying flat. I finally clasped my hand around his ankle and dragged him towards my log, but I realised it was all for nothing. His eye was shot out and the rear of his head was missing. I was angry with him. I cursed him for dying like that, so stupidly, and for making me try to rescue him when he was already dead. I stayed a moment looking at him until I heard something heavy and metallic drop behind me. I rolled over Yucca, raised him on his side and pressed into him tightly, closing my eyes while opening my mouth wide. His body shuddered as it absorbed the blast from the mortar. My ears were ringing now, but there was no longer time to be angry at Yucca because bullets were raining hard and I had to roll back over him to return to my log.

Alfa 1 was still ordering the troops to move north; soon, most had moved past us, drawing fire away. The bullets stopped. Palillo and I were now free to concentrate on the hatch. Looking through my scope, I thought I saw it lift. I was about to ask Palillo whether he saw anything when Alfa 1 gave a new order over the radio.

'*¡Devuélvanse!*' he said. 'Retreat!'

'I think I saw movement at the hatch,' I protested. 'Permission to remain in position?'

'Pedro, I said *retreat*.'

I pointed at Ñoño and said to Palillo, who was now standing, 'Take the platoon and get him to the first-aid station.'

Palillo's hands went to his hips. 'And what about you?'

'You're now in charge. I'll follow you shortly.'

I knew it was dangerous to remain alone. But I wanted to stay until the last possible moment. If it were only the two of us, Palillo would probably stay and argue. But Ñoño was groaning and losing blood, and since MacGyver was dead, Palillo was the highest ranking commander below me. He shot me a dirty look, slung four rifles over his left shoulder, scooped Ñoño into his arms and stumbled south-east to join the retreating mass of Autodefensas.

As for me, I lay back down flat under our fallen tree trunk and put my eye to my scope just in time to see five men dragging three canoes to the water's edge. They boarded the first canoe and paddled off. I could hardly believe what I was seeing. Were these Santiago's bodyguards initiating the first phase of his escape? It made no sense for him to flee or expose himself now – not when they had us on the run – but I had little time to think. I scanned back fifty metres to the *zorro solo*'s tree and, sure enough, the hatch flipped open and two soldiers emerged, one of them a young girl carrying a flat object the size of a laptop. They sprinted towards the canoes and launched the second canoe, which was smaller than the first, onto the water while I kept my scope hovering over the hatch. It opened again and five more men emerged. One of them had to be Santiago. In the darkness, however, they were difficult to distinguish. All of them were wearing camouflage and I couldn't see a moustache. Which was Santiago? They moved swiftly and my view was obscured briefly by a tree.

Five minutes earlier I would have allowed them to reach the water where the light was brighter and two other sniper teams would be covering their canoe crossing and downriver landing point. But I was now on my own and had to make a split-second decision as the group dashed in a tight huddle towards the last canoe.

The silhouette in the centre of the group was taller than the others. Santiago was six foot two; it had to be him. But his guards prevented me from getting a clear shot. I fired anyway and one fell immediately. In the seconds it took the others to realise he hadn't simply tripped, I shot a second guard. Santiago dropped flat to the ground and his remaining two protectors piled on top of him. But they were out in the open – halfway between the hatch and the canoe – and they seemed undecided about whether to continue on or return.

I kept firing, striking Santiago in the leg. He tried to stand but stumbled. His men gripped his upper arms and dragged him back towards the hatch. Three figures limping awkwardly made a simple target. I shot both guards easily but missed Santiago – he continued on his own, crawling in a zigzag, and dragged himself to safety behind a tree, where I could no longer see him.

I was certain it was Santiago. He was alive but injured. He was also without protection or the ability to move far, or even call for help. And I had another small advantage – he knew a sniper was targeting him so probably wouldn't risk changing positions. I fired two more shots either side of the tree to make him believe his escapes were blocked. And then I stripped off my ghillie suit, dived into the raging water and began swimming diagonally against the current, harder than I'd ever swum in my life.

The man who'd ordered Papá's death was only a hundred metres away, bleeding and unable to move. I had to finish the job.

102

I WAS HALFWAY across the river when several flares streaked high into the air, lighting up the sky above the Guerrilla base. It was strange that they'd been fired from our side of the river, but I had little time to wonder why. I was now a brightly lit target struggling across a waist-deep river. I ducked underwater, still gripping my Galil, and dug my free hand into the rocky riverbed, holding my breath for as long as I could. I had to come up for air several times before the flares died out.

When I reached the far bank, another set of flares went up and I heard the sound of low-flying aircraft, their engines growling. Bombers.

Later, I learned that once General Itagüí had heard the base contained no hostages, he'd changed his mind about crossing the border.

'*¡Que se jodan los socialists!*' he exclaimed, slamming his fist on a table. *Fuck the socialists!* Then he'd instructed army bombers to take off while Trigeño directed Alfa 1 to keep the Guerrilla contained inside their base to maximise their casualties. The pilots already knew the base's coordinates, but the flares gave them a visual lock on their target and ensured they wouldn't accidentally bomb the retreating Autodefensas.

The arrival of bombers also explained why Santiago had risked exiting his hatch. His aircraft scanners probably gave him five minutes' warning, and he must have decided to take his chances in a canoe. Of course, I knew none of this at the time. I only knew that I was at the edge of an enemy base, scrambling across an open riverbank with bombs about to drop.

I sprinted towards Santiago's tree. Suddenly, I saw a girl running, slightly ahead of me, in the same direction. I glanced back to my left along the riverbank and saw the second, smaller canoe was drawn up on the bank once more. Santiago's girlfriend, the one with the laptop, had returned for him. She reached the tree first and then turned, yelling and signalling for me to get down.

I didn't hear the bomb that hit me, or feel its blast. I only remember being slammed forward, smashing face-first into the ground and wondering why I hadn't had time to put my hands out to break the fall. I must have been knocked out, because when I came to the girl was crouched over me. Even in the eerie half-light of the flares, I could see she was extremely beautiful. Her hair was tied back in a ponytail, and I remember thinking it surreal that she was wearing earrings and make-up in the middle of a war zone.

'Can you walk?' Her voice sounded as though it were coming from the end of a tunnel. She pointed to the sky where the bombers were circling around for a second run.

I nodded. However, when I made no attempt to move, she took my wrist and began dragging me towards the hatch, leaning backwards, digging her heels in and pulling with all her might. Through my hazy thoughts, I remembered she was the enemy and looked around for my rifle, which I must have dropped during the fall. Instead, I drew my pistol and pointed it at her, staggering to my feet.

She let go of my wrist and leaped back with fear in her eyes. She glanced from my boots to my belt and finally to my face, perhaps noticing too late that my uniform was wet and didn't bear the Guerrilla insignia. She raised her hands and, at my order, turned and walked towards Santiago's tree.

The man who lay before me, with his back propped up against the trunk, was no warrior. He was slim, pale and scholarly like a kindly philosophy professor, with gold-rimmed glasses and a neat moustache. He was clutching a beret with a red tassel.

'I surrender,' he said, dropping the beret and holding up his open palms. The words sounded distorted; my ears were ringing from the bomb blast. I patted him for weapons but found none.

He and the girl exchanged a glance. My bullet had indeed hit his left leg – his camouflage pants were soaked with blood. The girl crouched, removed her belt and began binding it as a tourniquet around his thigh.

'Get back!' I ordered. She stood and stepped aside, leaving Santiago to fasten it himself.

When he'd done so, he raised his head and looked me in the eye. 'My name is—'

'Simón Santiago,' I cut in. 'A man who hijacks planes, explodes car bombs, kidnaps innocent people and imports thousands of rifles to prolong this war.'

'I'm a man of peace. I've never killed a single person. As you can see, I don't even carry a gun.'

I smiled grimly. 'A pure pacifist whose words inspire others' bullets.'

I wanted to get this over with quickly. I could hear the bombers drawing closer. The girl, standing behind him, glanced anxiously upwards as yet another set of flares lit the sky. But Santiago seemed inclined to debate. Even with death staring him in the face, he was willing to defend his beliefs to his last breath.

'We had no choice but to take up arms,' he said earnestly. 'If only wars could be fought with words. But what are the words of poor men against the bullets and bombs of the oppressors?'

'My father oppressed no one. He was a humble farmer who rose before dawn, who sweated in the sun six days a week, and who paid his workers a fair wage. With so many deaths on your hands, I don't suppose you even remember the name Mario Jesus Gutiérrez Molina.'

Santiago thought for a moment. 'I do. From Llorona, a year and a half ago.' He adjusted his glasses on his nose in order to study me properly. 'You must be Pedro. But you're mistaken. I didn't order your father's death. I simply authorised it. The request to execute him was made by Caraquemada. I know nothing of his day-to-day field operations.'

'So you authorised the death of a man you'd never met, a man who did nothing to you, for a reason you don't even know?'

'Caraquemada is devoted to our cause. He must have had good grounds.'

The bombers were closing in quickly, but the fear I felt was distant compared with my frustration. Nothing was going to plan and there was no time to properly conduct my interrogation.

I believed Santiago; he'd simply rubber-stamped Caraquemada's request. But that almost made it worse. He seemed incapable of making the connection between his highbrow philosophies, his blind, long-distance radio commands and the consequences they had in the real world for real people.

Santiago lived in a bubble of ideas floating in the sky, whereas I now realised Papá had been killed by men standing on solid ground. They were the ones I should be going after, not this pitiful philosophy professor clutching a beret.

'Perhaps you didn't pull the trigger, but I will have justice for my father.'

I aimed my pistol at his chest, now thinking it might be better to leave him alive for the moment. Santiago wasn't directly responsible for Papa's death, but if I took him prisoner he could lead me to those who were.

Santiago stared me in the eyes.

'You might extinguish a man's existence,' he stated serenely, 'but never his ideals.'

'Please,' begged the girl, pointing desperately to the hatch. 'We need to get underground right now!'

'Stand!' I said to Santiago. 'You're coming with me.'

But then the girl looked skyward and threw herself over Santiago, before the world around me exploded in a blinding flash of light.

Slowly, I blinked back to consciousness. I'd been thrown forward by the blast, but somehow I was lying on my back. My arms and shoulders were numb; when I tried to move, I couldn't. The two of them were standing over me. Santiago was leaning on the girl's shoulder, his left leg slack. She was wincing in pain and blood streamed down her forehead. The tip of her rifle was digging into my chest; her finger was shaking on the trigger. 'Yes or no?' she asked Santiago.

Santiago shook his head. He crouched with difficulty and spoke softly into my ear. 'Pedro, this is the second time I've spared your life. I am sorry for your father. But if you're truly seeking justice, don't get it confused with revenge.'

I must have blacked out again because the next thing I remember it was daylight. I was slipping in and out of consciousness. Now that the shock was wearing off, it felt as though I'd been slapped hard from behind with a brick wall. I felt pressure on my chest and opened my eyes to see a large, heavy boot belonging to a soldier who was staring down at me with his rifle wedged into my neck.

'Don't move, you *hijo de puta*.'

Falling into enemy hands was everyone's greatest nightmare; it was better to shoot yourself. I felt for my pistol, but I now saw that it was tucked into the soldier's pants.

I struggled beneath him, but he only pressed down harder with his boot and called out to his superior, 'We've got a live one here, *mi sargento*. Shall I finish him?'

His commander's voice called back, 'He might know something. Bring him for interrogation.'

I passed out again, and the next time I awoke I was facedown with my hands bound behind my back. My wounds must have reopened when they'd moved me, because I was lying on a swaying metal floor in a slowly expanding pool of my own blood. The loud *wop-wop-wop* of rotor blades told me I was in a helicopter.

I wasn't sure who'd captured me, although I was at least glad it wasn't the Guerrilla – they didn't own aircraft. However, it might be the Venezuelan army, in which case I was in serious peril.

'I'm thirsty,' I croaked, feeling dizzy from the pain rocketing up my back.

'You need water?' asked the soldier kindly, unclipping a canteen from his belt. I smiled and nodded, relieved to hear his accent was Colombian. The patch on his right sleeve read: BRIGADA FUERZAS ESPECIALES. However, since I didn't know about General Itagüí's change of heart, I wasn't sure how much to say to him after Beta's dire warnings about the perils of being captured by the government.

The soldier twisted open his canteen and extended it towards my mouth. But at the last moment he tipped it upside down and I watched precious, life-saving drops fly from the helicopter.

'That's for all my friends you've killed, you Guerrilla *hijo de puta*.'

Since I'd been captured on the Guerrilla side of the river, he believed I was one of them. And I couldn't contradict him without giving away details about my group.

'Where are you taking me?'

'For interrogation. And then to prison.' He laughed and looked down at my pool of blood. 'That is, if you live.'

Unlike the Autodefensas, the army's official policy was to render medical attention to injured enemy combatants. In the field, however, individual soldiers' hatred for the enemy sometimes got the better of them. An overly lenient judicial system meant *guerrilleros* often walked free, strolling back into the jungle to rejoin the war. It would be convenient if a captured *guerrillero* happened to die on the journey to hospital.

Immediately, I decided that interrogation and prison were preferable to death.

'I'm an Autodefensa.'

The soldier laughed in my face. 'And I'm Father Christmas.'

'Check my tattoo. Please!' I wiggled my shoulder. The soldier cut away my shirt with his knife. The viper tattoo changed everything.

'*¡Mierda!*' He signalled frantically to his *cursos* in the helicopter and they sprang into action. One attached a saline drip to my wrist, another clipped an oxygen mask over my face, and a third cleaned and patched my wounds. 'Why didn't you say so earlier?'

He grabbed his microphone headset, but it was too late. The pilot had radioed ahead with news of a captured *guerrillero*. A prosecutor from the *Fiscalía* was already on his way to meet the helicopter.

The *Fiscalía* was the Colombian Public Prosecutor's office – an agency separate from the army that was renowned for being incorruptible and for investigating and charging Autodefensas. It was they who'd initiated the capture warrant against Alfa 1 during the peace process.

'We can't stop them from taking you into custody,' the soldier told me.

But when we touched down in Villavicencio, one of his colleagues ran out with a bag of civilian clothes and changed me out of my torn and bloodied uniform. They also returned my *cédula* and gave me a cover story: I was a field worker looking for work who'd been accidentally caught in the crossfire of a battle.

I doubted this story and my fake *cédula* would stand up for long, but I only had to follow Beta's instructions: 'If you're captured just sit tight and don't say anything. We'll find you.'

I was about to ask the soldier if he could get word to my base when suddenly a man with a scrunched-up face like a bulldog's was looming over me. He was panting heavily from his sprint across the landing pad.

'Stand back from my prisoner,' he ordered the soldier and then began barking questions at me. 'Which *frente* are you with? Who's your *comandante*?'

The soldier stood his ground, shoving his arm against the bulldog *fiscal*'s chest.

'This patient needs urgent medical attention.' And to save me from having to answer anything immediately, he injected me with an extra dose of morphine, which knocked me out again. The last thing I remember was his winking and mouthing two words: 'Good luck!'

But with the bulldog *fiscal* against me, I'd need a lot more than luck.

103

I WOKE IN a small, white-walled hospital ward, disoriented and shaking, but glad to be alive. I was dressed in a blue gown. A tube ran from my arm up to a metal drip stand beside my bed. A man with a shaved head lay sleeping in the bed opposite with one bandaged hand elevated in a sling.

The door was open but my wrist was cuffed to the bed's metal railing, and a green-uniformed *fiscal* policeman was stationed on a chair in the corridor. As soon as my cuffs rattled, he punched a number into his phone.

'Subject is awake,' he said and hung up.

Once the initial elation at being alive wore off, my thoughts turned to my platoon. Palillo. Ñoño. Piolín. Giraldo. Where were they now? Had they sustained injuries during their retreat? I also wondered what had become of Santiago and the girl. Had they been captured by the government, or had they managed to escape in their canoe? I took the remote control from the bedside table and turned on the TV, hoping for information. Surely a battle that big would make national headlines. But nothing was mentioned on the news. The wall clock read 1 pm. Only ten hours had passed since the battle – perhaps not enough time for news to filter through.

Lying there, I had plenty of time to go over what had happened with Santiago. To have been spared by a man I despised, a man I could have killed myself, or at least taken prisoner, was humiliating. His false apology about my father, his condescending paternal advice, as though he were a school careers counsellor, was galling. I'd have much preferred his bullet to his mercy. As I lay handcuffed, ruminating in that hospital bed, Santiago's sparing me was the final insult.

But rather than making me disheartened, my encounter with Santiago sharpened my focus. At least I was alive. And that meant I was free to pursue Papá's real killers. In fact, by telling me about Caraquemada, Santiago had given me a gift.

I'd always believed that Santiago – as the highest ranking *comandante* who'd given the order – bore the greatest responsibility for Papá's death. I'd believed that with his demise, I might feel some relief and calm. It would be all over. But how could I continue hunting a man who'd spared my life, twice? Besides, now that I knew the truth about Santiago – that he was a delusional communist who cared more about ideas than people, my anger towards him turned to disdain, and even pity. From now on, I resolved, I would concentrate my energies on the men who'd actually carried out Papá's murder.

Caraquemada was my ultimate target. Of course, I'd get Zorrillo and Buitre too. I'd kill them both. But before I did, I'd force them to lead me to Caraquemada.

Presently, a surgeon arrived – a tall, bookish type in his early thirties, with a steady voice. He explained that they'd operated on me for five hours and had removed thirty-two *esquirlas* – shards of metal – from my back and legs. I'd have scarring, he told me, but should consider myself lucky.

'If you'd moved a centimetre to the left or right,' he said, rattling a plastic jar containing the *esquirlas*, 'any one of these could have severed a major artery and we wouldn't be having this conversation.'

'How long will I be stuck here?'

'A week at least. Perhaps longer.'

My first feeling on hearing this was relief – surely that would be enough time for my group to find me. However, on further reflection, that relief became tinged with trepidation. When my platoon had regrouped and realised I was missing, had they gone back looking for me, or simply assumed I was dead? It would take the Autodefensas at least two days to trek out from Río Jaguar via the shortest route, and even then I couldn't rely on them looking for me. I needed to find a trustworthy person to convey a message back to La 50 as soon as possible.

The doctor seemed friendly, so I thanked him for saving my life and attempted to engage him in conversation, trying to assess whether he might do me a favour. He could at least tell me whether other injured Autodefensas were in the hospital ward.

'May I keep the *esquirlas*?' I asked. 'I think I'll make them into a necklace.'

'Of course.' He laughed and held out the jar, but a hand shot out of nowhere and snatched it from him.

'This is evidence.'

It was the investigator from the *Fiscalía* who'd met my helicopter. His icy stare sent the mild-mannered doctor shuffling from the room. I now got a proper look at him – a podgy, balding man with cavernous nostrils like the muzzle of a double-barrelled shotgun.

The *fiscal* – who introduced himself as Eduardo Mendez – was reasonable at first. He drew up a chair, enquiring how I felt and whether I needed anything. I was polite in return but gave monosyllabic answers.

'Is there anyone you'd like me to contact on your behalf? Relatives or friends?'

'No, *gracias*.'

'So you have no parents or siblings? Not even a distant aunt who might want to know you're here? You were raised by wolves, I suppose?'

When I didn't answer he opened a notepad, took a pen from his pocket and his voice became gruffer. He demanded to know my name and how I'd sustained my injuries.

I gave the name from my *cédula* and stuck to my fieldworker-looking-for-employment story, even though it had more holes than a spaghetti strainer.

When I finished, he reviewed his notes. 'So you're telling me you went looking for work in the middle of Guerrilla territory, where there's not a factory, not a farm, not even a fucking *shop*. Pure jungle. And you were walking through that jungle when you just happened to wander into a battle between the Guerrilla, the Army and the Air Force?'

He had his pen poised over the paper. I said nothing.

He tried again. 'You say you were injured in an explosion. Where were you hit?'

'From behind.'

'And you were wearing these clothes?' He held up a bag containing my new civilian clothes.

'A blind man could see my blood on them. Test my DNA if you want.'

'Then where are the tears from the shrapnel?' he shouted. 'Are you suggesting these clothes stitched themselves back up? Perhaps you believe in witchcraft, Señor *Jhon Jairo García Sanchez*. Because I hear people from your region worship the Big Red Boy.'

I looked out the window. Defending my story against further questions would be like trying to block bullets with tissue paper.

Fiscal Mendez breathed out heavily through his nose and switched down a personality.

'I'm an honest prosecutor. I don't care whether a man is Guerrilla or Autodefensa – they're both terrorist organisations. But that ID isn't genuine and you don't look a day over seventeen. If you tell us who you really are and co-operate, we'll release you as a minor into the custody of your parents. If you can't return home, you'll stay in a safe house with kids your age, get a monthly living allowance and receive technical training at college. But if you sign your statement as an adult, you're facing up to twenty-five years in prison for *subversión* and *terrorismo*.'

He'd painted a pretty picture of the government's program for captured underage combatants. But the Autodefensas could get to me anywhere. I knew what they did to *sapos*, and I'd rather my commanders found me here, handcuffed to a bed for refusing to talk.

'I'm not signing anything.'

The *fiscal* stood and slapped his notebook closed with annoyance. 'Today I've been as soft as a kitten. But when I come back tomorrow, you'll give me answers or you'll see what I'm really made of.'

He departed and for the first time I began to seriously regret disobeying Alfa 1's order. I now needed the Autodefensas more than ever. Without them, I felt completely helpless and isolated.

My roommate opened his eyes and sat up. 'You resisted well. He tried similar threats on me this morning. I was worried about you at first. Looked like you got hit badly . . .' He raised his bandaged hand. 'We both did. Rocket-propelled grenade took three of my fingers. Fucking Guerrilla.'

'I don't know what you're talking about.'

I hadn't yet decided whether to trust him. He was being a little too friendly.

Besides, for now at least, being in hospital wasn't so bad. I was alive. I had food and water. And whatever the *fiscal* could dish out was better than what I'd believed I was facing ten hours earlier – falling into the hands of the Guerrilla.

The time to start worrying would be in two days, when my group returned to camp. What if they searched hospitals and prisons but didn't find me? What if they found me but suspected I'd been a *sapo*? My biggest worry, however, was that they'd assume I was dead and not look for me at all. How long before my squad dug up the jar containing our goodbye messages and made a heartbreaking phone call to Mamá and Camila?

Over the course of the afternoon, I rang the buzzer repeatedly, hoping to encounter a sympathetic face among the hospital staff. However, each time the same nurse entered – a humourless woman with steel-rimmed glasses, upright posture and a disposition to match. As my hopes of getting a message out faded, my thoughts returned to escaping. I asked to use the bathroom. However, the guard handcuffed my wrists together, accompanied me directly to the cubicle door and stood outside. At night, when my roommate was asleep, I tried picking the cuffs using a plastic fork I'd stolen from the dinner tray. It was not as easy as in the movies. Finally, I rolled my bed to the window and considered smashing the drip stand through the glass. But how would I leap from the second-storey with a bed attached to me? And how far would I get on foot in a blue hospital gown before they recaptured me?

Around midnight, I heard talking from the bed opposite. My roommate was using a cell phone. I only caught snippets of his conversation because he muffled the sound using a blanket. 'You need to get me out of here now . . . Yes, there's one other guy here . . . They're threatening us both with prison . . .'

The fact that he didn't offer to lend me his phone reduced my suspicions. If all else failed, tomorrow night I'd ask to borrow it.

The morning news contained nothing about the fate of Santiago or my companions. At 9 am, a new nurse slipped quietly through the door. She was pretty – a *paisa* girl from Medellín – with blonde hair, green eyes and large breasts that fought the buttons on her white cotton uniform.

'Señor Sanchez! How are you feeling today?' She fussed over me, measuring my blood pressure and fluffing up my pillow.

Then she touched one finger to her lips, undid the top two buttons of her uniform, leaned forward and lowered her bra. Across her left breast was written FISCAL. Across her right was an arrow that pointed to my roommate. So I'd been right not to trust him – he was an undercover government agent pretending to be an injured Autodefensa in order to extract information from me.

All the while the *paisa* nurse, who must have been on the Autodefensa payroll, kept up the polite, sing-song prattle that was typical of her region. 'Señor Sanchez, please be so kind as to sign this for the public health insurer.' She handed me a pen and tapped a fluorescent pink fingernail against a blank post-it note affixed to a form. I wrote, 'I'm Pedro' and then Culebra's phone number. Before leaving, the nurse touched her finger to her lips again and I nodded.

Although tempted to confront my roommate and expose him as a fraud, I refrained. I was now in an excellent mood. I'd just survived a major battle, the antibiotics flowing into my veins were shuttling me along the road to recovery, and I had food, water, a warm bed and television. I only had to keep my mouth shut and maintain my self-control until my group came for me.

An urgent newsflash appeared on the TV. The Caracol reporter claimed that a carefully planned, joint operation between the Colombian army and Air Force had, in recent hours, successfully destroyed a major terrorist training base in the south-eastern province of Vichada, leaving scores of Guerrilla casualties. Army casualties: zero.

The reporter flew over a destroyed patch of jungle in an army helicopter but was told it was too dangerous to land, owing to landmines. Instead, Caracol relied on shaky footage provided by the army.

I recognised the camp but the report didn't mention Santiago, and the rest of it was misinformation and propaganda. The date was false – our mission had occurred a day earlier. The location was false – the camp was across the Venezuelan border. The army hadn't formed part of the ground force; it was only us – the Autodefensas. But when it suited the army, the Autodefensas didn't exist. And since we didn't exist, our deaths didn't count either – the reporter made no mention of the men we'd lost. However, that was not what angered me most.

When the camera panned across a long row of Guerrilla casualties laid out on black plastic sheets, I sat up like a catapult. The bodies shown with Guerrilla insignia were *ours*. I recognised several bloodied companions – MacGyver, Terminator, Manzana and Yucca – laid out flat and displayed like fish at a market.

Furious, I grabbed my water glass and hurled it at the TV. It missed, smashing against the wall. The guard rushed in.

'What's wrong?'

I rattled my cuff. 'Unlock me now!'

He cuffed my other wrist. I thrashed and bucked. As punishment, he unplugged the television and threatened to cuff my ankles as well.

I lay there seething. It felt like my friends had died for nothing. They had given their lives as part of a monumental lie. The army dressing them up in Guerrilla uniforms to bolster their war statistics was the ultimate indignity.

My roommate offered his consolation.

'That's not even the correct river,' he said. 'It was Río Jaguar. Which unit are you from? I'm in Bloque Centauros.'

I should have kept my calm, but I was angry at him and angry at the government. I couldn't listen to any more falsities. 'Then unwrap the bandage.'

'What?'

'Unwrap the bandage on your hand.' Of course, he couldn't. Despite his claim of being hit by a grenade, he had no real injuries. 'I didn't think so.'

He fell silent and when I woke that afternoon his mattress was stripped bare. But I'd made a mistake – blowing the pretty *paisa* nurse's cover.

The bulldog *fiscal* stormed into the room and told the policeman to take a long coffee break. He closed the door, wedging a chair beneath its handle.

I reached for the buzzer but he knocked it out of my hand with a wooden baton, which he then used as a lever to twist my cuffs. They dug excruciatingly into my skin.

'She's gone,' he said, smiling.

'Who's gone?'

'Your friend. The one with the tits. She's been arrested.'

If he was telling the truth, I was sunk. But perhaps he was bluffing in order to secure my confession before help arrived.

'Your friend's gone too.' I nodded at the empty bed. 'The one with all ten fingers.'

'Today I'm sending you to prison.'

'You can't. I'm injured.'

'The prison has an infirmary. You can recover there. A long way from pretty little girls who try to send out messages.' He twisted the cuffs tighter.

'Then hurry up and sign the transfer. Because these painkillers are wonderful – I can't feel a thing.'

'*¡Bien!* You know how La Picota prison works? There's one wing for the Guerrilla and one for the Autodefensas. You came in listed as a *guerrillero*, so I'm sending you to the Guerrilla wing. I'm sure the communists will love your tattoo.'

The door handle rattled and we both looked up as the chair flew across the room and a middle-aged man in a blue suit and garish yellow tie barged in, rubbing his shoulder. He pondered the fallen chair and raised an eyebrow at the *fiscal*.

'Is the government short-staffed?' He snatched up the evidence bag of clothes and tossed it onto my chest. 'Get dressed, *muchacho*.'

'What's going on?' demanded the *fiscal*.

'I'm his attorney. Unlock him.'

'Not so fast.' He snatched back the clothes. 'He's in my custody and this is evidence of—'

'Of your incompetence.' He drew documents from his briefcase. 'The circuit judge just signed a conditional release order. Read it and grieve!'

The bulldog *fiscal* was beaten. But before returning my clothes and unlocking the cuffs, he held out his business card to me. 'Call me about *you know what*.'

Flushing with anger, I ripped the card to shreds and told him to go to hell. It was a malicious attempt to make me look like a *sapo*. And it must have worked because the attorney immediately turned on me.

'What did you tell him?'

'Nothing. I promise.'

'Good. Get downstairs to the car and don't say another word.'

I detached the drip, snatched up the packet of painkillers from the bedside drawer and walked along the corridor, rubbing my wrists and smiling from ear to ear. I felt elated. I'd survived everything the world had thrown at me and I'd made it. I was free. Now that I was returning home to the Autodefensas, nothing could touch me. I was invincible – a man made of steel.

I waved sarcastically to the returning police guard and two duty nurses. 'See you next time!'

They shook their heads and frowned. Downstairs at the hospital entrance, I saw the Blazer from La 50 parked at the kerb with its back door open. Inside, I expected to encounter Culebra, Beta or a familiar face. I'd ask them who'd survived the battle and then borrow a phone to call Mamá and Camila.

Standing outside the sliding doors, however, were three men in plain clothes who I'd never seen before. One dug a pistol into my ribs.

'Get in!' he ordered while another bound my hands. I asked who they were and what the hell was going on, but they gagged me and pushed me into the back of the Blazer.

And from their forbidding expressions and silence during the drive back to La 50, I realised that although I'd just survived hell, my ordeal was far from over.

104

WE REACHED LA 50 at dusk. After all the unseasonable rain, the creek was now a swirling, thundering river. One of the men untied my hands and ordered me to strip to my boxers. Then they bound me again with thicker rope. My painkillers had worn off, my wounds were stinging, but I didn't fight. A two-hour battle. Being hit by a bomb. The bulldog *fiscal*. And now this. If I'd had the energy, I might have laughed.

They carried me out into the creek towards the cascade, lowered me onto the metal pole that we used to hang onto during bathing time. And then they left me there.

But even with my wrists and ankles tied to a pole behind my back and the angrily rising creek reaching chest height, I considered myself lucky. La Quebrada was not the worst torture in the Autodefensas. It at least offered a sporting chance.

There were two ways you could die – drowning or hypothermia. But if you survived long enough and had proven to be a good soldier in combat, commanders sometimes took pity on you, as they had with MacGyver, and returned you to be retrained.

Part of the torture was not knowing whether the commanders intended it as a slow form of execution or merely as a protracted punishment. Another part was not knowing how quickly or how high the creek would rise.

I looked to the sky and then to the mountains behind me. Although the morning's lashing rain had abated, the run-off would keep coming, causing the river to continue rising. Worse still, more black clouds had begun their sinister migration from the horizon, leaching like an oil spill across the sky.

At first I wasted a lot of my strength trying to escape my bindings. I wriggled. I rubbed my wrists together, hoping the rope would fray. I shimmied up the pole, only to slide back down. Alfa 1 had left no guards.

A guard might have shared my suffering. However, with no one within earshot, I felt even more alone.

My body gradually grew numb while I formulated the excuses and promises I'd make to Alfa 1 in exchange for another chance. Not knowing what I was accused of made it difficult. Perhaps Alfa 1 believed I'd made a statement to authorities. But if so, why not ask me directly and let me defend myself?

After several hours, four boys arrived with coffee, hot soup and orders to lift me out. But twenty minutes later, they lowered me back in. The food was a good sign, I reasoned. It wasn't logical to waste food on a condemned man. Then again, it might have been an effective means of prolonging my agony.

At dusk, Alfa 1 appeared on the bank. He stood in silence, hands on hips, watching me. I shouted to be heard over the rushing water.

'What? What have I done?'

'As if you don't know.' He bowed his head like a Roman soldier commiserating with Jesus on the cross.

'I don't. I swear.'

'Try being honest with yourself.'

When he left, the water licked against my chin. Tiny splashes entered my mouth and nostrils, throwing out my breathing. I stood on tiptoes, trying to avoid sucking water into my lungs. As I spluttered desperately, a dark figure slipped through the bushes.

'What are you doing? Go away!'

But Palillo didn't listen. He stripped off and swam out. Then he dove down with two river stones, placing them under my feet. I was now twenty centimetres clear of the water.

'You're only prolonging this.'

'Drink lots of water,' he ordered, stuffing a Snickers bar in my mouth. He waited for me to finish chewing. 'Give me time to get dry and be seen. Then use this.' He wrapped my fingers around my penknife with its blade open.

When Palillo left, I could breathe again. But I couldn't feel any part of my body. I became drowsy and disoriented, and I returned to the question of why I was here. I went through every infraction I'd committed since joining the Autodefensas. The list was long.

Without a doubt, my two most reckless acts had been shooting Ratón and crossing the Jaguar River in pursuit of Santiago. Not for a moment did I regret pursuing either of them. However, the *way* I'd done it was completely wrong. I'd ignored the warnings of others. I'd gone ahead and risked my life. And in doing so, I'd risked other people losing me – people who loved me.

I'd also taken a series of smaller risks such as stealing bullets, the Taurus and the Galil. I'd made phone calls, taken the Blazer and photocopied the intelligence files, all without authorisation. If discovered, any one of these could have gotten me executed. Did it really matter which one I'd finally been caught for? They were all part of a pattern. But what exactly was I doing wrong? Not the list of infractions I might've been caught for but the *real* causes.

At first light, the water reached my chin once more. I stopped guessing and I stopped thinking. I was about to drown. What did it matter why? And perhaps it was because I was so broken and had given up on analysing that the reason finally came to me.

In truth, I'd repeated the very same mistake over and again: I had tried to do everything completely on my own and refused to rely on anyone else.

This, I realised, was the oath I'd sworn on the day of Papá's death. I had kept that oath. But in keeping it I'd acted against the Autodefensas whenever their interests diverged from mine. This was the true cause of my undoing.

I still had the knife in my hand – my last chance of escape. But they'd guess immediately that Palillo had brought it. As I felt myself losing consciousness, I opened my hand. The last thing I saw was the knife see-sawing underwater as the current dragged it away.

105

IT WAS LATE morning when I came to, and the creek's angry flow had slowed. The sun had muscled its way through the oil-spilled clouds, and the renewed light allowed me to see the creek bed clearly.

The river had peaked, and the water had wiped from me everything it could – all the anger, hatred, blame and regret.

I was ready to apologise for everything I'd done. I was ready to obey the rules. I was ready to be truly loyal. That is, if I got the chance. If not, I'd accept whatever came to me. Whether it was death or more torture, I would accept all consequences.

'Had enough?'

Alfa 1 stood on the bank with his arms folded. As the same four boys lifted me out, I kicked away Palillo's river stones so they wouldn't be discovered in the dry season.

My hands were white and my fingers wrinkled and blue. They dragged me to the parade ground and tied me to the new flagpole as the much-diminished troop began assembling.

I scanned their faces for my platoon and located my men at the back. It felt strange not to see Tortuga, Yucca or MacGyver there. I couldn't rid myself of the sensation that they might simply be late for parade. Any second they'd come running from the new bathroom block calling their apologies. But they didn't.

Alfa 1 arrived with Trigeño. I didn't know whether this signalled the end of my punishment or whether Alfa 1 now intended to execute me publicly as an example.

Trigeño's speech to the troop that day was sombre.

'We paid heavily at Río Jaguar,' he said, pointing to the gold, red and blue flag above me, hanging at half-mast. 'But the Guerrilla are on notice – we've trodden where no government soldier has stepped foot in thirty years. And we will do so again!'

He talked about duty and courage and the sacrifice of those who had not returned.

'Rest assured,' he said, 'their families will be looked after.'

He insisted that The Company was expanding into neglected parts of Colombia. Another intake of two hundred and fifty recruits would begin training next week. The tide of communism would be stopped.

Then he stepped down from his crate and turned his attention to me.

With Alfa 1 now standing on one side of me and Trigeño on the other, I felt like an accused criminal trapped between prosecutor and judge while the troop before me acted as the packed public gallery, hanging on every word.

If this was indeed a trial, there was hope. I'd been a good soldier in combat – killing two men at Puerto Pescador and taking out the Guerrilla M60s at Río Jaguar, not to mention Santiago's four bodyguards, which Alfa 1 didn't know about yet. That surely counted for something. And although I wasn't popular or funny like Palillo, I had my peers' respect. After the disastrous battle, our soldiers looked crestfallen and defeated. Publicly executing a commander in front of them would decrease morale further. Perhaps Trigeño would be merciful; I simply had to give him a reason – or an excuse – to let me live.

Clearly, Alfa 1 wanted me dead. His disgust with me was so great that I was no longer worthy of eye contact. I also sensed tension between him and Trigeño. Perhaps they blamed each other for our losses at Río Jaguar – Alfa 1 for his poor planning and Trigeño for giving the order to cross – and that might also work to my advantage.

'You know why you were in La Quebrada?' Alfa 1 asked me sternly.

'I didn't tell the *fiscal* anything. I promise.'

'Then why was this in your pocket?' He produced a business card belonging to the bulldog *fiscal*.

'It's a trick. I tore up the one he tried to give me. He must have slipped in a second card as payback.'

'Then why did he tell you to phone him about *you know what*?'

'Because I refused to talk and he wants to make you think that I did.'

'He's lying,' Alfa 1 said to Trigeño, drawing his Colt from its holster. 'Why should we believe any of this?'

'Because it's the truth,' I insisted.

Alfa 1 flipped the card and read aloud a hand-written note on its back: '*Pedro Juan Gutiérrez González. Signed statement taken on May 2.*'

Somehow, the bulldog *fiscal* had found out my full name and then written it on his card to make me look like a *sapo*. That was the bulldog's final trick, and it was effective.

Alfa 1 flicked the Colt off safety and cocked it. 'You have three seconds to change your story.'

'I can't change the truth. But I can prove it, if you lend me your phone.'

Trigeño nodded. Alfa 1 freed my hands and reluctantly passed me his phone.

I dialled the number on the card and put the phone on loudspeaker as the bulldog *fiscal* answered.

'It's me. Pedro. From the hospital.'

'*¿Sí?*'

'I've been thinking about what you offered . . .'

'And?'

'And I've changed my mind. I'm ready to talk.'

There was a pause. 'I knew you'd come around. Who can you give me?'

Trigeño snorted and snatched the phone. 'Me, you *hijo de puta*.'

'Who's *me*?' asked the *fiscal*, apparently confused by the change of voice.

'The invisible man. Enjoy your transfer.' Trigeño hung up, removed the phone battery and then snapped the SIM card between his fingers. For good measure, he hurled the phone into the river. Alfa 1 was not impressed; he'd just purchased a new phone and having it destroyed gave him one more reason to hate me.

'Even if Pedro didn't talk, that doesn't change the reason he was captured,' he persisted. 'He was rescued *inside* the Guerrilla base. I have witnesses who saw him swimming across after I gave the retreat order. How can he possibly explain that?'

Alfa 1 was right, but I knew begging for mercy would be useless. Men of power don't respect that. They respect displays of strength, particularly when there is little strength left to display.

'I had Santiago in my sights and took the shot, but I only hit his leg. So I risked everything trying to finish him. Our original plan was to go after Santiago, and that's what I did.'

'No,' boomed Alfa 1. 'What you *did* was disobey an order. You knew that your second-in-command was dead and you put your remaining platoon members' lives in danger by depriving them of a leader. You were *this* close to being captured by the enemy. But instead you got yourself captured by the government. Hundreds of my men died in that battle doing what they were told to do. But you decide to play the hero and then you expect us to come and save you. Do you have any idea of the strings we had to pull to get you out, not to mention the girl whose job you lost and how much it all cost us?'

I latched onto this final comment as a positive sign. Surely they wouldn't expend money and effort to rescue me only in order to kill me afterwards?

The issue of my disobedience at Río Jaguar, however, remained unresolved, owing to an interruption from Beta. Evidently, Alfa 1 had sent him to fetch something and he now returned smiling menacingly and casting dark, triumphant looks at me. He covered his mouth with his hand while whispering to Alfa 1. I only heard the final part as he handed over several papers: 'My contacts in the *Fiscalía* are certain it's Pedro.'

While my mind raced to think what this new information could possibly be, Alfa 1 took the papers, skim-read them and shook his head gravely.

'Bad news, *comando*,' he said, addressing Trigeño again. 'Your vehicle has been implicated in a double homicide committed in Villavicencio in March of last year. The Blazer was used as the getaway vehicle. At the time, Pedro was entrusted with the keys. Now that the government has his photo on file, it's been matched to an eyewitness's description of the driver, who they also believe was the shooter.' He swivelled towards me, leaned in close enough for me to smell his sweat and shook the papers in my face. 'Answer me straight! Did you make use of the Blazer without permission? And did you have anything to do with these homicides?'

I was trapped. There was nothing I could tell him except the truth.

'I did, *comando*, but—'

Alfa 1 raised his pistol and pushed it hard against my temple. My mouth opened but no sound came out. Trigeño held up his hand and pushed the Colt lightly aside.

'Wait! I want to hear him out.'

Alfa 1 turned on him and spoke with a fierceness that I'd never heard anyone use toward Trigeño. 'With all due respect, *comando*, there's nothing more to hear. Maybe he didn't talk to the *fiscal*. Maybe he did try to kill Santiago like he said. But he's admitted to stealing the vehicle. Now let's get this over with.'

'You can shoot him in a minute. But I want to know who he killed and why.'

I gulped and spoke as clearly as my chattering teeth allowed. 'Both were *guerrilleros*, *comando*,' I said, lifting my chin high and meeting his gaze. 'Alias Ratón was the head of the *Milicia Bolivariana* attached to the Guerrilla's

34th Unit operating out of Puerto Galán. The other one was his bodyguard.' I told Trigeño how I'd discovered the Guerrilla battery supplier using radio catalogues and the intelligence files. How I knew Ratón's political alias and used it to lay a trap. 'You can check their identities with the *Fiscalía*,' I finished. 'And I didn't steal your vehicle, *comando*. I repaired it while on leave and returned it with a full tank of fuel.'

Alfa 1 stamped his foot angrily.

'These shootings were not authorised by *La Empresa*. His actions go against the statutes that you wrote, *comando*.'

Trigeño jerked his head to indicate he needed a word in private with Alfa 1. While they stepped away to confer, I stood there thinking like crazy. My life hung by a thread. There was no longer a chance in hell that Alfa 1 would be swayed. I'd betrayed his trust.

For eighteen months, Alfa 1 had been my mentor. After my disobedience at the obstacle course, he'd spared my life and promoted me against his better judgment, telling me that I needed to be a team player. I'd promised him I *would* be a team player and yet, all along, right under his nose, I'd done exactly the opposite: I'd acted purely for myself. I'd stolen a pistol and bullets. I'd taken a vehicle registered in Trigeño's name, used it to commit murder and then escaped with the numberplates in full view of witnesses. I'd also stolen a Galil that they didn't know about. And at Río Jaguar, after Alfa 1 had kept his promise to me about Santiago and specifically reminded me that my position was one of great trust and responsibility, I'd disobeyed his direct order. Normally, any one of these infractions would earn me the death penalty. But with all of them combined, by what possible right could I ever ask him to spare my life?

I could see Alfa 1 slicing and chopping his hands violently through the air as he made his case privately to Trigeño; judging by Trigeño's nods, Alfa 1's arguments were gaining traction.

When they returned, I drew on every grain of sincerity I had within me. 'Give me a second chance, *comando*. Please. I've admitted to what I did and explained why. In both cases, I did it to kill our enemies. I've been a good soldier and I promise that if you give me another opportunity, you won't regret it.'

Trigeño closed his eyes. He was thinking. After a long deliberation, his eyes reopened and he spoke quietly. It was time for my sentencing.

'Pedro, I'm afraid Alfa 1 is correct,' he said sadly. 'Although you may have had the right reasons for doing the wrong thing, how could we ever trust you again?'

I was completely desperate now. I'd burned up every ounce of goodwill and exhausted every argument in my arsenal. I had only one piece of ammunition left – one I'd repeatedly resolved never to use. I lowered my voice so as not to be overheard by the troop.

'I can help you. You need money, right? I can get you money. And you said you've always wanted to enter Llorona. I can get you into Llorona too.'

Trigeño's ears seemed to prick up. 'Money? How?'

I pointed to Beta's cell phone, which hung on his belt, and signalled my desire to borrow it. When Trigeño nodded, it was Beta's turn to mumble about how much it had cost him.

I called Mamá and asked for Javier Díaz's number. He answered straightaway and I put the call on loudspeaker.

'Pedro, what a pleasant—'

'Javier, remember that three million dollars you offered me?'

'It was only one million.'

'It's three. Or it's nothing. Your choice.'

There was a long pause. 'Okay, then. Three. When do we get to—?'

'I'll phone you back with the date.'

I hung up and looked at Trigeño for his reaction.

He stood with his hands on his hips, probably wondering what exactly I might be offering in return for so much money, but also trying his hardest not to look impressed.

Alfa 1 watched Trigeño, matching his commander's increasing curiosity with his own increasing disbelief – surely Trigeño would not let me bribe my way out, especially not with someone else's money. Alfa 1 snarled sarcastically. 'And how do you propose to get us into Llorona?'

I should have offered only the money. Mentioning Llorona had been a stupid, impulsive boast caused by my desperation. But now I had to make good on it.

I dialled Colonel Buitrago at the Garbanzos Battalion. This was a far greater gamble than my previous calls to the bulldog *fiscal* and Javier. Buitrago had repeatedly sent word via Mamá not to contact him, but everything now depended on his taking my call.

Buitrago's secretary answered. She insisted the colonel wasn't in his office. I insisted it was an emergency. She said she'd do her utmost to have him phone me back if I left a number. I told her that was not an option. '*¡Por favor!* My life depends on him taking this call right now.'

The secretary sighed, there was a long pause, and then finally the phone line clicked and she patched me through.

'Pedro, what can I do for you?'

'We need to meet, Colonel. I have a proposal that I think will interest you.'

'What kind of proposal?'

'A proposal to save Llorona and your job along with it.'

There was another lengthy pause, this one lasting as long as a hangman's rope.

'Okay, I'm listening.'

PART SEVEN

SOCIAL CLEANSING

106

AFTER MY TRIAL at La Quebrada, I was carried to the infirmary on a stretcher. I was dehydrated, hypothermic and at risk of serious infection. Nevertheless, I was ecstatic. Every microscopic cell of my body rejoiced at being alive and every second that passed felt like a miracle.

Although exhausted, I needed to thank Palillo for bringing the river stones that had saved my life. I had a hundred things to ask him. What had happened after he and Ñoño left me by the Río Jaguar? Had they seen the news coverage? And, of course, had they made that dreaded phone call to my mother or Camila?

After all I'd suffered, I hoped Palillo would help me process things and put them in perspective. But when he arrived, he stood with his hands on his hips, fuming.

'Palillo, thank you so much for—'

'We thought you were dead. *Dead*, you understand? Just like MacGyver, Tortuga and Yucca.'

'I almost was. But I—'

'We were devastated. Grieving for four days. And then you turn up here in La Quebrada. I cried with joy when I saw you alive. I didn't know what you'd done wrong and I didn't care. I swam out with your knife, but you didn't escape.'

'I'm sorry. I—'

'And then I find out from Culebra that you went across that river on your own. Against orders.'

'But I shot and injured Santiago. I couldn't let him escape.'

'I don't care! You weren't there to carry the stretchers. You weren't there to hear Tiburón screaming. Or to see Beta shoot Mango to put him out of his misery.'

I sat up with my head bowed. Palillo had every right to feel betrayed. He'd warned me about my obsession and we'd agreed to take Santiago down together.

'I'm sorry. I've learned my lesson.'

'No you haven't. You go after your father's killers the first time, you almost get caught. You go after them again, you almost get killed. They capture you, arrest you and almost drown you, but you haven't learned a *puta* thing.'

Palillo left, slamming the door so hard it bounced back open.

'At least tell me one thing,' I called after him. 'Did you phone my mother?'

But Palillo didn't answer. He wanted me to think about it. Maybe he had. Maybe he hadn't. And while I did, he wanted me to suffer.

Ñoño and Piolín came to see me next. Ñoño threw himself on the bed and hugged me. 'I'm so glad you're alive!'

He proudly showed me his patched buttock. Doctors had removed the round and the wound was healing quickly. He told me that the evacuation of the injured had taken three days. Dozens of soldiers were still recovering in small clinics.

'Don't worry,' Piolín said. 'Palillo didn't phone your mother.'

Through an anonymous intermediary, Trigeño would deliver the news and pay three months' salary to the families of those who'd sacrificed their lives for Colombia. We'd still need to dig up the jar and send our friends' final messages to their loved ones, but we wouldn't have to break the news ourselves.

According to Piolín, Venezuela hadn't yet lodged a complaint about the bombing, and it was too early to know whether Santiago had perished or been captured. After my trial, Trigeño had praised Alfa 1's leadership and bravery and held a ceremony for the dead. As I suspected, it had been Trigeño's decision to cross the river. He claimed the battle was a grand victory; however, looking at the empty spaces in the ranks, few believed him.

'You're a hero, Pedro,' said Ñoño excitedly. 'Trigeño's saying you're the bravest soldier in the Autodefensas. He said you kill *guerrilleros* while on vacation!'

I laughed, but I didn't feel like a hero, and I couldn't bring myself to tell them about our dead friends being displayed dressed as *guerrilleros* on the Caracol report.

Before Ñoño and Piolín left, I asked them what to do about Palillo.

'Give him a few days,' said Piolín, squeezing my hand.

Phoning Mamá and Camila felt strange. To them, nothing had changed since we'd last spoken. I'd just undergone the most traumatic events of my life since Papa's execution, but I couldn't tell the two people I loved most, and I couldn't expect comfort from them.

I slept for twenty-two hours and the following day was transferred to La 35 to the home of Trigeño's mother, the kindly *señora* I'd passed several times in the chapel during our sniper course. She had a soft voice and a gentle manner, and tended to me in a room with lace curtains, urging me to rest and get strong, just like Mamá used to do when I was sick.

'Drink this chicken broth,' she said, placing a steaming bowl beside my bed along with a Bible. 'You need to build up your strength.'

When Trigeño entered the room, however, she muttered excuses to me and departed without looking at him. Trigeño seemed embarrassed but didn't offer an explanation. Instead, he gave me a signed copy of his recently published memoir – already a bestseller.

I received two more visits: the first was from Alfa 1. Thanks to Trigeño, Alfa 1 couldn't touch me, but our relationship would never be the same. I couldn't forget how he'd looked me in the eyes, placed a pistol to my temple and stated unequivocally that he wanted me dead.

'Proud of yourself?' he asked sarcastically.

'I was stupid.'

'No, *I* was stupid, deciding to forgive you and trust you.' He shook his head and left me drowning in a deep well of disappointment.

My second visitor was Beta, who would oversee the operation to take over Llorona, assuming details could be finalised with Buitrago and the Díaz brothers.

'Three million dollars?' he said approvingly. 'Quite some friends you have there. And I don't believe for a minute that you killed Ratón on your own. But you said nothing about your *negro* friend, even when you were half-dead. Those classes on resisting torture I gave you must have worked.'

My recovery took three weeks. I spent days alone in bed, thinking. At first, I fretted about Colonel Buitrago. During our phone call, he'd agreed to meet. But when I'd hinted at a possible alliance, he'd cut me short, saying, 'Not over the phone! I'll meet with you, but only you.'

What if he refused to co-operate with Trigeño? What if he didn't like our proposal?

I also worried about the upcoming deal with the Díaz brothers. For months, I'd deliberately downplayed my family's closeness to the Díaz clan. However, once he met them it wouldn't take long before he learned of their previous offers and that my mother was living with them.

But the wheels were now set in motion, so I tried to focus on the positives, such as what life would be like if we ousted the Guerrilla from Llorona.

Mamá would no longer need to rely on Javier's charity. We could reclaim rightful ownership of our *finca*, restoring it to its former glory. Uncle Leo could rebuild his hardware business. Don Felix could operate his bus routes. Don Mauricio's wife and children might return. The townspeople would be happy, no longer living in fear of extortion, murder and kidnapping. And most importantly, Camila might decide to stay.

When my strength returned, Trigeño took me fishing and I saw my opportunity to pre-empt any surprises. He'd sent to Llorona for my fishing rod and I ran my hands over the cane shaft, savouring its smoothness and remembering blissful days spent fishing with Papá on the sparkling river. As I turned the cedar handle to inspect the initials of my father, grandfather and great-grandfather, I noticed a fourth set burned into it – my own.

'I hope you're not offended that I look this liberty,' Trigeño said, 'but you're the man of the family now.'

I was touched. It was what Papá would have done for me on my sixteenth birthday.

'*Gracias, comando*. But there's something you should know,' I said. 'Last Christmas, the Díaz brothers wanted me to vouch for them to you in exchange for setting up an ambush against Zorrillo. I didn't accept because they're not brave and honourable people like you.'

Of course, I didn't mention my attempt on Zorrillo's life using the stolen Galil or that I'd read the intelligence file listing Humberto Díaz as a *traficante* – Trigeño was thorough and would likely read the files himself. Instead, I spontaneously chose to reveal my life's biggest secret: that Papá and I had buried Díaz.

'Papá was the one who suggested my mother place flowers on Humberto's grave. Later, Mamá received a threat from Zorrillo, and Javier offered her his house and bodyguards as protection.'

I was nervous about how Trigeño would react, but when he finally spoke, he wasn't angry at all.

'Thank you for your honesty,' he said. 'I never met Humberto myself, but he contacted me three years ago. He wanted our assistance against the Guerrilla. Back then, we had few soldiers and resources, and he claimed not to have the money to finance the plan, so it fell through. I think his sons know this and now want to resurrect the deal. But if we do go into Llorona, you need to know what you're getting into.'

Trigeño's face clouded over.

'When I declared war on the Guerrilla, they marked me and my four brothers for death. A month later, my two older brothers, David and

Ricardo, were driving to the cattle markets with their bodyguard when their truck was stopped at a Guerrilla roadblock. David refused to accompany them, so they shot him. My eldest brother, Ricardo, had no choice but to go with them. I paid Ricardo's ransom not once but twice. However, instead of releasing him, the Guerrilla killed him and strung up his body from that guayacan tree at the turnoff from the highway to La 50. It was meant as a threat to all those who'd joined my crusade. Ever since, I've been determined the Guerrilla will never take me alive. I keep my "emergency grenade" attached to me at all times, even when I sleep.

'After my brothers' deaths, five years ago, my mother vowed never to speak to me again, blaming their loss on my decision to go to war. She spends her days tending her vegetable garden and reading the Bible. She used to love going to church in town. But I won't risk her leaving the property, so I had the little wooden chapel built for her. She tells her friends that living on La 35 is like being in prison. I know keeping her here is the right decision, but she loathes me for it.'

'I think my mother resents me too.'

'Women don't always know what is best for them, Pedro. Part of being a man is doing what is right, no matter what people think of you. That is the sacrifice you must make.'

I was deeply moved by his confiding in me these excruciating experiences, which he'd omitted from his book. Trigeño dug his rod into the muddy bank and turned to face me.

'Pedro, I've lost almost everything I love. My father, two brothers and the sanctity of my home. My two remaining brothers are depressed. My whole family hates me . . .'

His voice trailed off, but I understood. I understood how it felt to have your father executed and left like a dead dog in the dirt. To have your own mother resent and blame you. I understood more than he could know.

'We need to get these bastards,' he said with a sudden flash of anger. 'I have my own score to settle with Zorrillo for murdering my cousin Jerónimo. But if this meeting is successful, the honour of killing him will be yours.'

I couldn't help but notice that while I'd earned the admiration of Trigeño and Beta – two men capable of the most brutal acts I'd ever witnessed – I'd simultaneously provoked anger in Palillo and Alfa 1, the two people whose esteem I most valued. Nevertheless, I chose to ignore these needling doubts when, a week later, Trigeño and I departed for Javier Díaz's hacienda to discuss the strategy for invading Llorona.

107

I CLIMBED APPREHENSIVELY into the co-pilot's seat of Trigeño's tiny four-seater Bell 204 helicopter and watched with trepidation as he flicked switches and twisted dials. My fingers gripped the seat as the engine pitch rose and the rotors began humming. Then my stomach dropped through my legs as we shot skyward.

Once my adrenalin settled I was able to appreciate the magnificent sights whirring past hundreds of metres below – broad, sweeping wetlands dotted with clumps of trees, snaking rivers and large lakes.

As we flew south, the Llanos floodplains gave way to vertiginous ridges and vast mountain ranges blanketed with dense, green jungle. From the air, my country seemed so peaceful and beautiful; it was hard to imagine a vicious, bloody war raging below. At the same time the aerial perspective emphasised our enemy's advantage: thousands of square kilometres of uninhabited territory to hide in and from which to launch guerrilla attacks.

I had two meetings that day: the first to introduce Trigeño to the Díaz brothers; the second on my own with Colonel Buitrago. The Díaz brothers had already signalled their willingness to pay and to trap Zorrillo, but the logistical and military details required negotiation. If both meetings were successful, the Díazes would convene a third meeting of the region's prominent citizens.

I looked down suddenly and recognised the Garbanzos plaza and church spire. The journey, which normally took fourteen hours along winding mountain roads, had lasted only an hour. Before touching down on the immaculate lawn of Javier's hacienda, we passed low over Camila's *colegio*. Since these meetings were secret, I'd phoned her to let her know I'd be in Garbanzos briefly for work but that I wouldn't be able to see her.

The Díaz brothers rushed out to greet us while the rotors were still spinning. Javier shook my hand. 'We knew we could rely on you, Pedro. You're like family to us.'

I bit my tongue. I wasn't sure I wanted to be treated as his family; my corpse might end up abandoned on a riverbank.

'And that goes for your mother too,' said Fabián unctuously, although his eyes gleamed with malice.

Mamá was at work, but if Fabián thought mentioning her in front of Trigeño might give him bargaining power, he was wrong. I'd already defused the threat.

We sat under an umbrella by the pool. Eleonora Díaz emerged from the house and offered Trigeño whisky from a crystal decanter.

'*Gracias*,' said Trigeño dryly, 'but it's too early to be celebrating. Ousting the Guerrilla will be more difficult than it would have been three years ago.'

Javier glanced at me, realising this meant I was aware of his father's proposal. I could see him recalibrating his assessment of my closeness to Trigeño. After the formalities, we got down to details.

'War is expensive,' stated Trigeño. 'Your funds will cover troops, uniforms, weapons, bullets, vehicles, food and bribes. We'll also need to set up a base near Llorona to prevent the Guerrilla returning. Right now your mother's *finca* is in Guerrilla territory – that means it's worthless. So we use that as our headquarters, then hand it back to you when the area is pacified.'

'But that's our childhood home,' complained Fabián. 'Is there nowhere else—?'

'No, there isn't. Do you want us here or not?'

Javier and Fabián exchanged wary glances. Clearly, they were used to setting terms themselves and had expected a friendly negotiation.

'Of course we do,' Javier conceded meekly.

'Then don't question me again or this whole deal is off.'

They shook hands with Trigeño to seal the agreement, and that concluded our initial meeting.

Javier nodded sternly to his brother, who disappeared. Then he offered Trigeño a personal tour of the hacienda while I departed for Buitrago's barracks to attempt a far more difficult negotiation.

108

THE TAXI DROPPED me at the battalion gate, which was directly opposite Camila's *colegio*. It was lunch hour and I stole a quick glance into the yard full of students, knowing she'd be sitting somewhere in the shade with her group of friends. It felt strange being back in town, so very close to Camila and yet unable even to establish contact.

In Buitrago's office I found the colonel looking wearier than I'd ever seen him. He was unshaven and had dark circles under his eyes. Clearly, the intense scrutiny from his superiors and public calls for his resignation were taking their toll.

'Thanks for meeting me, Colonel,' I began respectfully. 'I know that you haven't always approved of our methods.'

'I still don't,' he responded tersely. 'But my superiors leave me little choice. Two weeks before you phoned, they denied my meagre request for three trucks and one hundred more men. And then this happened.' He slid two photos across his desk, the first showing the mangled, charred shell of an exploded car, the second showing the warped battalion gates and the surrounding concrete strewn with twisted metal and broken glass. 'Three of my men killed on my doorstep. Two in hospital on life support. How can I fight barbarians when my own bosses have tied one hand behind my back?'

'I'm sorry for your men, Colonel, but I believe we can work together. My commander, Trigeño, would like to discuss our security proposal, man to man.'

Buitrago shook his head. 'After his book, that's impossible. He's a fugitive from justice. We can't even be seen in the same room.'

This came as a shock. I knew Trigeño's book had divided the nation. To many, he was a celebrity; to others, a pariah. However, I didn't know of any charges against him.

I pushed on with a description of our proposed military plan for ousting the Guerrilla. Phase One: ambush Zorrillo. Phase Two: establish our headquarters near Llorona and conduct patrols and reconnaissance. And Phase Three: occupy Puerto Galán and the river villages in order to weaken the Guerrilla logistics and intelligence networks in preparation for a coordinated attack on their temporary bases.

'However, to do this we'll need your assistance,' I concluded.

'What sort of assistance?'

I began to list Trigeño's requirements, which I termed 'requests' in deference to Buitrago. 'We're hoping to use your base to house our off-duty men and store supplies.'

'Completely illegal and out of the question.'

'What about granting us access to the Garbanzos airfield?

'Can't do that either. The Americans use it for their coca fumigation program.'

'Can't you move them elsewhere?'

The colonel laughed. 'Where do you think our helicopters come from? Who do you think pays for their maintenance? And provides our new weapons?'

'At a very minimum, we need you at tomorrow's community meeting about local security with Trigeño. If you don't give your backing, we simply can't operate.'

'Let me make this perfectly clear, Pedro. Even if I did agree, I wouldn't be *giving* you my backing. I would be *lending* you my permission, which I could withdraw at any time. And that's only provided your boss accepts my conditions: No mistreatment of civilians. No massacres. No torture. You hand over prisoners to us for processing. If you have suspicions but no proof against sympathisers, then you simply warn them to leave. I'm not agreeing yet, but I'll need your word on this, Pedro.'

Clearly, he'd read the magazine articles filled with allegations about Autodefensa massacres.

'Even if reports of those atrocities are true, they were committed by other *bloques* not under Trigeño's control. That's not how he operates, I can assure you.'

'I'll need his assurance too.'

'Then come to the meeting at Javier's. Many prominent citizens will be there.'

When the colonel still hesitated, I used my riskiest argument. 'You need us, Colonel. The communist cancer is spreading. Isn't any cure worth trying?'

Having secured Buitrago's reluctant agreement to attend the meeting, I detoured via the officers' mess and asked for Señora Gutiérrez.

Mamá emerged from the kitchen wearing pink washing gloves, with soapsuds on her brow. When she saw me a joyful smile lit up her face. 'Pedro! When did you get here?'

'I came with my boss this morning,' I said, kissing her cheek. 'He's visiting Javier on business.'

'You should have phoned. I'll ask the chef for an hour's break.'

'I'm sorry, Mamá. I'm on duty. But next time, I'll stay much longer. And you'll soon be able to quit this job.'

I returned early to Javier's hacienda to see him and Trigeño strolling back towards the mansion, deep in conversation. They shook hands firmly, and when Javier tried to withdraw his fingers, Trigeño squeezed harder so the muscles on his forearm stood out. He pointed at Javier threateningly.

'May I ask what that was about?' I asked Trigeño later, on the flight home.

'About how we'll run things afterwards,' he answered. 'And also about the Díaz brothers' participation in Phase One – the operation against your soon-to-be-departed friend, Zorrillo. It'll be dangerous, so Javier needed considerable persuading.'

This sounded plausible, but I couldn't shake the feeling there was something he wasn't telling me. Trigeño had trusted me with everything else. Why not include me in the part that was most personal to me?

Everything now hung on obtaining Colonel Buitrago's final agreement at the Community Security Meeting, which Javier was arranging for 5 pm the next day.

The following afternoon, twenty prominent ranchers and businessmen, including Don Felix and Don Mauricio, attended the meeting in Javier's spacious living room. Four servants dragged out the heavy teak dining table, carried in additional chairs and sofas, served drinks and then discreetly retired. To operate effectively, we needed every powerful person in the region on side, or at least no one making high-level complaints. All the guests knew why they'd been invited and who Trigeño was, but if they were made nervous by his presence, they covered it with noisy conversation.

Colonel Buitrago was the last to arrive. He entered Javier's living room looking like a man attending his own funeral. Silence fell over the group and all eyes turned to him. It was a bad sign that he was without his usual aides and dressed in civilian attire.

Buitrago removed his hat, kissed Eleonora gravely on the cheek and shook hands loosely with her sons. He nodded to me but averted his eyes from Trigeño and deliberately moved away from us, sitting tensely on the edge of his seat.

Trigeño stood immediately and took control.

'We are united here today for a just and patriotic cause. We have a common enemy – the communist Guerrilla. Unfortunately our individual efforts to date have been unsuccessful. Divided we remain weak. But together we will triumph.'

After a nod from Javier, Eleonora Díaz followed.

'The communist subversives demanded a million dollars for my late husband's safe return. That's in addition to the dozens of land plots we were forced to "donate" or sell to their collaborators at reduced prices, and the cash, cattle and crops they extorted from us. I'm now prepared to offer that money to the cause.'

Trigeño's eyes lit up. That made four million dollars for his war chest. Perhaps the Díaz family expected this to inspire other, albeit smaller, donations; however, after a respectful silence, everyone wanted his say and no one was offering money.

One after another, the attendees rose to their feet to decry the Guerrilla and list their numerous crimes. With each new tale of woe, people nodded and murmured approval. Some even glanced at Trigeño and cried out that it was time for 'a new military solution'.

Suddenly, Colonel Buitrago stood and called for silence. He now expressed his scepticism, explaining the difficulty of controlling thousands of square kilometres of mountainous jungle against a highly mobile enemy.

'I've been fighting these criminals for twenty-five years, and there's one thing I've learned: this war will not be won with military campaigns alone. The Guerrilla thrives on poverty. This region needs business investment, cell phone coverage and services like health, education, roadways and electricity.'

Fabián jumped in. 'Infrastructure is the government's responsibility, not ours.'

'Private companies need to reinvest profits and create employment,' countered Buitrago. 'People with jobs don't join revolutions.'

'Companies can't invest here when there's so much criminality,' Fabián persisted, ignoring a quelling look from his normally dominant brother, who was keeping himself unusually quiet.

'If you're referring to cocaine trafficking, preventing it is the responsibility of the National Police. If the army were in charge, young man, things would be very different . . .'

This pointed mention of cocaine was the closest Buitrago had come to acknowledging what he surely must have known about the Díazes. It stopped Fabián like a stick between two bicycle spokes. But we were veering into dangerous territory.

Trigeño stood once more. 'There will be no cocaine trafficking,' he said forcefully. 'We'll discourage pickers and planters and create alternative legal employment. Through my agricultural co-operative, I'll donate seeds, fertiliser and herbicides to farmers willing to destroy their coca crops.'

I scrutinised the brothers' faces. They hadn't invited the Autodefensas into the region and donated three million dollars only to destroy their main source of income. But their expressions were impassive.

'Now,' continued Trigeño, 'who will stand in the senate elections next March? Once the Guerrilla is ousted, the region can hold its first fair ballot in years.'

'I'd like to nominate Fabián,' Javier said coolly, looking around at the attendees. I now understood his earlier reticence; he'd wanted Fabián to occupy centre stage.

Grumbling came from across the room until Don Felix Velasquez stood to vocalise the group's opposition. 'Then I nominate Don Mauricio,' he stated.

After a long pause, Mauricio assented reluctantly and humbly. 'If the group agrees that it needs me, then I will stand.'

With the exception of Fabián, Javier and Trigeño, the gathering applauded.

Trigeño now presented a document. It was entitled REFOUNDING THE GREAT NATION OF COLOMBIA, with a rambling text below that made no mention of the Autodefensas or anything illegal. This was to be Trigeño's masterstroke – his solution for locking Buitrago into the pact and his insurance policy in case he tried to pull out.

Trigeño signed first and then offered the document to the colonel for signature. But Buitrago had little to gain by signing. In fact, if the document ever became public, he could go to prison.

Staring at the paper in front of him, he stated categorically, 'I will not sign.'

'Then there is no pact,' responded Trigeño menacingly, 'and you will go down in history as the man who lost Garbanzos. These patriots here are witnesses to your refusal.'

Never had I seen a man so pained as Colonel Buitrago. It was as though he'd been asked to sell his soul to the devil. The others' stares rattled him. He glanced towards heaven, made the sign of the cross and then kissed the crucifix on his necklace. Finally, he stood and extended his arm.

'As a gentleman, I prefer handshakes.'

Trigeño hesitated but saw that if he refused and Buitrago called his bluff the entire deal might fall through. Scarcely concealing a scowl, he shook Buitrago's hand. There were murmurs of relief and another spontaneous round of applause. My clapping was by far the loudest. I'd felt like my skull was in a vice, with Trigeño and Buitrago taking turns to screw it a notch tighter. But with their handshake, the pressure was suddenly alleviated.

Many months later, when the dark alliance I'd helped to found descended into chaos, I recognised Buitrago's wisdom in not signing. Reluctantly, he'd permitted the presence of the Autodefensas because he needed them to win the war. However, at the appropriate time, he would also need to kick them out.

109

'DON'T FUCK ME around, Pedro,' said Palillo after we'd touched down at La 35. He waved his long, black finger across my face like a windscreen wiper in violent weather. 'Just tell me straight. My sister phoned. She saw you in Garbanzos plaza.'

I stopped walking. We were out of earshot.

'We're going to take back Llorona. And the river towns.'

'And you organised this?'

'Parts of it, yes.'

Now that I was in the mood for honesty, I told Palillo everything. I told him about the intelligence files, the true circumstances of Humberto Díaz's death and my conversations with Buitrago. I told him about the child *vacuna* collectors, my attempts to assassinate Zorrillo and how I'd nearly been captured at the Guerrilla roadblock. And I told him about the Díaz brothers being cocaine traffickers, their approaches to me and the offer I'd made to Trigeño after La Quebrada.

The conversation took over an hour and Palillo was initially exasperated by my revelations, and incredulous that the Autodefensas wanted to retake Llorona.

But he was a pragmatist and was quick to grasp the possible benefits. If the Autodefensas cleaned up Puerto Galán, they'd ban coca-leaf pickers, wife-beaters and public drunkenness. Palillo's stepfather would have to curtail his nasty habits and find legitimate work, or leave.

'And now we have our ticket for a clean exit from the Autodefensas,' I told him. 'Trigeño's grateful for all I'm doing, and I'll ask him to release you, me and Piolín once it's done.'

For several seconds, Palillo was left speechless. Then his grin stretched as wide as the keys on a grand piano. He raised his hand to give me a high five. 'Genius, Pedro! Absolute genius!'

I laughed and he hugged me.

This warm embrace ushered in a fresh era in our friendship, one of complete co-operation in which there were no more secrets. We were one hundred per cent in this together, and when it was over, I was confident we'd be one hundred per cent out.

A week later, I found myself once more touching down with Trigeño on Javier's lawn, this time to begin the operation against Zorrillo.

Our plan was for one Díaz brother to attend a meeting with Zorrillo, luring him down from the Guerrilla's mountain camps, while the other brother stayed with Trigeño as 'insurance' in case the first wanted to back out. Trigeño was more than happy with my request to send Fabián.

Nevertheless, once we were seated in their living room and Trigeño had outlined the plan, he initially let the brothers think they had a choice, and we both enjoyed observing their cowardice as they bickered over who should go in the Mercedes.

'Why do *I* have to drive?' Fabián whined when Trigeño finally informed him he was to go. He knew he'd be risking his life in an ambush operation that could turn into full-scale combat.

'Because Pedro says you've had your licence for years.'

I'd told Trigeño about Fabián's insults at the Díazes' party, and I now struggled to suppress a grin.

Fabián looked at me imploringly. 'You've done this before, right? You know how to shoot?'

'Of course! I hit my mark about sixty per cent of the time,' I lied, relishing the reversal of our positions. 'Although wind or humidity can bring down my average.'

Javier pretended to be sympathetic towards Fabián, but his face showed relief at not being chosen, until Trigeño cocked his pistol and handed him the cordless phone.

'Javier, make the call. If anything goes wrong, you're both dead.'

I'd never expected this from Trigeño, and neither had they. Javier had viewed his pact with the Autodefensas as a partnership. In their own world, the Díaz brothers may have been princes with bodyguards and a court packed with famous models and wealthy hangers-on. But in our world – the world of war – they were like schoolboys.

Javier began sweating, and with good reason. If our plan worked, Caraquemada would list the brothers as military targets and there'd be no turning back. But he made the call exactly as Trigeño had coached him.

'I want to make peace,' he began, referring to the recent bombing of his bus and the price placed on his head after he protested Zorrillo's rising *vacunas*. Trigeño had instructed him to sound nervous and desperate, but Javier didn't have to pretend. With a pistol trained on him, his voice quavered. 'Our family can't afford the current *vacunas*, but neither can we afford any more buses or trucks being torched, nor our employees being kidnapped and murdered. I'm prepared to consider your demands provided my brother can speak to you face to face at our hacienda in Garbanzos.'

Trigeño knew that Zorrillo would never agree to enter Garbanzos, and Zorrillo reacted exactly as expected, by proposing a meeting deep in their territory. 'He can meet us in Puerto Princesa. I'll call with the time and place.'

'No! I need Fabián to feel safe. He'll be in our armoured Mercedes and he'll bring our bodyguards. He'll also bring the overdue payments. But the renegotiation of our deal needs to take place somewhere he knows, closer to Garbanzos.'

It was unusual for civilians to make demands of the Guerrilla, but the bait was attractive – a large amount of cash, a kidnappable businessman and his older brother still free to organise the ransom. Zorrillo was probably chuckling at Javier's insistence on an armoured vehicle. Tyres could be shot. The exit road could be blocked with logs. And even the Mercedes level III's reinforced glass windows would splinter and shatter after several successive impacts from 5.56mm rounds.

Nevertheless, these demands would reassure Zorrillo it wasn't a trap. More importantly, they prevented him from deducing the true location we were angling for.

In fact, Zorrillo waltzed into the trap by suggesting it himself. 'Your father's old *finca* then. We'll phone back with the time.'

He hung up.

Six snipers, including Palillo and me, were to embed at the meeting place immediately.

Zorrillo would undoubtedly send an advance party to sweep Humberto Díaz's old *finca*, but travelling from the Guerrilla camps to the meeting place would take at least a day. And on arrival the scouts would be looking for a government army platoon with thirty men, whereas we'd be as visible as six mossy rocks on a riverbank.

Trigeño patted me on the back and looked at his watch. It was 4 pm and there was just enough light left to get into position. 'Good luck!'

Although we'd performed dozens of mock insertions and ambush operations, I had butterflies in my stomach. Trigeño assured me this was normal: I was like a groom on his wedding day. Provided the bride showed up, nothing could go wrong.

110

OUR OPERATIVES WERE divided into three sniper teams: Fredys and Piraña, Coyote and Indio, Palillo and me. Once embedded on Hacienda Díaz, we'd be camouflaged in our hides. However, reaching our destination – fifteen kilometres inside enemy territory – was the risky part.

Since Buitre had a semi-permanent checkpoint outside Garbanzos, highway travel wasn't an option. Neither was a helicopter insertion, which would be noisy and visible. We couldn't travel by boat because of enemy controls on river traffic. The simplest way to infiltrate Guerrilla territory was also the most dangerous – trekking through the fields that I'd known since childhood.

We exited Javier's hacienda at irregular intervals with plans to rendezvous at my own family's *finca*. In order to pass for a *campesino* boy, I carried chickens in a wicker basket, while Palillo hauled plastic bags filled with groceries. The others lugged sacks of corncobs in which our rifles were concealed. Meanwhile, Colonel Buitrago sent out multiple helicopter sorties over the Santo Paraíso side of the river so it would appear as though the army were conducting an operation in a different location.

We made it safely to our rendezvous point, and when I passed Papá's unmarked grave and entered my house for the first time in fifteen months, I needed no further reminders of Zorrillo's crimes. The exterior walls were now whitewashed, but inside the house, the sight of the shredded and smashed fragments of our precious possessions filled me with pain and anger. This time, though, I'd finally make Zorrillo pay.

We freed the chickens, buried the corncobs and removed our rifles and suits from the sacks. Then we walked the short distance to Hacienda Díaz, stopping in a cluster of trees on the property's edge. It was just before sunset, allowing us an hour of fading light for observation.

The old ranch contrasted starkly with Javier's luxury mansion. The main house, which I'd visited several times during my childhood, was a sturdy two-storey building of stone, adobe and wood built in Spanish colonial style with fourteen high-ceilinged rooms arranged around a tiled central patio. Since Humberto's death, the dwelling had fallen into disrepair. The faded paint had peeled off completely. The large wooden entrance door now hung at an odd angle, and the surrounding grass had grown thick and tall.

Seventy metres to the west stood a milking shed. A little further away to the northwest was a large barn. On the other side of the main house was a tin-roofed caretaker's cottage with cracked windows and a large verandah bordered by rotting wooden railings. With some defences added, I thought, all four buildings could serve nicely as our new headquarters.

Suddenly, Palillo stiffened. He'd heard a noise. We turned our scopes back towards the main house just in time to witness a sow emerging through the servants' door with six piglets trailing behind and a gaggle of twenty hens in angry pursuit.

These animals might belong to squatters living inside, or they may simply have turned wild after Eleonora abandoned the ranch. Either way, we had no plans to sweep the place. Even if Zorrillo had already embedded observers, confronting them would ruin the mission. Our priority was to remain concealed and wait for our target to arrive.

Once darkness fell, we crawled towards the farmhouse to take up position in the hides we'd identified. We rejected the optimal firing locations as they'd be the first checked by enemy scouts. Instead, we selected three sub-optimal positions that formed a triangle around the farmhouse, camouflaging ourselves in slightly indented gullies in the rocky fields, only one hundred and twenty metres from the main building. Because we were so exposed, we'd be relying on surprise and fast, accurate shooting.

If the Guerrilla came at night with infra-red goggles, the surrounding rocks would hopefully retain enough of the sun's heat to throw up confusing temperature patterns. We could also use water from our water bottles to streak our faces with mud and dampen our ghillie suits, temporarily lowering our body heat emissions.

'No police on the highway,' Palillo said over the headset, our code for having embedded safely.

The response came through: 'Stand by for delivery of the *gallinita*.'

The *little chicken* was Fabián. We had no way of predicting when Zorrillo would phone back to specify the meeting time. I hoped it would be sooner than later, although we had enough water and energy bars to last up to five days.

Palillo and I spent that night motionless in our hide, one observing while the other slept, alternating every two hours. The cool night passed comfortably with no movement or sound apart from stray animals, and I spent the quiet hours mentally reviewing our plan.

I would take the first shot. Zorrillo, of course, was the main target. But Trigeño and Buitrago hoped the *guerrilleros* would come in considerable numbers. Buitre might even be among them since he was now in charge of kidnapping. However, even if he wasn't, I had Zorrillo's farewell planned in detail.

Army intelligence files listed him as 162 centimetres tall and left-handed – valuable information for a sniper since a target's split-second movements can make the difference between his life and death. And I wanted Zorrillo *alive*. Injured, but alive. This time I had authorisation not to kill him immediately. I'd aim at his trigger arm and then we'd finish off his men. Buitrago had two Blackhawks on standby to pursue any who escaped.

My main fear was that Zorrillo would shoot himself before I could force him to surrender. But if he did give himself up, I'd offer him bandages. And then I'd hand him Padre Rojas's Bible, make him kneel and circle him, just as Caraquemada had circled my father.

The following morning's sky was blue and cloudless. The frenzied hum of insects portended a wretchedly hot day. Lying in position, I felt safe and composed. Even Trigeño's precautions against a double-cross by the Díaz brothers filled me with confidence.

Right then, committing wholeheartedly to the Autodefensas seemed like the best decision of my life. But with Trigeño's trust had come much responsibility. He was counting on me. I couldn't let him down.

By midday the sun blazed overhead, heating my suit until it felt like a furnace. We endured a further three hours of scorching heat, until 3 pm, when my faith was finally rewarded.

'I've got a flat tyre,' said Palillo into his headset as he nudged me. My eyes followed the direction in which his binoculars were pointed. Human figures were moving slowly at the edge of the woods.

The enemy was arriving.

111

THE GUERRILLA'S ADVANCE squad of ten men looked rested and relaxed. They walked close together, laughing as though this were a routine visit. Another twenty *guerrilleros* came shortly afterwards, making a total of thirty. Zorrillo was not among them, although he may have been hanging back among the trees.

The *guerrilleros* spread out, searching the homestead and surrounding hills. One of them walked briskly towards our hide. He stopped at the rock directly in front of us and looked down.

Since the whites of eyes reflect a very distinctive light pattern, I followed proper procedure, even though it was the opposite of what my survival instincts were screaming – I closed my eyes and trusted my camouflage. Holding my breath while listening to enemy urine splashing onto the dirt only one metre away was absolutely terrifying. The tensest few seconds came after the splashing stopped. Had the *guerrillero* suddenly seen us, or simply finished? I thought I heard him zipping up his pants. Or was he reaching for his weapon? Then I heard footsteps receding. I opened my eyes and looked at Palillo. Our camouflage had held.

Eventually, the searchers must have given Zorrillo the 'all clear' because a transmission came from Trigeño: 'We'll save you some beers,' meaning Javier had just received Zorrillo's phone call and sent Fabián off in the car.

Twenty minutes later, the Mercedes arrived, its wheels crunching slowly up the gravel driveway, a cloud of dust hovering in its wake. Fabián circled and the brakes squealed as the vehicle pulled to a stop in front of the farmhouse, facing downhill with the engine idling.

The platoon surrounded the vehicle immediately. Its leader tapped on the hood, signalling for Fabián to exit. I began fretting. There was still no sign of Zorrillo. Had he sensed our trap and decided not to appear? To Fabián's credit, he followed our instructions not to drive off. If Zorrillo didn't show within three minutes, he was to make a hasty exit. They must have been the longest three minutes of Fabián's life. One minute passed. And then another. With ten seconds to go, he began revving the engine and thirty rifles were raised and pointed at the car windows. I pictured Fabián and his bodyguards trapped inside, cowering in anticipation of the volley of bullets that would surely follow his emergency retreat.

'There,' whispered Palillo, pointing to the far side of the clearing where another twenty *guerrilleros* had emerged from the trees.

Although Zorrillo frequently changed his appearance, that day he wasn't difficult to spot. Among dozens of soldiers, he was the only one wearing brown leather shoes and a gold watch. My heart beat faster as he sauntered towards the Mercedes with a bodyguard either side and tapped his knuckle against the window, signalling for Fabián to get out.

Finally, I thought. *This is actually happening.*

I took aim and nodded to Palillo, who gave two clicks on the radio – the signal that I was about to fire.

I breathed in deeply, and then released the air slowly. I squeezed the trigger. The Galil barked. Zorrillo clutched his upper left arm and then dropped to the ground. Half a second later, the report from the gunshot reached his companions and they dropped also, rolling towards the nearest cover – the Mercedes. Zorrillo's two bodyguards curled up on either side of him, beneath the front and rear axles. Nothing happened for a full five seconds. I'd forgotten to give the follow-up order. But I did now, just as the Mercedes sped off around the corner of the farmhouse, crunching over Zorrillo's ankle and depriving his men of their cover.

'*¡Dale!*'

We fired at the *guerrilleros* and they fired back wildly in all directions, also shooting at the Mercedes until it reached safety behind the homestead. Not knowing our positions, however, they were firing blind. Deprived of cover, they spread out and lay flat, crawling towards the trees.

We were now three highly trained sniper teams with thirty-round Galils against fifty *guerrilleros* bearing AK47s with similar firepower. But we had two advantages: first, they couldn't see us; second, they believed that lying flat and being spread out made it difficult for us to see *them*. We fired calmly and quickly on semi-automatic. Fifteen were down, including Zorrillo's bodyguards, before the remainder realised they were up against snipers and scampered for the trees. Our three spotters, including Palillo, changed to offensive mode, switching their rifles to automatic to join me and the other two snipers. The noise and muzzle flashes finally gave away our positions, but by then we had them divided and on the run. More than an entire platoon fell, one soldier after the other, while maybe a dozen managed to flee into the trees, leaving their commander writhing and abandoned in the centre of the field.

Palillo and I sprinted towards Zorrillo as quickly as our heavy ghillie suits permitted. Palillo kicked away his rifle and I confiscated his radio.

'Alias Zorrillo,' I stated calmly, throwing him a bandage and first-aid kit. 'Real name Edgar Hurtardo Junín, kidnapper and extortionist.' I pronounced his name in the same formal tone as Caraquemada had used to read out Papá's name from his *cédula*, as though it were proof of a crime.

Like a true coward at the moment of reckoning, Zorrillo tried to hide behind someone else. In this case, a dead person.

'I'm not Zorrillo.' After wrapping the bandage tightly around his upper arm, he pointed at a slain comrade. 'That's him right there. I'm just an ordinary soldier.'

I glanced at his wrist and raised my eyebrows. 'Wearing a Rolex?'

Just then, two of Buitrago's helicopters flew overhead in pursuit of the fleeing *guerrilleros*, and Zorrillo gave up the pretence, probably assuming I was from the army.

'I want a doctor and one of those helicopters here right now. I'm an important prisoner. You need to get me to hospital.'

'Do I? Do you know who I am?'

'A pathetic *campesino* boy with a gun licence from the oligarchy. But you've kept me alive for a reason. I'm too valuable to the government. Now get me your superior.'

'I'm the superior.'

'Then you know that you have to take me in.' He laughed. 'We have good magistrates. I'll be out in a week.'

'I believe your friend – I mean *your former friend* – Alias Ratón might disagree. I killed him.'

His eyes widened, although more in confusion than fear. His arrogant countenance remained. I was enjoying this game, so I teased it out some more.

'How's Santiago's left leg?' I smiled slowly. 'Yes, that was me too.'

I felt immense satisfaction watching his expression change once more as his arrogance faltered and his confusion turned to fear. 'But I still have rights,' he stammered.

'Not with me you don't.' I removed the hood of my suit so he could better see my face. 'You killed my father, prohibited his burial and banished us from our *finca*. What about *our* rights? What about the rights of everyone you've extorted, threatened and kidnapped?'

At last, recognition flickered in his eyes.

'Ah, yes. The liar, Pedro Gutiérrez González. You claimed to be a little sardine of fifteen. But I see you joined the capitalist army after all.'

'I'm seventeen now, and *no*, I didn't join the army.' I paused to let that sink in. 'You may recall the graffiti I painted over yours, with the same letters as these.' I peeled back my ghillie suit to reveal the black armband emblazoned with the white lettering of the Autodefensas' initials: AUC.

My words had the desired effect. Finally, the full horror of Zorrillo's predicament flooded in upon him.

Suddenly, he panicked. He scrambled to his feet and hobbled towards the trees, clutching his bandaged upper arm. Palillo took only four long strides to catch up. Clasping the nape of Zorrillo's neck, Palillo dragged him back to me like a mother cat lifting a helpless kitten. He pushed him flat to the ground and placed his knee on his head. I caressed the muzzle of my rifle along his cheek, and then dug it in hard against his teeth, just as he had once done to me.

Zorrillo began sobbing. Unclipping his watch, he held it up to me.

'Take this,' he said with difficulty. 'And I have cash. Lots of it buried in the jungle. I'm worth millions.'

'I'm not doing this for money.'

In his face, I finally saw the arrogance and narcissism shatter completely. His usual tricks weren't working. He was desperate now, begging me, imploring me to spare him. He looked pitiful, with his arms flailing in the dirt, trying to clasp my boot.

'Wait! Wait! Santiago and Caraquemada. They were the ones who killed your father, not me. I can take you to the base of those communist bastards.'

'I doubt that very much.'

I held up his radio handset – the one I'd confiscated. Since a dozen or more *guerrilleros* had escaped, word of our operation would already have reached his commanders anyway. And so I'd permitted myself a minor departure from Trigeño's script. This whole time, I'd had the TRANSMIT button depressed. The Guerrilla had listened to our every word.

Zorrillo blanched as he realised his commanders had heard his offer to betray them. For him, there was no going back to the Guerrilla now and he knew it.

I spoke into the handset, firmly and dispassionately.

'Buitre and Caraquemada. You've heard how much your cocaine cash cow loves you. Now hear this: I am Pedro Juan Gutiérrez González. I am an Autodefensa. I killed Ratón. I will now kill Zorrillo. You two are next.'

Then, as I nodded to Palillo, who raised Zorrillo unsteadily to his knees, I forced them to listen, just as they had made me watch my father's execution. They didn't see Zorrillo toss away the pocket Bible I offered him, but they did hear his pleas and his final, childish tantrum: 'Fuck you! Fuck your father. And fuck you all to hell.'

For an instant he looked at me as though I wasn't man enough to pull the trigger.

But I was.

I stepped behind him, raised my pistol and fired into the tiny spot I'd chosen. The Smith & Wesson cracked. I turned and walked away as Zorrillo swayed on his knees. I had my back to him so I didn't witness his complete fall. I only heard the thump – the perfect thump – of his body hitting the ground.

It had all gone exactly to plan. He'd even fallen face-forward like Papá. I kept walking without turning back or even looking over my shoulder. It had been a long time coming, but justice had been done. Justice had been perfectly done.

112

PALILLO RACED AFTER me. When he caught up, he patted my back in approval, although he did have one mild reproach.

'Why didn't you ask for the location of his cocaine millions? Then I could buy more of these.' He raised his wrist, displaying Zorrillo's Rolex, which he'd exchanged for his fake one.

I tried to coax Fabián from the shattered Mercedes, which was dotted with dents and tears from the bullets. At first he was too traumatised to unlock the door.

'It's okay,' I comforted him when he finally emerged, placing my hand on his shoulder and leading him to the porch where he could sit and breathe easily. I'd punished Fabián enough; I now considered us even. 'You're safe. You can go home to Bogotá. They won't touch you there.'

Buitrago's Blackhawk landed near the farmhouse. The sight of the colonel reassured Fabián further, but when Buitrago went to inspect Zorrillo's corpse, Fabián hardly knew where to cast his eyes. Twenty-six blood-soaked bodies lay sprawled in the yard of his boyhood homestead. There were five more near the trees. Fabián couldn't bear to look at any of them. Zorrillo had murdered his father, but he didn't seem happy the man was dead.

Witnessing Fabián's distress reminded me of how, in only eighteen months, I'd become accustomed to guns and battles and blood and dead bodies. During that first skirmish at Puerto Pescador, I'd been petrified. At the Jaguar River, I'd been revolted and, afterwards, depressed by all the killing. But this ambush elated me.

Trigeño's helicopter touched down with Javier aboard. When they saw each other, Trigeño and Buitrago raised their hands uncertainly, like secret lovers who didn't know whether to acknowledge each other at a party.

Javier sprinted across to Fabián. The brothers hugged. Their mutual terror during this incident seemed to have brought them closer together, and I was glad. They'd kept their word and would spend the coming months with their mother in the capital. After some pressure from Trigeño, they'd agreed to leave their bodyguards behind with Mamá, who would stay on at Javier's hacienda. Mamá would be completely protected there until I could safely reclaim our *finca*.

Buitrago approached me by the farmhouse. He must have been pleased, but he veiled his delight. We were professional soldiers, and victories that involved the extinguishment of human life had to be chalked up privately on blackboards in our minds.

Buitrago mustn't have heard my transmission on the Guerrilla frequency because he congratulated me for an operation that had been executed flawlessly.

'No civilians injured. No army soldiers killed. Thirty-one *guerrilleros* dead and, as I instructed, no one tortured.'

An army cameraman filmed the bodies strewn around the ranch as soldiers packaged them in black plastic. Of course, we six snipers, still in ghillie suits, were careful not to be caught on camera, but this time I didn't mind that the images of the dead would be broadcast – these were all genuine *guerrilleros*. Buitrago would have preferred to parade Zorrillo alive in front of television cameras at a press conference, but it was still the first time a mid-level *comandante* had been killed in decades.

After years of continual losses, this operation would give the Garbanzos battalion a much-needed boost in morale and public prestige. Accolades would be heaped upon Buitrago by his generals and the North Americans. As a result, Buitrago's trust in me and in the Autodefensas enjoyed a manifold increase.

The colonel called to the cameraman, 'Enough filming. Turn that thing off!'

While we stood there, a corporal arrived bearing a radio backpack. He relayed the message that Buitrago's soldiers had rappelled into the jungle from helicopters to intercept the fleeing *guerrilleros*. They'd managed to capture seven, who were being marched back to us with their wrists bound and bags over their heads.

'They're already blaming each other,' the corporal said with satisfaction. 'They claim they hate Zorrillo and have wanted to desert for a year. And they're promising to reveal everything they know about Caraquemada.'

Leaving me, Buitrago signalled to Trigeño for a private word. As I climbed aboard Buitrago's Blackhawk to be airlifted back to the battalion, I saw Trigeño and Buitrago – the illicit lovers – hugging in the shadows. It was the first and last time that I saw the army and Autodefensas embrace.

The dark alliance I'd helped form was now on a fast-moving upward trajectory. And although the journey ahead would be long and arduous, I felt like I was on a steam train accelerating quickly away from the station. We had a fresh victory behind us. We had confidence. And our momentum was unstoppable.

113

HAVING KILLED ZORRILLO, I was now confident that we'd succeed in reclaiming Llorona and the river villages. For Phase Two of our operation, I'd be second in command under Beta, supported by thirty Autodefensas from La 50, including Ñoño and Mona, who'd arrived in two tarpaulin-covered trucks.

Palillo still hated Beta for forcing Piolín to witness torture. But I didn't mind the idea of serving under him. Now that he'd seen my resilience in La Quebrada, my successful implementation of the Zorrillo operation and also how much Trigeño relied on me, he showed me greater respect.

That night, having been permitted by Buitrago to house my soldiers in a disused corner of his army barracks, I thought again of Camila, sleeping barely eleven kilometres away. It was painful being so close to her and yet being unable to visit. Since our upcoming mission was clandestine, I couldn't even call her.

With the successful operation against Zorrillo, my confidence was at an all-time high; we'd proven that the Guerrilla commanders weren't invincible. And once the Autodefensas were firmly entrenched in the region, we'd be within striking distance of Buitre and Caraquemada.

At dawn the following day, Beta and I met with Buitrago in his office, where he supplied us with two military maps and told us that the seven fleeing *guerrilleros* captured by the army the previous afternoon had already revealed the location of some temporary Guerrilla bases.

Of course, with only a single platoon, we had no intention of attacking these bases. But we could at least make an incursion into the area to shake the Guerrilla up, oust their civilian supporters and interrupt their supply chains. Beta estimated that the mission would take five days.

'Having lost a platoon, Caraquemada will be on the defensive,' Buitrago told us. 'He'll move these bases further back into the mountains, temporarily reducing his capacity for patrols and attacks. But you'll only have a small window before he decides to avenge Zorrillo. So be quick. And be careful.'

The colonel provided us with a list of known members of Zorrillo's Bolivarian Militia, each with a corresponding photo.

'These men recruit *campesino* children, ferry supplies to Guerrilla camps and terrorise peasant families so that they're too scared to talk to us. They don't wear uniforms, but they're armed and are not to be considered civilians. Yesterday, before we captured the seven *guerrilleros* from Zorrillo's platoon, I would have told you to confirm their identity then bring them in for questioning.'

'But today?' asked Beta, smiling in anticipation.

'Shoot them on sight.'

Buitrago airlifted our platoon of thirty-two Autodefensas in two Bell UH-1 helicopters to a point south of Puerto Princesa, half a day's march from where the roads ended. We trekked over hills, beside escarpments and along streams, wearing full combat webbing, face paint and black armbands with white AUC lettering. We wanted no confusion. We were not the army. We were a new force – a more committed and ruthless force – not bound by the ordinary rules of war.

Here, *campesinos'* lives were inextricably intertwined with the Guerrilla. Guerrilla patrols expected to sleep in their huts. They took a third of their crops, demanded information about army movements and expected their children to join the ranks once they were big enough to hold a rifle.

'Good day, *señores*,' Beta would say gruffly to the inhabitants of each dwelling. 'We're from the Colombian United Self-Defence Forces. This area is no longer under Guerrilla control.'

We granted the illegal squatters three days to leave. While two squads formed a security ring around each hut, five soldiers forced the inhabitants to lie flat with their noses touching the dirt while the rest of us smashed their furniture, tossed out pots and pans, cut their mattresses to shreds and prodded the surrounding earth for weapons.

A further day's trek from Puerto Princesa, the huts were little more than a few wooden boards nailed together and covered with rusted iron sheets. We were greeted by malnourished children who barely spoke. Even Ñoño, who'd grown up in the rough frontier country of Northern Antioquia, was appalled at how peasants here lived so primitively.

On the fourth day, we finally struck gold. We were now deep in enemy territory; these mountains led to Caraquemada's temporary bases. We had to tread slowly in this area with our eyes scanning the earth because Buitrago's maps indicated that the Guerrilla had laid *quiebrapata* landmines.

The knowledge that we were so close to the Guerrilla camps made us tense. I suspected most of the others now wanted to turn back. We'd complied with our orders. Why not return to Garbanzos? But Beta drove us on, determined to find something.

As we approached one small wooden hut, a man sprinted out through its door. Palillo ditched his pack, gave chase and tackled him to the ground.

I scanned Buitrago's list and saw the man's photo. 'He's one of them.'

In order to be sure, Beta ordered Giraldo to search the hut. Giraldo emerged, triumphantly holding aloft a heavy satchel. 'Looks like he was packing to leave.'

'What are these for?' Beta asked the man, opening the satchel and removing a handheld radio transceiver and a box containing fifty AA batteries.

The man broke free and ran for the cover of the jungle. Beta shot him twice in the back and he fell instantly. I fired the *tiro de gracia* into the back of his head.

'Find a shovel and bury him,' I ordered Tarantula, a broad-shouldered soldier who'd make light work of it.

'We haven't got time for this shit, Pedro!' said Beta. 'If they heard those shots . . .'

I knew Beta was no coward. To him, the mission was complete; we needed to turn back immediately. If the Guerrilla surrounded us, there would be no escape.

'Give me three minutes,' I said.

Tarantula and I hacked into the ground, while the others fanned out with their rifles covering the densely wooded mountains. These were the tensest moments of our trek. I felt exposed in the clearing. But I kept digging.

As we rolled the man into his shallow grave, Mona suddenly waved her hands for everyone to stop what they were doing. She placed her finger to her lips and pointed to the house.

Beta signalled for us to surround the dwelling. Ñoño whispered, 'I'll go in.'

He slipped his pack from his shoulders, flicked his Galil off safety and crept inside. He came out leading a little boy by the hand who looked about ten. He'd been hiding under the bed.

Beta berated Giraldo for not checking the hut properly.

'What's your name, little man?' asked Mona, bending down to the boy's height.

His lip trembled. 'Iván.'

'And where's your mother, Iván?'

He pointed up the hill; she'd probably fled to the Guerrilla.

'Where's my *papá*?' the boy asked.

Beta and I looked at each other, not knowing what to tell him, but Ñoño took control.

'He's dead,' he said softly, taking the boy's hand again and leading him towards the grave. 'You need to say goodbye to him quickly.'

'We can't take him,' stated Beta. 'The rules are clear. He's too small for the Autodefensas.'

'That's what you said about me. La 50 is the best place for him. He can do camp duties until he's big enough to carry a pack and rifle.'

'We don't take kids.'

'But the Guerrilla will. Then he'll grow up despising us and wanting revenge. That's one more enemy soldier we'll have to kill. But if we take him ourselves, that's one more soldier for us.'

Beta continued to argue, but Ñoño had already made up his mind.

'I'll take responsibility for Iván,' he said, and without looking back he began dragging the crying boy down the hill, away from his dead father.

'Get down!' Silvestre crash-tackled Beta as a volley of shots struck the hut behind us. Silvestre covered Beta and returned fire. Out in the open, and with no clear view of the enemy, we had no option but to scamper down the hill as fast as we could.

We marched all day and all night, and the following day we reached the thin woodlands on the outskirts of Puerto Princesa.

I looked up when I heard Trigeño's helicopter flying overhead; a cloud of leaflets fluttered down like confetti. I bent down to pick one up.

THE AUTODEFENSAS ARE HERE
YOU HAVE THREE DAYS TO LEAVE
YOU HAVE BEEN WARNED

Reading this filled me with pride. I'd painted similar words on my house eighteen months earlier when they represented little more than a dream. But now my words had come true; the Autodefensas were actually taking over, driving out the Guerrilla.

Suddenly, a hundred metres ahead of us, at the edge of a clearing, a man in camouflage uniform emerged from behind a tree, holding his rifle horizontal and high above his head.

'Pedro, take the shot,' ordered Beta. 'It might be a trap.'

But the man knelt, slowly laid his rifle on the ground, placed his hands behind his head and yelled out for us to please spare his life.

His name was Rafael. He was handsome and looked about twenty. He was a *guerrillero* and had assumed we were the army. He wanted to hand himself in and would co-operate in every possible way. In fact, he claimed to be a member of the team protecting Zorrillo when he went to meet Fabián Díaz. But when we opened fire and they'd fled in confusion, he'd become separated from his squad and decided to hide in woodlands to avoid his pursuers, thinking he'd return alone to camp later. However, after days of hiding, he'd had second thoughts – he now wanted to desert.

'If you have to kill me, please make it quick. But I'll never go back. My commander executed someone very close to me. I know I'm next on his list. I hate him. I want to join your side and kill him.'

'Who's your commander?' demanded Beta, disbelievingly.

Rafael's answer set my pulse racing: 'Buitre.'

114

BETA STILL WANTED Rafael dead. 'The only good *guerrillero* is a dead *guerrillero*,' he said. But I insisted we radio in the capture of an enemy soldier to Trigeño.

When our platoon arrived at Hacienda Díaz, Trigeño's helicopter was already parked next to the bullet-pocked farmhouse. Trigeño had disembarked and Alfa 1 was standing beside him. They'd flown down that morning from La 35 to drop the warning leaflets. Beta and I talked to them near the spot where I'd killed Zorrillo. Bullet casings and glittering shards of mirror from Fabián's destroyed Mercedes were littered across the grass.

Beta recounted the details of our operation, recommending that Rafael be turned over to his intelligence team. But after our recent successes, Trigeño was in a compassionate mood.

'Get this boy's story,' he ordered. 'Investigate it thoroughly. If it checks out, he can join the Autodefensas.'

'What?' cried Beta in utter disbelief. 'You made the law yourself. Captured enemy get killed. No forgiveness. No exceptions.'

'This one wasn't captured. He isn't even a deserter. He's a *defector*. We pay him cash for the rifle he brought. He gets no weapon for a month. When we trust him fully, give it back to him and he's one of us.'

Alfa 1 and Beta were on the verge of mutiny; there was no way they'd ever accept a member of the enemy standing beside their own loyal men.

Trigeño's new policy, however, was both logical and strategic. Rafael had brought his own rifle, and he was already battle-savvy, which would save us money and training time. His joining our ranks meant one more soldier for us and one fewer for the enemy – an advantage of two. And he was highly motivated – apparently, conditions in the Guerrilla were appalling. Rafael was grateful to be alive and pleased he'd eventually be doing a similar job to before, only he'd get paid for it and also be permitted to take leave.

He knew enemy trails, supply routes, radio codes, commanders' habits and their camps' locations.

He could identify *milicianos* in the river villages. And, because he was an orphan, he wouldn't need to conceal his identity with a balaclava to prevent reprisals against his family. Besides, he *wanted* the Guerrilla to know he'd changed sides. The psychological blow to his former *camaradas* would be immense. And it would also extend a small olive branch to the foot soldiers of our enemy. *Guerrilleros* knew when we captured them that a gruesome death ensued. But now there was an alternative: changing sides. Trigeño was a long-term thinker. In the bigger picture, a single defection was far more damaging to the Guerrilla than any number of losses in combat.

In time, Rafael would go on to become a trusted and valuable Autodefensa commander. His defection inspired dozens more. The conversion of enemies into allies was pure genius by Trigeño and also the high-tide mark of my surging wave of esteem for him.

Although this war is to the death, he was saying, in effect, *everyone has a choice and no one has to die.*

According to Rafael, Buitre was still at large, roaming the dense jungles we'd just trekked through. He had multiple camps and never announced to underlings which one he'd visit next. This would make locating him difficult. However, he did know Buitre's real name – Kiko Fuentes – and that he had a brother in a town called Barrancabermeja, who had blond hair and worked as a mechanic. That was sufficient for Trigeño to give the next order to Alfa 1.

'Call the Northern Bloque commander. Get them to find Buitre's brother!'

115

I WAS OVERJOYED to have Buitre almost within our sights. I had no idea how his brother, living in a faraway city, might be of use. Surely Buitre wouldn't be stupid enough to visit him, even if he were allowed to. Nevertheless, the knowledge that Trigeño was dedicating significant resources from *La Empresa* to my personal quest made me feel special.

Once more, I felt we were progressing in leaps and bounds.

Trigeño flew back to La 50 with Alfa 1, Beta and Rafael, leaving me with a shoebox full of cash and orders to construct our local headquarters.

He'd given no specific instructions about what to do with Iván, the young boy whose father we'd killed, leaving it to my discretion. Iván never strayed far from Ñoño, trotting after him with the grateful, adoring eyes of a rescued puppy.

When I suggested we find a family to adopt him, Ñoño rebelled. 'Iván's going nowhere,' he said, snatching up the boy's hand. 'He's already got a family, right here.'

Meanwhile, we set up camp at the old Díaz *finca* and began converting it into a proper base. Humberto Díaz's former home was unliveable. Squatters had used the ground floor to shelter livestock; the carpets were soaked with pig and chicken faeces. But the caretaker's cottage had fared better. The peeling green wallpaper had darker, rectangular patches where pictures once hung, but some furniture remained. This is where Beta and I would sleep. Our supply room would be the barn. The milking shed, where we hung twenty hammocks, would house our soldiers and be the communications and command centre.

Around the shed's perimeter we erected a one-and-a-half-metre high brick wall and, over the coming week, my soldiers cleared low-growing shrubs out to a radius of four hundred metres and cut the grass using machetes.

For additional security, I stationed *puntos* with handheld radios in strategic places to give warning if anyone approached, and set up four guard posts on the fence line. Four German shepherds were chained at the hacienda's perimeter in the spaces between each guard post, and were trained to bark at the slightest disturbance.

Surveying our defences, I felt happy with what we'd achieved. But when I thought of my own family *finca* just over the hill, I also felt sad. I missed Mamá, but she was hopeless at keeping secrets and I needed to be discreet until the Autodefensas were properly established. I also missed Camila. During one of my supply runs into Garbanzos, I phoned to tell her that I'd soon be working permanently in Llorona.

'That's incredible!' she said excitedly. 'Did Javier offer you a job?'

'Not exactly.'

'But you did quit?'

'No, we're moving here to make the town safe.'

'I see,' she said sceptically. 'But where exactly will you be?'

'Near our *finca*. We can't see each other yet, but I'll phone you soon.'

Camila, however, was stubborn and determined.

Around sunset, as I was making my new bed, Pantera, the *punto* I'd stationed on the dirt road leading uphill to our base, announced over the radio: 'Pedro, you have an incoming visitor. Pretty. Five foot five. School uniform.'

Camila had ridden up from Llorona on her bicycle. She threw her arms around me.

'I've missed you so much, baby,' I said, hugging her back. 'But you can't be here.'

'I guess you know about Zorrillo,' she said, glancing around at the bullet-pocked farmhouse. 'Is this where it happened?'

'Yes,' I said tentatively, worried she'd ask for details about my role.

But Camila had already moved on and was looking around with interest. 'So this is your new office?'

I nodded. 'But I'm still on duty and—'

'And I'm still your girlfriend, so don't you dare ask me to leave!'

I took a deep breath and led her back to my quarters, away from the curious glances of my men. When Camila saw the photos of us I'd hung above the bedhead, her hand went to her chest and she smiled. We kissed for minute and I felt myself becoming aroused.

Suddenly, she stiffened and pushed me away. I followed her shocked gaze and realised, to my horror, that she'd spied a list of five names taped to the wall beside the desk – Ratón, Zorrillo, Buitre, Caraquemada and Santiago – all of them except Buitre and Caraquemada accompanied by a photo. The names of the two dead men were crossed out in red.

'You put photos of these . . . these *murderers* . . . next to mine?'

'I'm sorry – I wasn't thinking. I didn't know you'd come here.' I stared at the ground, feeling stupid for not remembering the list I'd put up only yesterday.

'That's not the point! When, Pedro? When will you see that what you've started never ends?'

She burst into tears and beat her fists against my chest. I caught her wrists and drew her close to me.

'It *will* end,' I said grimly, 'when Papá's killers are gone.'

She looked at me aghast. 'But you promised you wouldn't. Under my house that night, you promised.'

'*Ssshh. Ssshh.*'

She let herself be embraced. She put her arms around me. I kissed her tears and then her nose and then her lips. And although she was angry and initially resisted my caresses, eventually I felt her heartbeat quicken and heard her breathing shorten and I managed to coax her towards the bed.

Afterwards, lying naked, I didn't want her to leave, although I knew she had to.

'You shouldn't be here, Camila. I love seeing you but it's too dangerous. Caraquemada probably knows we're here by now. What if he launches a counter-attack?'

'I want to stay.'

'You don't know what it's like. Bullets ricocheting everywhere. You could be kidnapped or killed.'

'Or *you* could be,' she retorted. Then, snuggling up to me, she added, 'If they take you, I'm coming.'

Two weeks after Zorrillo's death and the capture of seven of his *guerrilleros*, I met with Buitrago to finalise the military plan for Phase Three: the occupation of Puerto Galán to eliminate the remaining nine members of the Bolivarian Militia plus another twenty members of the Guerrilla's secret logistics, intelligence and recruitment networks who'd been identified by the captured *guerrilleros*.

After our successful trekking mission and the leaflet drop, Buitrago's trust in us had deepened. Enemy sympathisers had now been given fair warning. Anyone who chose to stay had sealed his own fate.

'Here's the full list of enemy collaborators,' he said, 'along with their last known addresses.'

Buitrago also agreed to temporarily hand over three of the *guerrillero* prisoners, bound and gagged. Their role would be to identify the *milicianos*. With Rafael also giving us valuable intelligence, Beta and Trigeño became hopeful that Caraquemada's entire underground network could be wiped out in a single, devastating strike.

For thoroughness, Puerto Galán would need to be occupied by a large force of Autodefensas for two or three days, during which time questions could be asked and witnesses called in order to thwart any attempt by the guilty men to disguise themselves within the village's population. To isolate the village during the occupation and make it difficult for the collaborators to escape or phone for help, a large tree would be felled across the highway between Llorona and Garbanzos behind the advancing Autodefensas, and the electricity and telephone wires would be cut.

Buitrago reluctantly agreed. He knew these were illegal tactics – mass detentions, interrogation of civilians without judicial basis, house-to-house searches without official warrants and summary executions without trial. However, provided it was done thoroughly, it would only have to be done once.

To ensure he could later deny any collusion, Buitrago arranged to have trusted men place explosives on a distant oil pipeline and then call in a sighting of 'hundreds of enemy'. On Friday morning he'd then lead three-quarters of his men away to deal with the 'attack'. By the time he returned, the Autodefensas would be long gone, leaving him a village cleansed of insurgents.

I fully expected to be part of the occupying force, but when Trigeño called me on the Friday morning, he told me I would not be included in the mission.

'*Bloque Norte* will do the job. Afterwards, you and Beta will be running these towns. I don't want blood on your hands.'

'My girlfriend, Camila, lives in Llorona. Will she be safe?'

'Warn anyone you care about living south of Garbanzos to depart for a few days. Be discreet. Tell them to keep their mouths shut.'

Anyway, that was the plan.

116

PALILLO IMMEDIATELY WARNED his mother to take his siblings and flee. Diomedes wasn't there to oppose her – he was off picking coca leaves in the Guerrilla-controlled fields.

'Maybe he'll get killed in the crossfire,' Palillo said wryly.

When I visited Old Man Domino, he refused outright to leave. 'I'm a *viejo* with only a few years left in me. I've already run once when Bogotá burned in 1948, and we settled here. I'm not running again.'

On my way to conceal two chainsaws in the bushes near the large Brazil nut tree that was to be felled, I also stopped at Camila's place.

When Señor Muñoz answered my knock, he was shocked to see me in uniform and tried to slam the door in my face. I blocked it with my boot.

'Don't act so surprised,' I said, still resentful towards him for opposing my relationship with Camila. 'You already know what I do.'

'What do you want?'

'To warn you. To protect you and your family. Something heavy is about to happen.'

'What do you mean "heavy"?'

'I don't have details. But lock up your store and take a week's vacation. And not a word to anyone.'

'It's only two-thirty. Camila's still at school.'

'Then pack her suitcase and meet her outside the school gates.'

An hour later, Palillo and I met Beta at the Garbanzos airstrip, an expanse of dried grass and compacted earth with three large corrugated iron hangars. Dark clouds were gathering as we handed over the three handcuffed *guerrilleros* who'd be used to identify the *milicianos*.

'Buitrago wants them back without a scratch,' I said, handing him three black balaclavas for concealing their faces.

Beta nodded grimly. 'And the chainsaws?'

'Hidden near the tree like you wanted.'

Lightning flashed on the horizon and thunder growled in the distance as two Antonov airplanes carrying the *Bloque Norte* troops touched down one after the other and taxied to the nearest hangar.

'Return to your base,' Beta ordered us. 'Don't leave for any reason until I radio you.'

As Palillo and I drove off, I turned to see ramps lowering from the back of the planes and row after row of battle-ready Autodefensas descend. Each carried a rifle, grenades and four magazines. None of them wore face paint. Instead, every man held a balaclava.

As we passed the army's permanent checkpoint in Garbanzos – already deserted – I felt a strange sense of foreboding. But my doubt was only momentary. We were committed now and there was nothing I could do.

117

CAMILLA CALLED ME on my way back to base. She'd locked herself in the bathroom of her aunt's house in Garbanzos – where Señor Munoz had taken the family – so that her father wouldn't overhear.

'Why did you tell us to leave, Pedro?' she whispered. 'I'm scared.'

'Don't be! It's just a precaution. Once the Guerrilla are gone, you'll be safe and we won't have to hide our relationship anymore, I promise.'

In spite of the storm raging outside, I slept soundly, secure in the anticipation of the new phase of my life that was about to begin. With Caraquemada's network of collaborators eliminated, perhaps Camila might change her mind about Llorona being such a shitty town. Perhaps she'd defer university. She might even decide to stay permanently.

I awoke refreshed on Saturday, blissfully ignorant of events that had begun the previous night and were still transpiring several kilometres to the south. We worked intensively finalising the headquarters, joking around and teasing each other. During breaks, I sat on an upturned wooden crate, sipping *tinto* by the small VHF radio and awaiting news. I had no inkling that anything was amiss until mid-morning on Sunday when I received a frantic radio transmission from Pantera: 'Army truck approaching rapidly. Be ready!'

A moment later, a green truck screeched to a halt by our headquarters. Colonel Buitrago got out, slammed the door and charged towards me like a wounded bull.

'*Hijueputa* liar! We had an agreement! No innocent people were to be touched.'

'What do you mean?'

'I've just come from Puerto Galán. Your men were drunk and torturing people in the abattoir. They cut up corpses and threw limbs into the river!'

'That's impossible, Colonel. You must be wrong.'

'Wrong, am I?' Buitrago's rage spiralled out of control. He seized me by the throat and marched me backwards, ramming me against the cabin of his truck.

'What's this then?' he said, indicating something in its tray.

I prised his hands away and doubled over, gasping for breath, before I was finally able to look.

It was the body of a dead woman. She was slightly bloated, her hair was wet and her skin a greyish blue. At first I assumed she'd drowned. But then I noticed two entry wounds – one in her stomach, the other above her left eye.

'This woman was an innocent seamstress with a six-year-old daughter. And witnesses say a small boy was killed by gunfire from a helicopter.'

'I don't know what to say, Colonel. I haven't moved from here or spoken to my superiors since we delivered your informants to Beta.'

When he saw that my astonishment was genuine, Buitrago calmed down slightly.

'Then get changed and get in the truck!' he ordered. 'When we reach Garbanzos, call your boss. I want answers.'

We drove full speed to Garbanzos Hospital, where I phoned Trigeño, who called me back on a landline at the nurse's station so that our conversation wouldn't be intercepted. I described the dead woman and repeated Buitrago's claims about the helicopter and the drunken bloodbath.

'I've had no reports back on this yet, Pedro, since this *limpieza* was conducted by *Bloque Norte*,' Trigeño said. 'But none of it sounds accurate. First, the Autodefensas don't own a military helicopter. Second, it's against our statues to drink alcohol on duty. As to the woman, having a child doesn't automatically make her innocent. I seem to recall a seamstress on Rafael's list who was supplying the Guerrilla with camouflage uniforms.'

Trigeño was confident that there had been no mistakes. Every 'disappeared' person fell into one of three categories: they were on our list; they were named by Rafael in advance or pointed out by the three captured *guerrilleros*; or they were fingered by other villagers interrogated during the *limpieza*.

'But what do I tell Buitrago?'

'Tell him that I'll investigate this thoroughly. If excesses were committed, the perpetrators will be severely punished.'

From the nurse's station I wandered the white-tiled corridors, searching for the colonel. I found him seated inside a ward with the door closed. When I entered, I saw three beds occupied by two men and a little girl of about seven years old. Two nurses tended to their wounds, attaching saline drips and heart-rate monitors.

Buitrago raised his eyebrows and came outside. I conveyed Trigeño's denials.

'And you really believe your boss?'

'I do, Colonel. I trust him with my life.'

'Well, I don't. The Autodefensas have a military chain of command. How could your top commander not have ordered this?'

'But, Colonel, this was not our unit, this was—'

'Enough!' Buitrago held up a tape recorder and pointed sternly to a chair inside the ward, indicating I should sit. My explanations could wait; he wanted me to hear these witness accounts first-hand as he recorded them.

The first bed was occupied by a middle-aged man with a bandaged hand, a broken nose and two black eyes that were so swollen he could hardly see. When he gave his name and profession I turned away in shame. He was Juan Ricardo, our family mechanic from ever since I could remember.

The second bed was occupied by a pale-skinned but badly sunburned man named Pablo Ruben, a cabinet-maker with a bullet still lodged under his clavicle. Buitrago's men had discovered him lying injured in a field, beneath the body of a woman.

In the third bed was the small girl, Margarita, who was wearing steel-rimmed glasses. Shaking and crying, she was being treated for shock.

It took two hours for these witnesses to give their statements.

I sat listening with increasing dismay and then revulsion. Not for a moment did I doubt their testimony. The details were so graphic and gruesome that not in a million years could they have invented the description of the suffering they were forced to endure over a harrowing thirty-six hours.

Combining their testimony with my own knowledge of the mission preparations, and other evidence from witnesses Buitrago had spoken to in Puerto Galán, I was able to form a stark mental picture of how the horrific events unfolded.

118

ALTHOUGH THE PEOPLE of Llorona and Puerto Galán don't know it yet, their fates are sealed at 7 pm on Friday, when a convoy of five SUVs and four mini-vans drives south from Garbanzos through the abandoned army checkpoint. For anyone caught beyond this point, there is no escape – they are about to endure the most terrifying two days of their lives. Many will not survive.

No one is present to witness the passage of the vehicles, but their numberplates have been removed and their headlights are off, despite the fact that dusk is falling.

The vehicles speed towards Llorona but, several kilometres before the town, the last SUV in the convoy screeches to a halt. Soldiers wearing balaclavas alight and use chainsaws to cut down a huge Brazil nut tree. It crashes through telephone and electricity wires and falls across the highway, blocking the only road connecting Garbanzos to Llorona and the river villages to the south.

Shortly afterwards, thunder cracks overhead and torrential rain pours down. The wife of Juan Ricardo, our family mechanic, is cooking dinner in Llorona when the lights go out. Power outages are common and Juan Ricardo fetches candles and peers out the window.

There is just enough light from the rising moon to illuminate the convoy of vehicles travelling slowly down Avenida Independencia. One stops on the opposite side of the street. Four men knock on his neighbour's door. Juan Ricardo is shocked to hear the loud pop of a pistol. The men drag a body to their vehicle, hurl it in the tray and then do a U-turn.

Juan Ricardo yanks the curtains closed, but when he tries to phone the police the line is dead. He tells his wife and children, 'Crawl underneath the house and don't come out until I get back.'

Meanwhile, the convoy continues south. Puerto Galán is now shrouded in darkness. At the food market, the men in balaclavas exit their vehicles.

They illuminate the riverbank with a searchlight and greet other soldiers arriving by boat. The men spread out and sweep from door to door with torches and typewritten lists.

'Is your father in?' the men ask Margarita, the little girl with glasses.

'Papá! Some men are here to see you.'

'Are you Señor Gilberto Piñeda?'

'*Sí.*'

Bang. Bullet to the face. Next house.

Margarita screams and runs, and she doesn't stop running until she reaches the abattoir, where she squeezes through a gap in the fence and hides in an unlocked cupboard.

Confusion and panic spreads through the village. Pablo Ruben, the sunburned man, now wishes he'd heeded the warning pamphlets dropped from a helicopter a week earlier.

Some villagers run for the tropical jungle on the outskirts of town, where they hide, petrified. Others lock their doors. But the men carry crowbars and the flimsy locks provide little protection.

Isolated pistol pops are heard. Then gunfire erupts in longer, automatic bursts. The rules appear to be simple:

Those on the lists are guilty.

Those who resist are guilty.

Those who flee are guilty.

And those who stay behind have little chance.

Pablo Ruben is one of those who try to run. He and his wife sprint hand-in-hand through the fields behind their house. They do not know that teams of soldiers have spread out to form a security ring one kilometre outside the town. When the men begin shooting, Pablo Ruben's wife is hit. A bullet lodges beneath Pablo's clavicle, and he survives by playing dead, lying in a ditch beneath the body of his wife, who bleeds to death while he tries not to make a sound.

Back in Llorona, Juan Ricardo sets out to drive to Garbanzos for help. Once on the highway, however, he finds a line of vehicles banked up at the first curve north of Llorona, unable to advance because a huge tree has fallen across the road.

Assuming the uniformed men near the tree are army soldiers, motorists honk and lean out their windows. 'Something's happening in Puerto Galán,' one shouts. 'We heard gunfire.'

Juan Ricardo exits his car and runs towards the soldiers. They signal angrily for him to go back.

'You need to help us!' he pleads. 'They're shooting people.'

But he quickly realises his mistake. Government soldiers don't wear balaclavas.

One of the men smashes a rifle butt across his face. Juan Ricardo falls and, before he can shield himself, is hit again. Dazed, he crawls and stumbles towards his car, but the men demand his ID. Fortunately, his name is not on their list. However, he sees a line of five kneeling motorists who've been separated from the others.

He's permitted to drive away, but in the rear-view mirror he witnesses the gunmen spraying automatic fire along these motorists' backs. They slump forward.

At Llorona, the same SUV from before is now blocking the town entrance. Juan Ricardo abandons his car and runs into scrubland, skirts wide around the fallen Brazil nut tree and, battling concussion, manages to stagger several kilometres north to his sister's house on the outskirts of Garbanzos.

At dawn, the men in balaclavas conduct a sweep through the jungle surrounding Puerto Galán, to round up anyone who is hiding. The male citizens of Puerto Galán are herded into the marketplace and forced to file slowly past three handcuffed informants who are wearing balaclavas. Those men identified by the informants are led away to the abattoir for interrogation.

There, a silent boy and his assistants tie them up by the wrists to an overhead meat hook. Little Margarita, hiding in the cupboard, watches in horror. Operating with the chilling precision of a surgeon, the boy makes tiny incisions in his victims' skin with a razor blade, which he then sews up before starting again. It seems to matter not how much pain he can inflict, but how long he can make it last. Margarita screws up her eyes and turns her head away. But even with her fingers in her ears she can't entirely block out the victims' screams and denials.

Finally, a group of twenty men are brought out of the abattoir. They look like scarecrows, their faces and bodies covered in sewn-up incisions oozing blood. They huddle together in terror. A soldier with a python tattoo on his forearm forces them to dance in the plaza, while he fires at the concrete under their feet. Bullets ricochet into their shins, bringing them down, and the soldiers crush their skulls with crowbars and bricks. Meanwhile, the next group of men are being led into the abattoir.

The sun is now high in the sky, and a helicopter hovers overhead. The villagers exit their houses waving, believing rescue has arrived. However, the helicopter fires .30-calibre rounds at the tin roofs, killing a small boy who is hiding beneath a mattress.

By midday, it is too hot for balaclavas, and the men remove them, even though this means that anyone who sees their faces must be killed. Vultures circle silently. Cicadas buzz in the heat. Above the low hum of flies come moans, groans and whimpers from the slowly dying.

The soldiers bring machetes from their mini-vans. The corpses from the highway and Llorona are added to the line of dead villagers outside the abattoir. The soldiers hack the bodies into pieces. However, cutting through bones using machetes is tiring work. They start up chainsaws and use them to cut up the bodies.

The soldiers have also brought garbage bags and shovels. But digging a grave seems like too much effort in the stifling heat.

'The river,' one gunman suggests.

Weighed down by stones, most of the body-filled bags sink. Some bags tear open and float. By late afternoon on Saturday, the river is awash with floating limbs.

At nightfall, several of the gunmen break into the general store and emerge brandishing bottles of *aguardiente* and rum. They ransack houses and terrorise anyone they find. Dogs and cats are killed. Slogans are drawn on walls with paint: *Guerrilla Out!* Later, the same slogans are written in blood. Now drunk, the men laugh at their own depravity.

On the third day – Sunday – the army returns from its mission. The guards have abandoned the fallen tree, and Colonel Buitrago's men saw through it and speed towards Puerto Galán. Before they arrive, the boats leave suddenly and the soldiers pile quickly back into the SUVs and mini-vans and head north. There is only one highway connecting Garbanzos to Puerto Galán, and the convoy of vehicles must pass the army vehicles headed in the opposite direction. But Buitrago does not yet know of the carnage and does not stop them.

119

FOR THE NEXT few nights, I found sleep difficult, imagining the suffering of the men in the abattoir. I was shocked and revolted by the wanton cruelty of the Autodefensas. The soldier with a python tattoo on his forearm sounded suspiciously like Beta, although he claimed he'd remained in Garbanzos the entire time. What bothered me most was that many of the victims had apparently been innocent. I hoped that those reports were mistaken. But to know for certain I'd need to wait for the results of Trigeño's investigation.

On the third day after the Puerto Galán *limpieza*, I met my mother in a restaurant in Garbanzos.

'Mamá, I have some good news: My boss is transferring me to Llorona. I wanted you to hear it from me first, since people will probably start talking.'

'You mean when they see you in uniform.'

This stopped me dead. I was astonished to hear Mamá speak of my being an Autodefensa so openly.

She must have read my expression. 'I never mentioned it before because I didn't want to interfere, *hijo*. I just wanted you to be safe.'

I squeezed her hand. 'And I never mentioned it because I didn't want you to worry. But I *am* safe. And you are too.'

I told her Javier had promised she could remain on his *finca* for as long as she needed. Although, hopefully, that would not be long.

'Soon enough, we'll be back where we belong.'

Mamá, Uncle Leo and Camila knew I had nothing to do with the *limpieza*. Of course, they had acquaintances in Puerto Galán, so news of multiple deaths filtered through to them. Luckily, however, the details did not.

On the Sunday, a week after the *limpieza*, the magazine *La Semana* published an article that called it a *massacre*. The account, based on multiple anonymous sources, contained far graver allegations than those I'd heard.

One witness claimed the Autodefensas had held sprinting races in the plaza, making bets on how far a man could run with an arm chopped off before he stumbled. Afterwards, the soldiers played football with a severed head. And worst of all were the chainsaws, possibly the very same chainsaws I'd left near the Brazil nut tree. The article claimed that when they were used to chop up victims, many of those victims were still alive.

Reading this, I felt sick to my stomach. I couldn't eat all Sunday. I couldn't even swallow water. What had I done? What had we set in motion? Were the Autodefensas really capable of such inhumanity?

On the Monday, a week after the *limpieza*, Trigeño flew down in his helicopter. When I confronted him with the article, he was outraged. According to him, this wasn't simply a case of lazy journalism; it was negligent, defamatory, left-wing propaganda.

Trigeño had made inquiries via the commanders of *Bloque Norte*, who protested there had been no excesses.

He wanted me to appease Buitrago.

'But how? He's livid.'

Trigeño produced a summarised list of information gathered during the *limpieza*, including names of sympathisers and suppliers in other regions.

I passed Trigeño's further denials about the *limpieza* on to Colonel Buitrago. He didn't believe them. He refused to read the intelligence list.

'Nothing can justify this. *Nothing!* You hear me?' He slammed his fist on his desk. 'Not even if you brought me Tirofijo and Santiago in matching body bags would I ever, *ever* sanction anything like this atrocity.'

The colonel was under investigation by international human rights agencies. They wanted him charged with 'Neglect of Duty' and 'Homicide by Omission and/or Deliberate Failure to Render Assistance'. In coming months, the victims' families, led by a human rights attorney, Yolanda Delgado, would consider formulating a class action against the government, seeking millions of dollars in compensation.

Two days later, the colonel had more terrible news.

'I need you to look at this closely and think hard about whom you work for and why,' he said, producing a photo of a naked dead man lying on a metal table. The body was so swollen that at first I didn't recognise it. Then, with a shock, I realised it was Don Mauricio.

'My men found him washed up two kilometres downriver,' said Buitrago grimly. 'He was shot in the head. How could this be an accident?'

In spite of everything I'd already absorbed that week, the news of Mauricio's death stunned me.

After we'd retaken control of Llorona, I'd dreamed that Don Mauricio's wife and children, including Cecilia – the one who had been kidnapped – might return from Medellín and live prosperously. Mauricio would be elected to the Senate. Instead, his family would now be grieving and, without Mauricio working to repay the money he'd borrowed for Cecilia's ransom, would be struck down by brutal poverty. Trigeño's explanation by telephone was flimsy.

'This was a tragic mistake. An oversight by men in the field,' he said. 'They were acting on confirmed information that Mauricio frequently passed cash to Zorrillo and supplied the Guerrilla with meat.'

Strictly speaking, this was true. But we all knew they were extortion payments. And if others on our side had been warned beforehand to leave, why not warn Mauricio?

After the heinous *limpieza*, I asked myself over and over: *why should I continue with the Autodefensas?* But I couldn't undo a past mistake and, having come this far, I decided I should finish what I'd started. Walking away from Puerto Galán after promising to liberate its inhabitants would make us just as bad as our enemy.

Undoubtedly, Colonel Buitrago underwent a similar period of painful introspection. He had no reason to continue any association with the Autodefensas. We'd lied to him, betrayed him and massacred the very citizens he'd sworn to protect. I fully expected him to kick us out.

Surprisingly, he sent a message back to Trigeño: 'I'll cover up your role in this, provided you fulfil your promise to make Puerto Galán safe. Using a small force, and without using torture.'

The colonel ordered his soldiers at the army checkpoint south of Garbanzos to turn back journalists and even forensic investigators sent by the government.

'There have been multiple Guerrilla sightings around the river villages,' the soldiers told them. 'Beyond this point, we cannot guarantee your safety.'

Buitrago did, however, have one final stipulation. He did not believe Beta's claim that he had not been involved in the *limpieza* and insisted he be banned from stepping foot in Garbanzos ever again. His continued support for the Autodefensas was contingent upon someone he could trust being in charge of the soldiers controlling the villages: me.

'Making war is easy, Pedro. Now try keeping the peace.'

120

ONE ROADBLOCK, SIX Yamaha motorbikes, a 7 pm curfew, twelve radio handsets and nineteen boys under the age of twenty-two. That was how we controlled Llorona and the river towns of Puerto Galán, Puerto Princesa and Santo Paraíso.

Heading south from Garbanzos towards the Amazon, there were now three checkpoints from three different armed groups. First was the army checkpoint just south of Garbanzos. Second was our Autodefensa checkpoint on the only road leading from Llorona to the three river villages. Third was an intermittent Guerrilla checkpoint near the car ferry wharf in Puerto Princesa. Whenever the *guerrilleros* manning the checkpoint heard rumours of my men's approach, they fled. We lacked the manpower to pursue them, but their turn would come.

'Security check,' we announced upon boarding passenger *colectivos* and *chivas* at our checkpoint – two forty-four-gallon drums on either side of the road with a pull-up chain between them. 'Off the bus and form a single queue, please.'

As I'd hoped, Don Felix's bus company was in business again. Rápido Velasquez and Transportadores Díaz buses now ran the route from Garbanzos to Puerto Princesa and back ten times daily. Private vehicles no longer paid Guerrilla road taxes, although we searched them thoroughly. Hollowed-out *caletas* in seats or false bottoms beneath spare tyres could mean only one thing – contraband. Concealed weapons or munitions could have only one beneficiary.

After patting down passengers, we noted their name, age, ID number, address and purpose of trip, which we recorded in a logbook to analyse patterns of behaviour.

'How many in your family?' Ñoño would ask as Giraldo rifled through bags of groceries.

We limited rice to two cups per person per day. If families carried excess cooking oil, we visited them a week later to see what remained. Any supplies that might be destined for the enemy – phone cards, batteries and cooking gas – we confiscated. Outsiders were turned back. Journalists, charity workers and human rights attorneys had no business in those villages other than to cause us trouble.

Local taxis now became our eyes and ears, reporting suspicious people and activities via radio. River traffic had to register at the Autodefensa checkpoint at the Puerto Galán wharf. Boats that didn't stop were threatened with impoundment or doused with gasoline and warned they would be set alight if they continued. However, it was trucks we scrutinised closest. Limited to two runs per week, drivers had to identify the purchaser of their goods in advance and show us signed invoices on their way back from making a delivery. When one truck driver attempted a third run using switched numberplates, we detained him and radioed Beta at La 50.

'I'll send some men,' he said. The next morning, members of Beta's intelligence unit arrived in an SUV and took him away. This was in line with Trigeño's policy of separating reporting from enforcement. Although my unit carried weapons, our job was to keep our hands clean, maintain good community relations and report to him via radio.

After that, only approved truck drivers with police and DAS checks were allowed through, one of whom was Uncle Leo. Thanks to me, he was able to resume his hardware deliveries unmolested.

Only one person was openly unhappy with the new state of affairs. 'This ain't right,' grumbled Palillo's stepfather, weaving his way home from the cantina. 'Kids running the town like they own it.'

But there was nothing he could do. We controlled everything.

During the first week, I visited Señor Muñoz, this time in plain clothes with no weapon. His greeting was cordial.

'Pedro, please come in.'

I remained standing on his doorstep. 'I'm sorry I lied to you about my job, Señor Muñoz.'

'I'm sorry too, Pedro. When my sons told me about your job, I probably should have come to you directly rather than pressuring Camila to stay away from you.'

'I also want you to know that I had nothing to do with events that occurred . . . further south.'

'We never thought otherwise. In fact, we're grateful you warned us. Especially considering what happened to poor Mauricio Torres.'

'That was a mistake.'

'But it made me worry. If they think anyone who has ever paid money to the Guerrilla is a voluntary supporter, then . . .' He looked down at his feet. 'Pedro, there's something I want you and your bosses to know. When I sold your cattle—'

I held up my hand. 'I know all about that. And I don't blame you. Zorrillo has paid for his sins and your family will always be safe as long as I'm around.'

We shook hands and he smiled.

I now had more than his permission to see his daughter; I had his blessing and encouragement. This was to be my happiest period with Camila since Papá's death – our honeymoon period. We spent long Sundays in my dinghy, with my men nearby protecting us. I dismissed them to make love to her by the rope-swing tree, this time on a picnic blanket.

By then, Camila was halfway through her final year at high school. With buses now running, attendance at her *colegio* was back up. The students felt safe, and Camila held her head high when I dropped her at the school gates each morning on a Yamaha.

In February, she was due to commence university. I'd hoped that she'd change her mind and decide to stay once Llorona was safe, but her heart was still set on studying and me going with her. That gave me seven months to finish off Papá's remaining killers and request a discharge from Trigeño. Having that deadline looming over us made every moment together more valuable.

Mamá was overjoyed to have me home. Now that we'd driven out the Guerrilla, it was safe enough for her to move out of Javier Díaz's home and into her own small apartment in Garbanzos. She cooked me dinner once a week and I accompanied her to the Llorona church for Mass on Sundays. On my few rest days, I toiled to restore our *finca*. My platoon became a work crew, painting the walls, mending blocked pipes and rewiring the chicken coop. I had a carpenter repair the floorboards in my room and nail together furniture.

I bought new frames for the cherished photos I'd kept in my locker at La 50 and Camila retrieved Papá's bullet-pocked cross from under her house.

Javier Díaz made good on his promise of promoting investment, accompanying a caravan of architects, engineers and national politicians on a tour of the region. The Díaz brothers won a government contract to build a new asphalt highway to replace the dirt road leading south from Llorona to Puerto Princesa. A Telecom tower was erected on the crest of the hill a kilometre and a half from our headquarters to provide cell phone coverage for Llorona and parts of Puerto Galán. Trigeño also trucked in a VHF repeater antenna, which we attached to a tall tree outside the camp's perimeter where it was guarded by a fifth German shepherd. This gave us direct communication with the army and local taxis.

Iván, the young boy Ñoño had brought back from our trek, fitted into camp life like a bolt into a nut. He slept when we did, in a hammock next to Ñoño's, and woke when we woke. During the day, he performed camp duties – sweeping the sheds, peeling potatoes and fetching firewood. He was a hard worker and, while it may be difficult for people born in cities to believe, his quality of life actually improved.

When I complimented him on the trenches he'd drained of water, Iván replied, 'This is easy compared to *el monte*.'

Life in the mountains, as the son of subsistence farmers, had been tough. He'd worked all day, from dawn to dusk. His father went away for days on end and Iván often went hungry and was filled with anxiety, not knowing when – or if – his father would return.

Even those of my men who'd initially begrudged Iván's presence as a trifling nuisance, mumbling that he was a *garrapata* – a tick that had latched on and knew where his food was coming from – were eventually won over by having their dirty plates washed and their hammocks aired out in the sun.

In July, for my next rotation of men, I had Coca-Cola transferred back into our unit. His limp prevented him from being a front line soldier, but he'd always dreamed of being an *urbano* with plain clothes, a pistol and a motorbike. Well, now he was.

After Coca-Cola's successful transfer, it was only a matter of time before Palillo came to me with a special request.

'You've got Camila. Other commanders get to live with their *novias*, so . . .'

'I'll try.'

Palillo was still only a squad commander, but after the successful Zorrillo operation and trekking mission, his star had risen. Trigeño sent us Piolín the following week.

'Discretion,' I told them on the first day. 'No distractions. Are we clear?'

They were still smitten with each other, but rather than hugging in front of the others, they nodded their greetings. This time, they gave me no trouble and I allowed them one privilege – a screen partition in the corner for privacy.

It felt good. Our old team was back together, minus Tortuga, MacGyver and Yucca, who were sadly missed. But together, we now ruled the town.

To restore security we behaved like new schoolteachers stamping authority on unruly students – strict at first with plans to ease off later. Drunks and brawlers were fined half a month's wages or, if unemployed, were required to perform a month's community service digging drainage canals and filling potholes. Theft ceased. Locals said if you left your car's engine on and doors wide open, it would run out of gas. Domestic violence was severely punished.

Piolín was particularly adept at earning victims' trust. She had a calm, open nature – like a counsellor you immediately wanted to confide in. The abuse she'd suffered at her father's hands made her sympathetic to battered women, but also passionate about preventing further violence.

'We'll talk to your husband,' she'd say. 'Don't worry, he won't be harmed. But he needs to know that *we* know.'

'If he discovers I've spoken to you, next time might be worse.'

'*Señora*,' she'd say earnestly, 'there won't be a next time.'

While we weren't able to stamp out cocaine production entirely, we limited its effects in the villages. Anyone smoking drugs was given three days to leave. Rapists and child molesters were sent to La 50 for a protracted death. Married men were forced to be faithful. The Autodefensas believed affairs broke down social order, eventually leaving women destitute and causing abandoned children to skulk around the streets looking to steal something. Broken families were ripe fruit for Guerrilla recruiters.

Unfortunately, nothing could be done about promiscuity. Womanisers like Uncle Leo would always find some foolish girl to believe their false promises. But for the unfaithful husbands who Piolín identified, Palillo added personalised touches to their punishments. For a cheater's first offence, Palillo would tie him to a fence post all day in the sun, wearing only his underwear. Local women could taunt him.

'Are you *caliente*?' they'd ask, hurling buckets of water to cool him off. During Fashion Week in late July – when the nation stopped to watch television coverage of models strutting in bikinis along Medellín catwalks – one man reoffended. Palillo got inspired, parading the cheater through the plaza in high heels with his lover's G-string over his face. Old Man Domino was the only man not whistling.

'Not enjoying fashion week, *viejo*?'

'Are you a policeman?' he demanded grumpily, glancing at my pistol. He was drunk and it seemed he'd forgotten his normally impeccable manners. I still owed him for his bravery and kindness, so I was courteous.

'No, *señor*. I'm not.'

'Didn't think so. Haven't seen a policeman around here for some time.'

Sober, Old Man Domino was delightful – often betting against Ñoño in checkers and beating him using the D'Orio triangle opening. Drunk, he became cantankerous. But he was right – villagers had never enjoyed a proper police force. However, as their trust increased, complaints to us soared.

Once villagers circulated our phone numbers, trivial neighbourhood disputes and age-old family grudges bubbled to the surface. Every downtrodden citizen wanted a piece of justice – preferably local justice, Palillo-style.

Palillo had found his niche. He'd always wanted to be a soap actor. But this was better. This was *real life* acting. He was now director and writer of his own show. The plaza was his set, villagers were cast members and Ñoño his best supporting actor.

On payday in August, as his stepfather stumbled home from the cantina, Palillo trailed alongside like he used to as a skinny thirteen-year-old on a pushbike, trying to protect his mother. Only now, he rode a Yamaha 200cc, wore designer sunglasses and kept a Taurus clipped to his hip.

'What do you want?' grumbled Diomedes, the engine's growl visibly taxing his nerves.

'Nothing,' replied Palillo, revving the Yamaha harder. 'Just out for a ride.'

'I ain't done *nada*. You got rules to follow too. I ought to report you to someone.'

'Let me call my boss.' Palillo unclipped his radio then slapped his forehead as though he'd just remembered. '*¡Ay!* Here he is right behind me!'

Riding pillion passenger, I fluttered my fingers in a wave. Diomedes knew we couldn't act without cause, but he didn't trust Palillo not to invent an offence. So he bowed with begrudging courtesy. 'Señor Pedro.'

But Palillo wasn't finished.

'What are you cooking for your family tonight? Look!' He handed him two bags of groceries that were dangling from the handlebars.

'This simply ain't right,' grumbled Diomedes turning into his house. 'World's turned upside down.'

'You're free to leave,' Palillo called after him. 'Doubt anyone will miss you.'

Late at night, Palillo sat revving the Yamaha outside his stepfather's house. 'Just try it!' he seemed to be saying. 'Lay one finger on her and you'll see who I am now.'

His motorbike vigils wasted fuel, but I couldn't complain. I owed Palillo big time.

121

AFTER TWO MONTHS we exchanged the checkpoint's pull-up chain for a proper boom gate with concrete ballast. Although we patrolled Puerto Galán by day, it was too dangerous to do so at night so we closed the highway at 7 pm and re-opened it at 7.30 each morning.

Earth movers, tractors, excavators and graders arrived on semi-trailers to begin work on the Díaz brothers' new highway. We believed the Guerrilla would try to destroy the machinery, so it was parked each night on Old Man Domino's property, where it was protected by its proximity to our headquarters.

The Díaz brothers were flourishing – Javier returned permanently to his luxury hacienda and Fabián came on regular flying visits from the capital in his new Cessna. Now that a respectful period had passed since Don Mauricio's death, Fabián announced his candidacy in Vichada's senate elections the following year – the outcome that he, Javier and Trigeño had probably wanted all along.

I couldn't help but wonder how our efforts to eradicate cocaine production were affecting the Díaz brothers. US fumigation planes were doing three runs per day from Buitrago's airfield to destroy coca plantations, no longer fearing the Guerrilla would shoot them down. Trigeño assisted those *campesinos* who wanted to sow legitimate crops, setting up a similar Agricultural Co-operative to the one run out of La 35. The barn beside our headquarters acted as a storage depot for seeds and fertilisers. From time to time, trucks arrived loaded with yellow barrels of herbicides. They were collected by Lulo Martínez, a trusted *campesino* boss from Puerto Princesa, who ensured they reached the right people.

Colonel Buitrago seemed happy with me running things south of Garbanzos. In September, the destroyed police garrison at Llorona was rebuilt.

Of course, we'd been expecting retaliation from Caraquemada for the *limpieza* and killing Zorrillo, and it was not long in coming. His men set up a surprise roadblock between our Llorona checkpoint and Puerto Galán and kidnapped a Telecom engineer who was planning the construction of a second cell phone tower further south.

'Secure the highway,' I ordered Palillo as soon as we learned of the kidnap. 'And block access to the river.'

I radioed Colonel Buitrago, who sent two platoons – eighty soldiers – into the jungle in pursuit.

A Blackhawk flew overhead, its gunners firing .30-calibre *ráfagas* into the canopy at the Guerrilla's estimated location. Although unlikely to hit them, this would slow their progress. A second chopper flew five kilometres ahead. Soldiers rappelled into two clearings and spread out, forming a loose net to block the kidnappers' escape, while the army and Autodefensas closed in from behind.

Buitrago's men found the engineer abandoned in a clearing. When he'd sprained his ankle the *guerrilleros* had been forced to leave him behind. The army airlifted him back to safety. The Guerrilla squad got away, but the thwarted kidnap made national headlines. Colonel Buitrago felt vindicated. Footage showed him in a flak vest assisting the limping engineer onto a transport helicopter. When the helicopter landed in Bogotá, cameramen filmed the engineer hugging his wife and children.

Victories like this were a boost to national morale. Buitrago's message to the Guerrilla was clear: *Whatever move you make, we will block you. Wherever you go, we will chase you. At any cost, we will stop you.*

'Finally!' said Alfa 1, who'd come down to join us for celebrations. He'd lived his life by that creed and for once was not jealous of the army taking credit. He even patted me on the shoulder. 'Good work.'

For several days, the family reunion footage played on loop. After watching it many times, I punched the OFF button. I was glad for the engineer but also glum.

'That should have been you, Papá,' I said. 'That should have been *us*.'

To have risked kidnapping the engineer so close to my checkpoint, Caraquemada's *frente* must have been desperate for funds or a military triumph. But they'd failed, making the rescue another turning point – a far happier one than the *limpieza*. The Autodefensa takeover of Llorona was flourishing. After yet another news feature portraying Buitrago as a fearless rescuer, he rang me.

'Caraquemada is still far from defeated,' said the colonel. 'But thank you, Pedro. Now I think it's just a matter of time.'

Field by field, farm by farm, person by person, we were wresting the country back from the Guerrilla's clutches. Every kidnap we prevented meant one fewer family devastated and one fewer Guerrilla bargaining chip against the government. Every bag of rice confiscated from Buitre's logistics network made the Guerrilla hungrier and more demoralised. And every enemy or collaborator we captured brought me closer to my father's killers.

A week later, I was at our base at sunset when Coca-Cola radioed me from Llorona Plaza. Two brothers who were well-known carpenters had stopped him on his motorbike, claiming they needed to see me urgently. They would talk to me, and only me. I agreed to meet them at our Llorona checkpoint and rode straight down.

'We didn't want to burden you with this,' said the younger brother, toeing the dirt. 'It's a delicate matter – a *family* matter that we'd normally have dealt with ourselves.'

The elder took over, leading me away from my men. 'It's our sister. She's pregnant. The father won't recognise the child.'

'But how does that involve us?'

'We reasoned with him. We even begged. Then my brother here almost punched him, but we know you prohibit fighting. He taunted us, saying how could we be sure it was his anyway? But our sister's not like that. She's only seventeen. He said if we didn't leave his shop, we'd have you to deal with.'

'Who did?'

'Your uncle.'

122

UNCLE LEO WAS behind his counter. The brothers arrived and politely invited Leo to accompany them to the civil registry where their sister was waiting. Leo jeered and pointed them to the door. His face dropped when he saw three Autodefensa soldiers gesturing for his customers to leave. A small crowd gathered, as Uncle Leo exited and then locked his shop. Of course, the townspeople didn't know what was happening, although later, when his young wife's bump showed, they would realise. When his eyes met mine, he flushed with embarrassment.

Coca-Cola stood there as witness while Leo signed the marriage certificate with Amelia.

Palillo didn't approve. 'Better to have no father than one who doesn't want you.'

'You really believe that?' I countered.

Palillo's stepfather had finally skipped town. His mother would no longer let Palillo near the house.

'You should be glad to be rid of him,' Palillo had said to her indignantly. But she wasn't glad. Yes, he'd been a violent drinker. Yes, he'd been a womaniser. But he'd had a steady job, sometimes he helped with the kids and, on the nights he did come home, he stopped her from feeling lonely.

'Eventually she'll realise she's better off without him,' Palillo declared. Fortunately Piolín got on well with Palillo's mother and had bonded with his siblings. I had no doubt she'd eventually reconcile mother and son.

Even at fourteen years old, Ñoño had the sense to remain neutral. He enjoyed inspiring fear in men three times his age, not to mention the side benefits with high school girls.

'Jump on!' he'd say to a girl walking along the road.

'Thanks, but I'm only going to the *supermercado* for my mother. It's two hundred metres.'

'Doesn't matter. I'll take you.'

Whether out of fear or daring, the girls agreed. Ñoño would speed off and circle the plaza three times before depositing them at the store.

In his spare time, Ñoño taught Iván how to disassemble and oil a Galil. He dragged up old planks from Uncle Leo's timber yard and constructed a set of monkey bars, which he used to train Iván every evening, between sit-up and push-up sessions.

'He's only a kid,' I said. 'He's not a soldier.'

'Just in case he has to go to La 50.'

Thirteen was the earliest age Iván could commence basic training. That gave us three years to find a way for him not to join the war.

In the meantime, we tried to make his childhood as 'normal' as possible. Camila brought him her brothers' old clothes. Piolín taught him to use a toothbrush and Mona helped him memorise the alphabet. On his days off, Ñoño took Iván to make friends with Old Man Domino. They played checkers in Llorona plaza and fed the pigeons.

When Palillo gave Iván his old BMX, the smile on the boy's face was as wide as if he'd won the lottery.

After Iván had been with us a full three months, something Ñoño said struck me in the heart. 'We made the right choice, Pedro. If we hadn't taken Iván, he would have become a *guerrillero*. We might even have faced off against him in battle. What if we shot him? What if *I* shot him?'

It was strange to think that a quick decision taken in the heat of a single moment could change the course of a boy's life. And that it could also make the difference between a person being your best friend or your mortal enemy.

In October, an itinerant worker in Puerto Galán accidentally drowned. Nobody knew how to reach his family, so his colleagues sent for us and the priest. We arrived at the wharf and transported the body to the local burial ground. But Padre Guzmán sent back a message: *'Sorry, very busy.'*

'I'll go,' said Palillo, kicking the Yamaha stand.

He returned doing wheelies along the main street with Guzmán behind him, his robes flailing and his chubby white fingers clutching Palillo's waist. Braking suddenly, Palillo skidded out the back tyre.

'Well? Off you get,' he ordered. 'Do your job!'

The priest, ashen-faced, stared at the compacted earth in the corner of the cemetery where we'd marked out a rectangular area and began sprinkling holy water on the body.

'What are you doing? Give me that!' Palillo snatched the leather gourd of holy water out of his hands and held out a shovel.

'Now dig!'

I pulled Palillo aside. 'You can't threaten a priest!'

'I didn't threaten anyone.'

'Then how did you persuade him to come?'

'I simply knocked on the church door holding a piece of paper and said, "Are you Orlando Guzmán?" He started shaking and said he'd do anything. I told him he didn't have to do *anything*, just his job.'

The next day, the priest applied for a transfer back to Bogotá. However, his *mulata* maid had settled into town life and would remain behind.

I phoned Padre Rojas immediately. He was delighted to hear from me.

'Perhaps you should apply for your old position,' I suggested.

Rojas laughed but I was serious, and after I explained that I could guarantee his safety, he agreed – not because of me, but because the town needed a priest.

Two weeks later, we stood together beside Papá's grave, where I'd arranged for a new granite gravestone to replace the bullet-riddled cross.

'I'm sorry I wasn't here for your father's passing,' he said. 'But you need to forgive the men who did this, Pedro. Or you will have no rest.'

War was an expensive business. The Díaz family's funds had covered initial operations and would last well into the future. But if everyone benefited, why should only they continue paying?

I wasn't sure about charging *vacunas* at first, but Trigeño convinced me.

'Pedro, I don't like charging taxes,' he said, 'but businesses and land values region-wide have appreciated much more than what we're requesting as donations. We've added value to the community. We've reignited the economy. We're maintaining a presence down here, keeping the peace and upholding justice. But that costs money, just like running a government does, and people are happy to pay to keep the Guerrilla away. Besides, citizens need to get used to paying taxes as their civic duty. When we hand over control to the army and politicians, they'll be paying much higher rates to the government.'

Unlike Guerrilla *vacunas*, our taxes were fair – based on turnover rather than a commander's whim. We charged 1,500 pesos – or one US dollar – per hectare of arable land; 5,000 pesos per *canasta* of beer; 15,000 pesos per harvested bag of rice, cassava, corn or African palm;

50 pesos per gallon of gasoline and 20,000 pesos per head of cattle sold. I assigned Ñoño and three boys to collection duties for smaller *fincas*, where they also monitored crop yields and counted cattle and poultry to ensure nothing was diverted to the enemy.

In November, Fabián Díaz commenced his election campaign. His supporters erected billboards and glued posters to walls. Fabián now looked the part – mature, serious and purposeful. In his VOTE 1 DÍAZ photo, he had short hair, wore a suit and had even removed his earring.

But that didn't fool me. In Colombia, *políticos* like Fabián don't seek office to transform the country – they do it to get richer. Once elected, they skim a percentage from government-awarded contracts, hire non-existent workers whose salaries they pocket themselves, and then siphon off health funds and workers' pensions. They half-build roads with low-grade materials, steal the remaining money and then get awarded the repair contract when the roads collapse. In the rare event they are exposed, they share their ill-gotten gains with investigators and judges, and then drum up political protection by threatening to expose those who brought them to power.

Fabián moved back to Javier's hacienda to re-establish his presence in Garbanzos. Caraquemada's response was immediate: the Guerrilla sprayed over Fabián's posters with FASCISTA and phoned Eleonora in Bogotá with death threats against both her sons. Trigeño's counter-response was lightning quick.

'I'm sending Beta down with three trucks and thirty men,' he told me. 'Fabián needs twenty-four-hour protection.'

'But Colonel Buitrago won't be happy. Remember he said—'

'Fielding a candidate was part of our pact. If Buitrago doesn't like Beta, then the army needs to guarantee Fabián's safety. If they can't, closer to the elections I'll send extra troops and establish a base in Puerto Princesa for when Fabián is campaigning in the villages.'

Of course, Buitrago protested, but his resources were already stretched so he tolerated it. As for me, I hoped Trigeño's setting up a second base further south might be part of a secret offensive against the Guerrilla camps. The sooner more troops came the better. I couldn't wait for Trigeño's long-promised attack against Caraquemada.

A week after Beta's arrival, we received good news. Don Felix announced that, after considerable reflection, he'd changed his mind – he'd stand independently in the elections. Privately, he told me it would be a tough race, particularly since Fabián was the Autodefensa-sanctioned candidate, but he couldn't let him win unopposed.

Buitrago and I were overjoyed. Felix had integrity and grit. Although he couldn't match the Díaz clan's campaign funding, his goodwill among townspeople gave him a chance of victory. Everyone knew the Velasquez name from his buses and also how Felix had stayed loyal to the region, when a weaker man would have fled.

November 17 marked the second anniversary of Papá's death. I still felt his loss keenly.

We marked the date by celebrating Mass at Llorona church. Since the return of Padre Rojas, attendance at Mass had soared.

Afterwards, I invited Mamá, Camila, Uncle Leo, Amelia, Palillo and Piolín to a special lunch and memorial ceremony at our *finca.* Mamá was overcome with emotion. She cried when she saw the renovated *finca* and our old photos in new frames. Uncle Leo brought back Mamá's glassware for the new bureau. Camila had baked a cake. Piolín made *limonada* while Palillo barbequed fish I'd caught.

Following lunch, we stood at Papá's new granite tombstone under the oak tree and I said a prayer for him. Mamá scattered flowers. Uncle Leo held Mamá's hand.

'You're looking more and more like him,' Mamá said. 'People in town say you're the only man around here with enough guts to do what's right.'

Pleased she no longer referred to me as a boy, I put my arm around her. 'And what do you say, Mamá?'

'I say: thank you, *hijo.*'

It was the first time in two years she'd set foot on her own property. And it was the first time she'd been able to properly farewell Papá. He was her true and only soul mate, just as Camila was mine.

'I was thinking of having him moved to the cemetery,' I suggested quietly.

'I think he likes it just fine where he is. And besides,' she said, tapping my shoulder lightly with the remaining flower, 'since you no longer listen to me, someone has to keep an eye on you.'

That afternoon, sitting with my family and friends, sipping *limonada*, and inhaling the fresh country air while soaking up the magnificent view over our majestic town, I felt that all the risks, hard work and painful sacrifices had been worthwhile.

'It won't be long before we can live here again,' I told Mamá. 'I think maybe after the elections next March.'

Once the Autodefensas had reinstalled legitimate governance with an honest leadership, hopefully under Felix Velasquez, the Guerrilla's power would continue to wane and social order would be restored. The Autodefensas would hand over control to the army and government. Llorona would return to normal; it might even be better than before.

In early December, Camila, who was now sixteen, graduated from high school a year early. She'd come top in her exams yet again.

Christmas that year was particularly special. At the start of the *Novena* prayer period, I erected a five-metre Christmas tree in the plaza. At night, my men ran a soup kitchen for the homeless. Villagers no longer hid the little wealth they had. Women wore jewellery. Parents bought presents for their children at market stalls. Couples walked in their finest clothes, blinking their eyes at the bright fairy lights as though waking up from a decade-long coma.

'Good news,' said Trigeño as we walked through Llorona markets. He'd flown down to congratulate me on what we'd achieved. 'We've located Buitre's brother.'

'Did he talk?' I asked excitedly.

'No. He doesn't know we're watching him,' said Trigeño, stepping aside for a pigtailed girl on a tricycle. 'We'll wait until he leads us to Buitre. Patience, Pedro. Keep working hard. We'll bring Buitre to you.'

'And Caraquemada and the Guerrilla bases?'

'Everything at its right time. The enemy is still strong, so stay on guard.'

On the morning of December 24th, Mamá and I attended Mass. We sat in our old pew. I was sad Papá wasn't there beside us. But I knew he was watching and I imagined he was proud.

'We were right, Papá,' I said to him afterwards. At midday I went fishing in our dinghy, imagining him beside me. 'No one else will have to go through what we did.'

In the afternoon, Camila and I made love, not in a hotel but at our *finca*, in my own bed – just as I'd always envisioned. Afterwards, I rang Mamá and suggested the three of us attend evening Mass.

'Twice in one day?' she exclaimed happily.

Wandering towards the church through Llorona's December plaza with Mamá on one arm and Camila on the other, I no longer imagined a time when my town would enjoy peace and prosperity. I was seeing it with my own eyes.

PART EIGHT

THE DARK ALLIANCE

123

FOR THE FIRST three weeks of the new year my life was clear blue skies. The only cloud on my horizon was Camila's approaching departure for university. I didn't like the idea that she might run into Fabián Díaz in the city with their mutual friend Andrea. But Camila had trusted me when I'd been away, and now I needed to show her that same trust. At least she'd finally stopped begging me to leave the Autodefensas and give up my pursuit of Papá's killers.

In fact, Camila had grown accustomed to the pistol on my belt and the arsenal of weapons my men kept by their hammocks. Strictly speaking, civilians weren't permitted on Autodefensa bases, much less to spend the night. But with Camila leaving soon, we treasured every moment together. Sometimes I'd awake in our caretaker's cottage to find a dandelion inserted into the muzzle of my rifle or a pink ribbon tied around the grip of my Smith & Wesson. She enjoyed talking to Piolín, and they'd fast become friends.

Of course, I wanted a future with Camila more than ever, and as soon as I'd eliminated Buitre and Caraquemada, I'd request a discharge and join her in Bogotá.

But while I waited impatiently for us to attack the Guerrilla's mountain strongholds, Trigeño was busy flying around the country, meeting with the candidates he was backing in the March elections and capitalising on his book's success by doing media interviews.

'Quite the celebrity,' Colonel Buitrago commented cynically at one of our regular security briefings. 'How truly committed is your boss to going after Buitre, Caraquemada and their camps? Looks to me like he's happy to hold Llorona, and that's it.'

Recently, Beta's 'electoral security' unit, provided by Trigeño to protect Fabián Díaz as he campaigned, had doubled in size. Two platoons were camped in the grounds of Javier's hacienda outside Garbanzos. Fabián now paraded through the villages in his bulletproof vehicle accompanied by five utility trucks, each with eight soldiers seated in the tray. Beta drove a red SUV that he referred to as his own, wore a thick gold chain and ate at restaurants that were beyond a soldier's salary.

Buitrago's doubts made me uncomfortable. I wanted to trust Trigeño, but as Camila's departure date drew nearer with still no action from him, my anger and impatience grew, and the assurances he fired back at me seemed as hollow as spent cartridges.

In late January, Don Felix Velasquez sent a message through Iván, asking me to meet him inside the Llorona church at 3 pm, alone.

As I rode my Yamaha down the bumpy dirt road, trying to ignore the oppressive heat, I wondered why Felix hadn't contacted me directly.

Only a month earlier, he'd welcomed me joyfully to his staff Christmas party. He was no longer being extorted by Caraquemada's eleven-year-old henchmen and his buses were once again travelling their full routes. Local polling placed Felix as the leading candidate for senator with seventy per cent of the likely votes. Fabián Díaz trailed on twenty-five per cent, while Yolanda Delgado, the human rights attorney who was running a class action on behalf of the *limpieza* victims, was placed third.

At the church, Padre Rojas ushered me inside, frowning at the pistol on my belt. 'Pedro, *por favor*, hide that *thing* in the urn,' he said, gesturing to an empty brass vase. 'Let's hope God can look the other way for five minutes.'

Inside, the only illumination came from an eerie stream of sunlight piercing the round stained-glass window above the altar. The fateful 9mm bullet hole that had prompted the padre's departure over two years earlier had been repaired, although the shade of blue didn't quite match the surrounding panels.

Felix was kneeling in prayer in the second pew. He'd removed his trademark fedora and was resting his forehead against his interwoven hands.

'Don Felix, why all the secrecy?' I asked, sitting down beside him.

Felix crossed himself and looked up.

'I'm sorry to break this so suddenly, Pedro, but I'm pulling out of the elections. Those Díaz brothers are as dirty as sewer rats. I've been through this *mierda* before when I stood against their father. Only he wasn't backed by a private army.'

'What do you mean?'

'It began a month ago, after I moved into the lead. When Fabián campaigns in the river villages, my buses are stopped on the way south by his security team – led by your colleague Beta – and my passengers intimidated with aggressive searches. Meanwhile, the Díaz buses are waved past undisturbed. During the rallies themselves, soldiers go knocking door to door, herding villagers into the plaza to attend.'

Although these allegations were new, I wasn't entirely surprised.

'Don Felix, I assure you none of this is coming from me or Trigeño.'

'Of course not. Your *patrón* phoned me personally in December to congratulate me on my success. But last week I received a very different phone call. "For your own good health," said the caller, "withdraw from the elections." And yesterday morning I found *this* hanging by a noose from the rafters of my porch.'

He handed me a rag doll in tattered trousers and shirt, its face and limbs roughly fashioned from coarse canvas. Upon its head perched a miniature fedora. And pinned to its shirt was a printed card inviting Don Felix to his own funeral.

I was shocked. If Fabián Díaz had sent this, it was a new low, even for him.

'I'll assign you two of my soldiers during the day, and another two to watch your house at night,' I said. 'But you can't pull out. You know Fabián won't run the local government honestly.'

Felix laughed bitterly. 'He'll rob the region blind like he has with that highways contract. For six months those earth-moving machines have been driving down to Puerto Princesa. Yet less than a kilometre of road has been asphalted. People are scared, Pedro. The Díazes want power at any cost. And Beta is their personal puppet. If you can guarantee my safety, I'll stay in the race. But you need to do something about those brothers. They have to be stopped.'

After Felix left, I sat for ten minutes in the pew, considering my next move. I felt responsible. I'd created this situation by introducing the Díaz brothers to Trigeño, despite knowing they were dirty. And now they were corrupting Beta. Villagers would make no distinction between Beta's actions and mine – we were all Autodefensas. My good reputation and all the positive work we'd done for my hometown were being dragged down by association.

For the first time since the *limpieza*, I felt ashamed to be a member of La Empresa. Felix was right: the Díaz brothers had to go.

But how?

The Díaz money made them Teflon. A journalist might throw accusatory mud, but none would stick. And although authorities like Buitrago scoured deeply into their affairs, the brothers emerged without a scratch.

The villagers would never denounce Beta's men, especially not to other Autodefensas. As for the threats against Felix, even if I could prove the Díaz brothers were behind them, I doubted Trigeño would break up our successful alliance over a patchwork doll hanging from a porch, and my accusations might well backfire, making me some powerful enemies.

I rode my motorbike to Garbanzos to consult with Colonel Buitrago.

The colonel's office was stuffy, and the corners of his moustache seemed to droop in the heat. A blue plastic fan swivelled slowly from side to side, blowing tepid air across the desk.

'Your colleague Beta is walking down a very dark path,' commented the colonel when I finished recounting Felix's revelations.

'I can't go to Trigeño with this,' I concluded. 'But perhaps if I could prove to him something even worse. For instance, that the Díazes have stepped into their father's dirty shoes . . .'

The colonel stared at me hard for several seconds, no doubt remembering the night at the Díaz fiesta when I'd revealed my knowledge that Buitrago had the combination to Javier's safe. We'd never openly acknowledged that the only place I could have obtained that information was from army intelligence files.

'That would be difficult,' he said at last. 'They're far smarter than Humberto.' He extracted a manila folder from a filing cabinet beside him and flipped it open on the desk. Reading it upside down, I saw it was a log of phone calls; some had been circled in blue, and one in red.

'As you clearly know, I monitored Javier and Fabián's calls for six months after their father's death. I found no direct evidence of trafficking. Only this.' He tapped the red-circled item. 'A call from Javier to Humberto's best friend and former business partner, Miguel Hernández.'

I realised Buitrago was referring to Don Miguel, the *patrón* from Flora's Cantina.

'I saw him with Javier. They were friendly—'

‘Friendship doesn’t prove they’re partners,’ interrupted Buitrago. ‘But expose them with evidence, and the Díaz charade is over.’

If the Díaz brothers were unmasked as *narcotraficantes*, not only would Fabián be forced to withdraw from the election but Trigeño would sweep them from our alliance, like leaves in the full force of a hurricane.

124

PALILLO WAS THE one person in whom I confided Felix's revelations and my plan to expose the Díaz brothers as *narcotraficantes*.

It was dusk and we'd walked to the wooden barn on the western side of our base, where we stored sacks of seed and the yellow barrels of chemicals for Trigeño's agricultural co-operative.

'Don't think for a moment that Beta will give up his luxury car and cavalcade of personal centurions without a fight,' Palillo warned. 'If you want to take on the Díaz, you'll have to get past their vicious guard dog first.'

After seven peaceful months, Palillo was no longer desperate to leave the Autodefensas. He visited his mother and siblings frequently, slept every night beside Piolín and received a regular wage. He'd grown complacent, firm in the belief that Caraquemada would never come down from the mountains to attack us. Ñoño, too, was happy. Iván still followed him around like a kid brother. Ñoño helped him train on their improvised obstacle course, and together they fed and walked the five guard dogs.

An hour after dawn the next morning, I was eating breakfast with Camila and fourteen of my men in our makeshift outdoor mess hall: two tables set up under the spreading branches of a jacaranda tree. The skies were cloudless and the horizon was tinged with pearly pink.

My platoon now numbered thirty. Mona fed us breakfast in two sittings with corn flatbreads and *huevos pericos* made from eggs she'd gathered from the chickens she kept in the old henhouse.

Palillo was entertaining the masses with his latest election joke.

'What's the difference between a politician who is *ignorant* and a politician who is *indifferent*?'

Ñoño, who'd heard him tell it before, proclaimed, 'Don't *know* and don't *care*. Either way voters are fucked.'

We were all laughing when I felt an urgent tug on my shirtsleeve, and turned to see Iván hovering beside me. His eyes darted hesitantly towards the others before he slid a folded piece of paper onto my lap.

I unfolded it and my heart seemed to stop. In the centre of the page was a large black-and-white photo of me. Above it, printed in huge black letters was: WANTED! And below the photo: PEDRO GUTIERREZ: FOR CRIMES AGAINST HUMANITY! BY ORDER OF ENRIQUE BOLIVAR, COMMANDER 34th UNIT. A reward of one hundred million pesos was offered for bringing me to 'justice' on 'behalf of the people'.

Furious, I crumpled the paper in my fist. Enrique Bolivar was the political alias used by Caraquemada!

'Iván, into the office. Now!' I whispered, glancing towards Camila, who didn't seem to have noticed anything.

I met Palillo's eyes. He rose silently and followed.

The 'office' was simply a corner of the milking shed screened off from my men's sleeping quarters. There was a white plastic table pushed against one wall, which boasted a radio, a conical lamp and an old laptop from which I sent Trigeño my accounting spreadsheets via email. I dismissed Cobra from radio duty.

'Iván, where did you get this?'

'In Puerto Galán. They're everywhere, *comando*. On the electricity poles, the bus stop and all along the walls of the abattoir. Someone must have put them up last night.'

Apparently, Iván had ridden his bike to Puerto Galán at dawn; he liked watching the fishermen bringing in their early-morning catch. Then he'd seen the posters. Most of them were too high for him to reach, but he'd managed to jump and grab one.

'I'm scared, *comando*,' said Iván, his spindly arms encircling my waist.

'You were very brave taking this down.' I placed a reassuring hand on his shoulder. 'But people might have seen you. So I don't want you cycling down to Puerto Galán anymore.'

'Let's go,' I said to Palillo, who looked worried. 'I need to see this for myself.'

I returned briefly to the table and told Camila that something had come up. She seemed to be about to demand details when Piolín, always the sensitive one, said, 'I'm happy to drive you home, Camila.'

Eight of us on four motorbikes sped from the base, covering the ten kilometres of dirt highway at breakneck speed. When we screeched to a halt beside the riverside food market, nothing could have prepared me for the sight that confronted me. Hundreds of posters covered every available surface. Beside the river, where the worst atrocities of the *limpieza* had occurred, white sheets fluttered against the boughs of the trees. In the side streets surrounding the market, they stretched as far as the eye could see. The effect was overwhelming; it was like walking into a hall of mirrors and seeing a thousand versions of my own face, distorted and grotesque, staring back at me.

It was 7 am on market day. Normally the village would be stirring early, but the covered stalls were deserted. Across the street I saw the baker ripping down posters from his store window. Seeing us, he darted inside and slammed the door. The few other villagers scurried away, perhaps terrified that the posters would unleash a wave of retaliatory violence.

'Spread out,' I ordered. 'Tear down every last fucking poster! Then check Puerto Princesa.'

As I yanked posters from the bus shelter and stripped them off the abattoir wall, my anger grew fiercer. Caraquemada had done this to undermine my authority, and he'd chosen market day to maximise my humiliation.

Palillo placed a hand on my shoulder. 'Why not chill out, *hermano*? We've got this under control.'

I finally stopped and looked around. Paper was strewn everywhere in my wake. Instead of systematically removing posters as my men had been doing, scrunching them up and tossing them into piles to be bagged and removed, I'd shredded them. Tiny pieces of paper were tumbling across the deserted cattle market, blown by a light breeze.

'It's a lie. Villagers know I had nothing to do with the *limpieza*!'

'Even so, a hundred million pesos is a lot of *plata*. Perhaps you should bunker down at La 50 until things cool off.'

'That's exactly what Caraquemada wants me to do,' I said. 'He's trying to get under my skin.' I interpreted these posters as a sign of Caraquemada's frustration. He was too weak to attack me militarily. This pathetic provocation was the best he could muster.

Upon our return to base, I found Piolín standing by the milking shed, waiting for me.

'I'm sorry,' she said, nodding towards the cottage. 'I drove her home earlier but she returned in a taxi.'

Camila was sitting on the corner of our bed amid the colourful feminine touches she'd added to the bedroom – vases of flowers on the windowsills and colourful sarongs hanging from the walls. She held a copy of the WANTED poster in her hands. She didn't look up and her voice was quiet. 'This was slipped under the door of my father's store last night. And Carolina phoned to say they're all over the villages.'

'Don't worry,' I said, sitting down beside her and putting my arm around her shoulders. 'We've collected all of them. And I promise Caraquemada won't touch you.'

'Pedro, it's not me I'm worried about,' she said. 'I'm not the one with a price on my head.'

'No one is going to kill me. The villagers know me. They respect me.'

'What if you're wrong? Caraquemada wants to *murder* you. And you act like it's nothing.'

'What would you have me do?'

'Come with me to Bogotá! Piolín told me you were on good terms with your boss. You could ask for a discharge.'

'If I run, Caraquemada will have won. People will lose faith that we can protect them. Patience, *mi amor*,' I said, offering her the same excuse Trigeño had given me for not attacking the Guerrilla camps. 'The time isn't right.'

'When *will* the time be right, Pedro?' she asked testily. 'When we're all dead?'

'When Llorona is safe. When Papá's killers are brought to justice.'

She shrugged out of my grip and stood. 'This isn't about Llorona. This isn't about justice. This is about *you*.'

Camila stalked away, while I remained on the bed feeling misunderstood and beset on all sides by enemies, as well as friends who should have been supporting me.

125

SINCE THE POSTERS were everywhere, I had no choice but to inform Trigeño. He was deeply concerned.

'Why not come back to La María and take leave, Pedro? Have a vacation on me until the situation settles down. Swim, jog, relax. You've been working eight months without a break. Palillo can take over while you're away.'

'I can't, *comando*. Stepping back now would send the wrong message to Caraquemada. With all due respect, what I need is more men. We need to go after him.'

'I'll see what I can do,' responded Trigeño. 'Meantime, avoid Puerto Galán and reinforce your headquarters in case he attacks.'

Trigeño sent cash and Alfa 1 transferred twelve more recruits. My unit now numbered forty soldiers, plus the two guarding Don Felix. I set about increasing our fortifications. Not only would this protect us in the event of an attack, it would also reassure my soldiers and placate Camila.

I had Tarantula, Montoya and R6 fill old tyres with dirt and stack them against the walls of my quarters and the barn to protect against heavier calibre rounds. They also built a second wall around the milking shed, punctuated with defensive firing positions, and covered it with barbed wire.

'Palillo, have Buitrago send me anti-mortar netting,' I ordered. 'Coca-Cola, get a radio handset to every house within five kilometres so they can report suspicious movements. And Giraldo, I want ten men working to dig four trenches, two metres deep, fifty metres back from the guard posts. We also need a connecting trench from the milking shed to the farmhouse. If Caraquemada attacks, we can't let him catch us divided.'

The two-storey farmhouse, with its thick walls, was the most defensible position. But it was seventy metres from the milking shed and soldiers needed to be able to reach it safely under enemy fire.

Meanwhile, I had Piolín print a WANTED poster for Caraquemada, with a sketch of him instead of a photo, and ordered two thousand copies taped on every surface in Puerto Galán, Puerto Princesa and even across the river in Santo Paraíso. I smiled to myself. Two could play at this game.

On our third day of work, when the sun was high overhead, I was on a ladder, fixing netting across the ground-level windows of the farmhouse while Palillo and Ñoño worked nearby. They'd dragged aside the old henhouse, having shooed out Mona's hens, and were working on the trench, their picks and shovels crunching into the dirt. Suddenly, I heard a muffled yelp and looked over to see Ñoño disappearing into the earth while Palillo dived to his side before he, too, disappeared completely.

I sprinted over, lay on my stomach and peered over the edge of a deep pit. They were three metres below, side by side on their backs in a square of sunlight. Dirt continued to pour down on top of them. Ñoño coughed and spluttered. Palillo turned on his side, groaning.

I looked around, hoping someone could bring a first-aid kit, but no one was in sight.

'Are you hurt?' I called down. 'Keep still! I'll get some rope!'

Palillo looked around and, strangely, burst into laughter.

'No need!' he said, standing up and stepping out of the light. I heard rattling and then the top rungs of an aluminium ladder appeared in front of me. 'Climb down. You've got to see this for yourself.'

Gingerly, I descended the rungs until my foot struck something solid. When my eyes adjusted, I saw I was standing in a four-by-four-metre bunker. Stacked around the walls were hundreds of white blocks covered in plastic. They almost reached the ceiling. A few blocks had toppled down and smashed open, their contents spilling out in white chunks. At first I couldn't quite believe what I was seeing.

Palillo was still laughing. He was covered in grass and soil, but also clumps of white rock.

'*¡Cocaína!*' we exclaimed at the same time.

'Holy Mother of God!' said Ñoño, standing and dusting himself off. He began counting the bricks in each row. 'If each block weighs two kilograms, there must be four tonnes here!'

Behind the blocks, the concrete walls were painted with waterproof sealant. The roof of iron girders above us was boarded over with wooden planks. A trap door dangled by its hinges; it must have rotted through during the rainy season and then buckled under Ñoño's weight. Beneath our feet, a layer of plastic covered more blocks that were stacked one metre high on a pallet in the centre of the floor. These bricks had luckily broken Palillo and Ñoño's fall.

'What do we do now?' asked Ñoño.

'Buy a month's supply of import-quality whisky,' suggested Palillo gleefully. 'Combined with this export-quality *perico* and some home-grown hookers, can you imagine the party?'

He scooped up two handfuls of powder, throwing one clump at me and rubbing the other in Ñoño's hair. Ñoño retaliated and soon cocaine was flying everywhere.

However, when Palillo caught my eye, he sobered up abruptly. 'You think these bricks belong to—'

'The Díaz brothers,' I finished for him. 'Who else? This must have been their storage point.'

It made sense. At their fiesta, I'd seen Fabián and his friends with a similar brick. And after their mother abandoned the property, the brothers had access to it for at least a year. But last April, when the Guerrilla suddenly demanded more money and torched one of their buses, it became too dangerous for them to step foot on the property. This load must have lain here ever since.

I smiled, remembering back to the initial meetings between Javier and Trigeño. No wonder the brothers had objected so strongly to granting us this *finca* as our headquarters. I could only imagine Javier's frustration, knowing his drugs were here but not being able to get to them.

Now I had the brothers in my crosshairs. This cocaine was exactly the evidence I'd been praying for.

'All I have to do is phone Trigeño,' I declared with satisfaction. 'He'll banish the brothers from the area. Javier will have to give up trafficking, and Fabián's career in politics will be over.'

Ñoño frowned. 'Trigeño won't banish the Díazes. He'll gut them like fish. Is that really what you want? I mean . . . Javier looked after your mother.'

'Then I'll call Javier first. I'll demand both brothers leave Vichada forever. Once they've gone, Beta and his army will have no reason to remain.'

'Dangerous plan,' Palillo warned. 'Don't underestimate the Díazes. People get killed for less than a single brick of this shit.'

'You have a better suggestion?'

He shrugged. 'Drag the henhouse back over the top, divert the trench and pretend nothing happened.'

But I couldn't. Fate had placed a sword in my hands; it was begging to be wielded. I told Palillo and Ñoño to cover the trapdoor loosely with a plywood sheet and alter the line of the trench. If any of my men asked why, they were to say they'd struck rock.

Then I phoned Javier. He claimed to be busy, even when I told him that he needed to come up urgently. While digging I'd found 'evidence of illegal activity'.

Only thirty minutes later Pantera announced, 'We have visitors.'

'*¡Mierda!*' said Palillo. It was not Javier who had arrived but Beta, with three trucks and thirty soldiers.

126

I WALKED TOWARDS the gate, suddenly fearful. I'd assumed that Beta would never tolerate *narcotraficantes*. But then, why was he here?

Beta was unpredictable. Once I told him about the cocaine, he was quite capable of phoning Trigeño and then slitting the Díaz brothers' throats. On the other hand, if he was here on Javier's behalf, he might be just as capable of slitting mine.

'Let Beta in. His men stay at the gate.'

Beta strolled up the drive with a self-satisfied swagger. He'd grown fatter since we'd last met and now wore a gold Omega watch. He stomped to a halt and planted his feet apart, aviator sunglasses hiding his eyes.

'What's going on?' he demanded. 'If there's illegal activity occurring anywhere in this region, you should inform *me* before anyone else.'

'I wanted to hear Javier's explanation first. Besides, it's on *my* base.'

'What is?'

'Cocaine.' I pointed across the grassy field to the henhouse. 'It's over there—'

Beta held up his palm to silence me and deliberately looked away from where I was pointing.

'You're not going to take a look?' I asked.

'I see only what I need to see, and nothing more.'

'But you will inform Trigeño?'

Beta removed his sunglasses and looked me in the eye. 'Pedro, our job is to protect our *patrón* – not only from danger, but also from damage to his reputation. If this gets out, it could taint Trigeño by association. Is that what you want?'

'Of course not.'

'How many people know?'

'Me, Palillo and Ñoño.'

'And Buitrago?'

'Not yet.'

'Then I suggest you keep it that way.'

It was unbelievable – I had hard evidence implicating the Díazes but Beta was asking me to cover it up. Not for a moment did I swallow his arguments about protecting Trigeño's reputation. Trigeño could shoot the brothers and no one would ever know about the cocaine. Or he could hand them and their merchandise over to the police. Of course, I knew Beta wasn't involved in trafficking, but it seemed he was prepared to turn a blind eye.

'So you're saying I should ignore what I saw? Is that an order?'

'No, it's not an order. It's a decision you have to make with your own good conscience. I suggest you think it over and choose wisely.'

He turned, walked back down the drive and sped off in his red SUV, taking his phalanx of bodyguards with him. I stood there, staring after him, marvelling at how he'd turned the tables on me.

Beta had intervened to protect the interests of his new benefactors. But he'd also covered his own backside by declaring he was acting in the interest of his official boss, Trigeño. All this without actually seeing the cocaine or making a decision himself. Whatever I chose to do about Javier's cocaine, and whatever the consequences, all the risk was on me.

Only thirty minutes later, two vehicles pulled up to the gate: a new champagne-coloured armoured BMW, driven by Javier, and the repaired Mercedes Fabián had driven on the day of the Zorrillo operation. Javier drove directly to the bunker where I stood waiting and emerged wearing leather shoes, pleated trousers and a crisply ironed white shirt. I studied his face, but Javier displayed no anxiety. In fact, he appeared curious, almost excited.

'Cigar?' said Javier, nonchalantly flipping open his silver case.

'I told you already; I don't smoke.'

'I shouldn't either. But it helps me relax.'

I descended the ladder and Javier followed. When his foot touched the cocaine, he reached into a concealed cavity in the wall and flicked a switch. A bulb on the wall lit the bunker. That confirmed it! If Javier knew about the switch, he knew about the bunker.

Standing with his hands on hips, he surveyed the walls of cocaine in apparent wonderment and emitted a low whistle.

'Beta said you'd found contraband,' he said. 'I was expecting a few kilograms. But this . . .'

He stabbed his car key into one of the broken bags, sniffed some powder from its tip and then dabbed the remainder on his tongue.

'Like a true professional,' I said. 'Well?'

'Uncut.' He stabbed the key in again, holding it out to me provocatively. I slapped his hand away.

'Then you admit it?'

'That I've tried cocaine . . .' He raised his hands in fake surrender. 'Guilty. But doing an occasional bump at a fiesta doesn't mean I'm the head of a cartel or that I have anything to do with this.'

Javier was a consummate actor, but I wasn't buying tickets to his show.

'It's on your property.'

'My father's property.'

'Which your mother inherited and which you had access to for a year before we set up this base.' I flicked the light switch off and on. 'You knew about this bunker.'

'About its existence, yes. About its current contents, no.'

'I don't believe you.'

'I don't care what you believe.'

Javier vaulted from the pallet, went down on one knee and removed a brick from against the wall, which he tossed to me. In the gap was a layer of yellowed newspaper. He removed more bricks and ripped away newspaper until a small wooden door became visible. The bricks above the door remained stacked on its lintel. Javier twisted the doorknob, revealing a narrow cavity with a blue sports bag at its entrance.

'This tunnel begins in the house behind a false panel in the cellar. My father built this bunker when I was five. He made us do regular drills, crawling in here to practise in case the Guerrilla came to kidnap us. These were our supplies.' He unzipped the sports bag to reveal torches, candles, tins of tuna and bottles of water.

'That proves its original purpose. Not what you've used it for since.'

'I've told you already, this cocaine is not mine.'

'And I've told *you* already, I don't believe you.'

Javier looked around the bunker in genuine exasperation. Then his eyes lit upon the torn newspaper. He picked it up, read it and smiled victoriously.

'Clearly, you're determined to think the worst of me, Pedro. But perhaps you still trust the news.'

He stood and handed me a page. The newspaper was dated two weeks before Humberto's death. I'd made a gross miscalculation – the cocaine had been here *before* Javier took control of the *finca*. But I was still convinced in my gut that Javier was a trafficker and that this bunker was strong leverage.

'Even if this belonged to your father, it won't make a difference. I've seen Trigeño execute two brothers just because they were related to a *traficante*.'

'And you'd do that to us? You'd have us killed? But . . . we . . . your mother . . .'

'And I'm grateful to you. But I can't keep this from my commander.'

'Trigeño doesn't need to know. I'll move this stuff elsewhere. And you'll receive a reward for finding it.'

'I don't want your dirty money.'

'Then what *do* you want?'

'What I want from you . . . no, what I *require*, is for Fabián to withdraw from the elections. I want no more threats against Felix Velasquez. And I want Beta and his growing army of men on your payroll to leave your hacienda for good.'

Javier clicked his tongue. 'So that's what this is about. I know nothing about any threats, but as for the rest, you've overplayed your hand. Trigeño not only needs Fabián as senator, he needs our money. We agreed to pay him three million dollars over three years in monthly instalments. If you turn him against us, our alliance will disintegrate and he'll lose the outstanding payments. Your *patrón* is spending *our* funds to keep the Autodefensas functioning – not just here, but in other regions too. Once that tap is turned off, you'll have to abandon Llorona. And we both know Buitrago can't hold this region on his own.'

This time I could not disguise my shock. I thought I'd had Javier. Four tonnes of immovable evidence lay before us, but he'd spun it around on me a hundred and eighty degrees.

If the Autodefensas withdrew from Llorona, Caraquemada would retake control. I could only imagine the Guerrilla reprisals against those who'd helped us. But even worse, I'd lose my shot at Papá's remaining killers. All those years of sacrifice and suffering – completely wasted.

I was defeated and Javier knew it.

'Board this up,' he said magnanimously. 'I'll have the contents removed under cover of dark so you're not compromised . . . any more than you already are.'

Presumably, he intended to sell it, which would compensate him for every dollar he was spending on the alliance, plus a few million more. Javier extended his hand, but when I didn't shake it he patted my back like we'd made a deal anyway.

'You're losing sight of what's important here, Pedro. We're not your enemy. It's Caraquemada and Buitre you want. We promised to help you, and we will.'

'Help me how?'

'In two days, Beta will bring you a gift as reward for your silence. Something that will be very useful to you. You have my word of honour as a man.' When I looked sceptical, he added, 'Then I swear to you on my mother's life. And one more thing: I saw those wanted posters. You obviously need protection from Caraquemada, so I'm lending you the Mercedes.'

For the next two nights I slept in twists and knots. Of course I was grateful for the armoured vehicle, but I still didn't trust Javier. His word was as solid as smoke. As for Beta, I had more faith in a mirage.

Four tonnes of pure cocaine lay hidden beneath my base and I hadn't informed Trigeño. I'd done as Javier suggested, boarding the bunker up and dragging the henhouse back into position above it, although not before crawling through the tunnel and locating the false panel in the cellar.

Were Javier and Beta setting a trap for me, planning to tell Trigeño or Buitrago about the cocaine themselves? I was wary when, two days later, Beta's caravan reappeared in the late afternoon. This time I authorised the entry of his men and he drove to the main farmhouse, accompanied by two utility trucks, each with eight soldiers seated in the tray.

The steely-eyed soldiers formed up in four lines. I didn't recognise any of them. They'd begun calling themselves the *Escorpiones Negros* and now wore an upper-arm patch with a black scorpion insignia.

'I have a little present for you,' Beta said. 'In appreciation of your loyalty to *La Empresa*.'

He waved towards his SUV and two of his men sprang forward to open the rear door. They dragged out a male prisoner whose head was covered with a pillowcase and whose hands were cuffed in front of him. He was dressed in faded blue overalls streaked with motor grease.

'Look familiar?' said Beta, grinning slyly as he yanked off the pillowcase. When I saw the gagged and blindfolded man beneath, blood surged to my temples.

He had blond hair.

127

WHEN I RAISED the blindfold, however, it revealed a young man of about sixteen, with the same emerald-green eyes as Buitre but too young to be him. The boy blinked a few times and then, without looking directly at any of us, closed his eyes.

'Who's he supposed to be?' I asked, unable to mask my disappointment.

'Buitre's brother. The one we've had under surveillance in Barrancabermeja.' Beta told me his men had kidnapped the boy from work, marching him away from his colleagues at gunpoint. As I began removing the boy's gag, he added, 'I wouldn't do that if I were you.'

Immediately, the boy's mouth opened and words chugged out in bursts, like water from an upside-down bottle.

'I'm innocent! I'm not responsible for what my brother does. I haven't seen or spoken to him in seven years. I'm an apprentice mechanic, not a *guerrillero*!'

'*¡Oye!*' Beta slapped him lightly across the cheek and leaned in close. 'Have we mistreated you? Have we denied you food or water? Have we tortured you?'

The boy shook his head.

'So shut up then.' Beta replaced the blindfold. 'I know you're not Guerrilla.'

My mind began racing. Having his brother might result in a sudden leap forward in my hunt for Buitre, but I was shocked that Beta had kidnapped a civilian in contravention of the Autodefensa statutes – and that he'd done this entirely for me, to buy my silence.

'Does our commander know?' I asked.

Beta put his finger to his lips and shook his head.

'What do you want me to do with him?'

'Ransom him. Let him go. Chop him up and feed him to the fish, for all I care,' he said loudly. Then he motioned me out of the boy's hearing and lowered his voice. 'But I suggest using him as bait to reel in Buitre.'

'How?'

'Remember Rafael, the *guerrillero* who defected after the Zorrillo operation? At first I didn't trust that son of a bitch, but his information was gold. He insists the brother is so important to Buitre that he'd give up his own life to save him.'

He handed me a copy of a property deed, tapping his finger against the name of its owner.

'That's Buitre's mother. He sent her the money to purchase this house two years ago. And he paid his brother's apprenticeship fees.'

The deed was evidence of two things: that Buitre cared about his family and that his mother, at least, was likely in contact with him. The latter was essential since Beta was adamant that we couldn't contact Buitre via the Guerrilla's network.

'Buitre will need to keep this from his group. If Caraquemada finds out, he'll prohibit Buitre from negotiating. This needs to be personal, Pedro, between you and him. This is family.'

I was still slightly stunned, knowing the kidnapping of a civilian was wrong, not to mention that we were going behind Trigeño's back. But Beta told me this was *my* decision and, despite some misgivings, I didn't hesitate for long.

I walked over to the boy. 'Can you get word to your brother?'

Nodding his head frantically, he said, 'I can try.'

By this time a crowd of my soldiers had gathered around, wondering who this new arrival was. Beta drew his pistol, grasped the boy's shoulder and marched him into the farmhouse and up the stairs.

Over the past months, we'd gradually been restoring the dilapidated building for use as an additional barracks when Trigeño sent more soldiers. We'd stripped the putrid carpets, sanded the floorboards and plastered over the holes in the walls. The broken hinge on the front door had been fixed and the missing slats on the wooden shutters replaced.

Beta shoved the boy, who was still blindfolded, into a bedroom on the second floor.

'You get one phone call,' he said, slamming the door behind us and grinding his Colt .45 into the boy's temple. 'No fucking around. If you're telling the truth about not being able to contact your brother, I suggest you phone your mother.'

I cringed, seeing the boy's cuffed hands trembling, but Beta enjoyed this sort of thing. He reached into the boy's pockets and tossed me his wallet. 'I've already checked it, but take a look for yourself.'

I flipped through it, looking for business cards or phone numbers. It contained a small amount of cash and two photographs: one black-and-white shot of an older woman – presumably his mother – and the other of a young pretty girl.

Meanwhile, Beta coached the boy on the phone call script, warning him not to say anything stupid.

The boy told Beta his mother's number and Beta dialled, turning on speakerphone so we could all listen.

'*Hola*, it's me. How are you, Mamá?'

By asking a question, he'd already departed from the script. Beta kicked the boy in the shin.

'*Hijo*, where are you?' his mother demanded. Crying and rambling, she was out of her mind. 'I was so worried. Your boss said bad men took you away. When are you coming home?'

'Mamá, I need you to get word to Kiko. Tell him the Autodefensas will contact you two weeks from today with a number for him to call.'

There was a long silence. Finally, she whispered, 'But I haven't heard from Kiko in years.'

This next part would be the most difficult part for the boy – confronting his mother with evidence that she'd accepted financial benefits from her *guerrillero* son.

When he hesitated, Beta ground the Colt in harder to his temple and clicked the safety off.

He took a deep breath. 'Mamá, they have a property deed with your name on it. They say Kiko gave you money for our house and paid for my studies. I said it wasn't true, but . . .'

There was another long silence, then sobbing. I could imagine his mother sitting on the other end of the line, her face crumpled with anguish.

'*Mijito*, I'm so sorry. I . . . I just wanted to protect you. Keep a roof over your head and pay for your education.'

'It's okay, Mamá. It's not your fault. But please, whatever you do, don't contact the authorities.'

'Or they'll kill me,' Beta reminded him in a whisper.

But the boy paraphrased, 'Or there'll be consequences.'

Beta hung up and struck him across the face. 'Cheeky little *hijo de puta*, aren't you?'

'I have a name,' he said with dignity. 'It's Ernesto.'

I was thankful Ernesto was still blindfolded. That way I didn't have to meet his eyes. Hearing his mother's distress had shaken me. I'd sent Mamá my salary, bought her groceries and paid her rent. I thought also of Trigeño's mother, trapped on La 35 'for her own safety'. What son didn't want to put a roof over his mother's head? And what mother wouldn't go to any lengths to protect her son?

Beta leaned out the window and ordered Ñoño to come up and guard the prisoner. When Ñoño entered, he stared at Ernesto, but he knew better than to ask questions in front of Beta.

'I'm sorry, *comando,*' I said to Beta as we exited the farmhouse. 'I don't think I can do this.'

'Of course you can.' He signalled to two of his soldiers. 'Do you want your father's killers or not?' From the back of a cattle truck, they removed chains and padlocks, a metal window grille and a steel cattle gate, hurling them to the ground. 'Secure that bedroom properly. You've seen how it's done.'

Beta clearly intended for me to keep Ernesto prisoner no matter what, but the sight of all this hostage paraphernalia only compounded my unease. Beta had even brought the same type of wall hooks I'd seen in his own bunker on La 50, only now I'd be the jailer.

'What do I say when I phone back in two weeks?'

Beta patted me on the back paternally. 'You'll figure it out as you go. But to make sure you don't fuck it up, I'm transferring Rafael to your unit.'

128

AS BETA'S CARAVAN roared through the gates, I felt a wild rush of motivation. In a single afternoon I'd gone from complete despair to *this*: my first real shot at Buitre.

Palillo was waiting for me beside the pile of equipment left behind by Beta's men. He'd just returned from a meeting with Don Felix about his new security arrangements.

'I heard you got Buitre!' he declared joyfully. 'Did he talk? Will he help us get Caraquemada?'

I shook my head. 'It's Buitre's brother.'

'Also a *guerrillero*?'

'Apprentice mechanic.'

Palillo's judgment blazed into my eyes like a spotlight. 'You're holding a civilian?'

'We'll be giving Buitre a taste of his own medicine.' Palillo started to speak. 'And whatever you're about to say, don't.'

'Camila won't like it,' he said flatly, picking up an armful of chains.

'Then we'll just have to make sure she doesn't find out.'

We spent the rest of the afternoon fitting out Ernesto's cell. We attached the barred steel gate inside the door. The metal grille we fitted to the inside window frame, keeping the outside shutters closed with the slats angled open for light. We furnished the room with a bed and a jug of water.

We chained Ernesto to the wall by his ankle. He had enough slack to reach his bed but not to get as far as the window or gate. A tear rolled down his cheek as I padlocked his ankle restraint.

All my soldiers would do guard shifts on the chair outside Ernesto's cell. 'But they're not to talk to him,' I instructed Palillo. 'Only you, Ñoño and I are to go inside.'

If Ernesto had been cheeky to Beta, with me he was outright rebellious, steadfastly rejecting eye contact.

He insisted on being unchained for meals, saying, 'Kill me if you have to, but please don't treat me like an animal eating off the floor.'

This meant I had to watch him eat. I didn't like him holding a knife and fork, but he pushed his point, saying, 'I am a peaceful person.' His tone left no doubt as to his true meaning: *I am not like you.*

Whenever we spoke about Buitre, Ernesto also insisted that I use his brother's given name, Kiko. 'Buitre is a horrible name. One day, I will tell you how he got it.'

'Don't bother,' I shot back. 'The name "Vulture" suits him perfectly.'

Despite his stubbornness, once he'd adjusted to his new living arrangements, Ernesto remained upbeat and found ways to be helpful.

'Excuse me, but I think that starter motor's going to short,' he advised Ñoño, hearing one of the Yamahas spluttering outside. Ñoño ignored him. Ernesto shrugged. 'I'm a mechanic and I'd like to do something useful, if you'd please trust me.'

Later that afternoon, Ñoño returned to base panting, having pushed the broken-down Yamaha two kilometres uphill. 'All right, *señor* know-it-all,' he said, unlocking Ernesto's cell door. He'd wheeled the bike into the farmhouse's central courtyard and fetched a toolbox.

'Give me half an hour, please. I promise not to escape,' Ernesto said and proceeded to fix the bike.

After this incident, Ñoño became my prisoner's fiercest advocate.

'This is wrong, Pedro! Ernesto is a kind person. His brother being a Guerrilla is not his fault. You should let him go.'

I guessed some of my other soldiers shared Ñoño's views but dared not voice them. And deep down I knew Ñoño was right.

As I waited for Rafael to arrive, we continued reinforcing the base. I decided to show Iván the hidden tunnel in the cellar, where he could hide if there was danger above, careful to emphasise that he was never to go far into the passage. I also convinced Mamá to move back in with Javier Díaz, citing heightened security concerns. After sending me Ernesto, Javier could hardly refuse my mother a space in his guesthouse.

Meanwhile, Ernesto made it harder and harder for me not to sympathise with his predicament – a predicament for which I was wholly responsible. When I unlocked the gate to bring him breakfast, he'd brighten, keeping up a brave prattle of jokes and pleasantries. Somehow he started calling me Little Pedro, and I didn't stop him. 'Pedrito,' he'd say, 'how did you sleep last night? It was so hot, don't you think?' or, 'Pedrito, thank you for the food at lunch; it was delicious. Please convey my compliments to the cook.'

He even told me about his fiancée – the girl from the photo. He'd asked her to marry him only two months ago, tricking her into climbing up to a lookout since he couldn't think of anywhere romantic in his *vereda*. He'd given her a pink plastic ring from a Corn Flakes box, with a love letter promising a proper ring later, once he got his pay rise.

I knew the Guerrilla never spoke to their hostages for good reason, but I foolishly thought myself stronger. When I asked his fiancée's name, Ernesto said, 'Astrid,' and begged me to let him call her. He said her only information would be from his mother, who was hopeless in a crisis.

Of course I couldn't allow that – if Buitre found out, he'd interpret it as weakness – but after seeing Ernesto's desolation, I relented. 'If you like, I could call her myself and tell her I'm a friend, and that you are definitely alive.'

Ernesto shook his head but sat there in silence for a minute, pondering. 'We would be friends, Pedrito. Don't you think?'

During that first week holding Ernesto, I thought more and more about Papá. Normally, in dark moments, I felt him standing behind me with his hands outstretched, ready to guide me through tough dilemmas and catch me if I fell.

But now, my shoulders felt heavy with the burden of his disapproval. In my heart of hearts, I knew he didn't condone what I was doing.

On the seventh afternoon of Ernesto's captivity, I left his cell convinced I was making a mistake keeping an innocent boy chained with absolutely no moral justification. But now that I'd made the decision, I had to stick to it.

129

THE FORMER *GUERRILLERO* Rafael arrived at the main gate early the following evening as the sun was setting. I waited for him at the top of the drive in front of the farmhouse, in the exact same spot where Zorrillo had been standing just before I shot him.

Clearly, word had passed around since a number of my soldiers lingered nearby, pretending to work. Many of them remembered Rafael from when he'd surrendered on the final day of our trek to oust the Guerrilla and now voiced their objections.

'No way I'm sleeping under the same roof as him,' protested Tarantula.

'Once a *guerrillero*, always a *guerrillero*,' Pantera declared.

Rafael didn't seem to care. Neither did the girls. Mona nudged Piolín and both stared open-mouthed as he strolled up the drive wearing his pack, with a guitar in a soft case slung over one shoulder and his Galil strapped to the other. Rafael was tall, well-built and strikingly handsome with chiselled features, a square jaw and brown eyes that glinted with sadness. He was dressed in camouflage with an AUC armband. A tattoo of a coral snake on his wrist indicated he was now a junior commander.

'*¡Comando!*' he said, saluting me before shaking my hand firmly. 'An honour to meet you. Alfa 1 and Trigeño speak very highly of you. I know you have no reason to like or trust me, but I feel we have a lot in common.'

Rafael seemed sincere, and Alfa 1 and Trigeño promoting him was a strong vote of confidence. But he was right: I was indeed wary. After all, he'd been a member of Caraquemada's unit under Zorrillo and Buitre. What if he'd been one of the *guerrilleros* present on the day of Papá's execution? He'd also spent the past seven months in Beta's power, and I was still unsure of whether his transferring Rafael to my unit was part of an elaborate trap.

'Welcome, soldier,' I replied tersely.

I was bursting with so many questions that I didn't know where to start. What did Rafael know about the inner workings of the Guerrilla?

What could he tell me about Caraquemada? And most importantly, how did he think holding Ernesto prisoner would help us capture Buitre? But I didn't want to give anything away myself. Luckily, Rafael seemed eager to win my confidence, and when I invited him to speak privately in my quarters, he did most of the talking.

'I'm sorry for your father, *comando*. Truly I am,' he said, stepping into the living room and immediately spying the framed photo of Papá mounted above the sofa. 'I'm told he was a good man. But I know little about his death. I was away on a mission that week.'

I nodded, relieved to hear it.

Rafael had moved on to the photos of Camila hanging beside those of my parents. 'Your girlfriend?'

'Camila. She lives in Llorona.'

'She's *hermosa*!' He brightened, turning back to face me and taking a seat in one of the faded blue armchairs. 'You're lucky to have her, and to be able to see her and touch her. I miss Beatriz every day. All I have now is this photo.' He reached into his breast pocket and handed me a photo of a pretty girl with wavy dark hair and brown eyes, dressed in camouflage.

I was silent, sensing he wanted to continue.

'I met Beatriz when I joined the Guerrilla. She was beautiful and vivacious and I was totally in love with her. We were recruiters who would travel together to tiny *veredas* to persuade other teenagers to join. Buitre was our commander and the three of us were the best of friends; in fact, it was thanks to him that we were allowed to become *socios*. That decision gave me the happiest years of my life.'

A smile briefly lit Rafael's face, and then just as quickly faded. 'One thing you need to understand, *comando*, is that when you join the Guerrilla you lose your family forever. Visiting them, or even contacting them, earns you the death penalty. We're not given cell phones or leave periods. We're not even allowed to carry cash. It's "Revolution or Death", and commanders control every aspect of our lives. So Beatriz and Buitre were my new family, and I loved him like a brother. But Buitre wasn't willing to give up contact with his real family. He was rarely able to leave the jungle himself, so he asked us to take packages secretly to his hometown and give them to his mother. Buitre admitted he was skimming from Caraquemada's cocaine money. Eventually he asked us to take a backpack bulging with cash so his mother could buy a house and pay for his brother's apprenticeship. And we did it.'

'What if you'd been caught?'

'Instant execution. All three of us. And Caraquemada probably would have killed Buitre's family. But we were always careful, and without Buitre's protection, senior commanders would have separated me and Beatriz for being too much in love. Once, Beatriz asked Buitre what he would do if Caraquemada noticed he'd been skimming cash. Buitre said, "I'd shoot him and run." Beatriz pointed out that he wouldn't get ten paces before Caraquemada's bodyguards riddled him with bullets. And you know what Buitre replied? "But my family would go on living." When I heard that and saw the steely resolve in his eyes, the way his teeth clenched with determination, I knew he wasn't lying. Don't you see, *comando*? He'll risk execution to send them letters. He'd steal from his own trusted commanders. He'd kill anyone he had to before he'd let harm come to his family. If it came down to it, he'd rather die himself. And that's why I'm one hundred per cent certain that he'll surrender to save his brother.'

Rafael paused for a moment to let his words sink in then asked with sudden fierceness, 'Where are you holding our hostage? I need to see him.'

'Maybe tomorrow,' I said, glancing at my watch. 'It's late. You can lay your pack there and sleep in my cottage tonight.'

'You don't believe me,' Rafael stated flatly.

'I *do* believe you,' I said, 'but I'm tired and need time to think.' Truth be told, I sensed Rafael wasn't telling me everything about Buitre. Plenty of people will say they would die, or kill, for their family. But, as they say in Colombia, 'Words are beautiful.' So Buitre simply claiming he'd die for his family didn't explain Rafael's absolute conviction. There had to be more to the story.

'Okay. Fine. Maybe you believe me,' he said. 'But you don't *trust* me. To be completely honest, *comando*, I wasn't sure how I'd feel meeting you. On that day you ambushed Zorrillo, you also killed a lot of my friends. But the fact is, I don't bear you any ill will. This is war, and it might well have been the other way around. Besides, I'm eternally indebted to you.'

'Indebted how?'

'When I surrendered, Beta wanted to kill me. You stopped him. If not for you, I'd have been cut up into little pieces with a chainsaw. I've been given a second chance at life. That's a debt I intend to repay with every ounce of my ability.'

Rafael's mention of the day he defected reminded me of something. 'You told us that Buitre wanted you dead. And that you wanted to join us so you could kill him. What happened?'

Rafael bowed his head. 'That's something I'll share when I know you better.'

'At which point, Rafael,' I said, 'maybe I'll let you talk to Ernesto.'

Rafael nodded slowly, smiling ironically, conceding defeat. He leaned his head back against the sofa and closed his eyes. He was silent for such a long time that I was about to go into my bedroom when he began speaking again in a low voice that quavered with emotion.

'One day Beatriz came to me in tears. She was pregnant. It should have been the best news of our lives. Instead, we were petrified. Every *guerrillera* is given a monthly contraceptive injection, but if it fails she's sent to a horrible, dirty clinic and forced to abort. We didn't want them to kill our baby so we planned to desert. Buitre immediately gave us three thousand dollars, enough to get away, but the army was in the area. All missions were suspended. We'd have to wait.

'As her bump began to show, Beatriz begged Buitre desperately to get us out of camp. She began raising her voice at him, reminding him that we'd helped his mother, and cried every day until finally he agreed to invent a mission for us. But the very next morning, during bathing time, one of the older girls blurted out, "*¡Dios mío!* You're pregnant!" Beatriz was hauled before Caraquemada. She denied her pregnancy but they searched her pack and found the money. Caraquemada put her on trial for "stealing from the revolution". She was loyal to Buitre and didn't tell Caraquemada where she'd got it. But Caraquemada is a tyrant who'd shoot a child before he'd swat a fly. His order was immediate: "Execution."

'I almost died when I heard that. I went crazy and began yelling. Luckily, Buitre intervened. "Keep quiet, *hermano*! Trust me on this!" He offered to personally carry out the execution. As the three of us walked to the camp's perimeter Buitre explained his last-minute escape plan. While I dug her "grave", he'd let Beatriz slip away and then fire a shot in the air. I'd desert on my next mission and join her in an agreed location. She kissed me goodbye. She turned, smiling, to hug Buitre and thank him, but he drew his pistol and shot her, first in her stomach where our baby was growing, and then, when she fell to her knees, in her head. "You bury her," he said to me kindly. "I'll go tell Caraquemada it's done."

'I just stood there, reeling in shock as the ghastly truth dawned on me. "You set this up! You told that girl Beatriz was pregnant!" I said. He nodded. "I did it for *us*. She'd never have made it and her big mouth would have gotten us all killed. You, me, my mother and brother." He put his arm over my shoulder. "I thought you'd understand . . . I had no choice." I don't know how I could even utter a word, but somehow I did. "*Understand?* You killed my unborn child. You killed the person I love most in the world." His response was chilling. The memory of his cold green eyes will be imprinted on my brain forever. "I could have tried you as well, comrade," he said, "but your ingratitude now makes the situation between us very clear."

'After that, I knew he was looking for a way to kill me. I wanted him dead too, but I was so stunned and grief-stricken that Caraquemada confiscated my rifle and tied me up, believing I was a danger to myself. On the day Zorrillo called for volunteers to kidnap Fabián Diaz at this *finca*, Buitre was out of camp. I raised my hand, smiling as though I was better, and Zorrillo returned my rifle to me. The rest, Pedro, you already know . . .'

Rafael was silent for a long, long time. His head was bowed, tears in his eyes. Rafael had indeed convinced me he was no threat to me or my men. He'd also convinced me that his hatred for Buitre was genuine. Now that I'd heard about Beatriz's death, I no longer doubted his sincerity. I felt we had something in common, the pain of losing a loved one.

Rafael's eyes glittered. 'Pedro, the only way people truly learn anything is through suffering, by losing or fearing to lose the thing they value most. For Buitre, that is Ernesto and his mother. And I'm convinced that for either one of them, he will give his life.'

I hardly slept that night. My mind buzzed with possibilities, churning over the new information Rafael had imparted. His first-hand depictions of Buitre and Caraquemada made them seem real, and that meant the possibility of capturing them suddenly felt real also. Knowing now how much Buitre loved his family, Rafael's plan to use Ernesto seemed plausible.

At breakfast the following morning, the atmosphere remained tense. The only one to break ranks was Iván, who remembered Rafael from when the Guerrilla would pass his father's shack. 'You used to give me sweets!' he exclaimed.

Everyone else ate in subdued silence, interrupted only by the clinking of cutlery and occasional grumbling. Rafael rose and confronted their misgivings head-on.

'Yes, I was a *guerrillero*. And I know you hate what they have done to your fallen comrades, your families and your villages. But I also hate the Guerrilla now. Their commanders killed many of my *compañeros* too, and they killed a person very dear to me. Trigeño promoted me to commander, but if you still don't trust me . . .' He removed the cartridge from his rifle and handed it to Palillo. 'Please return this when you do.'

That night, Rafael played his guitar, a melancholic communist ballad, deliberately strumming the final chord out of tune.

'Anyway, that's the romantic bullshit they brainwashed us with,' he said.

Now that he had their attention, Rafael began regaling them with stories about his life in the Guerrilla, which made our own brutal organisation seem much better by comparison. He also reminded us who the real enemy was. According to him, the Guerrilla commanders were hypocrites.

'Maybe when the insurgency first formed, our commanders had ideals. I know Santiago still does; I've heard him speak at the annual assembly. But he's from the old guard. For the younger commanders, war is a business. It's about money and cocaine.'

At this, Palillo pricked up his ears. 'So, is it true what Zorrillo said about the *caletas*?' he asked. 'Is there really cash buried out there in the jungle?'

Rafael grinned. 'It's true, *amigo*, every word.'

Palillo laughed. 'Then we definitely need to talk.'

Over the next few days, the others in the camp learned Rafael's sad story one by one. He would always choose his moment. Not because he wanted anyone's sympathy but because he needed them to understand. It was a strange quality in a supposedly hardened soldier. I found it unsettling at first but nonetheless entrancing.

Quickly, the initial scepticism faded. The men thought he was funny. The girls thought he was cute. They felt sorry for him, with his sad eyes and melancholic ballads. Three days after his arrival, it was agreed: Palillo should return Rafael's rifle magazine.

Rafael achieved what I had failed to do – he made the others resolute about our prisoner. Once Beatriz's horrific death at the hands of Buitre was common knowledge, Rafael's determination to fight the Guerrilla became infectious. The mood of my soldiers shifted. Of course, they still didn't know exactly what was planned, but Rafael inspired trust and his presence gave Ernesto's imprisonment a purpose.

Despite all this, I wasn't yet ready to introduce Rafael to Ernesto. I was worried that since the brothers looked so similar and Rafael's hatred for Buitre was so overwhelming, he might lose control.

And besides, Rafael didn't need to meet Ernesto to advise me on how to use him to get to Buitre. I declined his request several times until finally he confronted me in my office.

'*Comando,* I was sent here for one reason and one reason only – to help you get Buitre. I want exactly what you want – to avenge the person I loved most in the world. I can't do it on my own. And neither can you. Now, where is Buitre's brother?'

Finally, I relented. It was time for Rafael to meet Ernesto.

130

WHEN RAFAEL FIRST laid eyes on Ernesto, he stood stock-still, hands on hips, appraising him.

'You even have the same green eyes.'

'Please,' said Ernesto. 'I'm Kiko's brother, but I'm innocent. I have a girlfriend.'

'So did I,' Rafael replied coldly. 'And she was innocent too . . . until your charming brother killed her.'

'Who are you? What do you want?'

'I'm Rafael. And I'm here to help you understand.'

Rafael sat on Ernesto's bed and began explaining why Ernesto had been kidnapped and what his brother had done to make it justified, setting out patiently and compassionately the many reasons Buitre had to die.

Ernesto tried to interject, claiming that Kiko had always been a good person until circumstances changed his life.

Rafael cut him off. 'You haven't seen him for seven years. He's different now to the brother you knew.'

After we returned to my cottage, Rafael outlined his plan to reel Buitre in.

'Buitre is ruthless and he's experienced,' he warned me. 'If we don't prepare, he'll run rings around us.'

Beta had already briefed Rafael on our phone call to Buitre's mother two weeks earlier. It would soon be time to make the follow-up call.

'Just remember,' Rafael said, 'any hint of weakness and Buitre will sense it. *You* make the demands. *You* set the time limits – he is to call us back at midday tomorrow, then you give him three days to surrender. Don't let him speak to Ernesto. Don't allow him to distract you. If you let Buitre string this out, we completely lose our position.'

I nodded. All this sounded completely logical.

'Your most important leverage is the threat to Ernesto. In fact, the threat is all we have. I've heard you're fond of Ernesto, but for Buitre to hand himself in, I'm sorry, Pedro . . . you need to threaten to kill Ernesto. And you need to mean it.'

No way, I thought. *I will never kill Ernesto.* I'd rather let Buitre get away.

Rafael picked up on my hesitation. 'If you don't have the stomach for it, I can handle the calls.'

His suggestion had merit. I was no kidnapper whereas he'd seen firsthand how it was done. However, I couldn't predict how he might react talking to the man who'd killed his pregnant girlfriend. He might become emotional and derail everything. Besides, I wanted Buitre to know it would be my hands meting out his justice.

'I'll do it. You can listen and signal if I go wrong.'

'Fine. But Buitre needs to believe you, one hundred per cent. And to maximise the pressure, we need Buitre's mother to believe it too.'

It was now up to me to phone Ernesto's mother. After only one ring she answered.

'Ernesto?'

My stomach tensed immediately at the sound of her plaintive voice. 'No. The Autodefensas. Did you pass on our message?'

'I did,' she said shakily. 'Kiko tried to phone me, but I could hardly hear a word he said. Please don't hurt Ernesto!'

'Write this down.' I read out my number. 'Tell Kiko he's to call Pedro at precisely noon tomorrow. If you value Ernesto's life, *señora*, make sure your older son complies. The choice is his. Right now, I believe Ernesto is still alive . . .'

That afternoon I was sitting in the shade of the jacaranda tree with Palillo. We were relaxing with a cup of *tinto*, surveying the broad sweep of dry fields surrounding our base. Rafael had gone to Garbanzos to buy our weekly supplies. Ñoño was helping Iván practise on the monkey bars, and Piolín had driven down to Llorona to pick up Camila on one of the Yamahas.

A call came in from a blocked number. Buitre wasn't due to phone until tomorrow, and I answered it without thinking.

'I believe you know who this is,' came a cool, calm voice: Buitre's.

I leapt off my chair, adrenalin rushing through my veins. I intended to follow Rafael's advice – remain composed, use short sentences, control the conversation and not let Buitre get under my skin. It all sounded so simple. In theory.

Palillo mouthed, 'Is it him?' I nodded.

I focused my concentration and tried to take slow, deep breaths. 'Ah, yes. How could I forget that voice? Kiko Fuentes, murderer of elderly motorists and kidnapper of schoolgirls. The man who held me down and forced me to watch my father be executed. I bet it feels different now that the pistol's pointed at someone from your own family.'

'Killing my brother won't bring your father back.'

'But it will make you suffer. And the only way you can prevent that is by surrendering to us.'

'What makes you think I'd do something so stupid?'

'Because you're phoning me.'

He chuckled. 'I'm a communist, not Jesus Christ. I haven't seen Ernesto in years.'

'And yet you care enough to pay his tuition and buy him and your mother a house. You care enough to steal from Caraquemada and murder one of your best friends to cover it up.' I paused to let that sink in. 'Rafael told me everything.'

'*¡Hijo de puta!* Tell him he's dead! I should have shot him the same day I killed his crazy bitch. I saved his fucking life.'

'By executing his pregnant girlfriend. He sends his regards. But that doesn't change your only option: hand yourself in or Ernesto dies.'

'To you, never. To the army? That, I might consider. At least your friend Buitrago understands the principle of surrender. Accepting defeat doesn't result in cold-blooded murder.'

'Buitrago isn't an option. It's me you're dealing with. You have three days to surrender at our highway checkpoint in Puerto Galán.'

Buitre laughed again. 'Listen, Pedro, there's no way I'm handing you my head on a plate. But there's a head I know you want more than mine. And he has a girlfriend. A civilian girlfriend. You arrange for me to speak to Ernesto, and I'll send you a photo of her . . . with Caraquemada.'

I knew I'd already lost my cool and talked for way too long. My heart had been beating fast, but now, at the mention of Caraquemada, it nearly burst out of my chest. This was exactly what Rafael had warned me of: Buitre would try to play me and negotiate. But I'd never expected this, that he might offer something on Caraquemada instead. And my pause told Buitre he'd thrown me.

'That's right,' he continued. 'Caraquemada. Your war is with him, not me. That day he executed your father I had no idea what he was going to do. You've got it all wrong, Pedro. I'm innocent here, as is Ernesto. So it's very simple. You let me speak to him and I send you the photo.'

Again I paused. In reality, he was offering next to nothing. Nevertheless, since it was Caraquemada, next to nothing was tempting.

'We're holding Ernesto a long way from here. And besides, what would a photo prove?'

'That I'm not lying. That she can be tracked and lead you to Caraquemada.'

'The photo first then. If I'm satisfied, I'll arrange for you to talk to him.'

'How do I know you'll keep your word?'

'It's the word of one kidnapper to another.'

Buitre swore under his breath but realised he was in no position to bargain.

'Log into this email.' He spelled out a Hotmail username and password. 'I'll call back in five minutes.' He hung up.

Palillo, meanwhile, had been listening to my side of the phone call intently. 'What did he say?' he demanded.

'He's going to email me a photo of Caraquemada's girlfriend.'

'Are you sure that's a good idea? Didn't Rafael tell you not to bargain with him?'

Palillo was right, but I brushed off his concerns and strode towards the command centre, angry at myself for even being tempted. Of course, I knew a photo alone would never lead me to Caraquemada, but if this girl could be located, her phone tapped and we could somehow track her . . .

I dismissed Coca-Cola from radio duty. Trembling with anticipation, I sat down at my desk, opened my laptop and entered the login details. The Hotmail account's inbox showed only one email with no subject heading or text. I clicked on it and saw it contained an embedded jpeg, which took shape painfully slowly until the full image resolved on my screen.

The first thing I saw was the sculpted back of a young woman, completely naked apart from a lacy black G-string. Her face, turned in profile, was obscured by a mane of blonde hair. She was straddling a man who was leaning back on a chair with his shirt off, holding a half-full bottle of whisky, and her arms were draped around his neck. I recognised him immediately. Caraquemada.

My chest constricted painfully. I hadn't seen that hellishly scarred face since the day of Papá's death, and it brought everything back to me. The image in my head was flawless as a photo: Caraquemada pulling the trigger, Papá's knees buckling and his skull striking the hard, dry earth.

I right-clicked 'save' on the image and watched anxiously as the blue 'percentage complete' bar inched across the screen, but before it finished saving the photo disappeared and the email closed itself, leaving an empty inbox. Hotmail was shut down, and when I tried to log back in I couldn't.

My phone vibrated, its sharp ring piercing my thoughts.

'Satisfied?'

'You deleted it.'

'You saw what you needed to see.'

'Where did you get it?'

'I stole it from the laptop of a man called Baez. He's Caraquemada's head of security. I've kept my end of the bargain. Now let me talk to Ernesto. Before this discussion goes any further I need to know he's alive.'

I tried to think quickly – difficult when I had the feeling Buitre was right there, watching me. Letting Buitre speak to his brother was a small risk provided I didn't give away Ernesto's location. Besides, if Buitre *was* playing me, the situation wouldn't change; we still had Ernesto. In the desk drawer we kept a bundle of new, untraceable SIM cards, each in an envelope with the phone number on the outside. I took one out.

'Here's the number where you can reach him. But wait ten minutes; I have to let them know to expect your call.' Then I read out the phone number of the new SIM.

I radioed Palillo while fumbling to insert the SIM into a phone that we'd never used before. When he arrived in the office, I instructed him to take Buitre's call and pass it briefly to Ernesto.

'I don't want any part in this,' said Palillo.

But I persuaded him, and we raced upstairs to Ernesto's cell. When Buitre phoned back, Palillo said 'Wait!' then held out the phone on speaker. 'Tell your brother you're alive.'

'I'm here, Kiko,' said Ernesto. 'But don't—'

I snatched the phone from Palillo and hung up.

My own phone rang again two minutes later.

'Did you talk to him?' I asked innocently.

'Yes,' said Buitre, sounding resigned and much calmer. In fact, he sounded almost smug, which puzzled me.

'I told you. He's fine.'

'Very well. I'm not handing myself in, but I'll help you get Caraquemada.'

'And why would you do that? Why sell out your commander?'

'I think we both know the position you've put me in.'

I would never let Buitre off the hook – not in a million years – but every photo, every clue he gave me on Caraquemada might be useful. And when I finally did force him to surrender in return for Ernesto's life, I would extract every tiny bit of information he possessed. However, to do that I needed to know how much he knew, so I played along.

'How do I know your information about his girlfriend will help me track Caraquemada?'

'Because that photo wasn't taken on a Guerrilla base. She isn't a local. Caraquemada takes risks and goes off base to see her. I know her name and phone number. With that information your army friends can put her under surveillance and track her to their rendezvous points.' Buitre paused. 'If you want to know more, I'll trade the information, instead of my life, for Ernesto's freedom. You have twenty-four hours to think about it. I'll call back tomorrow for your answer.'

Then he hung up, leaving me completely convinced that I was now hot on the trail of not one, but both of Papá's remaining killers. Convinced, that is, until Rafael returned to base.

131

RAFAEL RETURNED LATE in the afternoon in the pick-up truck with Mona, Tarantula and Montoya, who'd just closed our highway checkpoint for the evening. They parked by the milking shed next to the Mercedes and began unloading the week's food supplies. I was sitting at the wooden table under the jacaranda tree with Camila, soaking up the last rays of sunshine as she excitedly discussed her university plans and how much I was going to love Bogotá when I joined her.

Once the sun had set, Camila left to help Mona in the kitchen, and I called Rafael over. I was eager to update him on Buitre's pre-emptive call and knew he'd be disappointed to have missed it.

Rafael was concerned that Buitre had defied our instructions by calling a day early. He thought I'd made a tactical error by allowing Buitre to change the rules.

'Why did you take the call? You should have waited.'

'It made no difference,' I assured him. 'He wants to give us Caraquemada instead of surrendering himself. He sent me a photo of him with his civilian girlfriend. Of course, I'd never accept, but this proves that once we have Buitre we can force him to divulge the girl's identity. She might lead us to Caraquemada.'

I thought Rafael would be happy with this. After all, Caraquemada had given the order to execute Beatriz. But he folded his arms, unconvinced.

'Why would Buitre send you a photo? You didn't bargain with him, did you?'

'Don't worry!' I told him. 'I stuck mainly to the script. He sent it to me for virtually nothing.'

'What do you mean *virtually* nothing? Please tell me you didn't let him speak to Ernesto!'

'Only for five seconds. I had Buitre call Palillo on a phone we've never used with a new SIM. There's no way he could have figured out Ernesto is here.'

'I wouldn't be so sure. The Guerrilla scan our radio frequencies. Buitre might know Palillo's voice . . . So if Palillo spoke even a few words during that phone call . . .' He stood, squinting as he surveyed the camp perimeter. 'We need to be very careful, Pedro.'

At that moment, Pantera came running from the milking shed. 'We have an emergency! Puerto Princesa. The caller said he sighted six *guerrilleros*. They've blown up the ferry. And one of them is shouting through a megaphone that if villagers turn out to vote, the Guerrilla will come back and do much worse.'

'*¡Mierda!*' I said angrily. The Guerrilla often tried to sow chaos in the lead-up to elections. If we didn't respond immediately, villagers would never trust our ability to protect them. I radioed Palillo with the news and asked him to call his most trusted contact in Puerto Princesa. He ran over with the man on speakerphone.

'It's true!' rasped an elderly male voice. 'The ferry's ablaze and sinking. They're dynamiting all the boats and torching the wharf. Please come quickly!'

'Caraquemada's cutting off river transport to Santo Paraíso,' I said to Palillo. 'I want your squad and four of Pirata's men. Load ammunition into the pick-up truck. We'll take the Toyota, the Mercedes and two bikes. Meet me back here in two minutes!'

'Wait!' said Rafael to me as Palillo raced off to rally his men. 'Something's not right here, *comando*. Buitre calls you this afternoon. Now there's an emergency in Puerto Princesa for the first time in seven months. What if it's not Caraquemada? What if it's Buitre making a move? Drawing you to Puerto Princesa so he can ambush you on the way, or trying to reduce the number of men here on the base in order to attack it?'

Rafael's words made me uneasy. I glanced towards the barn, where Palillo and his men were frantically loading the pick-up truck with RPGs and extra magazines.

'Why would Buitre attack, after proposing we negotiate?'

'Because he's figured out Ernesto is here.'

Four of Pirata's men roared over on the Yamahas. A minute later Palillo pulled up in the Toyota with his eight soldiers – including Giraldo, Mona and Coca-Cola – sitting anxiously in the back tray, clutching their rifles.

'Let's go!' Palillo said. 'While you *señoritas* stand here gossiping, Caraquemada might be killing people.'

I, too, was itching to confront Caraquemada's troop; however, before making my final decision, I radioed the four perimeter posts myself and had Coca-Cola radio Buitrago's base.

The perimeter guards reported no suspicious movements. But when Buitrago's base responded that they were aware of the emergency – in fact, twenty *guerrilleros* had been sighted and Buitrago was sending two platoons – I heeded Rafael's advice.

'Palillo, stand your men down. Keep the ammunition in the pick-up and your squad on standby. If the army needs us, we go.'

On Palillo's signal, his soldiers leaped from the Toyota and gathered by the henhouse to await orders. It was now fifteen minutes after sunset. The temperature was dropping and the light fading. Pantera returned to the command centre. I walked with Rafael and Palillo to the open space in front of the farmhouse. It afforded an almost uninterrupted view of the camp's southern, eastern and western perimeters. I turned in a slow arc. Rafael now had me thinking.

Only a minute later, Ñoño and Iván came running towards me, carrying one of the German shepherds on a blanket. Her tongue was lolling out of her mouth, and her lips were encrusted with dried white saliva.

'It's Coco!' Ñoño said as they laid the dog at my feet. Normally, we kept her chained to a tree near the VHF repeater cabinet at the far west of the camp. 'She was lying semi-conscious at her post.'

Hearing the commotion, Mona and Camila rushed out of the farmhouse.

'Oh, the poor thing!' exclaimed Camila. 'Looks like dehydration.'

Piolín stroked the dog's head. Iván looked on anxiously while Ñoño rang the vet.

Rafael folded his arms. 'Could be poisoning.'

He now had my full attention. If he was right, that meant Buitre was close by.

'Ñoño, take Camila, Iván and the dog to the cottage!' I ordered. 'Piolín and Mona, go to the command centre.' I radioed Johnnie Walker. 'I want your squad manning the trenches – three men per trench.' Then I radioed the perimeter guards a second time: 'Be alert! Check the dogs. Possible enemy attack.'

'All clear,' they each reported back. Apparently, the four other dogs tethered between each post were fine.

Palillo's phone rang. 'What? Mamá . . . now's not a good time. Why are you whispering?' He frowned in annoyance, but then suddenly clutched his forehead and responded in a fierce whisper. '*¡Jesucristo!* Keep the kids hidden in the bushes! Pedro's right here. I'll put him on speakerphone.'

Palillo held out his phone, its screen glowing. Dusk was now falling rapidly; within minutes it would be dark. His mother spoke so softly that Palillo, Rafael and I had to lean in to hear.

'Help us!' she whispered. 'Men with guns surrounded our house and ordered us outside. We obeyed, but now I can see one of them stomping on the roof, splashing gasoline everywhere – it's trickling down the walls. They're yelling obscenities, saying Palillo's a kidnapper and we have to pay the price. What's going on, Pedro? I don't understand. Please come! They're going to burn our house to the ground.'

'It's a bluff,' said Rafael with absolute certainty. 'Buitre is *here*. He's watching us *right now*. He's seen that we didn't fall for the ferry trick. This is his next move to draw your soldiers off the base.'

'What the fuck do you mean a *bluff*!' yelled Palillo, turning viciously on Rafael. 'My mother's not lying. The Guerrilla are ten fucking metres from my brothers and sisters. Pedro, we need to go *right now*.'

I felt panic rising within me. There was no longer any doubt – Buitre was behind this. Whether he was taking revenge against Palillo for holding Ernesto or planning an ambush on me or an attack on the base, I couldn't be sure. I couldn't leave the base unprotected, but there was no way I could leave Palillo's mother in danger either. This was my fault. I'd fucked up by letting Buitre speak to Ernesto.

'*Comando*,' said Rafael calmly. 'He's here for you and Ernesto. I know him. He's got every angle covered. Divide your troops and we all die.'

Torn, I looked from Rafael, whose understanding of Buitre I trusted, and who I knew, logically, was probably right, to Palillo, my most loyal friend, who'd been there on the day of Papá's death and who'd offered to transport Papá to the cemetery and take the blame himself. The friend who'd done everything since to protect me and the people I loved most in the world. It was a tough call to make. If Buitre had set an ambush, then we might never reach Palillo's mother, and many more lives might be lost.

'Tarantula, drive the Toyota back to the barn and unload the ammunition. You four,' I said to Pirata's men, 'man the defensive firing positions surrounding the command centre. Everyone else inside,' I said, walking briskly towards the milking shed. 'I'm sorry, Palillo. I need to assess the situation.'

'Fuck your assessments!' said Palillo, grabbing my elbow and ripping me to a halt. 'This is my family we're talking about.'

'It's not that simple.'

'To me it is. I'm going. At least give me my squad and the Toyota. But if not, fuck you, Pedro. I'll do this *on my own*. Just remember this: if me or my family dies, you're the one who let Buitre hear my voice.'

He was right. This situation wasn't about military logic. This was my best friend and his family. I changed my mind.

'You, me and four men,' I said to Palillo, tossing him the keys to the Mercedes. 'We take the armoured vehicle in case it's an ambush.'

'Mamá.' Palillo spoke into the phone. 'Stay out of sight. We're on our way.'

'Come quickly, *hijo*,' his mother replied, 'they're—'

But the call cut out. A few seconds later we heard an explosion from the direction of Llorona. The ground rumbled. Some of my men raced out of the milking shed, and Camila, Ñoño and Iván came running from the caretaker's cottage.

'What was that?' Camila cried, huddling against me.

Palillo held his phone up. 'No signal!'

'The Guerrilla must have blown the cell phone tower in Llorona!' Ñoño said. The tower was located on the crest of the hill, about a kilometre and a half down the road.

'*¡Mierda!* I keep telling you!' said Rafael. 'Buitre's about to attack.'

Without explanation, he sprinted to the generator by the barn, heaved a twenty-litre barrel of diesel into a wheelbarrow, tipped the barrel on its side and ripped off the cap. He then wheeled the barrow frantically in a circle around the farmhouse, dousing the dried grass with fuel.

'Radio the army again!' I shouted to Coca-Cola in the command centre. No sooner had I said the words than a bullet whizzed past my ear. I hurled myself against Camila, pulling her to the ground.

The camp lights went out and then, from the southern and western perimeters, more bullets rained in on us.

'Go! Go! Go!'

Taking advantage of the darkness, I dragged Camila to the milking shed. Palillo, Ñoño and Iván crawled along beside us.

Inside the command centre, by the dim light of two torches held by Pantera and Piolín, I counted about twenty men, all lying flat on the concrete floor.

I had to think quickly. If I'd listened to Rafael, I would already have more men in each trench.

'Pirata, situation report.'

'Twenty-six men accounted for here,' said Pirata, grim-faced, 'including four manning the defensive positions. Three men in each trench. No word from the southern and western guard posts. They've cut the power. Our hand-held radios are working. But the VHF repeater is dead. Landline too.'

Buitre had cut us off completely. Without radio or phone, there was no way to get word of this attack to Beta or the army. We were on our own.

Since the firing had come from the south and the west, and those guard posts weren't responding, I reasoned that Buitre's forces were already coming in from those perimeters.

'Coca-Cola, hand out the extra radios. Giraldo, I want you and thirteen men defending this shed. Indio, send reinforcements to the southern and western trenches. Stay low!' I yelled. 'But get to your positions quickly. *Go!*'

As my men fanned out through the door, a rocket struck the diesel generator by the barn. Camila clutched my hand in terror. Then two more explosions rocked the area near the Mercedes and the Toyota pick-up truck. Heavy sustained gunfire rained in on us from the western perimeter, along with lighter fire from the south.

'Palillo, Ñoño and Piolín, come with me upstairs! Bring the RPGs. We need to stop their advance.'

I turned to Iván. 'You remember that secret place I showed you?' In my torchlight, I saw him nod. 'When we get to the farmhouse take Camila down to the cellar. You know where to go if the *guerrilleros* get inside the house.'

With Palillo, Ñoño, Piolín, Camila and Iván, I dropped into the connecting trench to the farmhouse. We raced the fifty metres, ducking our heads beneath the parapet of sandbags as bullets whizzed above. Once inside, Iván and Camila headed for the cellar while the rest of us sprinted upstairs to the bedroom at the south-west corner, which had almost 270-degree coverage through its four large windows.

Rafael was already there, crouching by an open window. He had a rag in his hands, which he was wrapping around a small rock. It stank of gasoline. I wanted to apologise – he'd been right all along – but his wink made this unnecessary. 'Come take a look,' he said. 'Their forces are concentrated in the west, with backup from the south.'

I dropped to my knees and crawled over. I saw muzzle flashes as Giraldo's squad returned fire from the barricades surrounding the command centre. The soldiers in our southern and western trenches added their firepower.

Keeping my head low, I fired my RPG towards the enemy's most concentrated firing positions. As soon as the rocket left my rifle, gunfire shattered the glass above me and strafed the interior wall behind us. I ducked and moved to the adjacent window. Ñoño handed me a second RGP, and

I fired again while he reloaded the first. Meanwhile, Palillo, supported by Piolín, was firing rockets from the western windows.

Suddenly, the enemy guns went silent.

After a lengthy pause, Buitre's voice came over a megaphone from the south-western perimeter.

'Pedro Gutiérrez, we have you completely surrounded. You have thirty-eight men left. I have one hundred.'

'He's lying,' said Rafael. 'I counted their rifle fire. I'd say he has no more than thirty.'

'My brother is innocent,' boomed Buitre's voice again. 'A sixteen-year-old boy you kidnapped from his workplace. How many lives should be lost because of Pedro's cruelty? Tarantula, will you give your life for a vendetta that doesn't involve you? Pantera and Mona. Piolín and Ñoño. Try to make Pedro see sense. If not, as Palillo can confirm . . . we'll find your families . . .'

'It's not true,' Rafael said. 'Everyone in the river villages knows your aliases. This is a common Guerrilla tactic. Don't let it get to you.'

'Release Ernesto now and no more lives will be lost. Just yell "yes" from your upstairs window.'

Of course, I didn't dare show my face. Ten seconds later, we heard the first of three mortars launch. The first two landed on open ground, but the third crashed through the roof of the milking shed with a thunderous explosion.

'Ernesto!' Buitre shouted. 'If you can hear me, yell out now. Tell me you're alive.'

From the northern bedroom, I heard Ernesto yelling, 'Kiko! I'm here! I'm here!'

'*Mierda*,' I muttered. He was locked safely in his cell, but I should have gagged him.

'Pedro, just let Ernesto walk out the front door and towards this light.'

A spotlight came on near the western guard post.

'*Comando*,' said Rafael. 'This doesn't make sense; he knows you won't send Ernesto out. Radio the eastern trench.'

I tried. There was no reply.

'It's a trick,' said Rafael decisively. 'They're sneaking in from the opposite side. Go and look for yourselves!'

Clutching the gasoline-soaked rag, he sprinted from the room.

Palillo and I raced to the window of the eastern bedroom and scanned the ground below – Palillo with night optics and me with my scope.

'There!' said Palillo. 'There. And there.'

Sure enough fifteen silhouettes were belly-crawling across the grass, their rifles flat in one hand. They were approaching from widely different angles, moving stealthily but quickly towards the house.

Before I could even line up a shot, I spotted Rafael crawling out directly into the path of the approaching *guerrilleros*. Ten metres from the farmhouse he sparked a lighter against the gasoline-soaked rag and rolled sideways, lobbing the flaming projectile onto the grass where he'd earlier laid the circle of gasoline. The grass lit up and flames licked along the line of fuel, spreading left and right like two startled snakes and creating a metre-high blazing wall of fire that encircled the farmhouse and radiated outwards. Agonised yelps went up from the attackers. Four of them had caught fire and they rolled from side to side, trying to extinguish the flames. I shot at one. I hit him. Then I hit another, and then the remaining two. Even through the clouds of smoke, the fire produced enough light to illuminate my fleeing targets. Rafael began firing from where he'd taken cover behind a wall of tyres as the enemy scurried away. I raced back to the south-western bedroom.

Below me I could see Johnnie Walker and Pirata and their men holding the western and southern trenches. Giraldo, Indio, Pantera and their soldiers were hanging on at the far side of the milking shed but were completely cut off because the section of roof nearest the farmhouse had collapsed thanks to Buitre's mortar bomb. The connecting trench had also been hit – there was a giant crater in the middle of it, the sandbag parapet had fallen and it could no longer be used for cover.

'We have to counter-attack,' I said, 'but Buitre hears every word I say on this radio. I need human messengers. Ñoño and Piolín, get word to Johnnie Walker and Pirata: when I launch the RPGs, they're to fire all at once and storm out of their trenches. Palillo, I need you to get the same message to the men cut off in the milking shed. Without the connecting trench, you'll be exposed.'

'Assuming I reach the milking shed,' said Palillo, 'counter-attack *how*?'

'Do you think the Mercedes is driveable?'

Palillo shook his head. 'Engine's blown.'

'Then release the handbrake, put it in neutral and have your men push it towards the enemy. There's a slight slope so it should roll. Use the vehicle as cover and hit them with everything you've got. This is all or nothing.'

I held my breath as I watched the barely visible shadows of Piolín and Ñoño belly-crawl towards the southern and western trenches. They made it. Then it was Palillo's turn. His role was the most hazardous, and I ordered the southern trench to fire at Buitre's position as a distraction. Palillo crawled out, but halfway across a hail of bullets rained in and he had to dive and roll to reach the milking shed, and then squeeze under the collapsed roof. Two minutes later, Palillo and six others crawled out near where the Mercedes was parked. Its bulletproof glass and heavy armouring would provide them with some protection. When they were ready, Palillo waved to me and I fired my first RPG at Buitre's position. That was the signal.

Palillo, Giraldo and their men began pushing the Mercedes downhill towards the enemy, using it as cover as they fired their rifles and hurled grenades. I attached another RPG and scored a direct hit on Buitre's spotlight. The squads in the southern and western trenches had waited for the explosions before scrambling over the rubble and collapsed sandbags in front of their trenches and sprinting towards Buitre's men, Galils blazing. I saw the muzzle-flashes from the enemy as they fled towards the trees, their shots becoming more sporadic.

Over the PA system, I heard an announcement in a deep voice I didn't recognise but which sounded strangely familiar: 'Pedro, this is Lieutenant Alvarez. We received your emergency call. Hold your positions. We're approaching fast.' Then a pause before a different-sounding, and yet very similar, voice responded: 'Copy that, *mi teniente*.'

Then I recognised the voice and burst out laughing. Coca-Cola! He was trying to trick the fleeing Guerrilla into believing we'd reconnected our VHF antenna and that the army were on their way.

I was out of RPGs but by then I was hopeful; my men had at least reached the perimeter.

There was no more return fire from the retreating enemy.

'They've gone,' Pantera announced over his hand-held radio.

We'd repelled them completely.

I went downstairs and outside to give follow-up orders for my men. And it was not until Iván ran out and hugged my waist joyously that I remembered: Camila.

132

CAMILA WASN'T IN the cellar. Nor was she in the downstairs bedrooms, but I knew she would not have crossed the dark open ground to return to our cottage. I bounded back up the stairs and stopped suddenly, seeing her at Ernesto's door, her hands clutching the bars. I didn't know how long they'd been speaking, but when Camila turned towards me, her face said it all. Her eyes were filled with unfathomable disappointment. Of course, she'd already heard Buitre's demands on the megaphone, but now she knew everything.

'I can explain,' I began, beckoning her away from Ernesto's door to indicate we should talk privately.

'How could you possibly—'

'Not here!'

Camila brushed past me, swept down the hall and entered an unoccupied bedroom. I barely had time to follow her in and close the door before she rounded on me.

'Tell me this isn't true! That these past three weeks, while I've been making love to you in our cottage, you haven't been holding a civilian you captured up here.'

I knew I needed to stay calm but I immediately felt my anger rising, burning hot under Camila's judgmental gaze.

'He's the brother of the man who caused Papá's death. And I didn't capture him – Beta did,' I added defensively. 'I've treated him well. You can ask him.'

Camila folded her arms. 'Ernesto is not responsible for what his brother did. And Beta brought him here for *you*. For you to *chop him up and feed him to the fish* or *let him go* as you pleased – that's what Ernesto told me. So don't try to twist the facts. This is you.'

'It's the only way to get Buitre,' I insisted. 'I have to make him pay for what he did to Papá and so many others. Have you forgotten how he kidnapped Cecilia, that girl from your *colegio*? When we have Buitre, I promise I'll release Ernesto.'

I tried to put my arm around her shoulder but she shrugged me off. 'That's not good enough. Do you have any idea what he's going through? And how do you think his mother and fiancée feel right now? Or don't you care? After all, you've never let your mother's or my feelings stop you from doing whatever you wanted.'

'That's not fair,' I protested. There was some truth in what she was saying – I hadn't put our relationship first – but maybe if she'd actually seen Papá lying there, the trail of ants and the vultures trying to get at him, her attitude might have been different. 'These men aren't human, Camila. They need to be punished. No one else is going to do it. I'm sorry it's affecting you, but for Papá's sake, this is something I have to do.'

Even as I spoke Camila was shaking her head.

'Listen to yourself! It's always about *you*. What they did to your father was abominable, but you haven't learned from it. Instead, you're multiplying your own suffering ten times over in others. At the beginning, when the Guerrilla was destroying our town, I could at least see some point to what you were doing. I told myself that once Llorona was peaceful, you'd put the past behind you. But you haven't. And I can see now that you won't.'

'I just need more time. And you agreed you'd wait. I'll join you as soon as Buitre and Caraquemada are dead.'

Camila was silent for a minute. When she spoke again her voice was soft but emphatic. 'I *was* willing to wait. And I've been patient. I've tolerated and compromised on things I never imagined I would. But it's no longer a question of waiting; it's a question of the person you've become while I've waited. Keeping Ernesto prisoner is wrong, Pedro. Purely and simply *wrong*. I can't turn a blind eye to things that I know in my heart are wicked. So I'm asking you for the very last time: give up this life, release Ernesto and come with me to Bogotá. It's your decision.'

'You're the one making this decision. You're the one who's changing things. You can't do this. You can't ask me to choose between you and Papá.'

Camila stared at me, tears welling in her eyes. I stared back at her, hoping to break her will. The fact that she was still standing there meant maybe, like me, she felt we were divided, like two cars on a dual carriageway, travelling in opposite directions, wanting and yet unable to turn around.

'Your Papá is dead, Pedro. I'm alive. I want a boyfriend who has passions and dreams – and hobbies other than killing people! And if you can't do as I ask,' Camila continued, a tear trickling down her cheek, 'then this is goodbye. It's over. But when I'm gone, I hope you'll look closely at your own reflection. And I pray you'll see how much you've changed. Because what you're becoming is a monster, no better than the men you hate.'

Camila turned and opened the door. Palillo was standing there; he'd overheard our yelling.

'And *you*!' she said to him. 'You know I'm right. But you're too much of a coward to say it, even to your best friend.'

Palillo looked at me, open-mouthed, as she pushed past. I heard Camila's footsteps rapidly descending the stairs. She'd never have said those words if she'd known about Palillo's family. I expected Palillo to be angry with me too – it was my fault they'd attacked his mother's house. He didn't know whether they'd burned it down or whether his mother and siblings were even alive. But he must have been in shock, because all he said was, 'I came to tell you that I'll wait until first light. And then I'm taking one of the Yamahas and going to look for my family.'

I nodded, wracked with guilt at how I'd brought more suffering into his family's already difficult life. 'I hope they're all fine, *hermano*. I'm sorry I involved you.'

Palillo lingered in the doorway. 'You okay?'

'She's demanding I release Ernesto.'

'So what are you going to do? It was one thing to do this when Camila didn't know, but is it worth losing her over? If you do what she asks, maybe it's not too late . . .'

'So I should just leave the Autodefensas, go to Bogotá and forget Buitre and Caraquemada ever existed? No way.'

'You're no monster, *hermano*,' Palillo said before leaving. 'But maybe Camila has a point. This obsession you have . . . it's getting you nowhere, and we're all paying the price.'

After Palillo left, I fell back against the wall and slid to the floor, my head buried in my hands. I knew Camila had meant every word – we were definitely over. I never thought I'd lose her. I didn't want to lose her. But I had.

How could she end a four-year, loving relationship with an ultimatum that she knew was impossible for me to fulfil? She and her family had reaped all the benefits I'd battled to win for Llorona. We'd made the town peaceful enough for her to continue her studies in safety, for her parents to run their store and for her brothers to return. It was now easy for her to turn things around on me and take the moral high ground.

As for her final stabbing insult, comparing me to the Guerrilla – how pathetic and ridiculous! I couldn't stand the thought of being with someone who had such a low – and unjustified – opinion of me, nor someone who could interpret the same facts so differently.

Even after all our years together, Camila was clearly incapable of understanding the most fundamental force that drove me: my love for Papá. That I should forget what they had done to my family in order to live in Bogotá – something that *she* wanted, not me – showed how truly selfish she was. What I was fighting for was bigger than her, bigger than me, bigger than us. And if she couldn't see that, then maybe I was better off without her.

133

AT FIRST LIGHT I emerged from the farmhouse and stood, hands on hips, surveying the carnage. Six hours had passed but the sulphurous odour of gunpowder still lingered in the air, together with the smell of singed grass, burnt rubber and what I assumed was charred human flesh.

The thick walls of the farmhouse were pocked with bullet holes. Broken glass littered the ground; every window was shattered. The milking shed roof had partially collapsed and its four support columns were tilted at precarious angles. The generator was twisted, blackened metal. Around our defensive trenches, tyres had fallen, sand spilled from the sacks and thousands of shell casings littered the ground.

I sent Indio's squad to scout the perimeter.

'They're definitely gone,' he said on returning. 'I've sent Coca-Cola to fix the VHF antenna.'

I nodded. Once that was done we could radio Colonel Buitrago to come up.

Another team was collecting the corpses, lifting them by the ankles and wrists and lining them up in front of the farmhouse. We'd lost six men in total – Gafas and El Mago at the guard posts; Condor when the mortar bomb hit the milking shed; and Montoya, Zeus and Batman in the northern trench, their throats slit by Buitre's covert rescue squad.

The media would probably report Buitre's attack as 'a minor skirmish with few casualties', if they reported it at all. But these were men I knew, men whose lives I'd been responsible for. All of them were dead because of my decision to hold Ernesto.

The five German shepherds were also dead, including Coco, who'd passed away during the night.

'Call Padre Rojas when the phone lines are back,' I told Pantera. 'These men deserve a proper burial. And bury the dogs beyond the northern perimeter.'

'What about the nine dead *guerrilleros*?' he asked.

'Leave them for Buitrago.'

Camila, accompanied by Piolín, emerged from our cottage, which, being furthest from the fighting, had escaped major damage. Her eyes were red and puffy, and she refused to look at me. There was nothing more to say.

My own anger had also dissipated, replaced by resignation. I'd accepted that Camila might even be right about Ernesto, yet I couldn't change my position or my nature and therefore we were definitely over.

Spotting the line of dead bodies, Camila averted her eyes. 'I've asked Piolín to take me home.'

'It's too dangerous,' I said. 'Buitre may still be out there. He may have the road covered.'

She finally faced me. 'How long do I have to wait?'

'Until we fix the antenna, radio the army and they've secured the area. Maybe another hour.'

Palillo approached me, wheeling one of the bikes. 'I'm going for my mother.'

'If it's safe enough for Palillo, why can't I go?' demanded Camila.

'I told you. It's *not* safe. Palillo's going because he has to.'

Suddenly, we heard a commotion and the sound of children's voices at the gate. Palillo dumped the bike and sprinted down the drive. 'Mamá!' he called out in disbelief.

Palillo's mother had arrived, bedraggled, carrying her youngest child in her arms. Her four other children were trailing behind, shell-shocked and hugging close to her skirts. Their legs were dusty and they looked ready to drop from weariness.

Palillo hugged them all, apologising profusely for not coming to their rescue. 'Mamá, you walked all this way?'

She nodded. 'We hid with the neighbours and watched while those men burned our house down. None of us could sleep. But at dawn we got scared they'd come back. So we came here.'

While Piolín took charge of the kids, herding them to my cottage to wash, feed and send them to bed, Palillo put his arm around his mother. 'I'm just glad you're alive.'

She looked around in amazement at the devastation. 'And I'm glad you are.'

Camila glared at me. 'I guess that means the road is safe. *Now* can I go?'

My instinct was still to wait for the army, but after the constant flurry of urgent decisions made under extreme pressure I felt depleted.

Over the previous twenty-four hours I felt like I'd been caught up in a spiralling series of mistakes and consequences that I'd never intended or imagined were possible but had somehow just happened. So I relaxed and let go. I was simply glad that Camila was alive, that Palillo's family was alive, that Buitre had been repelled, and that together, as a team, we'd all fought so valiantly.

Above all my selfish considerations, what I wanted most right then was what Camila wanted for herself – for her to be with her family, where she'd feel safe.

So when Pantera called out that the VHF antenna was fixed and the army was on its way, there seemed little to be gained by waiting.

But my grey-dawn decision, made in the bubbling wake of waves of adrenalin, with my judgment skewed by tiredness, grief and guilt, turned out to be one of the worst of my entire life, and one that meant everything would be far from over.

'Let's take her home.'

134

SIX OF US would travel on three bikes – Camila, me and four others. When I called for volunteers Ñoño immediately raised his hand.

'You're behind me on the lead bike,' I said. Next was Tarantula. 'You take Camila on the middle bike.'

When Hector volunteered to ride rear-guard with R6, our convoy was set.

As we motored downhill along the bumpy dirt road, it was a clear day, with a pink dawn sky and a scattering of clouds. As always, I had my pistol. But since it's impossible to fire a rifle while driving a bike, only Ñoño and Hector carried their Galils. Nevertheless, with Palillo's family having walked this route safely and Buitrago on his way and likely to cross our path any minute, my lingering fears about Buitre had vanished.

We passed my *finca* and then Old Man Domino's white fence. Just as we rounded a bend and entered the thicket before the road dipped more steeply to the town centre, I spotted a severed tree trunk blocking the road. My heart raced.

'Ambush! Turn around!' Even as I braked heavily, several *guerrilleros* raised their heads from behind the tree and took aim with their rifles. Yanking the handlebar, I spun the bike into a desperate 180-degree turn. The other bikes skidded and spun too, sending up showers of tiny pebbles.

Ñoño's fingers dug tightly under my ribcage as I sped back uphill. But it was too late. Another tree was already falling ahead of us, thumping onto the road. More *guerrilleros* crawled out to take up positions behind it. I skidded us to a halt again and glanced sideways at Camila. She was clutching Tarantula's waist and looking at me in terror. We spun our bikes again.

From the trees to our left, I heard Buitre's voice thunder through his megaphone, 'Throw down your weapons!'

Ñoño let go of my waist and began firing, as did Hector from the back of R6's bike. When the enemy returned fire, I screamed, 'To the right! Go!'

We were at the lower reaches of Old Man Domino's property, and provided we made it off the road, we'd be protected by the trees and have a chance of making it to the open fields behind.

Tarantula and Camila went first, exiting under heavy fire. They headed diagonally into scrubland. The instant they'd made it I followed, with Ñoño gripping my shoulder with one hand while firing with the other. As we zigzagged through the trees, low-hanging branches whipped against my legs and face. The engine screamed and my tyres spun wildly in the dirt. To my right, R6 and Hector were keeping pace – until I heard a shout and glanced sideways in time to see R6 fall off, hit, and Hector's body being buffeted by bullets.

Camila and Tarantula were almost clear of the thicket when, fifty metres ahead of us, two *guerrilleros* emerged from the trees and began firing. Tarantula was struck. His head jerked sideways and their bike veered off course, tilted, then fell. Camila screamed as the Yamaha landed on her leg.

I changed course, accelerating towards her, when I heard a pop from my front tyre and lost control of the steering. We struck a ditch at speed and Ñoño yelped as he was thrown into the air. I held on, squeezing the brake, but my momentum caused me to slide forward until my front wheel hit a tree root and I was catapulted over the handlebars.

I sat up, dazed. Fifteen metres behind me, Ñoño lay on the ground, unconscious. His rifle was nowhere to be seen. Fifteen metres ahead of me, Camila was trapped beneath the Yamaha, screaming for help. Both were completely exposed to the enemy. I had to make a quick choice with the Guerrilla closing in: I could likely save one, but not both.

I raced to Camila and pulled the bike off her, firing my pistol at the two *guerrilleros* as I dragged her to safety behind a tree. I pushed her into the woodlands behind me. 'Run to the river,' I yelled. 'Don't stop! And don't turn around.'

I sprinted towards Ñoño, intending to drag him to safety and hold off the Guerrilla while praying for the army to arrive. But I'd barely made it five paces when a hail of gunfire forced me to dive behind another tree. Peering around it, I saw Buitre's men swarm around Ñoño. He must have regained consciousness because I heard a panicked shout of 'Pedro!' as they lifted him and spirited him away.

Within seconds, figures were scurrying through the thick forest to my left and right. I fired at them but couldn't get a clear shot. They were rapidly closing off my avenues of retreat.

This is it, I thought to myself as they edged closer. I fired sporadically, preferring to die fighting than be captured, but with only two magazines

I had to conserve ammunition. Finally, with absolute dread, I realised the reason they weren't shooting back: Buitre wanted me alive.

He shouted through his megaphone, 'I tried to do this the friendly way, Pedro. You asked me to surrender. Now it's your turn.'

Meanwhile, his men moved nearer and nearer. One would scurry closer in front of me; I'd fire. Then another moved behind me; I'd turn and fire again. They were well trained and gradually formed a circle around me, which grew tighter and tighter.

My panic continued to mount. If captured, ordinary commanders could expect a protracted, agonising death. But I wasn't an ordinary commander – I'd killed two of their leaders, held Buitre's brother hostage and sworn death to Caraquemada.

My second magazine was almost empty. I'd been counting the shots, just as Culebra taught me. Evidently, so had Buitre.

'Don't move, Pedro!' he yelled. His voice was closer and he was no longer using the megaphone. I caught sight of him behind a tree. 'You have one round left. Hands behind your head!'

I raised the pistol to my temple, my finger resting on the trigger. I was breathing in short gasps, my heart racing. Sweat poured down my neck. I was terrified by what I now had to do. I didn't want to die, but the alternative was unthinkable.

Fifteen of Buitre's men closed the circle, their rifles trained on me.

'You threaten to shoot my innocent brother,' Buitre called out. 'Yet you're too scared to pull the trigger yourself?'

'I'm not the one hiding behind a tree,' I yelled back. 'Yes, I have one bullet left. Come out and let's see who I use it on.'

In the distance, I heard the faint howl of engines. Buitrago's trucks! I couldn't be sure but I took a gamble.

I aimed the pistol at my left boot, closed my eyes and pulled the trigger. Pain exploded in my foot, like a blow from a hammer, and lightning shot up my spine. My vision blurred as I fell backwards, my pistol falling from my hand.

'Stupid move,' he said, kicking it aside and walking smugly towards me.

My aim now was simply to stall for time. 'I can't walk,' I taunted him from the ground. 'So you can't march me anywhere. Go ahead and finish me.'

'You idiot.' Buitre laughed. 'We can *carry* you. I know many people who will be extremely interested to meet you back at camp.'

'You won't get far carrying me,' I said. 'Not with only three minutes' head-start on the army.'

Buitre now heard the trucks too. '*¡Chulos! ¡Hijos de putas!*' he said bitterly. 'Saved by the *chulos* from the slow death you deserve.'

Buitre took a running kick at my ribs, and his men piled in behind, landing brutal kicks and punches.

'Go ahead and kill me!' I spat. 'It will be much less painful than what Beta will do to your brother in response.'

This stopped Buitre in his tracks, and his men stopped too. I had his attention.

'The *limpieza* took three days. I'm sure with the right razorblades Beta could make Ernesto's pain last much longer . . .' Buitre said nothing, so I drove home my advantage. 'He might even let you listen via radio before he sends Ernesto's fingers to your mother, assuming Beta's men don't pick her up too . . . in Barrancabermeja.'

'You son of a bitch!' Buitre kicked me again. I heard my ribs crack.

'Think about it!' I wheezed, wincing in pain. 'You'll never get Ernesto back unless you let me live.'

'Not true,' said Buitre, drawing a serrated hunting knife and pointing towards the forest. 'I have your little friend, Ñoño.'

'A skinny fourteen-year-old who's worth nothing. No way Beta would trade Ernesto for Ñoño. Not when he sees you've killed me and the soldiers on the base.'

I could hear the army trucks drawing closer.

'You get me my brother back,' Buitre said, crouching and holding his knife to my throat. 'Or I'll come for you again. You and your whole family. In case you forget, let this serve as a reminder.' He slashed his knife down the side of my face, cutting deep.

Then he stood and booted me in the head.

When I came to, Camila was leaning over me, looking aghast and sobbing. 'What have they done to you?'

Groggily, I turned my head and saw Buitrago's men fanning out in a protective ring.

'Please don't say anything about Ernesto,' I croaked.

After that, my recollections are hazy; I was bumping along a road – the army soldiers were conveying me somewhere in a truck. I was barely conscious when someone stabbed my thigh with a syringe, and after that I felt nothing.

135

I AWOKE, DAZED and disoriented, blinking my eyes to regain focus. I saw Colonel Buitrago standing over me. I looked around. Bright light streamed through a window, a pair of crutches leaned against a bare white wall, and I realised I was in a bed in the army infirmary.

I tried to sit up, instantly aware of tightness in my cheek and numbness when I tried to move my leg. I lay back against the pillow and closed my eyes, my mind racing back. Buitre had Ñoño!

And Camila . . . I remembered Camila leaning over me. She was safe, but had she said anything about Ernesto? I panicked momentarily, convinced Buitrago was here because he'd found out everything. He would free Ernesto, depriving me of my only leverage over Buitre. Then Trigeño would find out. The base would be searched, the cocaine found and my life would be over. But when I opened my eyes again the colonel was peering down at me sympathetically.

'How do you feel?' he asked.

I reached for my left check and felt padding.

Buitrago grabbed my wrist. 'It's deep, Pedro. Thirteen stitches. The doctor said not to touch the wound until it's healed.'

'Did you rescue Ñoño?'

Buitrago shook his head gravely. 'They got away. I'm sorry, Pedro. I know how it hurts to lose good men. You have ten down – six on the base, three in Caraquemada's ambush on the road and one captured. I lost three men myself responding to the ferry explosion.'

'Then you saw what they did to my base?'

He nodded. 'If I'd known Caraquemada was coming for you, I'd have sent you a platoon. But we had our hands full all night in Puerto Princesa. Caraquemada blew all the towers and hit everything at once. Santo Paraíso is completely cut off. I'll give the Guerrilla this: they're clever.'

From the way he was talking, it was clear Buitrago didn't know about Ernesto. And he too had fallen for Buitre's ruse that Caraquemada had instigated the attacks. I felt relieved, although slightly uncomfortable deceiving the colonel after all the faith he'd invested in me.

'And Camila? Is she okay?'

'She's in the next room with her parents.'

I raised myself gingerly onto my elbows, feeling light-headed. Looking down, I noticed my left foot was bandaged tightly, with a round patch of blood soaked through in the centre.

'I need to speak to her.'

'Now's not a good time. She's hardly said two words. She's still in shock—'

Buitrago was interrupted by a knock on the door. It was one of his lieutenants with an urgent message: 'Fabián Diaz's Mercedes is at the gates, *mi coronel.* Beta and his soldiers are with him – around thirty of them, *mi coronel,* in five vehicles. They're requesting permission to enter.'

'Show Señor Díaz to my office,' said Buitrago. 'But tell that *hijo de puta*, Beta, that if he doesn't withdraw his men immediately I'll inform Trigeño and throw him out of this town for good.' The colonel looked at me and shook his head. 'Thirty soldiers! Why didn't Trigeño station those troops where they should have been – on *your* base? Then none of this would have happened.'

I sat up and swivelled my legs from the mattress, then paused to let a dizzy spell pass. Through the window I now saw that the ward was on the second floor with a view over the car park and main gate. Fabián's Mercedes rolled through the entrance while several vehicles behind turned and departed. What the hell was Fabián doing here anyway?

'Pedro,' Buitrago said gently, 'I've informed your mother that you're here. I told her to wait until this afternoon to visit. She wants you to leave Llorona.'

'Never,' I said, turning to face him.

'Just think: first those wanted posters, now this. You're a target.'

'*You* haven't left,' I retorted. Through the window I saw the smarmy Fabián exit his Mercedes and then saunter towards the building, carrying a bunch of orange flowers. Suddenly I realised the real reason for his visit – he was here to see Camila! He'd wanted her ever since his fiesta. She'd been fifteen then – too young for him – although that hadn't stopped him from asking for her number. Now that she was seventeen he was trying again, using this accident as a way in.

I stood giddily from my bed, grasping the metal antibiotics stand as support before hopping on my good foot to reach the crutches.

'Pedro, wait,' the colonel called out. 'The surgeon said—'

The crutches squeaked on the linoleum floor as I launched myself through the doorway into a bare white corridor. I paused to gain my balance. Luckily, I didn't have far to go. Camila was sitting up in bed wrapped in a blanket. Her father was standing beside her, one hand placed comfortingly on her shoulder while her mother sat on the edge of the bed holding her hand.

'Pedro!' Camila turned to me, taking in my patched cheek and bandaged foot. 'I'm *so* sorry. I should have listened to you.'

Her mother stood and hugged me. 'We owe you our thanks.'

Mr Muñoz shook my hand. 'Camila told me you saved her life,' he said, although his look implied something different: *if not for you, she wouldn't have been in danger in the first place.*

There was a knock at the door. I turned to see Fabián Díaz. It had been over eighteen months since the party at the Díaz hacienda, but Camila's parents welcomed him as though they'd spoken yesterday. Fabián bowed respectfully then beamed at Camila and held out the flowers. 'A small present for the patient.'

Fabián now addressed Señor Muñoz. 'I'm sorry to arrive like this unannounced, but I heard what happened and would like to offer whatever assistance I can. My friend Andrea told me Camila commences university in two weeks. However, if she's now a target it might be best if she leaves immediately.' He outlined his plan, offering to transport Camila to the airport in his bulletproof Mercedes with armed escorts and then fly her directly to Bogotá in his Cessna. Meanwhile, her mother could pack her bags, which he'd forward the following day on a Transportadores Díaz bus.

My blood boiled. Fabián was using his wealth and power to get closer to Camila. Surely Camila and her parents would see through him. However, they seemed grateful.

'The rental contract on her student room starts in ten days,' said her mother tentatively. 'Where would she stay until then?'

'That won't be a problem, *señora*,' Fabián said smoothly. 'We own a building in the best part of town. Camila could take one of the empty duplexes.'

I could say nothing against this without looking foolish. I could only watch in horror as Camila's mother raised her eyebrows at her husband. Both parents exchanged looks with Camila, who nodded.

'That's extremely generous of you, Don Fabián,' Señor Muñoz said.

'Then it's settled. I'll wait with your parents in the Mercedes,' Fabián said to Camila. 'I imagine you two need a moment of privacy . . . ' He turned to me. 'To say goodbye.'

After Fabián left with Camila's parents, she stood, still holding her flowers, and I rushed to her side.

'Don't go with him! *Please!*' I whispered.

'I need to leave. I need to feel protected. I told you we're through. Not just because of what you've done, but because with you I'll never feel safe.'

'Fabián and his brother are drug traffickers. I can prove it!'

'And you're a kidnapper!' she snapped. 'Don't worry, I kept your dirty little secret. Just promise me you'll get Ñoño back.' She squeezed my hand and tears welled in her eyes. 'It was my fault he was taken. Just promise me!'

'I promise.'

And with that, Camila left, still clutching the blanket around her shoulders.

No sooner was she gone than Fabián re-entered the room. He'd lied about waiting in the Mercedes; he'd remained in the corridor and overheard everything.

'Think carefully about what you say publicly, *muchacho*,' he snarled. 'Once again, Javier is generously looking after your mother. And now I'll care tenderly for your girlfriend – or, should I say, your *ex*-girlfriend – who you almost got killed. We're doing this for *you*, Pedro. We're on *your* side. But if you're not on ours, then that might well affect our ability to protect the two people you love most in the world.'

136

I RETURNED FOUR days later to my camp, hobbling on crutches. The doctors had told me my foot would require redressing every four days, weeks of antibiotics and regular X-rays.

My men looked shocked by my injuries although relieved to have me back. Palillo, Indio and Johnnie Walker formed up the troop. They'd done a good job of maintaining order. The debris had been cleared from the burned grass, the tyres replaced and new sacks filled with sand, although the milking shed required structural repairs, and the wooden barn was now a pile of ash.

I stood in front of my men, thinking back to the aftermath of the disastrous battle of Jaguar River. At the time, I'd thought Trigeño a hypocrite for claiming we'd made great strides against the enemy. But now I put on a brave face and tried to make similar claims. Like Trigeño, I'd been responsible for our losses, but a commander's obligation was also to restore morale.

I praised Rafael for his quick thinking and bravery. I praised Giraldo for holding the milking shed, and Johnnie Walker's and Indio's squads for their fearless charge towards enemy lines. And I singled out Piolín and Palillo's heroism in reaching the trenches with my message to counter-attack.

Afterwards, we held a ceremony for our nine fallen soldiers, who were now buried in the Llorona cemetery. We played the national anthem over the PA system, and I had Pantera's squad fire a volley of shots into the air as a farewell salute while a tearful Iván erected five miniature crosses for the German shepherds.

'Don't cry,' I said. 'I'm getting you five more. And three puppies.'

'They were only dogs,' he said. 'Ñoño's a person. And he's my brother. I can't live without him. Please bring him back.'

As if I needed a reminder. I was already riddled with guilt over Hector, Tarantula, R6 and the others lost on my watch. I was also grieving over Camila. But now was not the time for self-pity. I put my own emotions aside and concentrated on keeping solidarity and focus within my unit. To keep their minds occupied, I immediately set my soldiers to work fitting out the farmhouse as their new barracks.

Rafael approached me and saluted. Of course, he would have been well within his rights to say, 'I told you so,' but he didn't. Instead, he seemed to intuit what I was feeling.

'Don't blame yourself, *comando*,' he said sincerely. 'Buitre will stop at nothing. But at least we still have Ernesto.'

'How is he?'

'Shaken. But holding up okay.'

Ernesto confirmed this when I visited him in his cell.

'I'm glad you're alive, Pedro,' he said. 'But does that mean Kiko is dead?'

'No,' I said, touching my finger to the patch on my cheek. 'He almost killed me.'

'I'm truly sorry, but you need to understand. All this, Kiko did for me. Of course he wants to rescue me. He did this out of *love*.'

As I watched Pirata's squad carry furniture to my new temporary office in a downstairs bedroom of the farmhouse, I was once more overwhelmed by the same depressing thought that had plagued me every waking minute since Buitre's ambush: Ñoño.

I knew Buitre wanted his brother back and would trade him for Ñoño. But that would mean Buitre escaping my clutches. I might never get another shot at him. He'd send Ernesto and his mother into hiding and never show his face again. And with Buitre's disappearance, I'd lose the chance at Caraquemada. On the other hand, how could I risk Ñoño's life? Buitre was vicious. Only that morning I'd faced the mirror and peeked under the gauze on my left cheek and cringed at the sight of the long, seeping gouge held together by thirteen tiny knots of black thread.

It had been four days since the ambush and still Buitre had not called. The longer he drew this out, the more I fretted about Ñoño and the angrier I became knowing that Buitre was deliberately provoking my desperation.

Sitting at my wooden desk, I radioed Palillo and Rafael to join me for a strategy meeting.

Palillo was the first to arrive. He'd visited me at the hospital with Mamá and already knew about my near-death encounter with Buitre. Following Buitre's attack on their house, Palillo's mother and siblings had been forced to move in with cousins in Garbanzos, but they couldn't stay there forever.

'What's the plan?' he asked, pulling up a plastic chair.

'The plan is to get Ñoño back.'

Rafael knocked on the door then sat beside Palillo. After the many occasions he'd proven me wrong, I was now willing to listen carefully to his advice.

'When Buitre calls, *comando*, don't deviate from the original plan. Nothing has changed. You still have Ernesto.' He glanced at my cheek. 'Only you now have proof of how desperately he wants him back.'

'What do you mean?' exclaimed Palillo incredulously. '*Everything* has changed. Buitre has Ñoño. He might kill him. Pedro, why are you even considering this *pendejo*'s advice? You've known him a week. Ñoño's in this situation because of *you*.'

I couldn't help but think that Rafael's assessment of Buitre's brotherly love was optimistic, bordering on delusional. If Buitre hadn't handed himself in the first time, why would he do so now that his position was so much stronger?

However his advice to continue to demand Buitre's surrender had merit. I'd consistently underestimated Buitre and he'd played on my flaws. At a minimum, I needed to ensure negotiations occurred on my terms. And the only way to do that was to convince him that Ñoño meant nothing to me.

It would be a dangerous gambit, and when hour after hour passed without word from Buitre, my anxiety deepened. I spent that afternoon in my new office, phone in hand, staring at it, willing it to ring. I didn't eat from worry. That night I hardly slept.

Finally, at dawn the next morning as I was lying in bed, a call came in from a blocked number. I sat bolt upright. I subdued my nerves, letting it ring five times before answering.

'Have you shaved recently?' asked Buitre.

'Kind of difficult with a patch across my cheek.'

'Good. Then you remember what I'm capable of when angry. Each of us knows the game has changed. We're both holding aces now. So if you want your squealing little friend back unharmed, we can make a fair and equal exchange: free Ernesto and then I'll release Ñoño.'

'No deal. And if you don't want your brother chopped up with a chainsaw and the pieces sent to your mother, then you'll do exactly as I say.'

'Harm Ernesto and I'll kill Ñoño.' Then he stated with confidence, 'You wouldn't let him die.'

'You're wrong. I didn't grow up with Ñoño. I'm not his brother. I'm his commander, and I've only known him for two years. He's a trained soldier who signed up voluntarily and accepted the risks. My demand is unchanged: you have three days to hand yourself in at our checkpoint.'

I hung up, my hands trembling. Of course every word I'd spoken was a bluff. Buitre was right – I'd never sacrifice Ñoño's life – but while I knew instinctively I'd made the right opening move, I also began to accept the inevitable. Unless we could locate and rescue Ñoño, the only way to save him was to swap him for Ernesto. Although, maybe all was not lost. Maybe there was room to bargain. After all, Buitre might still be persuaded to give up Caraquemada.

Five minutes later, as I was showering with plastic taped around my bandaged foot, the phone rang again. I wrapped a towel around my waist and hopped to my bed to answer. It was Trigeño.

'Pedro, thank God you're alive!' He sounded extremely concerned. 'I've been away and out of cell phone range so I just heard the news from Beta. I feel so ashamed. You said you needed more men and I didn't give them to you. I'm flying down tomorrow with Alfa 1. We'll hold a parade to honour the fallen soldiers. Have your men formed up at 6 am.'

With Humberto's cocaine and Ernesto concealed on my base, that was the last thing I needed. But I controlled my voice.

'That's not necessary, *comando*. I've already conducted a ceremony. You're busy with elections. Visit me once we've won.'

'At least come back to La 35 to recuperate. On full pay, of course. I'll have Beta take your place while you're on medical leave.'

Trigeño's sincerity I didn't doubt for a moment, but I now suspected the play Beta was making behind the scenes. He'd love nothing more than to have me out of Llorona and take over my base.

'Colonel Buitrago would never accept Beta being in charge of anything other than protecting Fabián, remember?'

'That's true. But this attack by Caraquemada can't go unanswered and I also promised the colonel that I'd protect you. I should have done this when you suggested it at Christmas. I'm sending down Valderrama with fifty soldiers – forty of his own plus ten to replace the men you lost. They'll set up base in Puerto Princesa. I'll transfer you funds to buy replacement vehicles.'

'Thank you, *comando*,' I said.

'I was wrong to leave you on the front line with only forty men. Not when Beta has almost sixty for Fabián's security.'

More like a hundred and twenty, it was on the tip of my tongue to say. If Trigeño didn't know Beta's true numbers, there was only one possible explanation: Beta was recruiting soldiers himself, and the Díaz brothers were funding their salaries. Who would these Autodefensa soldiers be loyal to, if it came down to it?

'Don't worry about me, *comando*, I'm down but not defeated. In fact, I'm more determined than ever to see this through. I'll see you in five weeks, after the elections.'

'I promise to squeeze in a visit before then,' said Trigeño. 'You're a brave soldier, Pedro. We need more like you.'

Although I'd managed to thwart Trigeño temporarily, he was spontaneous and I couldn't afford a surprise visit. Ernesto I could hide, move or, in the worst case, try to explain. Not so the four tonnes of cocaine.

Three weeks had passed since Javier had promised to move it. He'd ducked my calls and ignored repeated messages requesting he 'come with trucks and men to help move those heavy boxes as promised'. The need was now urgent. I wanted the cocaine gone.

I was glad when this time Javier picked up. 'Pedro,' he said. 'Don't say a word. I received your messages. I'm getting in my BMW right now.' I heard a car door slam. 'I'm on my way up.'

137

TO MY SURPRISE, Javier arrived in his champagne BMW with no trucks and no workers – only two bodyguards. I was standing by the henhouse, having expected that we were about to open the bunker. Javier pulled up in front of me and exited the car, looking tired and stressed.

'*Amigo*, you're one tough *berraco*,' he said, taking in my patched cheek and crutches. 'Beaten, shot, nearly killed but straight back to work. That *hijueputa* Caraquemada has it in for you. But at least your mother and Camila are safe with me and Fabián.'

'And I'm truly indebted to you both,' I said through gritted teeth. 'But that's not why I phoned.' I tilted my head towards the henhouse. 'You promised to move that white *mierda*.'

'I did promise. And I'm sorry, but I can't.'

'Can't? Why not?'

'Because I don't have a clue how to get rid of it. I've asked close friends and they've said it's worth millions, but I simply don't know how that industry works.'

'How can that be? I know for a fact that your father delivered barrels of sulphuric acid to the Guerrilla.'

'And as far as I know, that's all he ever did – divert chemical supplies from our fertiliser factory to Caraquemada under duress. How is that different to your own father handing over his hard-earned cash and crops? And it doesn't mean that I know anything about distributing the final product.'

'I'm standing on four tonnes of *perico*,' I said, tapping my toe against the henhouse. 'It's on your father's *finca*. And you yourself showed me the newspaper proving it was placed here two weeks before his death. So clearly he moved a lot more than chemicals. For all I know, your father was a cocaine *capo* and that's the reason Zorrillo killed him.'

'Impossible! How dare you—' Javier began, raising his fist and stepping towards me.

I jumped back and, with the sudden stab of pain from my wounded foot, it just came out: 'Then why else would Zorrillo demand the little white book?'

Javier froze, staring at me in shock. Then he frowned in puzzlement before unclenching his fist. 'Buitrago tapped our phones,' he stated flatly, dropping his hand by his side. 'I should have known.'

'So what was in the book?' I asked matter-of-factly.

'I have no idea. We never found it. Fabián and I have spent years wondering. If you're right, and our father was selling or transporting drugs, then maybe the book had a list of routes or buyers. Whatever it contained, Caraquemada wants it badly. Two months after they killed my father, he sent a squad here. They tied up our caretaker and tortured him, demanding the location of the book. They're animals, Pedro. Even with Caraquemada weakened I still have nightmares he'll kidnap me and do the same.'

'You have Beta. You're hardly in danger.'

'Beta? You think I like waking up and seeing an army camped on my lawn?'

'Tough price to pay. Your businesses are flourishing.'

'Money isn't everything. Look at me! I'm thirty-one and I look fifty. I'd love nothing more than to get married and have children. I didn't choose this life, Pedro. It was forced on me. I'm not a soldier like you. I'm not brave. I'm a businessman. But ever since Fabián and I helped you with Zorrillo, we also have prices on our heads.'

'Then why not leave?'

'We could! We have US passports. But I won't flee like a dog with its tail between its legs. Maybe you and Buitrago are right – maybe our father wasn't always strictly legal – but he worked like a packhorse his whole life. And I can't throw all that away. It would be like spitting on his grave.'

'That doesn't change the fact Trigeño is promising to visit here any day or that he'll kill me, you and anyone who's seen that white powder down there. You need to move it right now, Javier. What about your friends from the fiesta?'

'They're the ones I asked. They laughed and offered to buy a brick. For personal consumption. Although there is one person I didn't call – Don Miguel, my father's old business partner. He might know someone. But you need to trust me and keep this quiet a little longer. I've kept my word. I had Beta bring you Ernesto.'

There was not much I could say to this. Javier had indeed kept his promise to help me get Buitre. It wasn't his fault the situation had changed with Buitre now holding Ñoño captive in the jungle.

Prior to this visit I'd been certain Javier was involved in *narcotráfico*, but when he departed that certainty wavered and I began to wonder yet again whether I'd been wrong about him. His reactions seemed genuine. The way he'd puffed up so violently at my accusation against his dead father, and then his sudden deflated calm when confronted with the fact of the little white book. He'd seemed embarrassed, ashamed even, and with a drug trafficker for a father, who wouldn't be? He'd also been frightened by my mention of Trigeño's possible visit. Knowing Trigeño's deadly stance against trafficking, it simply wasn't logical for Javier not to move the cocaine if he were able to.

There was no doubt Humberto had been a large-scale trafficker who'd worked with the Guerrilla. However, it might just as well have been Zorrillo and Caraquemada, rather than the Díaz brothers, who'd taken over his operations after his death.

Perhaps Rafael knew something. I radioed him and asked him to meet me under the jacaranda tree.

'What can you tell me about the Guerrilla's involvement in drug trafficking?' I asked.

Rafael shrugged. 'Not a lot. That wasn't my job, *comando*. True, I've guarded coca fields and shot at the US Blackhawks and fumigation planes sent to poison the crops. I've even buried money in the jungle – millions of dollars in blue plastic crates – marking the spot on a map. What I do know is that cocaine is absolutely crucial to their financing. That's why Caraquemada has been prepared to give up Puerto Galán and Puerto Princesa, but never Santo Paraíso – it's like a money factory for him.'

'So they definitely protect the growers and producers, and tax them. But do they traffic it themselves?'

'It's possible. I've seen cocaine – mountains of it. We used to move it by foot and by boat to Flora's Cantina.'

'But how do they get it out? That's what I simply don't understand. We search every vehicle at our checkpoint and Buitrago's men inspect river traffic.'

Rafael shrugged. 'No idea, *comando*. But I just saw you talking to Javier Díaz. Does this have something to do with him?'

'You know what?' I said. 'I'm beginning to think it doesn't.'

138

THAT NIGHT AT dinner I received a text message that could only be from Buitre: CHECK THAT SAME ACCOUNT.

'Don't do it, *comando*,' urged Rafael. 'Buitre's trying to bargain. Remember what happened last time. As soon as you open that email, he'll know you're weak.'

Palillo disagreed. 'How can you not open it with Ñoño's life at stake? He's already had him for five whole days.'

I stood from the table and limped to my new office with Rafael and Palillo trailing behind, still arguing.

The inbox contained a single email with a blurry video clip that was four seconds long. Ñoño was hanging upside down, swinging from side to side. His face was bruised. The camera panned up, showing one of his ankles tied – he was suspended by a rope from a tree. A wooden pole struck him, he thrashed about, and Buitre's voice demanded, 'Speak!'

But Ñoño was brave. 'Pedro! I've said nothing. Don't—'

Then the video cut out. I played it again. And again.

Palillo glared at me. Rafael folded his arms.

'Ñoño's fine,' he declared. 'Those bruises are from the motorbike fall. I've seen that technique used a dozen times. More than thirty minutes upside down and the person can't thrash about like that. Buitre hasn't hurt Ñoño. But now he knows you've seen this, you've weakened our position.'

Palillo was ready to jump down his throat when Rafael insisted we now had to counter with a similar video of Ernesto. 'If you won't then I will,' Rafael offered.

'No way,' I said. I pressed REPLY and began typing.

'What are you doing?' demanded Rafael.

'Negotiating,' I said.

My message read, 'Resend the photo of Caraquemada. Or else . . .' I attached a photo of a chainsaw before pressing SEND.

Rafael was furious. '*Comando*, you're making a big mistake here. Provided you don't let him bargain, he'll hand himself in.'

Palillo disapproved also, but for a different reason. For him the choice was simple: we all wanted Ñoño back, and Ernesto's presence was a curse that had only brought misery upon us. 'Just do the straight exchange, one for one. I know how much you want Caraquemada, but you're bluffing using Ñoño's life!'

However, five minutes later, my bluff bore fruit. The same photo of Caraquemada with the blonde girl appeared in the inbox. This time, Buitre didn't delete it. I began downloading the file and then noticed Buitre had included a short reply: 'I'll help you get him, but time is limited. They meet once a month. Send this photo to Buitrago for authentication. You'll need him to track her. I'll swap Ernesto for Ñoño, as well as the girl's name and number.'

Again, Rafael was incredulous. 'It's a trick, *comando*. And even if it isn't, you said it yourself: once we have Buitre we can extract his information on Caraquemada.'

Whether it was a trick or not, I'd soon find out. I forwarded the photo in a fresh email to Colonel Buitrago with the following message: 'I recognise the face. But is this authentic?'

The colonel phoned me the next morning and I took a taxi to his office.

On Buitrago's desk, the photo of Caraquemada lay on top of a local gazette. I'd expected him to be happy, but he looked more frazzled than ever.

'Bad news?' I asked.

He slid the photo aside and held up the gazette. The front-page headline read: COLONEL FAILS TO PROTECT TOWNS. The article below detailed the recent attack on Puerto Princesa and called yet again for his resignation.

'Rather than providing me with more resources, my superior is reassigning my own soldiers to other units.'

'Don't worry. Don Felix will reverse that once he's elected.'

'I wouldn't be so sure,' he said. 'I'm hearing rumblings from the generals. Someone powerful wants me transferred. They won't say whom. But whoever is making these moves against me not only has political contacts at the highest national level but also strong influence over local media.'

I didn't have to think hard to figure out who he meant: the Díazes.

The colonel now turned his attention to the photo. 'Ugly motherfucker,' he said. 'Never seen him myself, but no wonder he doesn't like cameras. Where did you get it?'

'A *guerrillero* who defected to us has an inside source,' I said. 'So is it authentic?'

The colonel nodded. 'Pure gold if we knew where to dig. My analysts decrypted the EXIF metadata tags on the jpeg file. The image originated from a Canon model released in the US only five months ago. So it's recent. That red flower you see in that vase behind them – that's a haliconia, native to the region south of Santo Paraíso. The girl's hair appears to have been dyed professionally, so she's not likely a *guerrillera.* But our facial recognition software came up with no match; even if she's in our database, it would require a frontal shot.' Placing his forearms on the desk, Buitrago leaned forward assertively. 'So who is she?'

'Apparently, his civilian girlfriend. They meet regularly. If I can get her name and number, could you track her?'

'Into the jungle? Extremely complicated. There's no signal so I couldn't triangulate her phone. For a track-and-capture operation, at a *bare minimum* I'd need to know the terrain, the building layout, the enemy's weapons and security configuration. I'd also need authorisation from my generals. Without that, legally, I can't endanger my men's lives.'

'You won't have to,' I said, standing. 'When I get you this information, the insertion team will consist of me and Palillo.' I tapped my finger against the gazette. 'You need this, Colonel. We both do.'

139

ANOTHER EIGHTEEN HOURS passed with no further contact from Buitre. During that time the image of Ñoño hanging upside down had been replaying in my mind, and his screams echoed constantly in my ears.

While I waited for Buitre to make contact, I went over my strategy. I knew he would try to bluff and make new threats and counter-proposals. But by then I was tired of his games, and I'd learned to play them well myself.

I'd decided to feign reluctance to do the exchange, resisting at every turn, but once I'd extracted as much information as I could about Caraquemada and his girlfriend, I'd finally agree. I'd chosen Monday as the day to swap our prisoners – it was the quietest morning of the week after the Sunday markets and afternoon drinking sessions.

At last, on Saturday, when I was sitting in the waiting room of Garbanzos hospital for a follow-up X-ray on my foot, Buitre called.

'My sources inform me you just visited your beloved colonel,' he said. 'So you know the photo is genuine.'

'I also know the colonel can't track her deep into the jungle. So your offer of her name and number won't be enough. We need dates and a location.'

'I don't have them,' Buitre said testily. 'Not even the girl knows in advance.'

'Then I can't stop Rafael from making his sequel to your little video – this one starring Ernesto. Make sure you check your hotmail account in an hour! I'm sure you'll enjoy the show . . .'

'*Wait!*' Buitre said, and at that moment I knew I had him. He might have guessed I myself wouldn't harm Ernesto, but he knew with absolute certainty that Rafael would. In hostage negotiations, he was used to gripping the dagger's handle; but now its sharp tip was at his own throat. 'They meet in various peasant huts just outside of Santo Paraíso – a different one each time – so you won't have to track her far. Baez calls her five days before each meeting, and she travels from her home in Bogotá by plane to Villavicencio, and then to Puerto Princesa by bus using a fake *cédula*, alone and dressed down to avoid attracting attention. She changes clothes at Flora's Cantina, and then she's transported the rest of the way by donkey.'

'What about weapons and the security configuration around the hut?'

'Security is minimal. His superiors don't know about her. So he takes only Baez and ten trusted bodyguards. They carry AK47s, no RPGs. Four of them guard the corners of the hut. The other six form a security ring at five hundred metres.'

I believed Buitre. After my mentioning Rafael's name, he'd sounded desperate. While he talked, my mind worked furiously. If we could penetrate close enough to the hut, getting Caraquemada might be feasible.

'If we *were* to do this, what's to stop you from telling Caraquemada that his girlfriend is compromised once Ernesto is free?'

'And what's to stop you from kidnapping him again? Or my mother? Pedro, we at least need to trust each other on this. For the sake of our families.'

'Fine. Then we do the exchange Monday, 6 am. You know the tributary just south of Puerto Princesa, on the border of our territories? There's thick jungle on both sides. We each take ten men. Our prisoners search us and the boats, and confirm via radio that we have no weapons. Then we row out, meet in the middle and do the swap while our men cover us from the banks. I give you Ernesto. You give me Ñoño and when you get back to your side, you radio me the girl's name and number. You and I can walk away from this as enemies, but our families stay out of this – forever.'

Buitre paused for a long time. 'Monday, 6 am.'

It was Saturday night. The exchange was two days away but preparations needed to begin immediately. I told Palillo to gather his own squad, the two snipers – Coyote and Indio – plus Pantera and Barracuda for a briefing in my office. But first I felt I owed it to Rafael to break the news to him face to face. His advice on negotiating with Buitre had been invaluable. Without it, Buitre would never have agreed to give up Caraquemada. I knew he'd be disappointed, but I thought I'd make it up to him by inviting him to join Monday's team.

However, when I told Rafael I'd be exchanging Ernesto for Ñoño, he protested. 'How can you possibly *do* this? To your father. To me and Beatriz.'

'It's done,' I said.

'Not yet, it's not! You could call it off. Or simply not go.'

'My decision is made. And if you want to be a member of Monday's team, I need to know your emotions won't cloud your judgment.'

'With all due respect, *comando*, right now, that's an assurance I can't give,' Rafael said, saluting me before he turned and slammed the door.

Thirty minutes later, just as I was about to commence the briefing, Rafael knocked on the door, repentant and apologetic. 'I'm sorry, *comando*. I *did* get emotional, thinking about Beatriz. But I want to be there. I'm with you one hundred per cent.'

The others were excited when they heard my plan to exchange prisoners, until I explained that it would take place mid-river on the border of Guerrilla territory.

'I'm in, but I don't like it,' Palillo stated bluntly. 'Buitre's already attacked you twice. Take a look in the mirror. He wants you dead.'

'I'm in too,' said Piolín, 'but I don't like it either. Call it women's intuition.'

'We don't have a choice,' I said. 'Palillo, I need you to transfer Papá's dinghy to the wharf at Puerto Princesa. On the morning itself, you'll row the boat around to the tributary. The ten of you will be along the bank covering me. Palillo, Coyote and Indio will have their scopes on Buitre. If they shoot me, the snipers shoot Buitre, and the rest of you fire at his men on the opposite bank. You'll need to shoot quickly; they'll also be trying to kill Ñoño.'

'But that's suicide!' said Piolín. 'If one person dies, you all die.'

'Exactly.' I looked hard at her and then at the rest of my men. 'It's the only way.'

140

BEFORE FIRST LIGHT on Monday, I handcuffed Ernesto and transferred him from his cell to one of the two new pick-up trucks.

'You're going free,' I said. 'I'm swapping you for Ñoño.'

'Really?' His face lit up. 'And Kiko?'

'He'll escape me this time. But I need you to stay calm and do exactly as instructed or it might end in bloodshed.'

Eight of us piled into the pick-up. Palillo and Coça-Cola would follow directly behind us on a Yamaha. Fortunately, I could now walk without my crutches, although my foot still ached and was now encased in a heavy plastic moon boot.

As we drove the twenty kilometres towards Puerto Princesa, the darkness gradually dissolved to reveal an unseasonably gloomy day. We passed the sunken ferry and burned-out *lanchas* at the wharf, and Coca-Cola peeled off to drop Palillo at Papá's dinghy. We then continued half a kilometre further south to where the dirt road ended abruptly in a wall of thick jungle.

While the rest of us waited in the pick-up, Mona and Pantera went down the narrow track used by fishermen that led to the tributary with orders to scout the bank.

Ten minutes later Mona's voice came over my hand-held radio. 'All clear.'

I radioed Palillo to start rowing around, and our team began walking along the track with Ernesto, our rifles raised and our senses on full alert. Despite Mona's reassurance, I wouldn't put it past Buitre to attempt another rescue.

The air was filled with the piercing shrieks of parakeets and macaws. From the trees high above we heard the eerie cries of howler monkeys as they shook the branches, raining leaves upon us. At a sudden rustling in the undergrowth, I froze and held my breath until a family of capybaras waddled across our path.

The track opened suddenly to reveal a tributary sixty metres wide with slow-flowing, muddy water. Its steep banks were covered with low ferns and shrubs. On the other side, a lone dinghy sat at the water's edge. Even from this slight elevation, snipers would have no trouble picking off the occupants of a boat. Once out on the water, there would be no escape and no refuge.

While Coyote guarded Ernesto, the rest of the squad scouted through the jungle, choosing optimal firing positions behind the larger trees and boulders. Piolín crouched down behind the spreading buttress roots of an enormous ceiba tree and began scanning with binoculars. 'No sign of enemy movement,' she reported. 'But something's not right. I can feel it.'

To my left I saw Palillo one hundred metres away, rowing towards us through the mouth of the tributary. Behind him the sun was rising, shrouded in dark clouds.

When he drew level with our position, Palillo dragged the dinghy out of the water and scrambled up the bank carrying a black vest.

'At least wear this,' he said. It was Kevlar body armour borrowed from the army and would protect me from body shots.

'Where's mine?' asked Ernesto.

Palillo shook his head. 'You're not the target.'

'No,' he said with disgust. 'I'm a human shield.'

Finally, Piolín reported, 'They're arriving.'

I looked through my own binoculars and saw movement among the trees, but Buitre's men were careful not to come out into the open. They, too, concealed themselves amid the thick vegetation. Ñoño and Buitre emerged onto the bank.

My radio crackled. 'Pedro, it's me.' It was Ñoño's voice. He sounded happy, excited even. 'Can you see me waving?' He raised his hand in the air. 'I've checked Buitre for weapons.'

I waved back, handed my rifle and pistol to Piolín, and passed my handset to Ernesto, who patted me down. 'No weapons this side either.'

My men took up their positions as I headed down the bank with Ernesto and Palillo. Once beside the dinghy I unlocked the cuff on Ernesto's wrist, recuffed it to my own left wrist and slipped the key into my breast pocket. We would row with one oar each.

'What's this for?' he asked, rattling our cuffs.

'A precaution.' The handcuffs would deter Buitre's snipers from firing on me. If they did, Ernesto couldn't dive in the water and would be shot in turn. Our fates were literally interlocked.

We sat side by side in the dinghy and I radioed Buitre a final time. 'No weapons in the boat,' Ernesto confirmed to his brother. Then, as instructed, he added, 'But you should know I'm cuffed to Pedro.'

Palillo shoved us off, and with a light drizzle spraying our faces, Ernesto and I began rowing out into the murky river. Ernesto seemed relaxed. But I wasn't. Not at all. It would only take one nervous man and one accidental trigger pull for both riverbanks to erupt into automatic fire, with our dinghy trapped in the crossfire.

I glanced over my shoulder and saw Buitre's boat pulling out from the opposite bank. Ñoño was rowing while Buitre was crouched low behind him.

Clever, I thought. But it was too late to copy his tactic. I felt completely exposed, rowing with my back towards the enemy.

Once our dinghies drew up alongside each other, Buitre and I grabbed the gunwales. There was a long moment of calm as we drifted, side by side. Buitre and I stared at each other. We were so close I could see the pores of his skin and the eyelashes fringing his cold green eyes.

It felt surreal; I was once more face to face with the man I'd been hunting for months, the man who'd killed my soldiers, scarred my face and kidnapped Ñoño.

Buitre glared at me defiantly then glanced at my cheek. 'Not even time will heal that wound.' But when he turned to Ernesto his expression softened. 'You've grown up, little *hermano*.'

Ernesto smiled. 'Is Mamá okay? They wouldn't let me call her.'

'She's hanging in there, *hermanito*,' Buitre said, before pinning me with another icy stare. 'Although she's too afraid to leave the house. I'm sorry you both got dragged into this because of me.'

'Are you okay?' I asked Ñoño as he stood, preparing to change boats. 'This *hijo de puta* didn't harm you?'

'I am – thanks to you, Pedro. I thought I was dead. You saved me.'

'Celebrate when your foot touches land,' I said, suspicious that Buitre might yet be laying a trap.

I unlocked the handcuffs and Ernesto stood also. 'You're a good person, Pedro. I always knew you'd do the right thing.'

'I hope one day you can forgive me,' I responded.

'I already have.'

While Buitre and I continued holding the boats together, Ernesto and Ñoño stepped across the gunwales then hugged. 'Don't take this the wrong way,' said Ernesto, smiling. 'But hopefully I won't ever see you again.'

My eyes remained locked with Buitre's. 'If you don't radio me with the girl's details as soon as your boat touches the other bank,' I told him, 'I have snipers ready. You and Ernesto won't make it one step. After that if you breathe a single word to Caraquemada, a thousand copies of your emails will rain down on the jungle with that photo you sent – taken by Baez on a late-model Canon, I believe.'

Buitre nodded, and with the trade completed we thrust the boats apart. I began rowing furiously, my heart racing from the exertion but also from fear that I was now an easy target. Buitre had kept his word so far, but that didn't mean I trusted him.

'Lie flat in the bottom,' I ordered Ñoño. 'Don't lift your head.'

I kept my eyes firmly on Buitre. From his long, relaxed strokes, I finally accepted there was no trick.

With Ñoño safe and Ernesto free, my adrenalin subsided. I felt tired. But not from rowing. I was tired of war. Tired of fighting. Tired of being angry.

When we reached our bank, Buitre was still ten metres from his. Ñoño leaped from the dinghy and Palillo bundled him behind the gigantic ceiba tree. Crouching low, I followed quickly behind.

Piolín threw her arms around Ñoño. 'We thought we'd lost you.'

Palillo, Mona, Coca-Cola and Giraldo joined their embrace. Rafael was the only one not rejoicing. Instead, he appeared distracted, watching the tributary where Buitre was still rowing slowly. I followed his progress through binoculars.

Suddenly, the sound of rifle fire came from the jungle on the opposite side. The river's surface around Buitre's boat burst into vivid orange flame. Buitre dropped his oars and hurled himself into the hull with Ernesto, covering him with his body.

I pressed myself against the tree while Coyote and Giraldo fired blindly across at the jungle. At first I was convinced this was a trick by Buitre. But it couldn't be: he was trapped in his boat and no bullets had struck our side.

'Cease fire!' I shouted.

Across the river I saw muzzle flashes to the left and right of the Guerrilla position. Figures darted between the trees, closing in on Buitre's men from both sides, rifles blazing. Within a minute, the fighting ceased. Buitre's squad was dead.

An engine roared to life and I looked downstream towards the Llorona River to see a large speedboat shooting into the tributary's mouth.

It descended upon Buitre's dinghy in a matter of seconds. When I saw Beta at its helm, I realised immediately what had happened.

'You did this,' I said, rounding on Rafael. 'You went to Beta behind my back and betrayed me.'

Rafael squared his shoulders defiantly. 'I did my job. I did exactly what I was sent here to do.'

'I trusted you!'

'You did,' he said, 'and I sincerely apologise, *comando*. But there was no other way.'

In the meantime, Beta had forced Buitre and Ernesto onto his speedboat. I had a sinking feeling. If Beta killed Buitre, I'd never get the girl's number. They sped towards us, running aground on the muddy bank. Beta leaped proudly from the bow, smiling victoriously. His men dragged Buitre and Ernesto from the boat, forcing them to kneel at the water's edge. I ran down to them. Buitre looked at me with utter hatred, convinced I'd set this up.

Beta slapped me on the back. 'In spite of your best efforts to fuck things up, mission accomplished.' He saluted me sarcastically then kicked Buitre in the back, knocking him forward. 'You have your man. With the compliments of Javier and Fabián Díaz.'

I stood there, shocked.

'Rafael wanted the honour, and he probably deserves it, seeing as you went so soft . . .' Beta drew his pistol, flicked off the safety, cocked it and held it out to me. 'But I promised you it would be yours.'

'Not here,' I managed to say.

'Fine, you get to kill him wherever you want, in whatever way you want to. You get the credit. I won't say a word. I'll leave both prisoners in your capable hands. Take your time, but don't fuck this up again.'

141

IN EXCHANGE FOR my silence, Javier and Fabián Díaz had given me what I wanted: Buitre, the *hijo de puta* who'd held me down and forced me to watch my father's murder; Buitre, who possessed the key to capturing Caraquemada; Buitre, to do with as I pleased.

'You son of a bitch,' Buitre said as we tied him up and hurled him into the back of the pick-up. 'I knew I shouldn't have trusted you.'

'I didn't organise that ambush,' I responded, signalling to Palillo that Ernesto should ride in the cabin.

'Maybe not,' he said, 'but you should still keep your word. Ñoño is safe. Release me and Ernesto.'

I had indeed benefited from Rafael and Beta's trickery. Rafael, I could hardly bear to look at. But any dishonour I felt vanished the moment we reached the base and I remembered the nine men Buitre had slain during his attack and ambush on the road.

Despite his being tied, it took five soldiers to subdue Buitre, remove him from the Toyota and carry him up to Ernesto's former cell.

Palillo had gone ahead and was now standing, arms folded, at the metal gate. Kicking and screaming obscenities, Buitre refused to enter.

'I didn't harm your family,' he said, suddenly noticing Palillo.

'That's true,' said Palillo. 'And yet—' he punched Buitre in the face, knocking him to the ground '—you did torch my mother's house.'

Coca-Cola dragged him roughly into the cell while Pantera removed the magazines, lamp and radio we'd permitted Ernesto. Even the ordinarily compassionate Piolín became fiery as she padlocked the shackle around Buitre's ankle. 'Those kids are traumatised because of you!'

A line of volunteers snaked up the stairs. They all wanted to guard Buitre and taunt him, or at least catch a glimpse of the man who'd killed their friends. Even little Iván stared indignantly at him through the bars. 'This war is between humans,' he said. 'Why would you kill dogs?'

The only soldier to defend Buitre was Ñoño, who had pushed to the front of the queue. 'He treated me well, Pedro.'

'He hung you upside down.'

'Only for a few minutes. He didn't harm me.'

'Ñoño, you're dismissed.' Then I yelled at the men on the stairs: 'All of you are!'

'See. I did the right thing by Ñoño,' said Buitre calmly when I entered his cell. His hands were still cuffed behind his back and he was looking up at me from the floor. 'You should do the right thing too and hand me over to Buitrago.'

'I might have considered it before you attacked my base, killed my soldiers and shot at my girlfriend. The best you can hope for now is a quick death. I want the girl's name and number.'

'Never. Caraquemada will come for me. He'll wipe this base from the map, and all of you with it.'

'Unlikely. Beta tossed your men's bodies into the river for the caimans. Caraquemada will think you're all dead. Tell me the girl's name and I'll release Ernesto, just as we agreed. I won't touch your mother. She and Ernesto can keep their house. But don't forget that you need Caraquemada dead as much as I do. If he finds out about the money you stole, your mother and Ernesto will never be safe.'

I slammed the iron gate and locked it, leaving him alone on the bare wooden floor.

'Think about that. But don't think too long.'

By far Buitre's biggest advocate was Ernesto. He was temporarily under guard in my cottage while a comfortable upstairs bedroom was being prepared for him. When I entered I found him sitting peacefully in one of my faded blue armchairs, holding a screwdriver and tinkering with a broken lamp.

'I'm sorry, Ernesto, but we might have to keep you a little longer. Your brother isn't cooperating.'

'So you're keeping *me* prisoner until he does.'

Ernesto's reproach was fair; there was nothing I could say. Standing there, looking at him – an industrious boy who liked to fix things – I wondered how two brothers could turn out so differently.

Without looking up again, he asked, 'Why do you hate my brother so much?'

I hesitated. 'He helped murder my father.'

Ernesto paused for a long time, thinking. 'Then I understand. You're wrong to do this, but I understand. Please sit down, Pedro. I want to tell you how my brother got his alias.'

I had no desire to learn further details of Buitre's history – his misdeeds spoke for themselves – but after all I'd done to Ernesto, I felt I owed it to him to listen. So I pulled over the other armchair and sat beside him.

'When I was eight and Kiko thirteen, our father was killed,' Ernesto began. 'He was a public ombudsman who denounced the paramilitary assassinations of trade unionists. Kiko and I were both there when armed men broke down our door at 3 am. We didn't know who they were at the time; we only knew that our mamá was crying because these men in balaclavas were taking Papá away. Kiko jumped on my father's back and I hung from his wrist, thinking that if we weighed him down they couldn't take him. But Papá made us get off. He said he loved us very much but there was nothing we could do. The Autodefensas took him away, hacked him to pieces and left him strewn throughout our *vereda*.

'They gave us three days to leave town. We collected his arms, legs, hands, feet and torso for burial, although we never found his head. The vultures had got to him and Kiko killed them using a slingshot. That's how he got his name: Buitre. They said he was a "little vulture killer". Guerrilla recruiters approached us and promised that if Kiko joined they'd look after Mamá and me – giving us food, medicine and cash and helping us find a new house. But they never did.'

'Why are you telling me this?'

'Despite what the Autodefensas did to our family, I forgive them. And I want you to forgive Kiko. I'm sorry for your father and whatever part my brother played. Rafael is right. I don't know my brother well, but I'm sure he's sorry too.'

On Tuesday morning, when Buitre had been in captivity for twenty-four hours, Valderrama's platoon and my ten new men arrived from La 50, just as Trigeño had promised. Two F350 trucks pulled up at the gate, each containing twenty-five soldiers. I limped down the drive to meet them. I'd removed the dressing on my cheek on my doctor's orders, and these would be the first outsiders to look upon my scar. The surgeon had told me it would fade with time to a thin white line, but at the moment the wound was still angry and red.

I remembered Valderrama from my training days at La 50 when he'd been doing the promotion course. He was an experienced soldier, ten years my senior, and his group would be independent of mine and Beta's; he would report directly to Trigeño.

'Pedro, I'm not here to get in your way, or Beta's. The three of us have separate jobs to do. This is your home town, and Trigeño told me the steep price you've paid to claw it back from the enemy.' He glanced at my cheek and automatically averted his eyes. 'My base will act as a buffer against further Guerrilla incursions from the south. I'm here to take the pressure off you. If the Guerrilla so much as cross that river, you'll be the first to know. And if you need assistance on anything, I'm only a radio call away.'

Valderrama departed immediately to set up his new base on a plot of land Trigeño had acquired. This was exactly what was needed. A stronger Autodefensa presence – overseen by a commander with direct accountability to Trigeño – would restore the necessary stability to the region and set the stage for crossing the river and retaking the Guerrilla's final civilian stronghold: Santo Paraíso.

Knowing Buitre was in captivity and a full additional platoon was stationed in Puerto Princesa, I rang Mamá and told her it was safe for her to leave Javier's hacienda and move back in with Uncle Leo.

All that was required now was for Buitre to give me the girl's name.

That afternoon, however, when I looked in on Buitre, I couldn't help but see Ernesto in his face. As people, they were nothing alike, but Buitre had the same nose and identical green eyes – eyes that had also looked upon their father's dismembered body. I thought back to what Papá used to say: when you know a man's story, you're less likely to judge him. Knowing that Buitre's father had been stolen from him and left for the vultures, just like Papá, made me feel sad and torn. It dampened my will to execute him. He'd joined the war at thirteen – two years younger than I had – and he had done so to help his family.

I'd expected to relish having Buitre in my power and to enjoy protracting his ordeal, but now I just wanted this over as soon as possible.

'Are you ready to give me her name?' I asked him through the bars.

'I'll do that once you agree to hand me over to the army, not murder me in cold blood. I don't deserve to die. I'll spend years in prison and Ernesto and my mother can visit me. Isn't that justice?'

'For what you did to my father, no, it isn't.' I looked around the bare room and spied nothing but the bed and water jug. I unlocked his cell door, entered and snatched up the jug. 'Perhaps a day without water will persuade you to talk.'

'Pedro, wait! I didn't kill your father.'

'No, you just held me down and made me watch while Caraquemada pulled the trigger.'

'I had no idea what he was going to do. Our commanders tell us nothing. Questions are forbidden; we're there to obey orders. All I know is your father had done something to anger Caraquemada. If you'd interfered, he would have shot you too.'

'My father did nothing. I was the one who spoke to the Autodefensa recruiters in the plaza, yet after his death they called Papá a *sapo*. Zorrillo painted that lie all over our *finca*.'

'Zorrillo was a spoilt *narco* with no self-control. But not Caraquemada. He's swift. He's brutal. And he overreacts. But he always obeys our statutes. So your father couldn't have been completely innocent. Caraquemada wouldn't have executed him for something *you* did.'

I knew Buitre was mistaken. I was responsible. And his attempts to explain my father's death by insisting on Papá's guilt only made me angrier. I wanted answers, not more questions and doubts.

I returned his water jug. 'You can keep this . . . for now. But you *will* give me that girl's name. In the meantime—' I dragged the mattress off his bed and hurled it into the corridor '—it's your choice how much you want to suffer.'

142

FOR THE NEXT three days – Wednesday, Thursday and Friday – Buitre continued to resist my demands for the girl's name and number.

'Are you ready to talk?' I'd ask each time I went to his cell.

'Have you released Ernesto?' he'd reply.

'I will once I'm certain I can get Caraquemada.'

Frustrated by his obstinacy, I gradually increased his discomfort, hoping to break him. From the day of his capture I'd kept him handcuffed at all times. I'd then begun removing his privileges one by one: on the second day, he'd lost his bed and blankets. On the third, I stopped letting him out for toilet breaks, giving him a bucket to use instead, hoping he'd eventually tire of his own rotten smell. On the fourth day, we nailed the shutters closed, blacked out the windows and reattached the door in front of the metal bars with only an eyehole drilled through it so guards could observe him. I knew Buitre had no conscience, but I hoped that as he sat alone in silence and total darkness his own thoughts would drive him crazy. Finally, on Friday morning, I cut off his meals.

Physical torture I couldn't abide, but that wouldn't stop me making his life a living hell. Whether it took a day, a week or a month, Buitre would eventually see that his predicament was hopeless.

To my surprise, Palillo approved of these privations. 'Free accommodation is already way more than that house-burning motherfucker deserves. As for Ernesto, a few more days with us won't kill him.'

The rest of my men, including the ten new arrivals, seemed motivated and happy, barring Rafael, whose rifle I'd confiscated after his treachery. He wisely stayed out of my way. Guarding an important Guerrilla commander imbued the camp with a renewed sense of pride and purpose.

Aside from Camila's unwavering silence, I had every reason for optimism: I had Ñoño back, my foot and face were healing, and I was once more properly mobile since the new pick-ups were automatic. Best of all, Buitre was in my custody and I'd soon have the information I needed to go after Caraquemada.

Meanwhile, I was looking forward to the elections in three weeks. Felix was still on track to being elected senator – his approval rating was now seventy-five per cent. That might dull the shine on Fabián Díaz's smile, but I didn't care.

Once Fabián was no longer a candidate, he'd have no justification for retaining his battalion of 'bodyguards'. Beta and his Black Scorpions would have to return to La 50, and the towns would return to the peace they'd enjoyed for the first six months after our takeover. A sense of change was in the air, not only in our camp but also in the streets, markets and plazas.

'Whatever you said to Beta or the Díazes, it worked,' Felix told me when I met him for lunch in Garbanzos on Friday. 'The harassment of my passengers has stopped. We're getting word to voters in the villages and mountains. Despite Caraquemada's intimidation, they're determined to vote.'

There were still disturbing reports, however, about the Black Scorpions extorting small businesses in the river villages. Felix had also heard that the Díaz brothers were buying up land well below market value, using threats and intimidation when they encountered resistance.

'One landowner who refused to sell simply disappeared. Men in balaclavas took him away in a truck and he hasn't been seen since,' Felix reported.

'Who was taken?'

'I trust you, Pedro, but for his family's sake I can't tell you. However, once I'm sworn in I'll make sure Colonel Buitrago receives adequate men and resources to protect people's rights.'

After lunch I visited the Llorona church to say a prayer for Papá.

Crossing myself and opening my eyes as I finished my prayer, I saw Padre Rojas standing beside the pew.

'How are you, my son?'

'Healing quickly, Padre. The stitches are out. I'm back driving again and I'll have this thing off in a week.'

I pointed to my moon boot, but rather than glancing down, Rojas gave me one of his deeply religious stares – looking into my eyes as though he were peering at the very depths of my soul. 'True healing involves the spirit not the flesh. Anything you want to talk about? My confession box is always open, if you feel you have lost your true path.'

'*Gracias*, Padre, but I have no sins to report . . . anyway, none that are new.'

Rojas shook his head gravely and turned away before I could catch him trying not to smile.

Coming out of the church, I found Old Man Domino in the plaza playing checkers with Iván. His wife, Gloria, was tugging at his wrist, trying to cajole him into coming home for lunch. He was drunk and belligerent, insisting he was about to win and that she was interrupting his concentration.

'Time to go home, *viejo*,' I said. 'I'll give you a ride.'

He looked up at me with glazed eyes. 'You children think you've changed things in this town. You haven't changed *ni mierda*. Let us play two more games, then you can drive me home. We'll have a meal and I'll show you the cesspit you're drowning in.'

When I insisted we leave immediately, Old Man Domino swiped the board clean, sending pieces flying and smashing the bottle of *aguardiente* on the concrete.

Gloria began crying as I bent down to clean up the mess. 'I'll accept your invitation when you're not blind drunk,' I said.

'You do that, *muchacho*,' he said angrily. 'Then we'll see who's blind.'

Friday also marked two weeks since Camila's premature departure from Llorona in Fabián's Cessna. I hadn't heard a word from her since. By then, I guessed she must have moved into her shared student accommodation. Bogotá was only a three-hour drive beyond Villavicencio, but considering her coldness and silence she might as well have been on the moon.

Although we'd gone for much longer stretches than this without talking when I was away at La 50 or out patrolling the savannah, this was different. I'd always known she was there, loving me, ready and waiting for me to come home. Finally, I understood how Camila had felt – waiting, not knowing, and wondering whether she would ever see or hear from me again.

The next morning I was reading the Saturday paper in the sunny courtyard of the farmhouse while Piolín was in a nearby bedroom, organising books onto shelves for her new classroom and library. Flicking past the social pages, a photo caught my eye.

It had been taken at a *farándula* event, and there were celebrities in the background. The photo was centred on Fabián, who had one arm around Camila. She was bright-eyed and smiling, with her long hair styled in large glamorous curls, and wearing a red dress with a plunging neckline. On Fabián's other side stood Andrea.

'I'll kill him,' I said. 'I'll fucking *kill* him.'

Hearing me, Piolín came out, and when she saw the newspaper she tried to calm me. 'Look! He's got his arm around Andrea too. They're just huddling together for the photo. Don't read into it, Pedro. She still loves you.'

'I don't trust him. I've seen how he operates. He'll get her drunk. He'll drug her.'

'They're friends, Pedro,' insisted Piolín. 'She tells me every time.'

'Every time when?'

Piolín flushed. 'Camila has been calling. She claims she's checking in on me. But that's not the real reason. She's calling to find out about *you*.'

'Then why not call me?'

'I don't know, but I can promise that after all Camila has been through she's definitely not looking for a new relationship. She's happy being single.'

I knew Piolín meant this as reassurance. But to me it wasn't. Single meant Camila was *available*. Maybe nothing had happened with Fabián Díaz. Maybe instead Camila was out meeting many guys and having lots of fun, but with 'no commitments'. I was not sure which felt worse.

Camila had asked me never to contact her again. So far I'd respected her position, but after seeing that photo my will crumbled.

I texted her: 'Camila, I miss you. I love you with all my heart.'

My phone beeped and my heartbeat quickened. Her response contained an address in Bogotá followed by: 'If you truly love me, you know what you have to do . . .'

143

ON SUNDAY, THE sixth day of Buitre's captivity, Mamá called early and asked me to go with her to the ten o'clock Mass at Llorona.

I was still upset after seeing the photo of Camila, and told her I was busy.

'Then meet me afterwards. Surely you can spare fifteen minutes for your old mother?' she insisted.

Later, as I waited on the church steps, I surveyed the town and looked up the hill, admiring our restored *finca*. After the elections it would be safe enough for Mamá to start living there again. My birthday was in ten days and that would be my present to myself – seeing her happily restored to our home.

At the end of Mass Mamá emerged from the church with Uncle Leo. She was holding a bunch of sunflowers.

'I promised to lay these for Eleonora,' she said, hugging me with less than her usual warmth. Clearly, something was bothering her. 'Her sons were so good to me, taking me in again like that after the recent trouble. Will you accompany me?'

Leo waited in the truck while Mamá and I walked arm in arm through the cemetery. Mamá placed the flowers at the base of Humberto Díaz's tombstone.

'I'm sorry you were in danger again, even for a few weeks,' I said. 'I know it was because of me.'

'It wasn't because of you.'

'You don't blame me?'

'Not at all,' she said. 'I blame myself. Maybe if I'd helped bury my husband, like you said. Maybe if I'd insisted Leo bring Papá's body here to the cemetery. Maybe if I hadn't snapped at you for what you said to Zorrillo, you wouldn't have left and you wouldn't be doing this.'

'Doing what? We've banished the Guerrilla. Since that last attack, we've driven them back across the river. Llorona is at peace.'

'It's not the town I'm worried about. It's you, Pedrito. I'm afraid for *you.*' Mamá paused. 'You were so brave the day Mario died. I couldn't see it at the time, but afterwards I was so proud of you. You did everything a son could possibly do. Everything a *man* should do. You looked after me. And you saved this town. But what you're doing now . . .' She hesitated. 'Is it true you're holding a prisoner? An innocent boy?'

I was shocked. My own men were loyal; they wouldn't have told her. No one could have seen Ernesto on the base. The only person who knew, and who Mamá was in regular contact with, was Javier Díaz. Unless . . .

'You've been speaking to Camila!'

Mamá flushed. 'She phoned yesterday from Bogotá. She misses you, Pedro. But she's a strong girl and she's not coming back.'

'Then why is she even calling you?' I said angrily.

'So it *is* true. Is that why they shot you and did this to your cheek?'

I didn't answer, but a mother knows her son's face better than her own.

'Pedro, how could you? Your father would be so ashamed.'

Her words were like a stab to my heart. 'He's the brother of one of the men who killed Papá. That blond one! The one who held me down!'

'I don't care who he is. Release that boy now! If you don't, you're no son of mine. Call me when you decide to do what's right,' she said. Then she turned her back. 'But not before.'

144

MAMÁ DEPARTED IN Uncle Leo's truck, leaving me tangled in a net of shame. One minute I'd been happy, contemplating the prospect of returning to our *finca*. The next Mamá was claiming I'd disgraced Papá's values and telling me I was no longer her son. All because I had Ernesto.

And the reason I still had Ernesto was simple: Buitre refused to open his mouth and enunciate one single name. If he'd revealed the identity of Caraquemada's girlfriend six days earlier, his brother would be free by now.

I'd already decided I wanted this over. Well, now it had to be. I wanted Buitre and Ernesto out of my life forever. Buitre's grave was already dug; he was merely teetering on its edge.

I leaped into the pick-up, slammed the accelerator flat and sped in a blind fury towards the base. The engine's roar was merely a buzz, drowned out by my deafening anger. The passing vegetation was a green blur against the sharp focus of my rage.

I hurtled through the gate and skidded to halt by the farmhouse.

'What's wrong?' asked Palillo as I stormed inside.

'What's *wrong*?' I grabbed a crowbar from the tool cupboard in the downstairs hall. 'I'll show you what's wrong. Just watch!'

'Don't do anything stupid!' Palillo chased after me as I clomped awkwardly up the stairs. The pain shooting through my foot at every step, far from crippling me, only spurred me on.

I dismissed a startled Coca-Cola from guard duty, turned the key in Buitre's door, opened the gate and burst into the room.

Buitre was asleep on the floor, his hands cuffed behind him. I kicked him awake using my hard plastic boot. Then I prised open the shutters with the crowbar, flooding the darkened room with sunlight. Shielding his eyes, Buitre squinted at me with surprise and sudden fear.

I stooped over him and, gripping both ends of the crowbar, hooked it under his chin. Buitre cried out in pain as I pulled upwards, yanking him to his knees and dragging him backwards to the window.

'Take your last look at the sky,' I said. 'I'm done with your games. You'll attack a base and murder nine men. You'll let your own *compañeros* die. You'll kidnap and torture a fourteen-year-old kid. All supposedly to save Ernesto. But when it truly comes down to it, you're willing to gamble with your brother's life if you think there's a chance it will save your own. Well, there isn't. Today you die. I'll give you and Ernesto ten minutes to say your goodbyes.'

I released one hand from the crowbar, and when Buitre collapsed to the floor I swung it down hard, belting his thigh.

'Finally!' said Palillo as I slammed the door.

'Transfer Ernesto into Buitre's cell,' I told him. 'Then leave. You said you wanted this obsession of mine to end. Well, it ends here today, one way or another.'

I found Rafael in the kitchen scrubbing pots. Since the day of his betrayal, I'd assigned him permanently to kitchen duties and barely spoken to him. He now looked up uncertainly, spying the Smith & Wesson in my hand.

'You gave me Buitre,' I said. 'Now I'm giving him back to you. You wanted to make him understand suffering. Time to make him suffer.'

Rafael's uneasiness vanished and his eyes glinted. 'With pleasure, *comando*. But why the change of strategy?'

'You're not here to ask questions!' I snapped. 'You're here to obey my orders. Come up to Buitre's cell in ten minutes. Ernesto is with him.' I unclipped the magazine, emptied it of bullets then reinserted it. 'I need the name of Caraquemada's girlfriend. I don't care what you have to do to Buitre to get it, but under no circumstances is Ernesto to be harmed. Is that clear?' I handed him the pistol.

'Completely, *comando*.'

I returned to Buitre's cell and stood quietly at the door, looking through the eyehole. Buitre was now sitting by the window with his back against the wall. Ernesto had his arms around his brother and their foreheads were touching. They were murmuring, so I could only hear snippets of what they said.

'I thought when I joined . . . but it's only brought you and Mamá more misery,' Buitre was saying. 'Once I was in . . . couldn't get out . . . would have killed all three of us . . . could only protect you from afar.'

'We missed you . . . we never stopped loving you,' Ernesto replied. 'We wanted you home. Couldn't you have . . . ?'

'Impossible. Maybe another year or two . . . enough money for all three of us to escape the country . . . but then this happened. The only good thing I ever did was buy that house. You wouldn't believe the terrible things they made me do . . . I've made a mess of my life.'

'You were only thirteen. They tricked you. It's not right. It's not fair.'

'*Fair!*' Buitre said loudly. I could now hear his every word. 'You think fairness has anything to do with it? Since when has life ever been fair? But it's not too late for you. When I die, promise me you'll finish your apprenticeship. Promise me you'll look after Mamá.'

'No!' said Ernesto. 'I won't let you die. I'm not leaving you here.'

'You don't have a choice. Those men out there are killers!'

I was so deeply immersed in their sorrowful farewell that I didn't realise Rafael had come up behind me until he gently tapped my shoulder.

'I'm ready, *comando*,' he whispered.

I had tears in my eyes, but I pushed them back and swallowed the knot in my throat. After seeing what I'd seen, after hearing what I'd just heard, I should have stopped it there. But I didn't. I handed Rafael the keys.

When Rafael opened the door and entered with the pistol behind his back, at first the brothers didn't look up. The door clicked closed and I felt a shiver down my spine.

'*Hola*,' said Rafael. 'It's been a long while, *hermano*.'

Buitre looked up in shock then scrambled to his knees. 'What do you want?'

'I came to say goodbye.' Rafael pulled out the pistol, tapping its barrel against his palm. 'Your ten minutes are up. Admittedly not a lot of time. Although far longer than you gave me to farewell Beatriz.' He tossed a pair of handcuffs to Ernesto. 'Put these on.'

Buitre leaped to his feet and stood in front of Ernesto, shielding him with his body. 'My brother has nothing to do with this.'

Rafael clicked his tongue then grabbed the chain linked to Buitre's ankle with both hands and wrenched it, pulling Buitre off his feet. He dragged him, thrashing, across the floor, shortened the chain and tethered it to the wall.

'You were almost right, *hermano*. This *was* between you and me. It could have been,' he said, now cuffing Ernesto himself, pulling him backwards against his chest and pressing the pistol under his chin. 'If only you hadn't also involved someone innocent.'

'I'm sorry!' cried Buitre, regaining his feet and stepping forward only to be jerked back by the chain. 'Beatriz was going to give us away to Caraquemada. He'd have killed me, you and my family. Don't do this,' he pleaded, his voice breaking. 'Ernesto doesn't deserve to die.'

'No one *deserves* to die, and yet . . . everyone does. The only question is when. There's a grave out there already dug. Whether it ends up containing one body – or two – is entirely up to you.'

'Where's Pedro?' demanded Ernesto, glancing at the door. 'Pedro's a good person. He wouldn't allow this.'

Hearing Ernesto defend me was a knife in my heart.

'Pedro *is* a good person,' said Rafael calmly. 'He would have let you both go free at the river. I stopped that happening. You're both here because of me. But Pedro's patience has run out. He wants the girl's name.'

'You're lying,' said Ernesto, tears running down his cheeks. 'Pedro would never harm me.' He twisted out of Rafael's grasp, ran to the door and kicked at it furiously, crying out, 'Pedro! Pedro, help us!'

I stepped aside, pressing myself against the wall so he couldn't see me. I heard scuffling inside and looked again through the peephole. Rafael had a hold of Ernesto once more, but he only screamed louder. 'Pedro! Please come quickly. Please, anyone who can hear me. Rafael's in here. He has a gun!'

Through the open window everyone in the camp would have heard those cries. Palillo. Piolín. Ñoño. And little Iván. I imagined them gathering on the grass below, then searching the camp frantically, looking for me, thinking I was the only one who could stop this. When all the while I was right outside the door, allowing it to happen.

'Pedro's not going to save you,' said Rafael. He held up my Smith & Wesson and raised his eyebrows. 'Who do you think gave me this pistol? But Pedro's soft. That's why he sent me to do his dirty work.'

I bristled at the jab. I knew Rafael was acting, but he'd said it with such conviction. Besides, the last part was completely true. I was the one doing this, although I was pretending it wasn't me.

'This is it, *hermano*,' said Rafael. 'Beatriz had no choice. But you do. So, do you love your brother or not?'

Buitre hesitated; withholding the girl's name was the only thing keeping him alive. Once he gave it, he was dead.

'I'm going to count to three,' said Rafael. 'And as I count, I want you to think about what you did to Beatriz. Our baby would be six months old right now. We would have been happy.'

He grabbed Ernesto's shoulder, forced him to his knees and pressed the pistol against his forehead. When Ernesto began sobbing, Rafael laughed and wiggled his finger on the trigger. '*Oooone* . . . One is for Beatriz.'

Witnessing Ernesto's terror was excruciating. Rafael had promised no physical harm, but that didn't mean it wasn't violent – emotionally violent. I placed my hand on the doorknob.

Ernesto didn't deserve this, but *Buitre did.* And I could also see the effect it was having on him. Only a minute more and he would surely cave and say the girl's name.

Buitre strained against his chain, thrashing wildly, trying to reach Ernesto and kicking out with his free leg. Then, defeated, he dropped to his knees and bowed his head. 'Please don't do this! I'm begging you . . . Please!'

'Do you love your brother or not?' Rafael shouted. 'I said, *one*!'

Ernesto began hyperventilating.

In the next instant I realised Rafael wasn't acting; he had snapped completely. *Crack!* went the pistol beside Ernesto's ear. Even in the corridor the gunshot was deafening.

'Stop!' I yelled, ripping open the door. 'That pistol wasn't loaded.'

Rafael pointed it at me. 'I loaded it,' he said. 'Stay out of this, Pedro. It's between me and him.'

I pushed at the iron gate then realised with horror that it was locked. I could only stand there, watching, gripping the bars and shaking.

'Two is for our unborn baby. *Twoooooo*.' Rafael fired a second time next to Ernesto's left ear.

Rafael turned to Buitre and smiled. 'And three is for me. *Thr—*'

'Stop! Stop! I'll tell you.' Buitre collapsed back onto his heels, sobbing. 'Tita! That's her working name.' The words flooded out of him quickly between desperate gasps. 'Her real name is Ofelia Vanegas. Her number is on a folded slip of paper in a slit in the sole of my left boot.'

Rafael ripped off Buitre's boot and gleefully plucked out the paper. 'Got it!'

'You win,' said Buitre, looking up at me. 'Both of you win. You got what you wanted. I deserve it. Let Ernesto go and then kill me.'

Rafael unlocked the gate, keeping the pistol trained on Buitre.

'Get up on your knees,' he ordered.

Buitre raised himself up. 'Pedro.' He sniffed. 'I don't want this sick son of a bitch to do it. I want *you* to. But not in front of Ernesto. Let him go. Then please make it quick.'

'Go downstairs and wait,' I said to Ernesto, uncuffing him. He was pale and shaking as he left, looking over his shoulder at his brother.

Rafael placed the pistol in my hand. I pointed it at Buitre and raised it. I hesitated. I lowered it. I raised it again.

Rafael winked at me. He seemed to think I, too, was acting in order to protract Buitre's suffering, and he was revelling in it. When I flicked the safety on, he realised I wasn't.

'I'll do it,' he offered.

But I couldn't let him do it either. I couldn't explain why. I just couldn't.

'Not yet,' I said, gesturing Rafael out of the cell and closing the door behind us.

It was noon when I emerged into the fresh air and the open ground surrounding the farmhouse. I could breathe properly again. It was like any other ordinary day in the camp. Birds twittered in the jacaranda tree. Mona was serving lunch. But something had changed within me. Stepping from the dark farmhouse with the midday sun above me, it felt as though I'd escaped from the depths of midnight only to find myself under a blazing spotlight.

Everyone was gathered around Ernesto, comforting him. He was shaking and sobbing so much he could barely speak. Piolín looked at me in disgust.

'Fetch Ernesto's clothes,' I told Ñoño.

'Shouldn't you first verify the girl's name?' said Rafael.

'No. Ernesto's going home.'

While Ernesto changed I rang Buitrago and passed on every detail Buitre had revealed about the girl. Whether the name and number were authentic, and whether or not they would lead me to Caraquemada, hardly seemed to matter. What I'd done was wrong. Purely and simply wrong.

Those were Camila's words, and I now knew she was right. Holding Ernesto hostage had been wicked from the very beginning. And I'd compounded my original wrong by continuing to keep him once I had his brother, to use him as a tool to torment Buitre.

Even my promise not to harm Ernesto I'd broken. He'd been psychologically terrorised and almost killed. True, I hadn't known Rafael was so deranged or that he'd go much further than I'd imagined. But I'd given him the pistol and I'd ordered him into that room. I'd preyed upon the love between two brothers; I'd trespassed and defiled a bond no less sacred than my own bond with Papá.

It took witnessing them both breaking down completely to finally snap me from my self-justification. I'd facilitated this, I'd allowed it to happen, and in doing so I'd turned into the monster Camila had accused me of being.

The troop gathered to farewell Ernesto. He was dressed in the same overalls he'd been wearing on the day of his capture. There was no danger he'd tell authorities. Rafael's final threat had made sure of that.

'Not a word to anyone,' he warned Ernesto. 'We'll be watching you.'

Ernesto patted Iván's puppies and hugged Ñoño before turning to the others. 'Look after each other.'

'Shall I drive him to the bus terminal?' offered Coca-Cola.

'No,' I said. 'That's my job.'

I watched him cast one last glance up at the farmhouse where we'd left his brother locked in his cell. After the trauma we'd put him through, could he ever return to a normal life? How many years would he spend looking over his shoulder? What would he tell his mother and Astrid?

Ernesto and I drove in silence. There was no point in apologising. What could I tell him? That the gun hadn't been loaded? That I'd wanted to stop it but couldn't? What kind of excuses were they?

On the way to Garbanzos, I lent him my phone to call his mother. As he told her of his release I could hear her crying with joy and couldn't prevent tears from welling in my own eyes. When we reached the terminal and I gave him money for his ticket home, Ernesto thanked me, opened the door then turned towards me.

'Are you going to kill him?' he asked. 'I need to know.'

'You're free. That's all that matters. It's over. You and your mother are safe.'

'Pedro.' As he shook my hand, his expression vacillated between joy at his own release and terror of what that meant for his brother. 'I know you'll do the right thing.'

Driving back towards the base, I felt cleansed. In leaving Ernesto at the bus terminal, I'd also shed the skin of the cruel monster I'd become over the past few weeks.

Maybe I hadn't done the right thing, but I'd finally stopped doing the wrong thing. And at least I'd taken one step off the dark path I'd been stumbling blindly down for so long. So when my phone rang – Buitrago had good news – it was almost like God was rewarding me.

'We got a match!' the colonel declared, his voice brimming with excitement.

Buitrago had pulled in a favour from a police major in the anti-narcotics intelligence unit. His search for 'Ofelia Vanegas' and 'Tita' had received an instant match in their classified system. The major had sent Buitrago the file, which contained a photo of a fake blonde.

'It's the same girl,' he told me. 'Come to my office tomorrow at 9 am to discuss the operation.'

I was overjoyed – all this might soon be over. Immediately, I texted Camila: 'Ernesto is free.' I waited for a response, but receiving none I called Mamá at Uncle Leo's hardware store where I knew she was now working.

'Mamá, the boy is free. He's on his way home to his mother.'

'I'm glad, Pedro. You've always been a good boy. I knew you'd make the right choice,' she said cautiously, although not with the tone of unconditional forgiveness I'd expected. 'His mother deserves to have him home.' Mamá paused for a long time. 'But, Pedro, your own mother also wants her son back. You said it will soon be safe to return to the *finca*. I hope then you can leave this life behind and start building the kind of future your father and I always knew you were capable of.'

I hoped so too. I wanted to start trying. But then there was a problem: Buitre. What would I do with Buitre? How exactly would I now kill him? March him outside and coldly, rationally pull the trigger on a completely defenceless man. This situation was different to that of Ratón and Zorrillo. I'd killed them in the heat of anger, charged with adrenalin or following a hail of bullets. With Buitre utterly at my mercy, my temper had cooled. Gradually over the past week, ever since Ernesto had told me about their father's death, Alias Buitre, an enemy soldier, had become Kiko Fuentes, a twenty-year-old boy with a family. A boy who'd had a father he'd loved and lost, just like I'd lost Papá. Killing him would leave his sixteen-year-old brother and his mother grieving and devastated, their lives forever scarred, just like mine and Mamá's.

When I reached the base I was surprised to see three trucks with a platoon of Black Scorpion troops.

Beta.

He was standing next to Rafael. I had no way of knowing whether he'd called Beta. Both their faces were impassive. But the timing was too much of a coincidence. And when I saw Buitre, cuffed and kneeling behind Beta's red SUV, I knew they'd been waiting for me.

145

BETA SCOWLED AT me. 'You've had your fun, Pedro. And now you've released the brother. So why is this scum still alive?' He kicked Buitre in the stomach, causing him to double over.

I had no answer.

'Don't be weak. It's time to finish the job.'

Beta was right. Buitre had served his purpose; I had the information I needed. I'd insisted I wanted to capture and kill him. Beta and Javier had kept their word to help me. My dogged determination to get to this point had cost many lives and caused Ernesto and Ñoño incalculable suffering. It had ended my relationship with Camila and prompted Mamá to disown me.

To turn around now and *not* do it would mean I'd made others pay a steep price, all for nothing. I knew there was no logical reason not to kill him, so why was I hesitating?

Beta plucked my Smith & Wesson from its holster, tightened my fingers around the grip, cocked it for me and pointed it at Buitre. I breathed deeply, lining up the front and rear sights with the back of his head. I willed myself to recall the feeling of powerlessness as Buitre held me down to watch Caraquemada shoot Papá, but instead my mind cast up an image of a thirteen-year-old Buitre shooting rocks at vultures with his slingshot as he collected the parts of his father's dismembered body.

I lowered the pistol.

Beta's hands shot to his hips and he shook his head angrily. 'Do you know how many families this *hijo de puta* has destroyed? I should have gift-wrapped him for El Psycho. But you insisted you wanted justice and that you wanted to do it yourself. I captured him for you, Pedro. This is what you've dreamed of and planned for. But if you won't accept the honour, Rafael or a dozen patriots over there will.'

I raised the pistol again and Buitre squeezed his eyes shut, tears running down his cheeks.

Beta grabbed him by the hair and twisted his face towards me. 'Open your eyes, *hijueputa*, so before you go to hell you can see who's killing you and remember why.'

Buitre obeyed. But when he looked at me with those emerald-green eyes, pleading, the face I saw was Ernesto's.

When I didn't pull the trigger, Beta stood behind me, locked his forearm under my chin and pulled my neck back tight while holding my head forward. Choking, I felt my adrenalin surge and my fury rise. Beta was the cause of my anger, but I tried to channel it towards Buitre.

'Right in front of you is one of the men who killed your father. Have you forgotten? Do it!'

I was now giddy and off balance. But his words worked, adding fuel to the fire of my forgotten anger. Next he struck a spark.

'What kind of son are you? This is your duty to your father.'

I felt myself being sucked back to the day of Papá's execution. 'Okay,' I yelled, breaking out of the chokehold and shoving Beta in the chest. 'I'll do it.'

I aimed the pistol. I didn't circle. I didn't read the charges. I didn't make my speech.

'Wait!' yelled Buitre. 'Think of my mother.'

I fired two shots. Buitre toppled forward.

'*Adiós*, Guerrilla *hijueputa*.' Beta spat on the body. He put me in another headlock, half friendly and half deadly serious, and dragged me away. 'Don't *ever* touch me again! Especially not in front of my soldiers,' he said. Then he ruffled my hair and relinquished his grip slightly. 'Cheer up, Pedro. Take pride in being a man.'

But something was wrong. Suddenly seized with anger, I twisted out of Beta's hold, ran back to Buitre and fired and fired and fired. Although he was already dead, I emptied an entire clip into him, all the while yelling, 'You're not sorry. Say sorry. Say sorry.'

But I knew it wouldn't bring Papá back. Nothing would bring him back. And then I heard a voice behind me.

'Put the gun down, Pedro. It's over.'

It was Palillo. When I turned towards him, he raised his hands in surrender, afraid I hadn't recognised him. He looked at me as though I were a man possessed.

'It's me! Palillo. Your friend. Put the gun down, please.'

I lowered the pistol.

Palillo placed an arm across my shoulder and hugged me tightly. I felt him prise the pistol from my fingers and toss it aside. Then he turned me to face him and looked into my eyes. 'How do you feel?'

Palillo never asked anyone how they felt. He always claimed he could deduce people's feelings from their behaviour. But this time he seemed genuinely perplexed.

'I don't know,' I answered.

I'd killed three of my father's murderers, but I no longer felt anything. The first time with Ratón I had shaken and almost vomited. With Zorrillo there had been adrenalin but no fear. However, this time there was no sickness in the stomach. No guilt. Nothing.

'Why are you looking at me like that?' I demanded.

'You're crying,' Palillo replied matter-of-factly.

'No, I'm not.'

Palillo touched a finger to my face and showed me the glistening tear on its tip. 'It's okay to cry.'

'Why would I be crying?'

'Because you didn't feel what you wanted to feel.'

Palillo had always been smart at reading me, but this was one of the most perceptive things I'd heard him say. I felt no remorse that Buitre was gone, but no satisfaction either. If anything, I felt strangely hollow. When I mentally replayed Buitre's execution, the moment I pulled the trigger was a blur. Instead, the clearest image was that of Beta's powerful hand forcing the pistol into mine. I'd wanted Buitre to die by my own hand. But would I have actually gone through with it? Beta's interference meant I'd never know.

Palillo hugged me tightly again but I stood stiff, my arms limp. Finally, I heard car doors slamming. Beta and his men were leaving.

Palillo picked up my Smith & Wesson and led me to my cottage. 'Get some rest, *hermano*,' he said. 'Then you can start to focus more clearly on the future you really want. But I know you won't do that until it's completely over.' He placed the pistol beside my pillow. 'And for that to happen, you'll need to pull this trigger one last time.'

He was right. On the day of Papá's execution, Buitre had merely been following orders. Caraquemada had not only given those orders, he'd planned them beforehand, made the decision and then pulled the trigger himself. Throughout Vichada he was a potent, almost mythical symbol; his repeated escapes from death made him emblematic of the Guerilla's supposed invincibility. I remembered Trigeño's words: cut the head off a snake and its body might thrash around wildly, but eventually it would die. Killing Caraquemada would be the true end to all this. And the death of a single man would prevent thousands more.

PART NINE

THE WORK OF OTHER MEN

146

IF I'D DOUBTED Rafael had phoned Beta, by morning parade I was sure of it. Rafael had been on guard duty at the northern post. He wasn't answering his radio.

'He's gone,' reported Pantera.

At first I assumed he'd defected to Beta's camp. But then Pantera found Rafael's uniform folded neatly under his rifle. He'd deserted. It all made sense. He'd never believed in the Autodefensas. He'd simply wanted revenge on Buitre.

With Rafael's departure, my mood seemed to lift. I realised I'd been spending too much time on the base, focused on Buitre with my own claustrophobic thoughts clouding the lens of my judgment.

Once out on the open highway on my way to visit Colonel Buitrago, with fresh air whipping my face, seeing ordinary citizens going about their daily business, the lens pulled back and the bigger picture opened up. These people could now walk freely, talk freely and live without fear because of what we'd achieved.

When I reached Garbanzos plaza I saw a crowd gathered around a temporary wooden stage covered with Don Felix's electoral posters. Technicians were mounting speakers and sound testing a microphone while Felix's supporters distributed flyers. Felix himself was leaning against the stage holding a sheaf of papers and practising his speech. Coca-Cola and Pantera – his assigned bodyguards that day – stood on either side of him, scanning bystanders attentively.

I honked my horn and waved.

This was what we'd been fighting for: the right of ordinary citizens to vote and decide for themselves how they wanted society governed rather than having a doctrine imposed on them at gunpoint.

Why had I begun doubting myself over the death of one man? Now was not the time for last-minute questioning. We were almost there.

'So have you located the girl?' I asked eagerly when I was seated across the desk from Buitrago in his office.

The normally dour Buitrago's eyes were sparkling with excitement. 'We have. We're already intercepting her phone and have her apartment under physical surveillance.'

Tita, he told me, belonged to a stable of high-class prostitutes – once-were, hoping-to-be and 'just-while-I'm-studying' models and TV presenters known as *prepagos* or 'pre-paids'. Police had been monitoring Tita's 'modelling agency' for years in pursuit of high-level cocaine traffickers.

Wealthy clients chose their girl from a catalogue of photos and then phoned for home visits. Jungle delivery to known terrorists or fugitive cocaine *capos* incurred a danger surcharge. If a client really liked a girl, she could turn *exclusiva*, like Tita had for Caraquemada. Her university tuition fees and the rent on her luxury apartment in the prestigious suburb of Rosales would be paid in cash by a corrupt Bogotá attorney. She would need to be ready to drop everything and travel when notified. The rest of her time would be her own.

Thanks to the information provided by Buitre, we knew Tita's next meeting with Caraquemada would be near Santo Paraíso and that Caraquemada's head of security would phone her five days in advance to specify the date. We also knew that she would have to arrive via the Garbanzos highway – the only road into the jungle.

'But how do we track her, Colonel?'

'For that, we'll need the North Americans. I'm seeking their permission to use their hardware and technology. They could provide us with a miniature GPS transponder and a Beechcraft surveillance plane to receive the signal. Provided they agree to help, my undercover operatives will follow Tita on her way to the rendezvous with Caraquemada, looking for an opportunity to plant the transponder on her. If we can get a good signal, we can direct you and Palillo to her final coordinates. But Pedro, there's a condition. I've worked with the North Americans before. They'll need this operation to remain small and will want to keep their hands clean, so no one can know, especially not the Autodefensas' high commanders. And that means you can't tell Trigeño.'

I nodded, disappointed I couldn't immediately share the good news with Trigeño but convinced that once we got Caraquemada his happiness would help him forgive me for keeping this a secret.

Our meeting was interrupted by a sharp knock at the door. It opened to reveal the concerned face of Buitrago's lieutenant, who beckoned the colonel over. 'I'm sorry, *mi coronel,* but it's an emergency.'

They spoke in whispers and then Buitrago turned to me, looking as though he'd seen a ghost. 'Six shots fired in Garbanzos plaza. Felix Velasquez was hit.'

While Buitrago went to the plaza, I sped to the hospital on my Yamaha, where Coca-Cola met me in the bare white waiting room of the emergency department. He was distraught and blaming himself.

The rally I'd passed earlier had been a resounding success. Felix's speech was met with cheers and applause. The *sicarios* had waited until Don Felix was at his most vulnerable – climbing down the small wooden ladder from the stage.

'There were two of them on a red motorbike, both wearing helmets,' said Coca-Cola. 'We didn't see them until the very last second, when their engine revved. People screamed and they mounted the sidewalk and sped towards the stage, shouting, "Death to Fascists." We drew our pistols and yelled to Don Felix, but he was on the ladder above us with his back turned and couldn't react in time. As soon as the shots were fired people scattered everywhere, running for their lives. We couldn't fire at the assassins – we might have hit a civilian. And we couldn't give chase because we had to apply pressure to Felix's wounds and bring him here.'

Felix was now in the operating theatre. He'd been hit twice – one bullet had entered his right lung and another was lodged in his left wrist. He'd suffered massive internal bleeding and lost consciousness within minutes. The nurses at reception didn't know whether he'd make it.

'Pantera is beside himself,' said Coca-Cola. 'He's in there right now, donating blood for Felix's transfusion.'

'It wasn't your fault,' I told him.

I sat in the waiting room, fretting over Felix. That day in the Llorona church, when he'd told me about the patchwork doll and invitation to his own funeral, I'd persuaded him to remain in the race and given my word to protect him. I'd taken the threat seriously, but I'd never imagined such a brazen daylight attack – not in the centre of Garbanzos, only four blocks from the army base. If he died it would be entirely my fault.

Buitrago arrived an hour later, also blaming himself. 'I should have assigned Felix some of my own men in addition to yours,' he said grimly.

He told me he'd called Yolanda Delgado – the left-wing candidate – and offered her around-the-clock protection. It would have been a tough call for Buitrago to make; she was also the human rights attorney who'd pushed for charges against him for neglect of duty.

'What did she say?'

'She responded sarcastically, "*Gracias*, Colonel. Just like you protected the villagers during the Puerto Galán massacre?" Then she hung up.'

Finally, after three hours, the surgeon came out in a blue robe, removing his rubber gloves and smiling. He told us Felix had been lucky. They'd removed the bullets and drained his lung of blood. He would be on a respirator for five days. He'd likely suffer nerve damage in his left hand but could otherwise expect a full recovery.

'Colonel,' said the surgeon. 'You can go in and interview him now. But five minutes only. My patient needs rest.'

Buitrago and I looked at each other; the colonel's face mirrored my own relief. Of course, on a personal level we were overjoyed Felix had survived, but while his life hung in the balance we'd remained silent on the drastic political ramifications for our region that were also at stake. It was only ten days before the elections. If Felix had died, Fabián would have won easily. However, his survival meant he could now turn this attack to his advantage. Attempted assassinations generate significant political capital.

On entering the intensive care unit, I was shocked to see the normally tanned and smiling Felix lying flat on his back, pale as death, with tubes connecting him to various machines.

'Don Felix,' I said, 'I'm so sorry this has happened. I feel responsible.'

'Don't! I took on the risk,' he said. 'But I now accept that it's over. After what happened to Mauricio and then that death threat they sent me, I was stupid to think I could run. I'm out. I'll stick to what I know: buses. It's a quieter life, but in these troubled times old age is a blessing.'

'But if you drop out, Fabián will win,' I said, my relief turning to alarm.

Buitrago grimaced. 'The region needs you, Don Felix. Please, I beg you to reconsider.'

'Yolanda Delgado would be Fabián's only remaining opposition,' I added. 'And she can't possibly win.'

'Maybe she deserves to,' Felix said. 'I don't like her, personally. And I disagree with her politics. But at least she's honest. And taking on the government and Autodefensas as she did after the *limpieza* – and even going after you, Colonel – proves she's brave.'

Buitrago, who'd bristled at the mention of Delgado's name, said nothing. I wanted to argue but couldn't keep pushing a man who'd nearly been killed to risk his life again.

The assassination attempt made national headlines. That night, as I sat depressed on the sofa watching TV with Palillo, the news flashed to a shot of the immaculately groomed Fabián Díaz flanked by supporters wearing matching yellow T-shirts with his slogan: Together We Will Triumph. He'd convened a media conference outside the gates of Javier's luxury hacienda.

'Today we're lucky not to be attending yet another funeral,' he declared, his delivery at once polished and passionate. 'Make no mistake – the cowardly Guerrilla did this! And they will try to destroy democracy again and again. But I am here to tell you that I will *not back down*. I will *not* be intimidated. I will *not* abandon my home town in its hour of need.'

I turned the television off and hurled the remote across the room.

The assassins' shout of 'Death to Fascists' had been a clever ruse, creating the impression that this was an attack by the Guerrilla. Publicly, even Buitrago was sticking to this official version, although we both knew that was unlikely. Caraquemada's *miliciano* network had been destroyed completely. The Guerrilla used bombs and ambushes to kill people, not *sicarios* on motorbikes. And besides, Caraquemada had little to gain by killing Felix – of the two pro-Autodefensa candidates, Felix was the more moderate. Taken together with Mauricio's 'accidental' death during the *limpieza*, the pattern was now obvious.

We had no proof, but as people say: when seeking the perpetrators of a carefully orchestrated crime, look no further than its main beneficiaries.

147

MARCH 12 MARKED my eighteenth birthday and two and a half years' service in the Autodefensas. The elections were four days away. Voting would be held over two days, on the Saturday and Sunday. It would be my first time casting a ballot, but with Felix recuperating in hospital, it was hard to become enthusiastic. As for my birthday, even though my moon boot had come off and I was now able to walk normally – albeit with a slight limp – I struggled to find anything worth celebrating.

Over the past week, a legion of new Autodefensas had flocked into Garbanzos to join the Black Scorpions under Beta's direct command. They camped on Javier's lawn, called Beta *patrón* and had no idea who I was, or what I'd done. Dozens of experienced soldiers had defected from other *bloques*, strengthening my suspicion that they'd been lured here by the higher salaries paid by the Díazes. The majority, however, were young soldiers rushed through training, who knew very little about the sacrifices we'd made to wrest back control of the river villages. They simply treated the Autodefensas as a job, following Beta's instructions to make it known that every adult resident must register and vote. The more Beta's troop numbers increased, the more convinced I became that he might be planning to break away from Trigeño and form his own *bloque*.

With Don Felix no longer campaigning, Yolanda Delgado was Fabián's only remaining competitor. Her electoral slogan was *Por La Verdad* – For the Truth. At first, however, Beta hadn't seen her as a threat.

'She'll be lucky to get five per cent of the vote,' he'd told me wryly. 'But it's important for Fabián to have competitors, at least on paper.'

Clearly, Beta believed Felix's supporters would automatically transfer their allegiance to Fabián. But that didn't happen. The latest telephone polls indicated Delgado's support had surged to thirty per cent, making her a possible contender. She also had strong backing in the mountains and the river villages – people who didn't own phones and weren't represented in the polls.

I'd planned to spend the morning of my birthday at a security meeting with Buitrago. Since the Guerrilla were notorious for intimidating voters and disrupting elections, Buitrago planned to run extra patrols around the outskirts of Llorona and Puerto Galán starting the following day. With my forces and Valderrama's in the south, the Autodefensas would provide an additional layer of security. However, the colonel had called late the previous evening to cancel; he'd been summoned to Bogotá for an urgent meeting with his generals.

'It sounds important,' he'd said. 'I'm not sure whether they're going to grant my request for more men, or fire me.'

Instead, I went to the town hall with my birth certificate to register on the electoral roll. *Perhaps I'll vote for Delgado,* I thought. Technically, she was the Autodefensas' political opposition. But anyone would be better than Fabián Díaz and his lapdog, Beta.

Mid-morning I visited Don Felix in the hospital. Thankfully, his condition was now stable. As I was leaving the ward I received a phone call from Old Man Domino. I hadn't seen him since his drunken checkers tirade, but he now sounded lucid.

'You promised to visit me two weeks ago,' he said. 'But this time you can't back out. Iván and Gloria have baked you a birthday cake.'

I accepted the invitation.

Turning in at the gap in the white fence, I saw Gloria kneeling by a rose bush, clipping pink blooms. Iván stood nearby, emptying a huge watering can onto the garden bed. They both waved as I dismounted. The smell of baking wafted from the kitchen window.

Eating calmly under the oak tree surrounded by friends reminded me of happy days on our *finca* when Papá and I would return from fixing the irrigation pipes, our appetites sharpened by hours of work, to share a delicious lunch served by Mamá.

After they'd sung me 'Happy Birthday', Old Man Domino led me behind the house, past his dilapidated wooden barn to a tall, recently constructed aluminium-roofed shed.

'This probably isn't the birthday present you had in mind,' he said, 'but you're eighteen now, and that means you could go to prison.'

He rolled open the door. Inside were five massive bright yellow vehicles – a bulldozer, steamroller, grader, dump truck and cement mixer, each with huge, thick pneumatic tyres that came up to my shoulder. Since August

I'd witnessed these same vehicles coming and going from Puerto Princesa, though much less frequently in recent weeks.

'At first I was happy to let Javier's subcontractors store their valuable machinery on my land,' Old Man Domino said. 'After all, it was to help the highway get built, and they promised to pay me rent. But apart from what they spent on this shed, I haven't seen a peso. And I don't see any highway either.'

I nodded, waiting for Old Man Domino to get to his point. So far, this was nothing new; everyone knew the Díaz brothers had pocketed the funds and probably had no intention of building the road.

'You have to open your eyes, *muchacho*, and see what sort of men you're involved with before it's too late,' he said.

'But what did you mean by prison? I have nothing to do with the Díazes stealing government money.'

'This goes way deeper than fraud.'

Old Man Domino explained that for the first few months the heavy machinery had driven out every morning and returned at dusk to his shed. Once a month the vehicles were loaded onto semi-trailers and sent to Bogotá for maintenance.

'Then two months ago, the routine changed,' he said. 'The machines still drive down to Puerto Princesa, but only on Tuesdays. So if they're not being used to construct the highway, why are they now being transported north for service *once a week*?'

I looked at Old Man Domino, realising what he was trying to tell me without saying it directly: the machinery was being used to transport cocaine.

'Whatever decision you make, Pedro, please keep me out of it. This is occurring on my land, but I'm old and I'm not moving again. I intend to die in my own house, in my own bed and of natural causes.'

'*Gracias*,' I said. 'Leave this with me.'

After dark I pulled back into Old Man Domino's driveway, this time armed with a torch and toolkit. If there was contraband hidden in the machinery, I was determined to find it. But it wouldn't be easy. It might be anywhere – deep within the engine or in a compartment behind a false panel. However, all the components were welded or bolted into place, and it would require specialised tools to remove them.

First I pried open the grader's fuel cap, shone my torch inside and peered into the tank but saw only gasoline. Next I lay flat on my back beneath the bulldozer – its belly plating was impenetrable steel.

Positioning a nail between the treads of the steamroller's rear tyre, I hammered it in. The nail penetrated only three centimetres before striking metal and bending. I was no mechanic but it didn't take a genius to know pneumatic tyres don't contain steel inserts. I tried the same tyre again, only this time from the inside rim with a Stanley knife. The rubber was dense and after several minutes of twisting and gouging, the blade bent and then snapped. I'd almost given up when I saw a cordless drill on a workbench. I inserted the long spinning drill bit slowly into the tyre, watching as it spat out thin curls of shredded rubber and then plastic. When I pulled the drill bit out, its tip emerged flecked with white powder.

I stood there, astounded. If every tyre on the five vehicles was stuffed with narcotics, it might amount to tonnes. And who knew what other components might be filled?

Ever since my conversation with Rafael, I'd been wondering how the Guerrilla transported their cocaine. Now I knew; they were packing it into these vehicles in Puerto Princesa.

Later, I discovered exactly how their system worked. The cocaine, compressed into blocks and vacuum-wrapped in layers of industrial plastic, was collected from the processing laboratories south of Santo Paraíso. It was transferred across river to Puerto Princesa and camouflaged within the machinery then driven to Old Man Domino's *finca*. The semi-trailers then collected the vehicles for transport to coastal ports for international shipping and to private runways for flights to Central America.

The scheme was simple yet ingenious. At inland checkpoints, anti-narcotics police would have little reason to suspect machinery owned by the subcontractors of a legitimate construction company that had been awarded the tender for an important government highway. In the event that the semi-trailers were waved into a weighing station, the additional cargo would be negligible among tonnes of heavy equipment. A thorough inspection would take forever, requiring customised tools to remove the tyres, belly plates and fuel tanks.

Of course, right then, I didn't realise the full extent of the operation. I only knew that Caraquemada could not be doing this alone. At a minimum it would require the complicity of the drivers, supervisors and management of the construction company. And how could Javier and Fabián not be involved? Javier's protestations of innocence and performance of dismay at not knowing how to get rid of the four tonnes in the bunker had been masterful, but I would never again be fooled.

I pressed the chips of rubber back into the hole, hoping it wouldn't be noticeable during the next 'maintenance check', and I dialled Buitrago.

Unfortunately, since the machinery belonged to their subcontractor, this wasn't the absolute proof we needed to bring down the Díazes. And of course, Buitrago couldn't impound the vehicles immediately without implicating Old Man Domino. However, he could at least search the semi-trailers when they next moved north through his checkpoint and discover the cocaine 'by accident'. Having the vehicles impounded with multiple arrests and national media coverage mentioning the Díazes might provide the scandal we needed just in time to prevent Fabián from winning the election.

When Buitrago's phone went straight to voicemail, I kicked the ground in frustration and racked my brain, wondering who else I could turn to. Only then did Don Felix's words come back to me about someone who was brave. Someone who was honest. Someone who, maybe, deserved to win.

148

YOLANDA DELGADO'S CAMPAIGN 'headquarters' was a tiny, cramped office off the main plaza in Llorona. At 7.30 pm I rode past it, parked the bike three blocks away, put on a cap and walked back briskly, wary of being seen.

I didn't know Delgado. I'd never met her. She'd been born in Puerto Galán but left for Bogotá to practise law. Following the *limpieza* she'd returned and set up office in Llorona, gathering witness statements for her class action, and then decided to run for office.

I wasn't even sure she'd talk to me. By contacting her, I knew the risk I was taking – Delgado was our political rival. But by then I didn't care. My cause was the Autodefensas, not Fabián Díaz and Beta. Nevertheless, if news of my visit got back to Trigeño the consequences would be dire.

The door was open but at first I thought I'd come to the wrong place. There were no glossy posters in the windows. Inside, there were no festive streamers, no banners, no bustling team wearing brightly coloured T-shirts. Delgado had no electoral security team, only a single staff member – a young man in jeans and a collared shirt photocopying pamphlets.

A plump, earnest-looking woman in her mid-forties sat behind a desk dressed in a faded blue business suit. She wore thick spectacles but no make-up or jewellery. Her black curly hair was tied back tightly in a bun. Three towers of manila folders on her desk were stacked higher than her head.

Based on appearances and resources, she was no match for the well-heeled, photogenic Fabián Díaz. But I realised quickly what she may have lacked in beauty, armed bodyguards and campaign funding, she made up for in intelligence, courage and efficiency, as well as fearless supporters.

She was pounding the keys on a laptop so furiously that at first I believed she hadn't noticed me enter.

'Señora Delgado?' I inquired politely, standing in front of her. When she didn't look up, I continued. 'My name is Pedro Juan—'

'I know *exactly* who you are,' she said, tapping a small monitor beside her laptop then pointing to two CCTV cameras mounted on the walls before resuming her typing. 'And if you're here to kill me then you should know you're being recorded remotely and the witness statements in these folders are already with the *Fiscalía*.'

'I'm also filming,' said the young man, and I turned to see that he was aiming a mini video camera at me. 'So you'll have to shoot me too.'

'You've got it wrong!' I said defensively. 'I'm here to help you. I believe we're fighting for the same thing.'

'Are we?' she said acidly, finally looking up. 'I highly doubt that. But since your mother and I attended primary school together . . .' She tapped her watch. 'I'll give you sixty seconds of my time. Speak.'

I glanced at her assistant. He lowered the camera but it was clear he wouldn't leave his boss on her own, so I was forced to speak in front of him.

'*Señora*, I have something that may be of interest to you. I'd like you to come up with me now, and please bring that camera. The evidence is located near my family's *finca*.'

'Which is right next to your illegal paramilitary base on the Díaz property.' She laughed ironically and glanced at my Smith & Wesson. 'Will I also be meeting with your boss, Beta?'

'Beta's not my boss. Neither are the Díazes. In fact, the evidence I have is against them.'

'*Gracias*,' she said, 'but I have all the proof I need linking them to the massacre.'

'But not enough to stop Fabián winning the election. Your court case will take years. By then it will be too late.'

'True justice takes time. I can wait.'

'*Señora*, please. I promise you no harm.' I laid my pistol on her desk. 'Come with me now. Take this and return it to me afterwards.'

'Danilo,' she said, pulling her office keys from the drawer and tossing them to her assistant, 'you can lock up and go home.'

Then she stood, stepped into a pair of low heels with black bows and turned to me.

'Señor Gutiérrez, my own death I accepted years ago.' She handed me back my pistol. 'But that doesn't mean I believe in violence.'

Delgado followed me to Old Man Domino's property in her rusted-out white sedan, its single headlight flickering intermittently. Inside the shed,

I explained the dubious maintenance runs, and then she began recording. Holding my torch in my mouth, and being careful not to show my face in the frame, I once again drilled into the tyre, and once again the drill bit came out tipped with white powder.

Delgado stood there shaking her head, although hardly surprised.

'Stealing from their own country. Exporting misery to another. The very definition of multinational efficiency.'

'So you think you can use this?' I asked.

'As evidence, it's thin as smoke,' she said, now filming the vehicles, their plate numbers and subcontractors' logos. 'But that doesn't mean I can't shout *fire*.'

'What exactly will you do?'

'Fabián is so confident he'll win that he challenged me to a live radio debate this Friday. I didn't respond.' She ejected the tape and held it up. 'But now I will.'

149

THE FOLLOWING MORNING – Thursday – I received a call from Colonel Buitrago's assistant. 'The colonel has returned from Bogotá. He's requesting a meeting with you at his private residence.'

I'd never been to the colonel's home; it was a small, austerely furnished apartment within the army barracks. I almost did a double take when Buitrago greeted me at the door dressed in jeans and a white T-shirt. I'd never seen him out of uniform. In fact, as he led me inside past framed photos hanging on the wall – of his children at different ages and the colonel in uniform at various promotion ceremonies – I realised I knew nothing of his personal life.

'Your wife's beautiful,' I said, pausing to admire a picture of a young Buitrago kissing his bride on the steps of a church.

'Ex-wife,' he corrected me. 'I don't need to tell you that military life is tough on women.'

In the dining room, a bottle of single malt whisky was sitting on the table.

'Are we celebrating?' I asked. 'Are the generals sending you more men?'

Buitrago shook his head and pointed to the bedroom where empty moving boxes lined the carpet. 'Quite the opposite,' he said despondently. 'Twenty-seven years of loyal service and they give me my marching orders. I'm being transferred effective ten days from now.'

'What?' I said in dismay. 'They can't do that!'

'They can and they did. I was saving this for when we got Caraquemada,' he added, reaching for the whisky bottle. 'But we might as well open it now.'

My heart sank as I contemplated the consequences. If Buitrago left and Fabián seized power, he'd ensure Beta took charge of Llorona and the river villages. I'd have no control – that is, if I were even allowed to stay on. The pressure on farmers to sell land to the Díazes below market value, the disappearances of dissenters and the abuses against civilians would continue completely unchecked.

All wasn't yet lost. Fabián's seat in the Senate was no longer assured – not after my meeting with Yolanda Delgado. But even if elected, she was unlikely to help save Buitrago's job; she was the one who had pushed for charges against the colonel for 'neglect of duty' over the *limpieza*.

Before he could twist the cap off the whisky, the colonel's phone rang. 'Excuse me for a minute,' he said, stepping into the bedroom to take the call.

I heard him talking in a low voice. When he returned, standing erect, it was as though I were looking at a new man.

He snatched the whisky off the table. 'Looks like this bottle's fate will be decided five days from now – along with our own!' he said, shelving it in a cabinet then pulling on his khaki shirt. 'That was my colleague in Bogotá. Caraquemada's lover, Tita, just received a phone call. The rendezvous has been arranged for Tuesday night. The North Americans have agreed to send us a Beechcraft surveillance plane and lend us three Blackhawks. We have only one shot at this, Pedro. This is make or break.'

Bringing down the region's highest Guerrilla commander would make him a national hero; his generals couldn't transfer him. In fact, after such a victory he could demand whatever resources he needed. And with Delgado's interview the following evening, the scandal could be enough to tip the election. Buitrago might find it difficult working alongside Delgado, but Fabián would be defeated and Beta ejected from the towns for good.

'And your own news?' asked Buitrago. 'Your voicemail said it was urgent.'

I told him about the earth-moving equipment. The colonel doubted it would be enough to bring the Díazes down. 'An investigation would take months. A court case could take years.'

But it was worth a try. The colonel promised to search and then impound the machinery on its next journey through his checkpoint in Garbanzos.

However, riding back to the base, I checked in on Old Man Domino and the barn and phoned Buitrago back immediately.

'It's gone! The shed's empty. They've moved it.'

'Let's hope they're not on to us,' he said grimly. 'We've underestimated the Díazes and Beta before. One of my lieutenants is dating a kitchen hand at Javier's hacienda. She said that every mealtime she washes three hundred plates. Pedro, you need to watch your back.'

On the Friday at 6 pm, Yolanda Delgado went on local Garbanzos radio for her joint interview with Fabián Díaz. It was supposed to be a civilised, supervised debate in which the announcer asked each candidate for their respective views on various topics. Delgado knew it was all a grandiose, well-orchestrated show in which she was cast as a dull background prop to make its star, Fabián, shine brighter.

'Why should people vote for you?' asked the interviewer.

'Because I'm not a cocaine trafficker,' she said, 'and, if elected, I am offering to work without a salary. If people open their eyes, they'll see work promised by my opponent – and paid for with our hard-earned taxes – has hardly begun. Bulldozers, steamrollers and graders sit idle next to widening potholes. Meanwhile, Fabián's head of electoral security, the same man who supervised the Puerto Galán massacre, is parading around town without a single charge against him. Armed men under his control escort those same vehicles up from Puerto Princesa to Llorona, and I have evidence proving the machinery is laden with tonnes of cocaine—'

Suddenly, the interview was interrupted by a beer advertisement. Afterwards, the station played a song. I continued listening, hoping for an explanation but the announcer returned as though nothing had happened.

An hour later the station ceased broadcasting local news, switching instead to a live feed from a national station.

That was the Friday night. The elections would be conducted over the next two days. Thousands of people listened to the radio. Those who didn't would quickly hear the news. I prayed to God that Delgado's on-air accusation might just be enough to tip the balance against Fabián. Because if it didn't, I'd risked my life fighting to evict the Guerrilla from our region, only to help two cocaine traffickers and their malignant private army take their place.

On Saturday I walked to the polling booth at our old primary school in Llorona, where green-uniformed policemen and Buitrago's soldiers stood guarding the perimeter, searching bags for weapons and explosives. Transportadores Díaz had offered free bus rides for those travelling to vote, and I watched as a caravan of *colectivos* and *chivas* – festooned with gold, blue and red streamers and posters of Fabián on their sides – ferried in scores of *campesinos* from the river villagers and outlying regions.

As passengers disembarked, an army of yellow-shirted supporters thrust *How To Vote* flyers into their hands. A sixteen-year-old with a military crew cut – one of Beta's soldiers – blocked my path.

'Here!' He reached into a sack and held out a cellular phone. 'Take this!'

'What for?'

'Once you've filled out the form correctly, you point the camera lens and press this button here. Show the photo to my colleague over there on your way out. Then collect your *recompensa*.'

The *reward* was either ten dollars cash or fifteen dollars' worth of groceries. I waved the boy away, disgusted that Fabián was now resorting to outright bribery. However, once I was in the privacy of the partitioned booth, I was pleased to see the name of Felix Velasquez still on the ballot. He'd withdrawn from campaigning, but evidently his candidature had not officially been deregistered. Surely people weren't stupid. Seeing Felix's name would be yet another reminder to them of the sequence of dirty tactics used by Fabián. I ticked the box next to Delgado's name, praying other voters would see sense and do the same.

At 6.15 pm, when polling stations had closed for the day, Palillo called me from the Llorona bridge.

'Get down here now! You need to see this.'

Dusk was falling as I sped downhill from our base in the pick-up. In the fading light, a lone policeman was trying to disperse a crowd that had gathered around a body propped up against a rock beneath the bridge. It was riddled with bullet wounds, staining the victim's white shirt and green polyester jacket with vivid splashes of blood. The lips were sewn together with blue thread and the head lolled back to one side. In fact, the face was so covered in blood as to be unrecognisable.

'Who is he?' I asked Palillo. But even as I spoke I went cold as I recognised the low heels with black bows, one of which had come off and lay several feet further down towards the water. And then I saw the card with the Black Scorpions logo placed beside what I now realised was the body of a woman.

'Who do you think?'

150

DELGADO'S HORRIFIC DEATH was the final straw for me. Of course, I felt responsible; I'd furnished her with the information that led to her death. But this was not about me. Beta had gone too far. The Black Scorpions were as bad as the Guerrilla, if not worse. Allowing opposing political candidates to stand was supposed to be proof that the Autodefensas believed in democracy and free speech.

Beta had done this out of spite. And he'd done it openly and brazenly, using his own logo as a message to the public that from here on in there would be absolutely no opposition permitted. Not a single word of criticism would be tolerated. The Black Scorpions would rule the region with iron fists and lead bullets for anyone who spoke out. He'd also left that card because he *wanted* the authorities to know he was above the law and could not be touched.

Everyone knew the Black Scorpions were a branch of the Autodefensas. And that meant Beta was defiling everything we stood for. I had to inform Trigeño. He needed to know he had traitors within his fold. But I would have to be careful. After the elections I still needed to live in Llorona, and without Colonel Buitrago I would have little protection against Beta. I decided I would cast my suspicions directly on the Díazes, mentioning Beta only in passing.

'Is it urgent?' said Trigeño when he picked up.

'Several things have been weighing on me lately, *patrón*.'

'Then speak your mind. You and I, we have no secrets, remember? Speak!'

'I can't, *patrón*. Not over the phone.'

He sighed. 'If it's that serious, I'll come to you first thing tomorrow.'

'I need our talk to be confidential. Can we meet at my Papá's *finca*, *patrón*? And if anyone finds out afterwards, please tell them it was a friendly surprise visit.'

Despite my intention to implicate the Díazes rather than Beta directly, I realised that Beta would still get word. And since he knew about the cocaine on my base, he wouldn't have to slit my throat. He could turn things around on me by telling Trigeño himself.

I needed to get rid of the cocaine immediately. But how?

Suddenly, an idea occurred to me. How could I have been so blind? Perhaps it was because the cocaine had seemed so valuable. And when you're guarding an asset that is worth more than any amount of money you've ever contemplated, you assume that asset should not, in fact *cannot*, be destroyed.

I phoned Javier Díaz. 'You need to get up here right now. I don't care what you do with this shit, but I want it off my base.'

'But it's elections,' Javier protested. 'There are police and officials everywhere.'

'Exactly! After what Delgado said on radio about Fabián being a trafficker, Buitrago is making noises. This is your property and there are rumours from Bogotá of an independent raid. So you've got two choices: either you come up here with your men before midnight and remove it, or I'll have my own men slit every brick open and toss it all into the river.'

'You can't! It's worth millions!'

'Maybe it is . . . to *you*. But to me it's worth nothing.'

Javier arrived at 11 pm with three trucks and ten workers wearing balaclavas. By then my men were asleep and I refused to help. Javier stood near the henhouse watching them load the trucks, smoking a cigar. I kept my distance, knowing he'd only grumble and complain, playing dumb and trying to convince me he was still innocent. I doubted he had anything to do with Delgado's death – he was a businessman and murder was bad for business. However, I didn't care either way. Whether he knew or not, they were all in this together.

As Javier departed I felt cleansed, and with a four-tonne weight lifted from my chest I could breathe much easier. It had taken Javier barely an hour to load and move the cocaine, and I now knew he could have done so at any time.

For months he'd refused to remove it in order to keep it as an insurance policy against me breaking my silence. I'd kept my word and held my tongue, even as I'd accumulated suspicions, heard accusations and witnessed crimes that could no longer be ignored. But with the cocaine gone, Javier's insurance policy was now torn to shreds and I was free to speak my mind. All of it could now come out. And all of it would.

The following morning, I walked a kilometre over the fields to my own family's *finca*. Only two weeks earlier, after I'd captured Buitre and before the assassination attempt on Felix, I'd hoped Mamá would very soon be able to return and live here. But all that was now in doubt. Delgado's assassination meant Fabián's victory was assured. And with Beta's escalating military power and Buitrago's transfer imminent, it might not be safe to remain in the region after the elections – neither for me nor my family. There was still a faint hope. Once Trigeño knew what was happening locally, he could remove Beta. He could also force Fabián to stand aside. But all that depended on convincing Trigeño to take action – no small feat when I had little direct proof and enemies who eliminated anyone who spoke a single word against them.

At 8 am Trigeño's helicopter touched down on the freshly mown lawn at my *finca*, and he emerged, smiling and friendly.

'Walk with me, Pedro,' he said, putting his arm over my shoulder and leading me away from his men towards the barn. 'What's troubling you?'

'I'm concerned that Beta is getting too close to the Díazes. He's rarely out of their sight.'

'Because I told him to keep a close eye on them. I trust these brothers less than you do.'

'I saw a woman yesterday who'd been executed and had her lips sewn together. She was an independent candidate, running against Fabián Díaz.' I hesitated, knowing that once I voiced my accusations there would be no turning back. '*Patrón*, I think the Díazes are eliminating their political and business rivals. Not just the Guerrilla like we planned, but also loyal men from our own alliance and anyone who stands in their way. First Mauricio, then Felix, now this woman Delgado.'

Trigeño stopped walking. 'And you think Beta is assisting them? That's a very serious allegation.'

'True, but I'm not sure what else to believe. This was found beside the body,' I said, handing over the Black Scorpions card. '*Patrón*, I think the Díazes are dirty. There were rumours about Humberto Díaz trafficking cocaine and working closely with the Guerrilla. His sons always seem to have a lot of money.'

'What exactly are you insinuating? We trust each other more than this, Pedro. Be direct!'

'Delgado claimed on-air that Beta was responsible for supervising the *limpieza*. She implied that Fabián has stolen money paid to him to build the highway and that he was using earth-moving equipment to transport tonnes of cocaine—'

'She said *what*?'

I repeated Delgado's accusation. Trigeño frowned with annoyance.

'Then Beta is more hotheaded than I thought. Delgado has made defamatory and ridiculous claims before. But killing her will make them appear true and bring the spotlight onto Fabián.'

'I'm sorry to have dumped all this on you, *patrón*. Maybe I'm being paranoid. It's simply that I saw Beta behaving so . . . independently.'

'Beta is loyal,' said Trigeño. 'Both to me and to the Autodefensas. And also to you. He brought you Ernesto, didn't he? And he asked me to transfer Rafael to your unit, which allowed you to catch Buitre.'

Somehow I managed to contain my shock. So Trigeño had known all along! Beta and Javier had lied to me, making me think these were secrets they'd deliberately kept from Trigeño at great danger to themselves, and to me. And it had worked. I'd spent weeks tiptoeing around Trigeño and pushing back his visit, fearing it would all come out. But there had been no danger whatsoever; Trigeño had not only known, he'd authorised it.

My anger at them knew no bounds. In fact, it was compounded by anger at myself for being so stupid. The only true leverage they'd had was Humberto's cocaine, which they'd cleverly made me feel complicit in guarding. Although even that now seemed foolish; I could have told Trigeño the day I found it and none of this would have happened.

Fortunately, I'd saved my most damning insinuation for last.

'That's true, *comando*. Perhaps I've been worrying unnecessarily. It's just that I've heard of internal wars in other *bloques* where one of the commanders turns rogue, splitting away and taking his men with him. I didn't want that to happen to you. With Beta having accumulated three hundred soldiers on Javier's hacienda who are more loyal to him than to the Autodefensas, I thought maybe . . .'

Trigeño froze. 'I only authorised one hundred.'

He stood riveted to the spot. Dark storm clouds passed over his face, but he controlled them and spoke calmly.

'Thank you for sharing this, Pedro. I only wish my other commanders were so conscientious and loyal. I'll phone Beta now to make enquiries.

Don't worry! I'll make sure they won't lead back to you. And if I find a hint of evidence that the Díazes are involved in the drug business or killing people behind our backs, our deal is over. They'll be dealt with severely. As soon as I know something, you will too. You're my eyes and ears down here. I'm as proud of you as if you were my own son.'

As Trigeño's helicopter took off, I waved goodbye, completely reassured that Beta would be reined in. I couldn't have been more wrong.

151

ON SUNDAY EVENING, as polling booths were closing, Buitrago called me with an urgent request.

'I need you to bring Old Man Domino and his wife to my base immediately. Beta's men have just dragged Delgado's assistant at gunpoint from his parents' home. If they're murdering anyone who could corroborate Delgado's accusation about the cocaine, then Beta may already be on his way up.'

'Shit!' I threw the Toyota keys to Palillo. 'We're leaving right now.'

'And Pedro . . .' The colonel paused. 'I've also sent men to collect your mother. The Díazes may not simply be *killing* witnesses. If they're now searching for the source of the leak, Beta may interrogate them first.'

I hadn't told Buitrago about my secret meeting with Delgado, but he must have guessed.

I felt myself go cold. Delgado's assistant, Danilo, had been present when I'd visited her campaign headquarters. Given Beta's predilection for torture, it would only be a matter of time before he discovered that I'd offered to give her evidence against the Diazes and told her to bring her camera. And then we'd all be in danger – not just me, but my whole family.

As Palillo and I sped down the road, my heart raced and I prayed we'd reach Old Man Domino's in time. I had no idea what Trigeño had said to Beta that morning, but it clearly hadn't worked. In fact, it had only inflamed him and made him more determined to resolve problems the way he knew best – by eliminating anyone who posed a threat.

On the way I phoned Trigeño. The call rang out and went to voicemail. I left a frantic message: 'Buitrago just phoned. Beta kidnapped Delgado's assistant! You need to stop him, *patrón*.'

At first Old Man Domino refused to leave, even when I apologised profusely – it was my fault they were both in danger – and Gloria began crying and imploring her husband not to be stupid.

'Let them come,' he declared drunkenly, grabbing his shotgun from the cupboard, loading it with two cartridges and sitting in his armchair with a bottle of *aguardiente*. 'I've lived a good life.'

'Sorry, *viejo*,' said Palillo, scooping him up, 'but this town has had enough martyrs for one weekend and your wife needs you alive a little longer.'

In case Beta was on his way and crossed our path, we needed to conceal our passengers. We bundled them onto a layer of blankets in the tray of the pick-up between drums of gasoline, with Old Man Domino still protesting and refusing to relinquish his shotgun. Then we stretched a blue tarpaulin over the top and tied it down.

I sped downhill, relaxing slightly as we turned onto the long, smooth, straight highway. But my relief was short-lived. I tensed again at the sight of three vehicles ahead, approaching us at speed. I gripped the steering wheel tighter as they drew closer, and I saw precisely what I'd feared: Beta's red SUV.

Beta must have recognised my vehicle in turn because he extended his arm through the window, signalling me to stop.

There was no point in speeding past him – the two rear vehicles loaded with soldiers could easily swerve in front of me and block my path. I slowed and pulled up alongside Beta, winding down my window and then easing my hand towards my pistol. I assumed that he was on his way to Old Man Domino's farm, but if Delgado's assistant had already talked he could just as easily be coming for me.

'Where are you racing off to,' said Beta, cocky as always, 'on a lovely, quiet Sunday evening like this?' He craned his neck and peered into the cabin of my truck.

I had to think quickly. Beta was sly; he'd detect any lie immediately. There was no point in playing stupid. So I decided to be open and go on the attack.

'It *was* a quiet evening until you ruined it. Murdering Delgado was stupid enough. But kidnapping her assistant only makes us, and Fabián, look much worse.'

Beta didn't even bother denying it. 'News travels fast.' He chuckled then leaned through his window aggressively. 'What business is it of yours?'

'Buitrago made it my business. He just called, furious; he's threatening to raid Javier's hacienda and call the media. I'm on my way to his base. I need to calm him down and you need to return Delgado's assistant.'

'That's not going to happen.' Beta laughed and pointed over his shoulder. 'But you can say hi to him if you want.'

Danilo was in the back seat. My gaze locked with his, and his terrified eyes widened with recognition. His mouth opened, his face pleading for help. I swallowed hard, sweating now, and clicked my pistol off safety, all the while trying to act casual. Clearly, Beta had no suspicion I'd ever met his hostage. But one word from Danilo and that could change in an instant.

I was trembling and my mouth was dry, but I had to keep up the act. 'So what do I tell Buitrago? And what happens if Trigeño finds out?'

Beta's eyes narrowed. 'He won't, but you've raised a good point. This morning I received a curious phone call from Trigeño. We made sure nothing about Delgado's unfortunate accident came out in the media. But Trigeño already knew. You wouldn't happen to know how he found out so quickly?'

I'd dug myself into a hole and hardly knew how to respond. Luckily, my phone vibrated on the dashboard and its screen lit up: Trigeño. Beta and I stared at the phone.

'You want to answer that?' he said, eyeing me suspiciously.

I pressed ACCEPT CALL.

'Pedro,' said Trigeño. 'I got your message. What's going on—?'

'I'm fine, *patrón*. I'm here with Beta,' I interjected, hoping Trigeño would take the hint and realise that I couldn't speak freely. 'Buitrago's threatening all-out war against the Autodefensas. Beta and I are working together to defuse the situation.'

'Put him on.'

I handed the phone through the window to Beta, so I could only hear his side of the conversation, which Trigeño repeatedly interrupted.

'Yes, *patrón*, I'm aware it's the elections—'

'Yes, *patrón*, but Buitrago's mistaken. I swear to you I don't have him.'

'Copy that, *patrón*. Sending Pedro now.'

He hung up and stared confidently into my eyes. He'd just lied openly to the highest commander of the Autodefensas – my boss and his own. He knew I'd heard that lie, and yet he was unapologetic and unafraid.

'Your orders are to reassure the colonel that we have nothing to do with this boy's disappearance but we're doing everything in our power to locate the perpetrators and liberate him,' he said. Then his voice dropped and his tone became menacing. 'Just remember, Pedro, you have everything here. Your *finca*, your family and a job. Seven days from now, Buitrago won't be here to protect you. Trigeño's troops are stationed far away. So before you make that next call, think about where your loyalty is best placed.' He tossed the phone back through my window and yelled to the second vehicle, 'To the old man's farm.' Then he waved his arm forward and sped off.

I looked in my rear-view mirror, watching the tail-lights of Beta's convoy receding.

'You can't save that kid,' said Palillo. 'So for fuck's sake drive!'

I accelerated, my whole body shaking. I was relieved Beta hadn't found Old Man Domino and Gloria. At the same time I was trying not to panic. Now that Danilo had seen me, how long would it take him to talk? *Not long,* I thought. Not if he believed it was his only chance to bargain for his life. Although, since he'd heard my demands to release him and knew I was on my way to Buitrago, maybe he'd be brave enough to hold out.

'We're fucked,' said Palillo. 'Completely *jodido*. Whether you tell Trigeño or not, this is going to be war.'

Thirty seconds passed with the gap between us and Beta's convoy continuing to widen; I began to think that maybe we were safe.

'*¡Mierda!*' said Palillo, looking back through the rear windscreen. 'They've stopped! They're turning. Go! Go! Go!'

I pressed the accelerator to the floor and we flew towards Garbanzos with Beta's caravan closing in on us from behind.

I had Palillo phone Buitrago. 'Emergency, Colonel,' he said. 'We're heading your way in a white pick-up with Beta and his men in pursuit. Three vehicles. Twelve men that I counted.'

When we reached the plaza and sped towards the T-junction where the base was located, I could see the gates to the army barracks in front of us were open and I thought we'd made it. But Beta must have radioed ahead to his men in Garbanzos, and at the same moment a black SUV shot out from the street to our right and swerved in front of the gates to block our path. Six of Beta's Black Scorpions leaped out and pointed their rifles at us.

I slammed on the brakes; the wheels locked and we skidded to a stop, not twenty metres from safety.

Beta's caravan screeched to a halt behind us and his men piled out, also pointing their rifles.

I honked my horn and waved frantically to the gate guards. Then I heard Buitrago's voice over a loudspeaker.

'Leave your weapons in the vehicles. Exit slowly with your hands behind your heads, then lie flat on the ground.'

I looked for Buitrago and saw him emerge from the armoured booth beside the gate. Over fifty of his soldiers had Beta's men covered from multiple angles – from reinforced brick turrets high up on the walls and .50-calibre machine gun emplacements behind sandbags at both ends of the street.

Sullenly, Beta's men obeyed. Only Beta remained standing, still brandishing his pistol until Buitrago walked briskly towards him, rifle raised.

Beta laid his pistol on the road calmly, still cocky, smiling, and with no intention of lying down. He saluted Buitrago sarcastically.

'We'll leave peacefully, *mi coronel*,' he said. 'None of us wants a bloodbath on your doorstep.'

Palillo and I got out of our pick-up. 'Delgado's assistant is in the red truck,' I told the colonel.

Buitrago's men opened the door and pulled Danilo to safety.

'We rescued him for you, *mi coronel*,' said Beta facetiously.

'I'll bet you did,' said Buitrago. 'Tell your *patrón* our deal is over. I have six hundred soldiers. You have three hundred. You and your men have until 5 pm tomorrow to leave Garbanzos.'

'Maybe I will leave,' said Beta. 'But I'll be sure to return in a week, so Fabián Díaz and I can wave you – and Pedro – goodbye.'

Buitrago turned to me. 'Did you bring the others?'

I glanced nervously at Beta then tapped the side of the pick-up. 'You can come out now.'

Palillo stripped back the tarpaulin and Old Man Domino and Gloria sat up.

Shaking his head, Beta looked at me murderously and said very slowly, 'Son of a bitch.'

152

THE COLONEL USHERED us through the gates into the safety of his base. After ordering his lieutenant to organise beds for Old Man Domino, Gloria and Danilo, he led me and Palillo to his office where a cardboard box was already packed with his personal effects.

My nerves were still trembling. 'Is Mamá okay?'

'Your family is resting. They can all stay here until next Sunday, but after that they'll need to leave Garbanzos when I do . . .'

'But, Colonel! Beta just kidnapped Delgado's assistant. Surely that's enough to have him arrested and charged.'

'You think that kid will talk? He's shaking like a leaf. They murdered his boss. They know where he lives. His parents have already packed their suitcases. It's over, Pedro. The Díazes have won.'

Buitrago sat solemnly at his desk and pointed to the television screen. The polling booths were closed. Officials were finalising the tallies. In their excessive zeal, the Autodefensas had overdone it slightly, achieving a one hundred and seven per cent voter turnout in Vichada. Not only that, Fabián Díaz had received the highest percentage of votes in the region's history, with the dead Yolanda Delgado coming in second and Felix Velasquez third. Fabián's was not the only landslide victory. In provinces all around Colombia, his feat was being emulated by dozens of Autodefensa-backed candidates.

'But Fabián's been paying cash for votes and voting under the names of dead people. He had Beta shoot Felix Velasquez then assassinate Delgado. The brothers are traffickers. Colonel, we need to have these elections annulled.'

'Without proof, how?'

'At least denounce it to the authorities.'

Buitrago laughed. 'I'm one of them. Should I report myself for turning a blind eye? Should I report you for everything you've done?'

'Then we'll report it to Congress.'

'They *are* Congress,' said Buitrago, pointing again to the television where the new president, covered in confetti with his hand on his heart, was proclaiming victory and a new era of Democratic Security ahead.

'I'll testify. Go to prison if I have to. At the very least, Trigeño needs to know Beta lied to him outright about having kidnapped Delgado's assistant. I warned him about Beta this morning.'

'That wasn't so wise.'

'Why not?'

'You still believe Trigeño isn't aware of what's happening down here?'

'I'm positive. Not until I told him. But he now knows Beta is acting behind his back, funded by the Díazes. I told him they were traffickers. Trigeño could force Fabián to step down and concede the election to Felix Velasquez.'

'That won't happen. You're naïve, Pedro. We've both been played from the very beginning. This was their plan all along. They kept us while they needed us. But I was right – the cure was far worse than the cancer. And now I'm being transferred and you . . . You should get out safely, if you can, and move to Bogotá with your family.'

'Bogotá? What would I do in Bogotá? Where would we live? How would we survive? What would happen to our *finca*?'

I refused to believe it was over. I wanted to phone Trigeño – he could stop this – but Buitrago became angry and told me his base was in communications lockdown.

'Then what about Caraquemada? You said your generals and the North Americans would have to support you if we bring him down.'

The colonel nodded gravely. 'And they still might. But that's our only hope now. And it's a long shot. Even then it would take a minor miracle to prevent my transfer. Delgado brought those charges against me. The case was almost buried. But after her mentioning the *limpieza* on radio then being murdered the next day, they've reopened the investigation.' Buitrago glanced at me briefly, although there was no recrimination in his voice. Then he buried his face in his hands. We'd tried our best, but we were both responsible for bringing this plague upon our town.

Finally, he looked up wearily. 'Both of you should pray and then get some rest. Your kits are packed. You fly out tomorrow at dusk.'

153

IT WAS 5.45 pm on Monday when Buitrago began the mission briefing in a hangar at the airport. Palillo and I stood beside three sleek Blackhawk helicopters with our sniper rifles and backpacks as the sun went down beyond the sliding doors, casting an orange glow onto the colonel.

Tita, Caraquemada's lover, had phoned to reserve a taxi for 5.30 the following morning, her destination: El Dorado Airport. She was listed as a passenger under the name on her fake *cédula* on the 7.30 flight to Villavicencio.

From there, we assumed that she'd travel the same route to Santo Paraíso that Buitre had described, then be led by donkey to a *campesino* hut. But this time with one critical difference – Buitrago would have her bus pulled over at his checkpoint and, during a 'routine' bag search, a minuscule GPS transponder would be secreted in the lining of her handbag. A Beechcraft surveillance plane circling high above the cloud line would then relay the transponder's precise coordinates as she moved.

Palillo and I would be inserted in advance as close as possible to Santo Paraíso. When the transponder started moving out of the village – signalling that Tita was on her way to the meeting place – we'd track her stealthily but quickly, wearing our night optics.

'Remember, men,' Buitrago said, 'this is a capture or kill mission. If you can do so safely, immobilise and hold the target. These three Blackhawks will be on standby, each with fifteen soldiers. I'll have boots on the ground within twelve minutes.'

'And the girl?' I asked Buitrago.

'Avoid civilian casualties if possible,' he responded tersely. 'But she should know – when you lie down with dogs, you wake up with fleas.'

At nightfall Palillo and I slipped across the river from Llorona in a canoe and trekked south through the jungle for fifteen kilometres, hacking our way through thick undergrowth, swiping off ants and leeches while sidestepping tubular tarantula nests.

At midnight we buried ourselves in thick scrub two kilometres east of Santo Paraíso and rested until the sun began to rise. We awoke sweating under a blanket of humidity. Our instructions were to remain hidden, listening to the encrypted situation reports over our headsets.

At 7.15 am, Buitrago's agents at El Dorado Airport sighted Tita at the boarding gate. As expected, she was dressed scruffily to downplay her beauty – old jeans, red canvas sneakers and a grey hooded sweater. This description allowed Buitrago's undercover officer at the Villavicencio transport terminal to report her boarding a bus to Llorona at 9.30 am. At 4.30 pm she passed through the Garbanzos checkpoint, and one of his soldiers inserted the transponder into her bag. The Beechcraft took off immediately. Technicians aboard the plane reported that the transponder's signal was strong and clear. By 5.15 pm she'd crossed the river and was in Flora's Cantina.

Darkness fell at 6.30. Fifteen minutes later the transponder began moving slowly south-east. Palillo and I set off on a parallel bearing at a distance of one kilometre. The clouds parted, revealing a half moon; diaphanous light filtered through the dense vegetation. Since there was no rain to mask the crunch of our footfalls, we deviated frequently to avoid *campesino* huts.

'The furthest she can go is five kilometres to a tributary of the Tuparro River,' Buitrago informed us over our headset. 'If the rendezvous point is one of those fishermen's huts near the water, she'll reach it within the hour.'

We arrived at the river at the same time as the girl, one kilometre upstream.

'Her transponder has stopped. Hold your position,' Buitrago said. Then his voice registered alarm. 'Something's wrong! The signal's changed direction and sped up. She must be on a boat. She's heading straight towards you!'

To our right, we heard the low growl of an outboard engine. We lay flat and watched in disbelief as a *lancha* cruised past us with two figures silhouetted: the boatman standing and a woman in a hooded sweater seated in the bow.

At night, in thick, muddy jungle, cutting our way through vines, it would be impossible to keep pace. Abandoning caution, we trekked upriver quickly and noisily.

Twenty minutes later, another surprise came from the Beechcraft. 'We've lost her. No signal.'

'Either the canopy is blocking it,' said Buitrago, 'or the battery has failed.'

'*Mierda*,' hissed Palillo, shaking his head.

There was another possibility: the Guerrilla had discovered the transponder and we were heading into a trap.

'Avoid the river,' said the colonel. 'Too many huts. Move inland. Set your bearing towards her last known coordinates.'

During those twenty minutes, the transponder had travelled nine kilometres. In unknown terrain, it would take us two hours to cover that distance. But there was nothing for it but to keep going.

Whenever we detected movement, we froze. First it was for a thigh-thick *guiri* snake dangling overhead, then for a herd of short-tusked jungle boar that thundered across our path, their retinas reflecting green through our night-vision goggles.

One kilometre from the transponder's last known location we slowed our pace. We knew Caraquemada would have six sentries in his outer security cordon. They would be motionless behind trees, sitting in branches or lying camouflaged. If they saw us before we saw them, we'd be dead.

We needed elevation to see what we were moving towards. We climbed a ridge, then lay flat and belly-crawled to a log and peered over.

'Lights ahead at four hundred metres near the river,' whispered Palillo. 'Possibly the hut.'

By following the ridge around to the east we were able to get two hundred metres closer. Once there, we dropped to our knees and crawled a further twenty metres down the slope through the undergrowth. I tasted spider's web on my tongue then felt tiny legs clawing across my cheek. Finally, we emerged into a small clearing where a large tree had fallen. From here, our view down the hill towards the lights was now unobstructed.

'You're not going to believe this, Colonel,' said Palillo.

'What do you see?' Buitrago's excited voice came over the headset. 'Is it the hut?'

'No,' Palillo responded. 'About thirty of them. It's a gigantic base.'

154

I'D SEEN MANY astounding things in my life, but this was by far the most incredible. More than a Guerrilla camp, what I was observing through my binoculars was an absolute marvel of jungle engineering. Backing onto the river, a small citadel was laid out in concentric circles lit by hundreds of solar cells wired to trees that made it shimmer like a fairground in December.

Wooden boardwalks forked out like bicycle spokes from a central hub to an inner circle of tin-roofed dormitories with wooden walls and then to an outer circle of large square tents of khaki canvas. I also saw an office containing radio units, aircraft scanners and a satellite dish on a trolley.

Ten metres up, a roof of black insulation plastic explained how the camp avoided detection by blocking its emissions of electromagnetic radiation and also why the signal from Tita's transponder was obstructed.

Buitrago's next question snapped me out of my fascination. 'How many enemy?'

'Sixty, maybe eighty,' said Palillo, 'that I can see.'

My heart sank. Against that many soldiers, even if I could get a shot I'd never get into the camp to confront Caraquemada and escape in time.

'Do you have eyes on target?' asked Buitrago.

'Not yet.'

Getting a fix on any one of the many people moving within my field of vision was difficult since all were working furiously. On a jetty, a commander with a clipboard barked orders at a team of porters unloading supplies from a flat-bottomed boat. Bending forward as heavy boxes were hoisted onto their backs, the porters staggered like leaf-cutter ants towards the central hub. Finally, I saw ten heavily armed men standing around a large, separate hut close to the river.

'I see what looks like a master dormitory with ten guards.'

'Hold your position, but prepare to withdraw,' Buitrago said. 'I'm phoning the generals. We'll order a bomber.'

I looked at Palillo. Caraquemada would die and I'd never get to do my interrogation. Desperately, I scrambled down the slope. Palillo followed. I stopped on a rocky outcrop with an even better view over the camp. Palillo calculated the target's distance and I adjusted the clicks on my Remington.

'Prepare to evacuate,' Buitrago said.

'Wait! I think I've got eyes on the girl.'

The guards turned away respectfully as a young blonde woman emerged from the dormitory dressed only in bra and panties. She lit a cigarette.

'Is the target with her?'

'No eyes on target.'

'He must be inside.'

'Negative. No sign of him.'

Starting from opposite ends, Palillo and I scanned the base more thoroughly, hut by hut. However, everything we saw only increased our confusion. Military discipline seemed extremely lax. Apart from the ten soldiers guarding the blonde's dormitory, I counted only five more men in camouflage carrying rifles. The remaining men were without weapons or uniform. Women traipsed around in bikinis, flirting and drinking.

Some of the men ate while others worked. From the western perimeter, I heard music; a party was underway. Metre-high speakers blared *reggaetón* across a sunken dance floor. Strangely, only the men were dancing, wearing rubber rain boots and stomping out of time. None of this made sense – the music, the alcohol, the lack of command and security.

A moment later a tent flap peeled back and a man emerged wearing elbow-length rubber gloves and a gasmask. Palillo realised what was happening at the same time I did.

'It's not a Guerrilla base!' he whispered. 'It's a big, fucking, *puta de dios*, cocaine laboratory.'

It finally all made sense. The dance floor was a pit for crushing coca leaves and leaching out the alkaloid. Since it was repetitive, exhausting work, music was permitted for motivation. Women entertained during breaks.

Once more the dormitory door opened. This time a man's silhouette filled the doorframe. Naked, he emerged briefly into the light. Caraquemada.

I tensed suddenly, filled with hatred. Then I drew a deep breath and remembered my mission.

'It's the target. Confirmed,' I said into my headset.

'Come home immediately. We're proceeding with the bombing.'

'Negative. It's a drug lab. It's filled with civilians.'

Buitrago paused a moment. 'Then take the shot. I'm sending the Blackhawks.'

But Caraquemada had returned inside. Palillo and I breathed out at the same time. We curled our toes and stretched our fingers. I kept my Remington trained on the doorway.

Five minutes later, the commander with the clipboard looked skyward. He raised his hand for silence. Movement ceased. Pointing for the music to be switched off, he scrambled to the office and snatched up headphones attached to a scanner. Barking instructions, he pointed repeatedly in our direction. Women rushed into dormitories to grab clothes. Powerful spotlights came on, illuminating a clearing at the bottom of our hill.

'We may be compromised,' whispered Palillo. 'We need to go silent.'

Hearing all the fuss, Caraquemada reappeared momentarily in the doorway wearing pants but no shirt. However, before I could take the shot he stepped back.

I heard helicopter rotors. Could Buitrago's Blackhawks have reached us this quickly?

The rotors got louder and suddenly a small helicopter skimmed the jungle canopy behind us. Descending rapidly, it passed only metres above our heads and landed in the spot-lit clearing. The rotors slowed. Four men got out – two wearing suits, the other two in uniform and carrying rifles.

Caraquemada re-emerged, buttoning his shirt. I looked through my scope.

'Target back in sight.'

'Neutralise him,' said Buitrago.

I breathed in deeply. Palillo threw a distraction grenade towards the helicopter. I breathed out a long, slow breath. I took the shot. It was the hardest of my life. The bullet flew straight and true, hitting precisely where I aimed: his left knee.

155

CARAQUEMADA CRUMPLED. The bullet report reached his security contingent a second after the distraction grenade exploded near the helicopter. Five bodyguards raced to cover their fallen commander.

The two soldiers by the helicopter, believing themselves under attack from the Guerrilla, dropped flat with their rifles pointed towards the laboratory while the men in suits ran into the jungle.

Meanwhile, the ten *guerrilleros* not protecting Caraquemada fired at the helicopter, perforating the windscreen and fuel tank. The helicopter soldiers fired back. While both sides fought each other mistakenly, camp workers fled in all directions and I picked off Caraquemada's bodyguards one by one.

Following thirty seconds of automatic fire, the last of fifteen *guerrilleros* – the clipboard commander fleeing with a backpack – was down and the two soldiers from the helicopter were also dead.

Bounding down the hill with Palillo close behind, I ran towards Caraquemada, praying that he was still alive.

By the time I reached him, his workers and remaining soldiers had scattered into the jungle. Clutching his rifle, he was dragging himself to a tiny canoe moored at a jetty, leaving a wake of red behind him like a blood-soaked bridal train. Not ten metres away, tied to a tree, a German shepherd was barking and thrashing wildly against its leash.

As I approached, Caraquemada took aim with his Kalashnikov, but I fired first and my bullet shattered his hand. Keeping my pistol trained on his chest, I kicked away the rifle then confiscated his pistol and satellite phone. I hurled them into the river before crouching to study him.

In the two and a half years since murdering Papá, Caraquemada had grown thicker around the middle. His most distinctive features were unchanged – the burn-scarred left cheek, the flap of skin over his glass eye and the nose of a boxer who'd fought a decade beyond his doctor's advice.

However, his gel-plastered hair was now thinning and his clipped moustache was flecked with grey.

Caraquemada regarded me with animal cunning. Although haemorrhaging from his hand, he was still strong and his will was unshakeable. To prevent him bleeding out before I got my answers, I tossed him a bandage. He flung it into the river then flapped his arm, causing small fountains of blood to surge from his palm.

'Go get your chainsaw, you fascist slave. I'll be dead before you're back.'

I threw him a second bandage. 'I'm not here to torture you.'

He eyed me warily but must have believed me, or at least perceived an opportunity to stall for time. While he wrapped his hand, he seemed to be calculating the distance between us and assessing my size, muscle tone and potential brutality, as though they were measures of character.

He must have found me lacking because, when I leaned in to help tie off another bandage around his knee, he seized my wrist with his good hand and tried to dislodge my pistol with the other. Calmly, I ground my thumb into the bullet hole in his knee, all the while holding his gaze.

'Know who I am?'

'You could be anyone,' he growled contemptuously before relinquishing his grip. 'A man like me makes many enemies. I'd rather know who sent you. Was it the Díaz brothers or Trigeño, that two-timing *hijueputa*?'

Since Caraquemada didn't know about Buitrago tracking his prostitute, he might naturally assume Trigeño was behind this ambush, and that perhaps the Díazes had assisted, as they had with Zorrillo.

'I'm here on my own,' I said. 'You killed my father.'

Confusion knitted his brow. 'Like I said, *muchacho*. You could be anyone.'

I struck him hard across the face with the butt of my Smith & Wesson. 'You murder a man point-blank, you damn well better remember.'

Caraquemada shook his head and stared back impassively. His sensibilities were so deadened by war that violence was his remaining language. Luckily, after two years working with Beta, I spoke that language fluently.

'I am Pedro Juan Gutiérrez González, Autodefensa.'

'Trigeño, then.' He chuckled to himself ironically. 'I thought I recognised your voice. Congratulations. Now finish your master's work, capitalist puppet, and this time shoot straight.'

'Trigeño has nothing to do with this,' I retorted. 'You killed my father and banned us from our land. Why? Buitre said my father did something to anger you. Is that true? Or was it because I'd met with the Autodefensas in Garbanzos?'

'What?' He looked genuinely perplexed.

'My father giving the army water was simply an excuse,' I insisted. 'Your men saw me drinking beer with recruiters. So why not kill *me*?'

He laughed. 'Drinking beer is no crime.'

'Why then?'

He glanced across the small river, perhaps hoping to see a rescue party returning for him. 'Let me go and I'll tell you.'

'You're in no position to bargain!' I pointed my Smith & Wesson at him.

'Kill me and you'll never know.'

At this, I flew into an uncontrollable rage. Caraquemada was dangling the most painful event of my life right in front of my face, and using it to taunt me like a helpless infant. Looking around the compound, I seized a small gasoline tank and pitched its contents over him. As he squirmed and twisted sideways to avoid the splashes, his dog snarled viciously, gnashing at its rope.

When Caraquemada's clothes were soaked, I held up my lighter, flicked the flint twice so it sparked, and we stared at each other venomously. For the first time I saw fear lurking behind the bravado in his eyes. I'd always told myself I would never commit acts of torture, but at that moment I was prepared to light Caraquemada up like a bonfire.

'Okay!' He raised his uninjured hand to signal stop. 'I'll tell you. And you can decide, in your judgment as an honourable man, if I am truly to blame.'

I began to feel calm again. My interrogation was back on track: he was using flattery to feign submission; he would now downplay his own culpability, shifting responsibility onto others. But no matter what explanation he gave, he had pulled the trigger on Papá, and I was still determined to do the same to him.

'Against our orders, your father buried Humberto Díaz, who was an enemy of the revolution and had been cheating the people of taxes by lying to us about how much cocaine he was producing. Díaz was a rat. Your father should have left him to the vultures. For his disobedience, we had no choice but to kill him.'

A shaft of light punched through my dark clouds of guilt. For two and a half years I'd believed it should have been me they executed. I'd believed myself responsible for my father's death. *It's not your fault*, Mamá had said, despite me almost driving her to the grave with worry and shame. But hearing it from Caraquemada, I finally felt sure. Waves of relief flooded my body.

'Why banish us from our land?'

'That was Zorrillo. He always had a temper. But what could I do? He was my junior commander. I had to back him up.'

'And then use our *finca* as a lookout point.'

He shrugged. 'It was vacant.'

'Why should I believe you? You knew someone buried Humberto Diáz, but how did you know it was us?'

This threw him slightly. '*You?* We didn't . . . Our witnesses saw your father's Mazda driving at midnight with two men inside. Many of the villagers assumed it was the priest who helped him. For opposing the true and just will of the people's revolution, both had to be made examples of.'

'Examples?' I screamed, blood rushing to my head again. 'My father was the one setting the example. You left a human being to rot in the sun, and then you killed the only man who dared to do what was right.' My disgust was complete. 'Kneel!'

Caraquemada eyed my lighter and levered himself up onto his good knee.

I began circling. 'Son of Alvaro Alvarez, you have been accused, and found guilty, of the crime of murdering an innocent and good man on the trivial pretext of providing water to the government army, when, in fact, it was for defying your corrupt, cocaine-funded revolution—'

'Pedro, wait!' Caraquemada's gaze slid again towards the river. He obviously still expected his men to attempt a rescue and needed to stall for time. 'There's a way out of this for both of us. I can lift the ban on your property. We'll never come near you or your family again.'

It was a bankrupt offer; we ran every village up to Puerto Princesa.

'Not good enough.'

'What do you want then?'

'From you? Nothing. There is no way you can take back our suffering.'

'Don't you want to know who fingered your father?'

I hesitated and then shook my head. What did it matter which of the Guerrilla's numerous spies had informed on Papá? I resumed my circling.

'You have furthermore been accused and found guilty of using a good man's death to strike fear into the population, to terrorise innocent people and subjugate them to your will—'

'The *sapos* are the men you work for.' He paused, gloating. 'Fabián and Javier Díaz. They phoned Zorrillo to inform on your father.'

This stopped me dead in my tracks. Everything he'd said until then seemed credible, but this?

'Impossible!' I exclaimed. 'They detest you. Why would they do that?'

Surely the Díazes would be the last people on earth to report us, even if they had seen our Mazda that night. We'd done their family a brave service, which also prevented them from looking like cowards.

'Because at first we assumed *they* were the ones who'd buried their father. Zorrillo declared them military targets and they fled. But once they were safe in Bogotá, Javier phoned Zorrillo to name your father because he needed our permission to come back and take over his father's businesses.'

I struggled to absorb this new information. In my memory, I had recorded my own version of events surrounding Papá's death, and this new scenario forced me to confront my mistaken assumptions. Caraquemada's claims seemed incredible; however, they were also consistent with certain facts.

The four tonnes in the bunker established that Humberto was a cocaine trafficker. Javier had indeed phoned Zorrillo repeatedly after his father's death and, shortly afterwards, the brothers had returned to Garbanzos, clearly having struck a peace deal with the Guerrilla. The mountains of cash in Javier's safe and the cocaine in the earth-moving equipment indicated they'd since become large-scale distributors. Therefore, it was possible. And yet my mind rebelled. We'd known their family for years. Both our fathers had been killed by the Guerrilla. The sons had begged for my help. Why would they . . . ?

'Simply for a pile of cocaine?' I asked.

'No. For a *river* of cocaine.' Caraquemada gestured towards the compound. 'Who do you think owns this laboratory?'

'You do,' I retorted. 'To fund your corrupt cause through other people's misery.'

He shook his head. 'If rich gringos want to fund the liberation of our poor by snorting drugs, that's their choice. But you are wrong about the lab. The Díazes own and finance it. We're only minor partners, as we were with their thieving father . . .'

Across the narrow river I saw shadows darting between the trees. Soldiers, judging by the silhouettes of their rifles. They could only be *guerrilleros*, returning for their fallen commander. But I couldn't leave now.

'Humberto was cheating us so we kidnapped him to make his sons pay his debt. We also wanted him banished from the business forever, but we needed his routes and contacts. Humberto couldn't remember them all; everything was in a book he kept in his safe. We would have kept our word and released him in exchange for the book. Bankrupt and unable to traffic, but alive. However, Javier refused to hand it over, leaving us no choice but to kill Humberto.'

Caraquemada now had my full, shocked attention. What he was saying beggared belief: Javier could have saved his father *but chose not to.*

'You're lying! No son would do that. Especially not for a book.'

'Even if that book is worth tens of millions of dollars? Even if it contains the entire payroll for personnel along their trafficking routes? Transport companies and truck drivers. Highway police, army colonels, cargo boat captains and customs officials from Panama to Mexico. And friendly prosecutors and judges in case a load is impounded.'

I was stunned. That both sons might have deliberately let their own father be killed in order to take over his business was so despicable that I could barely contemplate it.

'You're wrong! I read the transcripts of Humberto's last phone call. His sons searched the safe twice for that book.'

Caraquemada shook his head sadly. 'They had it in their hands all along. They kept it to guarantee their role in our partnership. These are cold, cold men. They allowed their own father to be killed. When your father got in the way, they caused his death also so they could work with us. And then they used you to bring in Trigeño to protect themselves when they broke their promise to repay what their father owed.'

'I simply don't believe you,' I said, shaking my head. 'Why would you work with men you knew set up the ambush of Zorrillo?'

'Business,' he stated matter-of-factly. 'We couldn't work without their export routes. They couldn't work without our production. And because we are not animals. We are capable of forgiveness. Just as the Díazes were able to surmount the loss of their father.'

'I need proof. Where's the white book now?'

'If I knew that, I wouldn't be here bleeding with you.'

'You must have a hunch?'

'Somewhere very close to Javier – it contains too much information to memorise. He needs regular access to it and doesn't trust Fabián not to steal it and turn on him.'

'That's not proof.'

'Then go ask him yourself.' He pointed to the runway. 'You don't recognise their helicopter?'

In that instant, I knew it was true. Even without hard evidence, all of it was true. I lowered the Smith & Wesson.

'Well?' said Caraquemada in a soft, conciliatory voice. 'Now you know everything. Are you going to kill me, or is it the Díazes you want? I'll have them captured, bound and brought to you.'

I hesitated, then raised the pistol again. True, the Díaz brothers were abominations of humanity, but the Guerrilla were no better – killing innocent men and teaming up with their own enemies to trade cocaine, all the while proclaiming they were angel-winged communists striving for the good of the peasantry.

'You killed my father. Nothing the Díazes did changes that.'

'I'm sorry you lost your father. But this is war, *muchacho*. Don't take it personally.'

'Then you're not sorry at all!'

'I cannot apologise for what I know to be right. Our cause is just. There must be equality. The poor will rise and the people will triumph.'

Caraquemada was stuck like a scratched record, spouting communist platitudes about the proletariat fighting the bourgeois for the good of humanity. Capitalist landowners must be evicted for the greater good. Innocent men must die for the greater good. But what kind of good could he speak of if he had no regard for human life? It was like reasoning with a snake.

Realising I'd wasted my time, I resumed my circling. 'You have furthermore been accused of conspiring with men you despise to traffic cocaine, of funding your so-called revolution by destroying countless lives—'

'Go ahead and kill me!' yelled Caraquemada. 'Three men will proudly take my place. *¡Viva la revolución!*'

'And by the power vested in me by the United Self-Defence Organisations of Colombia—'

Suddenly, I stopped. The words of my speech sounded as broken and worn as his communist platitudes.

Caraquemada was right, I realised. After I shot him, his junior commanders would be promoted. To replace them, more children would be recruited from among poor, hungry and uneducated *campesinos*. And the cycle would continue. They kill ours, we kill theirs. It would go on forever. I could hardly look at Caraquemada – he filled me with such disgust – but my disgust with him was also disgust with myself. I too was part of an unthinking killing machine.

'Lost your nerve, *muchacho*?' he taunted, a smirk of victory curling at the edges of his mouth. 'Can't kill a man?'

I didn't bother answering. *Can't* kill a man is different to *won't* kill a man. Caraquemada was a man of war. Whether it was today or a year from now, he would eventually die at war. To a dead man with a thousand enemies, it makes no difference which one killed him. But to the man doing the killing, it means everything.

'You know what?' I lowered the pistol. 'You and your supposed cause disgust me. You're not worth it.'

His martyr's smirk collapsed in confusion. I tossed him the first-aid kit, stole a look to ensure his rescue party was not within firing distance and then cupped my hand upward against my ear at the thrumming of rotors.

'Paddle quickly. The army's about to land.'

As I walked away, Caraquemada's abuse flailed across my back: I was a fascist coward, an enemy of the people, the revolution would live on and the people would triumph – words that bounced off me like faint echoes.

What would happen to Caraquemada? I truly didn't care. Let him stay there for Buitrago to capture or let him escape in his canoe. Let him return to his decaying cause or let him seek retribution against me. For the first time since picking up a gun, I felt true power. Rather than killing the man I hated most in the world, I'd spared his life. Condemning him to continue his pathetic existence – that was my revenge.

156

BY THEN BUITRAGO'S three helicopters were landing. His soldiers spilled out onto the grass, lying flat and exchanging fire with Caraquemada's men across the river. In the dark and confusion, a blind battle ensued with me and Caraquemada in the middle. Bullets whizzed past me and I dropped flat.

'Buitrago!' I yelled into the headset. 'I'm near the river. Tell your men to stop firing.'

The shooting ceased within seconds, so the colonel must have heard me. But so had Caraquemada. Clearly, the army's arrival changed something for him.

'Pedro, wait!' I turned and saw he'd crawled behind a tree with his dog, whose neck he was hugging. 'You weren't lying, were you?' He began to laugh, at first in small chuckling fits and then uproariously. 'The Díazes and Trigeño have no idea you're here, do they?'

'So what?'

Caraquemada had already dealt me several startling blows. But his next revelation was to be the biggest; it would flip my world upside down. With the fighting stopped and his rescue party nearby, he clearly felt safe enough to take his time. He even seemed to be enjoying himself.

'You say I'm pathetic, but it is *you* who is a naïve, pathetic pawn who believes his master's lies. You say my cause is corrupted, but at least I have a cause. One I was born to. One whose oxygen I have breathed for three decades. And one I would die for. But the man you work for – your precious Trigeño, who you think is so clean – has no cause other than himself and his cocaine profits. That's right! Trigeño.'

'What? What do you mean?'

'I mean he is the biggest *traficante* of all! Long before he rebranded himself a counter-insurgent and pretended to become political, he was a *capo* in the Medellín cartel.' Seeing my utter disbelief, he pointed to the yellow barrels stacked inside the far tent. 'Who sells us those chemicals via your agricultural co-operative man, Lulo Martínez? Who buys our final product and has us hide it in his earth-moving machinery for international export? Trigeño is our true partner in this. The Díazes are simply minor intermediaries. After that infernal attorney exposed Trigeño's route, he sent them here tonight to negotiate new routes.'

I would later confirm Caraquemada's claims about Trigeño, but right then the certainty etched on his face and in his voice were proof enough. It made sense, as did Caraquemada calling Trigeño 'a two-timing *hijueputa*'. And yet, after everything Trigeño had said and done – writing a book decrying *traficantes* and executing the three brothers in front of me – part of me still refused to accept it was possible.

'Why should I believe you?'

'Look closely!' Caraquemada pointed to the soldiers I'd slain. 'Some of those men are mine, but most are Beta's, stationed here to protect the operation. You want more proof?' He reached into the dog's collar and withdrew a small memory stick, which he held out to me, beckoning. 'This video was to be my insurance policy, but now that everything has gone to *mierda* you can use it to bring down the Díazes.'

I was still struggling to take it all in. If Caraquemada's claims were true, it meant that Trigeño had agreed to invade Llorona, not out of patriotic duty, but to expand his cocaine empire. Three years earlier he'd almost struck an alliance with Humberto Díaz. In his sons, he must have seen the opportunity reborn. That second handshake I'd witnessed between Javier and Trigeño on Javier's *finca* was most likely a secret deal they'd struck behind my back – Trigeño had their three million dollars, but he also wanted a share of their drug business.

'But why would you help me?' I demanded. 'And why would you harm your partners?'

'Partners in what?' He snarled ironically at the compound that was now crawling with government soldiers. 'Trigeño and the Díazes are once more my enemies. Use this and you'll bring down both.'

He tossed me the memory stick and then signalled to his soldiers, who recommenced their shooting. 'Now run, capitalist pawn! Run!'

157

AS I CROSSED the makeshift runway, hands high in the air so Buitrago's soldiers wouldn't shoot, a maelstrom of thoughts and emotions spiralled within me. I felt like I'd been knocked off a precipice and was falling through a vast chasm.

Of course, I'd never liked nor trusted either Javier or Fabián Díaz. But not liking people based on intuition is far different to how I felt now, knowing that they had deliberately caused Papá's death. After such a betrayal, there was no patch in hell hot enough for their souls.

As for Trigeño, his betrayal was different, although far more agonising because I'd admired him, followed him and believed in him, almost like a father. He'd made me feel special and worthy, and seemed to recognise in me talents and strengths that no one else had.

I should have listened to Palillo; Trigeño had deceived me all along. Our entire relationship was a lie, and it rocked me deeply that anyone could be so callous, pretending I meant so much to them when I clearly meant so little. In truth, Trigeño had saved me at La Quebrada only because of the Díaz money I offered and because I had Colonel Buitrago's ear. I couldn't believe how wrong I'd been about someone I'd felt incredibly close to.

At the same time, I was truly proud of my decision not to kill Caraquemada. Trigeño had convinced me our war was between good and evil. But I saw now that it was just one big cycle of interconnected violence in a struggle for power, financed by cocaine trafficking. My quest for justice had been futile from the very beginning – what sort of justice can exist in such a corrupt, hypocritical system?

Killing Caraquemada would only have perpetuated the cycle of violence, entrenching me deeper within an unjust organisation that had no exit other than death. I'd mistakenly attributed Papá's death to five individuals: a radio operator, two low-level commanders, the triggerman and their high commander, when it was the entire basis of the war that was to blame.

I now understood why Papá had been so stressed on the night we buried Humberto Díaz. At the time, I failed to fully appreciate the danger. Papá had done his religious and moral duty at great risk to himself. He'd recognised that risk, considered it worthwhile and, when the Guerrilla came for him, Papá probably knew why. That's the reason he refused to run. He'd thought only of my safety, sending me inside and telling me to 'shut up' in case I revealed my own involvement.

The Guerrilla had not killed Papá because I'd publicly associated with the Autodefensa recruiters. Owing to my immaturity and youth, I'd gotten it wrong. In the intervening years, learning that the Guerrilla didn't usually kill for such trivial offences, I should have revised my interpretation, but guilt is not always rational or logical. Sometimes, an idea sticks so hard in your mind that almost nothing you see or hear afterwards can dislodge it.

I'd replayed Papá's execution in my mind a million times, torturing myself with the thought that his horror-struck glances towards me were *blame*. However, in his final moments of life, Papá had accepted the consequences of his own decision and was showing his love by shielding me.

Knowing this changed everything. It made me feel calm. The relief was so great that I no longer wanted to kill anyone. I'd allowed one obsession to consume my every waking moment. I wondered how much of my anger came from self-hatred that I'd turned outward against others. Shedding my guilt allowed me to complete my acceptance of Papá's passing.

I no longer thought of what I'd been doing as *justice*, instead I called it by its proper name: *revenge*. And upon renouncing my revenge, I felt immediately lighter, as though what had been driving me was not a powerful engine, but rather a loathsome burden.

There was a time I'd have given my life to avenge Papá's death, but that was no longer the case. Instead, I wanted to spend my life building and producing rather than waging war and visiting destruction upon others.

Like Caraquemada, who followed the tenets of an outdated, inflexible doctrine unquestioningly, I'd followed rules and orders, believing myself courageous because I would kill for them and die for them too. Rather than forging my own true path, I had done the bidding of my superiors. Rather than doing my own thinking, I had let others do the thinking for me. And in doing so, I had made my life a lie, blindly doing the work of other men.

The resolution to give up killing for revenge was the first decision I'd made for myself as a man, but as I approached Buitrago's Blackhawk, I could not have guessed how soon my resolve would be tested.

158

'WHERE'S CARAQUEMADA?' DEMANDED Buitrago when I'd crossed the runway and reached him.

'That way.' I pointed towards the river. The canoe was gone and Caraquemada's rescue party had slipped back into the shadows.

Buitrago signalled frantically for his men to give chase and then frowned at me. 'I thought you shot him?'

'I did. His reinforcements came. I couldn't hold them off.'

Any disappointment Buitrago felt at losing Caraquemada vanished when he looked around and realised what he'd seized. A thorough search would later reveal the laboratory's capacity to house a hundred and twenty men and produce nine metric tonnes of cocaine hydrochloride per week, dwarfing the largest impounded lab to date, Pablo Escobar's infamous *Tranquilandia*.

'Look at the size of this place!' he exclaimed.

Within minutes, Buitrago's men also captured the prostitute Tita, alive and already singing like a *loro*. A second group of soldiers returned with Javier and Fabián Díaz, who were covered in scratches from their attempted 'getaway' through the jungle. Apparently, they'd become lost after a kilometre and had begun arguing. When they heard a jaguar roar, they became fearful and turned back with their hands in the air, calling for help. Palillo had been hot on their trail and guided Buitrago's men via radio to the capture point.

As Palillo and the soldiers marched the handcuffed brothers towards us, I felt the hairs on my neck bristling.

'Pedro, my friend!' wailed Fabián as the soldiers jerked him to a halt. 'Colonel! Thank God you're both here! Tell these men there's been a big mistake. Tell them who we are.'

Javier added his own demands. 'You will release us. We have nothing to do with this!'

I struggled against my first instinct, which was to make the brothers suffer ten times more than they'd made me suffer. Javier and Fabián had caused Papá's death, yet, knowing this, they had looked me in the eyes each time we met, called me their friend, begged for my help that Christmas Eve, suckered in Camila by inviting us to their fiesta and also pretended to shield Mamá. All with the aim of meeting Trigeño, who was the only man who could save them from the Guerrilla's expanding power.

My anger against them was physical, but I quickly regained control.

'Colonel,' I said coldly, 'these men have *everything* to do with this. That helicopter is theirs. They were trying to escape.'

'Of course it's our helicopter!' scoffed Javier. 'We got shot down and were forced to land. You can see the bullet holes. We ran because people were shooting at us.'

'This laboratory is also theirs.' I leaned in close to Javier's face. 'You own and run it. The Guerrilla protect it.'

'Laboratory?' said Javier, looking perplexed and offended. 'Pedro, why are you saying this? You know we're good people. We protected your mother. We were on our way to a business meeting.'

'Exactly. A meeting here with Caraquemada. Probably to discuss new trafficking routes since Yolanda Delgado exposed the last one before you had Beta murder her. Just as you had Beta murder anyone who tried to stand against you.'

'Those are calumnious untruths,' said Javier, glaring at me viciously.

'You're crazy, Pedro,' added Fabián. 'As an elected congressman, I won't answer to you.'

'You'll answer to the courts and to God. And for far worse crimes,' I said. 'You allowed the Guerrilla to murder your own father so you could take over his cocaine business. And then you caused them to kill mine.'

All this while, Buitrago had quietly watched us trading insults, swivelling his head from one side to the other like a spectator at a tennis match. This time, however, he gasped and stared at the brothers in disbelief.

'That's preposterous!' cried Javier, puffing out his chest.

'I know everything,' I said and then repeated snippets from the brothers' final phone calls with their father and Zorrillo, the ones I'd read in Buitrago's transcript. '"7812B. I can't find it, Papá. It's not here. There's no white book . . . You'll have to kill him!"' I paused, looking from Javier to Fabián, and then reached into Javier's breast pocket and removed his silver cigar case. 'While all along you held it in your hand.'

It was a wild gamble, but Javier's look of alarm confirmed I'd guessed correctly. My fingers fumbled at the case's edges until eventually it split apart. Inside was a tiny booklet with a faded cream cover.

The brothers were too smart to say anything, but their guilt-ridden faces confirmed everything. They glared at each other, perhaps reliving the day of their father's execution and the horrendous decision they'd made together: to let him die. In their eyes I could see their old resentment rekindling.

Fabián spat in his brother's face.

Javier spat back.

'Sons of bitches,' said Buitrago. Taking the booklet and opening it, he saw lists of names and international phone numbers, which removed any remaining doubts. 'I've seen some twisted, inhumane *mierda* over my career. But that! There is only one word for that: *evil.* Pure fucking evil.'

Buitrago was a proud and controlled man who had played most of his life by the rules. I'd never seen him lose his temper or self-control. As he spoke, however, his face flushed with rage and the veins in this forehead bulged like worms beneath his skin. Suddenly, he punched Javier hard in the stomach, and then Fabián. They doubled over in pain and fell to their knees, winded.

Buitrago cocked his pistol and offered it to me. 'Certain animals don't deserve to inhabit the same planet as humans.'

Here was my chance for revenge, but I'd made that mistake before – playing judge, jury and executioner – and look where it got me. Of course I wanted justice to be done, but by the proper authorities, not me. I'd seen the alternative, where every individual wields his own brand of justice, and it was far worse. Instead of bypassing a weak legal system, my job was to believe in it and improve it.

Nevertheless, on the chance they did go free, I wanted to give the brothers something to think about in the meantime.

I kneeled down between them, speaking softly. 'I know you don't care about anyone else. So in whatever days are left to you, I want you to continue thinking *only about yourselves*. But be warned: Trigeño is aware of your and Beta's plotting against him.' The brothers looked truly horrified. 'And know this: none of this would have happened without what you did. Your father would not have been killed. My father and I would not have buried him. The Guerrilla would not have killed my father. I would not have joined the Autodefensas. You would never have met Trigeño or Beta or owned this laboratory. I wouldn't be here right now. And you wouldn't either. Anything you want to say to that?'

They bowed their heads. There was nothing they *could* say, but stunned silence can only last so long. Perhaps in prison they'd have time to come up with an answer. That is, if they lived.

159

PALILLO AND I touched down in the Blackhawk at first light and were immediately transported from Garbanzos airstrip to the XVIII Battalion. Although we were dead tired, a lieutenant escorted us through the gates and into an upstairs administration block, where she seated us in a drab debriefing room with grey concrete walls, a wooden table and three chairs.

'The colonel wants a full account of your actions,' she said, looking at her watch. 'He'll join you in exactly one hour.'

During the helicopter flight, Palillo had twitched with unusual excitement, as though bursting to tell me a secret. As soon as the door closed, he blurted it out. 'Guess what I found while doing perimeter protection for you?' he said. '*This*!' It was a small laminated piece of paper containing GPS coordinates, two compass bearings and distances marked in metres that led to a precise spot marked with an 'X' and named *El Abrazo*, meaning *The Hug*.

'It's a map leading to a *guaca*! I'm sure of it. I found it on one of Caraquemada's bodyguards I'd shot outside the camp. He was creeping along slowly, and I thought he was circling around to ambush you, but he had this in his hand, and a compass.' Palillo claimed he would have dug it up immediately except boarding the army Blackhawk carrying millions of dollars might have raised eyebrows. 'But we need to go back there right away.'

I laughed. 'Hugs and crosses don't make a map.'

'But distances, bearings and a landmark with a codename do.'

'Even if it is a map it might lead to cocaine or dead bodies.'

'Cocaine would be shipped out immediately. And why would they kill their own workers then draw a map to their graves? It's definitely money.'

'Then the army will find it, or the Guerrilla might return.'

'These distances and bearings lead to a location at least a kilometre from the lab. You think the army will dig that far out? Or that Caraquemada will limp back and find it without these precise directions?'

I disparaged his claims, but Palillo was adamant. 'You owe me, *hermano*. Besides, what exactly were you doing while I was busy protecting your *culo* and making us rich?'

I recounted my tussle with Caraquemada and how I'd deliberately let him go.

When he heard this, Palillo slammed his fist on the conference table. 'Are you completely *loco*? I spent two nights in the sweaty jungle ducking helicopters and dodging bullets to help you kill that fry-faced, glass-eyed *bastardo*. Why?'

'Because I'm not angry anymore. I thought you'd be happy. No more revenge. It's over, exactly as you wanted.'

Palillo's expression changed from anger to sympathy.

'You're right. I'm sorry.' He leaned across and hugged me. 'Truly, I'm glad.' Then he stood, punched both fists in the air and wiggled his hips. 'And that means we're one hundred per cent the fuck out of here.'

'Not one hundred per cent,' I cautioned. 'Asking Trigeño for a discharge will be delicate.'

When Trigeño heard about the laboratory raid he'd be furious at losing so much money, and also worried the Díaz might talk. He might put La 50 into lockdown again. And since he already had problems with Beta, he'd want every available commander and soldier on duty protecting him. At the same time, I was determined to keep my promise to Camila to leave the Autodefensas.

Camila had seen things about me that I couldn't see myself. Things I'd refused to see at the time, but now did. And in the meantime, I'd hurt her and I'd made her live in fear. I realised how hard it must have been for her to stay in love with me when she didn't know where I was or what I was doing and, knowing every time I left her, that I might never come home. And how it must have felt to be caressed by hands she knew had taken human life. It must have been difficult for her to be proud of being my girlfriend. She had defied her father's warnings, ignored her friends' advice and stayed with me through it all, until I finally proved myself to be just as bad as the men I was hunting.

After all I had done and all that she had suffered, I felt I owed her everything. Unfortunately, until I heard it from Trigeño's mouth, I would not be properly out of the Autodefensas. And until I was entirely out, I could not make us truly safe.

'Then how will we be able to leave?' asked Palillo.

'This might help.' I held up the memory stick.

Before Buitrago arrived, we requested a laptop from his lieutenant, purportedly to begin typing our statements. Even after all I'd seen and learned, the three photos and single video file it contained startled me.

The photos, taken during the day at some distance, showed uniformed Autodefensas I recognised from Beta's intelligence-gathering team playing football with a severed head. Another shot showed two soldiers dragging a corpse with no legs along behind them. The last and most damning photo proved Yolanda Delgado's allegation. It showed Beta standing in the middle of the plaza, pointing towards the river as he gave an order. Trigeño could no longer deny he was behind the Puerto Galán *limpieza*.

I was disgusted although not surprised. I'd always known the various tortures sounded similar to the work of Beta and El Psycho. However, I hadn't expected the level of open depravity they'd reached, not even attempting to hide their despicable crimes.

The brief video was from months earlier and must have been edited from a much longer recording, secretly filmed by the mistrustful Caraquemada during a meeting. It showed Javier and Fabián Díaz walking beside Beta as they inspected the partially constructed cocaine laboratory.

As they reached the yellow chemical barrels, Javier pointed and Beta made a radio call. '*Patrón*, I'm here with the partners. They require more yellow.'

'I'll send them more yellow,' came the clear reply, 'but we need the white in those earth-moving vehicles by next Friday.'

The recording stopped there.

'Holy Mother of God,' said Palillo slowly, turning wide-eyed to look at me.

We both knew that voice well: Trigeño's.

I'd known instinctively that Caraquemada was telling the truth, but seeing the evidence of Trigeño's duplicity for myself sent shivers down my spine. Caraquemada was right about it being an insurance policy. This video would bring down the Díazes and Beta. But Trigeño would be brought down too.

'Colonel,' I said as Buitrago entered the room. 'There's something you need to see.'

160

A GREAT DEAL HAPPENED over the next week, with one event knocking onto another like a series of closely stacked dominos. For several days we remained confined to the army barracks on Colonel Buitrago's orders, along with Mamá, Old Man Domino and Gloria.

Buitrago had been excited after seeing the video and photos. 'Providing they're authentic and Trigeño's voice can be matched by experts, these are the missing links we need. The photos establish the perpetrators of the massacre. The video connects the laboratory to the earth-moving equipment that my colleagues managed to impound on its way south through Villavicencio and establishes the Díaz brothers as the owners.'

By then, the Díazes were back in Garbanzos, albeit in a holding cell. Legally, they could be isolated for thirty days, but they must have bribed a guard to make a phone call. A horde of attorneys showed up, demanding their release.

Since the Díazes had not admitted anything, their attorneys embellished their fanciful defence with sworn depositions from reputable businessmen who were supposedly waiting to meet the brothers that night in Cali. Javier launched a counter-attack, demanding damages for his ruined helicopter and for being manhandled by the army and falsely accused of cocaine trafficking. Surrounded by suits and ties, he'd regained his arrogance.

'Release us or I'll instruct my counsel to sue for false imprisonment and defamation.'

'Do it,' said Buitrago. 'I've got you for thirty days.'

'Watch your step, Colonel!' said Fabián. 'I'm an elected congressman.'

'Elected,' responded Buitrago, 'but not inaugurated.'

Buitrago had the USB stick, of course, but didn't want to reveal his ace unless absolutely necessary. Over the next three days, the colonel's men meticulously combed the Díaz mansion, finding almost seventeen million dollars in cash that couldn't be explained. He now had enough to officially charge them. With their wealth and connections, they probably thought they could beat the charges. But there was one thing they feared far more than the law.

'Every person named here will be investigated,' said Buitrago, tapping the little white book. 'When I tell them you've informed on them, you'll need to be on my good side.'

Panicked, the Díazes began to talk. They blamed Beta for everything, claiming he'd extorted them, threatened their lives, installed his men on their *finca* and demanded use of their earth-moving vehicles. They also knew people who would testify that Beta was behind the attempt on Felix Velasquez's life and the murder of Yolanda Delgado.

Buitrago took down their statements. Their claim that Beta was responsible wouldn't do them much good. With the video on the USB showing them touring their own laboratory, along with the white booklet, Buitrago had enough evidence to put them away for a very long time.

When the brothers had signed, he ordered his men, 'Now bring me Beta.'

By then, however, Beta and his Black Scorpions had fled.

Five days later, Buitrago entered our room with a huge smile across his face and a full bottle of single-malt whisky dangling from his hand. He'd just returned from high-level meetings with his generals.

'Drink with me.' He poured three glasses. 'It worked.' He held up the USB. 'At first the generals said our own government might *lack the willpower* to pursue Trigeño, which probably means he could embarrass some very powerful people. But once we spoke to the North Americans, everything fell into place. They showed me this.'

He handed me a file marked CLASSIFIED, which had been translated from English.

> Carlos Trigeño. Former high-level member of the Medellín Cartel and close associate of Pablo Escobar Gavíria. He broke away from the cartel and assisted the Cali Cartel, PEPES and Search Block, notably Major Itagüí (now General) in the manhunt for Escobar.
>
> Following Escobar's death, Trigeño founded his own breakaway cartel, which was loosely protected by the government as repayment for his assistance as an informant. However, when confronted with extortion and kidnappings by the FARC-Guerrilla, Trigeño and other traffickers amassed private armies as protection. He united these private militias under the banner of the Colombian Autodefensas, hoping to achieve political legitimacy and legal status.

The Autodefensas are currently listed by the Department of State as a Foreign Terrorist Organisation. It is believed Trigeño continues to import chemical precursors and export cocaine hydrochloride to Mexico and Florida via cargo ships. He is protected at high levels of government. As yet, insufficient evidence is available to lay charges.

'Luckily,' Buitrago continued, 'the USB in combination with the white booklet was a game-changer. The North Americans have wanted to extradite Trigeño for years but lacked the proof. However, with this new evidence they can link Trigeño to crimes committed on US soil.'

He explained that this would take time and naturally involve the interrogation of less-important intermediaries, including the Díaz brothers.

'They'll have to admit their role in all this, implicate Trigeño and do some prison time here, or the North Americans will extradite them too,' added the colonel with satisfaction.

Since the Americans' extradition plans would take time, they'd pressured the Colombian government to use the evidence on the USB to imprison Trigeño in Colombia on lesser charges while they finalised their own evidence.

'Trigeño's government contacts informed his attorneys that they have clear evidence of his drug trafficking. When the attorneys expressed doubt, they were allowed to view the video contained on the USB. But the government has indicated that, provided he disarms his forces, surrenders voluntarily and pleads guilty to the lesser offence of being the intellectual author of the massacre in Puerto Galán, they can arrange a light sentence for him in a minimum-security facility in Colombia. Of course, before his sentence is over, the Americans will extradite him for drug trafficking, but Trigeño has no idea about this and has agreed to the deal.'

Best of all, the generals had finally granted Buitrago the resources he needed to rid the region of the Guerrilla forever. How could they refuse? Over the past twelve months he'd already made headlines for downing Zorrillo and rescuing the kidnapped Telecom engineer. Now he'd raided the largest cocaine laboratory in Colombian history.

Three hundred extra soldiers had already arrived and established outposts and daily patrols south of Puerto Princesa. Llorona and the river towns were safely back under government control.

Satellite images showed that troops belonging to Caraquemada's 34th Frente were withdrawing from their camps in the mountainous jungle around Santo Paraíso.

We toasted and then the colonel said, 'You're both free to go home.' With Beta gone, the Díazes still in army custody and Trigeño on the back foot, it was safe for Palillo, me, Mamá, Old Man Domino and Gloria to finally leave the barracks.

'But stay away from Trigeño,' warned Buitrago. 'Don't even phone him.'

For the time being, I obeyed. Instead, I asked Mamá and Uncle to meet me the following day for lunch at our *finca*.

161

THE *FINCA* LOOKED better than it ever had. Beds were made, food filled the refrigerator and Papá's granite tombstone had been polished until it shone.

Confident that Beta had left the area and no longer posed a threat, I'd refused Buitrago's offer of a bodyguard, although I thanked him. Without his go-ahead, Mamá would never have arrived with Uncle Leo and a heavily pregnant Amelia.

They looked serious, with their hands on the table, fingers interlocked, so I figured they had an inkling of why I'd invited them for lunch.

'It's over, Mamá. You can pack your things and come home. The Guerrilla are gone. So are the Autodefensas.'

'Ay, Pedro!' Mamá rushed to hug me, but I held up both hands.

'Mamá, there's something you need to know about Papá's death.' I glanced at Uncle Leo. He stood and took Amelia's wrist, making to leave, but I placed a hand gently on his shoulder and made him sit. 'Something you both need to know.'

I took a deep breath. 'Remember how no one would collect Humberto Díaz's body?'

I told them about the midnight trip in our Mazda to the river S-bend, the blue tarpaulin, the pen torches and our return trip via the cemetery. Before I finished, Mamá understood what I was really telling her – the cause of Papá's death – and she was weeping. We threw our arms around each other.

'I'm so sorry, Mamá.'

'But . . . all this time . . . I thought . . . I mean . . . why wouldn't he just tell me?'

'Papá was only trying to protect you. But you had a right to know.' Then I went further. 'And I should have told you afterwards.'

By keeping the burial secret we'd treated Mamá as a child. She'd suffered greatly, solely because of decisions made by the two men in her life.

'I thought *I* was to blame,' I continued. 'I was seen in the plaza with the Autodefensa recruiters. Papá warned me it was dangerous. So when he was killed, I didn't think of Humberto Díaz – I thought it was because of me.'

Uncle Leo nodded. He'd believed this as well.

'Then I owe you an apology,' he said, now on the point of tears himself. 'I've blamed you all this time. Whenever I saw my sister suffering, I— '

Mamá buried her face in her hands. Like Papá, she probably knew about Humberto Díaz's true vocation all along.

'Unfortunately, there's more,' I said sombrely. 'The Díaz brothers saw our Mazda that night. They were the ones who informed the Guerrilla. Afterwards, the Guerrilla turned against them and the brothers befriended us because they needed my boss's protection.'

Mamá gasped then sat there stunned. All along, Javier's generosity and probably Eleonora's friendship had stemmed from ulterior motives. Mamá finally had the truth, and it would help the healing.

I hoped Mamá would eventually reach the same calm place I had: Papá had lived by strong principles and died for doing what he believed was right.

Wiping away her tears, she whispered, 'Thank you, Pedro.'

Padre Rojas knocked. I had invited him too. I knew Mamá would have questions. And maybe Rojas, being Papá's best friend and confidante, could supply more answers and further words of comfort. After that, we'd all attend morning Mass.

'Uncle Leo.' I beckoned him aside after church. 'I have no right to ask any favours of you after all I've done. But . . .'

It was in Uncle Leo's blue truck that I sped out from Llorona, across Los Llanos and on towards Trigeño's *finca.*

162

THE FOLLOWING DAY, around noon, I finally reached La 50. I drove past without stopping and headed uphill in the direction of La 35. After nine months' absence I thought at first I'd forgotten the way and taken a wrong turn.

Instead of the pot-holed dirt track, I found myself on a paved road. Where the rusted cattle gate should have been, sandstone bricks arched over thick oak gates. There was a guard station, where a soldier stood behind bulletproof glass. I pulled up and wound down my window.

'Private property,' the guard barked through the intercom.

'*Perdón*. I'm looking for La 35.'

He nodded. 'Your name?'

After checking a list, he opened the motorised gates and I stared, stupefied. A gold-lettered sign announced the property's new name: Hacienda Ralito. Wild African palms had been uprooted and replanted along the driveway at measured intervals.

The dilapidated, wooden farmhouse had been razed and replaced by a complex of stylishly rendered and painted buildings clustered around a twenty-five-metre lap pool in which bikini-clad models now frolicked. Beside the pool stood a white marquee where a team of black-tie waiters carried silver platters of cheese, prosciutto, tuna carpaccio and fine wine. About fifty drivers and armed bodyguards sat at several round tables, some in police and army uniforms, others in suits and ties. Laughing and nudging each other, they admired the poolside entertainment.

Dotted throughout the grounds sat guest bungalows with thatched roofs, jacuzzis and bamboo privacy walls. An artificial lake boasted a wooden jetty, ski boat and an island sanctuary where pink flamingos stood. The small wooden chapel on the hill was the only structure that had not been altered. Even seeing it there, I couldn't shake the sensation I was in the wrong place. The transformation from my last visit was unbelievable.

Culebra stood up from one of the tables and we shook hands.

'What's been happening here?' I asked.

He chuckled. 'A few minor improvements.'

'A *few*. Who are these people? And where's Trigeño?'

Culebra nodded towards a brick conference room. 'He's tied up in meetings with political big-hitters. You'll have to wait.'

I walked up the hill and found the door locked. Cupping my hands, I peered through the glass. Inside, approximately thirty men sat around a U-shaped table. I recognised their faces from television, newspapers and recent *Vote 1* billboards – they were congressmen, senators, business leaders and colourfully decorated army generals, including Itagüí.

Pacing and turning, Trigeño was addressing the gathering with the same commanding presence as in his military briefings, pointing frequently to a whiteboard. His audience sat mesmerised and admiring.

Only a week earlier, I too had looked up to him and believed in him unquestioningly. He'd convinced not only me but thousands of loyal soldiers – children like Ñoño – to fight with fire and blood for a just and patriotic cause. But all the while he'd worked secretly with our enemy *in the interests of business.*

I did not hate him. I felt empty and betrayed, and also disappointed with myself for letting him fool me for so long. Right then, however, I simply wanted him out of my life with a minimum of conflict. I planned to ask courteously but directly for a discharge without mentioning what I knew. However, before I could knock, a strong hand gripped me by the back of my neck.

'What in *puta madre* are you doing?'

I'd never seen Alfa 1 without his uniform or weapon. Dressed in rain boots and muddy coveralls, he looked like a regular foreman from any *finca.*

'I need to talk to him. It's urgent.'

'So is this demobilisation meeting.'

If the disarmament Trigeño had agreed to in return for a short prison sentence was anything like the government's peace offer to the Guerrilla, Autodefensa soldiers who surrendered voluntarily wouldn't be charged or imprisoned. They would simply hand in their weapons and reintegrate into society as ordinary citizens. However, I didn't want Alfa 1 to know I'd heard anything about this in advance, so I raised my eyebrows questioningly, as though I were confused.

'You haven't heard the news?' he asked softly.

I shook my head.

'Apparently the war is over,' he said ironically. He mounted a motorbike and thumped the seat behind him. 'Get on and I'll explain. Then you can wait with me until his guests depart.'

We rode three kilometres downhill towards the fence that bordered La 50. A Constructoras Díaz crane was lowering two familiar forty-foot shipping containers from a Transportadores Díaz truck into a deep bunker. They were burying the La 50 armoury. Fifty recruits were mothballing uniforms, oiling weapons and plastic-sealing boxes of ammunition. I wondered what else they might be burying – tonnes of cocaine or barrels of chemicals perhaps – and whether Alfa 1 knew about *El Patrón*'s true profession.

'We'd always planned to demobilise in the future, after the war was won,' Alfa 1 explained. 'But Trigeño needs to disappear for a while. Meantime, he has to break all ties to his past, and that means us.'

'Why aren't you burying those?' A separate pile of old, rusted Galils was being loaded back onto the truck.

'We need them for the cameras. They're broken.'

Low-powered rifles, malfunctioning pistols and single-barrel shotguns would be handed over then crushed during a televised demobilisation ceremony. The good weapons they were keeping.

'What about our employees?'

'They go home, keep their mouths shut and receive a government salary. Some of the commanders need to demobilise too. Culebra will be in the first group.'

'And that's it?' I tried to hide my excitement. If all troops were being sent home, maybe I wouldn't have to request a discharge after all.

'Not exactly. Only two-thirds are demobilising. While Trigeño's away, I'll be in charge. If the government breaks the terms of our agreement, we have our men on speed dial and can dig all this up.'

'And me?'

'I'm glad you finally learned some loyalty, Pedro,' he said, patting my back. 'Trigeño is pleased with you for warning him about Beta turning rogue. We both are.'

I was glad Alfa 1 had finally forgiven me. I'd lied to him, used him to pursue my own self-interest and betrayed his trust. I now knew exactly how that felt.

Clearly, he was also trying to shore up my loyalty in case something went awry. The government might try to make Alfa 1 take the fall for the hundreds of bodies chopped and buried throughout Los Llanos in mass graves and fifty-by-fifty holes. War with the Guerrilla might flare up again, or an internal war might erupt among Autodefensa mid-range commanders, like Beta, who refused to disarm. Whatever the case, Alfa 1 wanted few enemies and needed to be ready with his own group.

We returned to the conference room from which senators, generals and businessmen had emerged, shaking hands and embracing. Cutting a swathe through the midst of his departing guests, Trigeño circled back around and manoeuvred them towards the gate like a barracuda corralling baitfish.

I had to hand it to him; with several atmospheres of pressure bearing down on him, his resilience was titanium. His world might be collapsing around him, but his façade remained intact.

When he noticed me waiting, his face lit up with pleasure.

'Thank you for coming, Pedro,' he said warmly, as though he'd invited me here himself. 'And your timing is perfect. I've had two days of stressful meetings with fucking *políticos* who wouldn't bother to smile unless there was a peso in it. They're such *falsos*! Now that I'm finally with someone real, I can relax. Come! We'll fish together.'

'*Comando*, I—'

'Walk with me.' He gripped my arm, pulling me towards the dam. 'As you can see, I'm making some big changes around here. I want you to be a part of them.'

He dismissed his bodyguards with orders to send us fishing rods, and then he turned to me in that old, confidential manner. 'You were right about Beta. I should have listened. But I assume everyone is like you and me – trustworthy, loyal and honest – but that also makes me vulnerable.'

When the caretaker arrived with rods, Trigeño tactfully changed subjects, informing me that the dam was stocked to capacity with vampire fish, a vicious predator he admired greatly because they put up an amazing struggle. Once the caretaker had departed, Trigeño cast his line and then leaned in close, speaking softly.

'What I'm about to tell you is in complete confidence. Somehow the government has photos of Beta and his men during the *limpieza* – playing soccer with severed heads, using chainsaws on men who are not yet dead. Disgusting, despicable acts that I can't bear to think about. Beta knows about the photos and has scurried to Monterrey, where he now hides like a rat in a drainpipe. I'm sending Alfa 1 to flush him out and exterminate him.'

Although he pretended to concentrate on his rod tip, Trigeño's lizard eyes flitted across at me, gauging my reaction. Perhaps he wanted to know how much of this I already knew and whether I'd continue participating in his fiction.

'What will happen afterwards?' I asked, again hoping his plans might make my request for a discharge unnecessary.

'Beta's junior commanders will be *disappeared*. His soldiers will be returned to the fold and retrained. Beta is a liar and a traitor, but unfortunately I am indirectly responsible for his actions. I ordered him to occupy Puerto Galán with the best of intentions. However, as his commander, I am responsible for the terrible atrocities he committed without authorisation. I must now fall on my sword.'

'What do you mean?'

'I've spoken to my friends in government and agreed to hand myself in. I will offer compensation to the victims' families, as they properly deserve. I will give a full and frank admission of my role as the intellectual author of Beta's crimes in exchange for a predetermined prison sentence.'

'For how long?' I asked. I didn't care that he was claiming this was by his own doing. With Trigeño locked up, I'd be safe.

'They say five years, although I could be out within two for good behaviour. Then we'll start back up.'

He seemed resigned, even philosophical, about going to prison. Clearly unaware of the manoeuvring by the North Americans to extradite him, he was in for a rude shock.

'Meanwhile, until the public furore dies down, I must maintain a low profile. Alfa 1 will take the helm. You will be his second in command and you'll—'

'*Comando*, I can't accept. In fact, I came to ask for a discharge. I'd like to include Palillo, Piolín and Ñoño in my request.'

'Impossible! Your friends can demobilise in the first parade, but I need you now more than ever.'

'Please, I've done over two years' service and helped you take Llorona as promised.'

'Our work is not done. Caraquemada and Santiago are still out there.'

'Please, *comando*. I've been loyal. I've been honest.'

'And I helped trap your father's killers. Does that count for nothing?'

'It does. But I must return to my family.'

'And you will. Only not yet.' For a second time, he leaned in close. 'There's something I should have told you earlier. You were also correct about the Díaz brothers. You're no doubt aware that Colonel Buitrago raided their laboratory. But what you don't know is that they and Beta were working intimately with the Guerrilla.' Trigeño spat noisily to emphasise his revulsion. 'There is only one thing I despise more than a cocaine trafficker and that is a lying, deceitful traitor. The Díazes were doing business with the enemy behind our backs. That, I can never forgive.'

This was too much for me. The flattery, the false modesty, the lying, the deceit and the shifting of blame, I could handle. But his double standard in moralising about unpardonable faults in others that were the very same faults he possessed himself sent me into a furious spin. With my next utterance, any possibility of a smooth farewell unravelled.

'We both know that isn't true. I saw a video of Beta and the Díazes at their laboratory talking to you about the yellow barrels.'

Trigeño's reaction was swift. He dropped his fishing rod and his left hand shot up to grip my throat while his right hand patted my chest and waist, presumably searching for a listening device. 'And I suppose you have your beloved colonel out there, waiting to arrest me so you'll both look like heroes.'

'I came alone,' I said calmly. 'Buitrago advised against it. I'm not recording anything.'

Trigeño released me and looked down at his boots, perhaps to conceal his embarrassment. It was out in the open now – I'd called him a liar to his face and he'd all but admitted it – so I continued.

'I also know you ordered every aspect of the *limpieza.* I know Don Mauricio's death wasn't an accident and the Guerrilla did not carry out the assassination attempt on Don Felix. Beta wasn't acting independently, just as the Díaz didn't betray you. You blame them now because it suits you, but you've been behind them all along.'

When Trigeño looked back at me, it was not anger I read in his face but genuine mortification, like that of a little boy finally caught with his hand in the cookie jar. But that didn't mean he was sorry.

'Although it left a foul taste in my mouth,' he said, 'those were deliberate strategies. We needed to get close to our enemy in the short term in order to defeat them in the long term—'

'Short term?' I said with disgust. 'I saw you and Javier shake hands during that first meeting a year ago. And killing Mauricio and Delgado – was that also part of your secret long-term strategy?'

'Everything I've ever done,' he stammered, 'was necessary for the good of Colombia. Everything our enemy did, we needed to do better, including financing our army. So when Javier—'

'I don't care who, or how, or why!' I interrupted. 'You lied to me. You manipulated me. And you used me.'

'I am truly sad that I had to deceive you, Pedro. You were still too young and idealistic to understand. But I now beg you to look to the future. Together with Alfa 1, we will run south-east Colombia. You will have a promotion. Triple pay. Two hundred men under your command. And if you want, a share from the agricultural co-operative.'

I could hardly believe it. He was attempting to bribe me with a share of cocaine profits.

'Did you ever understand me? Did you ever even care?'

'Of course I did. I saw a great deal of myself in you.'

'And I'm grateful for our similarities. You've shown me yours is not the path I want for myself.'

We had reached our final impasse. I'd accused him of lying, betrayal and hypocrisy, while I'd been sincere, loyal and transparent about my desire to leave and reasons for wanting to do so. But still he would not yield. There was only one thing for it. One final risk.

'Carlos, remember you once said I was like a son to you?' I had his full attention; I'd never called him by his first name. 'Would you shoot your own son?'

I turned and walked towards Uncle Leo's truck, waiting for the sharp, searing pain of a bullet between my shoulder blades. It didn't come. Trigeño chased after me, trying to wrench my shoulder around.

'Whether you believe it or not, you *are* like a son to me. I'd never touch a hair on your head. Pedro, I'll be genuinely sad, but you're free to leave.'

'Good.'

I continued walking, still half-expecting him to shoot. Behind me, I heard a sharp metallic clink. I turned, believing he was cocking his pistol. But instead he had pulled a pin from his waist belt – the pin belonging to the emergency grenade that he'd sworn to use on himself when cornered. He now flung the grenade into the lake.

Following a muffled underwater explosion, a mushrooming water cloud burst the surface, sending waves back and forth across the lake. Vampire fish floated up, dead and sideways. There must have been a tonne of them. They were a beautiful, magnificent fish with semi-transparent fins and iridescent silver scales down their elongated bodies. All of them were over two foot long with razor-sharp teeth and a pair of seven-centimetre fangs. I had never seen so many fish. Seconds earlier, all of them were in their prime. Now, most were dead. Others, half-alive, swam in circles.

'You see that!' he cried. 'You made me do that.'

I remembered Papá telling me about God's creatures being sacred, and I remembered how, a year earlier, on one of the afternoons we fished together, Trigeño had caught then released an armoured catfish. Back then, I had let myself be deceived. But with this final act of wanton destruction, he'd revealed the man within.

Jaw set hard, I turned and kept walking. And I wouldn't stop until I reached Camila's doorstep.

163

I STILL HAD CAMILA'S new address from her *if you love me* text. When I arrived in Bogotá it was only mid-afternoon, but already the sky was as dark as dusk, with grey storm clouds engulfing the city.

I drove north towards the centre. Apart from in the movies, I'd never seen such tall buildings. Beneath them I was a tiny, insignificant ant, ducking and weaving among ten million other ants.

Camila lived in a security apartment block with a twenty-four-hour *portero* on duty behind a desk. As I buzzed, holding a dozen red roses behind my back, I felt like the earth might open up at any moment and swallow me whole.

The *portero* trudged to the door and asked through the glass who I was.

'Pedro. For Camila Muñoz, *por favor*.'

It was 6 pm as I ascended the stairs and knocked on the door of apartment 202, hoping that Camila lived alone.

I'd wanted to surprise her, but now I regretted not phoning in advance. Imagine my embarrassment if Andrea, the simpering newsreader, was visiting. With her looking at me down her surgically sculpted nose, I wouldn't be able to say a single word. Or worse still, imagine if Camila had a new boyfriend who flung open the door wearing boxer shorts, only to find me concealing a bouquet.

Fortunately, Camila opened the door herself. She was wearing no make-up and simply dressed – in blue jeans and a tight-fitting white woollen pullover – yet radiantly beautiful. Her hair was tied back in a loose ponytail and she was wearing her reading glasses, which always made her look more serious and grown up.

We stood appraising each other awkwardly.

'Camila,' I began, 'I know you probably don't even want me here . . . but I just wanted to tell you . . .' I whipped out the flowers. 'I'm out! I quit.'

Camila's face brightened momentarily, but she suppressed her delight.

'Truly out?' Her hands went to her hips. 'Not just half-way, sort-of-but-not-really, maybe-later out?'

'No, *truly* out.' I felt myself on firmer ground now. 'I saw my boss and got my discharge. And I promise you I'll never go back.'

'What about the men who killed your father? Aren't some of them still alive?'

'Let them live. I need to move forward and start living again too.'

'I'm glad,' she said, mistrust still lurking in her eyes.

'I also want to say that I'm sorry for all the hurt and anxiety I caused you. I lied to you. I told you I would leave my job, but I didn't. And I know it made you scared. I was so obsessed, I probably seemed like a demented monster.'

She suppressed a chuckle. I saw this was getting through to her. Her hands slid slowly from her hips. 'Go on,' she said.

'But I still love you, Camila, and if you're not with anyone else, then I'm begging you for another chance. I know I've been selfish, but now I'll do anything you ask.'

She held herself back a moment longer and then, finally, she relented. It was like a dam bursting. She hugged me and I began crying. Tears of happiness flooded forth, but also tears of relief that it was all finally and properly over.

We stayed like that for a full minute, then Camila pulled back to look at me seriously, a finger on her chin. 'There is one thing you could do.'

'Anything!'

'That tattoo. It has to go.'

Her act broke, dissolving into a smile, and she threw her arms around me again.

164

I ARRIVED BACK AT Llorona having been absent less than a week, but the town was already abuzz with news of the Díazes' arrest.

Ultimately, both the Díaz properties were confiscated under anti-narcotics law. Eleonora's property was put up for public auction. But there were no bidders – no sane person would buy land that had been cursed by the Díaz family and which had also been the site of a battle and the local headquarters of an illegal army.

As for Eleonora herself, when she returned to visit her imprisoned sons, the townsfolk turned their backs on her, refusing her service in stores and ignoring her waves in the street. She was also shunned by *la gente de bien* – 'good society' – in Bogotá.

Since Fabián Díaz was in prison on cocaine trafficking charges, he was never sworn into public office. Instead, the election's runner-up was inaugurated: Don Felix Velasquez. Hearing this, I smiled, confident that Felix would run the region honestly. Under his leadership, the town of Llorona returned to relative tranquillity, as did Puerto Galán and Puerto Princesa. All three were now indisputably under army and police rule.

After his series of military triumphs against the Guerrilla, Colonel Julius Orlando Buitrago was an unimpeachable national hero. Caraquemada's 34th Frente abandoned the area completely.

Following Caraquemada's latest brush with death, I imagined him limping back to camp with his ego in tatters but his legend as an immortal escape artist grown even larger. The Guerrilla's reputation had reached an all-time low with proof of their direct involvement in cocaine trafficking, which they'd always vociferously denied.

For the time being, Buitrago remained in Garbanzos. But he'd made some powerful enemies and, like many senior army officers who had patriotically served two countries – Colombia and the United States – he and his family were offered resident visas by the North Americans. He told me he planned on retiring to Florida the following year.

As for Trigeño, he was set to hand himself in to the authorities when, on the eve of his imprisonment, he got word of the North Americans' extradition plan and reneged on the deal, becoming a fugitive. Over the coming years, some said he'd been killed by a US black-ops team, although rumours persisted that he'd undergone radical plastic surgery and was happily ensconced on his own Caribbean island.

With the disappearance of Trigeño, the various Autodefensas groups he had united under the aegis of the AUC fragmented. Alfa 1 abandoned La 50. Rather than surrender to the 'cowardly government', he vigorously pursued Beta, who remained holed up on a farm near Casanare with dozens of soldiers.

Hundreds of former Autodefensas, none of whom had spoken a word against Alfa 1, waited for the phone call that would return them to fight under their former commander and mentor. The unravelling process took many years to reach its conclusion, but that was the beginning of the end for the Autodefensas.

That same year, General Itagüí would receive medals and a fourth star for his 'heroic role in countering the communist insurgency'. His open sponsorship of the Autodefensas in Los Llanos was never made public, not even when the *Fiscalía* finally raided La 50 in response to my anonymous phone call to the bulldog *fiscal*.

The first sets of remains discovered belonged to Tango and Murgas – with the 200-peso coins I'd inserted in their graves setting off a metal detector. Using yellow plastic tape, CTI officers marked off a crime scene and began digging. The taped-off area was pushed further and further outwards as corpses and bone fragments in black garbage bags began to pile up. Fortunately, DNA testing by forensic investigators allowed many families of those 'disappeared' to finally get closure and put their loved ones to rest.

Back closer to home, things were much happier.

Uncle was now the doting father of a healthy baby boy. Mamá was thrilled to become an aunt, and also at my reconciliation with her brother. She moved back to the *finca* and spent her days tending her vegetable garden and attending Sunday Mass. She visited her neighbours Gloria and Old Man Domino regularly, never forgetting to bring sweets for the little boy they'd adopted: Iván.

In May, a month after my final conversation with Trigeño, my friends and I officially 'demobilised', handing in our weapons at a grand parade that included lots of reporters, television cameras and well-meaning handshakes. As part of our social reintegration process, we'd been debriefed by the army, received therapy from professional psychologists for the trauma we'd experienced and were now declared fit to be productive citizens.

For the next year, we'd be paid the minimum wage by the government while attending vocational workshops. I moved into Camila's tiny apartment. Meanwhile, Palillo, Piolín and Ñoño – who had a new puppy called Daffodil snapping at his heels – rented a small, shared apartment on the outskirts of Bogotá. On the night of the demobilisation parade, I invited my friends to Camila's place for a celebration.

We got drunk and relived our happy memories, making light of the horrific ones by teasing each other and satirising our commanders. Piolín had won a bet against the three boys, which meant she got to be Alfa 1.

'You!' She pointed at Palillo. 'Anaconda, give me fifty push-ups . . . naked.'

Coca-Cola spluttered as he took a sip of beer, spraying froth everywhere.

'And you!' she said to him. 'You like beer, do you? Then we'll change your name to *Cerveza*. Now, take this raincoat and give me ten pack runs up and down the fire stairs, drinking a beer each time.'

Piolín had Alfa 1's intonation and gestures down pat. Ñoño was beside himself until Piolín bellowed at him: 'Silence! Did I say you could laugh, Harry Potter? Give me a three-minute plank and then tie yourself to the balcony. You need a suntan.'

In the middle of all this play, Piolín stood, raised her beer can and clinked a fork against it repeatedly until the group fell silent.

'To good friends we've made,' she said, glancing at Camila so she'd feel included. 'And good friends we've lost.'

I looked around at the people who'd been my closest companions for the past two and a half years. We were brothers and sisters, bonded for life.

'Wait!' I stood. I had a toast of my own to propose. 'My heart knows for a fact that Camila and I will be spending the rest of our lives together. However, as you all know, I'm a very impatient man so . . . I'd like the rest of my life to start right now.' I bent down on one knee. 'Camila, will you—'

Before I could finish my question, she rushed forward and leaped on top of me, knocking me sprawling to the floor. 'I will! I will! I will!'

I didn't even have time to take the ring from my pocket, which was probably for the best as it was only a plastic Corn Flakes ring like Ernesto's. Our friends piled on top of us, hugging us, shaking our hands, patting our backs and kissing our cheeks.

We phoned Mamá, Uncle and Camila's parents with the news. Mamá was overjoyed, but then she sniffed. 'Your father would be so proud.'

'He *is* proud, Mamá.'

I'd prayed and spoken to him the previous night. He'd wished me luck and hoped that Camila and I would have plenty of children, with at least one boy who would grow up to become his own true man, just as I had.

EPILOGUE

PALILLO WORKED ON me for three months about returning to dig up what he insisted was a buried *guaca*. He never lost faith that money lay buried near the jungle laboratory.

'Not just thousands. *Millions*.'

'Even if you're right, it would be dirty money.'

'Of course it's dirty,' he said. 'But we'll clean it.'

'My answer is "no".'

It was July by then, eight weeks since our formal disarmament. Life after the Autodefensas was amazing. My friends were now making up for lost time, enjoying the freedoms that ordinary teenagers took for granted, like talking for hours on the phone, going to the cinema and not requiring permission to go to the toilet. They drank alcohol, played loud music, danced and stayed up late.

I was planning to live with Camila in Bogotá, at least until she finished university. In addition to the compulsory demobilisation classes, I was completing my final year of high school in order to receive the graduation certificate.

Once Camila had finished her degree, if she wanted to look for work in Bogotá, I would apply for university. However, I'd apply for Agricultural Economics, a course that would be useful for my true calling – running our *finca*. I knew Papá had wanted me to study business, but I made my own decisions now.

'You're being selfish, Pedro,' continued Palillo. '*You* mightn't need money, but your mother does. She could buy that neighbouring property and retire.'

Personally, I'd have been happy simply to be able to afford a few cattle. Mamá was still living alone on our *finca*, but without my income she had to catch a *colectivo* each day to work part-time at Uncle's hardware store.

'My mother is fine,' I insisted.

'Then do it for your friends. You owe me, *hermano*. This will solve all our problems. You can pay your university tuition. Ñoño can buy his mother a house. Coca-Cola can hire the best surgeon for his shattered knee. I won't even have to do acting school. I can buy a movie studio and star in my own production!'

'What if we run into a patrol?'

Although Caraquemada had been sighted in the faraway province of Neiva, the Guerrilla still used those mountains and rivers as supply routes.

'Exactly. That's why we go as a team.'

Of course, Palillo eventually wore me down. Which is why, three months after our mission against Caraquemada, I found myself in the middle of the jungle, back at the former laboratory, which had been dismantled and burned by the army.

We'd trekked arduously all day through the humid, insect-infested jungle. I was soaked with sweat and my muscles ached from carrying a heavy, rain-drenched pack. Not surprisingly, we had encountered no *guerrilleros*.

Now, as Palillo whipped the '*guaca* map' from his pocket, he buoyed my spirits by describing how our lives were about to change.

'I'll have an SUV with tinted windows. You can buy Camila a golf-ball-sized diamond ring to replace that plastic one. I'll put one of my apartments in my sister's name so my mother can receive money from the rent.'

From the starting coordinates, we followed the bearing for nine hundred metres towards the spot marked 'X' on the map, worrying all the while that we'd veer off course and end up digging in the wrong place.

'There!' Palillo pointed, laughing. We had indeed deviated, but the 'Hug X' was a literal symbol, unmistakable when we saw it. Two trees had fallen towards each other, coming to rest with their trunks crossing. They looked like they were hugging.

Using a tape measure, I paced exactly twenty-seven metres east of the trees. Then, sharing the tiny shovel, we took it in turns to break the earth, as we had on the day of Papá's execution, until blisters appeared on our hands.

'This is ridiculous!' I said once our third hole was two metres deep. 'I'm poor but happy. Let's go home.'

Suddenly, there was a dull thud as Palillo's shovel struck something plastic. We exchanged a look and dropped to our knees to scoop away the remaining dirt that covered the lid of a large blue crate.

GLOSSARY OF SPANISH TERMS AND SLANG

abrazo	hug
adelante	go! go ahead!
agallas	balls
aguardiente	aniseed-based liquor, literally 'firewater'
águila	Colombian beer
ajustícialo	execute him
auxiliar	assistant/helper
avenida	avenue
berraco	tough and gutsy person, a go-getter (slang)
bloque	unit
borracho	drunk
brigada fuerzas especiales	special forces brigade
buenas tardes	good afternoon
buñuelos	fried dough ball
busetero	bus worker
caldo	broth, soup
caletas	hidden compartment
caliente	hot
camaradas	comrades
campesinos	peasant farmers
canasta	a crate or box
capo	drug boss
Caracol	TV/radio station in Colombia
cariño	dear (term of endearment)
cédula	national ID card
cerveza	beer
chapa	alias
chica	girl, chick
chivas	rural buses, literally 'goats'

cojones	balls
colectivo	public mini-van
colegio	school
comandante	commander
compa	friend (abbreviation for *compadre*)
compañero	friend, colleague
contrabandistas	contraband traffickers
corazón	heart
culo	butt, bum, ass
cursos	fellow soldiers (slang)
dale	go! do it!
dios mío	my god!
farándula	the world of celebrities, people involved in show business
finca	farm, property
frente	in the FARC, a military unit (literally, 'front')
gallina/gallinita	chicken/little chicken
garrapata	tick
gente de bien	good society
gracias a dios	thank god
guaca	buried treasure
guerrillera	female guerrilla soldier
guerrillero	male guerrilla soldier
hermano	brother
hermosa	pretty
hijo	son
hijo de puta/hijueputa	son of a whore, son of a bitch
jefe	boss, chief
joder	fuck!
jodido	fucked
joven	young man
lancha	motorised boat
lárguese	get out of here
lechona	stuffed pork dish
limpieza	cleaning, cleansing
loco	lunatic
loro	parrot
lotería	lottery
mala	bad

mierda	shit
mijito	my little son (abbreviation for *mi hijito*)
milicianos	militia member
mi querido	my dear
monte	mountain
mosqueteros	musketeers
muchacho	boy
mulata	a woman of mixed black and white ancestry, especially one having one white and one black parent
novias	girlfriends
oiga	listen! hey!
paisa	a person from Antioquia region of
parqueadero	parking lot
pasteles	sweets
patrón	boss, chief
pelado	boy
pendejo	dickhead
perras	bitches
pillado	busted
planazos	strikes with flat side of machete
plata	silver (slang for money)
políticos	politicians
pollo	chicken
por dios	for god's sake
princesas intocables	untouchable princesses
punto	point guard/lookout
pura mierda	bullshit
puta	whore
puta madre	fucking hell
puteadero	whorehouse
qué bueno	great!
quiebrapatas	landmines (literally 'foot-breakers')
ráfagas	burst of gunfire
rápido	quick
raspachín	coca leaf picker (slang)
reggaetón	rap music from Puerto Rico
sapo	toad (slang for 'informant')
señorito	a young, unmarried man

sicario	hired killer
socio/a	romantic partner (guerrilla slang)
soldado	soldier
suba	get in, get up
suegro	father-in-law
supermercado	supermarket
taxista	taxi driver
tinto	coffee
tiro de gracia	coup de grâce
traficante	trafficker
urbano	member of urban militia
vacuna	guerrilla tax, literally 'vaccine'
vallenato	type of Colombian music
vámonos/vamos	let's go
vereda	rural village, settlement
viejo	old man (slang)

ACKNOWLEDGEMENTS

Readers see one name on the front cover, but not the silent army of supporters, hidden (and often long-suffering) between the pages.

My first debt of gratitude is to the dozens of child soldiers and members of the FARC, AUC and ELN who opened up and trusted me, often at great risk to themselves. Special thanks to 'Alias Pedro', 'Alias MacGyver', Jader, 'Alias Tarzan', Lenis, Abel, Andrea, Yineth, Diana and Leidy. To the many others – you know who you are and the reasons you can't be named.

To my friends and colleagues in the anti-kidnapping program, particularly JJ, Jorge Matallana and Tim Bulot, as well as the members of the Colombian National Police and Army whose bravery and patriotism helped their country turn the corner after a dark period in history, but who also wished to remain 'off the record'.

The biggest thanks by far, and my eternal gratitude, go to Simone Camilleri, who has been my literary agent, editor, story consultant, honest critic, believer in my ability and, dare I admit, sometimes co-author of this book, but above all else a caring friend. Her creativity, imagination, grasp of story and pace, as well as her assistance with plotting and deepening of the characters, made this book what it is.

To my beautiful sister, Rani, and wonderful parents, Marie and Peter, for their love, belief in me, patience as well as practical and financial support. *Muchas gracias* for helping your adolescent son, with pretensions of one day being a writer, become a middle-aged struggling artist, once more living back at home!

Huge love goes to Bradley Fraser, treasured friend and Tuesday-night confidant, who loaned me his ironing board as a desk, as well as a copy of his house key, and who provided open-ended, unconditional support. To my bestest of best friends, Scooter McGregor, sage advisor and critical reader, for his undying loyalty, open writer's house in Mumbai, and for keeping me on an even mental keel.

To the Fosters, whose 'Writer's Shed' and hospitality were given generously for many years. To Daniel Toomey, friend since childhood, for helping me visualise this project, for his beach house refuge and incredible website support.

I would also like to extend my warmest gratitude to everyone who read and commented on the manuscript over the years. Particular thanks go to Brian Camilleri, Sergio Barbosa and Ralph Glenny, who spent countless hours giving discerning and insightful feedback, and also to Enzo Congiu, Lucy Hughes, Mireille and Gary Hennessey, Orlando Savage, Carlo Giacco, Aiying Law, Cobie Dellicastelli and Isolde Martyn. Your detailed comments were greatly appreciated and helped polish the novel. Thanks also to John Purcell for sharing his wealth of knowledge about the publishing industry. Simone would also like to thank the members of the Turramurra Writers Group for their support.

To Rebecca Reed, personal cheerleader, amazing friend, and deliverer of soup, who always lent a sympathetic ear and provided a constant fount of laughter. To my gorgeous friend Belinda Pratten, for believing in me, reading many terrible drafts, and for her incredible humanitarian work in Colombia that inspired me to make a difference. To Toby Loneragan for planting seeds and playing with ideas. To Stella Duque, Steve Fisher and Greg Preuss for their dedication to helping child soldiers.

To Beverley Cousins, editor extraordinaire, for her talented, professional judgment, for shaping and cutting the story, and for gently removing my overwritten metaphors! Almost as importantly, for her unerring support, diplomacy and patience with an erratic writer who missed several deadlines and tended to disappear overseas to work on 'unrelated projects' at a moment's notice. To Nikki Christer, who championed the book and took a chance on me. To Brandon VanOver, my copy-editor, for his hard work, incredible attention to detail, and his eagle eye that spotted my many errors. To Jem Butcher – what an amazing cover design! To Jess Malpass for her dedicated campaigning and promotion, and to the wonderful team at Penguin Random House, whose passion and enthusiasm helped this book make its way into readers' hands. My apologies for giving you all grey hairs, but glad you're still smiling (I think).

Finally, to *mis parceros colombianos*: Don R. Escritor, Thomas McFadden, Vampiro Niels, Heals, Yency, Martha, Dan, Houses, Boyzy, German, Ali, AJ & Carrie, Giles, Carolina, Clare, Andre, Astrid, Consuelo, Sole, Matt, Maria, Rich & Diana, Pinky, Tom, Jordan, Jules, Carrie, Nando, and the crazy Bogotá *combo*.

And to the Sydney crew – John Pease, Alina, Mez, Rom, Bunk, Pen, Colonel D. Rothwell, Jules & Megs, Gui & Edwina, Bally, Damo & Poss, Dean, Simona, Rhys, Llewellyn, Marcus, Kath, Burge, Chris, Piers & Nirmal, Sam, Ed & Jules and Caz – as well as the many other friends and fans who believed in me, read my shitty drafts and kept asking, 'When will it be finished?' while never doubting it would be.

Simone Camilleri would like to extend her warmest thanks to her parents, Brian and Adrienne Camilleri, who inspired her love of reading, nurtured her creativity and who always encouraged her to dream. And, most importantly, she would like to thank her husband, Sergio Barbosa, for the unwavering love and the joy he brings into her life, his practical support and the countless hours he spent reading and providing insightful comments on the manuscript, and his extraordinary patience during the many years devoted to this project.

Penguin
Random House
Australia